A DARK CONSPIRACY

Universitas Press
Montreal

www.universitaspress.com

First published in January 2023

Library and Archives Canada Cataloguing in Publication

Title: A dark conspiracy : and other nineteenth-century Canadian short stories in English / edited by Henry M. Wallace.
Other titles: Dark conspiracy (Universitas Press)
Names: Wallace, Henry M., 1970- editor.
Identifiers: Canadiana 2023015249X | ISBN 9781988963419 (softcover)
Subjects: LCSH: Short stories, Canadian—19th century. | CSH: Short stories, Canadian (English) | CSH: Canadian fiction (English)—19th century.
Classification: LCC PS8325 .D35 2023 | DDC C813/.010804—dc23

A DARK CONSPIRACY

and

other 19th-century
CANADIAN SHORT STORIES
in English

Edited by Henry M. Wallace

Universitas Press
Montreal

CONTENTS

Introduction

Canadian fiction began in earnest in the 1820s, with the first novel (*St Ursula's Convent*) and the first short stories, which benefited from the periodical press founded in the new cities and towns of Nova Scotia, New Brunswick, Lower Canada (Quebec), and Upper Canada (Ontario). By the end of the decade, some authors were confident enough to put together the first volumes collecting their short fiction, either in the mother country (Thomas McCulloch published a book of novellas in Edinburgh in 1826) or in the colony (John Howard Willis had his *Scraps and Sketches* out in 1831 in Montreal). By the 1830s, not only did short stories start pouring in, thanks again to the multiplication of newspapers and periodicals (a relatively long-lasting magazine, *The Literary Garland* was also founded in 1838), but Canadian short fiction had its first international bestseller in Haliburton's *Clockmaker*.

To be sure, Canadian short-story writers were also looking to other venues, such as *Bentley's* of London or *Graham's* of Philadelphia (not only because contributing there was more lucrative, but also because these periodicals were usually more established, with a larger audience, which allowed them to survive much longer than the usually short-lived Canadian literary press) and, by the end of the 1860s, May Agnes Fleming of New Brunswick was a prolific contributor to the New York *Sunday Mercury*. However, new Canadian periodicals continued to appear and to encourage short-story writing: among those with the largest quantity of short fiction, the *Anglo-American Magazine* (Toronto) and *The Provincial* (Halifax), in the 1850s; or the *New Dominion Monthly* (Montreal) and the *British American Magazine* (Toronto) in the 1860s. These are, of course, just a few examples, and they do not account for the fiction that was being published in newspapers or in periodicals other than literary. Despite the early advances in the Maritimes and the rapid development of Upper Canada (despite also the fact that many authors were residents of these provinces), from at least the mid-1830s until at least the mid-1870s, the Canadian literary scene was dominated by Montreal, veritable cultural capital of English Canada. The balance began to shift in favour of Toronto in the last quarter of the century, when fiction also started to come from farther west, as new communities emerged in the prairies and on the Pacific coast.

A Century of Stories

Thousands of short stories were published in Canada in the 19th century (not including sketches, tableaux, and other semifictional pieces) and there was probably an equal number published by Canadian authors elsewhere in the English-speaking world. There was, obviously, a rather slow start, not dissimilar to what was going on in other places, whereas the production of short stories picked up the pace and it became quite plentiful in the last two decades of the century. This is illustrated in the selection here: of the thirty-five stories included in this anthology, eighteen were published after 1880.

Some of the first short stories written in Canada followed the device of a tale or, rather, a series of tales, disguised as letters to the editor. This device had been perfected throughout the 18th century in English and Scottish periodicals, in which it took either the form of what is known as an "essay-series" (when published within the pages of a magazine; this was still practised in the early 19th century, for example, by Charles Lamb, whose "Essays of Elia" began in 1820 in the *London Magazine*) or in the form of an "essay serial" (when a small magazine consisted entirely of these pieces; an early-19th-century example would be James Hogg's

The Spy). The latter model was largely followed by Samuel Hull Wilcocke, whose *Scribbler* and *Free Press* appeared in Montreal in the early 1820s, though his writings do not really qualify as short fiction. In fact, much of the material published in all these series or serials was, as the name suggests, nonfictional: essays were often interspersed with tales and anecdotes. The Nova Scotian practitioners included in this anthology (Thomas McCulloch and Thomas Chandler Haliburton), however, chose a new formula, which consisted of a series of interrelated short fictions (the part of the essays was simply played by the comments of the narrator, which never amounted to more than a few sentences), with recurring characters, either part of a small community (McCulloch) or moving about, in the guise of a travelogue (Haliburton). This formula (which anticipates the short-story cycles of the late 19th and early 20th centuries, practised in Canada, for example, by Duncan Campbell Scott and Norman Duncan) was also in its infancy in England, where it was being developed by authors like Mary Russell Mitford.

To the reader more used to the short-story cycles of the 20th century, the most striking feature of those written in the first decades of the 19th is probably the constant presence of a first-person narrator/character, through which (via the influential model of Washington Irving) 19th-century short-story writers were reaching back to their 18th-century models. In fact, many of them (including Mitford in England) intermingled their stories with essays, nature pieces, diaries, and other nonfictional genres. Haliburton did it himself after the first series of the *Clockmaker*, but the most notable Canadian practitioner of the salmagundi cycle is undoubtedly Susanna Moodie. Her *Roughing It in the Bush* and *Life in the Clearings*, both published in the early 1850s, are also quintessential examples of what may be the most typically Canadian fictional form of the first decades of the 19th century: the fact-based short story (represented here also by Joseph Howe and Mary Jane Katzmann, though it was resuscitated towards the end of the century by authors like Roger Pocock or Ernest Thompson Seton). Moodie's first-person narratives were, of course, based on her own experiences, but Howe's and Katzmann's were not; however, it matters less if the "facts" on which the story is based are accurately transmitted to the reader; like in the non-fiction novel, the pretext of factuality holds the story together. As one of the authors selected here put it (in 1866) in the preface to a collection of short stories: "although some of them may appear to matter-of-fact readers as the flourishes of fiction, I can give no better idea of their reality than by comparing them with a living person when clothed. They are embodied facts; but I have undertaken to dress and embellish a few of them in such a manner as I thought most suitable to my own fashion" (Spedon 9).

Canadian authors also adopted the "well-wrought tale," which necessarily ends with a twist, mostly in the 1860s (May Agnes Fleming is a good early example), but they remained at their best when they did not try to follow a recipe. Grant Allen or Robert Barr, who became successful practitioners of this form in the 1880s and 1890s, also chose to parody it. A very unusual, yet all the more specific, narrative form that cropped up in Canadian literature in the 1860s and 1870s is a kind of "medley," as if an entire short-story cycle had to be condensed in only one tale: the narrator/character becomes intimate with the hero of the account, which may or may not be a love story (parodied or not); this account is interrupted by humorous character sketches; dialectal speech is carefully reproduced; there are several scenes in which people of various social strata interact; naturally, it is set in a city or town and cityscapes play an important part; there is a mixture of genres involved (going from the sentimental tale to gritty realism, but sometimes poetry intrudes). The best examples of this are Allan's "Captain Ardmore" (1858) and Rutherford's "Charlie Chatterton" (1868), which have been selected here; but the form survived in some of John Arthur Phillips's fictions of the 1870s, and even later (Gilbert Parker comes close to it in "Frith Highland, Gentleman" from 1893). This should not be a matter of concern to the contemporary reader. It is true that many of us have been trained to expect short stories to exhibit a certain kind of rigour and to provide an unexpected turn of events; and that only recently has a cautionary note been sounded "about the enduring legacy of formalism within short story criticism" (March-Russell viii-ix). However, it is time to apply to the study of this narrative form the same tools that poststructuralism has taught us to use when reading other genres.

In fact, well-wrought structures were followed closely in short stories written by Canadian authors in the last decades of the 19th century, but they are not always as conspicuous or as salient to the story itself, since the focus (and the meaning) is veered towards the genre of the story, be it "local colour" (in the case of Duncan Campbell Scott or Edith Eaton), feminist naturalism (Lily Dougall) or the study of behavioural patterns (Lucy Maud Montgomery), all of which are synchronous with late-19th-century developments of the short story in the United States and Europe. In some other cases, the same structural mastery participates in the construction of more specifically Canadian genres: the animal story (represented in this anthology by Charles G.D. Roberts) and the humorous sketch as sublimated by Leacock. This last statement brings us to a question that has long marred the critical discourse on 19th-century Canadian literature, that is, which works and which authors can truly be considered Canadian—an issue which is itself specifically Canadian.

"Purely Canadian"

In its original manifestation, the issue involved the abundance of foreign (mostly British) literature in Canadian periodicals. Many early (and some more modern) commentators were concerned that this impeded the development of a "national literature" in Canada. Only recently has a different opinion been voiced, according to which this abundance was actually "key to the magazines' own understanding of their role as agents of national cultural development" (Rieley 130). A little later, in the 1840s and 1850s, the issue was upended: Canadian magazines published so much foreign literature because Canada lacked authors. Especially in the 1860s and 1870s, the (refurbished) issue was the necessity to persuade the actual, existing Canadian authors to use Canadian content: "O, ye Canadians! why will ye slumber in literary indolence and allow your noble rivers to roll on, year after year, 'unlettered and unsung?'" (Spedon 5). Almost at the same time, the issue became about Canadian authors finding (some degree of) fame elsewhere because the local audience was not ready for them: "The gifted pen of a Mrs. Moodie, whose whole life is characteristic of exemplary fortitude, has inscribed her genius upon the monument of fame in other lands; whilst the envious critics of Canada have done little more than to chalk her name upon the blackboard of censure" (Spedon 8); or because they could not make a living as writers in Canada: in one of the stories selected here (John Arthur Phillips's "Thompson's Turkey"), the hero "thought he would turn his talents to account and he sent some of his writings to the American papers, for the Canadian papers were willing enough to publish, but very unwilling to pay, and as Thompson was writing for bread and butter he could not afford that kind of business." Phillips was editor of *The Hearthstone*, a Montreal literary magazine, and, in June 1872, he printed a wanted ad "to the literary men and women of Canada," asking for contributions and offering prizes for "Canadian stories" (by which he meant both novels and short stories): "We ask for novels and stories founded on Canadian history, experience and incident—illustrative of back wood life, fishing, lumbering, farming; taking the reader through our industrious cities, floating palaces, steam-driven factories, ship-building yards, lumbering shanties, fishing smacks, &c." Referring to an older aspect of the same issue, Phillips explained that "We want to have an essentially Canadian paper, and gradually to dispense with selections and foreign contributions." Nevertheless, the prizes offered for the best and second-best short stories ($50 and $25, respectively) barely matched what was at the time the expected remuneration for any story published in an American magazine (see Cooper 279).

In the last two decades of the century, the issue became that of a "brain drain," as too many Canadian authors not only published elsewhere, but also took up residence either in the US, in Britain, or in another British colony. Writing about Canadian short-story writers towards the end of the 19th century and referring to such authors as Grant Allen, Gilbert Parker, Edward William Thomson, Robert Barr, and Sara Jeannette Duncan, one commentator complained that they "have practically ceased to be Canadians" (Brodie 335). With this, the last facet of the same issue emerged: which authors were (or were still) Canadian? Being foreign-born was certainly not a problem as long as the writer lived in Canada (Phillips, who was himself born in England, explained that, in the short-story competition he had organised, "any resident of Canada is eligible to compete, and the subject of birth or nationality will not be taken into consideration at all as long as the writer is a resident of Canada"). Even not being a resident of Canada was becoming acceptable towards the end of the century, when some authors moved to the countries where they were being published, as long as they continued to write about Canada. This view was reiterated more recently, when a commentator of 19th-century Canadian literature spoke about "the creation of a national literature that distinctively and appropriately referred to Canada" (Gerson ix). Such view, however, excludes those works of foreign-born Canadian authors (see Catharine Parr Traill or Edith Eaton in the present volume) that refer to their experiences before immigration or the country of their ancestors. It also excludes any interest in non-Canadian themes (this led, for example, to the poet Charles Heavysege being seen as "not Canadian in spirit" because he wrote mostly about religious subjects). A few years after Carole Gerson's statement, a subtler point was made about "the fundamental criterion that a work should be intended for Canadian readers" (MacDonald 14). This implies, quite reasonably, that it is enough for the work to be published in Canada, for a Canadian audience, even if the author's stay in the country had been brief (MacDonald gives, in fact, an example to this effect; there is also an example in this anthology—John Rutherford's "Charlie Chatterton").

However, this last view excludes those Canadian authors who were writing for British and American periodicals or had their books published in London or Boston. In some cases (e.g., Joseph Howe, Susanna Moodie, Duncan Campbell Scott, Stephen Leacock, Lucy Maud Montgomery), their writings were, sooner or later, reprinted in Canada. In others, they were not (see, for example, the stories by Ethelwyn Wetherald and Sara Jeannette Duncan, included in this anthology). Except for the last five years of her life, May Agnes Fleming (some of whose stories are actually set in Canada) continued to reside in Saint John, New Brunswick, while writing exclusively for American periodicals and publishing houses. Did she "cease to be Canadian," as Brodie suggested? Despite his unconcealed nationalism, Brodie asked a valid question. If people born elsewhere can become Canadian, then so can native-born Canadians become something else. Of the five authors he mentioned in his 1895 article, Thomson actually returned to Canada in 1902 (though he retired to Boston in 1922 and died there two years later); Gilbert Parker and Sara Jeannette Duncan never returned, but their most important works about (and for) Canada were produced while living abroad. The two that remain are the most problematic: Grant Allen and Robert Barr, both native-born Canadians who left and never returned and who were little concerned with addressing Canadian themes (both are included in this anthology with one story each). The fact is that, when it comes to 19th-century Canada, one has to remain very liberal with the criteria according to which an author qualifies as Canadian, because one has to deal not just with authors born elsewhere or authors publishing elsewhere, but also with authors relocating to other countries. There were also authors born in Canada, who left, came back, then left again; or authors born elsewhere who came, stayed for a longer or shorter period of time, then went somewhere else in the English-speaking world. It was, simply put, very easy to do so: there was no language barrier; and, just as immigration from the British Isles continued freely, Canadians themselves were relatively free to move both inside the large British empire and the United States. Consequently, it is easy to assume that both Allen and Barr never excluded the possibility of eventually returning to Canada or of writing about Canada, just as other had done.

Modernity

Of the 29 authors selected here, 17 were born in Canada; but of the twelve born elsewhere, five came to Canada when under the age of 7 (they were, in the words of their Scottish contemporary Francis Lathom, "born abroad and bred at home"); another two came as teenagers and another four when they were 30 years old or younger; the only exception is John Rutherford, who came and left, but whose departure might be explained by the fact that he felt in danger (he investigated the Fenian movement in Canada). Many of those native-born, in fact, also left Canada. Even Haliburton, the most celebrated Canadian author of the entire 19th century, moved to England and became member of the British House of Commons. The insistence of so many magazine editors, critics and other commentators on the importance of a "purely Canadian" literature (see McMullen v), which would have left behind stories about the mother country, was in the end salutary, because it likely contributed to the (slow) end of sentimental novels and short stories, and it encouraged the realistic, fact-based short story and the humorous sketch. However, both the abundance of foreign literature in periodicals (as Rieley, mentioned above, noticed) and the authors' constant movement from one literary field to another was ultimately beneficial. Thomas McCulloch (born in 1776) came to Canada as a 27-year-old born and educated in Scotland, of the same generation as Walter Scott and James Hogg, whom he wished to emulate and rival. Susanna Moodie and Catharine Parr Traill were already published authors in England when they settled in an unincorporated area of Upper Canada. John Arthur Phillips had already been a journalist in New York when he came to Montreal in 1870. Thanks to such circumstances, Canadian (short) fiction appears to emerge whole, like the fully armed Athena from her father's forehead.

Some of the first fictions published in Canada are perhaps excessively sentimental and some hark back to earlier developments. However, this was true in many other countries: Romanticism in fiction was everywhere at its peak in the 1820s and 18th-century models were still being followed. By the mid-century, Canadian short stories were moving towards realism, even sometimes fact-based realism, and, later, were borrowing the structure of the well-wrought tale and even developing new literary forms. That is why the Canadian literary-historical concept of "Early Canadian Literature" (which refers to all literature from beginnings to the end of World War I) seems largely inappropriate in the case of short stories, which clearly exhibit (as this anthology will hopefully prove) the features of a "modern" literature. Short stories, especially as they have been practised since the beginning of the 19th century, are precisely a modern genre; and, in the case of Canadian literature, they are manifestly a departure from the actual "early" period, with its own—nonfictional—genres, such as accounts of explorers, travellers, traders, hunters, soldiers, missionaries; guidebooks on emigration and farming; general descriptions of a province, etc. After a few decades of practising fact-based realism and recording the hardships and the pleasures of Canadian country life, short-story writers soon (much sooner than poets or novelists) discovered that they had entered a new era. One has to look only at "A Dark Conspiracy," a story from 1867 (halfway through the eight decades of fiction covered here) to notice how authors themselves were suddenly concerned with capturing the fleeting nature of modernity.

The risk of such an anthology is to obscure some obvious differences and to give the impression that the place occupied in the literary history of 19th-century Canada by each of the authors selected here is somewhat the same; its advantage, on the other hand, is that it shows that none of these authors was alone in their undertakings. With E.W. Thomson's "The Privilege of the Limits," we are going back to Thomas McCulloch and Haliburton: Thomson's McTavish is like McCulloch's Gosling if he had some of Sam Slick's astuteness. Edith Eaton's "Story of Iso" can easily be seen as a response to Catharine Parr Traill's "Autobiography of an Unlucky Wit." Lucy Maud Montgomery's two stories are so thematically similar that they could provide the object of a stimulating study of differences.

Most importantly, perhaps, this anthology is the most inclusive ever published: 35 stories (18 by women, 17 by men), written by 29 authors (15 men, 14 women). Some of the stories have never been reprinted since the 19th century. Among the predecessors of the present anthology, *A Book of Canadian Stories* (Ed. Desmond Pacey. Toronto: Ryerson Press, 1947) includes seven 19th-century stories; *Nineteenth Century Canadian Stories* (Ed. David Arnason. Toronto: Macmillan, 1976) includes fifteen stories; the two volumes of *Short Stories by Canadian Women* edited by Lorraine McMullen, Sandra Campbell in 1993 (Ottawa: University of Ottawa Press) together include thirty stories; finally, *Early Canadian Short Stories: Short Stories in English before World War I* (Ed. Misao Dean. Ottawa: Tecumseh, 2000) includes nine stories from the 19th century.

Henry M. Wallace

Works cited

Brodie, Allan Douglas Brodie. "Canadian Short-Story Writers." *The Canadian Magazine of Politics, Science, Art and Literature* 4: 4 (February 1895), 334-344.

Cooper, John A. "Editorial Comment." *The Canadian Magazine* 12: 3 (January 1899), 278-280.

Gerson, Carole. *A Purer Taste: The Writing and Reading of Fiction in English in Nineteenth-Century Canada.* Toronto: University of Toronto Press, 1989.

MacDonald, Mary Lu. *Literature and Society in the Canadas 1817-1850.* Lewiston: Edwin Mellen, 1992.

McMullen, John Mercier. *The History of Canada.* Brockville: McMullen, 1868.

March-Russell, Paul. *The Short Story: An Introduction.* Edinburgh: Edinburgh UP, 2009.

Rieley, Honor. "'Every Heart North of the Tweed.' Placing Canadian Magazines of the 1820s and 1830s." *Studies in Canadian Literature/Etudes en littérature canadienne* 42: 1 (2017), 130-153.

Spedon, Andrew Learmont. "Preliminary." *Canadian Summer Evening Tales.* Montreal: John Lovell, 1866. 5-9.

CHRONOLOGY OF EVENTS

1801

David Thompson attempts (and fails) to cross the Rocky Mountains ~ The first of about 10,000 Scottish immigrants (-1815) arrive ~ Aqueducts for Montreal opened ~ Founding of St Thomas, Upper Canada ~ Alexander Mackenzie's journal of *Voyages* is published ~ Royal Institution in Lower Canada

1802

King's College in Windsor (NS) receives a royal charter ~ Catholic Scots from the Hebrides start settling in Cape Breton ~ Legislation passed authorizing fines and prison sentences for striking employees~ Treaty of Amiens (temporary end of hostilities between UK and France)

1803

British parliament passes the Canada Jurisdiction Act to regulate conflicts between HBC and NWC ~ William Osgoode, chief justice of Upper Canada, declares slavery inconsistent with the laws of the dominion ~ Parliament passes legislation regulating transatlantic passage ~ Highlanders settle PEI

1804

XY Company absorbed by NWC ~ York has a population of 435 ~ Montreal's first theatre opened by Ormsby, a Scottish actor ~ Elisabeth Francis Hale paints *York on Lake Ontario, Upper Canada*

1805

First issue of *Quebec Mercury* (-1903), a weekly founded by Thomas Cary ~ Thomas Dunn administrator in Lower Canada ~ Founding of Chatham, NB

1806

Simon Fraser and John Stuart begin a journey west of the Rockies; Fraser names the region New Caledonia ~ William Cottnam Tonge expelled from the NS Assembly ~ Baltic trade closed by Napoleonic wars; new timber laws in Britain ~ Founding of Waterloo, Upper Canada ~ President Jefferson prohibits trade out of American ports; this will favour exports from the Maritimes ~ Henry Alline's journals are published posthumously

1807

Jewish merchant Ezekiel Hart is elected to the Parliament of Lower Canada but is expelled because of his religion ~ David Thompson crosses the Rockies with his family and names the Kootenai River; he discovers the Columbia River ~ Joseph Willcocks begins publishing the *Upper Canada Guardian* in Niagara-on-the-Lake ~ *The Royal Gazette and Newfoundland Advertiser* begins publication ~ James Craig governor in Lower Canada ~ John Rodgers Jewitt publishes *A Journal Kept at Nootka Sound* ~ George Heriot publishes *Travels through Canada*

1808

Simon Fraser begins exploring the river that now bears his name and descends it to the Pacific ~ A stagecoach between Montreal and Kingston begins operations ~ George Prevost lieutenant-governor in Nova Scotia ~ Thomas McCulloch publishes *Popery Condemned by Scripture and the Fathers*

1809

The Labrador Act reannexes Labrador to Newfoundland ~ The paddleboat *Accommodation* has its maiden voyage between Montreal and Quebec City ~ Reelected, Ezekiel Hart is expelled a second time ~ Drury Lane Theatre opens in Saint John, NB ~ Alexander Henry publishes *Travels and Adventures in Canada*

1810

The *Kingston Gazette* begins publication ~ The *Acachan*, the first Canadian steamboat, travels from Montreal to Quebec City ~ Proposal to unite the Canadas ~ Founding of Prescott, Upper Canada

1811

David Thomson travels down the Columbia River and claims the adjacent territory for Britain ~ Lord Selkirk buys 300,000 km^2 from HBC (for 10 shillings) in order to start the Red River colony (or Assiniboia); the first shipment of Selkirk colonists sails from Scotland and arrives in Canada ~ Johan Schiller plants the first Canadian vineyard ~ The *New Brunswick Courier* is founded by Henry Chubb in Saint John ~ Fur trade war begins in the west ~ Prevost governor in Lower Canada ~ Brock administrator of Upper Canada

1812

The Parliament of Upper Canada legislates on raising volunteers; the population of Upper Canada is 75,000 ~ Letters of British spy John Henry are read in the US Congress ~ US President James Madison asks Congress for a declaration of war; Congress declares war on Britain aiming to "liberate" Canada ~ American troops from Detroit invade Canada; Canadian troops invade Michigan; Huron living in the area ally with the British ~ Tecumseh, a Shawnee chief, attacks American troops; he is joined by General Isaac Brock and together besiege and capture Detroit ~ The Selkirk colonists arrive in the Red River colony and establish Fort Douglas (Winnipeg) ~ American troops cross the Niagara River but are defeated and pushed back by Brock in the Battle of Queenston Heights; Brock is killed by a sniper ~ American generals Dearborn and Pike invade Lower Canada but are defeated and driven back by Salaberry ~ Fort Astoria sold to the NWC ~ Cunard and Son founded ~ Legislatures in New England condemn the war; both New England and the Maritimes remain largely neutral during the War of 1812

1813

Tecumseh and General Proctor defeat the Americans at Frenchtown, Ohio ~ American troops capture York; the commanding general, Zebulon Pike, is killed when the retreating British blow up Fort York ~ Americans under General Jacob Brown win the battle of Sackets Harbour on Lake Ontario ~ British and First Nations troops win the Battle of Stoney Creek and capture two American generals ~ 570 American soldiers cross the Niagara River, but Laura Secord warns the Mohawk and British troops; they repel the enemy and 462 Americans soldiers are captured ~ US General Harrison forces the British to evacuate Detroit; Harrison enters Upper Canada and defeats Proctor at Moraviantown, where Tecumseh is killed ~ Against overwhelming odds, Salaberry defeats a new US force at Chateauguay ~ USS *Cheasapeake* in Halifax Harbour ~ A new British victory at Crysler's Farm forces the Americans to abandon their campaign in Lower Canada ~ John Murray sacks Buffalo and other cities in New York State ~ James McGill dies and leaves an endowment for the establishment of a college ~ Founding of Hamilton ~ Battle of Lake Erie

1814

The Pemmican Proclamation by Assiniboia governor Miles Macdonnell prohibits the exports of provisions of any kind; Macdonnell confiscates pemmican from the Metis ~ US General Wilkinson enters Lower Canada but is defeated in the Battle of Lacolle and retreats to Plattsburgh ~ US General Brown captures Fort Erie and defeats the British at Chippewa, but a new encounter at Lundy's Lane (one of the bloodiest of the War of 1812) is undecisive ~ Negotiations to end the war begin in Ghent (Belgium) ~ British troops land in Chesapeake Bay and march on Washington, where they burn the Capitol and the White House ~ Close to 2,000 freed slaves are carried by British warships to Canada (mostly around Halifax) ~ The Treaty of Ghent is signed and status quo ante is restored

1815

Métis led by Cuthbert Grant attack and burn the Red River settlement, whose colonists disperse; the settlement is restored four months later ~ Street lamps fueled by whale oil (the first in Canada) are installed on St Paul Street, Montreal by private citizens ~ Schemes to assist emigration for soldiers and sailors are set up ~ Newfoundland fishery begins to stagnate; sealing increases in importance ~ New Corn Law protects colonial production ~ Gordon Drummond administrator of Lower Canada ~ Founding of Drummondville ~ Assembly of Lower Canada provides for public vaccination against smallpox; the public remains distrustful ~ Some 800 Highlanders settle in Glengarry County, Upper Canada ~ Government helps several thousand Scots to settle in the Lanark area of Upper Canada ~ Newfoundland has a population of c.40,000 ~ William Smith publishes *History of Canada* ~ Thomas Cowdell publishes *A Poetical Account of the American Campaigns of 1812 and 1813*

1816

St. John's, Newfoundland, is destroyed by fire ~ The *General Smyth*, the first steamboat in the Maritimes, begins operating between Saint John and Fredericton ~ The *Frontenac* is the first steamboat on the Great Lakes ~ The Métis led by Cuthbert Grant defeat the Red River colonists in the Battle of Seven Oakes; the settlement is again evacuated ~ Lord Selkirk retaliates by seizing Fort William (Thunder Bay) from NWC with his mercenaries (turning point in the war between the two companies) ~ A Commission of Enquiry is formed to mediate between Selkirk, the HBC and the NWC ~ In London, Selkirk publishes *A Sketch of the British Fur Trade in North America* ~ Settlement of Lanark County begins ~ Sherbrooke governor of Lower Canada ~ Founding of Perth, Upper Canada ~ Ann Cuthbert Rae publishes *A Year in Canada and Other Poems*

1817

The Bank of Montreal (the oldest Canadian bank) is incorporated ~ Construction of the Lachine Canal begins ~ Rush-Bagot agreement ~ Harsh winter; Maria Louisa Beleau case ~ Founding of Galt, Upper Canada ~ Gourlay affair (-1819) ~ Founding of the Society for the Relief of Strangers in York (name changed to "Relief of the Sick and Destitute" in 1828), the first major public-welfare agency ~ Walter Bates publishes *The Mysterious Stranger*

1818

John Ross leaves London in search of the North-West Passage; he stops in Lancaster Sound when he thinks to have found mountains blocking his way ~ The Buchan-Franklin Arctic expedition ~ Epidemics of smallpox, measles, and whooping cough among First Nations (-1821) ~ Dalhousie University is established in Halifax ~ Convention of 1818 to fix boundary between BNA and US; the two powers agree on a joint occupancy of Pacific coast between Alaska (Russian) and California (Spanish) ~ Night watchmen introduced in Montreal ~ Founding of Peterborough, Upper Canada

1819

Parry sails towards Lancaster Sound to verify Ross's 1818 claim; his is the first expedition to spend winter with ships locked by ice on purpose, as well as the first expedition to use canned food ~ John Franklin leaves England to explore and chart the north coast of Canada and find the northwest passage ~ Selkirk settlers return to their homes in the Red River Colony ~ Gourlay is banished and leaves Upper Canada ~ *Albion* emigrants arrive in NB ~ First steam crossing of the Atlantic ~ Thomas McCulloch publishes *The Nature and Uses of a Liberal Education* ~ John Strachan founds the *Christian Examiner* (-1820)

1820

Construction of Dalhousie University begins ~ Cape Breton Island (a separate colony since 1784) is reunited with Nova Scotia ~ Lord Selkirk dies ~ Dalhousie governor ~ York has a population of 1,200 ~ W.L. Mackenzie arrives from Scotland ~ John Strachan publishes (under his brother's name) *A Visit to the Province of Upper Canada* in Aberdeen ~ Daniel Williams Harmon publishes *A Journal of Voyages and Travels in the interior of North America* ~ Ariel Bowman publishes *Hours of Childhood and Other Poems* ~ Charles Stuart publishes *The Emigrant's Guide to Upper Canada; or, Sketches of the Present State of that Province*

1821

NWC and HBC are merged; George Simpson placed in charge of North American operations; Montreal ceases to be the centre of the fur trade ~ The University of McGill College receives its royal charter ~ Construction of the Lachine Canal begins (-1825) ~ The Franklin expedition begins charting the Canadian coastline ~ Bank of Upper Canada chartered ~ Samuel Hull Wilcocke (as Lewis Luke MacCulloh) begins publishing *The Scribbler* (-1825) ~ *The Enquirer* is founded in Quebec (-1822)

Thomas McCulloch. "The Stepsure Letters" begin in *Acadian Recorder* 9: 51 (22 December 1821), 2.

1822

The St. Lawrence Steamboat Company is created ~ Americans have moved into Gulf of St Lawrence fishery ~ The Canada Trade Act ~ The *Literary Miscellany* is founded in Montreal (-1823) ~ Wilcocke writes *The Free Press* in Montreal (-1823; with an extra issue in 1824)

Thomas McCulloch. "The Stepsure Letters" run in the *Acadian Recorder* until May.

1823

James Monroe announces the Monroe Doctrine ~ Construction of the Quebec City fortifications begins (-1832) ~ Assisted Irish settlement begins in Upper Canada ~ The "Family Compact" (the elite of men ruling Upper Canada) gets its name (from Thomas Dalton, in the *Kingston Patriot*) ~ 49th parallel surveyed at Pembina ~ John Beverley Robinson submits plan for a Canadian confederacy to the Colonial Office ~ Public vaccination against smallpox in Lower Canada is ended due to lack of interest on the part of the populace ~ Newfoundland School Society founded ~ John Franklin publishes *Journey to the Polar Sea* ~ Thomas Chandler Haliburton publishes *A General Description of Nova Scotia* ~ George Nelson writes his memoir (published in 1988 as *"The Order of the Dreamed": George Nelson on Cree and Northern Ojibwa Religion and Myth*) ~ *Canadian Magazine and Literary Repository* is founded by David Chisholme (-1825)

Thomas McCulloch. "The Stepsure Letters." *Acadian Recorder* (the second run, January-March 1823).

1824

Parry begins a new expedition in search of the Northwest Passage through Lancaster Sound ~ William Lyon Mackenzie founds *The Colonial Advocate* ~ The Canada Company, proposed by John Galt, is incorporated ~ The parliament building of Upper Canada is destroyed by fire ~ Fort Vancouver established ~ New Brunswick has a population of c.75,000 ~ The Literary and Historical Society of Quebec holds its first meeting ~ Peter Fisher publishes *Sketches of New Brunswick* ~ Julia Catherine Beckwith Hart publishes *St Ursula's Convent; or The Nun of Canada*, the first Canadian novel ~ George Longmore publishes *The Charivari* ~ *Canadian Review and Literary and Historical Journal* is founded by H.H. Cunningham (- 1826; called *Canadian Review and Magazine* at the end of its run)

John Howard Willis. "Moonlight." *Canadian Review* 1:1 (July 1824), 93-103.
John Howard Willis. "The Fairy Harp." *Canadian Review* (December), 111-112, 342-345.
John Howard Willis. "Recollections of My Youth. No. I: The Haunted House." *Canadian Review* (December), 372-376.
Anonymous. "Narrative of an Escape from Drowning." *Canadian Magazine and Literary Repository* 3: 15 (September), 207-211.

1825

Second Franklin expedition to the Arctic begins ~ The Theatre Royal Company founded in Montreal; Montreal has 22,000 inhabitants ~ Forest fire destroys the Miramichi Valley; 15,000 left homeless ~ Robert Wilmot-Horton ~ Lachine Canal opens ~ 2,000 Irish immigrants are helped by the government to settle in the Peterborough area of Upper Canada ~ John Strachan attacks the

Methodists ~ Julia Catherine Beckwith Hart publishes *Tonnewonte, or the adopted son of America* ~ Oliver Goldsmith publishes *The Rising Village*

Levi Adams. "The Young Lieutenant." *Canadian Magazine and Literary Repository* 4: 24 (June 1825). 495-500.
Levi Adams. "The Wedding." *Canadian Magazine and Literary Repository* 4: 24 (June 1825). 523-524.
Anonymous. "The Matrimonial Dispute. A Tale." *Canadian Review* 2: 3 March).
John Howard Willis. "A Concert." *Canadian Review* 2: 3 (March), 202-204.
John Howard Willis. "The Faithful Heart." *Canadian Magazine and Literary Repository* 4: 23 (May). 416-418.

1826

The first paid police force in Canada is founded in Saint John, NB ~ George Simpson, governor of Northern Department of Rupert's Land, also becomes governor of the Southern Department (-1860) ~ Colonel John By arrives in Canada to build the Rideau Canal; founding of Bytown (Ottawa) ~ The Type Riot: 15 Tories disguised as First Nations vandalize the offices of Mackenzie's *Colonial Advocate* ~ Peter McGregor founds the city of London, Ontario ~ Hearings of Parliamentary Emigration Committee ~ Huron Tract (500,000 ha) granted to the Canada Company; the company receives, for a nominal price, another 500,000 ha elsewhere in the province ~ Egerton Ryerson replies to John Strachan ~ Catherine Parr Traill publishes *The Young Emigrants; or Pictures in Canada* ~ *The Acadian Magazine* is founded in Halifax (-1828)

Thomas McCulloch. *William and Melville* (Edinburgh: Oliphant).
R.S. "Nathaniel Smith." *Acadian Magazine* 1: 2 (August 1826), 53-55.

1827

John Strachan obtains a royal charter or an Anglican university (King's College, later U of Toronto) ~ John Galt founds the city of Guelph, Ontario ~ Joseph Howe buys *The Novascotian* ~ Thomas McCulloch founds the *Colonial Patriot* in Pictou ~ Naturalization Bill passed in Upper Canada ~ Fort Langley established near the mouth of the Fraser River ~ PEI has a population of 27,000 ~ *The Christian Sentinel* is founded in Montreal (-1829) ~ Thomas Johnston publishes *Travels through Lower Canada*

Anonymous. "Tales of a Winter Alongshore." *Acadian Magazine* 1: 7 (January 1827), 249-256

1828

Development begins on Huron Tract in Upper Canada ~ Corn Act of 1828 allows colonial advantage outside Europe ~ W.L. Mackenzie is elected to the Upper Canada assembly ~ Joseph Howe begins publishing his "Western Rambles" in the *Novascotian* ~ John Richardson publishes the poem *Tecumseh, or the Warrior of the West* ~ *The Weekly Observer* is founded in Saint John, NB ~ *The Canadian Miscellany* is published in Montreal

1829

King's College (University of New Brunswick) opens in Fredericton ~ First settlers arrive for the first commune in Canada (the "Toon O'Maxwell" in

Lambton County, Ontario) ~ Nancy Shawnawdithit, the last of the Beothuks, dies ~ McGill University opens ~ The Welland Canal is finished and the first vessels sail from Lake Ontario to Lake Erie ~ Black settlement established at Wilberforce, Upper Canada ~ Joseph Lancaster in Lower Canada; opens a school in Montreal ~ Joseph Howe publishes "Eastern Rambles" in the *Novascotian* ~ John Richardson publishes *Écarté; or The Salons of Paris*

1830

Upper Canada College (York) opens its doors ~ The Canadian Grand Orange Lodge is founded in Brockville, Upper Canada (90 lodges with 8,000 members by 1833) ~ Contentious boundary between New Brunswick/Lower Canada and Maine submitted to arbitration Founding of Brantford, Upper Canada ~ Kingston Penitentiary completed ~ The Methodist Press (and Methodist Book Room) established ~ Thomas Chandler Haliburton publishes *An Historical and Statistical Account of Nova Scotia* ~ John Galt publishes *Lawrie Todd* ~ Edward Lane publishes *The Fugitives; or, A Trip to Canada* ~ Adam Kidd publishes the poem *The Huron Chief* ~ W.L. Mackenzie publishes *Catechism of Education* ~ First art exhibit in Halifax ~ *The Halifax Monthly Magazine* is founded (-1833)

S. "Saint Monday. A Tale." *The Halifax Monthly Magazine* 1: 3 (August 1830), 105-114.

1831

James Clark Ross locates the North Magnetic Pole at Cape Adelaide ~ The first copyright law is debated in the Parliament of Lower Canada ~ A mob enters the Assembly of Upper Canada demanding that Parliament be dissolved ~ Election riot in PEI ~ New Brunswick Land Company founded ~ Osgoode Hall built in Toronto ~ Around 50,000 Irish immigrants arrive in Canada ~ Alexis de Tocqueville visits Lower Canada ~ Fort Simpson founded on the border with Alaska ~ John Galt publishes *Bogle Corbet* ~ *Canadian Casket* founded (-1832)

John Howard Willis. *Scraps and Sketches; or, The Album of a Literary Lounger* (Montreal, H. H. Cunningham).

Susanna Moodie. "My Aunt Dorothy's Legacy. A Tale of the Christmas Hearth." *The Comic Offering* 2, 1832 [1831], 118-128.

U. V. W. "The Reward of Envy." *Canadian Casket* 1: 2 (29 October), 9-10; and 1: 3 (12 November), 17-18.

1832

Quarantine Act in Lower Canada, establishing a quarantine station on Grosse Isle ~ Typhoid and cholera (brought by two ships, *Voyageur* and *Carrick*) kill 3,800 in Quebec City and 4,000 in Montreal ~ The Rideau Canal opens between Kingston and Bytown ~ Susanna Moodie arrives in Canada ~ W.L. Mackenzie presents grievances to Lord Goderich ~ John Lewellin publishes pamphlet on emigration to PEI ~ Petworth Emigration Committee established ~ York police force founded ~ Election "massacre" in Montreal ~ Bank of Nova Scotia founded ~ *The Montreal Museum, or Journal of Literature and Arts* is founded (-1833) ~ *The Canadian Garland* (later, *The Garland*) is founded in Hamilton (-1833) ~ John Richardson publishes *Wacousta* ~ William "Tiger" Dunlop publishes *Statistical Sketches of Upper Canada*

Charles Durand. "The Romantic Lovers." *Canadian Garland* 1: 3 (13 October), 17-18.

Charles Durand. "Jane Somers. A True Picture." *Canadian Casket* 1: 14 (2 June), 105-107.

C. S. "Viola. A Tale of Patriotism." *Canadian Casket* 1: 15 (16 June), 113-115.

1833

The *Royal William* is the first Canadian steamer to cross the Atlantic, from Pictou to Gravesend ~ British Parliament abolishes slavery in the colonies (with effect on 1 August 1834) ~ The Welland Canal is finished ~ *The Montreal Daily Advertiser*, Canada's first daily newspaper, is founded ~ Cholera epidemic in Lower Canada ~ Work on Chambly Canal begins ~ James Russell publishes *Matilda, or The Indian's Captive* ~ First art exhibit in Toronto ~ *The Canadian Magazine* is founded in York by William Sibbald ~ *The Canadian Literary Magazine* is founded in York by John Kent ~ *Carbonear Star and Conception Bay Journal* founded in Newfoundland (-1840; called *The Star and Conception Bay Journal* after 1834) ~ *Saturday Evening Magazine* is founded in Montreal (-1834)

Susanna Moodie. "The Sailor's Return. A Village Tale." *Canadian Literary Magazine* 1: 3 (October), 148-154.

Susana Moodie. "The Miser." *Lady's Magazine and Museum* 1: 2, 247-257.

Cinna. "A True Story." *Canadian Magazine* 1: 4 (April), 356-361.

John Howard Willis. "An Indian Warrior's Avowal of Love [Fragment]." *Montreal Museum* 1: 3 (February), 165-168.

Diana H. Bayley. "The Young Soldier." *Montreal Museum* 1: 4 (March), 201-211.

Diana H. Bayley. "The Recruit." *Montreal Museum* 1: 6 (May), 353-358.

Diana H. Bayley. "Enthusiasm; or Female Friendship." *Montreal Museum* 1: 8 (July), 488-497.

E. "Isabel Douglas; or, A Sketch from Real Life." *Montreal Museum* 1: 11 (October), 696-698.

1834

Chateau St. Louis in Quebec City is destroyed by fire ~ The building of the Parliament of Upper Canada in Toronto is destroyed by fire ~ The "92 Resolutions" are adopted by the Assembly of Lower Canada, demanding responsible government ~ York is renamed Toronto; it has over 9,000 inhabitants; W.L. Mackenzie is elected mayor ~ Journalist Francis Collins dies of cholera after visiting Irish patients ~ British American Land Company chartered ~ Reformers gain control of the assembly in Upper Canada

1835

Joseph Howe is tried for criminal libel because of an editorial against the magistrates of Halifax; he defends himself and is acquitted ~ The Kingston Maximum Security Penitentiary opens ~ Shiners (Irish gang) terrorize Bytown ~ PEI establishes a divorce court ~ Council of Assiniboia established ~ A commission headed by W.L. Mackenzie produces the "Seventh report on grievances" ~ *The Morning Courier for the Country* is founded in Montreal (-1841) ~ *The Weekly Mirror* is founded in Halifax (-1837) ~ *The Instructor* is founded in Montreal (-1836) ~ *The Bee* is founded in Pictou, NS (-1838)~ Daniel H. Mayne publishes *Poems and Fragments*

Thomas Chandler Haliburton begins *The Clockmaker* with "The Trotting Horse" in *The Novascotian*.

1836

A meeting of Patriotes urge people of Lower Canada to boycott British products ~ The HBC purchases the Red River Colony from Lord Selkirk ~ The Champlain and St Lawrence Railway, Canada's first passenger railway, opens, linking St Jean on the Richelieu River to La Prairie, opposite Montreal on the south shore of the St Lawrence River ~ Lt-gov Francis Bond Head proposes removing all First Nations peoples on Manitoulin Island ~ First steam vessel on the Pacific coast ~ British Parliament holds enquiry on treatment of aboriginal peoples in the empire ~ World economic crisis ~ William "Tiger" Dunlop founds the Toronto Literary Club ~ Catharine Parr Traill publishes *The Backwoods of Canada*

Susanna Moodie. "The Doctor Distressed." *Lady's Magazine and Museum* 9, 241-243.

1837

Britain rejects Lower Canada's "92 Resolutions" ~ Declaration of Saint-Ours ("Ten Resolutions"): a new meeting of Patriotes decides in favour of smuggling and once again demands responsible government ~ Banks in Lower Canada suspend payment for a year ~ Public meetings are prohibited in Lower Canada ~ Between 4,000 and 6,000 Blackfoot are killed by smallpox in the Upper Missouri area (from Montana to northern Saskatchewan) ~ A committee of patriotes in Lower Canada is formed, led by Papineau; a similar committee is formed in Upper Canada, led by W.L. Mackenzie ~ Mackenzie publishes "The Declaration of the Reformers of Toronto" and then a manifesto draft of a Canadian constitution in *The Constitution* ~ Rebellion in Lower Canada begins with the Assembly of Six Counties, meeting at Saint-Charles of 5,000 delegates led by Dr Wolfred Nelson ~ Near Longueuil, rebels are fired upon by government troops ~ 2,000 soldiers from Upper Canada are sent against the Patriotes in Lower Canada ~ Battle of Saint-Denis: Wolfred Nelson's Patriotes defeat the British troops; a week later, however, Wolfred Nelson is forced to flee ~ The Patriotes under Thomas Storrow Brown are defeated the following day in the Battle of Saint-Charles ~ W.L. Mackenzie's rebel forces begin the rebellion in Upper Canada, but are dispersed near Toronto and Mackenzie flees ~ Dr Charles Duncombe reignites rebellion in Upper Canada, but he, too, is defeated and escapes to the US ~ Mackenzie returns from the US, occupies Navy Island on the Niagara River, and proclaims the "Republic of Canada" ~ The Patriotes led by Jean Olivier Chénier and Amury Girod suffer a bloody defeat at Saint-Eustache ~ Financial crisis caused by the collapse of British and American banks ~ Petworth scheme ends ~ Upper Canada passes Seduction Act ~ George Arthur governor in Toronto ~ Government of Upper Canada establishes "houses of industry" to provide work for all "fit and able inmates" among the poor ~ Robert Davis publishes *The Canadian Farmer's Travels in the United States of America* ~ *The Colonial Herald and Prince Edward Island Advertiser* is founded in Charlottetown (-1844) ~ *The Halifax Pearl* is founded (-1840; called *The Colonial Pearl* after 1838) ~ Anne Langton arrives in Ontario; her journals will be published in 1950 as *A Gentlewoman in Upper Canada*

Thomas Chandler Haliburton. *The Clockmaker; or, The Sayings and Doings of Samuel Slick, of Slickville.* Halifax: Joseph Howe [dated 1836].

John Simpson, Ed. *The Canadian Forget Me Not for MDCCCXXXVII.* Niagara: Thomas Sewell, 1837.

1838

British Parliament suspends the constitution of Lower Canada and appoints Lord Durham as governor-general ~ Canadian patriots and American sympathizers occupy Pelee Island on Lake Erie but are defeated by regulars and militia ~ Lower Canada Patriotes return from exile in Vermont with American sympathizers but are pushed back ~ HBC receives a 21-year extension of its trading monopoly ~ Rebel leaders Samuel Lount and Peter Matthews are publicly hanged in Toronto ~ Lord Durham banishes Wolfred Nelson and 7 other Patriotes to Bermuda and forbids the return of 16 exiled Patriotes ~ *The Toronto Examiner* (with the motto "Responsible Government") is founded ~ A second rebellion in Lower Canada is led by Robert Nelson, who is proclaimed president of the Canadian Republic; the Patriotes are defeated at Odelltown and Nelson flees to the US ~ Upper Canadian and American rebels of the Hunters' Lodge are defeated in the Battle of the Windmill; 11 leaders are hanged; 60 rebels are transported to Australia ~ The rebellion in Lower Canada is similarly defeated in the Battle of Beauharnois; 12 leaders are hanged, 58 rebels transported to Australia ~ The *Saint John Morning News*, the first penny newspaper in Canada ~ William Cooper in London arguing for escheat ~ Jesse Happy case: extradition principles established in Canada ~ *The Literary Garland* is founded (-1851) ~ Anne Jameson publishes *Winter Studies and Summer Rumbles in Canada* ~ *Cabinet of Literature* is founded in Toronto (-1839) ~ *The Literary Transcript and General Intelligencer* is founded in Quebec City (-1839)

Thomas Chandler Haliburton. *The Clockmaker. Second Series*. London: Bentley.

Catharine Parr Traill. "The Mill of the Rapids: A Canadian Sketch." *Chambers's Edinburgh Journal* 7, 322-323.

Catharine Parr Traill. "The Autobiography of an Unlucky Wit." *The Gift: A Christmas and New Year's Present for 1839* (Philadelphia: E. L. Carey & A. Hart, 1838), 220-232.

John Gibson. "The Hermit of Saint Maurice." *Literary Garland* 1: 1 (December 1838), 5-15.

John Howard Willis. "Fragments of an Unpublished Indian Story." *Godey's Lady's Book* 16 (June 1838), 254-260.

1839

Maine is at war with New Brunswick as American volunteers occupy Aroostok; the Aroostok War in the disputed territory of Madawaska ~ Lord Durham submits his *Report on the Affairs of British North America* ~ Cunard Line established; it is awarded a contract to carry mail by steamships between Liverpool and Halifax ~ Public execution of several Patriote leaders ~ A resolution in British Parliament for the union of Lower and Upper Canada ~ The Parliaments of both provinces vote in favour of the union ~ Crown Lands Protection Act in British Parliament ~ Prostitution mentioned in Lower Canadian statute ~ Montreal has a population of 37,000

Joseph Howe. "The Locksmith of Philadelphia." *Bentley's* 5, 272-280.

Eliza Lanesford Cushing. "Deaf Molly." *Lady's Book* 18 (March), 104-107.

Eliza Lanesford Cushing. "A Canadian Legend." *Literary Garland* (March), 167-180.

Eliza Lanesford Cushing. "A Tale of the Richelieu." *Lady's Book* 19 (July-August), 13-19, 73-80.

Eliza Lanesford Cushing. "Grace Morley. A Sketch from Life." *Literary Garland* (August), 405-412.

Susanna Moodie. "The Gold Medal." *Literary Garland* (August), 385-388.

Susanna Moodie. "The Fugitive." *Literary Garland* (November), 566-570.
Moses Henry Perley. "The Camp of the Owl." *The Sporting Review* (September), 198-200.

1840

The Union Act: the two Canadas are united and have a single government and parliament; Upper Canada becomes Canada West; Lower Canada becomes Canada East; Kingston is the first capital of the new province of Canada ~ Benjamin Lett, a member of the Hunters' Lodge, blows up the monument dedicated to Isaac Brock ~ Nova Scotia miners go on strike ~ Carbonear riot in Newfoundland ~ John Richardson publishes *The Canadian Brothers; or, Prophecy Fulfilled* ~ W.A. Stephens publishes *Hamilton and other poems* ~ M.E. Sawtell publishes *The Mourner's Tribute*

Thomas Chandler Haliburton. *Letter-Bag of the Great Western; or, Life in a Steamer*. London: Richard Bentley.
Thomas Chandler Haliburton. *The Clockmaker. Third Series*. London: Bentley.
Moses Henry Perley. "The Forest Fairies of the Milicetes." *The Sporting Review* (March), 191-196.
Moses Henry Perley. "Ottowin and Lola." *The Sporting Review* (June), 427-432.
Moses Henry Perley. "The Stream-Drivers." *The Sporting Review* (August), 100-105.
John Abbott. "Border Legends: Three Gibbets." *Literary Garland* (September), 450-455.

1841

First elections to the united Assembly of Canada ~ The first session of the united Parliament is held in a Kingston hospital ~ A commission surveys the problems of Newfoundland ~ Education Act in the Province of Canada ~ Edward Theller publishes *Canada 1837-8* ~ John Richardson founds the magazine *New Era; or Canadian Chronicle* ~ Joseph Howe sells the *Novascotian* ~ Standish O'Grady publishes "The Emigrant, a Poem in Four Cantos" ~ *The Amaranth* is founded in Saint John, NB (-1843)

Moses Henry Perley. "The Lawyer and the Black Ducks." *The Sporting Review* (January), 25-30.
W. R. N. B[urtis]. "The Storm Spirit of the Milicetes." *The Amaranth* 1: 1 (January), 2-8.
M. W. B. "The Camp Meeting. A Tale of the South." *Literary Garland* (September), 460-470.
W. S. "The Emigrant. A Tale." *Literary Garland* (May), 273-275.
Catharine Parr Traill. "Barbara." *Literary Garland* (December), 21-26.

1842

The Imperial Copyright Act comes into effect ~ Gesner Museum, first public museum in Canada is founded in Saint John (NB) at the Mechanics Institute (today NB Museum) ~ Charles Dickens visits Canada ~ Webster-Ashburton Treaty establishes the boundary between US and Canada ~ Baldwin-Lafontaine is the first Liberal cabinet in Canada ~ Newfoundland gets its first legislature ~ Jean-Baptiste Meilleur takes over educational system in Canada East ~ N.P. Willis publishes *Canadian Scenes* ~ Standish O'Grady publishes *The Emigrant*

M. W. B. "Anne and Clara. A Tale." *Literary Garland* (October), 512-523.

Diana Bayley. "The Father and Daughter." *Literary Garland* (January), 76-77; (February), 122-123; (March), 185-186.
M. S. "Sketch from Real Life." *Literary Garland* (October), 526-529.
Catharine Parr Traill. "St. Margaret's Minster." *Literary Garland* (January), 49-54.
Catharine Parr Traill. "Helen." *Literary Garland* (September), 476-479.

1843

Classes begin at Mount Allison Wesleyan Academy ~ King's College (later, the University of Toronto) opens its doors ~ Troops are sent in to pacify mobs in Miramichi's "fighting election" ~ Fort Victoria is built on Vancouver Island ~ Metcalfe Crisis begins: the Baldwin-Lafontaine ministry resigns in protest over Governor Metcalfe's practice of granting government positions without consulting them (-1844) ~ Canadian School Act ~ Corn Laws and Timber Laws repealed ~ Conservative victory in Nova Scotia ~ Faculty of Arts opens at McGill University ~ John Richardson publishes *The Canadian Loyalist and Spirit of 1812* ~ Robert Fleming Gourlay publishes his autobiography *The Banished Briton and Neptunian* ~ Samuel Douglas Smith Huyghue publishes *Argimou: A Legend of the Micmac* ~ J.K. Liston publishes *Niagara Falls*

Thomas Chandler Haliburton. *The Attaché, or Sam Slick in England*. London: Richard Bentley.
Susanna Moodie. "The Broken Mirror." *Literary Garland* (April), 145-154.
Eliza Lanesford Cushing. "Heart Pond." *Literary Garland* (January), 4-15.
Mrs. [Diana] Bayley. "The Elopement." *Literary Garland* (January), 37-41; (February), 79-83.
Ned Caldwell. "Sam Horton's Last Trip." *Literary Garland* (November), 522-524.

1844

James K. Polk wins the Democratic nomination by calling for the annexation of Oregon (his slogan is "54-40 or Fight") ~ The capital of Canada is moved from Kingston to Montreal ~ Reformers found two newspapers: *The Globe* in Toronto (George Brown) and *The Pilot* in Montreal ~ The *Ottawa Citizen* is founded (as the *Bytown Packet*) ~ Political crisis in New Brunswick ~ Ryerson becomes superintendent of schools for Canada West (-1876) ~ Joseph Howe retakes the position of editor of the *Novascotian*

Thomas Chandler Haliburton. *The Attaché. Second series.* London: Bentley.
Susanna Moodie. "The Miner. A Tale." *Literary Garland* (January), 28-32.
Theoda Davis Foster. "Fortune's Favourite." *Literary Garland* (March), 129-138.
A. E. Lundy. "The Yorkshire Factory Girl." *Literary Garland* (Sep), 398-403.
J. W. Dunbar Moodie. "The Ould Dhragoon; or, A Visit to the Beaver Meadow." *Literary Garland* (August), 360-362.

1845

39 Patriotes are pardoned and return from Australia ~ John Franklin sails on his third Arctic expedition ~ More than two thirds of Quebec City are destroyed in two fires ~ Independent Order of Odd-Fellows brought to BNA ~ Cathcart administrator of Canada ~ F.X. Garneau publishes the first volume of *Histoire du Canada* ~ George Simpson publishes *Narrative of a Journey round the World in 1841 and 1842*

Emily Elizabeth Shaw Beavan. *Sketches and Tales Illustrative of Life in the Backwoods of New Brunswick*. London: Routledge.

Eliza Lanesford Cushing. "Katrina. A Simple Tale." *Literary Garland* (March), 123-135.
Ann Cuthbert Fleming. "The First Ewe." *Literary Garland* (October), 460-462.

1846

Britain announces the adoption of free trade ~ The Oregon Boundary Treaty is signed by President Polk and Queen Victoria establishing the boundary along 49°N latitude ~ Canadian geologist Abraham Gesner announces the discovery of kerosene ~ Last sighting of the Franklin expedition ~ John Richardson publishes the muckraking *The Weekly Expository or Reformer of Public Abuses and Railway and Mining Intelligencer* in Montreal ~ The first telegraph line in Canada is established between Toronto and Hamilton ~ Beginning of the asylum movement ~ Great fire in St John's ~ Reform victory in New Brunswick ~ Common School Act in Canada West ~ Lower Canadian School Act ~ The Theatre Royal opens in Halifax ~ Alexander McLachlan publishes *The Spirit of Love and Other Poems* ~ George Jehoshaphat Mountain publishes *Songs of the Wilderness* ~ The *Constitutionalist* is founded in Charlottetown ~ *The People's Magazine and Weekly Journal* is founded in Montreal (-1847) ~ *Barker's Canadian Monthly Magazine* is founded in Kingston (-1847) ~ Joseph Abbott publishes *Philip Musgrave; or, The Adventures of a Missionary in Canada*

Catharine Parr Traill. "The Bereavement." *Literary Garland* (February), 69-72.
Thomas Chandler Haliburton. *The Old Judge* begins serialization in *Fraser's Magazine* (until 1847).
Eliza Lanesford Cushing. "The Indian Maid." *Literary Garland* (May), 193-205.
Crispin, Junior. "The Deserted." *Literary Garland* (November), 490-492.
E. L. E. "The Sisters. A Tale of Canada." *Literary Garland* (January), 34-40.
E. L. E. "A Sketch from Real Life." *Literary Garland* (September), 421-423.
H[enry]. J[ames]. Friel. "The Misanthrope." *Literary Garland* (August), 343-357.
S. Jones. "An Old Man's Reminiscence." *Literary Garland* (December), 544-545.

1847

Franklin dies ~ 300 die in a hurricane off Newfoundland ~ The first zoo in Canada opens in Halifax ~ 98,000 Irish sail to Canada following the potato famine: 292 die at sea, 8,072 on Grosse Isle, 7,000 of diseases on their way to Montreal or Toronto ~ Telegraph lines are established between Montreal and Toronto, Montreal and Albany, etc. ~ Montreal Gas Company established to provide gas for the city's street lamps ~ Alexander Kennedy Isbister presents a petition against the HBC in the name of the Red River Métis in British Parliament ~ Riot in Woodstock, NB ~ 3,000 Irish immigrants settle in Bytown (Ottawa) ~ Societies of Arts are founded in both Toronto and Montreal ~ John Richardson publishes *Eight Years in Canada* ~ *The Maple Leaf, or Canadian Annual* is founded in Toronto (-1849)

Susanna Moodie. "Brian, the Still Hunter." *Literary Garland* (October), 460-467.
Susanna Moodie. "The Well in the Wilderness." *Victoria Magazine* 1, 54-58.
Susanna Moodie. "The Walk to Dummer." *Literary Garland* (March), 101-109.
Susanna Moodie. "Our Borrowing." *Literary Garland* (May), 197-205.
Susanna Moodie. "Tom Wilson's Emigration." *Literary Garland* (June), 283-286; (July), 293-303.
Susanna Moodie. "Uncle Joe and His Family." *Literary Garland* (August), 363-368; (September), 423-429.
Susanna Moodie. "Old Woodruff and His Three Wives." *Literary Garland* (January), 13-18.

Susanna Moodie. "Scenes in Canada. A Visit to Grosse Isle." *Victoria Magazine* 1, 14, 17.
Susanna Moodie. "A Detected Cheat." *Victoria Magazine* 1, 93.
Mary Anne Sadlier. "A Peep into the Dominions of Pluto." *Literary Garland* (November), 504-506.
W. P. C. "The Tale of a Recluse." *Literary Garland* (December), 559-562.
Theoda Davis Foster. "Aunt Patty's Day at the Sea Shore." *Literary Garland* (January), 41-48.
J. W. Dunbar Moodie. "Groot Vader's Bosch. A South African Sketch, with Verse." *Literary Garland* (February), 93-95.

1848

The first responsible government in Nova Scotia ~ The first responsible government in the Province of Canada ~ Old constitution restored in Newfoundland ~ Baldwin-Lafontaine second ministry ~ Edmunston, NB is founded ~ Vancouver Island a Crown colony ~ John Richardson publishes *The Guards in Canada; or The Point of Honour* ~ James Huston begins publication of *Le Répertoire National* ~ Royal Lyceum Theatre opens in Toronto

Susanna Moodie. "The Quiet Horse." *Victoria Magazine* 1, 265-268.
Mary Anne Sadlier. "The Fortunes of Brian Mulvany and His Wife Oonagh." *Literary Garland* (June), 279-285.
Harriet Vaughan Cheney. "Jacques Cartier and the Little Indian Girl." *Literary Garland* (October), 461-468; (November), 520-527; (December), 561-571.
Ned Caldwell. "A Night among the Thousand Islands." *Literary Garland* (September), 405-409.
Theoda Davis Foster. "A Haytian Day Dream." *Literary Garland* (June), 261-268.
Andrew L. Picken. "The Shark, a Recollection of the West Indies." *Literary Garland* (February), 59-62.

1849

Violence erupts between Orangemen and Catholics in Saint John (NB): 1,000 belligerents, 12 dead ~ The Parliament of Canada prohibits immigration of lunatics, idiots, the deaf and dumb, blind or infirm, who would thereafter be deported if they arrive in Canadian ports ~ Rebellion Losses Bill introduced by Lafontaine; Tories outraged; Governor-General Elgin assents; mass protests in Montreal, where the parliament building is burned down; Toronto declared capital ~ University Bill introduced by Baldwin; higher education becomes secularized ~ Most of Toronto is destroyed by fire ~ Britain repeals the British Navigation Acts; financial panic in Canada ~ Tory convention in Kingston; manifesto in favour of annexation to the US ~ Another "annexation manifesto" is published by the Rouges, French-Canadian liberals; annexation movement strong in NB ~ The term "Clear Grit" is popularized by George Brown of the *Toronto Globe* in reference to hardcore reformers in Canada West ~ Vancouver Island created Crown Colony but managed by HBC; Victoria is the western headquarters of the company ~ Canada legalizes segregation: law allows towns to establish separate schools for Black Canadians ~ Sayer trial opens Red River to trade outside the HBC monopoly ~ Gas lighting in Quebec City ~ King's College becomes the University of Toronto ~ British-American League launched in Kingston ~ The (Royal) Canadian Institute founded in Toronto ~ Cornelius Krieghoff paints *A Winter Landscape* ~ *Sinclair's Journal of British America* is published in Quebec City ~ *The Gaspé Magazine and Instructive Miscellany* is founded in New Carlisle (-1850) ~ Josiah Henson publishes *The Life of Josiah Henson, Formerly a Slave, Now an Inhabitant of Canada*

Thomas Chandler Haliburton. *The Old Judge, or Life in a Colony*. London: Colburn.
Catharine Parr Traill. "The Two Widows of Hunter's Creek." *Home Circle* (21 July 1849), 33-35.
Rosanna Mullins Leprohon [R. E. M.]. "Alice Sydenham's First Ball." *Literary Garland* 7: 1 (January), 1-14.
Harriet Vaughan Cheney. "Captain Hale." *Literary Garland* (October), 561-563.
Ned Caldwell. "Wild Wood Life." *Literary Garland* (January), 40-42, 74-78.

1850

New Caledonia is renamed British Columbia ~ US President Millard Fillmore signs the Fugitive Slave Bill ~ Keefer's *The Philosophy of Railroads* published ~ Clear Grit party founded ~ Samuel Douglas Smith Huyghue publishes *Nomades of the West; or, Ellen Clayton* ~ John Richardson publishes *The Monk Knight of St. John*

John Richardson. "The Sunflower, a True Tale of the North-West." *Graham's American Monthly Magazine* 37 (November), 285-292.
Harriet Vaughan Cheney. "The Emigrants." *Literary Garland* 8: 6 (June), 275-281.
Harriet Vaughan Cheney. "Cousin Emma. A Sketch from Real Life." *Literary Garland* 8: 8 (August), 365-372.
Harriet Vaughan Chaney. "The Condemned." *Literary Garland* (April), 169-178.
Harriet Vaughan Cheney. "Fortune Telling, a True Tale." *Literary Garland* (September), 417-420.
Joseph Abbott. "My Aunt Phoebe's Cottage." *Literary Garland* (October), 466-472; (November), 499-505; (December), 568-577.

1851

The Anti-Slavery Society is formed in Canada ~ Canada's first postage stamp, a 3-penny beaver ~ Battle of Grand Coteau: the Métis of Red River defeat the Sioux ~ The capital of Canada moved from Toronto to Quebec City ~ Great Exhibition in London: Canada shows its mineral wealth ~ Gold discovered in the Cariboo district of BC; gold rush begins ~ PEI gets responsible government ~ Frederick Wilkins (Shadrach Minkins) escapes to Canada ~ James Douglas becomes governor of Vancouver Island ~ The newspaper *The Voice of the Fugitive* founded in Windsor ~ New Brunswick has a population of almost 200,000 ~ Nova Scotia has a population of 275,000 ~ Thomas Chandler Haliburton publishes *The English in America* ~ John Richardson serializes *Westbrook, the Outlaw* ~ *The Mayflower; or, Ladies' Acadian Newspaper* is founded in Halifax (-1852) ~ *The Canadian Family Herald* is founded in Toronto (-1852)

Susanna Moodie. "Michael Macbride." *Literary Garland* (February), 49-55.
Harriet Vaughan Cheney. "A Legend of the Lake." *Literary Garland* (February), 74-79.
Harriet Vaughan Cheney. "The Daughter of the Congregation." *Literary Garland* (October), 460-471.
Robert Hamilton. "The Prophecy." *Literary Garland* (July), 322-328.

1852

First sewing machine in Canada; Toronto tailors go on strike ~ Stonecutters in Kingston go on strike ~ Mary Ann Shadd Cary founds *The Provincial Freeman* in Toronto ~ East side of Montreal destroyed by fire, 10,000 homeless ~ Toronto Stock Exchange established ~ Grand Trunk Railway incorporated ~ *Canadian Journal* (of the Royal Canadian Institute) begins publication ~ Catharine Parr Traill publishes *Canadian Crusoes* ~ *The Anglo-American Magazine* is founded in Toronto (-1855) ~ *The Provincial; or Halifax Monthly Magazine* is founded (-1853) ~ *The Maple Leaf; a Juvenile Monthly Magazine* is founded in Montreal (-1854)

Susanna Moodie. *Roughing It in the Bush; or, Life in Canada.* London: Bentley.
Susanna Moodie. "Jeanie Burns." *Bentley's* 32, 143-152.
Mary Jane Katzmann Lawson. "Tales of Our Village. No. 1." *The Provincial* 1: 2 (February 1852), 67-73; "Tales of Our Village. No. 2." *The Provincial* 1: 3 (March 1852), 109-113; 1: 4 (April 1852), 141-145; "Tales of Our Village. No. 3." *The Provincial* 1: 6 (June 1852), 215-221; "Tales of Our Village. No. 4." 7.5-8 *The Provincial* 1: 9 (September 1852), 352-358; "Tales of Our Village. No. 5." *The Provincial* 1: 11 (November 1852), 431-437; "Tales of Our Village. No. 6." 7 *The Provincial* 1: 12 (December 1852), 466-471.

1853

Bishop's College receives its charter ~ Alessandro Gavazzi, pro-Italian, anti-Catholic speaker in Montreal; riots ~ *Toronto Globe* becomes a daily ~ Land Purchase Act passes in PEI legislature ~ School Act of 1853: separate Catholic school system ~ Samuel Strickland publishes *Twenty-Seven Years in Canada West* ~ Bellini's opera *Norma* presented in Toronto

Susanna Moodie. *Life in the Clearings versus the Bush.* London: Richard Bentley.
Thomas Chandler Haliburton. *Sam Slick's Wise Saws.* London: Hurst and Blackett.
W. C. Chewett. "Tale of a Scrap." *Anglo-American Magazine* 3: 1 (July), 89-94.
W. C. Chewett. "The Thousand Isles." *Anglo-American Magazine* 2: 4 (April), 353-355.
Rhoda Ann Falkner. "An Hour in the Ice." *Maple Leaf* 2: 5 (May), 130-136.
Augustus Jukes. "Christmas Eve." *Anglo-American Magazine* 2: 1 (January), 65-70.
Catharine Parr Traill. "Cousin Kate; or, the Professor Outwitted." *Anglo-American Magazine* (May), 510-514.
Mary Jane Katzmann Lawson. "Tales of Our Village. No. 7." *The Provincial* 2: 4 (April 1853), 128-133; "Tales of Our Village. No. 8." *The Provincial* 2: 8 (June 1853), 211-217, 2: 7 (July 1853), 267-272, 2: 8 (August 1853), 289-304; 2: 9 (September 1853), 346-353; 2: 10 (October 1853), 379-388; 2: 11 (November 1853), 431-438; 2: 12 (December 1853), 459-469.

1854

Cholera kills 1,000 in Saint John (NB) ~ Fire destroys parliament buildings in Quebec City ~ Construction begins on the Victoria Railway Bridge in Montreal ~ The *Arctic* collides with another steamer; 370 dead ~ Abolition of the seigniorial system in Canada East (bill introduced by Lewis Drummond) ~ A Great Western train collides with a freight train at Baptiste Creek, Canada West; 52 dead ~ Liberals and Tories join forces to pass a bill secularizing Clergy Reserves ~ New Brunswick gets responsible government ~ Great Western Railway opens ~ Reciprocity Treaty negotiated between Great Britain and US ~ Catharine Parr Traill publishes *The Female Emigrant's Guide* ~ Susanne Moodie publishes *Flora Lyndsay* ~ Alexander Ross publishes *Fur-Hunters of the Far West* ~ Joseph Antisell Allen publishes *Day Dreams by a Butterfly*

Thomas Chandler Haliburton. *The Americans at Home; or, Byways, Backwoods, and Prairies.* London: Hurst and Blackett.

1855

Bytown is renamed Ottawa ~ The Niagara Suspension Bridge is opened ~ Reopening of trade between Canada East and France ~ Toronto becomes the new capital of Canada ~ Parliament abolishes postage on newspapers published in Canada ~ Newfoundland gets responsible government ~ Newfoundland

ratifies reciprocity with US ~ Responsible government in Newfoundland and PEI ~ PEI has a population of 72,000 ~ Susanna Moodie publishes *Geoffrey Moncton* ~ John Mercier McCullen publishes *The History of Canada* ~ Paul Kane publishes *Wanderings of an Artist*

Thomas Chandler Haliburton. *Nature and Human Nature*. London: Hurst and Blackett.

Clotilda Jennings [Maude]. "The White Rose in Acadia." *The White Rose in Acadia, and Autumn in Nova Scotia*. Prize Tale and Poem. (Halifax, James Bowes and Sons, 1855), 6-30.

1856

Canadian Lt. Alexander Roberts Dunn wins the Victoria Cross for gallantry in the Charge of the Light Brigade ~ The first passenger train travels from Montreal to Toronto ~ The second Brock Monument is built ~ Vancouver Island gets assembly ~ John A. Macdonald becomes leader of conservatives ~ Cartier introduces bill on centralized legal system ~ Legislative council of the Province of Canada is made elective ~ Alexander Ross publishes *The Red River Settlement* ~ Charles Sangster publishes *The St. Lawrence and the Saguenay and other poems* ~ Caroli Candidus publishes the play *The Female Consistory of Brockville* ~ *The Montreal Literary Magazine* (ed. John Reade) is published

1857

British House of Commons appoints committee to investigate HBC monopoly in the west ~ Steam engine *Oxford* derails in Canada West, over the Desjardins Canal near Hamilton; 59 dead ~ John Palliser is appointed by the British government to ascertain the feasibility of a transcontinental railway and to analyse the quality of the soil in western Canada ~ Canadian government hires Henry Youle Hind on a similar mission ~ The *Montreal* sinks near Quebec City; 157 dead ~ Macdonald-Cartier ministry ~ First commercial oil well in North America is dug at Oil Springs, Ontario ~ George Brown becomes leader of liberals in Canada West ~ Province of Canada begins recruiting immigrants in southern Germany ~ Survey of 49th parallel begins in Rocky Mountains ~ Opening of normal schools in Canada East ~ Tupper comes to power in NS ~ Newfoundland rejects Anglo-French fisheries treaty ~ Grit convention in Toronto ~ Ottawa chosen as permanent capital ~ Gold discovered on Pacific mainland ~ Nova Scotia becomes the only colony to allow legal divorce on grounds of cruelty ~ Robert Michael Ballantyne publishes *Ungava; a Tale of Esquimaux-land* ~ Charles Heavysege's *Saul: a drama in three parts* is performed in Montreal

May Agnes Fleming. "The Lady's Choice." *The Western Recorder and Carleton Advertiser and Home Journal* (Saint John, NB), 28 November, 1.

1858

The dollar becomes the official currency of the Province of Canada; first Canadian coins are minted (1 cent, 5 cents, 10 cents, 20 cents) ~ Fraser gold rush begins; 31,000 gold seekers invade BC ~ Alexander Tilloch Galt proposes the union of all British North America; he joins the Macdonald-Cartier ministry on condition that the union become part of the Tory platform ~ First underwater telegraph cable between Newfoundland and Ireland ~ New Caledonia (later, BC) is created a crown colony ~ Imprisonment for debt abolished ~ British Colonial secretary rejects Cartier's proposed union ~ Amor De Cosmos founds *The British Colonist* in Victoria (today, *Times Colonist*) ~ James Douglas becomes the first governor of British Columbia (-1864), while continuing as governor of Vancouver Island ~ Chinese immigrants arrive in BC ~ Mount Allison University allows women to attend classes ~ Mainland British Columbia becomes a separate crown colony ~ Robert Traill Spence Lowell publishes *The New Priest in Conception Bay* ~ Thomas D'Arcy McGee publishes *Canadian Ballads and Occasional Verses* ~ *The Grumbler* is founded in Toronto (-1869)

James McGrigor Allan. *Grins and Wrinkles*. London: James Blackwood.
Rev. R[obert] J[ackson] Macgeorge. *Tales, Sketches and Lyrics*. Toronto: A.H. Armour & Co.

1859

King's College (Fredericton) is established as the University of New Brunswick ~ MLA John Sheridan Hogan is assassinated ~ Ottawa official capital; construction of the Parliament building begins ~ Queensborough (renamed New Westminster) becomes capital of BC ~ Maurice Blondin, famous tightrope walker, crosses the Niagara Falls ~ William Hall, a black Nova-Scotian sailor, is awarded the Victoria Cross for bravery at the Siege of Lucknow ~ Americans occupy San Juan Island (today part of Washington State) ~ First steamship, first newspaper and first regular postal service arrive in Red River; the West's first newspaper, *The Nor'-Wester* (-1869) ~ Paul Kane publishes *Wanderings of an Artist among the Indian Tribes of North America* ~ William Kirby publishes "The U.E.: A Tale of Upper Canada" ~ Rosanna Leprohon serializes *The Manor House of De Villerai* ~ Augusta Baldwyn publishes *Poems*

Ellen Kyle Noel. *The Abbey of Rathmore and Other Tales*. Kingston: Creighton.
May Agnes Fleming. "Little Lilly." *The Western Recorder and Carleton Advertiser and Home Journal*, 21 May, 1-2.
May Agnes Fleming. "Nora; or, Love and Money." *Sunday Mercury* (New York), 26 June, 3.

1860

The *Hungarian* is wrecked off Cape Sable; 205 dead ~ The first oil gusher at Enniskillen, Ontario ~ The San Juan Islands (between Vancouver Island and the mainland) are occupied by both British and American marines (-1873) ~ Edward, Prince of Wales, tours Canada; in Montreal, he attends the official opening of the Victoria Bridge (26 people had died during its construction) ~ Joseph Howe becomes prime-minister of Nova Scotia ~ The *Lady Elgin* sinks in Lake Michigan; over 300 dead ~ Horse-drawn tramcars are introduced in Montreal ~ PEI Land Commission; free grants are recommended for those who could prove their Loyalist ancestors had been promised land ~ The extradition case of fugitive slave John Anderson is heard in Canada ~ University of New Brunswick in Fredericton (it had been a college under the control of the Church of England) ~ About 4,000 gold miners set off for the Cariboo regions in BC ~ Henry Youle Hind publishes *Narrative of the Red River Exploring Expedition of 1857 and of the Assiniboine and Saskatchewan Exploring Expeditions of 1858* ~ Cornelius Krieghoff paints *Merrymaking* ~ Charles Sangster publishes *Hesperus and other poems and lyrics*

Thomas Chandler Haliburton. *The Season Ticket*. London: Richard Bentley.
Susanna Moodie. "Our Lady's Well." *Family Herald* (15 February), 109-110.
Susanna Moodie. "The Wraith." *Family Herald* (22 February), 117-118; (21 March), 149-150.

1861

A resolution proposing the union of British North America is adopted by Joseph Howe and sent to all governors ~ Horse-drawn trams in Toronto ~ The Trent Affair: an American man-of-war arrests two Confederate agents on board a British steamer ~ Britain sends 14,000 troops to Canada ~ John Jessop introduces Canadian-style education in BC ~ Commission on the land question in PEI ~ Alexander McLachlan publishes *The Emigrant and other poems* ~ Peter Jones's posthumous *History of the Ojibway Indians* is published

Andrew Learmont Spedon. *Tales of the Canadian Forest.* Montreal: John Lovell.

1862

Smallpox epidemic among First Nations people in BC (-1864) ~ "Overlanders" (gold seekers) pouring into Cariboo, BC ~ Delegates from Canada, Nova Scotia and New Brunswick meet in Quebec City and agree on financing a transcontinental ("Intercolonial") railway ~ The Royal Highland Regiment (the "Black Watch") is organized in Montreal ~ A system for issuing passports is set in place, as the US requires identification from all Canadians during the Civil War ~ HBC reorganized ~ Gold strike on Williams Lake ~ Canadians reject imperial militia legislation ~ Thomas McCulloch's *Letters of Mephibosheth Stepsure* (1821-3) are published in book form (dated 1860)

May Agnes Fleming. "Accursed." *Sunday Mercury* (New York), 9 February, 2.
May Agnes Fleming. "For Spite." *Sunday Mercury* (New York), 27 April, 2.

1863

US President Abraham Lincoln signs the Emancipation Proclamation ~ The *Anglo-Saxon* is wrecked off Cape Race, Newfoundland; 237 dead ~ The HBC goes public and the International Financial Society buys controlling interest ~ Palliser's report published in British parliamentary papers; his conclusion is that much of Alberta and Saskatchewan is unfit for agriculture ~ Henry Yule Hind edits *Eighty Years' Progress of North America* ~ Conservative victory in Nova Scotia; Tupper's pro-confederation supporters form cabinet ~ Cariboo Road completed in BC ~ Isadore Gordon Ascher publishes *Voices from the Hearth and other poems* ~ James McCarroll publishes *Letters of Terry Finnegan* ~ *The British-American Magazine* is founded in Toronto (-1864) ~ J.M. LeMoine publishes *Maple Leaves: Canadian History—Literature—Sport* (a new series in 1873)

Susanna Moodie. "My Cousin Tom." *British American Magazine* 1, 12-20.
Thomas Hounsell Hodge. "A Tale of the Bay of Quinté." *British American Magazine* 1 (October), 569-579; 2 (November), 18-26.
Thomas Hounsell Hodge. "Leaves from the Life Romance of Merne Dillamer." *British American Magazine* 2 (December), 140-146.
Henry J. Ibbotson. "Policeman X." *British American Magazine* 1 (August), 345-354.
Ellen Kyle Noel. "The Beverleys." *The Churchman's Magazine* 1: 9-12 (March-June).
May Agnes Fleming. "My Folly." *Sunday Mercury* (New York), 5 July, 2-3.

1864

Proposals for a conference on Maritime union are accepted by legislatures in both Nova Scotia and New Brunswick ~ Chilcotin War between a road crew and First Nations warriors in BC ~ The "Great Coalition" government (federation of British North America as its program): noted reformers join the Conservative cabinet ~ The St Hilaire train disaster: 99 dead ~ Canada Temperance Act (the Dunkin Act) passed: each town can decide to be wet or dry ~ Charlottetown Conference discusses the union of Nova Scotia, New Brunswick, and Prince Edward Island; delegates from Canada attend ~ Quebec Conference with delegates from all provinces; Seventy-Two Resolutions about the union of British North America are adopted; they are sent to all provinces for examination and to the British government for approval ~ Canadian militia patrols the border after rumors of possible Fenian raids ~ St Albans raid (Confederate soldiers escaped to Canada organize an attack against Union troops in Vermont) ~ Rosanna Leprohon publishes *Antoinette de Mirecourt* ~ *Charlottetown Herald* founded (-1921) ~ *The Canadian Illustrated News* is founded in Hamilton (-1864)

Susanna Moodie. "The Accuser and the Accused." *British American Magazine* 2, 285-296; 350-355.
Susanna Moodie. "Dorothy Chance." *British American Magazine* 2, 569-577.
Henry Faulkner Darnell. "Chapter from the Life of a Threepenny Piece." *British American Magazine* 2 (November), 583-589.

1865

Joseph Howe publishes the "Botheration Letters" (against the proposed confederation) in the Halifax *Morning Chronicle* ~ The Legislative Council of Canada votes in support of Confederation and formally requests Britain to unite its North American colonies ~ Great Fire in Quebec City ~ Newfoundland rejects confederation ~ William Wentworth-Fitzwilliam, Viscount Milton and Walter Butler Cheadle publish *The Nort-West Passage by Land* ~ Charles Heavysege publishes the poem "Jeptha's Daughter" ~ *The Saturday Reader* is founded in Montreal (-1866)

Mary Eliza Herbert. *Flowers by the Wayside. A Miscellany.* Halifax: Citizen Office.

1866

The American Reciprocity Treaty is cancelled by the US ~ The Legislative Council of New Brunswick votes in favour of the union of British North America ~ The Newfoundland Assembly decides to postpone its decision ~ Irish Fenians invade NB, but are dispersed by the US military ~ Fenians cross into Canada from Buffalo and occupy Fort Erie; Battle of Ridgeway between Fenians and Canadian troops; Fenians retreat; they battle Canadian militia at Fort Erie and emerge victorious; they subsequently retreat to the US ~ 1,000 Fenians invade Canada East, plunder and retreat ~ British and Canadian troops meet another Fenian raid at Pigeon Hill and force them across the border ~ Conservative victory in New Brunswick; New Brunswick votes in favour of confederation ~ The new Civil Code of Lower Canada is approved by Parliament ~ Gold rush in Ontario ~ First railway on Vancouver Island ~ British Columbia and Vancouver Island are united ~ Delegates from Canadian provinces meet representatives of British government in London; London Resolutions are adopted ~ Transatlantic cable laid ~ Westminster conference ~ Fire destroys part of Quebec City ~ Tupper pushes confederation in Nova Scotia ~ Death of Susan Sibbald, whose *Memoirs of Susan Sibbald, 1783-1812* would be published in 1926

Andrew Learmont Spedon. *Canadian Summer Evening Tales*. Montreal: Lovell.
Ellen Kyle Noel. "The Secret of Stanley Hall." *Saturday Reader* (3 February-10 March).

1867

The British North American Act is passed in the House of Commons ~ An act proposing union between Canada and British Columbia is passed in the BC assembly; Britain rejects BC's request to join the union ~ BNA Act is proclaimed on July 1st; John A. Macdonald becomes Canada's first prime-minister ~ A resolution is adopted for the inclusion of Rupert's Land and the Northwestern Territory into the Dominion of Canada ~ New provincial premiers: Blanchard in Nova Scotia, Rainford in NB, Chauveau in Quebec, Sandfield Macdonald in Ontario ~ US purchases Alaska from Russia ~ Alexander Muir writes "The Maple Leaf Forever" ~ Henry James Morgan publishes *Bibliotheca Canadensis; or a Manual of Canadian Literature* ~ *The Progress Magazine* is founded in Summerside, PEI ~ *The New Dominion Monthly* is founded in Montreal (-1879) ~ *Stewart's Literary Quarterly Magazine* is founded in St John, NB (-1872; called *Stewart's Quarterly: An Original Magazine* after 1870)

May Agnes Fleming. "Miss Ingersoll's Story." *Sunday Mercury* 6 October, 2-3.
May Agnes Fleming. "Tom's Revenge." *Peterson's Magazine* 52: 6 (December), 413-417. Reprinted as "A Dark Conspiracy" in 1875.
May Agnes Fleming. "For Better or Worse." *Peterson's Magazine* (July), 23-26.
May Agnes Fleming. "A Woman's Story." *Peterson's Magazine* (September), 179-182.

1868

BC legislature and the governor-general of Canada Monck lobby the Colonial Office in favour of BC joining the confederation ~ Thomas Spence is elected president of the Republic of Manitobah; the Colonial Office does not recognize the new state ~ Thomas D'Arcy McGee is assassinated ~ Canada First is founded ~ The Rupert's Land Act is passed; Rupert's Land and the North-Western Territory become part of the Dominion of Canada ~ Schulz jailbreak in Red River ~ Regiment of Papal Zouaves raised in Quebec; they leave to defend the papal state in Italy ~ Wave of secessionism in Nova Scotia ~ Victoria becomes the capital of BC ~ James Anderson publishes *Sawney's Letters* ~ Rosanna Leprohon publishes *Armand Durand* ~ Charles Mair publishes *Dreamland and other poems*

John Rutherford. *Charlie Chatterton, a Montreal Story*. Montreal: John Lovell.
May Agnes Fleming. "Mr. Mounterville." *Peterson's Magazine* (May), 346-350.
May Agnes Fleming. "The Ghost of Lemon Lane." *Peterson's Magazine* (December), 460-464.
Helen Boggs. "Mind-Pictures." *The New Dominion Monthly* 3: 2 (November 1868), 97-100.

1869

Charles Mair publishes a series of articles critical of the Métis; Louis Riel responds in a Montreal newspaper ~ A Canadian survey crew arrives in the Red River region and announces the Métis that Canada has acquired Rupert's Land ~ Smallpox epidemic on the plains ~ Joseph Howe tours the prairies and writes a report favourable to the Métis ~ Riel declares to the Council of Assiniboia that union with Canada has to be the result of negotiation with the Métis ~ At Fort Garry, the Métis National Convention makes up a list of conditions for the union with Canada; Riel issues the Declaration of the People of Rupert's Land and the North West ~ The Métis capture several English-speaking Canadians, including Charles Mair ~ Riel becomes president of the Métis provincial government ~ Another *Canadian Illustrated News* (unrelated to the one from Hamilton) is founded in Montreal (-1883) ~ James De Mille publishes *The Dodge Club* ~ *The Churchman's Magazine and Monthly Review* is founded in Hamilton (-1871) ~ R.G. Haliburton delivers (then publishes) his lecture on *The Men of the North and Their Place in History*

John George Bourinot. "The Mystery at the Chateau des Ormeaux." *Stewart's Quarterly Magazine* 3 (October), 242-251.
Helen Boggs [as Nell Gwynne]. "The Box of Shells." *The New Dominion Monthly* (August 1869), 36-41.

1870

PEI rejects confederation ~ The *City of Boston* sails from Halifax with 191 on board and vanishes without a trace ~ Thomas Scott is tried by a Métis "council of war," found guilty of taking arms against Riel's government, sentenced to death and executed by firing squad ~ The government of Canada agrees with most demands of the Métis provisional government, but does not grant Riel amnesty for Thomas Scott's execution ~ With the passing of the Manitoba Act, the new province is admitted into the confederation ~ Fire destroys much of the St Roch suburb of Quebec City ~ Battle of Eccles Hill: Fenians are defeated by Canadian troops ~ Delegates from BC arrive in Ottawa to negotiate the terms for joining the confederation ~ The North West Emigration Aid Society is founded to help settlers in Manitoba ~ Riel and other members of his provisional government flee to the US ~ Canada First movement begins in Ontario ~ *The Canadian Literary Journal* is founded in Toronto (-1871)

Rosanna Leprohon. "My Visit to Fairview Villa." *Canadian Illustrated News*, 14, 21, and 28 May.
John Lesperance. "Rosalba; or, Faithful to Two Loves. An Episode of the Rebellion of 1837-1838." *Canadian Illustrated News*, 19 March-16 April.
John George Bourinot. "What Happened at Beauvoir on Christmas Eve." *Canadian Illustrated News*. 2 instalments.
Helen Boggs. "The Briers." *The New Dominion Monthly* (April 1870), 37-42.

1871

Britain and the US sign the Treaty of Washington ~ British Columbia joins the confederation as the sixth province; BC gets assembly and responsible government ~ The last British troops leave Quebec City; there are now no British soldiers anywhere in Canada except for the small garrison in Halifax ~ The Ontario School Act; attendance made compulsory at least 4 months a year in elementary school; Ryerson is behind it ~ Common Schools Act in NB triggers a crisis, as both religion and minority languages are banished from schools ~ Nova Scotia has a population of 387,000; New Brunswick, 285,000; PEI, 109,00 ~ Alexander Begg publishes *The Creation of Manitoba*

Susanna Moodie. "Washing the Black-a-Moor White." *Canadian Literary Magazine* 1, 163-165.
John George Bourinot. "Stories We Heard among the Pines." *Stewart's Quarterly* (October), 242-268.

1872

Canadian Archives established in Ottawa ~ Dominion Lands Office established ~ General strike in Hamilton ~ Trade Union Act; unions are legal and have now the right to strike but not to picket ~ Riel returns to Manitoba ~ Wild Bill Hickock performs in the first Wild West Show at Niagara Falls, Ontario ~ The Canadian Pacific Railway Company is formed with Hugh Allan president ~ Conservative victory in federal elections ~ Mowat reelected premier of Ontario ~ The *Canadian Monthly and National Review Magazine* is founded in Toronto (-1878) ~ *The Toronto Weekly Mail* is founded (-1895) ~ J.A. Phillips is editor of *The Hearthstone* in Montreal; *The Hearthstone* is replaced by *The Favorite* (-1874)

Bernard Bigsby. *"That Bowl of Punch!" What It Did, and How It Did It. Six Christmas Stories.* Toronto: Hunter, Rose & Co., 1872.
John George Bourinot. "Results of a Skating Adventure." *New Dominion Monthly*. 2 instalments.
Rosanna Leprohon. "Clive Weston's Wedding Anniversary." *Canadian Monthly and National Review* 2: 2 (August) and 2: 3 (September).
Ellen Kyle Noel. "A Night of Peril!" *Canadian Illustrated News*, 24-31 August.
Ellen Kyle Noel "The House-Keeper at Lorme Hall." *Canadian Illustrated News* 6: 20 (16 November), 315; 6: 21 (23 November), 331.
John Arthur Phillips. "My Reporter. A Story of an Elopement." *The Hearthstone* 3: 5 (3 February 1872), 1-2.
John Arthur Phillips. "A Perfect Fraud." *The Hearthstone* 3: 16 (20 April 1872), 1-2.
Christopher Crosscut. "My Birth-Day." *The Hearthstone* 3: 13 (30 March 1872), 8.
G. S. Barnum. "The Mystery of the Chateau Ramsay." *The Hearthstone* 3: 52 (28 December 1872), 5-6.

1873

PEI negotiates joining the confederation and is admitted as the 7th province ~ The Canadian Pacific Railway Company receives $30M in subsidies and over 20M ha of land; it is revealed that the company had paid $360,000 in campaign funds to Macdonald, Cartier and Hector Langevin (at their request); the "Pacific Scandal" forces the government to resign ~ Alexander Mackenzie and the liberals take power ~ *Manitoba Free Press* is founded in Winnipeg ~ The *Atlantic* sinks outside Halifax Harbour; 546 dead ~ Cypress Hill Massacre: American wolf hunters ambush and kill 30 Assiniboine; Parliament decides to create the North West Mounted Police; all the recruits of the NWMP arrive in Manitoba by the end of the year ~ Coal mine explosion at Westville, NS; 60 dead ~ Riel elected MP but does not go to Ottawa ~ Cyclone strikes Cape Breton Island; 500 dead, 1,200 ships lost ~ Gold rush in Cassiar, BC ~ International Bridge between Fort Erie and Buffalo, NY is opened to traffic ~ Winnipeg incorporated (the "Forks" area and part of the Red River colony) ~ Gabriel Dumont is elected president of the Saskatchewan Valley Métis ~ Canada-US boundary commission established to survey the 49th parallel ~ *Grip* is founded in Toronto as a 4-page weekly (-1894) ~ George Monro Grant publishes *Ocean to Ocean*

John Arthur Phillips. *Thompson's Turkey and Other Christmas Tales, Poems, &c.* Montreal: John Lovell.
Helen Boggs. *Acorn Leaves. A Series of Canadian Tales.* Toronto: Copp, Clark.
Mrs. M[ary]. E. Muchall. "In the West Wing of Barton Grange." *The Favorite* 1: 2 (18 January 1873), 21-22.
E. A. Sutton. "Cousin Tom: or, My First Attempt." *The Favorite* 1: 6 (15 February 1873), 91-92.
Isabella Valancy Crawford. "'Where the Laugh Came in.'" *The Favorite* 1: 15 (19 April 1873), 225-226.
Isabella Valancy Crawford. "'That Yacht.'" *The Favorite* 1: 17 (3 May 1873), 268-269.
Emma Naomi Crawford. "Buggins' Mare." *The Favorite* 1: 9 (8 March 1873), 130.

Emma Naomi Crawford. "Major Barker's Mistake." *The Favorite* 1: 14 (12 April 1873), 221.
Mrs. C. Chandler. "Who Was Right?" *The Favorite* 1: 10 (15 March 1873), 150.
Mrs. C. Chandler. "Mr. Winkins' House-Hunting." *The Favorite* 1: 13 (5 April 1873), 206.
Mrs. C. Chandler. "Maud Marchmont; or, The Victim of Fortune-Telling." *The Favorite* 1: 15 (19 April 1873), 231.
W. S. Humphreys. "How I Lost My Ear and How I Won a Wife." *The Favorite* 1: 16 (26 April 1873), 250-251.
Annie Rothwell. "The Shadow of Daneham." *Appleton's Journal* 10: 245 (29 November 1873), 675-679.

1874

Dominion Elections Act introduces vote by secret ballot ~ First Russian Mennonites arrive in Manitoba ~ *Manitoba Free Press* becomes a daily ~ Riel is reelected but does not go to Ottawa ~ First train robbery in Canada (bandits are dressed as KKK members) ~ Beginning of economic depression in Canada (-1881) with high rate of unemployment and high number of bankruptcies ~ Montreal Stock Exchange established ~ Decisive liberal victory in federal elections; the secret ballot used for the first time ~ Canada First movement enters politics ~ Alexander McLachlan publishes *The Emigrant and other poems*

John Reade. "Winty Dane's Transformation." *The New Dominion Monthly* (August), 87-89.
May Agnes Fleming. "How the 'Lone Star' Went Down." *The Favorite* 3: 15 (11 April 1874), 234.

1875

Caraquet Riots in New Brunswick over plans to cut funding to French-language schools ~ New Brunswick's Grace Annie Lockhart is the first woman in the British Empire to earn a university degree as she graduates from Mount Allison ~ Riel and other Métis leaders receive amnesty on condition that they first stay 5 years in exile ~ Fort Calgary founded

Helen Boggs [as Nell Gwynne]. "Mopsy's Venture." *The New Dominion Monthly* (January 1875), 4-8; (February 1875), 84-88.
Helen Boggs [as Nell Gwynne]. "Flossy's Gold Mine." *The New Dominion Monthly* (July 1875), 36-42.
Helen Boggs. "Baby Lion." *The New Dominion Monthly* (June 1875), 348-351.

1876

After a nervous breakdown Riel is admitted to a mental asylum in Montreal ~ The Royal Military College of Canada opens in Kingston ~ Little Big Horn; the Sioux led by Sitting Bull retreat into Canada where they live for 5 years but are denied a reservation and will surrender to American authorities in 1881 ~ The first telephone call between Alexander Graham Bell and his uncle in Ontario ~ Indian Act passed into law ~ Wilson Benson publishes *Life and Adventures of Wilson Benson* ~ *Belford's Monthly Magazine* is founded in Toronto (-1882; called *Rose-Belford's Canadian Monthly and National Review* after 1878) ~ Nicholas Flood Davin publishes *The Irishman in Canada*

Noma & Vorsa. *Tales, Essays and Poems*. Amherst, N.S.: Amherst Gazette Steam
.Helen Boggs [as Nell Gwynne]. "Falling among Thieves." *The New Dominion Monthly* (May 1876), 363-369.

1877

Fire in Saint John (NB) leaves 13,000 people homeless ~ University of Manitoba opens ~ Ordinance for the Protection of the Bison ~ William Kirby publishes *The Golden Dog*

John Arthur Phillips. *From Bad to Worse; Hard to Beat; and a Terrible Christmas. Three Stories of Montreal Life*. Montreal: Lovell.
Anna Theresa Sadlier. *The King's Page: A Legend of the Moorish Wars in Spain, and Other Stories*. New York: Sadlier.
John George Bourinot. "The Old Japanese Cabinet." *Canadian Monthly* 12: 2 (August), 139-152.
John Charles Dent. "The Gerrard Street Mystery." *Belford's Monthly Magazine* (May 1877), 761-781.

1878

Construction workers at parliament building in Quebec City go on strike; troops brought in; two workers killed ~ The *Saskatchewan Herald* is founded (first newspaper in what was then the North-West Territory) ~ Conservative victory in federal elections; John A. Macdonald is prime-minister again (-1891)

Grant Allen [J. Arbuthnot Wilson]. "Our Scientific Observations on a Ghost." *Belgravia* 36 (July), 45-59.
Grant Allen. "The Empress of Andorra." *Belgravia* 36 (September), 335-351.
Grant Allen [J. Arbuthnot Wilson]. "My New Year's Eve among the Mummies." *Belgravia Christmas Annual*.
Helen Boggs [as Nell Gwynne]. "Lotty Farwell's Duty." *The New Dominion Monthly* 22: 5 (May 1878), 622-628; 22: 6 (June 1878), 723-735.
Helen Boggs [as Nell Gwynne]. "A Mistake." *The New Dominion Monthly* 23: 6 (December 1878), 741-744.
Helen Boggs [as Nell Gwynne]. "A Footprint on the Sand of Time." *The New Dominion Monthly* 22: 2 (February 1878), 200-203.

1879

At the Canadian Institute in Toronto, Sandford Fleming proposes 24 time zones ~ National Policy; hike in tariff ~ Anti-Chinese demonstration in BC ~ Alexander Begg publishes *Ten Years in Winnipeg*

Grant Allen [J. Arbuthnot Wilson]. "Lucretia." *Belgravia Christmas Annual*, 87-101.

1880

"O Canada" performed for the first time ~ By imperial Order-in-council, all British possessions in North America (including the Arctic archipelago, but excluding Newfoundland) are part of Canada ~ Mine explosion at Stellarton, NS; 50 killed ~ The *Edmonton Bulletin* is founded (first newspaper in Alberta) ~ Founding of Canadian Pacific Railway Company ~ National Gallery of Canada is founded ~ Charles G.D. Roberts publishes *Orion and other poems* ~ Homer Watson paints *The Pioneer Mill*

Grant Allen [J. Arbuthnot Wilson]. "Ram Das of Cawnpore." *Belgravia* 43 (November), 87-90.
William Henry Withrow. "An Adventure with Wolves." *The Boy's Own Paper* (18 December).
Isabella Valancy Crawford. "'Let No Man Put Asunder.'" *Frank Leslie's Popular Monthly* 9: 5 (May 1880), 530-539.

1881

Classes begin at the University of Western Ontario in London ~ Manitoba's boundaries are extended by act of parliament ~ Paddle steamer *Victoria* sinks near London, Ontario; 182 dead ~ Rat Portage War begins (-1884), a quarrel over jurisdiction between Manitoba and Ontario ~ NWT assembly elected ~ Fisheries agreement with the US ~ Royal Society of Canada is founded ~ John Charles Dent publishes *The Last Forty Years: The Union of 1841 to Confederation* ~ Homer Watson completes *The Stone Road* ~ John George Bourinot publishes *The Intellectual Development of the Canadian People: An Historical Review*

Grant Allen. "Pausodyne." *Belgravia Christmas Annual*, 24-38.

1882

The Dominion Redistribution Act adjusts representation in the House on the basis of population ~ The North-West Territory is divided into 4 districts: Athabasca, Assiniboia, Alberta and Saskatchewan ~ Oscar Wilde visits Toronto ~ The *Moncton Transcript* is founded ~ John Lake of the Temperance Colonization Company selects the site of a new settlement which he names Saskatoon ~ Wascana is renamed Regina ~ Unmarried women of property are allowed to vote in Ontario municipal elections ~ Conservative electoral victory ~ *Picturesque Canada*, edited by Lucius O'Brien, is published

Grant Allen. "An Episode in High Life." *Belgravia Holiday Number*, 59-76.
Grant Allen. "Mr Chung." *Belgravia Christmas Annual*, 67-80.
John Lesperance. *Tuque bleue: A Christmas Snowshoe Sketch* (Montreal: Dawson Brothers, 1882), 5-35.
Ethelwyn Wetherald. "How the Modern Eve Entered Eden." *Rose-Belford's Canadian Monthly* 8: 2 (February), 131-146.

1883

The capital of the NWT is moved from Battleford to Regina ~ Ontario's first public library opens in Guelph ~ Fire destroys the Parliament buildings in Quebec City ~ Franz Boas studies the Inuit (-1884) ~ Horatio Emmons Hale publishes *The Iroquois Book of Rites* ~ Palmer Cox publishes his first *Brownie* story in *St. Nicholas Magazine* ~ *The Week* is founded in Toronto (-1896)

Robert Barr [Luke Sharp]. *N. B. Strange Happenings*. London: W.A. Dunkerley.
Grant Allen. "The Reverend John Creedy." *Cornhill Magazine* new series 1: 48 (September), 225-242.
Grant Allen. "The Backslider." *Cornhill Magazine* new series 1: 48 (August), 191-213.
Grant Allen. "The Foundering of the 'Fortuna.'" *Longman's Magazine* III (November), 94-108.

1884

Two trains collide in Toronto; 31 killed ~ Admission of women to University College, Toronto, becomes legal ~ The Toronto Public Library is established ~ Federal government outlaws the potlatch practised by British Columbia First Nations ~ Barbados asks to join the Canadian confederation but the offer is declined ~ Riel, who is living in Montana, is invited to return to Canada by other Métis leaders; he arrives in Saskatchewan, from where he petitions the federal government to recognize the new province and to grant it responsible government ~ 386 Canadian volunteers leave for Sudan to rescue general

Gordon; they will arrive too late ~ Unmarried women and widows are given to right to vote in Ontario municipal elections ~ William Brymner paints *A Wreath of Flowers* ~ Isabella Valancy Crawford publishes *Old Spookses' Pass: 'Malcolm's Katie" and other poems*

Grant Allen. *Strange Stories*. London: Chatto and Windus.
Grant Allen. "Dr Greatrex's Engagement." *Cornhill Magazine* ns 2: 49 (June), 561-583.
Grant Allen. "The Curate of Churnside." *Cornhill Magazine* ns 3: 50 (September), 225-258.
Grant Allen. "John Cann's Treasure." *Cornhill Magazine* ns 3: 50 (October), 337-366.
Isabella Valancy Crawford. "A Five-o-Clock Tea." *Frank Leslie's Popular Monthly* 17: 3 (March 1884), 287-291.

1885

Canada adopts standard time ~ The CPR telegraph from the Atlantic to the Pacific is established ~ The Chinese Immigration Act imposes a $50 tax on every Chinese immigrant ~ Riel with an armed force seize the Batoche parish church, forms a provisional government, and asks for the surrender of Fort Carlton by the NWMP ~ The Métis ambush the NWMP troops, then a unit led by the commander of the Canadian militia in the Battle of Fish Creek; First Nations warriors had joined the Métis ~ First Nations win the Battle of Cut Knife Hill against Canadian troops ~ In the final Battle of Batoche, Canadian forces defeat the Métis; Riel is captured by the NWMP; Gabriel Dumont flees to the US; at Steele Narrows, the Cree warriors are also defeated; Big Bear, the Cree leader, surrenders to the NWMP ~ The trial of Louis Riel begins in Regina; he is convicted of treason, sentenced to death and hanged; eight Cree warriors are also hanged ~ Protesters against mandatory smallpox vaccinations attack the city hall in Montreal; 1,391 die of smallpox ~ Great Labrador Gale; 300 dead ~ The last spike of the CPR driven at Craigellachie, BC ~ Electric streetlights in Charlottetown ~ Canada's first national park is established in Banff Hot Springs Reserve ~ The federal government bans the Sun Dance ~ Catharine Parr Traill publishes *Studies of Plant Life in Canada* ~ Theresa Gowanlock and Theresa Delaney publish *Two Months in the Camp of Big Bear*

Charles G. D. Roberts. "The Stone Dog." *Longman's Magazine* 7 (November 1885- 1886), 53-58.
Grant Allen. "The Two Carnegies." *Cornhill Magazine* ns 4: 51 (March), 292-324.
Robert Machray. "A Man and a Brother. A Western Episode." *Harper's New Monthly Magazine* 70: 418 (March 1885), 642-643.
Robert Machray. "Two Halves of a Life." *Atlantic Monthly* 56: 338 (December), 806-824.
Edward William Thomson. "Petherick's Peril." *The Youth's Companion* (23 April 1885).
Isabella Valancy Crawford. "Sevres Fulkes." *Frank Leslie's Popular Monthly* 20: 3 (September 1885), 351-356.

1886

Mohawks work on the Lachine Bridge; they become known for their skills while working at great heights ~ Fire destroys Vancouver; 50 dead ~ The first transcontinental passenger train between Montreal and Port Moody, BC, travels the distance in 7 days ~ Yoho National Park established ~ Ontario Factory Act forbids the employment of boys under 13 and girls under 14 ~ Charles Mair publishes the poem "Tecumseh" ~ Isabela Valancy Crawford serializes *A Little Bacchante* ~ Joseph Edmund Collins publishes *Annette, the Métis Spy*

Susan Frances Harrison [Seranus]. *Crowded Out! And Other Sketches*. Ottawa: The Evening Journal Office.
Robert Sellar. *Gleaner Tales*. Huntington: Canadian Gleaner Office.
John Arthur Phillips. *Out of the Snow, and Other Stories*. Ottawa: Free Press.
Charles G. D. Roberts. "Bear vs. Birch-Bark." *Wide Awake* 23: 1 (June), 47-50.
Grant Allen. "The Third Time." *Longman's Magazine* 7: 39 (January), 294-308.
Isabella Valancy Crawford. "Extradited." *The Globe* (4 September).
Roger Pocock. "A Useless Man." *The Week* 3:32 (8 July), 515-516.
Roger Pocock. "The Ice Cortege." *The Week* 3: 42 (16 September), 675.
James Macdonald Oxley. "The Professor's Last Skate." *Wide Awake* 22: 6 (May 1886), 339-342.
Edward William Thomson. "Told on a Pullman." *Youth's Companion* (13 May 1886).

1887

Riots in Vancouver against Chinese immigration ~ McMaster University founded ~ Coalmine explosion in Nanaimo, BC; 150 dead ~ Britain grants Canada the power to negotiate commercial treaties with foreign countries ~ Conservative victory ~ Laurier becomes leader of Liberal party ~ First interprovincial conference in Quebec City~ Thomas Phillips Thompson publishes *The Politics of Labor* ~ *Saturday Night Magazine* is founded ~ Graeme Mercer Adam and Agnes Ethelwyn Wetherald publish *An Algonquin Maiden* ~ Sarah Anne Curzon publishes *Laura Secord: the Heroine of 1812* (drama in 3 acts)

Grant Allen. *The Beckoning Hand and Other Stories*. London: Chatto and Windus.
Roger Pocock. "The Lean Man." *Toronto World*, 5 November.
Duncan Campbell Scott. "The Little Milliner." *Scribner's Magazine* II: 4 (October 1887), 493-498.
Duncan Campbell Scott. "The Desjardins." *Scribner's Magazine* 2: 4 (October 1887), 498-501.
Duncan Campbell Scott. "Josephine Labrosse." *Scribner's Magazine*, 2: 4 (October 1887), 501-504.
Duncan Campbell Scott. "The Ducharmes of the Baskatonge." *Scribner's Magazine* 1: 2 (February 1887), 236-243.
John Charles Dent. "Gagtooth's Image." *Arcturus* 1: 3 (29 January 1887), 40-44.
Edward William Thomson. "Little Baptiste." *Youth's Companion* (24 November 1887).

1888

Queen Victoria Park opens in Niagara Falls ~ Natural gas discovered in Kingsville, Ontario ~ Archibald Lampman publishes *Among the Millet and other poems* ~ James De Mille's *A Strange Manuscript Found in a Copper Cylinder* is published posthumously ~ *The Dominion Illustrated* is founded in Montreal as a weekly (-1895; as a monthly after 1892)

Roger Pocock. *Tales of Western Life*. Ottawa: C.W. Mitchell.
John Charles Dent. *The Gerrard Street Mystery and Other Weird Tales*. Toronto: Rose Publishing Company.
James Macdonald Oxley "In the Nick of Time." *The Golden Argosy* (21 July).
Edith Eaton. "A Trip in a Horse Car." *Dominion Illustrated* (13 October), 235.
Edith Eaton. "Misunderstood: The Story of a Young Man." *Dominion Illustrated* (17 November).

John Talon-Lesperance. "A Missisquoi Holiday." *Dominion Illustrated* 1: 1 (7 July), 7-10; 1: 2 (14 July), 22-23.
Susie Frances Harrison. "In the Valley of the St. Eustache." *The American Magazine* 9: 2 (December 1888), 181-190.

1889

Royal Commission on Labour in Canada ~ Foundation of the Equal Rights Association ~ Toronto customs seize and destroy copies of Emile Zola novels ~ Kathleen Blake Watkins (as Kit Coleman) begins he column "Fashion Notes and Fancies for the Fair Sex" in the *Toronto Mail* ~ William Wilfred Campbell publishes *Lake Lyrics and other poems*

Grace Dean McLeod. "The Light on Black Ledge." *Wide Awake* (December).
Edith Eaton. "The Origin of a Broken Nose." *Dominion Illustrated* (11 May).
Edith Eaton. "Robin." *Dominion Illustrated* (22 June).
Edith Eaton. "Albemarle's Secret." *Dominion Illustrated* (19 October).
Sarah Anne Curzon. "Betty's Choice." *The Week* (28 June 1889), 471-472.

1890

Manitoba School Act abolishes separate schools for Catholics and Protestants ~ Electric trams introduced in Toronto ~ Oil discovered in Alberta ~ Bishop's University admits women to the faculty of medicine ~ Sarah Jeannette Duncan publishes *A Social Departure* ~ James Macdonald Oxley publishes *Up among the Ice*

Agnes Maule Machar and Thomas Guthrie Marquis. *Stories of New France*. Boston: D. Lothrop.
Joanna Wood. "Unto the Third Generation." *All the Year Round* 67: 95 (25 October 1890), 396-404.
Grace Dean McLeod. "The Kaduskak Giant." *Wide Awake* (March), 68-72.
Louisa Murray. "A Story of a Christmas Rose." *The Week* 7: 5 (3 January), 72-74.
Marjory MacMurchy. "Mag's Children." *The Dominion Illustrated* 4: 95 (26 April 1890), 270-271.
Edward William Thomson. "Beset by Wolves." *Youth's Companion* (20 December 1890).

1891

Coal mine explosion in Springhill, NS; 125 killed ~ John A. Macdonald dies ~ Conservative victory; J.C. Abbott the new prime minister ~ The *Toronto Star* begins ~ First Ukrainian immigrants arrive in Canada ~ Goldwin Smith publishes *Canada and the Canadian Question* ~ Lady Hariot Dufferin publishes *My Canadian Journal* ~ Sara Jeannette Duncan publishes *An American Girl in London* ~ Lily Dougall publishes *Beggars All* ~ *Canada: A Monthly Journal* is founded in Halifax (-1892)

Grant Allen. "A Deadly Dilemma." *Strand Magazine* 1 (January), 14-21.
Grant Allen. "Jerry Stokes." *Strand Magazine* 1 (March), 299-307.
Gilbert Parker. "The Patrol of the Cypress Hills." *The Independent* (29 January).
Gilbert Parker. "A Castaway of the South." *English Illustrated Magazine* (December).
Agnes Maule Machar. "Parted Ways." *The Week* 8: 29 (19 June), 461-463.
Duncan Campbell Scott. "The Wooing of Monsieur Cuerrier." *Scribner's*. 9:3 (March 1891), 373-376.
Edward William Thomson. "The Privilege of the Limits." *Harper's Weekly* 35: 1805 (25 July 1891), 558.
Robert Barr. "Mrs. Tremain." *Black and White* 2 (29 August 1891), 3087-310.

1892

Fire destroys two-thirds of Saint John's, Newfoundland; 12,000 homeless ~ Abbott resigns; J.S.D. Thompson the new prime minister ~ Wilfred Grenfell begins his work towards improving the lives of Newfoundland fishermen ~ E. Pauline Johnson debuts on stage at the Association Hall in Toronto, reading her poems ~ Massey Hall opens in Toronto with a concert of Handel's *Messiah* ~ *The Lake Magazine* is founded in Toronto (-1893) ~ William Kingsford publishes *The Early Bibliography of the Province of Ontario* ~ George Parkin publishes *Imperial Federation: The Problem of National Unity*

Robert Barr. *In a Steamer Chair and Other Ship-Board Stories.* New York: Stokes.
Gilbert Parker. *Pierre and His People. Tales of the Far North.* London: Methuen.
Arthur Wentworth [Hamilton] Eaton & Craven Langstroth Betts. *Tales of a Garrison Town.* New York and St. Paul: Merrill.
Edward William Thomson. "Old Man Savarin." *Two Tales* 1: 1 (12 March), 279-304.
Gilbert Parker. "Pretty Pierre." *English Illustrated Magazine* (May).
Charles G. D. Roberts. "Do Seek Their Meat from God." *Harper's* 86: 511 (December 1892), 120-122.
Grant Allen. "That Friend of Sylvia's." *Short Stories* 11: 2 (October), 139-152.
Ethelwyn Wetherald. "A Modern Lear." *New England Magazine* (July), 603-606.
Louisa Murray. "Mr. Gray's Strange Story." *The Week* 9: 13 (26 February), 198-200.
Duncan Campbell Scott. "The Triumph of Marie Laviolette." *Scribner's Magazine* 12: 2 (August 1892), 232-241.
Frederick George Scott. "The Bible Oracle. An Invention." *The Dominion Illustrated Monthly* 1: 5 (June 1892), 259-264.
William Wilfred Campbell. "Deacon Snider and the Circus." *The Dominion Illustrated Monthly* 1: 2 (March 1892), 84-89.
Jessie A. Freeland. "The Renunciation of Grahame Corysteen." *The Dominion Illustrated Monthly* 1: 6 (July 1892), 323-334.
Kay Livingstone. "Brough's Daughter." *The Dominion Illustrated Monthly* 1: 10 (November 1892), 620-630.
Robert Barr. "The Predicament of de Plonville." *Black and White* 3 (18 June 1892), 780-783.

1893

The first wave of Dutch immigration to Canada begins in Winnipeg ~ The new Ontario parliament buildings are inaugurated ~ Algonquin Provincial Park established ~ Chateau Frontenac opened in Quebec City ~ William Lyon Mackenzie King begins his journal ~ The *Canadian Magazine of Politics, Science, Art and Literature* is founded in Toronto (-1921) ~ Bliss Carman publishes *Low Tide on Grand Pré* ~ Thomas Guthrie Marquis publishes *Stories from Canadian History* ~ Duncan Campbell Scott publishes *The Magic House and other poems* ~ Egerton Ryerson Young publishes *Stories from Indian Wigwams and Northern Campfires* ~ Sara Jeannette Duncan publishes *The Simple Adventures of a Memsahib*

Robert Barr. *From Whose Bourne, etc.* London: Chatto and Windus.
Grant Allen. *Ivan Greet's Masterpiece, etc.* London: Chatto and Windus.
Grace Dean McLeod Rogers. *Stories of the Land of Evangeline.* Boston: Lothrop.
Pauline Johnson. "A Red Girl's Reasoning." *Dominion Illustrated Magazine* (February), 19-28.
Charles G. D. Roberts. "Within Sound of the Saws." *Longman's Magazine* (June).
Grant Allen. "Unexpected Englishman." *Longman's Magazine* (February).
James Barr [Angus Evan Abbott]. "Sylvia Deane." *Arrowsmith's Annual* (summer).
Sara Jeannette Duncan. "Peter Linnet's Interview." *Cosmopolitan* 15 (October), 732-737.

Gilbert Parker. "Frith Highland, Gentleman." *Two Tales* 4: 46 (21 January), 155-168.

Gilbert Parker. "The Pilot of Belle Amour." *Cosmopolitan* (July).

Gilbert Parker. "The House with the Tall Porch." *McClure's Magazine* (November), 533-534.

Roger Pocock. "The Arrest of Deerfoot: A Tale of the Mounted Police." *Ludgate Monthly* (March).

Roger Pocock. "Shipmates." *Ludgate Monthly* (October).

James Macdonald Oxley. "Mademoiselle Angelique." *The Ladies' Home Journal* (February).

Charles G. D. Roberts. "The Perdu." *Current Topics* (March).

Frederick George Scott. "The Unpardonable Sin of Mr. Baggs." *The Dominion Illustrated Monthly* 2: 1 (February 1893), 52-55.

Stuart Livingston. "Told in the Ballroom." *The Dominion Illustrated Monthly* 1: 12 (January 1893), 715-724.

Stuart Livingston. "The Girl in Canada." *The Lake Magazine* 1: 6 (January 1893), 362-371.

Jessie A. Freeland. "John Bentley's Mistake." *The Canadian Magazine* 2: 2 (December 1893), 142-148.

Edward William Thomson. "The Ride by Night." *Youth's Companion* (14 December 1893).

Annie Rothwell. "How It Looked at Home: A Story of '85." *The Week* 10: 24 (12 May 1893), 560-564.

1894

Second Colonial conference held in Ottawa ~ Death of J.S.D. Thompson; Mackenzie Bowell the new prime minister ~ Alexander Begg publishes *History of the North-West* ~ The Montreal Symphony Orchestra founded ~ Margaret Marshall Saunders publishes *Beautiful Joe: An Autobiography of a Dog*

Arthur Hodgkin Scaife [as Kim Bilir]. *Three Letters of Credit and Other Stories*. Victoria, BC: The Province Publishing.

Robert Barr. *The Face and the Mask*. London: Hutchinson.

Ernest Thompson Seton. "Lobo, the King of Currumpaw." *Scribner's Magazine* 16 (November), 618-628.

Grant Allen. "An Idyll of the Ice." *English Illustrated Magazine* 11 (May 1893), 776-780.

James Barr [Angus Evan Abbott]. "Hawk's Een." *The Idler* (December).

Gilbert Parker. "Three Commandments in the Vulgar Tongue." *Atlantic Monthly* 73: 439 (May 1894), 615-624.

Jean Newton McIlwraith [Jean Forsyth]. "A Singing-Student in London." *Harper's New Monthly Magazine* (February).

Frederick George Scott. "The Soul-Snake." *The Canadian Magazine* 2: 4 (February 1894), 351-354.

Charlotte Augusta Fraser. "Who Was He?" *The Canadian Magazine* 3: 5 (September 1894), 480-488.

Annie Rothwell. "A Point of Contact." *The New England Magazine* New Series 11: 4 (December 1894), 504-509.

Charles G. D. Roberts. "'The Young Ravens that Call upon Him.'" *Lippincott's Monthly Magazine* 53 (May 1894), 675-677.

1895

A Woman's Suffrage Bill introduced in the New Brunswick Legislative Assembly is narrowly defeated by a vote of 18 to 17 ~ Joshua Slocum begins his solo voyage around the world ~ Clara Brett Martin becomes the first woman law graduate in Canada ~ Commercial treaty with France ~ Foundation of Trail, BC ~ Bliss Carman and Richard Hovey publish *Songs from Vagabondia* ~ William Henry Withrow publishes *Barbara Heck, a Tale of Early Methodism in America* ~ E. Pauline Johnson publishes *White Wampum* ~ D.W. Prowse publishes *A History of Newfoundland*

Edward William Thomson. *Old Man Savarin and Other Stories*. Toronto: Briggs.
James Macdonald Oxley. *My Strange Rescuer and Other Stories of Sport and Adventure in Canada*. Edinburgh: T. Nelson.
Grant Allen. *The Desire of the Eyes and Other Stories*. New York: R.F. Fenno.
Robert Sellar. *Gleaner Tales. Complete Edition*. and *The Summer of Sorrow, Abner's Device and Other Stories [Gleaner Tales: Part Two]*. Huntington: Robert Sellar.
Catherine Simpson Hayes. *Prairie Pot-Pourri*. Winnipeg: Stovel.
Emma Jeffers Graham. *Etchings from a Parsonage Veranda*. Toronto: Briggs.
Mary Anne Sadlier et al. *Stories of the Promises and Other Tales* (from *Canadian Messenger*) by Mrs. M. A. Sadlier and Her Daughters. Toronto: D. & J. Sadlier.
Lily Dougall. "Witchcraft." *Atlantic Monthly* 76: 453 (December), 740-747.
Stephen Leacock. "My Financial Career." *Life*. 25: 641 (11 April 1895), 238-239.
Stephen Leacock. "An Experiment with Policeman Hogan." *Truth* 14 (3 August), 10-11.
Stephen Leacock. "Telling His Faults." *Truth* 15: 454 (28 December), 15.
Grant Allen. "Joe's Rascality." *Cassell's Family Magazine* 22 (February), 203-205.
Grant Allen. "Léonard Léonie." *Cassell's Family Magazine* (January).
Gilbert Parker. "The Going of the White Swan. A Story out of Labrador." *Scribner's Magazine* 17: 1 (January 1895), 65-78.
Lily Dougall. "Thrift." *Atlantic Monthly* 76: 454 (August), 217-223.
Lily Dougall. "The Face of Death." *Atlantic Monthly* 76: 457 (November), 640-644.
Maud Ogilvy. "A Dangerous Experiment." *Canadian Magazine* 6: 1 (November 1895), 38-40.
Harriet Campbell Jephson. "The Judge's Widow." *Windsor Magazine* 1 (June), 709-712.

1896

Liberals win the election and Wilfrid Laurier becomes the first Liberal prime minister since 1874 ~ Klondike Gold Rush begins ~ The Laurier-Greenway compromise on the issue of Manitoba schools: Catholic schools will have French-language classes ~ Clifford Sifton, minister of the interior, announces plans to encourage immigration, with special attention given Eastern European farmers ~ M. Bowell resigns; Sir Charles Tupper the new prime minister (for 2 months) ~ Liberal victory in the federal elections; Wilfrid Laurier the new prime minister ~ New boundaries granted to Quebec ~ Robina and Kathleen M. Lizars publishes *In the Days of the Canada Company* ~ Ernest Thompson Seton publishes *Art Anatomy of Animals* ~ Edmund Morris exhibits *Girls in a Poppy Field* ~ Gilbert Parker publishes *The Seats of the Mighty*

Duncan Campbell Scott. *In the Village of Viger*. Boston: Copeland and Day.
Charles G. D. Roberts. *Earth's Enigmas*. Boston: Lamson, Wolffe.
Gilbert Parker. *An Adventurer of the North* and *A Romany of the Snows*. New York: Stone and Kimball.
Margaret Marshall Saunders. *For the Other Boy's Sake and Other Stories*. Philadelphia: C.H. Banes.
Roger Pocock. *Arctic Night*. London: Chapman and Hall.
James Macdonald Oxley. *The Hero of Start Point and Other Stories*. Philadelphia: American Baptist Publication Society.
F. Clifford Smith. *A Lover in Homespun and Other Stories*. Toronto: Briggs.
John Maclean. *The Warden of the Plains; and Other Stories of Life in the Canadian North-West*. Toronto: William Briggs.

Stephen Leacock. "The Awful Fate of Melpomenus Jones." *Truth* 15: 457 (18 January 1896), 10.
Stephen Leacock. "The Conjurer's Revenge." *Truth* 15: 460 (8 February), 10.
Gilbert Parker. "'I Was a Stranger.' A Tale of Pontiac." *Phil May's Annual* 6 (winter), 4-15.
Joanna E. Wood. "A Mother." *Canadian Magazine* 7: 6 (October), 558-561.
Lucy Maud Montgomery. "Our Charivari." *Golden Days* (9 May), 396.
Roger Pocock. "The Filibusters." *Chapman's Magazine* 4 (July 1896), 337-344 .
Roger Pocock. "The Mutineers." *Chapman's Magazine* 4 (July 1896), 317-337.
Edith Eaton. "Ku Yum." *Land of Sunshine* (June), 29-31.
Edith Eaton [Sui Sin Far]. "The Story of Iso." *Lotus* (August).
Duncan Campbell Scott. "The Mystery of the Red Deeps." *Massey's Magazine* 2 (1896), 232-240, 309-315.
Duncan Campbell Scott. "Ends Rough Hewn." *Massey's Magazine* 2, 276-282.
Duncan Campbell Scott. "John Greenlaw's Story." *Massey's Magazine* 2, 30-34.
Edward William Thomson. "Bill McKee's Tent." *Youth's Companion* (12 March).

1897

Queen Victoria celebrates her Diamond Jubilee ~ Pope Leo XIII issue *Affari Vos* on the issue of the Manitoba School question, criticizing the Laurier-Greenway compromise as insufficient ~ Compulsory vaccination in Quebec schools ~ Herbert Brown Ames publishes *The City below the Hill*

Lady Jephson. *A Canadian Scrap-Book*. London: Marshall Russell.
Edward William Thomson. *Between Earth and Sky and Other Strange Stories of Deliverance*. Toronto: William Briggs.
Lily Dougall. *A Dozen Ways of Love*. London: A. and C. Black.
Charles William Gordon [Ralph Connor]. "Tales of the Selkirks." *The Westminster*.
Grant Allen. "A Domestic Tragedy." *Illustrated London News* (4 September).
Grant Allen. "The Thames Valley Catastrophe." *The Strand* (December).
James Barr [Angus Evan Abbott]. "The Cry of Fate." *The Idler* (November).
James Barr [Angus Evan Abbott]. "Heaps of Lots." *Ludgate* (December).
Susan Frances Harrison. "The Holding Up of the Alhambra." *The Strand* (June).
Gilbert Parker. "The Tune McGilvray Played." *Pocket Magazine* (August).
Gilbert Parker. "The Man That Died at Alma." *Phil May's Annual* 7 (Winter).
Ella S. Atkinson. "The Widowed Stranger." *Canadian Magazine* 9: 6 (October), 464-467.
Stephen Leacock. "Self-Made Men." *[New York] Truth* 16: 511 (28 January), 11.
Lucy Maud Montgomery. "The Goose Feud." *Arthur's Home Magazine* 66: 4 (April), 225-230.
Lucy Maud Montgomery. "A Strayed Allegiance." *Arthur's Home Magazine* (July), 422-431.
William Alexander Fraser. "'Le Bretagne.'" *The Black Cat* (February), 26-30.
Roger Pocock. "The Haunted Island." *Chapman's Magazine* (April).
Roger Pocock. "The Noble Five." *The Peterson Magazine* 7 (August 1897), 757-771.
Edith Eaton. "The Daughter of a Slave." *Short Stories* (January–March 1897).
William Wilfred Campbell. "The Jesuit's Well." *Massey's Magazine* 3: 2 (February 1897), 134-137.
Edward William Thomson. "The Hole in the Wall." *Youth's Companion* (22 April and 29 April 1897).

1898

A national plebiscite is in favour of prohibition, but the result is too tight for Parliament to take any measure ~ Yukon Territory created out of the NWT ~ Preferential tariff for England ~ Susie Francis Harrison publishes *The Forest of Bourg-Marie* ~ William Brymner completes *Two Girls Reading* ~ Henry James Morgan publishes *The Canadian Men and Women of the Time*

Ernest Seton Thompson. *Wild Animals I Have Known*. New York: Scribner's.
Ralph Connor. *Black Rock*. Toronto: The Westminster Co.
Thaddeus William Henry Leavitt. *Kaffir, Kangaroo, Klondike. Tales of the Gold Fields*. Toronto: R.H.C. Browne.
Charles G. D. Roberts. "The Bewitchment of Lieutenant Hanworthy." *Saturday Evening Post* (19 November).
Stephen Leacock. "Insurance Up-do-date." *Canadian Magazine* 12: 1 November), 89-90.
Grant Allen. "The Adventure of the Cantankerous Old Lady." *The Strand* (March).
Grant Allen. "Isenberg's Regiment." *The Pocket Magazine* (October).
Grant Allen. "A Woman's Hand." *Cosmopolitan* (December).
Susan Frances Harrison. "A Social Anomaly." *Pall Mall Magazine* (August), 451-459.
Gilbert Parker. "The Gunner of Percé Rock." *The Strand* (January), 67-79.
Kathleen Blake Willis Watkins Coleman [Kit]. "Holy Saint Claus." *Canadian Magazine* 12 (December), 157-160.
Lucy Maud Montgomery. "A Pastoral Call." *Christian Herald* (13 and 20 April), 331, 356-357.
William Alexander Fraser. "King for a Day." *McClure's Magazine* (April).
James Macdonald Oxley. "Lovers of Mademoiselle Angelique." *Saturday Evening Post* (21 May).
Edith Eaton. "Sweet Sin." *Land of Sunshine* 8:5 (April 1898), 223-226.

1899

1,200 volunteers respond to an invitation to fight in the Boer War ~ Rock slide in Quebec City destroys Champlain Street and kills 45 people ~ Start of the Boer War ~ Canada sends a first contingent of 57 officers and 1,225 soldiers ~ Over 7,400 Doukhobors are granted land in Saskatchewan ~ Ralph Connor publishes *The Sky Pilots* ~ *Canada: An Encyclopaedia of the Country* (ed. J. Castell Hopkins) is published in five volumes

Robert Barr. *The Strong Arm*. New York: Frederick A. Stokes.
Robert Barr. *Revenge!* London: Chatto and Windus.
William Alexander Fraser. *The Eye of a God and Other Tales of East and West*. New York: Doubleday and McClure.
Henry Cecil Walsh. *Bonhomme. French-Canadian Stories and Sketches*. Toronto: William Briggs.
Grant Allen. *Twelve Tales*. London: Grant Richards.
William McLennan. *In Old France and New*. Toronto: Copp, Clark.
Grant Allen. "Joseph's Dream." *Cosmopolitan* (January).
Stephen Leacock. "Hoodoo McFiggin's Christmas." *Canadian Magazine* 12: 3 (January), 285-286.
Gilbert Parker. "The Eye of the Needle." *Collier's Weekly* (21 October).
Lucy Maud Montgomery. "A Double Joke." *Golden Days* (21 January), 145-146.
Lucy Maud Montgomery. "Kismet." *Canadian Magazine* (July), 228-232.
Lucy Maud Montgomery. "Miss Marietta's Jersey." *Household* (July), 5-6.
Lucy Maud Montgomery. "A Brave Girl." *Family Herald* (19 July), 5.
Lucy Maud Montgomery. "The Way of the Winning of Anne." *Springfield Republican* (10 December), 18.
William Alexander Fraser. "His Passport." *McClure's Magazine* (January).

1900

Canadian troops win the Battle of Paardeberg ~ Rioting in Montreal with clashes between McGill students and Laval University students (pro and con the Boer War, respectively) ~ Canadians take part in the Battle of Israel's Port ~ Much of Hull is destroyed by fire; 15,000 homeless ~ PEI adopts prohibition

(-1948) ~ Reginald Aubrey Fessenden performs the first radio broadcast from Cobb Island ~ Katherine Ryan ("Klondike Kate") becomes the first woman member of the NWMP ~ A promotional movie sponsored by the CPR encourages immigration to Canada ~ Liberal victory in federal elections ~ An amendment to the Copyright Act of 1875 gives Canadian publishers the right to negotiate agreements with foreign publishers ~ Charles G.D. Roberts publishes *The Heart of the Ancient Wood* ~ National Council of Women of Canada publishes *Women of Canada: Their Life and Work* ~ *The Poems of Archibald Lampman*, edited by Duncan Campbell Scott

Charles G. D. Roberts. *By the Marshes of Minas.* Boston: Silver, Burdett.

Sophia Margaret Hensley [as J. Try-Davies]. *A Semi-Detached House and Other Stories.* Montreal: Lovell.

Norman Duncan. *The Soul of the Street. Correlated Stories of the New York Syrian Quarter.* New York: McClure, Phillips.

Ethelwyn Wetherald. "An Embodied Conscience." *The Outlook* (14 July), 643-645.

Gilbert Parker. "'The Light of Other Days.'" *Pall Mall Magazine* (October).

Jean Newton McIlray [signed J. N. McIlwraith]. "On Georgian Bay." *Cornhill Magazine* (August), 179-195.

Lucy Maud Montgomery. "The Knuckling Down of Mrs. Gamble." *Good Housekeeping* (January), 3-8.

Lucy Maud Montgomery. "The Adventures of a Story." *Philadelphia Times* (28 October), 32.

Lucy Maud Montgomery. "Lillian's Business Venture." *Advocate and Guardian* (1 November), 335-337.

William Alexander Fraser. "The Home-Coming of the Nakannies." *The Ladies' Home Journal* (January).

William Alexander Fraser. "The Infatuation of Ackerly." *McClure's Magazine* (January).

Edith Eaton. "The Smuggling of Tie Co." *Land of Sunshine* (July 1900), 100-104.

Note on the Texts

Many of these stories were published only once, either in magazines or in books. They have been lifted from the pages of the original publications without change, except for the correction of the occasional typographical error. The spelling and, sometimes, the punctuation of these stories often depended on local or in-house editorial practices. These have been preserved here since, in the absence of manuscripts, there is no indication of the preferences of the authors themselves.

Some of the stories, on the other hand, were republished either in a different periodical (e.g., those by L.M. Montgomery) or, more frequently, in a book, and the authors operated various changes, which have been followed in this anthology, even though some of these changes (i.e., the spelling and the punctuation) clearly occurred because the story was being republished in another English-speaking country. Of more interest here have been significant changes, evidence of the authors' intention to improve on the way the story is told. Each time such editorial changes occur, they are discussed in the footnotes.

Information about the source of each text is provided in introductory notes.

Thomas McCulloch

[The Career of Solomon Gosling]

(1821)

Thomas McCulloch.

The author: Thomas McCulloch was born in 1776 in what is now Barrhead, a town in East Renfrewshire, in the Central Lowlands of Scotland, about eight miles south of Glasgow. He was the second son of six children of a master block-printer. He attended the University of Glasgow and was later trained to become a Presbyterian minister of the General Associate Synod (the so-called "Anti-Burghers," who had seceded from the Church of Scotland over the issue of the oath required of civil servants, which made them accept the official religion of the realm). He was ordained in 1799 in Stewarton, but four years later he applied for an appointment in North America and was sent to Prince Edward Island. He arrived in Pictou, Nova Scotia, with his wife and three children in November 1803, and was persuaded to remain in that town and minister to the congregation of Prince Street Church, today First Presbyterian, in Pictou. In 1808, McCulloch founded a grammar school, which became in 1815 the very successful Pictou Academy. In 1838, he accepted the invitation to become the first principal of Dalhousie University, which had been established two decades before but had not held a single class. McCulloch made it operational in the five years he had left to live (he died on 9 September 1843). Apart from his several publications on religion and education, McCulloch wrote letters to the *Acadian Recorder*, which he attributed to a "Mephibosheth Stepsure;" a volume of *Colonial Gleanings* (containing two novellas, "William" and "Melville," the first of which was based on a second series of Stepsure letters); and two historical novels, "Auld Eppie's Tales" and "Days of the Covenant," which were never published.

The text: This is the first instalment of McCulloch's *Stepsure Letters*. It appeared in the *Acadian Recorder* 9: 51 (22 December 1821), 2. The letters had a first run (or series), from December 1821 to May 1822, and a second one from January to March 1823. Some of the punctuation has been corrected following the *Letters of Mephibosheth Stepsure* (Halifax: H. W. Blackadar, 1860 [1862]), 5-11 (this has meant changing some of the original semicolons into commas, eliding a few unnecessary commas, adding quotation marks in one place). Spelling has been improved twice ("affraid" has become "afraid," following the Blackadar edition; "to sooth" has become "to soothe," following the Davies edition). Gwendolyn

Davies's edition (listed below) contains information about the publishing history of the letters. None of the letters had titles. The title used in this anthology has been suggested by George Patterson's *A History of the County of Pictou, Nova Scotia* (Montreal: Dawson Brothers, 1877), which cites the letter and introduces it as follows: "As to many others who attempted business, then and afterward, we cannot do better than give the picture, drawn by the author of the letters of Mephibosheth Stepsure, of the career of Solomon Gosling" (257).

Further reading: Thomas McCulloch. *The Mephibosheth Stepsure Letters*. Ed. Gwendolyn Davies. Ottawa: Carleton University Press, 1990.

Northrop Frye. "Introduction to *The Stepsure Letters* [1960]." *Northrop Frye on Canada*. Eds. Jean O'Grady and David Staines. Toronto: University of Toronto Press, 2003. 306-312.

Daniel Coleman. "The Enterprising Scottish Orphan: Inventing the Properties of English Canadian Character." *White Civility: The Literary Project of English Canada*. Toronto: University of Toronto Press, 2006. 81-127.

To the Editors of the Recorder.

Gentlemen,—

1821

Happening some time ago to call upon parson Drone, the clergyman of our town, I found him administering his old, standard consolation to my neighbour Solomon Gosling. The parson has been long among us, and is a very good sort of man; but, I believe, he has fared very hardly: for though my townsmen all respect him, and are the most active people in the world at selling watches and swapping horses, they have never made themselves rich; and, therefore, have little to give but good wishes. But the parson, except when he is angry, is very good natured, and disposed to bear with a great deal; and, having acquired a large fund of patience himself, he has become a quack at comforting, and prescribes it indiscriminately for all sorts of ills. His own life has been spent between starving and preaching; and having no resources himself, it never occurs to him, that, for the wants or troubles of others, there can be any remedy but patience.

My neighbour Gosling is completely an every day character. His exact likeness may be found at any time, in any part of the province. About thirty years ago, his father David left him very well to do; and Solomon, who at that time was a brisk young man, had the prospect, by using a little industry, of living as comfortably as any in the town. Soon after the death of old David, he was married and a likelier couple were not often to be seen. But unluckily for them both, when Solomon went to Halifax in the winter, Polly went along with him to sell her turkeys and see the fashions; and from that time the Goslings had never a day to do well. Solomon was never very fond of hard work. At the same time he could not be accused of idleness. He was always a very good neighbour; and at every burial or barn raising, Solomon was set down as one who would be sure to be there. By those means he gradually contracted the habit of running about, which left his own premises in an unpromising plight. Polly, too, by seeing the fashions, had learnt to be genteel; and for the sake of a little show, both lessened the thrift of the family, and added to the outlay; so that, between one thing and another, Solomon began to be hampered, and had more calls than comforters.

When the troubles of life arise out of idleness, a return to industry is usually the last shift. The habits which my neighbour had been gradually contracting, left him little stomach for the patient and persevering toils of a farming life: nor would urgent necessity permit him to wait for the sure but slow returns of agricultural exertion. But necessity is the mother of invention; and though the family of the Goslings were never much noted for profundity of intellect, Solomon by pure dint of scheming, contrived, both to relieve himself from his immediate embarrassments and to avoid hard labour. Though Goose Hill farm, from want of industry, had not been productive, it was still a property of considerable value: and it occurred to Solomon, that, converted into goods, it would yield more prompt and lucrative returns, than by any mode of agriculture. Full of the idea, accordingly, my neighbour went to town; and, by mortgaging his property to Callibogus,[1] the West India merchant, he returned with a general assortment, suited to the wants of the town. When I say a general assortment, it is necessary to be a little more explicit. It did not contain any of those articles which are employed in subduing the forest, or in cultivating the soil. These he knew to be not very saleable. He was aware, that, though old Tubal Thump supplies the whole town with iron work, he is so miserably poor, that he can scarcely keep himself in materials. The only article of the iron kind which he brought, was a hogshead of horse shoes; which a blacksmith in

---

[1] Callibogus (more commonly "calibogus ") is a Newfoundland term for a cocktail of rum (sometimes brandy or gin), spruce beer, and molasses.

Aberdeen, who knew something of America, had sent out upon speculation.—From the number of horses and young people in the township, Solomon knew that horse shoes would meet with a ready sale.

When a merchant lays in his goods, he naturally consults the taste of his customers.—Solomon's accordingly, consisted chiefly of West India produce, gin, brandy, tobacco, and a few chests of tea. For the youngsters, he had provided an assortment of superfine broad cloths and fancy muslins, ready made boots, whips, spurs, and a great variety of gum flowers[2] and other articles which come under the general denomination of notions.[3] In addition to all these, and what Solomon considered as not the least valuable part of his stock, he had bought from Pendulum & Co. a whole box of old watches elegantly ornamented with lacquered brass chains and glass seals, little inferior in appearance to gold and Cairngorms.[4]

When all these things were arranged, they had a very pretty appearance. For a number of weeks, little was talked of, but Mr. Gosling's Store; for such he had now become by becoming a merchant: little was to be seen, but my neighbours riding thither to buy, and returning with bargains: and during the course of the day, long lines of horses, fastened to every accessible post and pinacle[5] of the fences, rendered an entrance to his house almost impracticable. By these means, the general appearance of the town soon underwent a complete revolution. Homespun and homely fare were to be found only with a few hard fisted old folks, whose ideas could never rise above labour and saving. The rest appeared so neat and genteel upon Sundays, that even the Reverend Mr. Drone, though I did not see that his flock had enabled him to exchange his old habiliments for Mr. Gosling's superfine, expressed his satisfaction by his complacent looks.

Mr. Gosling, too, had in reality, considerably improved his circumstances. The greater part of my neighbours being already in debt to old Ledger and other traders about; and considering that if they took their money to these, it would only go their credit, carried it to Mr. Gosling's Store; so that by these means he was soon able to clear off a number of his old encumbrances, and to carry to market as much cash as established his credit.

[2] Hand-made flowers made of paper, cloth, silk, etc.

[3] Haberdashery.

[4] Also called smoky quartz.

[5] The phrase "and pin[n]acle" is not present in the 1862 edition.

Among traders punctuality of payment begets confidence in the seller; and the credit which this affords to the purchaser, is generally followed by an enlargement of orders. My neighbour returned with a much greater supply; and here his reverses commenced.—Credit could not be refused to good customers who had brought their money to the store. Those, also, who formerly showed their good will by bringing their cash, proved their present cordiality by taking large credits. But when the time for returning to the market for supplies arrived, Mr. Gosling had nothing to carry thither but his books. These, it is true, had an imposing appearance. They contained debts to a large amount; and my neighbour assured his creditors, that, when they were collected, he would be able to pay them all honourably, and have a large reversion to himself. But, when his accounts were made out, many young men who owed him large sums, had gone to Passamaquoddy;[6] and of those who remained the greater part had mortgaged their farms to Mr. Ledger, and the other old traders: and now carried their ready money to Jerry Gawpus,[7] who had just commenced trader by selling his farm. In short, nothing remained for Mr. Gosling, but the bodies or labours of his debtors; and these last they all declared themselves very willing to give.

About this time it happened that vessels were giving a great price; and it naturally occurred to my neighbour, that, by the labour which he could command, he might build a couple. These, accordingly, were put upon the stocks. But labour in payment of debt, goes on heavily; and besides, when vessels were giving two prices, nobody would work without double wages; so that the vessels, like the ark, saw many summers and winters. In the mean time peace came;[8] and those who owned vessels, were glad to get rid of them at any price. By dint of perseverance, however, Mr. Gosling's were finished: but they had scarcely touched the water, when they were attached by Mr. Hemp, who at the same time declared, that, when they were sold, he would lose fifty per cent

[6] Passamaquoddy Bay was known as a smuggling area, on the border between New Brunswick and the US state of Maine. The name was changed into "the Lines" in the intended Scottish edition, which was only published in 1990. "The Lines" (the border with the US) was another term for Passamaquoddy Bay.

[7] Gawpus or gaupus is a Scottish term for a simpleton.

[8] The year 1815 saw the end of both the Napoleonic Wars and of the War of 1812.

upon his account for the rigging. Such was my neighbour's case; when, happening, as I have already mentioned, to step into Parson Drone's, I found that Mr. Gosling had been telling his ailments, and was receiving the reverend old gentleman's ordinary, clerical consolation: What can't be cured, must be endured: let us have patience.

"I'll tell you what it is, parson," replied my neighbour, "patience may do well for those who have plenty; but it won't do for me.—Callibogus has foreclosed the mortgage; my vessels are attached; and my books are of no more value than a rotten pumpkin. After struggling hard to supply the country with goods, and to bring up a family so as to be a credit to the town, the country has brought us to ruin. I won't submit to it. I won't see my son Rehoboam, poor fellow, working like a slave upon the roads, with his coat turned into a jacket, and the elbows clouted with the tails.[9] My girls were not sent to Mrs. McCackle's boarding school to learn to scrub floors.—The truth is, parson, the country does not deserve to be lived in. There is neither trade nor money in it, and produce gives nothing.—It is fit only for Indians, and

emigrants from Scotland, who were starving at home. It is time for me to go elsewhere, and carry my family to a place that presents better prospects to young folks."

In reply, the parson was beginning to exhort Mr. Gosling to beware of the murmurings of the wicked; when Jack Catchpole, the constable, stept in to say that the sheriff would be glad to speak with Mr. Gosling at the door.—Our sheriff is a very hospitable gentleman; and, when any of his neighbours are in hardship, he will call upon them, and even insist upon their making his house their home. Nor did I ever know any shy folks getting off with an excuse. As it occurred to me, therefore, that Mr. Gosling might not come back for the parson's admonition, I returned home; and soon learned that my neighbour had really gone elsewhere, and made a settlement in the very place where Samson turned miller.[10]

This event has not added much to the respectability of the Goslings; nor is it calculated to brighten their prospects. My neighbour's children are as fine a young family as any in the town;

[9] Clouted means patched.

[10] Allusion to Judges 16:21, about Samson's imprisonment by the Philistines: "and he did grind in the prison house." This means that Gosling goes under arrest in the sheriff's house.

but it unavoidably happened, that the apparent prosperity of their father introduced among them habits, not very friendly to regular industry and saving. Hob Gosling, the oldest son, is really a smart young fellow; and in haying time or harvest, he can do more work in a day than any three labourers. But hard work requires recreation; and when a young man does any thing uncommon, he wishes to receive credit for it among his neighbours. Accordingly, it would sometimes happen, that it would take Hob a week to tell about the exertions of a day. He would also occasionally recreate himself by riding races, or playing a game at cards when he was drinking a glass of grog with other youngsters over Mr. Tipple's counter: and by these means, though Hob is not a quarrelsome young man, his name was frequently called over in court in assault and battery charges. This, it is true, was not without its advantages. Hob acquired a great knowledge of the law, and the character of being a 'cute young man.[11] But I am inclined to think that the gain ended here; for I remember that after one or two of these causes were tried, a few acres of Mr. Gosling's best marsh passed into the hands of Saunders Scantocreesh, a hard-faced, hard-working Scotchman, who, a few years ago, came among us with his stockings and shoes suspended from a stick over his shoulder, but now possesses one of the best farms in the town.

My neighbour's daughters, too, are very agreeable young ladies. Every body allows that Mrs. McCackle has done justice to their education. For painting flowers and playing upon the piano forte, they have few equals. Some of my neighbours, indeed, used to complain that, when Mr. Gosling asked them to dinner, the meat was always ill cooked; and the puddings and pies, mere dough: but the reason was that neither Mrs. Gosling nor the young ladies could get the black wench to do as she was bidden, unless they were always at her heels.

But this was not the only hardship which my neighbour suffered by the elegant accomplishments of the young ladies. To be genteel in the country is attended with difficulties and losses of which you townsfolks can have no conception. Morning visits in the afternoon, dressings and other things interfere so frequently with rural industry, that great show and sad accidents are usually combined. I recollect when Jacob Ribs married his fourth wife, Mr. and Mrs. Gosling were asked to the wedding;

[11] "Cute" (from acute) meant sharp, clever.

and as it happened to be on churning day, the young ladies were left to look after the butter making. But, when the chaise[12] which carried the old folks to the marriage returned, it occurred to the young ladies, that, before proceeding to domestic toil, they would have plenty of time to return Miss Trotabout's last morning visit; and off they set, leaving directions with the black girl to have the churn before the fire by the time they returned. During their absence, it unfortunately happened that the wench descried one of her black cronies passing; and, running down the lane to enjoy a little talk, left the kitchen door open; when Mr. Gosling's boar pig Mammoth, who was always a mischievous brute, finding a clear passage, entered without ceremony and upset the churn. My neighbour's kitchen was immediately converted into the country of the Gadarenes.[13] To guzzle up the contents was but the work of a moment. The succeeding scarcity also aroused that inquisitive disposition for which swine as well as ladies are noted, when one of the vile animals, perceiving something in the churn, as it lay upon its side, thrust in its snout to examine. In this state of things, the black wench, having descried the young ladies at a distance, returned to her post. Vengeance succeeded amazement; and the first object of it, and apparently the most guilty, was the individual whose fore quarters had already passed from observation. Now, it so happens that no way has yet been invented to drive a pig straight forward, but to pull it by the tail. As soon, therefore, as it found itself assaulted behind, the unclean beast made a fair entrance into the wooden tabernacle: and, when the young ladies returned to make butter, it was rolling round the floor, to the utter dismay of the girl, and complete discomfiture of the whole herd of swine. From such trials as these, yon townsfolks, who have nothing else to do but to be genteel, are altogether exempted.

After Mr. Gosling's unfortunate confinement, I went to call upon his family, imagining that the countenance of an acquaintance would help to soothe and keep up their spirits. Parson Drone, too, had prepared a long discourse upon patience, and was come to deliver it. But we found them all very cheerful; and the parson,

[12] A chaise was usually a light, two-wheeled carriage, for one or two passengers, and drawn by one or two horses. When bigger, it was normally identified by the number of horses, e.g., "chaise and four" or "chaise and six."

[13] Today the ruins of Gadara, in northern Jordan. In the New Testament, it was the place where Jesus encountered a man possessed by demons, which he had to exorcise.

unwilling to lose his labour, made his visit short, and carried his discourse to old Caleb Staggers, whose mare had just died of the botts.[14] Mr. Gosling's confinement they considered merely as a temporary inconvenience, arising from the spite of his creditors. But when his debts were called in, he would pay every body; and the whole family agreed that, then, with the rest of his property, they would go to a country better worth the living in. I found among them, however, a diversity of opinion about where this should be. Mrs. Gosling spoke of the Ohio; but Mr. Rehoboam declared that it was a new country, without roads, where a young man could not lay a leg over a saddle from the one year's end to the other. Miss Dinah preferred the Cape of Good Hope; but she was afraid of the Caffres,[15] who sometimes carry off white women. To elope with a lord or a duke, she observed, would be a very pretty incident; but, should any person ever write a novel about the Goslings, to be carried off by a Hottentot[16] would appear so droll. Upon the whole, they seemed to think the opinion of Miss Fanny most feasible: that it would be best to go to Botany Bay,[17] where every genteel family like the Goslings receives so many white nigers,[18] sent out every year from Britain by Government for the supply of the colony.

As your warriors for the winter have not yet opened their campaign, I hope you will find room in your paper for the preceding accounts of my neighbour and his family. It will not, I know, be very interesting to your readers in general; for they have all seen the like, and heard the like a hundred times before: and as it is no fable but a true story, they will not be able to deduce from it any sage moral for their own direction in life. Yet its insertion will oblige a great many of your readers. By looking over the list

[14] An infestation of a horse's stomach by the larvae of the botfly (*Gasterophilus intestinalis*). Staggers (the name of this neighbour) is also a disease affecting cattle and sheep.

[15] An obsolete (and today regarded as offensive) term for the Nguni (and other Bantu) people from South Africa.

[16] An obsolete (and today regarded as offensive) term for non-Bantu-speaking, nomadic pastoralist, indigenous people of South Africa, known as the Khoisan.

[17] The original British settlement in Australia (today, part of Sydney); for a time, the name referred to any and all British settlements in Australia.

[18] This is the original spelling (preserved in Davies, though Blackadar doubled the middle consonant). The reference is to British citizens who were deported to Australia and had to work as indentured labourers.

of your subscribers, you will see that the Gosling family have extensive connexions in every part of the province and in every kind of occupation; and I am sure, it will gratify them all to hear how their relation Mr. Solomon is getting on. Should you oblige them and myself thus far, I may be induced to send you, at some future period, the sequel of my neighbour's trading career.

MEPHIBOSHETH STEPSURE.

John Howard Willis

The Faithful Heart

(1825)

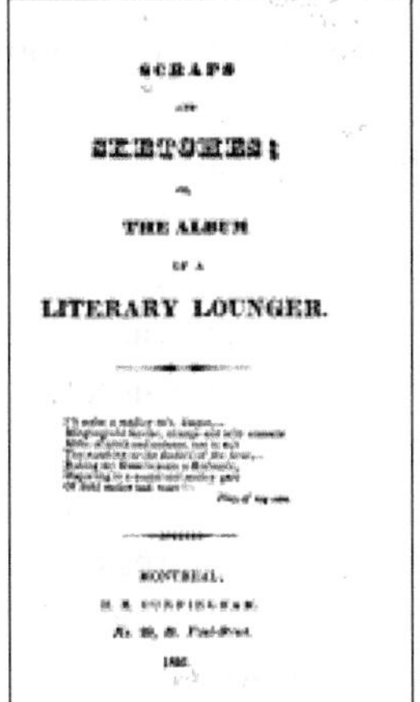

THE ALBUM

LITERARY LOUNGER.

The author: John Howard Willis was one of the most important Canadian poets of the 1820s and 1830s, an accomplished painter, and one of the first practitioners of the short story genre in British North America. He was born in 1802 or 1803, in or around Quebec City; he was the son of Robert Willis, barrack-master at Lachine. At a very young age, he was an ensign in the Lower Canadian militia at the end of the War of 1812 and was mentioned later as "supernumerary." His obituary in the *Quebec Mercury* of 3 July 1847 tells us that he died on 2 July 1847 at his residence on Couillard street in Quebec City, and that he had been "many years clerk in the Commissariat department." He contributed poetry and prose to several publications, especially from Montreal. He published one volume of *Scraps and Sketches* in 1831 and the publisher, H. H. Cunningham, bought the copyright, which may be the first such example in Canada. An anecdote related by him on "The Real Moose Hunter of Canada" (about an incident which occurred in the summer of 1841) was reproduced in Peter Hawker's 1844 *Instructions to Young Sportsmen* (274-276) and then reprinted in similar publications.

The text: First published in the *Canadian Magazine and Literary Repository* 4: 23 (May 1825), 416-418, where it was signed "H." It was included in Willis's anonymous 1831 volume *Scraps and Sketches; or, The Album of a Literary Lounger* (Montreal: H. H. Cunningham, 1831), 63-67, from which the following has been taken. In the book, punctuation has been improved (in the same spirit, we have eliminated a few superfluous commas), paragraphs have been multiplied, and typographical errors have been corrected. Some spelling changes from 1831 ("liliac" for "lilac" and "mandoline" for "mandolin") have been ignored and the originals restored. Content changes operated by Willis in the 1831 version are identified in footnotes.

Further reading: Mary Lu MacDonald. "Three Early Canadian Poets." *Canadian Poetry: Studies, Documents, Review* 17 (Fall/Winter 1985), 79-81.

Mary Jane Edwards. "Essentially Canadian." *Canadian Literature* 52 (Spring 1972), 8-23.

> Oh! she was true in life,—nor had the grave,
> Whose chilling damp so quickly makes a void
> 'Tween human hearts, however fond on earth,
> Power over one that loved as her's had done.
>
> *My own MS.*

It is the extreme height of absurdity to suppose, but for a moment, that the many high-wrought and impassioned details which so often adorn the florid pages of romanceful history, depicting the devotional intensity of the female heart in its affections, have not their counterpart in nature and truth. Yes,—thousands upon thousands are the instances which occur, and that with a circumstantial reality which speaks direct to the heart of the sneering and heartless sceptic;—and I will now quote one as a conviction in point of the truth of my affirmation.

I had occasion, a few years ago,[19] to stay some time at the singularly wild and lonely village of Bay St. Paul,[20] situated some distance below Quebec. In the garden attached to the house where I had fixed my residence,[21] I perceived a grave, rather large in size than common, and made in a corner among a group of lilac trees, and in whose thick shade it was scarcely perceptible by a casual observer. I naturally made enquiry about it, and these were the particulars as far as I could learn.—

In the summer of 1814,[22] one of the transports which had entered the river with troops from the Peninsula,[23] landed an officer in the last stage of a dangerous fever, and whose particular request it was that he might be put on shore to die. He was accompanied, or perhaps I might more properly express it, attended by an

[19] This was clearly dated 1824, since the original version from 1825 read "last summer," though it became, quite naturally, "a few years ago" in 1831.

[20] Baie-Saint-Paul is a small city on the northern shore of the St. Lawrence, about 100 km north-east of Quebec City.

[21] Here, Willis removed the following from the 1825 version: "and which jutted out to nearly the edge of a tremendous precipice, that rose abruptly an immense height from the raging surf which lashed its rocky base."

[22] The 1825 version has "1815."

[23] The Peninsular War, in which Britain had fought alongside Spain and Portugal against Napoleonic France, had ended in April 1814. Some of the troops that had taken part in this conflict were sent to North America to fight in the War of 1812.

interesting young woman, whose accent and manner[24] denoted her of foreign extraction—conjecture rumoured either Spanish or Italian.

The young man died in a few days, and was buried as I have before related. The house was then occupied by an English family, who had kindly received him when brought from on board the transport, and had been as attentively ministering to his comfort during his little span of existence among them, as though he had been an adopted relative.—But who was she who was thus left lone and desolate in a strange land?—None could tell.

She had not been, it was thought, attached by any legal obligation to him whose dying eyes she had so tenderly closed, and whose last breath was spent on her lips; but let that be as it may, she was bound by a tie paramount to every other—that of affection, fervid and lasting, and which seemed identified with her very existence.

The death of her lover, or if you choose to call him so—her protector, did not appear to elicit from her any extravagant display of sorrow. She had, it is probable, prepared herself for the event; for his illness had been long and tedious, and its termination might have been looked forward to with a degree of certainty.

Luckily for her, the family with whom she was placed as if by chance, were considerate as well as kind; and she was left free of intrusive civility (which, indeed, in some cases is a species of mockery) to muse and linger over a grief which was placid and calm in its ostensive appearance, like the surface of molten metal, but, like it, all cankering and consuming beneath.

She used to join, as far as she could make herself useful, in the domestic operations of those about her, but in a kind of torpid abstraction that too plainly denoted how little of interest her being had in what was now left it on earth. She lived for months with them, and she was yet a stranger. She barely knew enough of English to express a few ordinary wants in that language; and though it was evident that French was next to her native tongue, she was so reserved and silent, that she scarcely ever spoke, except when compelled by the mere obligation of her intercourse with those with whom she lived, and who were too delicately tender of her feelings to intrude interrogatories that it was palpable she wished to shun and avoid.

[24] In the 1825 version, this reads "whose accent and complexion."

Her face and form were alike beautiful, even though blighting care and the discomforts of a sea voyage must have worn them something—and which a hopeless sorrow was fast wasting with a fiery corrosion day after day, and she was becoming less like an inhabitant of this world.

Her only pleasure—for it must have been a pleasure to her, if her heart had the capability of feeling the sensation—was in the fall of evening to sit beside the grave of him she loved, and give the soft tones of her country's guitar to the stillness of twilight, accompanying them with her voice, that then breathing the accents of her native land, would pour forth in all its rich fullness of power some peculiar air that was, doubtless, the favourite of the one who slept unconscious of the once loved melody.

At a time like this, it was said her appearance would be almost supernatural. As she leant over her mandolin, her long dark hair would stream in the breeze and over her shoulders, and nearly hide the large black eyes which would now flash with a light more than mortal,—and together with this, her tall and pliant figure robed in its sable dress, would for the moment give her a wild and unearthly mien.

But this enthusiasm of impassioned sorrow would gradually subside, and bending her head down over the grave, till her fine tresses mingled with its long rank grass, she would silently weep for hours.

As I observed before, she wasted fast away. At the close of the fifth month from her arrival, she had been sitting out at the grave in the garden, one bleak autumnal evening, much later than was her usual custom; and the family, becoming uneasy at her absence, sent one of their number to ascertain the cause.—She was found stretched at length on the grave, with her face close pressed to its turf covering; and her beautiful arms extended, as tho' they had in life's departure—for she was dead—attempted to clasp to her bosom the cold earth which was so soon to admit her to the side of her beloved.

As she had been heard to express a wish[25] to be buried in the same grave with her lover—need I observe that such a wish was religiously complied with.

[25] The first part of this sentence was much longer and more sentimental in the 1825 version: "To the ribbon of her guitar, which lay at her head, was pinned a small scrap of paper, with a request on it in the French language."

And such was the end of a being, whose heart was embalmed[26] in its deep and absorbing grief—And that heart was broken under such circumstances too!—far from her country and her friends, where there were none to whom she could turn,—now that he was gone for whose sake she had dared and endured the encountering every ill to which life could expose her—None to whom she could look for solace in her loneliness of dreary despair.

Her friends—connexions,—and what were they? How heart rending to think[27] that one who must have been dear to them should in a foreign land breathe her silent agony of existence away, unpitied, comparatively, and unknown. And, doubtless, hers must have been rank and affluence in the country of her birth; for there was that elegance and refinement about her which they only can confer; and her manner was too complaisantly dignified not to proclaim them habitual.

Peace to her gentle spirit![28] She sleeps in death with him whose existence while on earth gave hers its only value.—And the hallowed spot which entombs a heart so faithful is to me far more sacred than if the unmeaning benediction of some pretender to piety had sanctified it to the inhumation of thousands of the mercenary and worthless, however eminent and highborn.

[26] The following phrase inserted here has been removed from the 1825 version: “if I might be allowed to trifle so far with a thing so sacred, as to use a poetical similitude.”

[27] These five words were added to the beginning of the sentence in the 1831 version.

[28] This exclamation was added in the 1831 version.

Thomas Chandler Haliburton

The Clockmaker

(1835)

The author: Thomas Chandler Haliburton was born on 17 December 1796 in Windsor, Nova Scotia, as a third-generation Nova Scotian (his grandfather had emigrated in 1761). Like his father and grandfather before him, Haliburton was a judge and a Tory. He graduated from King's College, Windsor, in 1815, and left for England, where he met his first wife. Back in Canada, he passed the bar (in 1820) and became a lawyer, a member of the House of Assembly (1826-1829), a judge in the Inferior Court of Common Pleas (1829-1841), and a Supreme Court judge (1841-1856). Immediately after retirement, he moved to England, where, in 1859, he became a Tory member of the House of Commons. He died on 27 August 1865 in Isleworth, West London. He published many books, essays, and pamphlets on Nova Scotia, Canada, and North America, but he became famous for the short-story cycles centred on the life and sayings of Sam Slick. For a while in the late 1830s, he was seen as a rival of Dickens (while the latter was known simply as Boz). In 1852, at the peak of his fame, he edited *Traits of American Humour, by Native Authors.* Haliburton was, during the last 30 years of his life, the most celebrated Canadian author and the only one enjoying worldwide celebrity.

The text: First published in *The Novascotian* on 23 and 30 September 1835 as the first two instalments of a series on Sam Slick. These became the first and second chapter of *The Clockmaker; or, The Sayings and Doings of Samuel Slick, of Slickville* (Halifax: Joseph Howe, 1836 [1837]), 5-10. The book was also quickly published in London by Richard Bentley the same year (1837), without copyright. The following is from the book published by Howe, which appeared in January 1837 (with the year 1836 on the title page). Although these are technically two short stories of the same cycle, they can function together as one story, since the first one simply introduces the character, whose first chance to exhibit his skills is in the second one. There are several spelling inconsistencies, but they have been preserved here.

Further reading: Frank M. Tierney, Ed. *The Thomas Chandler Haliburton Symposium.* Ottawa: University of Ottawa Press, 1985.

Matthew R. Laird. "Nativist American Humour: Sam Slick and the Defense of New England Whig Culture." *Canadian Review of American Studies* 23: 4 (Winter 1993), 71-88.

I. The Trotting Horse

I was always well mounted; I am fond of a horse, and always piqued myself on having the fastest trotter in the Province. I have made no great progress in the world, I feel doubly, therefore, the pleasure of not being surpassed on the road. I never feel so well or so cheerful as on horseback, for there is something exhilirating in quick motion; and, old as I am, I feel a pleasure in making any person whom I meet on the way put his horse to the full gallop, to keep pace with my trotter. Poor Ethiope! you recollect him, how he was wont to lay back his ears on his arched neck, and push away from all competition. He is done, poor fellow! the spavin[29] spoiled his speed, and he now roams at large upon 'my farm at Truro.'[30] Mohawk never failed me till this summer, I pride myself (you may laugh at such childish weakness in a man of my age,) but still, I pride myself in taking the concert out of coxcombs I meet on the road,[31] and on the ease with which I can leave a fool behind, whose nonsense disturbs my solitary musings. On my last journey to Fort Lawrence,[32] as the beautiful view of Colchester[33] had just opened upon me, and as I was contemplating its richness and exquisite scenery, a tall thin man, with hollow cheeks and bright twinkling black eyes, on a good bay horse, somewhat out of condition, overtook me; and drawing up, said, I guess you started early this morning, Sir? I did, Sir, I replied. You did not come from Halifax, I presume, Sir, did you? in a dialect too rich to be mistaken as genuine Yankee. And which way may you be travelling? asked my inquisitive companion. To Fort Lawrence. Ah! said he, so am I, it is *in my circuit.* The word *circuit* sounded so professional, I looked again at him, to ascertain whether I had ever seen him

[29] Enlargement of the hock (the tarsal joint of the hind leg) of a horse by a bony growth or fluid accumulation.

[30] Truro is a town in Nova Scotia, named by British settlers after the city of Truro in Cornwall.

[31] "To take the concert out of" is an expression that meant to ridicule, to make fun of.

[32] A village on the border with New Brunswick, in Cumberland County.

[33] A county in Nova Scotia (Truro is the largest town), east of Cumberland County.

before, or whether I had met with one of those nameless, but innumerable limbs of the law, who now flourish in every district of the Province. There was a keenness about his eye, and an acuteness of expression, much in favor of the law; but the dress, and general bearing of the man, made against the supposition. His was not the coat of a man who can afford to wear an old coat, nor was it one of 'Tempest & More's,'[34] that distinguish country lawyers from country boobies. His clothes were well made, and of good materials, but looked as if their owner had shrunk a little since they were made for him; they hung somewhat loose on him. A large brooch, and some superfluous seals and gold keys, which ornamented his outward man,[35] looked 'New England' like. A visit to the States, had perhaps, I thought, turned this Colchester beau into a Yankee fop. Of what consequence was it to me who he was—in either case I had nothing to do with him, and I desired neither his acquaintance nor his company—still I could not but ask myself who can this man be? I am not aware, said I, that there is a court sitting at this time at Cumberland? Nor am I, said my friend. What then could he have to do with the circuit? It occurred to me he must be a Methodist preacher.[36] I looked again, but his appearance again puzzled me. His attire might do—the colour might be suitable—the broad brim not out of place; but there was a want of that staidness of look, that seriousness of countenance, that expression, in short, so characteristic of the clergy. I could not account for my idle curiosity—a curiosity which, in him, I had the moment before viewed both with suspicion and disgust; but so it was—I felt a desire to know who he could be who was neither lawyer nor preacher, and yet talked of his *circuit* with the gravity of both. How ridiculous, I thought to myself is this; I will leave him. Turning towards him, I said, I feared I should be late for breakfast, and must therefore bid him good morning. Mohawk felt the pressure of my knees, and away we went at a slapping pace. I congratulated myself on conquering my own curiosity, and on

[34] A firm of Halifax tailors.

[35] Jesting reference to the distinction between the "outward man" and the "inward man," which originates in 2 Corinthians 4: 16, but was made famous in Protestant theology by its discussion in Martin Luther's treatise *On the Freedom of a Christian*.

[36] A "circuit" used to be a judicial division throughout which a judge travelled, holding court in different locations. Haliburton himself was such a judge, who used to ride through his "circuit." Similarly, Methodist preachers were often "circuit riders."

avoiding that of my travelling companion. This, I said to myself, this is the value of a good horse; I patted his neck—I felt proud of him. Presently I heard the steps of the unknown's horse—the clatter increased. Ah, my friend, thought I, it won't do; you should be well mounted if you desire my company; I pushed Mohawk faster, faster, faster—to his best. He outdid himself; he had never trotted so handsomely—so easily—so well.

I guess that is a pretty considerable smart horse, said the stranger, as he came beside me, and apparently reined in, to prevent his horse passing me; there is not, I reckon, so spry a one on *my circuit.*

Circuit, or no circuit, one thing was settled in my mind; he was a Yankee, and a very impertinent Yankee, too. I felt humbled, my pride was hurt, and Mohawk was beaten. To continue this trotting contest was humiliating; I yielded, therefore, before the victory was palpable, and pulled up. Yes, continued he, a horse of pretty considerable good action, and a pretty fair trotter, too, I guess. Pride must have a fall—I confess mine was prostrate in the dust. These words cut me to the heart. What! is it come to this, poor Mohawk, that you, the admiration of all but the envious, the great Mohawk, the standard by which all other horses are measured—trots next to Mohawk, only yields to Mohawk, looks like Mohawk—that you are, after all, only a counterfeit, and pronounced by a straggling Yankee to be merely 'a pretty fair trotter!' If he was trained, I guess that he might be made do a little more. Excuse me, but if you divide your weight between the knee and the stirrup, rather most on the knee, and rise forward on the saddle, so as to leave a little daylight between you and it, I hope I may never ride *this circuit again*, if you don't get a mile more an hour out of him. What! not enough, I mentally groaned, to have my horse beaten, but I must be told that I don't know how to ride him; and that, too, by a Yankee—Aye, there's the rub—a Yankee what? Perhaps a half-bred puppy, half yankee, half blue nose.[37] As there is no escape, I'll try to make out my riding master. *Your circuit*, said I, my looks expressing all the surprise they were capable of—your circuit, pray what may that be? Oh, said he, the eastern circuit—I am on the eastern circuit, sir. I have heard, said I, feeling that I now had a lawyer to deal with, that there is a great deal of business on this circuit—pray, are there many cases of importance? There is

[37] Bluenose is a nickname for a Nova Scotian.

a pretty fair business to be done, at least there has been, but the cases are of no great value—we do not make much out of them, we get them up very easy, but they don't bring much profit. What a beast, thought I, is this; and what a curse to a country, to have such an unfeeling pettifogging rascal practising in it—a horse jockey, too—what a finished character! I'll try him on that branch of his business.

That is a superior animal you are mounted on, said I—I seldom meet one that can travel with mine. Yes, said he coolly, a considerable fair traveller, and most particular good bottom. I hesitated, this man who talks with such unblushing effrontery of getting up cases, and making profit out of them, cannot be offended at the question—yes, I will put it to him. Do you feel an inclination to part with him? I never part with a horse sir, that suits me, said he—I am fond of a horse—I don't like to ride in the dust after every one I meet, and I allow no man to pass me but when I choose. Is it possible, I thought, that he can know me; that he has heard of my foible, and is quizzing me, or have I this feeling in common with him. But, continued I, you might supply yourself
1835 again. Not on *this circuit*, I guess, said he, nor yet in Campbell's circuit. Campbell's circuit—pray, sir, what is that? That, said he, is the western—and Lampton rides the shore circuit; and as for the people on the shore, they know so little of horses, that Lampton tells me, a man from Aylesford[38] once sold a hornless ox there, whose tail he had cut and nicked for a horse of the Goliath breed. I should think, said I, that Mr. Lampton must have no lack of cases among such enlightened clients. Clients, sir, said my friend, Mr. Lampton is not a lawyer. I beg pardon, I thought you said he rode the *circuit*. We call it a circuit, said the stranger, who seemed by no means flattered by the mistake—we divide the Province, as in the Almanack, into circuits, in each of which we separately carry on our business of manufacturing and selling clocks. There are few, I guess, said the Clockmaker, who go upon *tick* as much as we do,[39] who have so little use for lawyers; if attornies could wind a *man up again*, after he has been fairly *run down*, I guess they'd be a pretty harmless sort of folks. This explanation restored my good

[38] A farming community in Nova Scotia, on the eastern shore of the Bay of Fundy.

[39] To "go upon tick" was an expression meaning to take up goods on credit (in order to sell them).

humour, and as I could not quit my companion, and he did not feel disposed to leave me, I made up my mind to travel with him to Fort Lawrence, the limit of *his circuit.*

II. The Clock Maker

I had heard of Yankee clock pedlars, tin pedlars, and bible pedlars, especially of him who sold Polyglot Bibles (*all in English*) to the amount of sixteen thousand pounds. The house of every substantial farmer had three substantial ornaments, a wooden clock, a tin reflector,[40] and a Polyglot Bible. How is it that an American can sell his wares, at whatever price he pleases, where a blue-nose would fail to make a sale at all? I will enquire of the Clockmaker the secret of his success. What a pity it is, Mr. *Slick*, (for such was his name,) what a pity it is, said I, that you, who are so successful in teaching these people the value of *clocks*, could not also teach them the value of *time.* I guess, said he, they have got that ring to grow on their horns yet, which every four year old has in our country.[41] We reckon hours and minutes to be dollars and cents. They do nothing in these parts, but eat, drink, smoke, sleep, ride about, lounge at taverns, make speeches at temperance meetings, and talk about "*House of Assembly.*" If a man don't hoe his corn, and he don't get a crop, he says it is all owing to the Bank; and if he runs into debt and is sued, why says the lawyers are a curse to the country. They are a most idle set of folks, I tell you. But how is it, said I, that you manage to sell such an immense number of clocks, (which certainly cannot be called necessary articles,) among a people with whom there seems to be so great a scarcity of money.

Mr. Slick paused, as if considering the propriety of answering the question, and looking me in the face, said, in a confidential

[40] Better known today as a "reflector oven;" it had an open side facing the fire, allowing the food to be cooked or baked without being kept directly over the source of heat.

[41] Cows over three years old usually start gaining a ring on their horns every year.

tone, Why, I don't care if I do tell you, for the market is glutted, and I shall quit this circuit. It is done by a knowledge of *soft sawder*[42] and *human natur*. But here is Deacon Flint's, said he, I have but one clock left, and I guess I will sell it to him. At the gate of a most comfortable looking farm house stood Deacon Flint, a respectable old man, who had understood the value of time better than most of his neighbours, if one might judge from the appearance of every thing about him. After the usual salutation, an invitation to "alight" was accepted by Mr. Slick, who said, he wished to take leave of Mrs. Flint before he left Colchester. We had hardly entered the house, before the Clockmaker pointed to the view from the window, and, addressing himself to me, said, if I was to tell them in Connecticut, there was such a farm as this away down east here in Nova Scotia, they would'nt believe me—why there aint such a location in all New England. The deacon has a hundred acres of dyke[43]—seventy, said the deacon, only seventy. Well, seventy; but then there is your fine deep bottom, why I could run a ramrod into it—Interval, we call it, said the Deacon, who, though evidently pleased at this eulogium, seemed to wish the experiment of the ramrod to be tried in the right place—well interval if you please, (though Professor Eleazer Cumstick, in his work on Ohio, calls them bottoms,) is just as good as dyke. Then there is that water privilege, worth 3 or $4,000, twice as good as what Governor Cass paid $15,000 for.[44] I wonder, Deacon, you don't put up a carding mill on it: the same works would carry a turning lathe, a shingle machine, a circular saw, grind bark, and ——. Too old, said the Deacon, too old for all those speculations—old, repeated the clock-maker, not you; why you are worth half a dozen of the young men we see, now-a-days, you are young enough to have—here he said something in a lower tone of voice, which I did not distinctly hear; but whatever it was, the Deacon was pleased, he smiled and said he did not think of such things now. But your

[42] To "sawder" means to flatter; "soft sawder" (possibly coined by Haliburton) became a relatively popular expression in 19th-century North America (it comes from the actual technique of "soft solder").

[43] Dykelands are agricultural lands developed from marshes around the Bay of Fundy, in Nova Scotia and New Brunswick.

[44] Lewis Cass (1782-1866), the US Secretary of War at the time, had been Governor of the Michigan Territory between 1813 and 1831, overseeing several treaties with first nations and thereby acquiring lands in exchange for money (usually paid in perpetuity), though none matches the sum mentioned here by Slick.

beasts, dear me, your beasts must be put in and have a feed; saying which, he went out to order them to be taken to the stable. As the old gentleman closed the door after him, Mr. Slick drew near to me, and said in an under tone, that is what I call "*soft sawder.*" An Englishman would pass that man as a sheep passes a hog in a pasture, without looking at him; or, said he, looking rather archly, if he was mounted on a pretty smart horse, I guess he'd trot away, *if he could.* Now I find—here his lecture on "*soft sawder*" was cut short by the entrance of Mrs. Flint. Jist come to say good bye, Mrs. Flint. What, have you sold all your clocks? yes, and very low, too, for money is scarce, and I wished to close the concarn; no, I am wrong in saying all, for I have just one left. Neighbor Steel's wife asked to have the refusal of it, but I guess I won't sell it; I had but two of them, this one and the feller of it, that I sold Governor Lincoln. General Green, the Secretary of State for Maine,[45] said he'd give me 50 dollars for this here one—it has composition wheels and patent axles, it is a beautiful article—a real first chop—no mistake, genuine superfine, but I guess I'll take it back; and beside, Squire Hawk might think kinder harder, that I did not give him the offer. Dear me, said Mrs. Flint, I should like to see it, where is it? It is in a chest of mine over the way, at Tom Tape's store, I guess he can ship it on to Eastport.[46] That's a good man, said Mrs. Flint, jist let's look at it. Mr. Slick, willing to oblige, yielded to these entreaties, and soon produced the clock—a gawdy, highly varnished, trumpery looking affair. He placed it on the chimney-piece, where its beauties were painted out and duly appreciated by Mrs. Flint, whose admiration was about ending in a proposal, when Mr. Flint returned from giving his directions about the care of the horses. The Deacon praised the clock, he too thought it a handsome one; but the Deacon was a prudent man, he had a watch, he was sorry, but he had no occasion for a clock. I guess you're in the wrong furrow this time, Deacon, it ant for sale, said Mr. Slick; and if it was, I reckon neighbor Steel's wife would have it, for she gives me no peace about it. Mrs. Flint said, that Mr. Steele had enough to do, poor man, to pay his interest, without buying clocks for his wife. It's no concarn of mine, said Mr. Slick, as long as he pays me, what he has to do, but I guess I don't want

[45] Levi Lincoln Jr. (1782-1868) was Governor of Massachusetts (1825-1834); Roscoe Greene (1796-1840) was secretary of state of Maine (1831-1834).

[46] A city in Maine, on the border with New Brunswick.

to sell it, and beside it comes too high; that clock can't be made at Rhode Island under 40 dollars. Why it ant possible, said the Clockmaker, in apparent surprise, looking at his watch, why as I'm alive it is 4 o'clock, and if I hav'nt been two hours here—how on airth shall I reach River Philip[47] to-night? I'll tell you what, Mrs. Flint, I'll leave the clock in your care till I return on my way to the States—I'll set it a going and put it to the right time. As soon as this operation was performed, he delivered the key to the deacon with a sort of serio-comic injunction to wind up the clock every Saturday night, which Mrs. Flint said she would take care should be done, and promised to remind her husband of it, in case he should chance to forget it.

That, said the Clockmaker as soon as we were mounted, that I call '*human natur!*' Now that clock is sold for 40 dollars—it cost me just 6 dollars and 50 cents. Mrs. Flint will never let Mrs. Steel have the refusal—nor will the deacon learn until I call for the clock, that having once indulged in the use of a superfluity, how difficult it is to give it up. We can do without any article of luxury we have never had, but when once obtained, it is not '*in human natur*' to surrender it voluntarily. Of fifteen thousand sold by myself and partners in this Province, twelve thousand were left in this manner, and only ten clocks were ever returned—when we called for them they invariably bought them. We trust to '*soft sawder*' to get them into the house, and to '*human natur*' that they never come out of it.

[47] A village in Cumberland County, Nova Scotia.

Catharine Parr Traill

The Autobiography of an Unlucky Wit

(1838)

The author: Catharine Parr Traill was born on 9 January 1802 in Rotherhithe (today part of London, England) as Catharine Parr Strickland. She had four older sisters, one younger sister (Susanna Moodie) and two younger brothers. She spent most of her childhood in Suffolk. The death of her father in 1818 prompted her (and her sisters) to try for a career in writing. She published her first volume of stories in 1818. Several books followed (mostly didactic children's tales). After a two-year engagement was broken off by her fiancé in 1831, Catharine met a widowed Scottish half-pay officer, Lieutenant Thomas Traill, whom she married on 13 May 1832, despite family opposition. After a brief tour of Scotland, the newlyweds left for Canada in early July 1832. Her sister Susanna followed her the same month. Her brother Samuel (1804-1867) had already immigrated there in 1825 and lived in the Douro district in Ontario. In 1836, she published an account of her first experiences as a settler, *The Backwoods of Canada*, which remains her best-known book. In the meantime, she continued to contribute stories to British and American periodicals.

The text: First published in *The Gift: A Christmas and New Year's Present for 1839* (Philadelphia: E.L. Carey & A. Hart, 1838), 220-232. It was signed "by Mrs. Traill" and ended with an indication of her location: "Westover, U[pper] C[anada]." This is evidently a misspelling: it should read "Westove" (as the Traills named their first log cabin in Douro and, later, the house they purchased in 1862), which was the name of the estate of the Traill family on the Orkney Islands. The following year it was reprinted in *The Young Lady's Reader; arranged for examples in rhetoric: for the higher classes in seminaries* by Louisa C. Tuthill (New Haven: S. Babcock, 1839), 215-224, as an example of "fictitious narrative," after which is seems to have been out of print until its inclusion in Peterman and Ballstadt's selection *Forest and Other Gleanings: The Fugitive Writings of Catharine Parr Traill* (Ottawa: University of Ottawa Press, 1994), 20-30. The following is from the original published in 1838 in *The Gift.*

A woman had better be born with no more brains than a goose, than be heiress to that dangerous possession—wit.—In the former case she is sure, soon or late, to find some honest gander for her mate, and, perhaps, some good uncle or aunt to make his or her will in her favour; but in the latter she is destined to die an old maid, and cut herself out of the good graces of all her friends and relations, by the sharpness of her tongue.

Having suffered all my life from the ill effects of this mischievous propensity, I would, from motives of pure philanthropy to the rising generation, entreat—advise—admonish and implore all guardians of the young of my own sex, mothers, aunts and governesses to check, crush and exterminate all tendency to mimicry, satire, repartee, sauciness, smartness, quickness; in short, all lively sallies that may grow up to form what is usually termed a *witty woman*. Let their young charges be dunces—the veriest pieces of affectation that ever minced steps at a dancing-master's ball. Let them be pedants—stuff their poor brains with astronomy, geology, conchology, entomology,—but let them not be wits—and, above all, do not let them imagine themselves possessed, in any way, of this most offensive weapon, for, ten to one, they will make fools of themselves through life.

While I was yet in my cradle, my mother discovered an unusual precocity about me, and a love of the ridiculous, which made me laugh ten times more than any of her other children had done at the some age; nay, she even attributed a certain comical cast that was perceptible in one eye during my childhood, to the droll way in which I used to squint up at nurse's high-crowned cap, which was at least half-a-foot higher than that of any old dame's in the village. I always thought it was turning that eye in an oblique direction to watch the movements of the pap-spoon, which, I shrewdly suspect, oftener visited the old woman's lips than the open mouth of her hungry, squalling nursling.

By the time I was three years old I was the veriest imp of mischief that ever lived; unfortunately, my freaks were laughed at, all my smart speeches duly repeated by a fond and foolish mother, and when I deserved to be whipped, I was forgiven on the score that I was so clever and such a *wit*. Now I verily believe half what is called wit in a child is *folly*, and if timely discouraged, the world would be spared much trouble in chastising, mortifying and disinheriting grown up culprits of this description.

At four or five I could mimic the voice, tone, gait and manner of every one I saw—even a comical face in a picture-book was a study for me, and once I amused myself at a lady's house, where my mother had left me to spend the day, by moulding my little face into an exact resemblance of the brass lion's head on the handle of the bell-pull, to the great amusement of all the company. For one frolic I got a sound box on the ear from my father—(it is a source of regret to me I have so few of those valuable salutations to record.)

Our landlord was a stiff old major, who wore a single-breasted coat, flapped waistcoat, a three-cocked hat[48] and a big curled wig. At his quarterly visitations not a syllable must be spoken, but, ranged on our four-legged mahogany stools, my sisters and myself must sit as mute as mice, not a giggle must be heard, not a whisper, while politics (I remember it was Pitt and Fox time,)[49] were discussed between my father and the old major.

Oh, it was dulness of the most refined order to keep our tongues still, our hands in our lap, and our ears open.

I had somehow managed to secrete the clean-picked drumstick of a goose from the dinner-table one Michaelmas-day, to make what we call an apple-scoop. Well, I looked at my dry bone, and I glanced at the wig. The major was in the act of describing a chevaux-de-frise[50]—I thought what an admirable one I could make of his wig. Unseen, unheard, I cracked my bone into a hundred splinters, and, favoured in my retreat from the circle by my quietly mischievous companions, I succeeded in sticking the wig as full of the white shivers of the goose-bone as I have since seen a sponge-cake soaked in wine and custard, (called a hedgehog,) stuck full of blanched almonds.

Imagine the grave, withered, crab-apple face of the major, and then think of the wig and its adornments—he wore, besides, a

[48] Better known as a tricorne.

[49] William Pitt the Younger (1759-1806), British prime minister during the last two years of his life, was the political rival of Charles James Fox (1749-1806) after 1783.

[50] Actually, "cheval de frise" ("chevaux" is the plural form), a military defensive implement consisting of many spikes bound together so as to block cavalry charges.

pigtail coming from beneath the wig. I was just putting the coup de grace to his appearance, by fastening a long bit of rag to the end of this appendage—it was too much for the risible organs of my sisters—a universal burst of laughter took place—it was like the bursting of a long pent-up volcano—it rolled on in spite of the awful frown of my father and the agitated look of the poor major, who was only partly unconscious of the ridiculous figure he cut. I shall never forget the scene, or the suppressed expression of mirth that gleamed and twinkled in my poor father's eyes, as he assisted to recompose the ruffled wig, (no easy matter,) and, in a thundering voice, demanded who had played the trick.

"I was only making a chevaux-de-frise," I said, trying to laugh.

A thundering box on the ear sent me reeling to the further end of the room; given, I verily believe, more out of respect to the feelings of the offended major, than from genuine displeasure against the culprit—but it would not do—the dignity of the old soldier was mortally wounded; he never entered the house again, to the great mortification of my mother, who counted his few formal visits a great honour, and was wont to boast of the major as one of her grand acquaintance.

My next freak was a more fatal one to my own interests, as, by an unlucky speech, I made an implacable enemy of a maiden aunt who occasionally visited our house; sometimes in company with a younger sister. Aunt Martha seldom inflicted her society on us for less than a month at a time, to the infinite regret of every member of the household, from the tom-cat up to my honoured father.

Aunt Martha was a tall, lean, sour-faced woman of thirty-two; her nose had a sort of pinch at the top, which was very red, and her cheeks were somewhat of the colour of a red cabbage, only wrinkled a little more after the manner of a savoy-leaf;[51] moreover, to complete the pleasantness of her physiognomy, she wore what was then in fashion, a cropped head, called a "Brutus;"[52] no wonder that I should draw an unfavourable comparison between her young, pretty, good-natured, lively sister and herself—the latter I called my pretty aunt, by way of distinction.

[51] The Savoy cabbage, a winter vegetable with wrinkled leaves.

[52] Originally a hairstyle fashionable with men, inspired by the hairdos of late-18th-century French actors who played in a revival of Voltaire's *Brutus*: short hair, combed upward and outward; it was adopted by women (famously by Lady Caroline Lamb) in the early 19th century.

One day a coach stopped at the door—one of my aunts was expected—I eagerly ran to peep through the banisters of the hall-stairs, half-dressed as I was, and in no very low tone asked if it were my "pretty aunt or my ugly aunt that had come?"—A withering glance from Aunt Martha, as she hastily brushed past me on the staircase, proved she had heard the question; she curled up her little red nose, and looked ten times uglier than ever. She never forgot nor forgave the insult—nay, she carried it to her grave, for in her last will and testament the unlucky speech was recorded against me, as a sufficient reason for cutting me out of her will. Younger sisters and brothers, tom-cats, parrots, and cousins to the eight remove, being sharers of her wealth, to the exclusion of poor me, though I had been scolded, starved, whipped and lectured into obedience to her auntly authority, till she had not outwardly a more dutiful niece in the whole list of brother's and sister's brats than myself.

Experience should have taught me wisdom, but a vey small portion of that valuable acquirement fell to my share.

It was my misfortune to be the goddaughter of a proud, mean, vain old woman, some very, very distant relation of my father's, who graciously condescended to bestow upon me her own *beautiful* name, "Deborah Anne,"—horrible compound!—and when I had attained the mature age of sixteen, she benevolently signified her intention of taking me by the hand, and introducing me into company. In other words, I was to be her companion, *alias, white slave*, and if, on the supposition that I might in time become her heiress, I had the good fortune to marry some wretched old bachelor, ancient widower, or sickly dandy of family, I was to bless for ever the goodness and generosity of Mrs. Deborah Anne Pike.

In the meantime, till such eligible connexion could be formed, I must favour, flatter, and attend to the whims and caprices of my patroness and worthy godmamma; fill the important place of ladies' maid and milliner, butler and housekeeper, amuse morning visiters, play the amiable to evening ones, play backgammon till my head was bewildered by the rattling of the dice-box, or pursue the monotonous draughtsmen across the board, till the white chickens looked black and the black white; and, of a rainy day, play billiards or bagatelle.[53]

[53] A popular table game in the 19th century, somewhat similar to billiards.

Our mornings were passed in solitary dulness, till the carriage was at the door to take us our daily round of calls on people as dull as ourselves; from five till six the business of the toilet occupied out time, and I was expected to attend to admire a face that even rouge could not improve, and a figure that resembled two boards bound together.

"Hum—ha—how do you like me now, Miss, that I have beautified a little?" was generally the closing speech, as she cast a satisfied glance at her withered charms in the old japanned dressing-glass.[54]

Once I gave mortal offence by carelessly replying to "How do I look now?" "Much as you generally do, madam."

She was wont to make four things her boast: that she had never threaded a needle or set a stitch since she married the dear old general that was departed; never read any other newspaper than the John Bull, nor any books but the old Bath Guide[55] and her prayer-book; never omitted taking an advantage at whist, nor gave more than a penny to a beggar at a time.

The first month was intolerable. In it I had given offence to one old beau and two danglers,[56] and expressed my intention of pleasing myself in the choice of a husband—a glaring piece of folly and ridiculous assertion of my independence that could not be tolerated. The next—but happily my tongue for once did me a worthy service, and set me free from my worse than Egyptian bondage before the second month was out.

The old lady used to pester me to admire the beauty of a faded green stuffed parrot that stood in an old-fashioned hideous case, among Chinese mandarins, cups and saucers of old Dresden china, and other odd knick-knacks that filled up an ancient Dutch cabinet.

One day I unluckily was tempted to say, "I suppose, madam, you *starved* the parrot whilst it was alive, and *stuffed* it after it was

[54] A mirror with black lacquer.

[55] *John Bull* was a Sunday newspaper founded in 1820, published in London and seen as very conservative. Starting in 1762 (the year of its first publication) the most popular guide to Bath was called *The New Bath Guide*, and new editions were published annually. The "old Bath guide" either refers to an old edition of this book (which other people would have replaced with a new version) or to the original *The Travellers' Guide to and from Bath* (1742).

[56] "Dangler" was slang for a man who flirts with women and hangs around them, but has no interest in a serious relationship.

dead." I said it playfully and in joke, but an awful cloud gathered on the offended lady's brow—silence ensued for a moment; then came a torrent of rebukes, and reproaches, and invectives. I apologized—it was only said in joke. Joke!—to joke with a person of her wealth—her dignity—and I a poor country curate's daughter, that she had taken from obscurity and beggary to make something of. This was too much—the pride of all my race rose up to my aid, and I retorted. The carriage was ordered to the door, and the old woman flung into it, commanding me to go to my room and pack my trunk. Next morning I was duly installed on an *outside* place on the mail[57]—and—the right owners got me by six the same evening. The same mail brought a letter, the essence of spite, from my amiable relative, which, after dwelling on the heinousness of my enormities, concluded with these emphatic words:—

"Miss was too independent and too great a WIT for her station; humility had become the daughter of a poor curate better, and might have been rewarded with not less than £3,000."

I lost the chance of this fine fortune, but I did not lose my detestable name, for the infliction of which I was never remunerated, but I gained what was inexpressibly dearer to me than ever it had been before—my liberty. Nay, even to this hour, though something old, and poor, and single withal, I cannot help congratulating myself on my miraculous escape, convinced, as I am, that had I remained the abject dependant of my rich relative, I should have been left, after a life of slavery, with no better recompense than a broken spirit and an empty purse; the too frequent reward of a rich old woman's *companion.*

I was a little tamed for a while after I came home, but by degrees all my old propensities returned, and I now became worse than ever. I quizzed all my acquaintance, laughed at the old beaux and bachelors of our village, teased the young ones, ridiculed my female friends, with the exception of one or two whom I made my companions, these aped my fashions and manners, and repeated all my sayings. In short, I considered myself as a star among them.

So sharp was my wit at last that few dare enter the lists to answer me, and if I happened to be in one of my *brilliant* humours

[57] Short for "mail coach," a stagecoach that carried letters, packages, and travellers.

no one was safe from my raillery. I could not endure to pass by an opportunity of displaying my talent—friend or foe, young or old, were alike exposed to my sarcasm.

I had nick-names for all my acquaintance, and prided myself on their significance, though now I am inclined to think the practice is vulgar, illiberal and foolish to a degree, besides being excessively ill-natured. In more than one instance I had the mortification of finding these names had reached the ears of the only persons they were not intended for, and that they gave much offence.

The surgeon and apothecary of our village, a huge bachelor with large unmeaning glassy eyes and whiskers of no common size, with an extensive practice, a new white stuccoed dwelling, with vinery and green-house at the end of the village, a stud of horses,[58] and a kennel full of wretched cur dogs, was held in great esteem by the single ladies of the neighbourhood and their mammas, who did not fail to say the doctor would be a good *catch* for some one. One old maid, who had set her cap indefatigably at the good man during the space of eight whole weary years, was pleased to be very jealous of some attention he paid me at a race-ball, and in an audible whisper she said, stretching her scraggy neck across so as partially to eclipse the poor doctor:

"If Mr. L—— makes you an offer, I would advise you to *snap*!"

I coolly thanked her for her advice, but said—"I was not quite in so great a hurry to *snap* (as she elegantly expressed it,) as she might be."[59] The doctor laughed, and the scraggy lady withdrew her crescent-shaped face in evident wrath.

For some time the doctor was looked upon almost as my declared lover, but I happened to hear that he should say, if I had come in for my share of Aunt Martha's legacy, or had been the *certain* heiress of Mrs. D. A. Pike, he might have been *induced* to offer his hand, his house, his vinery, his horses and dogs to me, for I was very clever and a dashing sort of a girl, though, 'pon honour, rather too sharp for him. I was incensed at his mercenary

[58] "Stud" is a term used either for livestock or for an establishment where livestock are kept.

[59] A play on different meanings of "snap" that were more common in the early 19th century than today: the "old maid" asks the narrator to "share" the doctor (if he invites her to dance); the narrator replies that she does not speak foolishly and in haste, like the old maid.

conduct, and resolved to revenge myself in some way. As to my mother, she excused his foible and hoped for the best, and my sisters still thought something might yet be done to bring him on, if I would but be a little meek, and not tease his dogs, and talk very affectionately of my rich godmother.

But the doctor's dogs were my aversion, a set of wretched living skeletons, that followed yelping at his heels, scratching and whining at his patients' doors like fiends of ill omen.

The oft-repeated proverb of "love me love my dog," which he never failed to repeat with a tender squeeze of my hand and a languishing stare from his gooseberry orbs,[60] failed to win my admiration. One might have managed to tolerate one dog, but the doctor had six, though to be sure the whole half-dozen would not have made one respectable sized lady's spaniel. I called these miserable beasts the doctor's patients—himself the "*man of pills*," and the "gooseberry-eyed monster," while his assistant, the elegant, dandified Mr. C——, was the "stork"—he was six feet three inches, and slender to a degree—both were extravagantly proud of their perfections, and, though on the *fortified* side of thirty, the doctor was quite as vain as the youthful Adonis, his companion.

It was Valentine's day. I was resolved to revenge myself for the slighting manner in which of late the man of pills had treated me, and I dashed off a caricature, in which my quondam admirer, with huge bear's whiskers, and eyes as big as saucers, was in the act of drawing an old woman's tooth; his huge frame ridiculously contrasted with a crowd of half starved—not patients—but puppies of all sorts and sizes. Over the surgery door in legible characters was written TEETH DISTRACTED HERE. The centre figure was an admirable likeness of Mr. C. mounted on a stork's legs, and with a bird's head; on the *bill* were inscribed pills, draughts, powders, &c., with an enormous sum-total added up. The resemblances were excellent; in spite of the incongruous appearance of the unhappy doctor and his assistant, every one that saw the group, recognized the originals with shouts of laughter.

"Oh do let them have it," "Pray send it, they will never find out," "It is so clever they can't suspect," cried several of my *best* friends; and go it did, to be returned, not by the postman, but by the dignified, offended object of my satire, Mr. L——.

[60] Gooseberry orbs (or eyes) are round and bulging.

One of my treacherous bosom friends had betrayed me, for the sake of ingratiating herself in the doctor's favour. I was mortified, vexed, ashamed; forced to apologize; but all to no purpose. As I grew meek, the doctor grew more spiteful, and ended with telling me I should soon become an ill-natured, satirical, sour old maid. I lost my admirer, and had the mortification of seeing my treacherous acquaintance become mistress of the stuccoed house, vinery, &c., and flaunt past me at church, in a pink satin hat and feathers, with the six dogs prancing before and behind her.

After this adventure, I received an invitation to stay at —— Hall, with the aunt of Sir Charles S——. He was an elegant, sentimental young baronet; just recalled from his continental tour, by the death of his father. I had been ill, and was a little tamed by my misfortunes. Sir Charles was interested in me; was delighted with my singing, my drawing—I had been making sketches of the Hall, its old chapel, and the romantic scenes of his native village. I was proud, pleased, gratified at his praise. I began to indulge in visions of future bliss, to feel that I was not indifferent to the young baronet; I felt I could love him. Matters were in this train, when Sir Charles, one morning, announced his intention of taking his aunt and me to a race ball, at ——.

His good aunt presented me with a beautiful gauze and satin dress. I had never seen myself full-dressed, in such style. I was elated by my good looks. I should appear to advantage in the eyes of Sir Charles; my conquest would be complete; he had never seen me well-dressed, or in spirits. Sir Charles was a London-bred man. I must lay aside my country manners, and show him what I *could be*. I was all animation and gayety, full of repartee and lively sallies. I did not notice at first that as my spirits increased, so in proportion did Sir Charles become silent, abstracted, and grave. I rallied him at last, teased, quizzed; he looked displeased, and said little. I was blind to my danger, and when we reached the ball room, I flirted with the officer to whom I was introduced as a partner, with the hope of raising my lover's jealousy; but it would not do. I became reckless; pride would not allow me to notice Sir Charles's coldness and neglect. I exerted all my powers of wit to fascinate and charm. I heard my words repeated with admiration on all sides; but one voice alone was mute.

Sir Charles hated a spirited woman; a wit or female satirist was his detestation; he admired the soft, the gentle, the silent, the unaffected, simple country girl, more than the fashionable belle esprit.[61]

As we entered the supper room, I heard him say to his aunt, "I am disappointed, disgusted by her conduct, much as I admired her. I would not now make her my wife, for all the world! I abhor a witty woman!" I heard no more; my head whirled; I turned sick, giddy and faint.

Sir Charles never renewed his attentions, but left the Hall soon after; I saw him no more. Disappointed and grieved at my folly, I left a spot where I had been only too happy to mourn over hopes that my unfortunate propensity had blighted.

And now on the verge of fifty, I find myself with a narrow income, shunned and feared by a limited circle of acquaintance, that unfortunate person, a poor satirical old maid. The only reparation I can make to society, is by publishing this short memoir, as a warning example to my sex, to shun that too common error, a sarcastic temper, and flee from the reputation of being thought a WIT.

[61] Usually "bel esprit" (French for a witty, clever person), also used sometimes with the feminine adjective "belle" to denote a witty woman.

JOSEPH HOWE

The Locksmith of Philadelphia

(1839)

The author: Joseph Howe was born on 13 December 1804 in Halifax and died on 1 June 1873 in the same city. He was the last child of the second wife of John Howe, a loyalist printer during the American Revolution, who had taken refuge in Halifax in 1780. He became a journalist and made of the *Novascotian* the leading newspaper in the province. Apart from political reports, he contributed to his paper two series of travel essays about Nova Scotia: "Western Rambles" (1828) and "Eastern Rambles" (1829-1831). He also wrote poetry and became a publisher (he published *The Clockmaker*, written by his friend Thomas Chandler Haliburton). He is best remembered as one of the most influential politicians in Nova Scotia (he is often described as a "conservative reformer"), as a member of the House of Assembly (1836-1855) and as premier (1860-1863). He was initially opposed to the Canadian Confederation, but later joined Macdonald's cabinet. At the time of his death he was Lieutenant Governor of Nova Scotia. "The Locksmith of Philadelphia" is his only short story.

The text: The story appeared in *Bentley's Miscellany* (Vol. 5 [Vol. 3 for the American edition], March 1839), 272-280. It was signed "Peregrine." It went alongside more popular fiction, such as the serialised novel *Oliver Twist; or, The Parish Boy's Progress* by Boz (Charles Dickens), and it was popular enough to be reprinted in several other periodicals. It was inspired by the true case of one Patrick Lyon (1769-1829), a Scottish-born locksmith from Philadelphia, who was arrested on suspicion of robbery in 1798. Lyon published his own *Narrative* of the events in 1799, while Thomas Lloyd (1756-1827), the "Father of American Shorthand," lent his notes for the publication (in 1808) of an account of the subsequent civil suit. The following is from *Poems and Essays, by The Hon. Joseph Howe* (Montreal: John Lovell, 1874), a selection which (according to the introduction) was prepared by his family according to his wishes. It appeared there as "The Locksmith of Philadelphia. (A Tale)" (299-316), with slight changes of spelling and punctuation, which are adopted here.

In the sober looking city of Philadelphia, there dwelt, some years ago, an ingenious and clever mechanic named Amos Sparks, by trade a locksmith. Nature had blest him with a peculiar turn for the branch of business to which he had been bred. Not only was he skilled in the manufacture and repair of the various articles that in America are usually regarded as "in the locksmith line," but, prompted by a desire to master the more abstruse intricacies of the business, he had studied it so attentively, and with such distinguished success that his proficiency was the theme of admiration, not only with his customers and the neighbourhood, but all who took an interest in mechanical contrivances in the adjoining towns. His counter was generally strewed with all kinds of fastenings for doors, trunks, and desks, which nobody but himself could open; and no lock was ever presented to Amos that he could not pick in a very short time. Like many men of talent in other departments Amos Sparks was poor. Though a very industrious and prudent man, with a small and frugal family, 1839
he merely eked out a comfortable existence but never seemed to accumulate property. Whether it was that he was not of the race of money-grubs, whose instinctive desire of accumulation forces them to earn and hoard without a thought beyond the mere means of acquisition, or whether the time occupied by the prosecution of new inquiries into still undiscovered regions of his favorite pursuit, and in conversation with those who came to inspect and admire the fruits of his ingenuity, were the cause of his poverty, we cannot undertake to determine; but perhaps various causes combined to keep his finances low, and it was quite as notorious in the city that Amos Sparks was a poor man, as that he was an ingenious and decent mechanic. But his business was sufficient for the supply of his wants and those of his family, so he studied and worked on and was content.

It happened that in the Autumn of 18— a merchant in the city, whose business was rather extensive, and who had been bustling about the Quay, and on board his vessels all the morning, returned to his counting-house to lodge several thousand dollars in the Philadelphia Bank, to retire some paper falling due that day, when to his surprise he found that he had either lost or mislaid the key of his iron chest. After diligent search with no success he was led to conclude that, in drawing out his handkerchief he had dropped the key in the street or perhaps into the dock. What was to be done? It was one o'clock, the Bank closed at three, and there was no time to advertise the key, or to muster so large a sum as that required. In his perplexity the merchant thought of the poor locksmith; he had often heard of Amos Sparks; the case seemed one peculiarly adapted to a trial of his powers, and being a desperate one, if he could not furnish a remedy, where else was there a reasonable expectation of succor? A clerk was hurried off for Amos, and, having explained the difficulty, speedily reappeared, followed by the locksmith with his implements in his hand. A few minutes sufficed to open the chest, and the astonished merchant glanced from the rolls of bank notes and piles of coin strewed along the bottom, to the clock in the corner of his office, which told him that he had still three quarters of an hour; with a feeling of delight and exultation, like one who had escaped from an unexpected dilemma by a lucky thought, and who felt that his credit was secure even from a momentary breath of suspicion. He fancied he felt generous as well as glad, and determined that it should be a cash transaction.

"How much is to pay, Amos?" said he, thrusting his hand into his pocket.

"Five Dollars, Sir," said Sparks.

"Five Dollars? why, you are mad, man; you have not been five minutes doing the job. Come" (the genuine spirit of traffic, overcoming the better feelings which had momentary possession of his bosom,) "I'll give you five shillings."[62]

"It is true," replied the locksmith, "that much time has not been employed; but remember how many long years I have been learning to do such a job in five minutes or even to do it at all. A doctor's visit may last but one minute; the service he renders may be but doubtful when all is done, and yet his fee would be as great, if not greater than mine. You should be willing to purchase my skill, humble as it may be, as you would purchase any other commodity in the market, by what it is worth to you."

"Worth to me," said the merchant with a sneer, "well, I think it was worth five shillings, I could have got a new key made for that, or perhaps, might have found the old one."

[62] One US dollar was worth 8 shillings at the time; however, unlike in Canada, British currency was not in use in Philadelphia.

"But could you have got the one made or found the other, in time to retire your notes at the Bank! Had I been disposed to wrong you, taking advantage of your haste and perplexity I might have bargained for a much larger sum, and as there is not another man in the city who could have opened the chest, you would gladly have given me double the amount I now claim."

"Double the amount! why the man's a fool, here are five shillings," said the merchant, holding them in his hand with the air of a rich man taking advantage of a poor one who could not help himself; "and if you do not choose to take them, why, you may sue as soon as you please, for my time is too precious just now to spend in a matter so trifling."

"I never sued a man in my life," said Sparks, "and I have lost much by my forbearance." "But," added he, the trodden worm of a meek spirit beginning to recoil, "you are rich—are able to pay, and although I will not sue you, pay you shall."

The words were scarcely spoken when he dashed down the lid of the chest, and in a moment the strong staples were firmly clasped by the bolts below, and the gold and bank notes were hidden as effectually as though they had vanished like the ill-gotten hoards in the fairy tale.

The merchant stood aghast. He looked at Amos, and then darted a glance at the clock, the hand was within twenty minutes of three, and seemed posting over the figures with the speed of light. What was to be done. At first he tried to bully, but it would not do. Amos told him if he had sustained any injury, "he might sue as soon as he pleased, for his time was too precious just now to be wasted in trifling affairs," and, with a face of unruffled composure, he turned on his heel and was leaving the office.

The merchant called him back, he had no alternative, his credit was at stake, half the city would swear he had lost the key to gain time, and because there was no money in the chest; he was humbled by the necessity of the case, and handing forth the five dollars, "There Sparks," said he, "take your money and let us have no more words."

"I must have ten dollars now," replied the locksmith; "you would have taken advantage of a poor man; and besides opening your strong box there I have a lesson to give you which is well worth a trifling sum. You would not only have deprived me of what had been fairly earned, but have tempted me into a lawsuit which would have ruined my family. You will never in future presume upon your wealth in your dealings with the poor without thinking of the locksmith, and these five dollars may save you much sin and much repentance."

This homily, besides being preached in a tone of calm deliberation, which left no room to hope for any abatement, had exhausted another minute or two of the time already so precious; for the minutes, like the Sibyl's books,[63] increased in value as they diminished in number. The merchant hurriedly counted out the ten dollars, which Amos deliberately inspected to see that they belonged to no broken Bank, and then deposited in his breeches pocket.

"For Heaven's sake, be quick, man, I would not have the Bank close before this money is paid for fifty dollars," exclaimed the merchant.

"I thought so," was the locksmith's grave reply; but not being a malicious or vindictive man, and satisfied with the punishment already inflicted, he delayed no longer, but opened the chest, giving its owner time to seize the cash and reach the Bank, after a rapid flight, a few minutes before it closed.

About a month after this affair the Philadelphia Bank was robbed of coin and notes to the amount of fifty thousand dollars. The bars of a window had been cut, and the vault entered so ingeniously, that it was evident that the burglar had possessed, besides daring courage, a good deal of mechanical skill. The police scoured the City and country round about, but no clue to the discovery of the robber could be traced. Everybody who had anything to lose, felt that daring and ingenious felons were abroad who might probably pay them a visit; all were therefore interested in their discovery and conviction. Suspicions at length began to settle upon Sparks. But yet his poverty and known integrity seemed to give them the lie. The story of the iron chest, which the merchant had hitherto been ashamed, and Amos too forgiving to tell, for the latter did not care to set the town laughing, even at the man who had wronged him, now began to be noised abroad. The

[63] Also known as the sibylline books; according to legend, an old sibyl offered Tarquinius, the last king of Rome, nine very expensive books of prophecies. When he refused to buy them at that price, she burned three and offered him the remaining six at the same price. He refused again, so she burned three more and offered him the last three at the original price. Pressed by his advisors, the king accepted the last offer.

merchant, influenced by a vindictive spirit, had whispered it to the Directors of the Bank, with sundry shrugs and inuendoes, and, of course, it soon spread far and wide, with all sorts of extravagant variations and additions. Amos thought for several days that some of his neighbors looked and acted rather oddly, and he missed one or two who used to drop in and chat almost every afternoon; but, not suspecting for a moment that there was any cause for altered behaviour, these matters made but a slight impression on his mind. In all such cases the person most interested is the last to hear disagreeable news; and the first hint that the locksmith got of the universal suspicion, was from the officer of police, who came with a party of constables to search his premises. Astonishment and grief were of course the portion of Amos and his family for that day. The first shock to a household who had derived, even amidst their humble poverty, much satisfaction from the possession of a good name—a property that they had been taught to value above all earthly treasures—may be easily conceived. To have defrauded a neighbor of sixpence would have been a meanness no one of them would have been guilty of, but fifty thousand dollars, the immensity of the sum seemed to clothe the suspicion with 1839
a weight of terror that nearly pressed them to the earth. They clung to each other with bruised and fluttered spirits while the search was proceeding, and it was not until it was completed and the officer declared himself satisfied that there was none of the missing property on the premises, that they began to rally and look calmly at the circumstances which seemed, for the moment, to menace the peace and security they had previously enjoyed.

"Cheer up, my darlings," said Amos, who was the first to recover the sobriety of thought that usually characterized him,—"cheer up, all will yet be well; it is impossible that this unjust suspicion can long hover about us. A life of honesty and fair dealing will not be without its reward: there was perhaps something in my trade, and the skill which long practice had given me in it, that naturally enough led the credulous, the thoughtless, and perhaps the mischievous, if any such there be connected with this inquiry, to look towards us. But the real authors of this outrage will probably be discovered soon; for a fraud so extensive will make all parties vigilant, and if not, why then, when our neighbors see us toiling, at our usual occupations, with no evidence of increased wealth or lavish expenditure on our persons or at our board, and remember how many years we were so occupied and so attired, without a suspicion of wrong doing, even in small matters, attaching to us, there will be good sense, and good feeling enough in the City to do us justice."

There were sound sense and much consolation in this reasoning: the obvious probabilities of the case were in favor of the fulfilment of the locksmith's expectations. But a scene of trial and excitement, of prolonged agony and hope deferred, lay before him, the extent of which it would have been difficult if not impossible for him then to have foreseen. Foiled in the search, the Directors of the Bank sent one of their number to negotiate with Amos; to offer him a large sum of money, and a guarantee from further molestation, if he would confess, restore the property, and give up his accomplices, if any there were. It was in vain that he protested his innocence, and avowed his abhorrence of the crime; the Banker rallied him on his assumed composure, and threatened him with consequences, until the locksmith, who had been unaccustomed to dialogues founded on the presumption that he was a villain, ordered his tormentor out of his shop, with the spirit of a man who, though poor, was resolved to preserve his self-respect, and protect the sanctity of his dwelling from impertinent and insulting intrusion.

The Banker retired, baffled and threatening vengeance. A consultation was held, and it was finally decided to arrest Sparks, and commit him to prison, in the hope that by shutting him up, and separating him from his family and accomplices, he would be less upon his guard against the collection of evidence necessary to a conviction, and perhaps be frightened into terms, or induced to make a full confession. This was a severe blow to the family. They could have borne much together, for mutual counsel and sympathy can soothe many of the ills of life: but to be divided—to have the strongest mind, around which the feebler ones had been accustomed to cling, carried away captive to brood, in solitary confinement, on an unjust accusation, was almost too much when coupled with the cloud of suspicion that seemed to gather about their home and infect the very air they breathed. The privations forced upon them by the want of the locksmith's earnings were borne without a murmur, and out of the little that could be mustered, a portion was always reserved to buy some trifling but unexpected comfort or luxury to carry to the prison.

Some months having passed without Sparks having made any confession, or the discovery of any new fact whereby his guilt might be established, his persecutors found themselves reluctantly compelled to bring him to trial. They had not a tittle of evidence, except some strange locks and implements found in the shop, and which proved the talent but not the guilt of the mechanic. Yet these were so various, and executed with such elaborate art, and such an evident expenditure of labor that but few, either of the judges, jury, or spectators, could be persuaded that a man so poor would have devoted himself so sedulously to such an employment, unless he had some other object in view than mere instruction or amusement. His friends and neighbors gave him an excellent character; but on their cross-examination all admitted his entire devotion to his favorite pursuit. The counsel for the Bank exerted himself with consummate ability; calculating in some degree on the state of the public mind, and the influence which vague rumours, coupled with the evidence of the mechanic's handicraft exhibited in Court, might have on the mind of the jury, he dwelt upon every ward and winding, on the story of the iron chest, on the evident poverty of the locksmith, and yet his apparent waste of time, if all this work were not intended to ensure success in some vast design. He believed that a verdict would be immediately followed by a confession, for he thought Amos guilty, and he succeeded in making the belief pretty general among his audience. Some of the jury were half inclined to speculate on the probabilities of a confession, and, swept away by a current of suspicion, were not indisposed to convict without evidence, in order that the result might do credit to their penetration. But this was impossible, even in an American Court in the good old times of which we write. Hanging persons on suspicion, and acquitting felons because the mob think murder no crime, are modern inventions. The charge of the Judge was clear and decisive: he admitted that there were grounds of suspicion—that there were circumstances connected with the prisoner's peculiar mode of life that were not reconcilable with the lowness of his finances; but yet, of direct testimony there was not a vestige, and of circumstantial evidence there were not only links wanting in the chain, but in fact there was not a single link extending beyond the locksmith's dwelling. Sparks was accordingly acquitted; but as no other clue was found to direct suspicion, it still lay upon him like a cloud. The vindictive merchant and the dissatisfied bankers did not hesitate to declare, that, although the charge could not be legally brought home, they had no doubt whatever of his guilt. This opinion was taken up and reiterated, until thousands who were too careless to investigate the story, were satisfied that Amos was a rogue. How could the character of a poor man hold out against the deliberate slanders of so many rich ones?

Amos rejoiced in his acquittal as one who felt that the jury had performed a solemn duty faithfully, and who was glad to find that his personal experience had strengthened, rather than impaired, his reliance on the tribunals of his country. He embraced his family, as one snatched from great responsibility and peril, and his heart overflowed with thankfulness, when at night they were all once more assembled round the fireside, the scene of so much happiness and unity in other days. But yet Amos felt that though acquitted by the jury he was not by the town. He saw that, in the faces of some of the jury and most of the audience, which he was too shrewd an observer to misunderstand. He wished it were otherwise; but he was contented to take his chance of some

subsequent revelation, and if it came not, of living down the foul suspicion which Providence had permitted, for some wise purpose, to hover for a while around his name.

But Amos had never thought of how he was to live. The cold looks, averted faces, and rude scandal of the neighborhood, could be borne, because really there was some excuse to be found in the circumstances, and because he hoped that there would be a joyful ending of it all at some future day. But the loss of custom first opened his eyes to his real situation. No work came to his shop. He made articles but could not sell them; and, as the little money he had saved was necessarily exhausted in the unavoidable expenses of the trial, the family found it impossible, with the utmost exertion and economy to meet their current outlay; one article of furniture after another was reluctantly sacrificed, or some little comfort abridged, until, at the end of months of degradation and absolute distress, their bare board was spread within bare walls, and it became necessary to beg, to starve, or to remove. The latter expedient had often been suggested in family consultations, and it is one that in America is the common remedy for all great calamities. If a man fails in a city on the seaboard, he removes to Ohio; if a clergyman offers violence to a fair parishioner, he removes to Albany, where he soon becomes "very much respected;" if a man in Michigan whips a bowie knife[64] between a neighbor's ribs, he removes to Missouri. So that in fact a removal is "the sovereign'st thing on earth"[65] for all great and otherwise overwhelming evils. The Sparks' would have removed, but they clung to the hope that the real perpetrator would be discovered, and the mystery cleared up: and besides, they thought it would be an acknowledgment of the justice of the general suspicion, if they turned their backs and fled. They lived upon the expectation of the renewed confidence and companionship of old friends and neighbors, when Providence should deem it right to draw the veil aside. But to live longer in Philadelphia was impossible, and the whole family prepared to depart; their effects were easily transported, and, as they had had no credit since the arrest, there was nobody to prevent them from seeking a livelihood elsewhere.

Embarking in one of the river boats they passed up the Schuylkill and settled at Norristown.[66] The whole family being industrious and obliging, they soon began to gather comforts around them; and as these were not imbittered by the cold looks and insulting sneers of the vicinage, they were comparatively happy for a time. But even here there was for them no permanent place of rest. A merchant passing through Norristown on his way from the capital to the Blue Mountains,[67] recognized Sparks and told somebody he knew that he wished the community joy of having added to the number of its inhabitants the notorious locksmith of Philadelphia. The news soon spread, the family found that they were shunned, as they had formerly been by those who had known them longer than the good people of Norristown, and had a fair prospect of starvation opening before them. They removed again. This time there was no inducement to linger, for they had no local attachment to detain them. They crossed the mountains, and descending into the vale of the Susquehanna, pitched their tent at Sunbury.[68] Here the same temporary success excited the

[64] The Bowie knife is a fighting knife, originally designed for adventurer Jim Bowie (1796-1836), who died at the Battle of the Alamo.

[65] From Shakespeare's *Henry IV, Part 1* (I, iii, 56).

[66] Norristown is in the metropolitan area of Philadelphia, but on the opposite side of the Schuylkill River.

[67] The Blue Ridge Mountains, which are part of the Appalachians, and begin in Pennsylvania.

[68] Sunbury is a city in central Pennsylvania, on the Susquehanna River, about 175 km west of Philadelphia (as the crow flies).

same hopes, only to be blighted in the bud, by the breath of slander, which seemed so widely circulated as to leave them hardly any asylum within the limits of the State. We need not enumerate the different towns and villages in which they essayed to gain a livelihood, were suspected, shunned and foiled. They had nearly crossed the State in its whole length, been driven from Pittsburgh, were slowly wending their way further west, and were standing on the high ground overlooking Middleton,[69] as though doubtful if there was to be rest for the soles of their feet even there; they hesitated to try a new experiment. Sparks seated himself on a stone beneath a spreading sycamore—his family clustered round him on the grass—they had travelled far and were weary; and without speaking a word, as their eyes met and they thought of their prolonged sufferings and slender hopes, they burst into a flood of tears, in which Sparks, burying his face in the golden locks of the sweet girl who bowed her head upon his knee, joined audibly.

At length, wiping away his tears, and checking the rising sobs that shook his manly bosom, "God's will be done, my children," said the locksmith, "we cannot help weeping, but let us not murmur; our Heavenly Father has tried and is trying us, doubtless for some wise purpose, and if we are still to be wanderers and outcasts on the earth let us never lose sight of his promise, which assures us of an eternal refuge in a place where the wicked cease from troubling and the weary are at rest. I was, perhaps, too proud of that skill of mine; too apt to plume myself upon it above others whose gifts had been less abundant; to take all the credit and give none to Him by whom the human brain is wrought into mysterious adaptation to particular sciences and pursuits. My error has been that of wiser and greater men, who have been made to feel that what we cherish as the richest of earthly blessings sometimes turns out a curse."

To dissipate the gloom which hung over the whole party, and beguile the half hour that they intended to rest in that sweet spot, Mrs. Sparks drew out a Philadelphia newspaper, which somebody had given her upon the road, and called their attention to the Deaths and Marriages, that they might see what changes were taking place in a city that still interested them though they

[69] There are many townships called Middleton or Middletown in the area, but based on the description, this must be Middleton, in Wood County, Ohio.

were banished for ever from its borders. She had hardly opened the paper when her eye glanced at an article which she was too much excited to read. Amos, wondering at the emotion displayed, gently disengaged the paper and read "BANK ROBBERY—SPARKS NOT THE MAN." His own feelings were as powerfully affected as his wife's, but his nerves were stronger, and he read out, to an audience whose ears devoured every syllable of the glad tidings, an account of the conviction and execution of a wretch in Albany, who had confessed among other daring and heinous crimes, the robbery of the Philadelphia Bank, accounting for the dissipation of the property, and entirely exonerating Sparks, whose face he had never seen. These were "glad tidings of great joy"[70] to the weary wayfarers beneath the sycamore, whose hearts overflowed with thankfulness to the Father of Mercies, who had given them strength to bear the burden of affliction, and had lifted it from their spirits ere they had been crushed beneath the weight. Their resolution to return to their native city was formed at once, and before a week had passed they were slowly journeying to the capital of the State.

Meanwhile an extraordinary revulsion of feeling had taken place at Philadelphia. Newspapers and other periodicals, which had formerly been loud in condemnation of the locksmith, now blazoned abroad the robber's confession, wondered how any man could ever have been for a moment suspected upon such evidence as was adduced at the trial; drew pictures of the domestic felicity once enjoyed by the Sparks', and then painted, partly from what was known of the reality and partly from imagination, their sufferings, privations, and wrongs, in the pilgrimage they had performed in fleeing from an unjust but damnatory accusation. The whole city rang with the story; old friends and neighbors who had been the first to cut them, now became the loud and vehement partisans of the family. Everybody was anxious to know where they were. Some reported that they had perished in the woods; others that they had been burnt on a prairie; while not a few believed that the locksmith, driven to desperation had first destroyed the family and then himself. All these stories of course created as much excitement as the robbery of the Bank had done before, only that this time the tide set the other way; and by the time the poor

[70] A phrase originating in Luke 2: 10, but also used in sermons, hymns, and carols.

locksmith and his family, who had been driven like vagabonds from the city, approached its suburbs, they were met, congratulated and followed by thousands, to whom, from the strange vicissitudes of their lot, they had become objects of interest. In fact, their's was almost a triumphal entry, and as the public always like to have a victim, they were advised on all hands to bring an action against the Directors of the Bank; large damages would, it was affirmed, be given, and the Bank deserved to suffer for the causeless ruin brought on a poor but industrious family.

Sparks was reluctant to engage in any such proceedings; his character was vindicated, his business restored; he occupied his own shop, and his family were comfortable and content. But the current of public opinion was too strong for him. All Philadelphia had determined that the bankers should pay. An eminent lawyer volunteered to conduct the suit and make no charge if a liberal verdict were not obtained. The locksmith pondered the matter well: his own wrongs he freely forgave; but he thought that there had been a readiness to secure the interests of a wealthy corporation by blasting the prospects of a humble mechanic, which, for the good of society, ought not to pass unrebuked; he felt that the moral effect of such a prosecution would be salutary, teaching the rich not to presume too far upon their affluence, and cheering the hearts of the poor while suffering unmerited persecution. The suit was commenced and urged to trial, notwithstanding several attempts at compromise on behalf of the Bank. The pleadings on both sides were able and ingenious; but the counsel for the plaintiff had a theme worthy of the fine powers he possessed; and at the close of a pathetic and eloquent declamation, the audience, which had formerly condemned Amos in their hearts without evidence, were melted to tears by a recital of his sufferings; and when the jury returned with a verdict of Ten Thousand Dollars damages against the Bank, the locksmith was honored by a ride home on their shoulders, amidst a hurricane of cheers.

CATHARINE PARR TRAILL

A Canadian Scene

(1843)

Catharine Parr Traill

The author: Despite the success of *Backwoods of Canada* (1836), eleven thousand copies of which had been sold in England (the book was also translated into German and French), Catharine Parr Traill only received £125 in royalties. She taught in a school in Peterborough for a while, but mostly wrote stories and sketches for British, American, and Canadian magazines. Between 1833 and 1847, she also gave birth to nine children, seven of whom survived infancy. She found more success going back to her beginnings as an author of children's literature, with books like *Canadian Crusoes* (1852) and *Lady Mary and Her Nurse* (1856); and with nonfiction books like *The Female Emigrant's Guide* (1854-1855). She also became more and more interested in studying the flora of Canada and is now recognised as a pioneer Canadian botanist, due especially to her mature work, *Studies of Plant Life in Canada* (1885). A widow since 1859, Catharine Parr Traill spent the last decades of her life in her home in Lakefield, Ontario, where she died on 29 August 1899, surrounded by children and grandchildren, but not before publishing two more books, in 1894 and 1895.

The text: Traill knew very well Robert Reid (1773-1856), the character introduced here, who was the earliest settler in Douro, after emigrating in 1822 from County Down, Ireland, with his wife and nine children. In fact, Traill's brother, Samuel Strickland (1804-1867) had married Reid's eldest daughter, Mary (1805-1850) in 1827. This 1843 story should not be confused with a similar, shorter, and designedly nonfictional story, "The Lost Child," signed by "Mrs. Trail [sic]. Author of 'The Backwoods of Canada,'" which appeared in *Chambers's Edinburgh Journal* VIII: 397 (7 September 1839), 258. The 1839 text treated of two different cases of lost children, one in Ontario, the other in New Brunswick. It included an advertisement and a news story from the *Cobourg Star*. The first part (containing only the Ontario case) was reprinted in a Philadelphia journal, *The Ladies' Garland* IV: 11 (May 1841), 270-271. "A Canadian Scene" was first published in *Chambers's Edinburgh Journal* 12: 10 (25 March 1843), 79-80, unsigned. An enlarged version, including an introduction about Canada and a moral conclusion for children (probably added by the editor), appeared the same year with the title "Lost! Lost! A Scene in Canada," in *The Children's Magazine of General Knowledge and Instruction*, Ed. J.F. Winks (London: Simpkin, Marshall; Leicester: J.F. Winks, 1843), VI, 177-184. It was reprinted in *Chambers's Pocket Miscellany*

(Edinburgh: W. and R. Chambers, 1852), III, 173-177. It also appeared the next year in the American edition, *Chambers' Home Book, or Pocket Miscellany* (Boston: Gould and Lincoln, 1853), II, 165-169. It was reprinted a few years later as "The Lost Child—A Canadian Scene" in *The National Magazine* from New York, X: 3 (March 1857), 265-266. The following is the *National Magazine* version, in which several errors, perpetuated by all previous editions, were corrected.

On a raw Sabbath morning, after a night of heavy rain, in the month of August, we were assembled round the breakfast-table in our log-cabin, when the sound of a horse's hoofs, followed by a smart rap on the door, announced a visitor. It was Mr. Reid, who informed us that his child, which had been missing on the plains the night before, was not yet found, and begging of us, as we were near the ground, to turn out and assist in the search.

What are called plains in Canada are ranges of high ground, which stretch through the country, usually parallel to some lake or river, and extend in breadth from two or three to twenty or thirty miles. The soil is sandy, and except near a stream, thinly wooded; while the ground is covered with swarth,[71] intermixed with the most brilliant wild-flowers, and occasional beds of blueberries and wild strawberries; thickets of brush, frequently interspersed, rendering it difficult for a stranger to keep his course.

It is usual to make picnics to these fruit-gardens, and several of our number had been there the day before. On their return, they mentioned Mr. Reid searching for his child, but we had no apprehensions for its safety. Some immediately started for the appointed rendezvous, while those who were left behind to look after the cattle were not slow in following. Scarcely had we reached the foot of the ridge, which was about a quarter of a mile from our house, when a severe thunder-storm commenced, accompanied by heavy rain; and as we entered the forest, the roar of the storm, with the crash of falling trees, had a most awful effect. We thought of the terrors which must be felt by the poor lost one, and fervently wished it might be in some place of safety. Holding on our way, the smoke of a large fire soon brought us to head-quarters, where we found a number of people assembled, going about without any sort of organisation. The father had gone to seek some rest, after

[71] Variant of sward, i.e., land (turf) covered with grass.

wandering about the woods all night, calling on the name of his child, for they had got a notion that any noise or unknown voice would alarm the child, and cause her to hide.

Inquiry was now made for those who lived near and were best acquainted with the woods, and all of us were assigned different portions to search. My course lay through a dense cedar swamp, in the rear of our clearing. I wandered alone until towards evening, and never did I spend a Sabbath whose impressions were more solemn. My footsteps fell noiselessly on the deep moss, beneath which I could frequently hear the trickling streams, while the thunder roared above, and the hoary trunks of the gray cedars reflected the lightning's flash, or, shivered by its fury, fell crashing to the ground. After wandering for some time without success, I took shelter from the rain in a ruined log-house, which, by the remains of a rail fence, showed that a small clearing around had been once rescued from the forest; but the gloomy desolation of the scene seemed to have driven its possessor to seek a habitation nearer the society of men. We met at even, without success, but, on comparing notes, were not disheartened, as we had yet searched only the outskirts of the plains; the object of our search, we fancied, might have wandered deeper into the woods; but then came the awful reflection, that they abounded with wolves and bears, which often alarmed the settlers themselves; and stories were not wanting to render her situation more alarming. We were now, however, compelled to return, leaving a party to keep a look-out, and continue the fire. Next morning, the news having spread over the country, our number was increased to about two hundred. So great seemed the anxiety, that the store-keeper had left his store, as well as the farmer his hay unraked. All seemed to think only of the lost child. We first formed parties of ten or twelve, and ranged in different directions; then long lines were formed, each so near his neighbour, as to command the ground between. The Indians, belonging to a village eight or ten miles off, were sent for; every effort was used. Stretching far into the heart of the forests, not a bush was left, not a log unexamined. But again we returned without success. Some of our number were again left, thinking that in the stillness of the night they might hear the cries of the child and, wandering about, might thus discover it.

This morning was fine, and our number seemed increased to three or four hundred. Twelve or fourteen Indians were also there, on whom much dependence was placed. They, however, and with reason, would not search where we came. We again entered the forest, and traversed some of the heavily wooded parts. The scene was in many parts magnificent; and advancing in a straight line, we were led into many spots where human feet but rarely trod. The deer and foxes rushed affrighted from their lairs, and the sporting propensities of many of our friends were hardly restrained by fear of alarming the child. We began now to get disheartened, and instead of a steady search, often scattered ourselves over the beds of blueberries,[72] or feasted on strawberries, which were frequently scattered in cloisters along the ground. The wild flowers, too, in the thinner woods, were most brilliant; many of them are bright scarlet, and from the calmness of the atmosphere, their colour attains to great perfection. The joyous news was now spread that the Indians had found tracks; but on examining the spot, I felt certain they were my own footsteps around the old log-house; the ground being soft, they had contracted, so as to appear like a child's. These Indians fell far short of the intelligence with which they are usually painted. They were sullen and taciturn, not, seemingly, from a want of desire to converse, but rather, as I imagine, from sheer stupidity. The Indians having failed in following out the tracks, we were again thrown on our own resources, and leaving a watch, returned home.

This morning a large number again assembled, many from a considerable distance. But the search seemed carried on with less energy as the prospect of success diminished; the day was spent in traversing the woods in long ranks, but many seemed careless; and though the finding of a saucer which the child had carried seemed to revive hope, we parted at night fully persuaded that we should never find her alive.

Mr. Reid had now been out with us every day, and looked fatigued both in body and mind. This morning, on meeting in an altogether new quarter, he told us he had now no hope of finding his child alive, but it would be some satisfaction to ascertain her fate; and if we would use our utmost endeavour this day, he dare hardly ask to trespass further on our time.

[72] In the 1843 version, these are called "blaeberries," a Scottish term for the European bilberry. In North America, the equivalent fruit is the blueberry. In the second paragraph of the story, the 1843 version has "blackberries."

We now started with a determined energy, and beat round for some hours. At length we mustered the whole party to go back four or five miles to a burn,[73] beyond which we imagined she would not wander; every thicket was examined, and many places seen which had been missed before. It was beautiful to see the deer bound harmless along our track, as the old hunters raised their sticks, wishing they had been rifles; yet we reached the hill overhanging the burn without success. Here we at once stretched ourselves on the sunny bank, and soon stripped the blueberries of their black fruit. The younger part of us raked about the banks of the burn, while the elders lay down to rest, satisfied that our fruitless labour was now done. When the sun began to decline, we all started homewards, like the company breaking up from some country race-course. Many used praiseworthy endeavours to bring us to order, but in vain. Sometimes we formed line; again it was broken by a startled deer or a covey of pheasants; after which numbers, bounded, shouting and yelling with unseasonable merriment. Some trudged along, deep in conversation; while others, in short sleeves, overcome by heat, seated themselves on a log, or, leaning on their companions, jogged lazily along. At length we descended into a hollow thicket, in whose cool shade we again recovered a sort of line. Scarcely had we begun to ascend the opposite hill, when a faint cheer was heard; immediately the woods re-echoed the response of our whole line, and we rushed onward, heedless of every impediment, until we reached a large clearing, amidst which stood an empty frame of a house; and approaching it, there was Mr. Reid, with his child in his arms. I will not attempt to describe his joy; we all crowded round to get one glimpse, and then returned to our homes, elated with our success. After being in the woods from Saturday morning until Thursday evening, the child was found by a party of two or three who had straggled from the rest. They saw her standing on a log, and her first question to one of them who advanced was, "Do you know where Mr. Reid lives?" What had been the sufferings of the little creature for five days and four nights in the open forest, may be left to the imagination of the reader.

[73] Scottish term for a small stream, a brook.

Susanna Moodie

The Walk to Dummer

(1847)

The author: Susanna Strickland was born on 6 December 1803 in Suffolk, England, the youngest of six sisters, one of whom was Catharine Parr Traill. Like Catharine, Susanna sought to supplement the family income by writing, after the death of their father in 1818. She, too, began by writing for children, but then moved to stories and rural sketches like those of Mary Russell Mitford. On 4 April 1831, she married Lieutenant John Wedderburn Dunbar Moodie (1797-1869), an Orkney Scot who had served in the Napoleonic Wars and had been placed on half pay in 1816. Her husband had lived in South Africa between 1819 and 1829 and was now intent on immigrating to Canada. They left in July 1832 and first purchased a farm in Hamilton Township, near Cobourg, Ontario (in October), which they sold in order to move to uncleared land in Douro Township (north of Peterborough) in 1834. John Moodie served in the militia during the Upper Canada rebellion, after which he was appointed sheriff of Victoria District, and the family moved to Belleville. By then, Susanna had already contributed poems and sketches to British, American, and Canadian periodicals, most notably to the *Literary Garland* in Montreal.

The text: First published in *The Literary Garland* V: 3 (March 1847), 101-109, as "Canadian Sketches. No. II. The Walk to Dummer. By Mrs. Moodie." Reprinted in *Roughing It in the Bush; or, Life in Canada.* By Susanna Moodie (London: Richard Bentley, 1852), II, 222-258. The following is the version that appeared in the book form, for which Susanna Moodie made many changes regarding spelling and punctuation, also adding, subtracting, or rephrasing here and there. More important differences between the book version and the one published in 1847 are indicated in footnotes. Captain N— is based on Lieutenant Frederick Lloyd, who first settled in Dummer and later immigrated with his family to the United States. His wife's name was Louisa Sherin Lloyd, a native of County Cavan, Ireland.

Further reading: Carl Ballstadt. "Susanna Moodie and the English Sketch." *Canadian Literature* 51 (Winter 1972), 32-27.

We trod a weary path through silent woods,
Tangled and dark, unbroken by a sound
Of cheerful life. The melancholy shriek
Of hollow winds careering o'er the snow,
Or tossing into waves the green pine tops,
Making the ancient forest groan and sigh
Beneath their mocking voice, awoke alone
The solitary echoes of the place.[74]

Reader! have you ever heard of a place situated in the forest-depths of this far western wilderness, called Dummer?[75] Ten years ago, it might not inaptly have been termed "The last clearing in the world." Nor to this day do I know of any in that direction which extends beyond it. Our bush-farm was situated on the border-line of a neighbouring township, only one degree less wild, less out of the world, or nearer to the habitations of civilisation than the far-famed "English Line," the boast and glory of this terra incognita.[76]

This place, so named by the emigrants who had pitched their tents in that solitary wilderness, was a long line of cleared land, extending upon either side for some miles through the darkest and most interminable forest. The English Line was inhabited chiefly by Cornish miners, who, tired of burrowing like moles underground, had determined to emigrate to Canada, where they could breathe the fresh air of Heaven, and obtain the necessaries of life upon the bosom of their mother earth. Strange as it may appear, these men made good farmers, and steady, industrious colonists, working as well above ground as they had toiled in their early days beneath it. All our best servants came from Dummer; and although they spoke a language difficult to be understood, and were uncouth in their manners and appearance,[77] they were faithful and obedient, performing the tasks assigned to them with

[74] Moodie's own poem. The source of these lines is indicated in *The Literary Garland* as "Author."

[75] The first line was much shorter in 1847: "Reader, have you ever heard of a place called Dummer?" Dummer is now part of the township of Douro-Dummer, in Peterborough County, Ontario.

[76] The community of English Line is now part of the township of Trent Hills, Ontario.

[77] This phrase between the commas was added in the 1852 version.

patient perseverance;[78] good food and kind treatment rendering them always cheerful and contented.

My dear old Jenny, that most faithful and attached of all humble domestic friends, came from Dummer, and I was wont to regard it with complacency for her sake. But Jenny was not English; she was a generous, warm-hearted daughter of the Green Isle—the Emerald gem set in the silver of ocean. Yes, Jenny was one of the poorest children of that impoverished but glorious country where wit and talent seem indigenous, springing up spontaneously in the rudest and most uncultivated minds; showing what the land could bring forth in its own strength, unaided by education, and unfettered by the conventional rules of society. Jenny was a striking instance of the worth, noble self-denial, and devotion which are often met with—and, alas! but too often disregarded—in the poor and ignorant natives of that deeply-injured, and much abused land. A few words about my old favourite may not prove uninteresting to my readers.[79]

Jenny Buchanan, or as she called it, Bohánon, was the daughter of a petty exciseman, of Scotch extraction (hence her industry)[80] who, at the time of her birth, resided near the old
1847 town of Inniskillen.[81] Her mother died a few months after she
was born; and her father, within the twelve months, married again. In the meanwhile, the poor orphan babe had been adopted by a kind neighbour, the wife of a small farmer in the vicinity.

In return for coarse food and scanty clothing, the little Jenny became a servant-of-all-work. She fed the pigs, herded the cattle, assisted in planting potatoes and digging peat from the bog, and was undisputed mistress of the poultry-yard. As she grew up to womanhood, the importance of her labours increased. A better reaper in the harvest-field, or footer of turf in the bog, could not be found in the district, or a woman more thoroughly acquainted with the management of cows and the rearing of young cattle; but here poor Jenny's accomplishments terminated.

Her usefulness was all abroad. Within the house she made more dirt than she had the inclination or the ability to clear away.

[78] In the 1847 version, this was qualified as "the patient perseverance of the Saxon race."

[79] This sentence was longer in 1847: "A slight sketch of my old favorite may not prove uninteresting, and as it is drawn from life, I shall not hesitate in presenting it to my readers."

[80] The passage about Jenny's Scotch ancestry was added in 1852.

[81] Today spelled Enniskillen, it is a town in Northern Ireland.

She could neither read, nor knit, nor sew; and although she called herself a Protestant, and a Church of England woman, she knew no more of religion, as revealed to man through the Word of God, than the savage who sinks to the grave in ignorance of a Redeemer.[82] Hence she stoutly resisted all ideas of being a sinner, or of standing the least chance of receiving hereafter the condemnation of one.

"Och, sure thin," she would say, with simple earnestness of look and manner, almost irresistible. "God will never throuble Himsel' about a poor, hard-working crathur like me, who never did any harm to the manest of His makin'."

One thing was certain, that a benevolent Providence had "throubled Himsel'" about poor Jenny in times past, for the warm heart of this neglected child of nature contained a stream of the richest benevolence, which, situated as she had been, could not have been derived from any other source. Honest, faithful, and industrious, Jenny became a law unto herself, and practically illustrated the golden rule of her blessed Lord, "to do unto others as we would they should do unto us." She thought it was impossible that her poor services could ever repay the debt of gratitude that she owed to the family who had brought her up, although the obligation must have been entirely on their side. To them she was greatly attached—for them she toiled unceasingly; and when evil days came, and they were not able to meet the rent-day, or to occupy the farm, she determined to accompany them in their emigration to Canada, and formed one of the stout-hearted band that fixed its location in the lonely and unexplored wilds now known as the township of Dummer.

During the first year of their settlement, the means of obtaining the common necessaries of life became so precarious, that, in order to assist her friends with a little ready money, Jenny determined to hire out into some wealthy house as a servant. When I use the term wealth as applied to any bush-settler, it is of course only comparatively; but Jenny was anxious to obtain a place with settlers who enjoyed a small income independent of their forest means.[83]

[82] The end of this sentence is quite different in the 1847 version, and a subsequent sentence ("But God had poured into the warm heart of this neglected child of nature, a stream of the richest benevolence") was replaced in 1852 by all the lines from here until the sentence beginning "Honest, faithful and industrious..."

[83] The second sentence of this paragraph was added in 1852.

Her first speculation was a complete failure. For five long, hopeless years she served a master from whom she never received a farthing of her stipulated wages. Still her attachment to the family was so strong, and had become so much the necessity of her life, that the poor creature could not make up her mind to leave them. The children whom she had received into her arms at their birth, and whom she had nursed with maternal tenderness, were as dear to her as if they had been her own; she continued to work for them although her clothes were worn to tatters, and her own friends were too poor to replace them.

Her master, Captain N——,[84] a handsome, dashing officer, who had served many years in India, still maintained the carriage and appearance of a gentleman, in spite of his mental and moral degradation arising from a constant state of intoxication; he still promised to remunerate at some future day her faithful services; and although all his neighbours well knew that his means were exhausted, and that that day would never come, yet Jenny, in the simplicity of her faith, still toiled on, in the hope that the better day he spoke of would soon arrive.

1847 And now a few words respecting this master, which I trust may serve as a warning to others. Allured by the bait that has been the ruin of so many of his class, the offer of a large grant of land, Captain N—— had been induced to form a settlement in this remote and untried township; laying out much, if not all, of his available means in building a log house, and clearing a large extent of barren and stony land. To this uninviting home he conveyed a beautiful young wife, and a small and increasing family. The result may be easily anticipated. The want of society—a dreadful want to a man of his previous habits—the absence of all the comforts and decencies of life, produced inaction, apathy, and at last, despondency, which was only alleviated by a constant and immoderate use of ardent spirits. As long as Captain N—— retained his half-pay, he contrived to exist. In an evil hour he parted with this, and quickly trod the downhill path to ruin.

And here I would remark[85] that it is always a rash and hazardous step for any officer to part with his half-pay; although it is almost every day done, and generally followed by the same disastrous results. A certain income, however small, in a country

[84] There was no initial in the 1847 version and no reference to his service in India.

[85] The three-paragraph remark beginning here was added in 1852.

where money is so hard to be procured, and where labour cannot be obtained but at a very high pecuniary remuneration, is invaluable to a gentleman unaccustomed to agricultural employment; who, without this reserve to pay his people, during the brief but expensive seasons of seed-time and harvest, must either work himself or starve. I have known no instance in which such sale has been attended with ultimate advantage; but, alas! too many in which it has terminated in the most distressing destitution. These government grants of land, to half-pay officers, have induced numbers of this class to emigrate to the backwoods of Canada, who are totally unfit for pioneers; but, tempted by the offer of finding themselves landholders of what, on paper, appear to them fine estates, they resign a certainty, to waste their energies, and die half-starved and broken-hearted in the depths of the pitiless wild.

If a gentleman so situated would give up all idea of settling on his grant, but hire a good farm in a favourable situation—that is, not too far from a market—and with his half-pay hire efficient labourers, of which plenty are now to be had, to cultivate the land, with common prudence and economy, he would soon obtain a comfortable subsistence for his family. 1847
And if the males were brought up to share the burthen and heat of the day, the expense of hired labour, as it yearly diminished, would add to the general means and well-being of the whole, until the hired farm became the real property of the industrious tenants. But the love of show, the vain boast of appearing richer and better-dressed than our neighbours, too often involves the emigrant's family in debt, from which they are seldom able to extricate themselves without sacrificing the means which would have secured their independence.

This, although a long digression, will not, I hope, be without its use; and if this book is regarded not as a work of amusement but one of practical experience, written for the benefit of others, it will not fail to convey some useful hints to those who have contemplated emigration to Canada: the best country in the world for the industrious and well-principled man, who really comes out to work, and to better his condition by the labour of his hands; but a gulf of ruin to the vain and idle, who only set foot upon these shores to accelerate their ruin.

But to return to Captain N——. It was at this disastrous period that Jenny entered his service. Had her master adapted his habits and expenditure to his altered circumstances, much misery might have been spared, both to himself and his family. But he was a proud man—too proud to work, or to receive with kindness the offers of service tendered to him by his half-civilised, but well-meaning neighbours.

"Hang him!" cried an indignant English settler (Captain N—— was an Irishman),[86] whose offer of drawing wood had been rejected with unmerited contempt. "Wait a few years, and we shall see what his pride will do for him. I *am* sorry for his poor wife and children; but for himself, I have no pity for him."

This man had been uselessly insulted, at the very moment when he was anxious to perform a kind and benevolent action; when, like a true Englishman, his heart was softened by witnessing the sufferings of a young, delicate female and her infant family. Deeply affronted by the captain's foolish conduct, he now took a malignant pleasure in watching his arrogant neighbour's progress to ruin.[87]

The year after the sale of his commission, Captain N—— found himself considerably in debt, "Never mind, Ella," he said to his anxious wife; "the crops will pay all."

The crops were a failure that year. Creditors pressed hard; the captain had no money to pay his workmen, and he would not work himself. Disgusted with his location, but unable to change it for a better; without friends in his own class (for he was the only gentleman then resident in the new township),[88] to relieve the monotony of his existence with their society, or to afford him advice or assistance in his difficulties, the fatal whiskey-bottle became his refuge from gloomy thoughts.

His wife, an amiable and devoted creature, well-born, well-educated, and deserving of a better lot, did all in her power to wean him from the growing vice. But, alas! the pleadings of an angel, in such circumstances, would have had little effect upon the mind of such a man. He loved her as well as he could love

[86] The parenthesis was added in 1852. The model for Captain N— (Frederick Lloyd) was a native of County Tipperary, Ireland. He served as ensign in the 32nd Royal Regiment of Foot, then as cornet of the 21st Royal Dragoons at Salamanca, and as lieutenant of the 91st Royal Regiment of Foot in Jamaica. He met his future wife in Cape Town, South Africa. She was the eldest daughter of Captain Sherin of his regiment.

[87] The middle part of this paragraph (about the heart of an Englishman) was added in 1852.

[88] The parenthesis was added in 1852.

anything, and he fancied that he loved his children, while he was daily reducing them, by his favourite vice, to beggary.

For awhile, he confined his excesses to his own fireside, but this was only for as long a period as the sale of his stock and land would supply him with the means of criminal indulgence. After a time, all these resources failed, and his large grant of eight hundred acres of land[89] had been converted into whiskey, except the one hundred acres on which his house and barn stood, embracing the small clearing from which the family derived their scanty supply of wheat and potatoes. For the sake of peace, his wife gave up all her ornaments and household plate, and the best articles of a once handsome and ample wardrobe, in the hope of hiding her sorrows from the world, and keeping her husband at home.

The pride, that had rendered him so obnoxious to his humbler neighbours, yielded at length to the inordinate craving for drink; the man who had held himself so high above his honest and industrious fellow-settlers, could now unblushingly enter their cabins and beg for a drop of whiskey. The feeling of shame once subdued, there was no end to his audacious mendicity. His whole time was spent in wandering about the country, calling upon every new settler, in the hope of being asked to partake of the coveted poison. He was even known to enter by the window of an emigrant's cabin, during the absence of the owner, and remain drinking in the house while a drop of spirits could be found in the cupboard. When driven forth by the angry owner of the hut, he wandered on to the distant town of P——,[90] and lived there in a low tavern, while his wife and children were starving at home.

"He is the filthiest[91] beast in the township," said the aforementioned neighbour to me; "it would be a good thing for his wife and children if his worthless neck were broken in one of his drunken sprees."

This might be the melancholy fact, but it was not the less dreadful on that account. The husband of an affectionate wife—the father of a lovely family—and his death to be a matter of rejoicing!—a blessing, instead of being an affliction!—an agony not to be thought upon without the deepest sorrow.

[89] The size of the grant was added in 1852; it is only identified as "his lands" in 1847.

[90] Peterborough.

[91] "Most breachy" in the 1847 version ("breachy" was a term used for unruly cattle, likely to breach to fences).

It was at this melancholy period of her sad history that Mrs. N—— found, in Jenny Buchanan, a help in her hour of need. The heart of the faithful creature bled for the misery which involved the wife of her degraded master, and the children she so dearly loved. Their want and destitution called all the sympathies of her ardent nature into active operation; they were long indebted to her labour for every morsel of food which they consumed. For them, she sowed, she planted, she reaped. Every block of wood which shed a cheering warmth around their desolate home was cut from the forest by her own hands, and brought up a steep hill to the house upon her back. For them, she coaxed the neighbours, with whom she was a general favourite, out of many a mess of eggs for their especial benefit; while with her cheerful songs, and hearty, hopeful disposition, she dispelled much of the cramping despair which chilled the heart of the unhappy mother in her deserted home.

For several years did this great, poor woman keep the wolf from the door of her beloved mistress, toiling for her with the strength and energy of a man. When was man ever so devoted,
1847 so devoid of all selfishness, so attached to employers, yet poorer than herself, as this uneducated Irishwoman?

A period was at length put to her unrequited services. In a fit of intoxication her master beat her severely with the iron ramrod of his gun,[92] and turned her, with abusive language, from his doors. Oh, hard return for all her unpaid labours of love! She forgave this outrage for the sake of the helpless beings who depended upon her care. He repeated the injury, and the poor creature returned almost heart-broken to her former home.

Thinking that his spite would subside in a few days, Jenny made a third effort to enter his house in her usual capacity; but Mrs. N—— told her, with many tears, that her presence would only enrage her husband, who had threatened herself with the most cruel treatment if she allowed the faithful servant again to enter the house. Thus ended her five years' service to this ungrateful master. Such was her reward![93]

I heard of Jenny's worth and kindness from the Englishman who had been so grievously affronted by Captain N——,[94] and

[92] The weapon was added in the 1852 version.

[93] Instead of this last sentence, the 1847 version had: "This was all the thanks that she received for her unpaid labours of love. Oh! drink! drink!—how dost thou harden into stone the human heart!"

[94] The passage about the narrator's source was added in 1852.

sent for her to come to me. She instantly accepted my offer, and returned with my messenger. She had scarcely a garment to cover her. I was obliged to find her a suit of clothes before I could set her to work.[95] The smiles and dimples of my curly-headed, rosy little Donald, then a baby-boy of fifteen months, consoled the old woman for her separation from Ellie N——; and the good-will with which all the children (now four in number) regarded the kind old body, soon endeared to her the new home which Providence had assigned to her.

Her accounts of Mrs. N——, and her family, soon deeply interested me in her fate; and Jenny never went to visit her friends in Dummer without an interchange of good wishes passing between us.

The year of the Canadian rebellion came, and brought with it sorrow into many a bush dwelling. Old Jenny and I were left alone with the little children, in the depths of the dark forest, to help ourselves in the best way we could.[96] Men could not be procured in that thinly-settled spot for love nor money, and I now fully realised the extent of Jenny's usefulness.[97] Daily she yoked the oxen, and brought down from the bush fuel to maintain our fires, which she felled and chopped up with her own hands. She fed the cattle, and kept all things snug about the doors; not forgetting to load her master's two guns, "in case," as she said, "the ribels should attack us in our retrate."[98]

The months of November and December of 1838[99] had been unnaturally mild for this iron climate;[100] but the opening

[95] The two sentences about Jenny's lack of clothes were added in 1852.

[96] The first part of this sentence ("My dear husband was called away to help to defend the frontier, and") was left out of the 1852 version. The Upper Canada Rebellion occurred in December 1837; the last pockets of resistance were quelled in early 1838.

[97] In the 1847 version, the narrator speaks of "the usefulness of Jenny's manlike propensities."

[98] The 1847 version was modified here to include direct speech in Jenny's dialect. Jenny's peculiarities of speech were largely absent from the version published in the *Garland*.

[99] The year was added in the 1852 version. However, this should be 1837. Letters from Susanna Moodie to her husband confirm that the "walk to Dummer" took place in January or February 1838. Almost a year after the rebellion was defeated, in November 1838, rebels based in the US invaded southern Ontario but were prevailed against at the Battle of the Windmill. This might explain why Moodie is confused about dating the story.

[100] The "iron climate" is simply called "that season of the year" in the 1847 version.

of the ensuing January brought a short but severe spell of frost and snow. We felt very lonely in our solitary dwelling, crouching round the blazing fire, that scarcely chased the cold from our miserable log-tenement, until this dreary period was suddenly cheered by the unexpected presence of my beloved friend, Emilia, who came to spend a week with me in my forest home.

She brought her own baby-boy with her, and an ample supply of buffalo robes, not forgetting a treat of baker's bread, and "sweeties" for the children. Oh, dear Emilia! best and kindest of women, though absent in your native land, long, long shall my heart cherish with affectionate gratitude all your visits of love, and turn to you as to a sister, tried, and found most faithful, in the dark hour of adversity, and, amidst the almost total neglect of those from whom nature claimed a tenderer and holier sympathy.[101]

Great was the joy of Jenny at this accession to our family party; and after Mrs. S——[102] was well warmed, and had partaken of tea—the only refreshment we could offer her—we began to talk over the news of the place.

1847

"By-the-bye, Jenny," said she, turning to the old servant, who was undressing the little boy by the fire, "have you heard lately from poor Mrs. N——? We have been told that she and the family are in a dreadful state of destitution. That worthless man has left them for the States, and it is supposed that he has joined Mackenzie's band of ruffians on Navy Island;[103] but whether this be true or false, he has deserted his wife and children, taking his eldest son along with him (who might have been of some service at home), and leaving them without money or food."

"The good Lord! What will become of the crathurs?" responded Jenny, wiping her wrinkled cheek with the back of her hard, brown hand. "An' thin they have not a sowl to chop and draw them firewood; an' the weather so oncommon savare. Och, hone![104] what has not that *baste* of a man to answer for?"

---

[101] The last passage (beginning with "and, amidst") was added in 1852.

[102] Identified here only as "my friend" in the 1847 version. Emilia S. is based on Susanna Moodie's friend, Charlotte Emilia Shairp (1806-1895).

[103] Led by William Lyon Mackenzie (1795-1861), the Toronto rebels took refuge in the US, then returned and occupied the uninhabited Navy Island in the Niagara River, proclaiming the short-lived (13 December 1837-13 January 1838) Republic of Canada.

[104] Usually "ochone;" it is an Irish interjection expressing lamentation or regret.

"I heard," continued Mrs. S——, "that they have tasted no food but potatoes for the last nine months, and scarcely enough of them to keep soul and body together; that they have sold their last cow; and the poor young lady and her second brother, a lad of only twelve years old, bring all the wood for the fire from the bush on a hand sleigh."

"Oh, dear!—oh, dear!" sobbed Jenny; "an' I not there to hilp them! An' poor Miss Mary, the tinder thing! Oh, 'tis hard, terribly hard upon the crathurs, an' they not used to the like."

"Can nothing be done for them?" said I.

"That is what we want to know," returned Emilia, "and that was one of my reasons for coming up to D——.[105] I wanted to consult you and Jenny upon the subject. You, who are an officer's wife, and I, who am both an officer's wife and daughter,[106] ought to devise some plan of rescuing this poor, unfortunate lady and her family from her present forlorn situation."

The tears sprang to my eyes, and I thought, in the bitterness of my heart, upon my own galling poverty, that my pockets did not contain even a single copper, and that I had scarcely garments enough to shield me from the inclemency of the weather. By unflinching industry, and taking my part in the toil of the field, I had bread for myself and family, and this was more than poor Mrs. N—— possessed; but it appeared impossible for me to be of any assistance to the unhappy sufferer, and the thought of my incapacity gave me severe pain. It was only in moments like the present that I felt the curse of poverty.[107]

1847

"Well," continued my friend, "you see, Mrs. Moodie, that the ladies of P—— are all anxious to do what they can for her; but they first want to learn if the miserable circumstances in which she is said to be placed are true. In short, my dear friend, they want you and me to make a pilgrimage to Dummer, to see the poor lady herself; and then they will be guided by our report."

"Then let us lose no time in going upon our own mission of mercy."

[105] Spelled out "Douro" in the 1847 version.

[106] Married to her cousin Alexander Mordaunt Shairp (1802-1848), a lieutenant in the Royal Navy and then in the Coast Guard Service, Emilia was the daughter of Major Alexander Shairp of the Royal Marines.

[107] This whole paragraph from 1852 replaces a single sentence from 1847: '"Oh! if we could help her, it would give me the deepest pleasure—."'

"Och, my dear heart, you will be lost in the woods!" said old Jenny. "It is nine long miles to the first clearing, and that through a lonely, blazed path. After you are through the beaver-meadow,[108] there is not a single hut for you to rest or warm yourselves. It is too much for the both of yees; you will be frozen to death on the road."

"No fear," said my benevolent friend; "God will take care of us, Jenny. It is on His errand we go; to carry a message of hope to one about to perish."

"The Lord bless you for a darlint," cried the old woman, devoutly kissing the velvet cheek of the little fellow sleeping upon her lap. "May your own purty child never know the want and sorrow that is around her."

Emilia and I talked over the Dummer scheme until we fell asleep. Many were the plans we proposed for the immediate relief of the unfortunate family. Early the next morning, my brother-in-law, Mr. T——,[109] called upon my friend. The subject next to our heart was immediately introduced, and he was called into the general council. His feelings, like our own, were deeply interested; and he proposed that we should each provide something from our own small stores to satisfy the pressing wants of the distressed family; while he promised to bring his cutter[110] the next morning, and take us through the beaver-meadow, and to the edge of the great swamp, which would shorten four miles, at least, of our long and hazardous journey.

We joyfully acceded to his proposal, and set cheerfully to work to provide for the morrow. Jenny baked a batch of her very best bread, and boiled a large piece of beef; and Mr. T—— brought with him, the next day, a fine cooked ham, in a sack, into the bottom of which he stowed the beef and loaves, besides some sugar and

[108] In the 1847 version, Moodie capitalised the initials ("Beaver Meadow"). The "beaver meadow" is described in her brother, Samuel Strickland's memoir *Twenty-Seven Years in Canada West* (1852) as being created by beavers changing the course of streams: "These meadows are to be found within two or three miles of each other on almost every creek or small stream in Canada West. These industrious animals, the beavers, build their dams across the creeks in a very ingenious manner, with clay and brush-wood. . . . The size of these meadows varies from two or three acres to two or three hundred, and in some few cases is much larger" (44).

[109] Thomas Traill (1793-1859), married to Susanna Moodie's sister, Catharine Parr Traill (1802-1899).

[110] A small horse-drawn sled.

tea, which his own kind wife, the author of "the Backwoods of Canada,"[111] had sent. I had some misgivings as to the manner in which these good things could be introduced to the poor lady, who, I had heard, was reserved and proud.

"Oh, Jenny," I said, "how shall I be able to ask her to accept provisions from strangers? I am afraid of wounding her feelings."

"Oh, darlint, never fear that! She is proud, I know; but 'tis not a stiff pride, but jist enough to consale her disthress from her ignorant English neighbours, who think so manely of poor folk like her who were once rich. She will be very thankful to you for your kindness, for she has not experienced much of it from the Dummer people in her throuble,[112] though she may have no words to tell you so. Say that old Jenny sent the bread to dear wee Ellie, 'cause she knew she would like a loaf of Jenny's bakin'."

"But the meat."

"Och, the mate, is it? May be, you'll think of some excuse for the mate when you get there."

"I hope so; but I'm a sad coward with strangers, and I have lived so long out of the world that I am at a great loss what to do.[113] I will try and put a good face on the matter. Your name, Jenny, will be no small help to me."

All was now ready. Kissing our little bairns, who crowded around us with eager and inquiring looks, and charging Jenny for the hundredth time to take especial care of them during our absence, we mounted the cutter, and set off, under the care and protection of Mr. T——, who determined to accompany us on the journey.

It was a black, cold day; no sun visible in the grey, dark sky; a keen wind, and hard frost. We crouched close to each other.

"Good heavens, how cold it is!" whispered Emilia. "What a day for such a journey!"

She had scarcely ceased speaking, when the cutter went upon a stump which lay concealed under the drifted snow; and we, together with the ruins of our conveyance, were scattered around.

"A bad beginning," said my brother-in-law, with a rueful aspect, as he surveyed the wreck of the cutter from which we had

[111] The periphrasis, identifying Catharine Parr Traill as the author of *The Backwoods of Canada* (1836), was added in 1852.

[112] This passage about "Dummer people" and the one in the preceding sentence about "English neighbours" were inserted in the 1852 version.

[113] The second part of the sentence was added in 1852.

promised ourselves so much benefit. "There is no help for it but to return home."

"Oh, no," said Mrs. S——; "bad beginnings make good endings, you know. Let us go on; it will be far better walking than riding such a dreadful day. My feet are half-frozen already with sitting still."[114]

"But, my dear madam," expostulated Mr. T——, "consider the distance, the road, the dark, dull day, and our imperfect knowledge of the path. I will get the cutter mended to-morrow; and the day after we may be able to proceed."

"Delays are dangerous," said the pertinacious Emilia, who, woman-like, was determined to have her own way. "Now, or never. While we wait for the broken cutter, the broken-hearted Mrs. N—— may starve.[115] We can stop at Colonel C——'s and warm ourselves, and you can leave the cutter at his house until our return."

"It was upon your account that I proposed the delay," said the good Mr. T——, taking the sack, which was no inconsiderable weight, upon his shoulder, and driving his horse before him into neighbour W——'s stable. "Where you go, I am ready to follow."

When we arrived, Colonel C——'s family were at breakfast, of which they made us partake; and after vainly endeavouring to dissuade us from what appeared to them our Quixotic expedition, Mrs. C—— added a dozen fine white fish to the contents of the sack, and sent her youngest son to help Mr. T—— along with his burthen, and to bear us company on our desolate road.

Leaving the colonel's hospitable house on our left, we again plunged into the woods, and after a few minutes' brisk walking, found ourselves upon the brow of a steep bank that overlooked the beaver-meadow, containing within its area several hundred acres.

There is no scenery in the bush that presents such a novel appearance as those meadows, or openings, surrounded as they invariably are, by dark, intricate forests; their high, rugged banks covered with the light, airy tamarack[116] and silver birch. In summer

[114] Both the remark about "good endings" and the sentence about Emilia's half-frozen feet were added in 1852.

[115] Again, Emilia gets more lines: both her first sentence here and her wordplay about the broken cutter and the broken-hearted Mrs. N. were added in 1852. Also new is the narrator's comment about women's character.

[116] American larch, a coniferous tree native to Canada and some parts of the USA.

they look like a lake of soft, rich verdure, hidden in the bosom of the barren and howling waste. Lakes they certainly have been, from which the waters have receded, "ages, ages long ago;" and still the whole length of these curious level valleys is traversed by a stream, of no inconsiderable dimensions.

The waters of the narrow, rapid creek, which flowed through the meadow we were about to cross, were of sparkling brightness, and icy cold. The frost-king had no power to check their swift, dancing movements, or stop their perpetual song. On they leaped, sparkling and flashing beneath their ice-crowned banks, rejoicing as they revelled on in their lonely course. In the prime of the year, this is a wild and lovely spot, the grass is of the richest green, and the flowers of the most gorgeous dyes. The gayest butterflies float above them upon painted wings; and the whip-poor-will pours forth from the neighbouring woods, at close of dewy eve, his strange but sadly plaintive cry. Winter was now upon the earth, and the once green meadow looked like a small forest lake covered with snow.

The first step we made into it plunged us up to the knees in the snow, which was drifted to a great height in the open space. Mr. T—— and our young friend C—— walked on ahead of us, in order to break a track through the untrodden snow. We soon reached the cold creek; but here a new difficulty presented itself. It was too wide to jump across, and we could see no other way of passing to the other side.

"There must be some sort of a bridge here about," said young C——, "or how can the people from Dummer pass constantly during the winter to and fro. I will go along the bank, and halloo to you if I find one."

In a few minutes he gave the desired signal, and on reaching the spot, we found a round, slippery log flung across the stream by way of bridge. With some trouble, and after various slips, we got safely on the other side. To wet our feet would have been to ensure their being frozen; and as it was, we were not without serious apprehension on that score. After crossing the bleak, snowy plain, we scrambled over another brook, and entered the great swamp, which occupied two miles of our dreary road.

It would be vain to attempt giving any description of this tangled maze of closely-interwoven cedars, fallen trees, and loose-scattered masses of rock. It seemed the fitting abode of wolves and bears, and every other unclean beast. The fire had run through it during the summer, making the confusion doubly confused. Now we stooped, half-doubled, to crawl under fallen branches that hung over our path, then again we had to clamber over prostrate trees of great bulk, descending from which we plumped down into holes in the snow, sinking mid-leg into the rotten trunk of some treacherous, decayed pine-tree. Before we were half through the great swamp, we began to think ourselves sad fools, and to wish that we were safe again by our own firesides. But, then, a great object was in view,—the relief of a distressed fellow-creature, and like the "full of hope, misnamed forlorn,"[117] we determined to overcome every difficulty, and toil on.

It took us an hour at least to clear the great swamp, from which we emerged into a fine wood, composed chiefly of maple-trees. The sun had, during our immersion in the dark shades of the swamp, burst through his leaden shroud, and cast a cheery gleam along the rugged boles of the lofty trees. The squirrel and chipmunk occasionally bounded across our path; the dazzling snow which covered it reflected the branches above us in an endless variety of dancing shadows. Our spirits rose in proportion. Young C—— burst out singing, and Emilia and I laughed and chatted as we bounded along our narrow road. On, on for hours, the same interminable forest stretched away to the right and left, before and behind us.

"It is past twelve," said my brother T—— thoughtfully; "if we do not soon come to a clearing, we may chance to spend the night in the forest."

"Oh, I am dying with hunger," cried Emilia. "Do C——, give us one or two of the cakes your mother put into the bag for us to eat upon the road."

The ginger-cakes were instantly produced. But where were the teeth to be found that could masticate them? The cakes were frozen as hard as stones; this was a great disappointment to us tired and hungry wights; but it only produced a hearty laugh. Over

[117] From Byron's *The Siege of Corinth*. It is a reference to the term "forlorn hope," denoting a military unit sent on dangerous missions. The line had been misquoted in the 1847 version ("full of hope, unshamed, forlorn").

the logs we went again; for it was a perpetual stepping up and down, crossing the fallen trees that obstructed our path. At last we came to a spot where two distinct blazed roads diverged.

"What are we to do now?" said Mr. T——.

We stopped, and a general consultation was held, and without one dissenting voice we took the branch to the right, which, after pursuing for about half a mile, led us to a log hut of the rudest description.

"Is this the road to Dummer?" we asked a man, who was chopping wood outside the fence.

"I guess you are in Dummer," was the answer.

My heart leaped for joy, for I was dreadfully fatigued.

"Does this road lead through the English Line?"

"That's another thing," returned the woodman. "No, you turned off from the right path when you came up here." We all looked very blank at each other. "You will have to go back, and keep the other road, and that will lead you straight to the English Line."

"How many miles is it to Mrs. N——'s?"

"Some four, or thereabouts," was the cheering rejoinder. "'Tis one of the last clearings on the line. If you are going back to Douro to-night, you must look sharp."

Sadly and dejectedly we retraced our steps.[118] There are few trifling failures more bitter in our journey through life than that of a tired traveller mistaking his road. What effect must that tremendous failure produce upon the human mind, when at the end of life's unretraceable journey, the traveller finds that he has fallen upon the wrong track through every stage, and instead of arriving at a land of blissful promise, sinks for ever into the gulf of despair!

The distance we had trodden in the wrong path, while led on by hope and anticipation, now seemed to double in length, as with painful steps we toiled on to reach the right road. This object once attained, soon led us to the dwellings of men.

Neat, comfortable log houses, surrounded by well-fenced patches of clearing, arose on either side of the forest road; dogs flew out and barked at us, and children ran shouting indoors to tell

[118] The rest of this paragraph as well as the following one (except the last sentence, which was, however, paraphrased) were added in 1852.

their respective owners that strangers were passing their gates; a most unusual circumstance, I should think, in that location.

A servant who had hired two years with my brother-in-law, we knew must live somewhere in this neighbourhood, at whose fireside we hoped not only to rest and warm ourselves, but to obtain something to eat. On going up to one of the cabins to inquire for Hannah J——, we fortunately happened to light upon the very person we sought. With many exclamations of surprise, she ushered us into her neat and comfortable log dwelling.

A blazing fire, composed of two huge logs, was roaring up the wide chimney, and the savoury smell that issued from a large pot of pea-soup was very agreeable to our cold and hungry stomachs. But, alas, the refreshment went no further! Hannah most politely begged us to take seats by the fire, and warm and rest ourselves; she even knelt down and assisted in rubbing our half-frozen hands; but she never once made mention of the hot soup, or of the tea, which was drawing in a tin teapot upon the hearth-stone, or of a glass of whiskey, which would have been thankfully accepted by our male pilgrims.

1847

Hannah was not an Irishwoman, no, nor a Scotch lassie, or her very first request would have been for us to take "a pickle of soup," or "a sup of thae warm broths."[119] The soup was no doubt cooking for Hannah's husband and two neighbours, who were chopping for him in the bush; and whose want of punctuality she feelingly lamented.

As we left her cottage, and jogged on, Emilia whispered, laughing, "I hope you are satisfied with your good dinner? Was not the pea-soup excellent?—and that cup of nice hot tea!—I never relished anything more in my life. I think we should never pass that house without giving Hannah a call, and testifying our gratitude for her good cheer."[120]

Many times did we stop to inquire the way to Mrs. N——'s, before we ascended the steep, bleak hill upon which her house stood. At the door, Mr. T—— deposited the sack of provisions,

[119] The dialectal speech was added in 1852.

[120] This paragraph containing Emilia's sarcastic remarks replaces the following passage in the 1847 version: "All this was very tantalizing; as neither of us had thought of bringing any money in our pockets, (always a scarce article in the bush, by the bye,) we could not offer to pay for our dinner, and too proud to ask it of the stingy owner of the house, who was one of the wealthiest farmer's wives in the township, we wished her good morning, and jogged on."

and he and young C—— went across the road to the house of an English settler (who, fortunately for them, proved more hospitable than Hannah J——), to wait until our errand was executed.

The house before which Emilia and I were standing had once been a tolerably comfortable log dwelling. It was larger than such buildings generally are, and was surrounded by dilapidated barns and stables, which were not cheered by a solitary head of cattle. A black pine-forest stretched away to the north of the house, and terminated in a dismal, tangled cedar-swamp, the entrance to the house not having been constructed to face the road.

The spirit that had borne me up during the journey died within me. I was fearful that my visit would be deemed an impertinent intrusion. I knew not in what manner to introduce myself, and my embarrassment had been greatly increased by Mrs. S—— declaring that I must break the ice, for she had not courage to go in. I remonstrated, but she was firm. To hold any longer parley was impossible. We were standing on the top of a bleak hill, with the thermometer many degrees below zero, and exposed to the fiercest biting of the bitter, cutting blast. With a heavy sigh, I knocked slowly but decidedly at the crazy door. I saw the curly head of a boy glance for a moment against the broken window. There was a stir within, but no one answered our summons. Emilia was rubbing her hands together, and beating a rapid tattoo[121] with her feet upon the hard and glittering snow, to keep them from freezing.

Again I appealed to the inhospitable door, with a vehemence which seemed to say, "We are freezing, good people; in mercy let us in!"

Again there was a stir, and a whispered sound of voices, as if in consultation, from within; and after waiting a few minutes longer—which, cold as we were, seemed an age—the door was cautiously opened by a handsome, dark-eyed lad of twelve years of age, who was evidently the owner of the curly head that had been sent to reconnoitre us through the window. Carefully closing the door after him, he stepped out upon the snow, and asked us coldly but respectfully what we wanted. I told him that we were two ladies, who had walked all the way from Douro to see his mamma, and that we wished very much to speak to her. The lad

[121] A "tattoo" is either the rhythm (usually provided by drums) in military drills, or any kind of continuous drumming, rapping, or tapping.

answered us, with the ease and courtesy of a gentleman, that he did not know whether his mamma could be seen by strangers, but he would go in and see. So saying he abruptly left us, leaving behind him an ugly skeleton of a dog, who, after expressing his disapprobation at our presence in the most disagreeable and unequivocal manner, pounced like a famished wolf upon the sack of good things which lay at Emilia's feet; and our united efforts could scarcely keep him off.

"A cold, doubtful reception this!" said my friend, turning her back to the wind, and hiding her face in her muff. "This is worse than Hannah's liberality, and the long, weary walk."

I thought so too, and began to apprehend that our walk had been in vain, when the lad again appeared, and said that we might walk in, for his mother was dressed.

Emilia, true to her determination, went no farther than the passage. In vain were all my entreating looks and mute appeals to her benevolence and friendship; I was forced to enter alone the apartment that contained the distressed family.

I felt that I was treading upon sacred ground, for a pitying angel hovers over the abode of suffering virtue, and hallows all its woes. On a rude bench, before the fire, sat a lady, between thirty and forty years of age, dressed in a thin, coloured muslin gown, the most inappropriate garment for the rigour of the season, but, in all probability, the only decent one that she retained. A subdued melancholy looked forth from her large, dark, pensive eyes. She appeared like one who, having discovered the full extent of her misery, had proudly steeled her heart to bear it. Her countenance was very pleasing, and, in early life (but she was still young), she must have been eminently handsome. Near her, with her head bent down, and shaded by her thin, slender hand, her slight figure scarcely covered by her scanty clothing, sat her eldest daughter, a gentle, sweet-looking girl, who held in her arms a baby brother, whose destitution she endeavoured to conceal. It was a touching sight; that suffering girl, just stepping into womanhood, hiding against her young bosom the nakedness of the little creature she loved. Another fine boy, whose neatly-patched clothes had not one piece of the original stuff apparently left in them, stood behind his mother, with dark, glistening eyes fastened upon me, as if amused, and wondering who I was, and what business I could have there. A pale and attenuated, but very pretty, delicately-featured little girl was seated on a low stool before the fire. This was old Jenny's darling, Ellie, or Eloise. A rude bedstead, of home manufacture, in a corner of the room, covered with a coarse woollen quilt, contained two little boys, who had crept into it to conceal their wants from the eyes of the stranger. On the table lay a dozen peeled potatoes, and a small pot was boiling on the fire, to receive their scanty and only daily meal. There was such an air of patient and enduring suffering to the whole group, that, as I gazed heart-stricken upon it, my fortitude quite gave way, and I burst into tears.

Mrs. N—— first broke the painful silence, and, rather proudly, asked me to whom she had the pleasure of speaking. I made a desperate effort to regain my composure, and told her, but with much embarrassment, my name; adding that I was so well acquainted with her and her children, through Jenny, that I could not consider her as a stranger; that I hoped that, as I was the wife of an officer, and like her, a resident in the bush, and well acquainted with all its trials and privations,[122] she would look upon me as a friend.

She seemed surprised and annoyed, and I found no small difficulty in introducing the object of my visit; but the day was rapidly declining, and I knew that not a moment was to be lost. At first she coldly rejected all offers of service, and said that she was contented, and wanted for nothing.

I appealed to the situation in which I beheld herself and her children, and implored her, for their sakes, not to refuse help from friends who felt for her distress. Her maternal feelings triumphed over her assumed indifference, and when she saw me weeping, for I could no longer restrain my tears, her pride yielded, and for some minutes not a word was spoken. I heard the large tears, as they slowly fell from her daughter's eyes, drop one by one upon her garments.

At last the poor girl sobbed out, "Dear mamma, why conceal the truth? You know that we are nearly naked, and starving."

Then came the sad tale of domestic woes:—the absence of the husband and eldest son; the uncertainty as to where they were, or in what engaged; the utter want of means to procure the common

[122] The narrator's appeal to their similar backgrounds was added in 1852.

necessaries of life; the sale of the only remaining cow that used to provide the children with food. It had been sold for twelve dollars, part to be paid in cash, part in potatoes; the potatoes were nearly exhausted, and they were allowanced to so many a day. But the six dollars she had retained as their last resource. Alas! she had sent the eldest boy the day before to P——, to get a letter out of the post-office, which she hoped contained some tidings of her husband and son. She was all anxiety and expectation, but the child returned late at night without the letter which they had longed for with such feverish impatience. The six dollars upon which they had depended for a supply of food were in notes of the Farmer's Bank, which at that time would not pass for money, and which the roguish purchaser of the cow had passed off upon this distressed family.[123]

Oh! imagine, ye who revel in riches—who can daily throw away a large sum upon the merest toy—the cruel disappointment, the bitter agony of this poor mother's heart, when she received this calamitous news, in the midst of her starving children. For the last nine weeks they had lived upon a scanty supply of potatoes; they had not tasted raised bread or animal food for eighteen months.

"Ellie," said I, anxious to introduce the sack, which had lain like a nightmare upon my mind, "I have something for you; Jenny baked some loaves last night, and sent them to you with her best love."

The eyes of all the children grew bright. "You will find the sack with the bread in the passage," said I to one of the boys. He rushed joyfully out, and returned with Mrs. S—— and the sack. Her bland and affectionate greeting restored us all to tranquillity.

The delighted boy opened the sack. The first thing he produced was the ham.

"Oh," said I, "that is a ham that my sister sent to Mrs. N——; 'tis of her own curing, and she thought that it might be acceptable."

Then came the white fish, nicely packed in a clean cloth. "Mrs. C—— thought fish might be a treat to Mrs. N——, as she lived so far from the great lakes." Then came Jenny's bread, which had already been introduced. The beef, and tea, and sugar, fell

[123] The last part of the sentence was added in 1852. During the rebellions of 1837-1838 and the ensuing financial crisis, The Farmer's Bank (from Toronto) was not able to redeem the banknotes it had issued. The bank closed in 1854.

upon the floor without any comment. The first scruples had been overcome, and the day was ours.

"And now, ladies," said Mrs. N——, with true hospitality, "since you have brought refreshments with you, permit me to cook something for your dinner."

The scene I had just witnessed had produced such a choking sensation that all my hunger had vanished. Before we could accept or refuse Mrs. N——'s kind offer, Mr. T—— arrived, to hurry us off.

It was two o'clock when we descended the hill in front of the house, that led by a side-path round to the road, and commenced our homeward route. I thought the four miles of clearings would never be passed; and the English Line appeared to have no end. At length we entered once more the dark forest.

The setting sun gleamed along the ground; the necessity of exerting our utmost speed, and getting through the great swamp before darkness surrounded us, was apparent to all. The men strode vigorously forward, for they had been refreshed with a substantial dinner of potatoes and pork, washed down with a glass of whiskey, at the cottage in which they had waited for us; but poor Emilia and I, faint, hungry, and foot-sore, it was with the greatest difficulty we could keep up. I thought of Rosalind, as our march up and down the fallen logs recommenced, and often exclaimed with her, "Oh, Jupiter! how weary are my legs!"[124]

Night closed in just as we reached the beaver-meadow. Here our ears were greeted with the sound of well-known voices. James and Henry C—— had brought the ox-sleigh to meet us at the edge of the bush. Never was splendid equipage greeted with such delight. Emilia and I, now fairly exhausted with fatigue, scrambled into it, and lying down on the straw which covered the bottom of the rude vehicle, we drew the buffalo robes over our faces, and actually slept soundly until we reached Colonel C——'s hospitable door.

An excellent supper of hot fish and fried venison was smoking on the table, with other good cheer, to which we did ample justice. I, for one, never was so hungry in my life. We had fasted for twelve hours, and that on an intensely cold day, and had walked during

[124] In Shakespeare's *As You Like It* (II, iv), Rosalind exclaims "O Jupiter! how weary are my spirits!" to which the clown Touchstone actually replies "I care not for my spirits, if my legs were not weary."

that period upwards of twenty miles. Never, never shall I forget that weary walk to Dummer; but a blessing followed it.

It was midnight when Emilia and I reached my humble home; our good friends the oxen being again put in requisition to carry us there. Emilia went immediately to bed, from which she was unable to rise for several days. In the meanwhile I wrote to Moodie an account of the scene I had witnessed, and he raised a subscription among the officers of the regiment for the poor lady and her children, which amounted to forty dollars. Emilia lost no time in making a full report to her friends at P——; and before a week passed away, Mrs. N—— and her family were removed thither by several benevolent individuals in the place. A neat cottage was hired for her; and, to the honour of Canada be it spoken, all who could afford a donation gave cheerfully. Farmers left at her door, pork, beef, flour, and potatoes; the storekeepers sent groceries and goods to make clothes for the children; the shoemakers contributed boots for the boys; while the ladies did all in their power to assist and comfort the gentle creature thus thrown by Providence upon their bounty.

While Mrs. N—— remained at P—— she did not want for any comfort. Her children were clothed and her rent paid by her benevolent friends, and her house supplied with food and many comforts from the same source. Respected and beloved by all who knew her, it would have been well had she never left the quiet asylum where for several years she enjoyed tranquillity and a respectable competence from her school; but in an evil hour she followed her worthless husband to the Southern States, and again suffered all the woes which drunkenness inflicts upon the wives and children of its degraded victims.[125]

[125] Louisa Sherin Lloyd died in Chicago in 1883. Some of her children were quite successful in the US: one of them, probably the curly-haired son described by Moodie, who opened the door for her, was the future Dr. Frederick Lloyd (1826-1895), born in London (England). He became a surgeon with the US army both in the Civil War (on the Northern side) and later, but he had a practice in Iowa City. His younger brother Edward was a lieutenant colonel and commanding officer of the 119th New York Volunteers and was killed at Resaca, Georgia, on 15 May 1864. Frederick Lloyd wrote short stories, mostly for young readers.

SUSANNA MOODIE

Brian, the Still-Hunter

(1847)

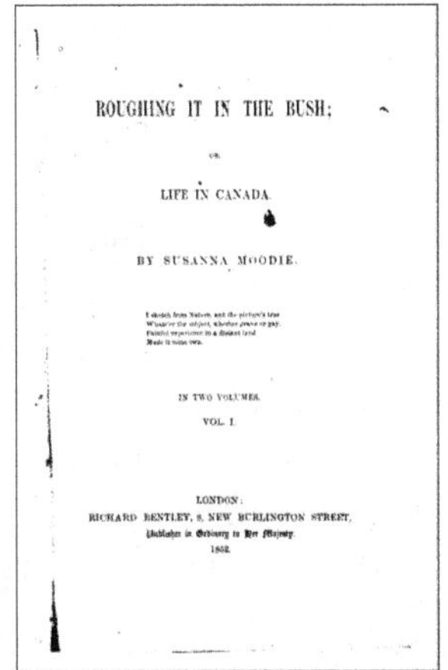
ROUGHING IT IN THE BUSH;

OR,

LIFE IN CANADA.

BY SUSANNA MOODIE.

IN TWO VOLUMES.

VOL. I.

LONDON:
RICHARD BENTLEY, 8, NEW BURLINGTON STREET,
Publisher in Ordinary to Her Majesty.
1852.

The author: In 1847, in Belleville, Ontario, Susanna Moodie and her husband began editing the *Victoria Magazine*. The first issue appeared in September 1847 and both spouses wrote stories and sketches, while at the same time trying to find subscribers. Susanna wrote or reprinted stories set in the Old World, essays, and nonfictional pieces about her first years in Canada, some of which ended up in *Roughing It in the Bush*: "A Visit to Grosse Isle," "Quebec," "[Dandelion Coffe]," and "The Whirlwind." She also serialised "Rachel Wilde; or, Trifles from the Burthen of a Life" (some of it was reworked later in her 1854 novel *Flora Lyndsay*). The *Victoria Magazine*, however, folded after only one year. She kept her Canadian stories for the *Literary Garland*: "Tom Wilson's Emigration," "Our First Settlement and the Borrowing System," "Uncle Joe and His Family," "Brian, the Still-Hunter," "The Walk to Dummer," and "Adieu to the Woods" (which became "Old Woodruff and His Three Wives." The "Canadian Skeetch" published in the *Garland* and reproduced below was based on one of their neighbours from the early 1830s (before their move to Belleville). His name was Brian Bowskill and he was an early English settler in the Hamilton township. His attempted suicide was reported in *The Coburg Star* in August 1831.

The text: First published in *Literary Garland* (October 1847), 460-467, as "Canadian Sketches. No. VI. Brian, the Still Hunter. By Mrs. Moodie." It was reworked as chapter X in *Roughing It in the Bush* (1852), I, 183-205, from which the following has been taken. The author corrected the punctuation and made many minor changes. More significant changes will be identified in the footnotes.

Further reading: Bina Freiwald. "Susanna Moodie. 'The Tongue of Woman:' The Language of the Self in Moodie's *Roughing It in the Bush*." *Re(dis)covering Our Foremothers: Nineteenth-Century Canadian Women Writers*. Ed. Lorraine McMullen. Ottawa: University of Ottawa Press, 1988. 155-172.

Michael Peterman. "*Roughing It in the Bush* as Autobiography." *Reflections: Autobiography and Canadian Literature*. Ed. K. P. Stich. Ottawa: University of Ottawa Press, 1988. 35-43.

O'er memory's glass I see his shadow flit,
Though he was gathered to the silent dust
Long years ago. A strange and wayward man,
That shunn'd companionship, and lived apart;
The leafy covert of the dark brown woods,
The gleamy lakes, hid in their gloomy depths,
Whose still, deep waters never knew the stroke
Of cleaving oar, or echoed to the sound
Of social life, contained for him the sum
Of human happiness. With dog and gun,
Day after day he track'd the nimble deer
Through all the tangled mazes of the forest.[126]

It was early day.[127] I was alone in the old shanty, preparing breakfast,[128] and now and then stirring the cradle with my foot,[129] when a tall, thin, middle-aged man walked into the house, followed by two large, strong dogs.

Placing the rifle he had carried on his shoulder, in a corner of the room, he advanced to the hearth, and without speaking, or seemingly looking at me, lighted his pipe and commenced smoking. The dogs, after growling and snapping at the cat, who had not given the strangers a very courteous reception, sat down on the hearth-stone on either side of their taciturn master, eyeing him from time to time, as if long habit had made them understand all his motions. There was a great contrast between the dogs. The one was a brindled[130] bulldog of the largest size, a most formidable and powerful brute; the other a staghound, tawny, deep-chested, and strong-limbed. I regarded the man and his hairy companions with silent curiosity.

[126] The fifth line was added for the book version. There are several other minor changes. In *Literary Garland*, the poem was followed by its source: "Author."

[127] The sentence continued in *Literary Garland*: "in the fall of 1832."

[128] The phrase "for my husband," present in *Literary Garland*, was later elided.

[129] A longer passage was eliminated from the version in *Literary Garland*: "to keep little Katie a few minutes longer asleep, until her food was sufficiently prepared for her first meal—and wishing secretly for a drop of milk, to make it more agreeable and nourishing for the poor weanling—"

[130] Gray or tawny (light brown) with streaks or spots of a darker colour.

He was between forty and fifty years of age; his head, nearly bald, was studded at the sides with strong, coarse, black curling hair. His features were high, his complexion brightly dark, and his eyes, in size, shape, and colour, greatly resembled the eyes of a hawk. The face itself was sorrowful and taciturn; and his thin, compressed lips looked as if they were not much accustomed to smile, or often to unclose to hold social communion[131] with any one. He stood at the side of the huge hearth, silently smoking, his eyes bent on the fire, and now and then he patted the heads of his dogs, reproving their exuberant expression of attachment, with—"Down, Musie; down, Chance!"

"A cold, clear morning," said I, in order to attract his attention and draw him into conversation.

A nod, without raising his head, or withdrawing his eyes from the fire, was his only answer; and, turning from my unsociable guest, I took up the baby, who just then awoke, sat down on a low stool by the table, and began feeding her. During this operation, I once or twice caught the stranger's hawk-eye fixed upon me and the child, but word spoke he none; and presently, after whistling
to his dogs, he resumed his gun, and strode out. 1847

When Moodie and Monaghan[132] came in to breakfast, I told them what a strange visitor I had had; and Moodie laughed at my vain attempt to induce him to talk.

"He is a strange being," I said; "I must find out who and what he is."

In the afternoon an old soldier, called Layton, who had served during the American war,[133] and got a grant of land about a mile in the rear of our location, came in to trade for a cow. Now, this Layton was a perfect ruffian; a man whom no one liked, and whom all feared. He was a deep drinker, a great swearer, in short, a perfect reprobate; who never cultivated his land, but went jobbing about from farm to farm, trading horses and cattle, and

[131] In the *Literary Garland* this passage reads: "as if they were not much accustomed to smiles, or, indeed, often served to hold communication with any one."

[132] John Monaghan was the Moodies' servant. His story is told in Chapter VIII of *Roughing It*.

[133] The War of 1812, which was often called "the American War" in Upper Canada. Ned Layton is based on William Latham, a Late Loyalist, i.e., an American who settled in Ontario after 1790. When the Moodies came to Canada, Late Loyalists were the majority of the Ontario population.

cheating in a pettifogging way. Uncle Joe[134] had employed him to sell Moodie a young heifer, and he had brought her over for him to look at. When he came in to be paid, I described the stranger of the morning; and as I knew that he was familiar with every one in the neighbourhood, I asked if he knew him.

"No one should know him better than myself," he said; "'tis old Brian B——, the still-hunter, and a near neighbour of your'n. A sour, morose, queer chap he is, and as mad as a March hare! He's from Lancashire, in England, and came to this country some twenty years ago, with his wife, who was a pretty young lass in those days,[135] and slim enough then, though she's so awful fleshy now. He had lots of money, too, and he bought four hundred acres of land, just at the corner of the concession line, where it meets the main road. And excellent land it is; and a better farmer, while he stuck to his business, never went into the bush, for it was all bush here then.[136] He was a dashing, handsome fellow, too, and did not hoard the money, either; he loved his pipe and his pot too well; and at last he left off farming, and gave himself to them altogether. Many a jolly booze he and I have had, I can tell you. Brian was an awful passionate man, and, when the liquor was in, and the wit was out, as savage and as quarrelsome as a bear. At such times there was no one but Ned Layton dared go near him. We once had a pitched battle, in which I was conqueror;[137] and ever arter he yielded a sort of sulky obedience to all I said to him. Arter being on the spree for a week or two, he would take fits of remorse, and return home to his wife; would fall down at her knees, and ask her forgiveness, and cry like a child. At other times he would hide himself up in the woods, and steal home at night, and get what he wanted out of the pantry, without speaking a word to any one. He went on with these pranks for some years, till he took a fit of the blue devils.

1847

[134] Uncle Joe has a chapter of his own (VII) in *Roughing It in the Bush*. He was based on Joe Harris, another Late Loyalist (a "New England Yankee," Moodie calls him) and the first settler in the Hamilton township. He sold his farm to the Moodies in September 1832 but refused to move out before May 1833.

[135] What follows after the comma till the end of the sentence was added in the book version.

[136] The explanation, "for it was all bush here then," was added in the 1852 version.

[137] In the 1847 version, the passage between the comma and the semicolon reads "and I whipped him."

“‘Come away, Ned, to the —— lake,[138] with me,’ said he; ‘I am weary of my life, and I want a change.’

“‘Shall we take the fishing-tackle?’ says I. ‘The black bass are in prime season, and F—— will lend us the old canoe. He’s got some capital rum up from Kingston. We’ll fish all day, and have a spree at night.’

“‘It’s not to fish I’m going,’ says he.

“‘To shoot, then? I’ve bought Rockwood’s new rifle.’

“‘It’s neither to fish nor to shoot, Ned: it’s a new game I’m going to try; so come along.’

“Well, to the —— lake we went. The day was very hot, and our path lay through the woods, and over those scorching plains, for eight long miles.[139] I thought I should have dropped by the way; but during our long walk my companion never opened his lips. He strode on before me, at a half-run, never once turning his head.

“‘The man must be the devil!’ says I, ‘and accustomed to a warmer place, or he must feel this. Hollo, Brian! Stop there! Do you mean to kill me?’

“‘Take it easy,’ says he; ‘you’ll see another day arter this—I’ve business on hand, and cannot wait.’ 1847

“Well, on we went, at the same awful rate, and it was mid-day when we got to the little tavern on the lake shore, kept by one F——, who had a boat for the convenience of strangers who came to visit the place. Here we got our dinner, and a glass of rum to wash it down. But Brian was moody, and to all my jokes he only returned a sort of grunt; and while I was talking with F——, he steps out, and a few minutes arter we saw him crossing the lake in the old canoe.

“‘What’s the matter with Brian?’ says F——; ‘all does not seem right with him, Ned. You had better take the boat, and look arter him.’

“‘Pooh!’ says I; ‘he’s often so, and grows so glum nowadays that I will cut his acquaintance altogether if he does not improve.’

“‘He drinks awful hard,’ says F——; ‘may be he’s got a fit of the delirium-tremulous.[140] There is no telling what he may be up to at this minute.’

[138] This is named “Rice Lake” in the 1847 version, here and afterwards. Rice Lake is in south-eastern Ontario, about 20 km south of Peterborough.

[139] The distance was “sixteen miles” in the 1847 version.

[140] F——’s funny suggestion was added in the 1852 version.

"My mind misgave me, too, so I e'en takes the oars, and pushes out, right upon Brian's track; and, by the Lord Harry![141] if I did not find him, upon my landing on the opposite shore, lying wallowing in his blood with his throat cut. 'Is that you, Brian?' says I, giving him a kick with my foot, to see if he was alive or dead. 'What on earth tempted you to play me and F—— such a dirty, mean trick, as to go and stick yourself like a pig, bringing such a discredit upon the house?—and you so far from home and those who should nurse you?'

"I was so mad with him, that (saving your presence, ma'am) I swore awfully, and called him names that would be ondacent to repeat here; but he only answered with groans and a horrid gurgling in his throat. 'It's a choking you are,' said I, 'but you shan't have your own way, and die so easily, either, if I can punish you by keeping you alive.' So I just turned him upon his stomach, with his head down the steep bank; but he still kept choking and growing black in the face."

Layton then detailed some particulars of his surgical practice which it is not necessary to repeat.[142] He continued—

1847

"I bound up his throat with my handkerchief,[143] and took him neck and heels, and threw him into the bottom of the boat. Presently he came to himself a little, and sat up in the boat; and—would you believe it?—made several attempts to throw himself in the water. 'This will not do,' says I; 'you've done mischief enough already by cutting your weasand![144] If you dare to try that again, I will kill you with the oar.' I held it up to threaten him; he was scared, and lay down as quiet as a lamb. I put my foot upon his breast. 'Lie still, now! or you'll catch it.' He looked piteously at me; he could not speak, but his eyes seemed to say, 'Have pity upon me, Ned; don't kill me.'

"Yes, ma'am; this man, who had just cut his throat, and twice arter that tried to drown himself, was afraid that I should knock

[141] Harry, Old Harry, or Lord Harry were all euphemisms for the devil.

[142] This sentence replaces the following from the 1847 version: "I then saw that it was a piece of the flesh of his throat that had been carried into his wind-pipe. So, what do I do, but puts in my finger and thumb, and pulls it out, and"—which links with the next paragraph in the 1852 version.

[143] This was followed by "dipping it first in the water to stanch the blood" in the 1847 version. The sentence also originally ended with the words "and pushed off for the tavern."

[144] Archaic term for gullet or throat (it was spelled "wizzand" in the *Literary Garland*).

him on the head and kill him. Ha! ha! I shall never forget the work that F—— and I had with him arter I got him up to the house.

"The doctor came, and sewed up his throat; and his wife—poor crittur!—came to nurse him. Bad as he was, she was mortal fond of him! He lay there, sick and unable to leave his bed, for three months,[145] and did nothing but pray to God to forgive him, for he thought the devil would surely have him for cutting his own throat; and when he got about again, which is now twelve years ago, he left off drinking entirely, and wanders about the woods with his dogs, hunting. He seldom speaks to any one, and his wife's brother carries on the farm for the family. He is so shy of strangers that 'tis a wonder he came in here. The old wives are afraid of him; but you need not heed him—his troubles are to himself, he harms no one."

Layton departed, and left me brooding over the sad tale which he had told in such an absurd and jesting manner. It was evident from the account he had given of Brian's attempt at suicide, that the hapless hunter was not wholly answerable for his conduct—that he was a harmless maniac.[146]

1847

The next morning, at the very same hour, Brian again made his appearance; but instead of the rifle across his shoulder, a large stone jar occupied the place, suspended by a stout leather thong. Without saying a word, but with a truly benevolent smile, that flitted slowly over his stern features, and lighted them up, like a sunbeam breaking from beneath a stormy cloud, he advanced to the table, and unslinging the jar, set it down before me, and in a low and gruff, but by no means an unfriendly voice, said, "Milk, for the child," and vanished.

"How good it was of him! How kind!" I exclaimed, as I poured the precious gift of four quarts of pure new milk out into a deep pan. I had not asked him—had never said that the poor weanling wanted milk. It was the courtesy of a gentleman—of a man of benevolence and refinement.

[145] The previous sentence was added in 1852, whereas the beginning of the current sentence read simply "and he lay bad there for six months" in 1847.

[146] This term replaces "monomaniac" from the 1847 version. In the early nineteenth century, "maniac" was a generic term for mentally ill patients, whereas a "monomaniac" was someone under the influence of an impulse that is stronger than his will, and consequently acts relatively normally between crises.

For weeks did my strange, silent friend steal in, take up the empty jar, and supply its place with another replenished with milk. The baby knew his step, and would hold out her hands to him and cry, "Milk!" and Brian would stoop down and kiss her, and his two great dogs lick her face.

"Have you any children, Mr. B——?"

"Yes, five; but none like this."

"My little girl is greatly indebted to you for your kindness."

"She's welcome, or she would not get it. You are strangers; but I like you all. You look kind, and I would like to know more about you."

Moodie shook hands with the old hunter, and assured him that we should always be glad to see him. After this invitation, Brian became a frequent guest. He would sit and listen with delight to Moodie while he described to him elephant-hunting at the Cape;[147] grasping his rifle in a determined manner, and whistling an encouraging air to his dogs. I asked him one evening what made him so fond of hunting.

"'Tis the excitement," he said; "it drowns thought, and I love

to be alone. I am sorry for the creatures, too, for they are free and happy; yet I am led by an instinct I cannot restrain to kill them. Sometimes the sight of their dying agonies recalls painful feelings; and then I lay aside the gun, and do not hunt for days. But 'tis fine to be alone with God in the great woods—to watch the sunbeams stealing through the thick branches, the blue sky breaking in upon you in patches, and to know that all is bright and shiny above you, in spite of the gloom that surrounds you."

After a long pause, he continued, with much solemn feeling in his look and tone—

"I lived a life of folly for years, for I was respectably born and educated, and had seen something of the world, perhaps more than was good, before I left home for the woods; and from the teaching I had received from kind relatives and parents I should have known how to have conducted myself better.[148] But, madam, if we associate long with the depraved and ignorant, we learn to become even worse than they are. I felt deeply my degradation—

[147] John Moodie was the author of *Ten Years in South Africa, including a particular description of the wild sports of that country* (London: Richard Bentley, 1835).

[148] Two passages were inserted in this sentence for the 1852 version: the one about Brian's travels and the one about his parents.

felt that I had become the slave to low vice; and in order to emancipate myself from the hateful tyranny of evil passions, I did a very rash and foolish thing. I need not mention the manner in which I transgressed God's holy laws; all the neighbours know it, and must have told you long ago. I could have borne reproof, but they turned my sorrow into indecent jests, and, unable to bear their coarse ridicule, I made companions of my dogs and gun, and went forth into the wilderness. Hunting became a habit. I could no longer live without it, and it supplies the stimulant which I lost when I renounced the cursed whiskey bottle.

"I remember the first hunting excursion I took alone in the forest. How sad and gloomy I felt! I thought that there was no creature in the world so miserable as myself. I was tired and hungry, and I sat down upon a fallen tree to rest. All was still as death around me, and I was fast sinking to sleep, when my attention was aroused by a long, wild cry. My dog, for I had not Chance then, and he's no hunter, pricked up his ears, but instead of answering with a bark of defiance, he crouched down, trembling, at my feet. 'What does this mean?' I cried, and I cocked my rifle and sprang upon the log. The sound came nearer upon the wind. It was like the deep baying of a pack of hounds in full cry. Presently a noble deer rushed past me, and fast upon his trail—I see them now, like so many black devils—swept by a pack of ten or fifteen large, fierce wolves, with fiery eyes and bristling hair, and paws that seemed hardly to touch the ground in their eager haste. I thought not of danger, for, with their prey in view, I was safe; but I felt every nerve within me tremble for the fate of the poor deer. The wolves gained upon him at every bound. A close thicket intercepted his path, and, rendered desperate, he turned at bay. His nostrils were dilated, and his eyes seemed to send forth long streams of light. It was wonderful to witness the courage of the beast. How bravely he repelled the attacks of his deadly enemies, how gallantly he tossed them to the right and left, and spurned them from beneath his hoofs; yet all his struggles were useless, and he was quickly overcome and torn to pieces by his ravenous foes. At that moment he seemed more unfortunate than even myself, for I could not see in what manner he had deserved his fate. All his speed and energy, his courage and fortitude, had been exerted in vain. I had tried to destroy myself; but he, with every effort vigorously made for self-preservation, was doomed to meet the fate he dreaded! Is God just to his creatures?"

1847

With this sentence on his lips, he started abruptly from his seat, and left the house.

One day he found me painting some wild flowers, and was greatly interested in watching the progress I made in the group. Late in the afternoon of the following day he brought me a large bunch of splendid spring flowers.

"Draw these," said he; "I have been all the way to the —— lake plains to find them for you."

Little Katie, grasping them one by one, with infantile joy, kissed every lovely blossom.[149]

"These are God's pictures," said the hunter, "and the child, who is all nature, understands them in a minute. Is it not strange that these beautiful things are hid away in the wilderness, where no eyes but the birds of the air, and the wild beasts of the wood, and the insects that live upon them, ever see them? Does God provide, for the pleasure of such creatures, these flowers? Is His benevolence gratified by the admiration of animals whom we have been taught to consider as having neither thought nor reflection?[150] When I am alone in the forest, these thoughts puzzle me."

1847

Knowing that to argue with Brian was only to call into action the slumbering fires of his fatal malady, I turned the conversation by asking him why he called his favourite dog Chance?

"I found him," he said, "forty miles back in the bush. He was a mere skeleton. At first I took him for a wolf, but the shape of his head undeceived me. I opened my wallet,[151] and called him to me. He came slowly, stopping and wagging his tail at every step, and looking me wistfully in the face. I offered him a bit of dried venison, and he soon became friendly, and followed me home, and has never left me since. I called him Chance, after the manner I happened with him; and I would not part with him for twenty dollars."

Alas, for poor Chance! he had, unknown to his master, contracted a private liking for fresh mutton, and one night he killed no less than eight sheep that belonged to Mr. D——, on the front road; the culprit, who had been long suspected, was caught in the very act, and this mischance cost him his life. Brian was sad and gloomy for many weeks after his favourite's death.

[149] In the 1847 version, Katie speaks here, saying "Oh! pretty, pretty flowers."

[150] This long question was added for the 1852 version.

[151] In the now archaic sense of knapsack.

"I would have restored the sheep fourfold," he said, "if he would but have spared the life of my dog."

My recollections of Brian seemed more particularly to concentrate in the adventures of one night, when I happened to be left alone, for the first time since my arrival in Canada. I cannot now imagine how I could have been such a fool as to give way for four-and-twenty hours to such childish fears; but so it was, and I will not disguise my weakness from my indulgent reader.

Moodie had bought a very fine cow of a black man, named Mollineux, for which he was to give twenty-seven dollars.[152] The man lived twelve miles back in the woods; and one fine, frosty spring day—(don't smile at the term frosty, thus connected with the genial season of the year; the term is perfectly correct when applied to the Canadian spring, which, until the middle of May, is the most dismal season of the year)[153]—he and John Monaghan took a rope, and the dog, and sallied forth to fetch the cow home. Moodie said that they should be back by six o'clock in the evening, and charged me to have something cooked for supper when they returned, as he doubted not their long walk in the 1847
sharp air would give them a good appetite. This was during the time that I was without a servant, and living in old Mrs. ——'s shanty.[154]

The day was so bright and clear, and Katie was so full of frolic and play, rolling upon the floor, or toddling from chair to chair, that the day passed on without my feeling remarkably lonely. At length the evening drew nigh, and I began to expect my husband's return, and to think of the supper that I was to prepare for his reception. The red heifer that we had bought of Layton, came lowing to the door to be milked; but I did not know how to milk in those days, and, besides this, I was terribly afraid

[152] The beginning of this paragraph was reworked for the 1852 version and the price of the cow was added then.

[153] The parenthesis was added for the 1852 version, undoubtedly for her British audience.

[154] The 1847 version gives the initial of the previous lodger: "Mrs. H——'s shanty" (that is, Mrs. Harris, wife of Uncle Joe, mentioned previously, and also named "Mrs. Joe" in the next paragraph) and is more specific in saying she was "without a female servant" (which is accurate, since John Monaghan was actually their servant at the time). The Moodies were in between female servants (two Scotswomen and one Irishwoman are named in the book).

of cattle. Yet, as I knew that milk would be required for the tea, I ran across the meadow to Mrs. Joe, and begged that one of her girls would be so kind as to milk for me. My request was greeted with a rude burst of laughter from the whole set.

"If you can't milk," said Mrs. Joe, "it's high time you should learn. My girls are above being helps."

"I would not ask you but as a great favour; I am afraid of cows."

"*Afraid of cows!* Lord bless the woman! A farmer's wife, and afraid of cows!"

Here followed another laugh at my expense; and, indignant at the refusal of my first and last request, when they had all borrowed so much from me, I shut the inhospitable door, and returned home.

1847

After many ineffectual attempts, I succeeded at last, and bore my half-pail of milk in triumph to the house. Yes! I felt prouder of that milk than many an author of the best thing he ever wrote, whether in verse or prose; and it was doubly sweet when I considered that I had procured it without being under any obligation to my ill-natured neighbours. I had learned a useful lesson of independence, to which, in after-years, I had often again to refer.[155]

I fed little Katie and put her to bed, made the hot cakes for tea, boiled the potatoes, and laid the ham, cut in nice slices, in the pan, ready to cook the moment I saw the men enter the meadow, and arranged the little room with scrupulous care and neatness. A glorious fire was blazing on the hearth, and everything was ready for their supper; and I began to look out anxiously for their arrival.

The night had closed in cold and foggy, and I could no longer distinguish any object at more than a few yards from the door. Bringing in as much wood as I thought would last me for several hours, I closed the door; and for the first time in my life I found myself at night in a house entirely alone. Then I began to ask myself a thousand torturing questions as to the reason of their unusual absence. Had they lost their way in the woods? Could they have fallen in with wolves (one of my early bugbears)? Could any fatal accident have befallen them? I started up, opened the door, held my breath, and listened. The little brook lifted up its voice in loud, hoarse wailing, or mocked, in its babbling to the stones, the

[155] The last sentence of this paragraph was added to the 1852 version.

Illustration to the 1871 edition (Toronto: Hunter, Rose), p. 25

1847

sound of human voices. As it became later, my fears increased in proportion. I grew too superstitious and nervous to keep the door open. I not only closed it, but dragged a heavy box in front, for bolt there was none.[156] Several ill-looking men had, during the day, asked their way to Toronto. I felt alarmed, lest such rude wayfarers should come to-night and demand a lodging, and find me alone and unprotected. Once I thought of running across to Mrs. Joe, and asking her to let one of the girls stay with me until Moodie returned; but the way in which I had been repulsed in the evening prevented me from making a second appeal to their charity.

Hour after hour wore away, and the crowing of the cocks proclaimed midnight, and yet they came not. I had burnt out all my wood, and I dared not open the door to fetch in more. The candle was expiring in the socket, and I had not courage to go up into the loft and procure another before it went finally out. Cold, heart-weary, and faint, I sat[157] and cried. Every now and then the furious barking of the dogs at the neighbouring farms, and the loud cackling of the geese upon our own, made me hope that they were coming; and then I listened till the beating of my own heart excluded all other sounds. Oh, that unwearied brook! how it
1847 sobbed and moaned like a fretful child;—what unreal terrors and fanciful illusions my too active mind conjured up, whilst listening to its mysterious tones!

Just as the moon rose, the howling of a pack of wolves, from the great swamp in our rear, filled the whole air. Their yells were answered by the barking of all the dogs in the vicinity, and the geese, unwilling to be behind-hand in the general confusion, set up the most discordant screams. I had often heard, and even been amused, during the winter, particularly on thaw nights, with hearing the howls of these formidable wild beasts; but I had never before heard them alone, and when one dear to me was abroad amid their haunts.[158] They were directly in the track that Moodie and Monaghan must have taken; and I now made no doubt that they had been attacked and killed on their return through the woods with the cow, and I wept and sobbed until the cold grey dawn peered in upon me through the small dim window. I have passed many a long cheerless night, when my dear husband was

[156] The last five words were added to this sentence in the 1852 version.

[157] The phrase "in the middle of the floor" appeared here in 1847.

[158] In the 1847 version, the passage after the last comma reads instead: "and my fear reached a climax."

away from me during the rebellion, and I was left in my forest home with five little children, and only an old Irish woman to draw and cut wood for my fire, and attend to the wants of the family,[159] but that was the saddest and longest night I ever remember.

Just as the day broke, my friends the wolves set up a parting benediction, so loud, and wild, and near to the house, that I was afraid lest they should break through the frail window, or come down the low wide chimney, and rob me of my child. But their detestable howls died away in the distance, and the bright sun rose up and dispersed the wild horrors of the night, and I looked once more timidly around me. The sight of the table spread, and the uneaten supper, renewed my grief, for I could not divest myself of the idea that Moodie was dead. I opened the door, and stepped forth into the pure air of the early day. A solemn and beautiful repose still hung like a veil over the face of Nature. The mists of night still rested upon the majestic woods, and not a sound but the flowing of the waters went up in the vast stillness. The earth had not yet raised her matin hymn to the throne of the Creator. Sad at heart, and weary and worn in spirit, I went down to the spring and washed my face and head, and drank a deep draught of its icy waters. On returning to the house I met, near the door, old Brian the hunter, with a large fox dangling across his shoulder, and the dogs following at his heels.

"Good God! Mrs. Moodie, what is the matter? You are early abroad this morning, and look dreadful ill. Is anything wrong at home? Is the baby or your husband sick?"

"Oh!" I cried, bursting into tears, "I fear he is killed by the wolves."

The man stared at me, as if he doubted the evidence of his senses, and well he might; but this one idea had taken such strong possession of my mind that I could admit no other. I then told him, as well as I could find words, the cause of my alarm, to which he listened very kindly and patiently.

"Set your heart at rest; your husband is safe. It is a long journey on foot to Mollineux, to one unacquainted with a blazed path in a bush road.[160] They have stayed all night at the black man's shanty,[161] and you will see them back at noon."

[159] This entire passage (after "cheerless night") was added in the 1852 version.

[160] The passage after "Mollineux" until the end of the sentence was added in the 1852 version.

[161] In the 1847 version, Brian says "at his shanty."

I shook my head and continued to weep.

"Well, now, in order to satisfy you, I will saddle my mare, and ride over to the nigger's,[162] and bring you word as fast as I can."

I thanked him sincerely for his kindness, and returned, in somewhat better spirits, to the house. At ten o'clock my good messenger returned with the glad tidings that all was well.

The day before, when half the journey had been accomplished, John Monaghan let go the rope by which he led the cow, and she had broken away through the woods, and returned to her old master; and when they again reached his place, night had set in, and they were obliged to wait until the return of day. Moodie laughed heartily at all my fears; but indeed I found them no joke.[163]

Brian's eldest son, a lad of fourteen, was not exactly an idiot, but what, in the old country, is very expressively termed by the poor people a "natural." He could feed and assist himself, had been taught imperfectly to read and write, and could go to and from the town on errands, and carry a message from one farm-house to another; but he was a strange, wayward creature, and evidently inherited, in no small degree, his father's malady.

During the summer months he lived entirely in the woods, near his father's dwelling, only returning to obtain food, which was generally left for him in an outhouse. In the winter, driven home by the severity of the weather, he would sit for days together moping in the chimney-corner, without taking the least notice of what was passing around him. Brian never mentioned this boy—who had a strong, active figure; a handsome, but very inexpressive face—without a deep sigh; and I feel certain that half his own dejection was occasioned by the mental aberration of his child.

One day he sent the lad with a note to our house, to know if Moodie would purchase the half of an ox that he was going to kill. There happened to stand in the corner of the room an open wood box, into which several bushels of fine apples had been thrown; and, while Moodie was writing an answer to the note, the eyes of the idiot were fastened, as if by some magnetic influence, upon the apples. Knowing that Brian had a very fine orchard, I did not offer the boy any of the fruit. When the note was finished, I handed it to him. The lad grasped it mechanically, without removing his fixed gaze from the apples.

[162] In the 1847 version, Brian says "and ride over to Mollineux's."

[163] The last sentence of the paragraph was added in the 1852 version.

"Give that to your father, Tom."

The boy answered not—his ears, his eyes, his whole soul, were concentrated in the apples. Ten minutes elapsed, but he stood motionless, like a pointer at dead set.

"My good boy, you can go."

He did not stir.

"Is there anything you want?"

"I want," said the lad, without moving his eyes from the objects of his intense desire, and speaking in a slow, pointed manner, which ought to have been heard to be fully appreciated, "I want ap-ples!"

"Oh, if that's all, take what you like."

The permission once obtained, the boy flung himself upon the box with the rapacity of a hawk upon its prey, after being long poised in the air, to fix its certain aim; thrusting his hands to the right and left, in order to secure the finest specimens of the coveted fruit, scarcely allowing himself time to breathe until he had filled his old straw hat, and all his pockets, with apples. To help laughing was impossible; while this new Tom o' Bedlam[164] darted from the house, and scampered across the field for dear life, as if afraid that we should pursue him, to rob him of his prize.

It was during this winter that our friend Brian was left a fortune of three hundred pounds per annum; but it was necessary for him to return to his native country, in order to take possession of the property. This he positively refused to do; and when we remonstrated with him on the apparent imbecility of this resolution, he declared that he would not risk his life, in crossing the Atlantic twice for twenty times that sum. What strange inconsistency was this, in a being who had three times attempted to take away that which he dreaded so much to lose accidentally!

I was much amused with an account which he gave me, in his quaint way, of an excursion he went upon with a botanist, to collect specimens of the plants and flowers of Upper Canada.

"It was a fine spring day, some ten years ago, and I was yoking my oxen to drag in some oats I had just sown, when a little, fat, punchy man, with a broad, red, good-natured face, and carrying a small black leathern wallet across his shoulder, called to me over the fence, and asked me if my name was Brian B——? I said, 'Yes; what of that?'

[164] A harmless madman; after the title (and the narrator) of an anonymous 17th-century poem (though the term predates the poem).

"'Only you are the man I want to see. They tell me that you are better acquainted with the woods than any person in these parts; and I will pay you anything in reason if you will be my guide for a few days.'

"'Where do you want to go?' said I.

"'Nowhere in particular,' says he. 'I want to go here and there, in all directions, to collect plants and flowers.'

"That is still-hunting[165] with a vengeance, thought I. 'To-day I must drag in my oats. If to-morrow will suit, we will be off.'

"'And your charge?' said he. 'I like to be certain of that.'

"'A dollar a day. My time and labour upon my farm, at this busy season, is worth more than that.'

"'True,' said he. 'Well, I'll give you what you ask. At what time will you be ready to start?'

"'By daybreak, if you wish it.'

"Away he went; and by daylight next morning he was at my door, mounted upon a stout French pony. 'What are you going to do with that beast?' said I. 'Horses are of no use on the road that you and I are to travel. You had better leave him in my stable.'

"'I want him to carry my traps,'[166] said he; 'it may be some days that we shall be absent.'

"I assured him that he must be his own beast of burthen, and carry his axe, and blanket, and wallet of food upon his own back. The little body did not much relish this arrangement; but as there was no help for it, he very good-naturedly complied. Off we set, and soon climbed the steep ridge at the back of your farm, and got upon —— lake plains. The woods were flush with flowers; and the little man grew into such an ecstacy, that at every fresh specimen he uttered a yell of joy, cut a caper in the air, and flung himself down upon them, as if he was drunk with delight. 'Oh, what treasures! what treasures!' he cried. 'I shall make my fortune!'

"It is seldom I laugh," quoth Brian, "but I could not help laughing at this odd little man; for it was not the beautiful blossoms, such as you delight to paint, that drew forth these exclamations, but the queer little plants, which he had rummaged for at the roots of old trees, among the moss and long grass. He sat upon a decayed trunk, which lay in our path, I do believe for a long hour, making an oration over some greyish things, spotted with

[165] Stalking and ambushing.

[166] Luggage.

red, that grew upon it, which looked more like mould than plants, declaring himself repaid for all the trouble and expense he had been at, if it were only to obtain a sight of them. I gathered him a beautiful blossom of the lady's slipper; but he pushed it back when I presented it to him, saying, 'Yes, yes; 'tis very fine. I have seen that often before; but these lichens are splendid.'

"The man had so little taste that I thought him a fool, and so I left him to talk to his dear plants, while I shot partridges for our supper. We spent six days in the woods, and the little man filled his black wallet with all sorts of rubbish, as if he wilfully shut his eyes to the beautiful flowers, and chose only to admire ugly, insignificant plants that everybody else passes by[167] without noticing, and which, often as I had been in the woods, I never had observed before. I never pursued a deer with such earnestness as he continued his hunt for what he called 'specimens.'

"When we came to the Cold Creek, which is pretty deep in places, he was in such a hurry to get at some plants that grew under the water, that in reaching after them he lost his balance and fell head over heels into the stream. He got a thorough ducking, and was in a terrible fright; but he held on to the flowers which had caused the trouble, and thanked his stars that he had saved them as well as his life. Well, he was an innocent man," continued Brian; "a very little made him happy, and at night he would sing and amuse himself like a child. He gave me ten dollars for my trouble, and I never saw him again; but I often think of him, when hunting in the woods that we wandered through together, and I pluck the wee plants that he used to admire, and wonder why he preferred them to the fine flowers."

1847

When our resolution was formed to sell our farm, and take up our grant of land in the backwoods, no one was so earnest in trying to persuade us to give up this ruinous scheme as our friend Brian B——, who became quite eloquent in his description of the trials and sorrows that awaited us. During the last week of our stay in the township of H——, he visited us every evening, and never bade us good-night without a tear moistening his cheek. We parted with the hunter as with an old friend; and we never met again. His fate was a sad one. After we left that part of the country, he fell into a moping melancholy, which ended in self-destruction. But a kinder, warmer-hearted man, while he enjoyed the light of reason, has seldom crossed our path.

[167] This appears as "even a chipmunk would have passed" in the 1847 version.

Mary Jane Katzmann

[The Hermit]

(1852)

The author: Mary Jane Katzmann was born in Preston, Nova Scotia, on 15 January 1828. Her mother came from a family of Loyalists, while her father was one of many Hanoverian officers in the British Army. Largely autodidact, Katzmann began publishing poems in the existing Nova Scotian periodicals and received praise from Joseph Howe for her poetical skill; then, at the age of 24, she began editing *The Provincial*, a literary magazine in Halifax. The magazine lasted two years. Its most important contribution to literature is Katzmann's own series of "Tales of Our Village," which included seven short stories and a novella. She opened a bookstore in Halifax, also called "Provincial," but she handed it over to her sister when she married William Lawson (with whom she had one daughter) in 1869. She used some of her writings from *The Provincial* to compile an award-winning *History of the Townships of Dartmouth, Preston and Lawrencetown, Halifax County, N.S.*, which was published posthumously, alongside a collection of her poetry (*Frankincense and Myrrh*), both in 1893. She died in Halifax on 23 March 1890.

The text: It was published, unsigned, in *The Provincial; or, Halifax Monthly Magazine* 1: 9 (September 1852), 352-358, as "Tales of Our Village. No. 4." It was not included in her posthumous historical work. The "Tales of Our Village" are all based on real people and real incidents, usually tragic, sometimes mundane, from an unspecified "village" in Nova Scotia, most likely in her native Preston Township. The title provided here seems like the most obvious choice, though one should stress the fact that Katzmann never gave titles (only numbers) to her "Tales of Our Village."

Further reading: Janet Guildford. "'Whate'er the duty of hour demands': The Work of Middle-Class Women in Halifax, 1840-1880." Histoire Sociale/ Social History 30: 59 (May 1997), 1-20.

A hermitage is a thing almost unknown in these busy bustling days, when railways intersect every land but our own Province,[168] and the Electric Telegraph sends its lightning message into the most retired nook. Goldsmith will not find an *Edwin* now, to restore an *Angelina* to, and Parnell would have to seek some other recipient of those moral and divine lessons imparted in his beautiful poem, the hero of which, a *Hermit*, having become rare in our day.[169] Yet now and then one of the species, (modified and different it is true) may be met with, and though not tender and sentimental, as he 'who sought a solitude forlorn' or 'reverent' as he who from 'youth to years' dwelt 'far in a wild, retired from public view,'[170] still to each, however humble or repelling, is some tale of interest attached, telling of a heart that if unconscious of the sympathies, has yet known the sorrows, of human life.

The Hermit of our story, however, does not dwell in a wilderness or cell, but in perhaps the most substantial house in our village, situated but a short distance from the highway, and placed on a pleasant spot that requires but taste and better cultivation, to make it a pretty country residence. A number of tall poplars are clustered around it, and there is a fine view of the broad ocean from its windows. There are bright green fields near it, and a fine grove of birch and maple in the back ground; it only wants the merry prattle and glad faces of a few rosy cheeked children, with the quiet neatness of a staid matron, to give it the appearance of a farmer's comfortable home.

Its only occupant for years has been a bent, shrivelled, decrepit old man, one who looks as if he had never known what it was to hear home voices or to feel the kindly emotions of human affections. His years now have outnumbered seventy. Toil and

---

[168] The Nova Scotia Railway, a pet project of Joseph Howe, received its charter in 1853, some six months after the publication of this story; the first railway lines were opened in 1858.

[169] Each of the two Anglo-Irish poets mentioned here—Thomas Parnell (1679-1718) and Oliver Goldsmith (1728-1774)—wrote a poem entitled "The Hermit." To avoid confusion, Goldsmith's is sometimes called "Edwin and Angelina," after the names of its heroes.

[170] The first quote is from Goldsmith's poem mentioned in the previous note; the others are paraphrases of Parnell's poem (they should read "Far in a wild, unknown to public view/ From youth to age a reverend hermit grew").

privations have made full havoc upon his wasted form; sickness has often visited him; the hardships and disappointments of life have also told their tale upon him, while the inward workings of an untoward and soured spirit have traced their record upon his forbidding countenance.

It seems difficult often, while gazing upon such a picture of dreary old age, to fancy that ever childhood or innocence belonged to it: those glad days of freedom and happiness, when we little dream of the rough places in life, or at least anticipate no encounter with them.

Isaac B—— was the son of Dutch settlers in the county of L——,[171] who, by their own hard labour, had secured a farm, and provided a maintenance for a large family of children. Frugal and industrious, they imparted these virtues to their family, who grew up in the dull, honesty stupidity that characterizes the German peasant.

Isaac, the elder son, was an active and busy fellow, a good mechanic as well as a plodding farmer, and soon accumulated a considerable portion of money; enough to purchase a small farm for himself, and commence life on his own account. Nature had not been very liberal to him either in personal or mental gifts, for his countenance even when young, wore the hard, forbidding expression that marks his age, and his temper was equally harsh and unyielding. Still kindness with him might have done, what it does with all to whom its influences are properly applied—softened down the rough places, and planted flowers in the stony soil—but poor Isaac was never fortunate enough to experience its regenerating effects.

He had not been long an occupant of the house he had erected on his newly acquired farm, when his thoughts ran upon matrimony; proving that his solitary feelings were but the growth of disappointed hopes and determination of later years. Strangely enough, however, his choice fell upon a girl of thirteen, the daughter of a neighbouring farmer, who with an eye to the comfortable property B—— had acquired, shewed that he regarded more the worldly advancement of his child, than her future happiness. Not to speak of the cruelty in allowing so young a girl to enter into

[171] Most likely Lunenburg County, Nova Scotia, home to many German (sometimes called Dutch) settlers. German immigration to Nova Scotia began as early as the 1750s.

a state of whose duties and claims she was necessarily ignorant, the great difference between her age and Isaac's made it a most unsuitable match. He was over thirty, and required a woman of experience as well as tact to manage his household and himself; not a child, who was capable of no more than gathering the bright strawberries from the green banks, or chasing the swift butterflies as they sported among the flowers.

Her own consent to the proposals of B—— was a thing easy to be gained or lost. With the volatile fancy of a child, she at one moment regarded her being married with delight; and then again, with the instinctive fear that haunts even the very young, she shrank from the grim face of her moody lover, and scampered off with her playmates to the more congenial occupation afforded by the birds and blossoms. Her parents, however, determined not to lose so good an opportunity of settling their child, and arranged the matter for her with her future husband; even her mother pressed the offer and persuaded her unheeding child to take upon herself the duty of being wife to an ill-tempered and peculiar man, who was old enough to be her father, and who had not one feeling in common with the weak and playful girl. 1852
B—— probably liked the child or he would not have sought her in marriage; possibly imagining that one so young would more readily yield to his wishes, and spare him the annoyance of argument or remonstrance. Doubtless it was with a view to his own comfort that he thought of taking her to his home; but it must have been a peculiar fondness for the girl herself, or one so far-seeing and thrifty as he, would have seen that a child of thirteen was not the most judicious person to choose, as a housekeeper, or a wife.

The marriage was at last completed, and the poor little thing left the home of her childhood, and her young brothers and sisters, for the lowly home of the 'cross old man,' as they termed him. He was kind to her in his own way, but the very kindness was irksome to her, and she frequently longed to escape from his dwelling, to her mother's home, or to the merry children with whom she had played through the glad hours of her young life. B—— was angry at this, and endeavoured by every means to induce her to stay at home, and attend to the duties he had imposed upon her. She rebelled still more at this restraint, and by her constant wilfulness aggravated the unhappy temper of the moody man, and made him still more exacting and imperious. He complained to her parents, and they used every endeavour to reconcile the poor girl to the husband they had forced upon her; but she was too young to see the importance of their counsel, and too heedless to feel that her husband and his house had claims upon her attention and care.

She played with the boys and the girls of the village as formerly; and he was often annoyed, when returning home from the field in the evening, to find her occupied in swinging, or hunting birds' nests with her young companions. His jealousy was almost equal to his annoyance; he even grudged her the society of her brothers, thus shewing that there were strong feelings in the man's heart, that a sensible and judicious woman might have turned to good account, making both him and herself happy.

Things went on in this way for nine years with no prospect of amelioration. They had a son born to them, but his birth was productive of little pleasure. The good feelings of both parents were destroyed by constant bickerings, and the life they led was most unhappy. Parents and friends had interfered to make peace, but failed. B—— was exacting and unyielding; his wife neither watchful nor conciliatory. She began to look upon him with dread and dislike: the feelings of the girl had merged into those of the woman. She saw around her in the young men she had grown up with, those with whom she might have been happy, and whose humours she might have borne and complied with, and she felt desolate and miserable as she reflected on her position: tied to a man whom she disliked and feared, compelled to live with him as his wife, feeling herself something between a prisoner and a slave, and cut off from all the anticipated pleasure of existence.

It was a dreary position for the young woman; and highly reprehensible were the parents who sentenced her to such a fate. Bitterly did they afterwards repent it, when sorrow was too late to remedy their child's condition, or to restore her to freedom.

B—— was also much to be pitied; he had hoped for a friend and comforter in taking a wife, and he had been grievously disappointed. The roughest nature has always some spot accessible to the sunshine. The gnarled bark of the most rugged tree woos winningly the vine to rest upon its harsh places; and so it is with human nature. Peasant or Prince yearns for something to love him; and rude as the heart or untutored as the mind may be, there is still some loophole that remains for a beam of kindness to enter by.

Thus it was that poor B—— doubtless had felt, and the blighting of all his hopes was hard to bear. It was sad to see the only being he had sought to love him, turn away in aversion, and thwart instead of please him. Though in low and unrefined life, it was still another proof of the wretchedness of ill-assorted marriages, be they from dissimilarity of age, feeling or affection.

At last the young woman could bear her condition no longer; and her parents, moved by her entreaties, consented to make the last reparation in their power, and take her again, with her infant boy, to their own home. B—— shewed no unwillingness now to consent to their proposal; he was either wearied of her, or the constant repetition of annoyance and discord. She went from the home he had prepared for her, leaving no relic of her presence, not even his boy, who might have been 'a spirit to soften and to bless;' and he was left alone—wifeless—childless. We seem to realize and deeply sympathize with Lord Byron's desolate condition, when he speaks of standing 'with all his household gods shivered about him,'[172] and yet this poor German peasant was equally desolate and aggrieved. The one was a peer and a poet, among the loftiest and most gifted of mankind; the other was a labourer and a clod, dull and dark in mind, and yet by that 'one touch of nature that makes the whole world kin,'[173] the peer and the peasant were reduced to the same level. Those who were his own to cherish and love, and whose right it was to bestow the same good offices for him, had gone out from his threshold, and he saw them no more.

No one knew how he felt or what he thought, for he wrapped himself in unsocial and gloomy silence: all were unwilling to molest or annoy him. But the change made a deep impression on him, notwithstanding, and the kindly emotions that may have slept within him were sealed and buried forever.

He soon announced his intention of selling his farm and leaving the country. He, however, told none of his plans, further than was necessary to their advancement. He disposed of his farm and left the place of his childhood, and scene of his domestic unhappiness. Though his neighbours were unacquainted with his

[172] This is not an exact quote. Byron uses versions of this line in *Don Juan*, in *Marino Faliero*, and in one of his letters. He was famously and controversially forced to separate from his wife and never saw his daughter again.

[173] From Shakespeare's *Troilus and Cressida* (III, iii, 175).

movements, it was to '*Our Village*' that his course was bent, many miles away from the place of his nativity,—to commence life anew, and set the world, its sympathies and companionship at defiance. He purchased here the farm described at the commencement of this sketch, and proceeded with the erection of the house, building the greater part himself; for, as before mentioned, his mechanical ability was considerable, and had been, indeed, often put in requisition by his neighbours. His dwelling was soon completed, and here he lived alone for a number of years—his own cook, laundress and dairymaid—associating with none, and asking help from none.

Why he renounced his solitary state is unknown, but suddenly he took to himself a woman, as his wife, *pro tem;* one of those homeless and friendless beings, who at last grow reckless as to whom their lot is cast with, so that the means of subsistence is supplied. This change was, eventually, anything but conducive to his comfort; instead of a housekeeper, she proved wasteful. Whatever her natural temper may have been, she ruined it by inebriety; and, what was worse, he at length found it more difficult to dislodge than to gain a tenant. He now lived over a second term of domestic martyrdom, and got worsted in the contest. Three children were added to his family—a boy and two girls: and these were objects of perpetual grievance to him. At last his ill-temper and violence grew so excessive, that a regard for her personal safety compelled his tormentor to take her departure, which she did, leaving behind her the three children to anything but the '*tender mercies*' of their father. The boy was, like himself, dogged, obstinate and ill-tempered; and from the time of his boyhood, outbreaks and contests with his father were frequent. The girls were stolid and untractable: brought up without encouragement or guidance, they were little more than civilized savages—untaught and unwomanly. Poor young creatures—it was well their feelings were blunted and unexercised, for theirs was a rough and dreary home, even to blinded and dull natures! They grew up to womanhood, ignorant and helpless, uncared for by their father, and destitute of moral or religious training. Nevertheless, while still very young, they were taken from a place miscalled home, and married to men fully double their ages. The eldest girl was the more fortunate. It was her lot to get the best of the two men, who took her to live with some of his own family; and there under womanly teaching and aid, she improved rapidly in all the duties which females in her station are called upon to perform. Though her husband was an elderly man, he was still active and industrious, and, when sober, was very kind. The youngest girl was more stupid and unteachable than her sister; while the man she married, the elder of the two brothers, was idle, ill-tempered and also intemperate. She had only gone from bad to worse,—to poverty and all the other ills she had ever encountered. Her lot in life will be a dark one, unless there may be yet some Samaritan, who will endeavour to illumine with a ray of light, the mind of this benighted and unfriended woman. After the marriage of his sisters, the boy continued to live with his father for some time; but they occupied different rooms, and sat at different tables, living on for weeks and months without interchanging a word, or apparently conscious of each other's presence—each acting as his own housekeeper and provider, and taking his own course, independent of the other. At last the boy left, and went to the adjoining town, to work at the carpenter's trade, and the old man was thus once more alone,—still plodding on, working as though a large family were dependant on his exertions for bread,—denying himself almost the comforts of life, and seeking assistance from none. He rarely went to church, and never entered a neighbour's house, unless sent for and requested to assist in some remunerative labour. Sickness often assailed him, but he took care of himself without the aid of doctor or nurse. Sometimes a kind and pitying neighbour who heard, by chance, of his ailments, would volunteer a visit; but the reception, if not ungracious, was of a forbidding character, and left no inducement to repeat the kindness. By his own unaided labour he built a small saw mill in the woods adjoining his house, and there, bending down by the hoary stream that dashed over the old green rocks, making wild music in the still noon-time, might the old man be seen, week day or Sunday, toiling at his work, looking like some elf of the forest, or goblin spirit, with his weird glances and shadowy stooping form. His son, to whom he had not spoken for many years, took a violent fever, and for a long time hovered between life and death.

It seemed then as if every touch of nature was not dead in the old man's breast, for he went to see his son, taking him, occasionally, presents of game, or anything from the farm he thought he might fancy. And at last, when his physician recommended his native air as a restorative, and his father had provided the means,—and when he was preparing to take him to his home again, he found the fever had taken a sudden turn, and that death had reached his boy's bedside before him. Those who saw the old man then, thought that nature once again was dominant, and knew that he trembled beneath, what indeed to him was, grief: another blessed assurance, that, hardened and darkened as human nature may be, there are some chords that will never forget their music,—some drops in the fountain of life that are not all bitterness.

Since that event the old man has gone on in his accustomed way, only looking more bowed and feeble, but still solitary in his hermitage, seemingly uncaring and uncared for. It were matter of interest to unravel, whether his 'sunset of life' is ever tinged by the memories of early joys and sorrows, and what his thoughts are with regard to past or future. Age has now darkened the windows of his mind,—and the solitude of his poor tenement will soon be exchanged for the narrower one of the grave. Surrounded by persons of his own class and degree in life, while all others have turned to the companionship of their families and friends, he has shut his nature up from the approach of all, and chosen to live alone. And when the dark hour comes, so hard to all, because it brings the severance of those ties so very dear to our hearts, he will have none to break, but he will have none to comfort him. Wife and child are far distant; daughters, early friends, are alienated or no more. To all appearance he must die—as he has lived—alone. It may be, perhaps, that some neighbour will miss him at his accustomed tasks, and, as day after day, passes on without his re-appearance, will cross his threshold to seek for him, and find the broken temple of our village hermit, lying motionless—inanimate, in the dreary loneness to which it has long been sentenced; and the tired, disappointed, but loosened spirit—where?

Susanna Moodie

Grace Marks

(1853)

The author: Susanna Moodie used her "Canadian Sketches" (including the two stories from 1847 selected here) to make up her first book published by Richard Bentley in London: *Roughing It in the Bush* (1852). This was followed by *Life in the Clearings* (1853) and *Flora Lyndsay* (1854). After her husband had to resign from his office as sheriff of Hastings County in 1863, he transferred his property to one of their sons and the parents moved in with this son and their daughter-in-law. However, the younger couple decided to immigrate to Delaware and the parents remained in Belleville, Ontario, moving into a small cottage. After John Moodie died in 1869, Susanna lived mostly with another son, Robert, in Toronto, where she died on 8 April 1885.

The text: It first appeared as part of Chapter X of *Life in the Clearings versus the Bush* (London: Richard Bentley, 1853), 215-232. The New York edition (DeWitt and Davenport) repeats the text, with different page numbers. It was republished as a standalone short story in *Anglo-American Magazine* 5: 6 (December 1854), 598-604. The story is based on the real-life trials of James McDermott and Grace Marks, held in Toronto, on 3-4 November 1843 (it further inspired Margaret Atwood's novel *Alias Grace*). The following is from the *Life in the Clearings*, though we are following the correction operated by the editors of the *Anglo-American Magazine* on the name of one of the victims. We have generalised the spelling of the name of the main narrator, which in both sources appears in two versions.

Further reading: Walton, George. *The Trials of James McDermott and Grace Marks*. Toronto: Star and Transcript Office, 1843.

Lorna R. McLean and Marilyn Barber. "In Search of Comfort and Independence: Irish Immigrant Domestic Servants Encounter the Courts, Jails, and Asylums in Nineteenth-Century Ontario." *Sisters or Strangers? Immigrant, Ethnic, and Racialized Women in Canadian History*. Eds. Marlene Epp and Franca Iacovetta. Toronto: University of Toronto Press, 2016. 209-230.

About eight or nine years ago—I write from memory, and am not very certain as to dates—a young Irish emigrant girl was hired into the service of Captain Kinnear, an officer on half-pay, who had purchased a farm about thirty miles in the rear of Toronto; but the name of the township, and the county in which it was situated, I have forgotten; but this is of little consequence to my narrative. Both circumstances could be easily ascertained by the curious. The captain had been living for some time on very intimate terms with his housekeeper, a handsome young woman of the name of Hannah Montgomery, who had been his servant of all work. Her familiarity with her master, who, it appears, was a very fine-looking, gentlemanly person, had rendered her very impatient of her former menial employments, and she soon became virtually the mistress of the house. Grace Marks was hired to wait upon her, and perform all the coarse drudgery that Hannah considered herself too fine a lady to do.

While Hannah occupied the parlour with her master, and sat at his table, her insolent airs of superiority aroused the jealousy and envy of Grace Marks, and the man-servant, MacDermot, who considered themselves quite superior to their self-elected mistress. MacDermot was the son of respectable parents; but from being a wild, ungovernable boy, he became a bad, vicious man, and early abandoned the parental roof to enlist for a soldier. He was soon tired of his new profession, and, deserting from his regiment, escaped detection, and emigrated to Canada. Having no means of his own, he was glad to engage with Captain Kinnear as his servant, to whom his character and previous habits were unknown.

These circumstances, together with what follows, were drawn from his confession, made to Mr. Mac—ie,[174] who had conducted his defence, the night previous to his execution. Perhaps it will be better to make him the narrator of his own story.

"Grace Marks was hired by Captain Kinnear to wait upon his housekeeper, a few days after I entered his service. She was a pretty girl, and very smart about her work, but of a silent, sullen temper. It was very difficult to know when she was pleased. Her age did not exceed seventeen years. After the work of the day was over,

[174] The defense counsel was Kenneth McKenzie.

she and I generally were left to ourselves in the kitchen, Hannah being entirely taken up with her master. Grace was very jealous of the difference made between her and the housekeeper, whom she hated, and to whom she was often very insolent and saucy. Her whole conversation to me was on this subject. 'What is she better than us?' she would say, 'that she is to be treated like a lady, and eat and drink of the best. She is not better born than we are, or better educated. I will not stay here to be domineered over by her. Either she or I must soon leave this.' Every little complaint Hannah made of me, was repeated to me with cruel exaggerations, till my dander was up, and I began to regard the unfortunate woman as our common enemy. The good looks of Grace had interested me in her cause; and though there was something about the girl that I could not exactly like, I had been a very lawless, dissipated fellow, and if a woman was young and pretty, I cared very little about her character. Grace was sullen and proud, and not very easily won over to my purpose; but in order to win her liking, if possible, I gave a ready ear to all her discontented repinings.

"One day Captain Kinnear went to Toronto, to draw his half-year's pay, and left word with Hannah that he would be back by noon the next day. She had made some complaint against us to him, and he had promised to pay us off on his return. This had come to the ears of Grace, and her hatred to the housekeeper was increased to a tenfold degree. I take heaven to witness, that I had no designs against the life of the unfortunate woman when my master left the house.

"Hannah went out in the afternoon, to visit some friends she had in the neighbourhood, and left Grace and I alone together. This was an opportunity too good to be lost, and, instead of minding our work, we got recapitulating our fancied wrongs over some of the captain's whisky. I urged my suit to Grace; but she would not think of anything, or listen to anything, but the insults and injuries she had received from Hannah, and her burning thirst for revenge. 'Dear me,' said I, half in jest, 'if you hate her so much as all that, say but the word, and I will soon rid you of her for ever.'

"I had not the least idea that she would take me at my word. Her eyes flashed with a horrible light. 'You dare not do it!' she replied, with a scornful toss of her head.

"'Dare not do what?'

"'Kill that woman for me!' she whispered.

"'You don't know what I dare, or what I dar'n't do!' said I, drawing a little back from her. 'If you will promise to run off with me afterwards, I will see what I can do with her.'

"'I'll do anything you like; but you must first kill her.'

"'You are not in earnest, Grace?'

"'I mean what I say!'

"'How shall we be able to accomplish it? She is away now, and she may not return before her master comes back.'

"'Never doubt her. She will be back to see after the house, and that we are in no mischief.'

"'She sleeps with you?'

"'Not always. She will to-night.'

"'I will wait till you are asleep, and then I will kill her with a blow of the axe on the head. It will be over in a minute. Which side of the bed does she lie on?'

"'She always sleeps on the side nearest the wall and she bolts the door the last thing before she puts out the light. But I will manage both these difficulties for you. I will pretend to have the toothache very bad, and will ask to sleep next the wall to-night. She is kind to the sick, and will not refuse me; and after she is asleep, I will steal out at the foot of the bed, and unbolt the door. If you are true to your promise, you need not fear that I shall neglect mine.'

"I looked at her with astonishment. 'Good God!' thought I, 'can this be a woman? A pretty, soft-looking woman too—and a mere girl! What a heart she must have!' I felt equally tempted to tell her she was a devil, and that I would have nothing to do with such a horrible piece of business; but she looked so handsome, that somehow or another I yielded to the temptation, though it was not without a struggle; for conscience loudly warned me not to injure one who had never injured me.

"Hannah came home to supper, and she was unusually agreeable, and took her tea with us in the kitchen, and laughed and chatted as merrily as possible. And Grace, in order to hide the wicked thoughts working in her mind, was very pleasant too, and they went laughing to bed, as if they were the best friends in the world.

"I sat by the kitchen fire after they were gone, with the axe between my knees, trying to harden my heart to commit the murder; but for a long time I could not bring myself to do it. I thought over all my past life. I had been a bad, disobedient son—a dishonest, wicked man; but I had never shed blood. I had often felt sorry for the error of my ways, and had even vowed amendment, and prayed God to forgive me, and make a better man of me for the time to come. And now, here I was, at the instigation of a young girl, contemplating the death of a fellow-creature, with whom I had been laughing and talking on apparently friendly terms a few minutes ago. Oh, it was dreadful, too dreadful to be true! and then I prayed God to remove the temptation from me, and to convince me of my sin. 'Ah, but,' whispered the devil, 'Grace Marks will laugh at you. She will twit you with your want of resolution, and say that she is the better man of the two.'

"I sprang up, and hastened at their door, which opened into the kitchen. All was still. I tried the door;—for the damnation of my soul, it was open. I had no need of a candle, the moon was at full; there was no curtain to their window, and it shone directly upon the bed, and I could see their features as plainly as by the light of day. Grace was either sleeping, or pretending to sleep—I think the latter, for there was a sort of fiendish smile upon her lips. The housekeeper had yielded to her request, and was lying with her head out over the bed-clothes, in the best possible manner for receiving a death-blow upon her temples. She had a sad, troubled look upon her handsome face; and once she moved her hand, and said 'Oh dear!' I wondered whether she was dreaming of any danger to herself and the man she loved. I raised the axe to give the death-blow, but my arm seemed held back by an invisible hand. It was the hand of God. I turned away from the bed, and left the room; I could not do it. I sat down by the embers of the fire, and cursed my own folly. I made a second attempt—a third—and fourth; yes, even to a ninth—and my purpose was each time defeated. God seemed to fight for the poor creature; and the last time I left the room I swore, with a great oath, that if she did not die till I killed her, she might live on till the day of judgment. I threw the axe on to the wood heap in the shed, and went to bed, and soon fell fast asleep.

"In the morning, I was coming into the kitchen to light the fire, and met Grace Marks with the pails in her hand, going out to milk the cows. As she passed me, she gave me a poke with the pail in the ribs, and whispered with a sneer, 'Arn't you a coward!'

"As she uttered those words, the devil, against whom I had fought all night, entered into my heart, and transformed me into a demon. All feelings of remorse and mercy forsook me from that instant, and darker and deeper plans of murder and theft flashed through my brain. 'Go and milk the cows,' said I with a bitter laugh, 'and you shall soon see whether I am the coward you take me for.' She went out to milk, and I went in to murder the unsuspicious housekeeper.

"I found her at the sink in the kitchen, washing her face in a tin basin. I had the fatal axe in my hand, and without pausing for an instant to change my mind—for had I stopped to think, she would have been living to this day I struck her a heavy blow on the back of the head with my axe. She fell to the ground at my feet without uttering a word; and, opening the trap-door that led from the kitchen into a cellar where we kept potatoes and other stores, I hurled her down, closed the door, and wiped away the perspiration that was streaming down my face. I then looked at the axe and laughed. 'Yes; I have tasted blood now, and this murder will not be the last. Grace Marks, you have raised the devil—take care of yourself now!'

"She came in with her pails, looking as innocent and demure as the milk they contained. She turned pale when her eye met mine. I have no doubt but that I looked the fiend her taunt had made me.

"'Where's Hannah?' she asked, in a faint voice.

"'Dead,' said I. 'What! are you turned coward now?'

"'MacDermot, you look dreadful. I am afraid of *you*, not of her.'

"'Aha, my girl! you should have thought of that before. The hound that laps blood once will lap again. You have taught me how to kill, and I don't care who, or how many I kill now. When Kinnear comes home I will put a ball through his brain, and send him to keep company below with the housekeeper.'

"She put down the pails,—she sprang towards me, and, clinging to my arm, exclaimed in frantic tones—

"'You won't kill him?'

"'By ——, I will! why should he escape more than Hannah? And hark you, girl, if you dare to breathe a word to any one of my intention, or tell to any one, by word or sign, what I have done, I'll kill you!'

"She trembled like a leaf. Yes, that young demon trembled. 'Don't kill me,' she whined, 'don't kill me, MacDermot! I swear that I will not betray you; and oh, don't kill him!'

"'And why the devil do you want me to spare him?'

"'He is so handsome!'

"'Pshaw!'

"'So good-natured!'

"'Especially to you. Come, Grace; no nonsense. If I had thought that you were jealous of your master and Hannah, I would have been the last man on earth to have killed her. You belong to me now; and though I believe that the devil has given me a bad bargain in you, yet, such as you are, I will stand by you. And now, strike a light and follow me into the cellar. You must help me to put Hannah out of sight.'

"She never shed a tear, but she looked dogged and sullen, and did as I bid her.

"That cellar presented a dreadful spectacle. I can hardly bear to recall it now; but then, when my hands were still red with her blood, it was doubly terrible. Hannah Montgomery was not dead, as I had thought; the blow had only stunned her. She had partially recovered her senses, and was kneeling on one knee as we descended the ladder with the light. I don't know if she heard us, for she must have been blinded with the blood that was flowing down her face; but she certainly heard us, and raised her clasped hands, as if to implore mercy.

"I turned to Grace. The expression of her livid face was even more dreadful than that of the unfortunate woman. She uttered no cry, but she put her hand to her head, and said,—

"'God has damned me for this.'

"'Then you have nothing more to fear,' says I. 'Give me that handkerchief off your neck.' She gave it without a word. I threw myself upon the body of the housekeeper,—and planting my knee on her breast, I tied the handkerchief round her throat in a single tie, giving Grace one end to hold, while I drew the other tight enough to finish my terrible work. Her eyes literally started from her head, she gave one groan, and all was over. I then cut the body in four pieces, and turned a large washtub over them.

"'Now, Grace, you may come up and get my breakfast.'

"'Yes, Mr. M——.' You will not perhaps believe me, yet I assure you that we went upstairs and ate a good breakfast; and I laughed with Grace at the consternation the captain would be in when he found that Hannah was absent.

"During the morning a pedlar called, who travelled the country with second-hand articles of clothing, taking farm produce in exchange for his wares. I bought of him two good linen-breasted shirts, which had been stolen from some gentleman by his housekeeper. While I was chatting with the pedlar, I remarked that Grace had left the house, and I saw her through the kitchen-window talking to a young lad by the well, who often came across to borrow an old gun from my master to shoot ducks. I called to her to come in, which she appeared to me to do very reluctantly. I felt that I was in her power, and I was horribly afraid of her betraying me in order to save her own and the captain's life. I now hated her from my very soul, and could have killed her without the least pity or remorse.

"'What do you want, MacDermot!' she said sullenly.

"'I want you. I dare not trust you out of my sight. I know what you are,—you are plotting mischief against me; but if you betray me I will be revenged; if I have to follow you to—for that purpose.'

"'Why do you doubt my word, MacDermot? Do you think I want to hang myself?'

"'No, not yourself, but me. You are too bad to be trusted. What were you saying just now to that boy?'

"'I told him that the captain was not at home, and I dared not lend him the gun.'

"'You were right. The gun will be wanted at home.'.

"She shuddered and turned away. It seems that she had had enough of blood, and shewed some feeling at last. I kept my eye upon her, and would not suffer her for a moment out of my sight.

"At noon the captain drove into the yard, and I went out to take the horse. Before he had time to alight, he asked for Hannah. I told him that she was out, that she went off the day before, and had not returned, but that we expected her in every minute.

"He was very much annoyed, and said that she had no business to leave the house during his absence,—that he would give her a good rating when she came home.

"Grace asked if she should get his breakfast?

"He said, 'He wanted none. He would wait till Hannah came back, and then he would take a cup of coffee.'

"He then went into the parlour; and throwing himself down upon the sofa, commenced reading a magazine he had brought with him from Toronto.

"'I thought he would miss the young lady,' said Grace. 'He has no idea how close she is to him at this moment. I wonder why I could not make him as good a cup of coffee as Hannah. I have often made it for him when he did not know it. But what is sweet from her hand, would be poison from mine. But I have had my revenge!'

"Dinner time came, and out came the captain to the kitchen, book in hand.

"'Isn't Hannah back yet?'

"'No,—Sir.'

"'It's strange. Which way did she go?'

"'She did not tell us where she was going; but said that, as you were out, it would be a good opportunity of visiting an old friend.'

"'When did she say she would be back?'

"'We expected her last night,' said Grace.

"'Something must have happened to the girl, MacDermot,' turning to me. 'Put the saddle on my riding horse. I will go among the neighbours, and inquire if they have seen her.'

"Grace exchanged glances with me.

"'Will you not stay till after dinner, Sir?'

"'I don't care,' he cried impatiently, 'a —— for dinner. I feel too uneasy about the girl to eat. MacDermot, be quick and saddle Charley; and you, Grace, come and tell me when he is at the door.'

"He went back into the parlour, and put on his riding-coat; and I went into the harness-house, not to obey his orders, but to plan his destruction.

"I perceived that it was more difficult to conceal a murder than I had imagined; that the inquiries he was about to make would arouse suspicion among the neighbours, and finally lead to a discovery. The only way to prevent this was to murder him, take what money he had brought with him from Toronto, and be off with Grace to the States. Whatever repugnance I might have felt at the commission of this fresh crime, was drowned in the selfish necessity of self-preservation. My plans were soon matured, and I hastened to put them in a proper train.

"I first loaded the old duck gun with ball, and, putting it behind the door of the harness-house, I went into the parlour. I found the captain lying on the sofa reading, his hat and gloves beside him on the table. He started up as I entered.

"'Is the horse ready?'

"'Not yet, Sir. Some person has been in during the night, and cut your new English saddle almost to pieces. I wish you would step out and look at it. I cannot put it on Charley in its present state.'

"'Don't bother me, he cried angrily; 'it is in your charge,—you are answerable for that. Who the devil would think it worth their while to break into the harness house to cut a saddle, when they could have carried it off entirely? Let me have none of your tricks, Sir! You must have done it yourself!'

"'That is not very likely, Captain Kinnear. At any rate, it would be a satisfaction to me if you would come and look at it.'

"'I'm in too great a hurry. Put on the old one.'

"I still held the door in my hand. 'It's only a step from here to the harness-house.'

"He rose reluctantly, and followed me into the kitchen. The harness-house formed part of a lean-to off the kitchen, and you went down two steps into it. He went on before me, and as he descended the steps, I clutched the gun I had left behind the door, took my aim between his shoulders, and shot him through the heart. He staggered forward and fell, exclaiming as he did so, 'O God, I am shot!'

"In a few minutes he was lying in the cellar, beside our other victim. Very little blood flowed from the wound; he bled internally. He had on a very fine shirt; and after rifling his person, and possessing myself of his pocketbook, I took off his shirt, and put on the one I had bought of the pedlar."

"Then," cried Mr. Mac—ie, to whom this confession was made, "that was how the pedlar was supposed to have had a hand in the murder. That circumstance confused the evidence, and nearly saved your life."

"It was just as I have told you," said MacDermot.

"And tell me, MacDermot, the reason of another circumstance that puzzled the whole court. How came that magazine, which was found in the housekeeper's bed saturated with blood, in that place, and so far from the spot where the murder was committed?"

"That, too, is easily explained, though it was such a riddle to you gentlemen of the law. When the captain came out to look at the saddle, he had the book open in his hand. When he was shot, he clapped the book to his breast with both his hands. Almost all the blood that flowed from it was caught in that book. It required some force on my part to take it from his grasp after he was dead. Not knowing what to do with it, I flung it into the housekeeper's bed. While I harnessed the riding-horse into his new buggy, Grace collected all the valuables in the house. You know, Sir, that we got safe on board the steamer at Toronto; but, owing to an unfortunate delay, we were apprehended, sent to jail, and condemned to die.

"Grace, you tell me, has been reprieved, and her sentence commuted into confinement in the Penitentiary for life. This seems very unjust to me, for she is certainly more criminal than I am. If she had not instigated me to commit the murder, it never would have been done. But the priest tells me that I shall not be hung, and not to make myself uneasy on that score."

"MacDermot," said Mr. Mac—ie, "it is useless to flatter you with false hopes. You will suffer the execution of your sentence to-morrow, at eight o'clock, in front of the jail. I have seen the order sent by the governor to the sheriff, and that was my reason for visiting you to-night. I was not satisfied in my own mind of your guilt. What you have told me has greatly relieved my mind; and I must add, if ever man deserved his sentence, you do yours."

"When this unhappy man was really convinced that I was in earnest—that he must pay with his life the penalty of his crime," continued Mr. Mac—ie, "his abject cowardice and the mental agonies he endured were too terrible to witness. He dashed himself on the floor of his cell, and shrieked and raved like a maniac, declaring that he could not, and would not die; that the law had no right to murder a man's soul as well as his body, by giving him no time for repentance; that if he was hung like a dog, Grace Marks, in justice, ought to share his fate. Finding that all I could say to him had no effect in producing a better frame of mind I called in the chaplain, and left the sinner to his fate.

"A few months ago I visited the Penitentiary; and as my pleading had been the means of saving Grace from the same doom, I naturally felt interested in her present state. I was permitted to see and speak to her; and Mrs. M—–, I never shall forget the painful feelings I experienced during this interview. She had been five years in the Penitentiary, but still retained a remarkably youthful appearance. The sullen assurance that had formerly marked her countenance, had given place to a sad and humbled expression. She had lost much of her former good looks, and seldom raised her eyes from the ground.

"'Well, Grace,' I said, 'how is it with you now?'

"'Bad enough, Sir,' she answered, with a sigh; 'I ought to feel grateful to you for all the trouble you took on my account. I thought you my friend then, but you were the worst enemy I ever had in my life.'

"'How is that, Grace?'

"'Oh, Sir, it would have been better for me to have died with MacDermot than to have suffered for years, as I have done, the torments of the damned. Oh, Sir, my misery is too great for words to describe! I would gladly submit to the most painful death, if I thought that it would put an end to the pangs I daily endure. But though I have repented of my wickedness with bitter tears, it has pleased God that I should never again know a moment's peace. Since I helped MacDermot to strangle Hannah Montgomery, her terrible face and those horrible bloodshot eyes have never left me for a moment. They glare upon me by night and day, and when I close my eyes in despair, I see them looking into my soul—it is impossible to shut them out. If I am at work, in a few minutes that dreadful head is in my lap. If I look up to get rid of it, I see it in the far corner of the room. At dinner, it is in my plate, or grinning between the persons who sit opposite to me at table. Every object that meets my sight takes the same dreadful form; and at night—at night—in the silence and loneliness of my cell, those blazing eyes make my prison as light as day. No, not as day—they have a terribly hot glare, that has not the appearance of anything in this world. And when I sleep,—that face just hovers above my own, its eyes just opposite to mine; so that when I awake with a shriek of agony, I find them there. Oh! this is hell, Sir—these are the torments of the damned! Were I in that fiery place, my punishment could not be greater than this.'

"The poor creature turned away, and I left her, for who could say a word of comfort to such grief? it was a matter solely between her own conscience and God."

Having heard this terrible narrative, I was very anxious to behold this unhappy victim of remorse. She passed me on the stairs as I proceeded to the part of the building where the women were kept; but on perceiving a stranger, she turned her head away, so that I could not get a glimpse of her face.

Having made known my wishes to the matron, she very kindly called her in to perform some trifling duty in the ward, so that I might have an opportunity of seeing her. She is a middle-sized woman, with a slight graceful figure. There is an air of hopeless melancholy in her face which is very painful to contemplate. Her complexion is fair, and must, before the touch of hopeless sorrow paled it, have been very brilliant. Her eyes are a bright blue, her hair auburn, and her face would be rather handsome were it not for the long curved chin, which gives, as it always does to most persons who have this facial defect, a cunning, cruel expression.

Grace Marks glances at you with a sidelong stealthy look; her eye never meets yours, and after a furtive regard, it invariably bends its gaze upon the ground. She looks like a person rather above her humble station, and her conduct during her stay in the Penitentiary was so unexceptionable, that a petition was signed by all the influential gentlemen in Kingston, which released her from her long imprisonment. She entered the service of the governor of the Penitentiary, but the fearful hauntings of her brain have terminated in madness. She is now in the asylum at Toronto; and as I mean to visit it when there, I may chance to see this remarkable criminal again. Let us hope that all her previous guilt may be attributed to the incipient workings of this frightful malady.

James McGrigor Allan

Captain Ardmore; or, The Rose of Chambly

(1858)

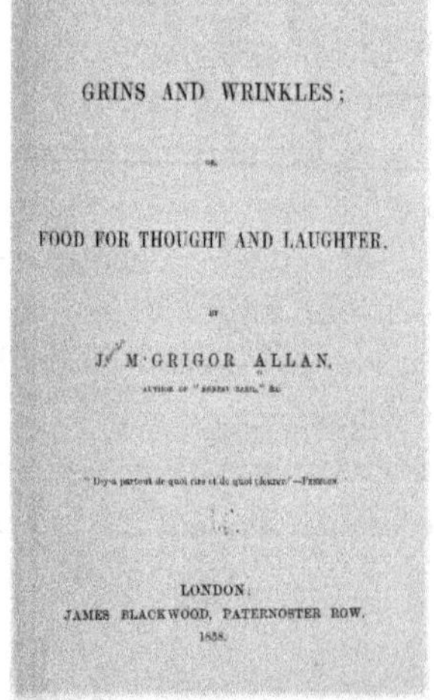

GRINS AND WRINKLES;

FOOD FOR THOUGHT AND LAUGHTER.

J. M'GRIGOR ALLAN.

LONDON:
JAMES BLACKWOOD, PATERNOSTER ROW.
1858.

The author: James McGrigor Allan was born in 1827 in Bristol, but came at an early age to Canada, where his father was chief medical officer of Halifax until 1836, when he retired and moved to Fredericton, New Brunswick. Leaving Fredericton in 1846, James McGrigor Allan lived in Montreal but he returned to New Brunswick when his older brother, the poet Peter John Allan (1825-1848) was dying. James collected his brother's poems in a volume and wrote the introduction. In the 1850s, he moved to Aberdeen, then to London. Between 1857 and 1888, he published seven novels (*Ernest Basil*, *The Cost of a Coronet*, *The Last Days of a Bacherlor*, *Nobly False*, *Father Stirling*, *The Wild Curate*, and *A Lady's Four Perils*) and one volume of short stories. He married in 1886 and died in 1916 in Epsom, Surrey. He was member of the Anthropological Society of London and was an opponent of women's suffrage. In the novels and stories he published in the 1850s and 1860s he often used Canadian characters and settings, which he explained in the dedicatory letter of *Grins and Wrinkles*: "A colonist by education, though not by birth, I still cling fondly to all my reminiscences of British America, and observe with interest the rising fortunes of that fair portion of the world."

The text: First published in Allan's *Gins and Wrinkles; or, Food for Thought and Laughter* (London: James Blackwood, 1858), 1-59, from which the following has been taken. The book is dedicated to Brown Chamberlin (1827-1897), who at the time was the publisher of the *Montreal Gazette* and who would marry Susanna Moodie's daughter Agnes in 1870. The book is divided into two parts ("In the New World" and "In the Old World") and this story is placed at the very beginning. Typographical errors have been corrected.

"Love is not love,
Which alters when it alteration finds,
Or bends with the remover to remove."
SHAKSPERE

The military sleighing-club of Montreal was in all its glory, when I was taking one of my accustomed long walks round the mountain, and had just arrived at a slight eminence, about a few hundred yards in front of which, the road, after a rather steep descent, made an abrupt and ugly turn, crossing a deep ravine over a wooden bridge. These natural difficulties were further increased from the fact, that the bridge, which was quite a new structure, had not yet received a balustrade. The risk, of course, to passengers whose horses were skittish and unruly, was imminent; and a fall from the bridge could hardly escape being fatal, as the height was not less than sixty feet.

Just as I had arrived at this spot, I was startled by the clear, shrill notes of a key-bugle,[175] followed directly by the jingling of the sleigh-bells, and then the brilliant *cortège* of the sleighing-club appeared, consisting of fourteen sleighs. I drew aside to let them pass, with a pulse considerably quickened as I thought of the unprotected state of the bridge. Cornet[176] Lord Royster, of the —— regiment of dragoons, led the van, driving four-in-hand,[177] in a sleigh more remarkable for its great height than for any particular beauty of shape or style. Surely he will pull up, at least his servant will get out and walk the horses over the dangerous pass, I thought, almost *said*. Not a bit of it. Lord Royster, either from not being previously aware of the actual condition of the bridge, or knowing it, and trusting fully to his own powers as a *whip*, and mastery over his horses, only slackened his speed sufficiently to round the ugly turn without risk of upsetting, and then passed the bridge at the full trot, the timbers quivering, and resounding under the tread of the four steeds, who were urged into a canter as the danger was left behind. The rest of the charioteers followed

[175] Also known as a Kent bugle, it has six finger keys, allowing the performer to play every key in the scale.

[176] The lowest rank of commissioned officer in a cavalry unit. It was replaced by the rank of second lieutenant in 1871.

[177] A "four-in-hand" is any vehicle drawn by four horses but driven by a single person.

his example, either equally indifferent to the risk, or disdaining to show more circumspection with a pair, or tandem, than Lord Royster had displayed with a four-in-hand. The only exception was the grey-haired colonel, who brought up the rear. He stopped his sleigh, got out, and crossed the bridge on foot, making his servant lead over the horses.

I confess my heart beat more freely when I saw the last sleigh disappear on the other side, and heard the last faint echo of the key-bugle. But, where then, was Captain Ardmore's elegant *cariole*, with its well-matched bay tandem (for I knew all the equipages by sight); why had he not joined the "meet" to-day? As I mentally asked myself this question, I stepped into the road, and prepared to renew my walk, when casting my eyes in the direction from which the sleighs had come, I perceived at a great distance, but advancing at a furious pace, two horses in a tandem dragging a light *cariole* behind them. I had an ample view of the road for a quarter of a mile, so that I could discern that the driver had lost all command over the horses, who were tearing along like mad things, and decreasing the distance between us with fearful rapidity. As

they approached I could discern that one of the occupants of the vehicle was a lady. The other person, a man, was making desperate but futile efforts to catch the reins, which appeared to be flying loose on the backs of the horses.

I remember in that moment asking myself the question—What was to be done? Could I—should I attempt to stop the horses, and peril my own life to save two strangers from almost inevitable death? for if the horses were not stopped before they reached the bridge, I knew that a fatal catastrophe must be the result. The sleigh would be sure to upset at the sharp turn, and slue over the bridge, precipitating its occupants into the ravine, and in all probability, by its weight, drag the horses after it.

It was a moment of fearful suspense. Without any fixed plan, when the infuriated horses had arrived at within one hundred yards distance, I stood in the middle of the road, extending my arms, and shouting with the whole force of my lungs. But frightened runaway horses are for the time *blind.* They came on with a speed little, if at all diminished. In a moment, had I preserved my position, I should have been trampled under foot. I cannot relate methodically what followed. I remember starting back instinctively, and then grasping at the loose rein which dangled from the head of the leader, as he almost brushed against me in passing. I clutched and clung to it with desperation—there was a severe strain—I was dragged some yards—then the leader fell heavily on his side—a moment more and the shaft-horse[178] had stumbled over him; the sleigh was stopped within ten yards of the sharp turn leading over the unprotected bridge. I had saved the lives of Miss Vane, and Captain Ardmore, of the —— regiment of dragoons.

In a few minutes the kicking and plunging horses were surrounded by a knot of persons (including the captain's servant), who had been in hot pursuit from the inn, where the animals had taken fright, and from whence they had started before the man, who had alighted to buckle a rein, could achieve his object. This, of course, accounted for the total want of command of Captain Ardmore over them. In due time the horses were got upon their legs, and after being soothed and patted, led carefully over the bridge. While this was taking place, Miss Vane and Captain Ardmore were profuse in their acknowledgements to me, for what they were pleased to term my heroic conduct; and Captain Ardmore pressed me so strongly to let him have the pleasure of taking me to town, that I at length consented. And thus it was that I became personally acquainted with Miss Vane and Captain Ardmore.

Captain Ardmore was well known to me by sight, I having frequently encountered him at evening-parties, although I had never made his acquaintance until the providential escape in which I had luckily been instrumental. I knew him by reputation to be one of the most agreeable and fashionable of the officers of any of the regiments then quartered at Montreal. A finer specimen of manhood I had never beheld. He was at least six feet two inches in height, but his figure united strength and symmetry in such just proportions, that I never suspected him to be above the ordinary standard, until I saw him in close proximity with other men. He was a genuine Saxon in appearance, with light hair and blue eyes, and his beard, whiskers, and moustache, which were worn in great profusion, were of the same golden yellow tinge, without the slightest tendency to red. His age might have been twenty-five or twenty-six.

[178] In a tandem of horses, the "leader" and the "shaft horse" are harnessed in front of each other, not side by side.

Common report had already informed me that Captain Ardmore was not a mere military Adonis, one of those faultless collections of thews[179] and sinews, without ideas, which so often pass muster as handsome men, both in the army and elsewhere. There was an expression of intellect on his finely formed features, of decision in the mouth, and reflection in the mild blue eye, which told of hours, not wasted over the wine-cup, or in the mischievous *liaisons* which so frequently disgrace garrison life, but devoted to study and improvement.

Captain Ardmore had returned some time ago from a country station, Chambly, where the admirable discipline he had maintained among his men, and his officer-like conduct in quieting some disturbances which had arisen between the *habitans* and the British Canadians, had won his golden opinions from all parties, and obtained for him on his return to the capital[180] a most flattering address from the inhabitants of the township.

Gay young subs[181] had pitied "Ardmore," for what they called his exile to Chambly; but it is probable that this officer did not consider in the light of a penance, a sojourn in a lovely Canadian

village, where he had ample leisure to cultivate his favourite literary and artistic pursuits; and it would appear that he had left Chambly even with regret. Gossip had indeed remarked, that he appeared pre-occupied and *distrait*, and went much less into company on his return to Montreal. To account for this, as usual, all sorts of conjectures had been started. Some said that the captain had lost his heart to a rustic beauty, though others thought it very unlikely that any mere country damsel could have made the slightest impression on a man so fashionable and accomplished as Captain Ardmore.

By degrees, then, as Captain Ardmore began to go again into company, these reports died away, and others took their place. It was now confidently asserted at a number of tea-tables that a match was pending between him and Miss Vane, only daughter of a rich merchant, and one of the acknowledged beauties of Montreal.

Miss Harriet Vane justly deserved her reputation of *a belle*, if not *the belle* of the capital. As far as *personal* beauty could

[179] An old term for muscles, especially if well developed.

[180] Montreal had been the capital of Canada between 1844 and 1849.

[181] Subaltern officers.

go, she certainly was a splendid woman. Tall, about five feet seven inches, and with a figure sufficiently inclining at one-and-twenty to *embonpoint*, to give promise of a portly woman at forty; her features were beautiful, without being monotonously regular; her nose was a decided aquiline, without being at all disproportionate; her eyes large, black, and lustrous, with eye-brows arched and distinctly defined, and long lashes; her brow fair and lofty, and shaded with luxuriant ebon-hued tresses; her complexion of that exquisite peachy tinge, so often seen in brunettes, in which there is no decided red, but a glow of health far removed from insipid pallor. The mouth was a remarkable and expressive feature; certainly beautifully shaped, though not so small as to be in strict proportion with the other features; and although the upper lip was short and finely chizelled, it too often displayed a scornful curl, which gave an ungentle and unfeminine look to the face.

Miss Vane, like many other young ladies in her sphere, turned all her matrimonial thoughts in the direction of the military; partly, because her taste led her to prefer handsome young officers, and because no other profession seemed to offer men of rank and wealth sufficient to be worthy of her hand. As a provincial belle, she well knew the power of her attractions on officers stationed in the colony, who, "*at home*," might even aspire to mate with the wealthy and titled daughters of the land. The hearts of young *militaires*, in spite of the prejudices of aristocratic education, and the reiterated advice of fond mammas, are not proof against the hospitable welcome of colonial society, and the bewitching influence of colonial beauty. Regiment succeeds regiment, and each laughs in turn at the matrimonial follies committed by its predecessors. Supercilious young ensigns and *blasé* captains and majors make valiant determinations only to amuse themselves at the expense of the colonists, and only to *flirt* with the colonial belles; but experience teaches them that the colonies are not quite so far behind the rest of the world as they had imagined, and the young ladies are so pretty, that after the usual quantity of balls and pic-nics, skating and sleighing parties, these stern resolves melt, and the departing regiment carries off its fair average of Benedicks.[182]

[182] A benedick is a newly married man, especially one who has long been a bachelor.

Nor would we infer from this any disparagement to the aforesaid quondam bachelors, on the score of infirmity of purpose; for good colonial society has no reason whatever to blush for itself, and contains as large a proportion of match-making mammas, who angle assiduously for rich sons-in-law, and marketable daughters, who dress and dance themselves into the affections of eligible men, as the highest "*ton*" of England.[183]

It was beautiful to see with what unanimity mother and daughter devoted themselves to acquire all the necessary information respecting the affairs of a new regiment. While Mrs. Vane inquired diligently into the private circumstances of all the officers, from the colonel downwards; and treasured up carefully in the chambers of her memory which were elder sons, with estates in prospect, Miss Vane was equally indefatigable in availing herself of all the license granted to a young lady of wealth and fashion, to walk, talk, flirt, dance, and ride on horseback, with a number of young officers, without injury to her reputation, and thus study the characters of her various admirers. Consequently, Miss Vane had been toasted at more than one mess-table as the boldest rider, the most indefatigable dancer, and, in short, the most beautiful, dashing, and fastest girl in Montreal. She had learnt to skate, and walk on snow-shoes, in addition to her other accomplishments; and compared herself to Die Vernon—with what truth we leave the reader to judge.[184]

Cornet Lord Royster was a complete contrast to Captain Ardmore, both in person and character. He possessed a short, squat, ungainly figure, with hair, eyebrows, and moustache of flaming red. As a child he had been spoiled and petted, allowed to learn just as little or just as much as he chose at school; had been expelled from college after one term; and the career of betting, horse-racing, gambling, and every species of dissipation, which he had run since, had amply sufficed to make him forget any learning which he might by chance have acquired. Reading was a penance he never inflicted on himself, unless, perhaps, a new novel, in compliance with the recommendation of some namby-pamby Miss, who secretly adored "his lordship." In spite of the openly immoral life he led, and the current reports respecting him (for he had no less than three illegitimate children by as many

[183] "Ton" was a term for fashionable society.

[184] Diana (Die) Vernon is a character in Walter Scott's 1818 novel *Rob Roy*.

poor girls whom he had seduced), he was an officer and a lord, and time-serving society could not stoop to censure faults which would have blasted the character of any civilian. Consequently, his escapades were passed over as incidental to "*blood*" and "*fashion*;" and mammas, who had marriageable daughters, quoted the old adage, that "reformed rakes make the best husbands," and thought that Lord Royster was certainly a "*little wild*," but that he would reform and settle down when he had a good wife.

It was a common occurrence for this noble young officer to leave the mess-table in a state of intoxication. He was to be seen frequently, with another congenial spirit, drinking in low taverns with red-shirted lumbermen, quarrelling and making up alternately with their companions. On the race-ground he would take the pipe out of the mouth of a black man, and smoke it; and when reproached by a brother officer for his ungentlemanly conduct, allege, that being in mufti,[185] he might do as he pleased. On one occasion, he was missing most unaccountably for a whole week; his turn of duty had come round, and surprise began to be converted into alarm. At length he was traced to a house of ill-fame, on the steps before the door of which his dog, a bull-terrier, was discovered sitting. On entering, Lord Royster was found drinking, without his coat, in the society of two women *en déshabillé*, and a bombardier;[186] embracing the latter most fraternally between the stanzas of a bacchanalian song.

My acquaintance with Captain Ardmore, made in the manner related, was destined to ripen into intimacy. The day after the adventure he called, and invited me to dine with him at the mess. We strolled together into the *Champ de Mars*,[187] to listen to the music of one of the regimental bands. Amongst other *belles*, Miss Vane was there, in a pony phaeton,[188] which she herself drove. Lord Royster had been talking to her, and sauntered away as we came up. She welcomed me with cordiality, and Captain Ardmore with more than cordiality. The manner of both appeared to me to confirm the report of their engagement.

[185] In civilian clothes (said about someone who usually wears a uniform).

[186] A noncommissioned artillery officer (below the rank of sergeant).

[187] Champ de Mars is a public park (and, in the past, also a parade ground) in Montreal.

[188] A small, open carriage, usually drawn by a single horse.

After some desultory conversation, Miss Vane said in a low voice, though perfectly audible, and with a significance plainly discernible,—

"Apropos, Captain Ardmore, of our narrow escape, I trust you took care to prevent any exaggerated or false reports from reaching the country."

In spite of Captain Ardmore's practised command of feature, I thought I could perceive a perceptible shadow pass over his face, as he replied calmly, "Why, pray?"

"Oh! are you not afraid that your rustic beauty, this fair Rosamond, who resides at Chambly, may have heard some alarming statement? But, of course, you will take care to anticipate all newspaper accounts."

Although Miss Vane spoke in a tone of badinage,[189] she scanned Captain Ardmore's features with a keen though covert glance, as she continued,—

"Oh, you men are sad creatures! But who would have believed that the gay and fashionable Captain Ardmore could have been interested for ever so short a period in a *rustic maiden*"—the latter words were pronounced in a tone of ill-concealed bitterness—"really, I long to see this paragon. Lord Royster says!"—

There was no mistaking the look of displeasure which now sat on Captain Ardmore's features.

"I am at a loss to understand you, Miss Vane. Pray, what has Lord Royster been saying?"

"Dear me!" exclaimed Miss Vane, bursting into a fit of laughter; "what a dangerous and excitable creature you are. Don't challenge poor Lord Royster, for he really said no more than what I knew already, that Captain Ardmore disregards us *belles* of the capital so far, as to prefer playing the gallant gay Lothario to rustic damsels in country quarters." Then, with female tact, changing the subject, she added, "How stupid that last piece was. I am so glad they have finished. Do, pray, Captain Ardmore, tell that dear delightful oddity, the German bandmaster, to play me my favourite from 'Norma;'[190] or rather let him come to me himself, he makes me laugh so with his mixture of German and English."

Accordingly, in obedience to a sign from Captain Ardmore, the bandmaster, Herr Schreitzner, a dapper little German,

[189] Playful banter.

[190] An opera (1831) by Vincenzo Bellini (1801-1835).

approached, bowing at every step, and lifting his hat repeatedly about two feet perpendicularly off his head, with a tremendous flourish.

"'Norma,' ya—as, Capitaine Ardmore. Ya—as, ya—as, Miss Fane, that should haff bin down in der programme. That giff me great pleasure to obey the commands of eine lady, who haff ein so goot taste in moosic. Ya—as, ein ver goot taste." And with another flourish of the hat, and repeated bows, Herr Schreitzner returned to his post; and soon after the sweet and plaintive melody was heard.

"Do not forget, Captain Ardmore," said Miss Vane, at the conclusion of the music; "and you, too, Mr.——," turning to me, "our little *reunion*, on Wednesday."

I had already received a card, and bowed my readiness to accept the invitation.

"Now, Harry, be quick," said Miss Vane, and the little boy-groom, who had till then stood at the horses' heads, jumped up into his place. "*Au revoir*, gentlemen;" and waving an adieu with her crimson-gloved hand, and touching her ponies lightly with the whip, Miss Vane drove off; the equipage and the fair charioteer 1858
both followed by the admiring looks of the bystanders.

As Captain Ardmore and myself passed through the barrack-square, we perceived a stranger, whose appearance bespoke him as belonging to that republic whose citizens are indiscriminately known to the British colonists as *Yankees*. Although there is no literal prohibition to the civilians, custom has made it the etiquette to confine the barrack-square exclusively to the military and their personal friends. Hence, I could not help being amazed on remarking this stray American, who with the utmost *naïveté*, and all the coolness and *insouciance* of his countrymen, was sauntering through the square, and admiring the *façade* of the barracks, evidently without the remotest suspicion that he could be trespassing, and quite as much at his ease as if he had been standing under the tree of American Independence on Boston Common.[191] Some of the junior officers, loitering about and waiting for the dinner-bugle to sound, had entered into conversation with the gentleman. Amongst these was Lord Royster, who very much to my surprise, though not at all to those who were better acquainted with his

[191] The Great Elm mentioned here, which used to stand in the centre of the Boston Common, was destroyed by a storm in 1876.

lordship, invited the former, though a perfect stranger, to dine at the mess; an invitation which was at once accepted.

Major Goliah Gallop (such was the portentous name of our American guest) was a type of a very large class of his countrymen, who always wear a full dress suit, whether because they think it the most fitting and agreeable travelling costume, or in order to be ready at any moment (as on the present occasion) to accept an unexpected invitation to dinner, or for some other reason or reasons which I will not undertake to determine. Major Gallop was a tall spare man, and might have been called handsome, but for the sallowness of his complexion, and the somewhat pointed character of his features. He had keen grey eyes, and wore a moustache and beard which completely covered his mouth and chin, and descended on his breast; his collars were turned down so as not to interfere with this volume of hair; a long and open black satin vest showed to great perfection his amble-plaited shirt-bosom, garnished with a heavy gold chain and studs; black trousers, made in the French fashion, and gathered in at the waist, and overlapping the boots of shining patent leather, the toes of which curled up an inch and a-half in front, as if emulating the extravagant fashion of the reign of Edward IV.;[192] a dress coat, with a very narrow collar, and a hat of the latest New York fashion, completed Major Gallop's *dress* or *travelling* costume, and marked him out to all British observers conspicuously as an American.

A significant look passed round the circle as this guest of Lord Royster was introduced, and took his seat at the mess-table; but as the dinner proceeded and the wine circulated, Major Gallop came out so very strong, told so many amusing anecdotes, and altogether appeared so very much at his ease, without any unbecoming familiarity, that looks of approbation began to sit on all faces, and even the seniors appeared to think that the stranger made up by his originality for any deficiency of polish. He was evidently one who had seen life in many phases, and could adapt himself with the utmost self-possession to any society into which chance might cast him. He called the officers by their respective titles of colonel, major, captain, *lef*tenant, &c., with the greatest gravity, and a *naïveté* which, coupled with his Yankee drawl, was inexpressibly comic; and when, after the cloth had been drawn and the decanters had made two or three rounds, Major Gallop

[192] King of England from 1461 to 1470.

was requested by Lord Royster to give a short sketch of his life and adventures, the proposal was so warmly seconded, that the American, after several preparatory "wells,"[193] and *guesses* and *calculations* "that it ain't much to tell," &c., did at last begin; and after being repeatedly interrupted by roars of laughter, occupied an hour at least in retailing the leading events of his life. To give it in his own words is impossible, and would moreover trespass too greatly on the reader's patience. I shall, therefore, insert here the following highly condensed

Summary of the Life and Adventures of Major Goliah Gallop, one of the most remarkable men in the United States.

Like a goodly number of Americans, Major Goliah Gallop has tried at everything, except, strictly speaking, the office of President. At nine years of age, he endeavoured to begin life on his own account by running away from home, and at twelve was kicked out by his father into the world to shift for himself. Being an American boy, this proved his first step to independence. He lost no time in associating himself in a commercial league with a peripatetic merchant, *vulgicé*,[194] a Yankee pedlar, who had realized a very good living by the sale of wooden hams, wooden nutmegs, and other pleasantly fictitious articles of commerce.[195]

1858

But as the deluded purchasers, on having consumed the veritable hams or nutmegs, and arriving at the deceptive articles, were naturally indignant, and cherished projects of revenge against those who had outwitted them, our adventurers never sold twice to the same customers, and were continually obliged to seek out new commercial paths in back settlements more and more remote; and, occasionally, to disarm suspicion, by adopting other

[193] Here, Allan inserted the following footnote: "A word which no English tongue could accent as he did."

[194] That is, "in common parlance" or "in vulgar terms."

[195] The term "Yankee peddler" was actually derogatory, referencing the perceived dishonesty of businessmen from the northern states. Unfounded stories of such peddlers selling unsuspicious customers wooden hams (painted pink) or, most famously, wooden nutmegs, abounded in the nineteenth century and were partly responsible for the apprehensiveness of others towards "Yankees," especially those from New England. To this day, Connecticut (whence the original wooden nutmeg peddlers were supposed to have come) is still sometimes called "The Nutmeg State." Haliburton uses the story about the wooden nutmegs in *The Clockmaker*.

professional avocations. So there is no great cause for wonder, if we find the junior partner opening a "whistling school," "on his own hook." This, though not exactly a successful speculation, was certainly not a failure, as far as Mr. Gallop was concerned. The scholars paid half the first quarter's salary in advance, and the teacher began his instruction by the command "begin to pucker," by which it is humbly suggested he meant "begin to form that muscular contraction of the lips indispensable to the act of whistling." This order was received with roars of laughter from the majority of the pupils.[196] In vain did some unsophisticated youth or maiden attempt to obey the injunction, "begin to pucker." It is a physical impossibility to whistle and laugh at once. Nothing disconcerted, Mr. Gallop dismissed his school for that evening, hoping that the *next time* they would be more docile. There was a gentle approach to a smile and a wink as he said this. On the following evening the pupils assembled, but no master appeared. Mr. Gallop had decamped with the profits to open school elsewhere.

He then *concluded* to teach singing and drawing, in which he persevered for some time, very much to his own satisfaction, but whether to the advantage of his pupils is uncertain. After he had given lessons in drawing for some time, he felt a desire to learn the rudiments of the art himself, as he wished to turn portrait-painter, observing, there was a considerable demand in "country parts" for being "drawed out," or "took," as the natives generally express the act of having a likeness painted. He accordingly came to "York," and took a few lessons in the art by hiring himself out as a decorator of omnibuses, or "*stages*," which in New York are perambulating picture galleries. On his return to the country, he was hailed as a genuine Apelles;[197] and by the commissions he received for portraits, joined to occasional sign-painting, and the profits of a small "*store*" for the sale of "*notions*," he managed to make a tolerable living.

Growing tired of *art* at length, he found his way to the South, and turned overseer on a plantation. After superintending the whipping and branding of a good many of his fellow-creatures, he all at once turned abolitionist; whether prompted by the stings of conscience, or his natural love of change, is unknown. Having

[196] In 19th-century slang, "pucker" meant "dishabille."

[197] Apelles was an ancient Greek painter of the 4th century BC.

eluded the vigilance of some anti-abolitionists, who were kindly taking measures to tar and feather him, he escaped to the North, carrying with him a negro, as a speculation, to move the sympathies of his hearers, in the capacity of an abolition lecturer. With his "*darkey*," as he emphatically styled him, Mr. Gallop made an "everlastin' sight" of dollars, by carrying him about to indignation meetings, where the florid eloquence of our philosopher, and the broken English of the escaped slave excited much sympathy.

The latter, however, beginning to think he might do better on his own account, decamped, having robbed the unsuspecting Gallop of all the ready money in his possession, and took a passage to England. When last heard of, he was electrifying a large audience at Exeter Hall[198] (and moving the female portion to tears), by a recited of his sufferings as a slave, and an exhibition of the scars of some wounds (accidentally received as a child), as the veritable tokens of his master's barbarous usage.

Mr. Goliah Gallop meanwhile joined a party of trappers and hunters, who were proceeding to the Far West; crossed the Rocky Mountains, and after enduring innumerable hardships, and many narrow escapes in skirmishes with Indians, reached the gold regions of California, where, after he had amassed a considerable quantity of the precious metal, he was robbed of everything, and left naked and nearly dead, with several stabs of a bowie-knife in different parts of his body, inflicted by a fellow-miner with whom he had quarrelled.

Disgusted with his ill luck and the country, as soon as his recovery permitted, he worked his passage before the mast in a vessel bound to Rio Janeiro, where[199] he landed just in the thick of the Mexican war.[200] As he was fond of fighting, and not particular on which side he enlisted, so long as he got pay and plunder, he joined the Mexican army, was taken prisoner by the Americans, volunteered into their ranks to avoid being shot for carrying arms against his countrymen, led a forlorn hope,[201] behaved with great gallantry, and returned home with the honourable rank of *major*.

[198] A large public meeting place in London (opened in 1831), in which many anti-slavery gatherings took place. It was demolished in 1907.

[199] Here, Allan may have meant to say "*but* he landed" instead of "where" (since Gallop landed in Mexico).

[200] The Mexican-American War (1846-1848).

[201] A "forlorn hope" is a military detachment that is ordered into very dangerous operations.

On the disbanding of the army engaged in the Mexican war, Major Gallop was by no means inclined to turn his sword into a ploughshare. He had found war a dollar-earning trade; he had got his hand in at fighting, and was disposed to do a little business on his own account rather than remain idle. Accordingly Major Gallop reaped fresh laurels as a Canadian sympathizer, and a Cuban invader,[202] besides numerous little filibustering expeditions and Indian massacres of too trifling a nature to be particularly noticed.

My limits only permit me to indicate the career of this enterprising and enlightened citizen. Suffice it to say, that after many vicissitudes of fortune, he is now at thirty-five an editor of a newspaper, a member of the state legislature, and has excellent prospects of being returned a member of Congress, and of course of eventually becoming President of the United States. In the course of his varied life, Major Goliah Gallop has sailed upon the waters of the Ottawa, the St. Lawrence, the Hudson, Mississippi, Missouri, the Amazon, the Ohio, and a number of lesser rivers, as well as on the great lakes and on the Atlantic and Pacific Oceans. He has fought a great many duels, three with revolvers, two with rifles, and one with bowie-knives. He has narrowly escaped being gouged and scalped more than once, has ridden for his life from a burning prairie, laid himself down in a stream to avoid destruction from fire in the woods, precipitated himself from the second-floor window of a house in flames, been in several railway collisions, once blown up in a steam-boat, lived six months alone in the primeval forest, visited the interior of a mine, been up in a balloon, and down in a diving-bell.

In spite of his active life, Major Goliah Gallop has not slighted the tender affection and the personal relations. He has married twice, been jilted five times, and has jilted himself, and made love to an indefinite number of the fair sex, besides having had three wives at once, when living after the patriarchal manner among the Mormons. In his literary capacity as editor of a paper, he has been led imperceptibly into other branches of the *belles lettres*, and has written a tragedy, a novel, and a book of sermons, besides innumerable political tracts.

Major Goliah Gallop is most desirous of visiting Europe; having, as he says, seen all on this side of the Atlantic, he wants

[202] Allusion to the filibustering Lopez Expedition (August 1851).

to see the *'tarnal* wonders of the old world that they brag so much of, such as Rome, Mount Vesuvius, and the Tower of London. He *reckons* he'll see nothing to "whip" the Falls. He has sketched out for himself a programme of his visit to the Old World, by which he calculates to leave New York, arrive in Liverpool, see London, England, and Europe generally, and "*do*" the sights of Asia and Africa, peep at the Pyramids, have a look for the source of the Nile, enter a harem and a mosque,[203] squint at the Chinese wall, and, to save the trouble of retracing his steps, *guesses* "it'll be about the quickest way to jump clean over Behring's Straits," and so return to New York within a couple of years, having made the tour of the globe.

I had not been long at Mrs. Vane's before Captain Ardmore was announced. A buzz ran round the room as he entered. He was dressed in plain clothes, in an elegant evening costume, and looked the *beau idéal* of a gentleman, certainly the handsomest and most *distingué* man in the room.

Miss Vane was talking, flirting I was almost going to say, with a Mr. Potter, a confidential clerk in her father's employ. Report said that this young man was most desperately enamoured of Miss Vane, and that he had even received her father's sanction to pay his addresses to her, but the daughter kept him off and on like a plaything, to gratify her own caprice. When she happened to be without her military admirers, poor Potter was taken into favour, but discarded without the slightest ceremony when brighter stars (*i.e.*, more eligible men) appeared in the horizon. Mr. Potter occupied near Miss Vane the convenient position of "*shoeing horn*" as it is defined in the "Spectator,"[204]—never intended to be accepted himself, but merely to urge tardy admirers forward. Such, however, was the infatuation of the unsophisticated young man, that he fluttered round the dangerous blaze, ever ready at the call of the perfidious beauty.

The instant Captain Ardmore was announced, Miss Vane, who had been delighting poor Mr. Potter with a show of graciousness, left him without ceremony. "Adieu, you bewitching creature!" she said to the latter, with an irony perceptible to all but her victim, too straightforward himself to suspect her of playing with his feelings.

[203] Both were famously inaccessible to infidels.

[204] By Joseph Addison, in the *Spectator* 536.

"How could you come so late?" she said, as she gave her hand to Captain Ardmore; "I have sulked the whole evening."

"Then you have not been singing?" replied the captain; "I have lost none of my favourites."

"How can you ask?" said she, with a look of sweet reproach; "you know I cannot sing without some strong inducement; without a listener who really cares to hear me, and who can appreciate music. Who was there to sing for till you came?"

Who could be indifferent to such flattering words spoken with an air of sincerity by so beautiful a woman? I saw that Captain Ardmore was not insensible to the compliment.

He led her to the piano. I expected, of course, that so fashionable a young lady would not condescend to sing any but a foreign language. I was then surprised and delighted when, in a full rich voice and with great feeling, Miss Vane sang a song which partook of the nature of a sacred harmony, "He doeth all things well."[205] I heard it for the first time, and it impressed me deeply. I watched Captain Ardmore's lip quiver and eye glisten as the melody proceeded:—

"My cup of happiness was full,
    My joy could none dispel;
And I blessed the glorious Giver,
    Who doeth all things well."

But the little child which made this hope and joy is taken away, and after a bitter wrestling with despair, her faith triumphs even in that hour of bereavement,—

"God gave; He took; He will restore:
He doeth all things well."

No fault could have been found with Miss Vane while singing. It would have been difficult to believe as she poured out the melody (giving to every note force and feeling) that she did not participate in the emotions which she evoked. But when she had finished, she looked up at Captain Ardmore, and the glance appeared to me to denote a desire rather to read the impression which she had made on him, than an appreciation of the pure and holy sentiments to

[205] A ballad by Edward M. Field, "He Doeth All Things Well: or My Sister," put to music and sometimes used as a hymn.

which she had just given utterance. His heart was evidently too full to permit him to pour out the idle words of compliment. As for Mr. Potter, he sate looking at Miss Vane as if she had been a superior being, while that young lady, as if anxious to dispel any melancholy which her song may have conjured up, dashed into a lively air with variations from "Il Barbiere di Seviglia."[206]

When she had finished she turned to Captain Ardmore, and requested him to sing. He assented at once, without any affectation of making excuses to enhance the value of his performance, and taking up a guitar, accompanied himself while he sung, in a rich and manly voice, that exquisitely beautiful song beginning—

> "Rome, Rome, thou art no more
> As thou hast been."[207]

I can recall him vividly in fancy as he stood on that evening, charming all with the grace of his person, and the skill with which he sung. Miss Vane was not the only young lady present whose admiration could be read very plainly in her looks.

In the course of the evening, Lord Royster was announced. 1858
To-night, then, it appeared music had more charms for him than the bottle, not that he appeared to have abandoned *it* too hastily either. As he advanced to pay his respects to the lady of the house, his heightened colour and a certain swagger in his gait showed that though perfectly competent to behave himself, he was certainly in the first stage of that mysterious condition which in the aristocracy is expressed by "*elevated!*" in the middling or respectable classes, "*intoxicated!!*" and in the mobocracy by the stern uncompromising word "*drunk!!!*" He had evidently imbibed enough to be mischievous, or inclined for a lark, certainly to remove all symptoms of the bashfulness which generally oppressed him in his perfectly sober moments in respectable female society.

As he found himself standing near me, he addressed me without any introduction, probably on the strength of having seen me at the mess-table, and his conversation, if not edifying, was certainly amusing. He spoke with a drawl, and in that peculiar slang which is characteristic of a large portion of the fashionable

[206] *The Barber of Seville* (1816), an opera buffa by Gioachino Rossini (1792-1868).

[207] A ballad based on the 1826 poem "Roman Girl's Song" by Felicia Hemans (1793-1835).

English (as much as *exasperating* their h's, confounding v's and w's is of the lower orders); for it is quite a mistake to fancy that incorrect speaking is confined to any one grade. This method of speaking consists in dwelling in an absurd manner on the last syllables of words, in cancelling the letter *r* altogether, or as far as possible, in dropping the final *g*, as in singin', bringin', and many other little peculiarities respecting which the sagacious reader will, doubtless, be independent of my information.

"Aw. So you ah hand and glo-ove with Awdmoah—aw—saved him from takin' a flyin' leap ova' the bwidge—a dooced[208] dangewous place—aw—and a deyv'lish bold thing of you to do. I knew a chap once who tried the very same thing—aw—and got an awm and leg bwoke for his pains. Well—now—aw—aw—what do you think of Awdmoah?"

"My acquaintance with Captain Ardmore has not been very long. From what I have seen and heard of him already, I think every one must like him."

"Aw—inde-e-d. Well now—do you know—I think Awdmoah a *doocëd* queeah fellah."

"How so, pray?"

"Aw—aw—because he's so different from other fellahs. He's always pokin' about doin' somethin' or otha'—he is, upon my honah—never idle, you know—that sort of fellah—eccentric—aw—got his rooms chawk full of books and paintin', and papahs—I mean MSS., and otha' wubbish of that sort—it's a fa-a-ct, I assuah you, he neva' has a moment to spaah—always on some crochet or otha'. Why—aw—aw—do you know what Awdmoah wawks at when he's not paintin', or readin', or writin', and when the weatha's not fine enough to go out? Haw! haw! you'll neva' guess—a turning la-athe. Haw! haw! fa-act, upon my honah."

Lord Royster's description of "*a queeah fellah*" amused me.

"By all accounts then, Captain Ardmore's time never hangs heavy on his hands?"

"Aw—cu-urse it, no—that's what I wonda' at. I say to him sometimes, Awdmoah, how the dooce can you who have aw—aw—seen life in England and on the Continent, manage to exist in this dismal hole of a provincial town? Aw—I think the colonies only fit to weah out old clothes in myself. There's only one thing in their favah that I know—aw—the brandy's so dooced good and

[208] Deuced, i.e., damned, confounded, devilish.

cheap. Haw! haw! But, dash me if I know how to kill time of an evenin'. There's nothin' goin' on,—no theatah—no opewa."

"Are there not plenty of private parties?"

"Aw—aw—I'm boahed (bored) to death with private pa-aties for aw—aw—tho' the ga'als are pwetty they haven't "*tin*"[209] enough to make it wawth a fellah's while to—aw—pay attention to them seriously—aw—aw—wa-all—I suppose it's no use frettin'. Montreal's a dooced deal betta' than that howid Chambly—aw—I'd have cut my throat if I'd stayed there a week longa'."

"Ah, what a loss to the world, my lord," said a waggish brother-officer who had overheard the last remark. "They would have mourned for you at Tattersall's,[210] and in the synagogues."

"Aw, Erskine," said his lordship, taking the new speaker by the arm, "I want to speak to you. This is deyv'lish slow, ain't it? Can't we contrive to—" Here Lord Royster's voice dropped into a confidential whisper so as to be inaudible.

That he was hatching some mischief I felt certain, and my anticipations were not disappointed, as the following events showed. In consequence of Lord Royster having expressed his conviction that "*the thing*" was slow, and his wish to enliven it a bit, the result of their consultation was that the officer in question took the earliest opportunity of informing Mrs. Vane that his lordship sung a very good song. The hostess, who was in a state of the highest delight at the opportunity of entertaining such fashionable company, and was only too desirous showing every attention to her titled guest, lost no time in requesting Lord Royster to sing.

Lord Royster declined, but so feebly, that the lady returned again and again to the task of persuasion, and at intervals throughout the evening might be heard entreating,—

"Oh do, pray, now, Lord Royster—if your lordship would only try—I'm sure your lordship isn't hoarse!" and—"*da capo.*"

Lord Royster, however, was deaf to the voice of the charmer, and persisted in declining until supper-time drew near. He then watched his opportunity, and hit it so cleverly, that he volunteered a song at the very moment that supper was on the point of being announced, when a servant had thrown the folding-doors wide open, and Mrs. Vane was on the point of marshalling the guests to the banquet. Common politeness required the lady of the house

[209] Slang for "money."

[210] The main auctioneer of racehorses in the United Kingdom.

to bow and smile, and express herself highly delighted. The guests also grinned as best they could, and resigned themselves to the infliction, murmuring "that they would be so happy to," &c., while, as the hot supper sent up its savoury steams from the adjoining room, there can be no doubt that one devout wish animated every bosom—that Lord Royster had been conveyed by some mysterious magic agency to Hong Kong, before he had chosen that critical moment for favouring the company. Nevertheless Mrs. Vane, and doubtless many others, consoled themselves with the idea that it would soon be over, and that the delay could not be of material consequence. Consequently, while a few resumed their seats, the majority of the company remained standing, the ladies hanging on the arms of their respective gentlemen, just as they had been when on the point of entering the supper-room; and this was the state of affairs when Lord Royster, leaning with *nonchalance* against the door-way of the forbidden apartment, began his song.

One, two, three, four, five, up to *ten verses!* and every listener decided that *this* would surely be the last; but no. Imagine the horror and consternation, the covert fury of the hostess and her guests, when ten, twenty, thirty verses were poured forth, and still no sign of termination. Just as the hope arose in the mind of some hungry individual, "*this verse must be the last*," Lord Royster, having inflated his lungs with air, would rush again into the burthen of his melody, *con strepitu, con amore*,[211] and with the most provoking gravity, as if he had not the slightest suspicion of the precious practical joke he was playing.

What the song was about, no one knew, no one cared. The most grateful odours found their way from the supper-tables, titillating the olfactories and whetting the appetites of the expectant guests, who were as completely paralyzed by the rules of etiquette as if some ancient mariner had seized each individually, and "held him with his glittering eye."[212] The supper was getting cold, and still the interminable song went on. At length, when fifty verses had been achieved, either because his lungs or his memory were tired, or that he was getting hungry himself, or that he thought he had carried the joke far enough, and that the growing symptoms of impatience warned him that his audience might summarily break the charm exerted by his impudence over their good breeding,

[211] As a musical direction, "con strepito" means "impetuously."

[212] "He holds him with his glittering eye" is a line from Coleridge's "The Rime of the Ancient Mariner."

or because the song was really at an end, Lord Royster took pity upon the famishing guests, and permitted them finally to enter the supper-room.

Here the master of the house was pointed out to me—*host*, I cannot call him. He was one of those meagre, insignificant, hen-pecked looking men, who, however, full of energy in business, leave their souls behind them in the counting-house, bank, or wherever may be the scene of their labours, and become in their own homes perfect nonentities. I should have fancied that his wife never regarded him with more contempt than at the present moment; for, at a time when most men become of some consequence in their own houses, Mr. Vane did nothing—*absolutely nothing*. He neither took the head nor the foot of the table, and you felt tempted to patronise him, and endeavour to make the poor man feel more at home. Lord Royster, who was now in his element, did so, and asked the *host* to take wine with him, an act of attention for which Mr. Vane seemed very grateful.

During the course of supper some alarm was created by one of the tables slightly giving way; happily, it was secured before any damage could be done. Those in the immediate neighbourhood
assisted; every one appeared more or less interested in the occurrence, 1858
with one exception—the master of the house. *He* merely looked on, without making the slightest effort to be useful, or seeming to think he had any concern in the matter. He only meekly murmured as he caught his wife's eye, "Mrs. Vane, my dear, the table seems to be coming down." Mrs. Vane replied with a *look* which seemed to say: "Only wait till the company have gone, that's all."

Under the influence of the punch Lord Royster grew exceedingly merry, and began talking quite confidentially to every one in his immediate neighbourhood. He proposed to me, on the breaking up of the party, to accompany him on a lark or spree; or, as he termed it, "to see what's up." I did not, however, accept his invitation to make a night of it, but preferred walking home with Captain Ardmore. It was a glorious winter evening, freezing hard, and the cold moon shone with a brightness never seen in England, lighting up the *façade* of the great French cathedral of Notre Dame, whose two gigantic towers loomed above us as we passed through the *Place d'armes*.[213]

[213] Place d'Armes is a square in Old Montreal. The Notre-Dame Basilica stands on of its sides. Its building began in 1824 and the two towers were finished in 1843. However, it has never been a cathedral.

Suddenly we heard a yelling and shrieking behind us,—sounds which we soon found proceeded from Lord Royster, and a parcel of kindred spirits, who were piled indiscriminately on a *cariole* (a kind of low sleigh which does duty for a public cab), and passed us at full speed, lashing the poor horse unmercifully, and wakening the echoes of the solemn cathedral with their shouts and senseless laughter.

Two days afterwards I read the following announcement in a Montreal paper:—"We draw attention to the reward of £50 offered for the detection of certain malicious and evil-disposed persons, who, on the night of the 20th December, removed all the fir-trees which marked out the road across the St. Lawrence to Longæul,[214] thereby endangering the lives of her Majesty's liege subjects, by rendering them liable to mistake the beaten track and wander into air-holes.[215] We can only say, if there be any truth in the rumour which has reached us that a certain lordling, holding a commission in the army, and remarkable for sundry escapades and breaches of the public peace, has had a finger in this disgraceful piece of rascality; and if it be owing to this that Cornet Lord R—st—r, of the —— regiment of dragoons has (as we have heard) decamped across the lines,[216] *his lordship* need not be in any hurry to return, as he will find that, if convicted of this grave offence, neither his commission nor his rank will screen him from the punishment he merits."

Nevertheless, in spite of this warning, Cornet Lord Royster did return after some time, and the matter blew over; either because it was hushed up through his influence, or that there was no evidence to prove him guilty.

My intimacy with Captain Ardmore ripened almost daily. The more I saw of him the more I liked him, and the more reason I found to admire him for his union of the most refined accomplishments and intellectual pursuits with the graceful ease and fashionable manners of a man of the world. A clue to his character was afforded on first entering his apartments. Instead of the meerschaums,[217] whips, portraits of ballet-dancers, and

[214] Actually Longueuil, which is on the south shore of the Saint Lawrence, opposite Montreal.

[215] A section of open water in a frozen surface.

[216] Across the border (with the US). See also note 6.

[217] Pipes (elaborately carved) made of a soft clay mineral called sepiolite, but better known at the time by their German name (meaning "sea foam").

race-horses, and the almost effeminate furniture of the toilette, which profusely decorated Lord Royster's rooms, the walls were covered with beautiful studies of English and American scenery, and drawings of heads and animals executed by himself; a large book-case displayed the best English and French authors, while his dressing-room contained all that was necessary, without any of the knick-knackeries or gim-cracks of a *petit-maître*.[218]

One evening, by the invitation of my friend (for by this name I was now entitled to call Captain Ardmore), I found myself at a large ball given by the officers of his regiment. Amongst the guests I noticed one couple who seemed quite out of their element, viz., a dapper little cockney shop or *store*-keeper, named Perkins, whom I knew very well by sight; and his wife, a portly, vulgar woman, with an extremely red face. I saw them enter, and no attempt was made to introduce them to Mrs. Floyd, the colonel's lady, but both were allowed to sit down near the door, blushing and looking extremely sheepish. As I suspected at the time, and afterwards learnt, Lord Royster had a hand in this also. He owed a large bill to Mr. Perkins, and was not proof against the request made by the husband at his wife's instigation, to invite them to the officers' ball. 1858

I do not know whether Mrs. Floyd saw them arrive, but I perceived that during the evening she became cognisant of their presence, as I saw her staring with artless and undisguised wonder at Mrs. Perkins's style of dancing. The latter lady did not walk through quadrilles.[219] Had she done so, she might not have attracted the notice of the colonel's lady, even though dancing in the next quadrille; but, alas! Mrs. Perkins's style of dancing was fearfully demonstrative. She bounced hither and thither, and hopped up and down, like a ship in distress. The expression on Mrs. Floyd's face said most plainly: "How did this woman gain admittance here?"

Whether from a wish to allay the feelings of awkwardness she had experienced in the early part of the evening, or because she was addicted to the use of stimulants, Mrs. Perkins had acquired a very evident supply of what is termed "Dutch courage;" and now, instead of shunning notice, she seemed to court it, and made

[218] A ladies' man, a fop. A "gimcrack" (as it is usually spelled) is a gaudy object of little use.

[219] A dance (a form of cotilion) performed by four couples in a rectangular formation.

several attempts to attract Mrs. Floyd's attention, by bowing and speaking to her, all which overtures the Colonel's lady *would not see.*

Dreading some *contretemps*, the ever-considerate Captain Ardmore took the opportunity of expostulating with Lord Royster, and urging upon him the propriety of using his influence with Mr. Perkins to remove his wife before she had committed herself further; to which Lord Royster made no other reply than—"Aw—cu-urse it, let her disgrace herself; she would come—aw—besides, if I were to insult Perkins by hintin' that his wife was drunk, I'd have him dunnin' me for money to-morrow—aw!"

Captain Ardmore appeared in excellent spirits this evening. He danced almost continually with Miss Vane. I had never seen a finer-looking couple than they appeared in the polka, which they performed to perfection. I had just concluded a quadrille with a young lady from the country, who had been boring me to death by her attempts to give our conversation a literary turn, and by the unmeaning platitudes which she uttered on Byron, Scott, and Longfellow;[220] I was very glad, therefore, when I felt myself at liberty to wander away into a dimly-lighted ante-room. I was listlessly stooping down to examine a screen covered over with engravings, and was completely hidden from view, when two people entered the room, whom I knew instantly from their voices to be Captain Ardmore and Miss Vane. They were speaking confidentially and in low tones, but every word was distinctly audible; and I heard enough to inform me that Captain Ardmore was the accepted lover of Miss Vane. I was relieved from my awkward and unintentional *rôle* of eavesdropper, by Miss Vane remarking as the music struck up, that she would not lose the next dance for the world; and the lovers hurried to the ball-room, where I in a short time followed.

It appeared as if Captain Ardmore would willingly have engrossed Miss Vane the whole evening. A polka had come to an end, and he was soliciting her hand for the ensuing dance; but she seemed to expostulate with him on the impropriety of paying her such marked attention. It was probably owing to this that Captain Ardmore danced the next quadrille with another lady, while Miss

[220] While Byron (1788-1824) and Walter Scott (1771-1832) were no longer alive, the American poet Henry Wadsworth Longfellow (1807-1882) was at the height of his popularity after publishing *Evangeline* in 1847 (Allan's sojourn in Montreal was in 1846-1848).

Vane accepted as a partner, Mr. Potter, already introduced to the reader as being an humble admirer of the haughty beauty.

Mr. Potter was certainly not calculated to make much impression on a young lady surrounded by regimental *beaux*. Though a capital accountant, he was totally devoid of those superficial graces, and that flow of small talk which young ladies love; and with every wish to make himself agreeable to Miss Vane, he either bored her to death, or served her when in a quizzing humour as a butt for her ridicule. I thought that under the present circumstances, when she had just plighted her troth to another man, Miss Vane might have had some compassion on the hopeless case of her admirer, and might have spared him. I was, however, mistaken.

During the quadrille, Mr. Potter hummed and hawed, and fumbled with his gloves, while Miss Vane appeared to be secretly enjoying his confusion.

"Did you speak, Mr. Potter?" said the young lady at length.

"I—I—no—that is—yes—I mean—not exactly," stammered Potter, growing very red in the face."

"The rooms are hot," continued Miss Vane, determined to 1858
draw him out.

"Well, yes—though—I must say—it didn't—though, of course, if you think so—yes, certainly."

"Have you no news for me of any kind, Mr. Potter?"

"Me, Miss; none, Miss—that is, I've not heard anything likely—to interest a young lady—of—of—I mean—a young lady of fashion like Miss Vane."

"You are complimentary, Mr. Potter," and Miss Vane deliberately made a low bow to her partner which considerably increased his confusion.

"No—really—Miss Vane—I didn't mean—" Mr. Potter hesitated and stammered.

"What, no news of any kind—nothing connected with trade?"

"Nothing really," began Mr. Potter, and then he stopped abruptly, and a ray of something like hope illumined the vacant waste of his countenance. "By the last accounts, flour is firm, cotton has declined, and sugar is up again."

Miss Vane burst into an unrestrained peal of laughter, without the slightest remorse or pity for her victim. When she had somewhat recovered from her paroxysm of mirth, she said,

"What gratifying intelligence you mercantile men have to bestow; so sugar is really *up*. How long would it have been before Lord Royster could have told me that?" and she began laughing again.

Poor Mr. Potter was dreadfully abashed. He did not utter another word while the quadrille lasted; but at its termination, after he had led the young lady to a seat, he did muster up courage to ask when he might have the honour and happiness of waiting upon her at her own residence. Miss Vane turned upon him her eyes flashing with mischievous mirth, and repeated his question slowly so as to raise some hopes in the mind of the unfortunate Potter that she was about to return a satisfactory answer to his request.

"When may you have the honour and happiness of waiting upon me. Why—really, Mr. Potter—I think—all things considered—you may call—*when sugar's down*."

Mr. Potter retreated in speechless confusion.

Just at this moment the attention of the company was drawn to an explosion which had been for some time pending. From the glimpses I had occasionally caught of Lord Royster, he seemed to me to be hatching some mischief or other. I had seen him standing apparently engaged in conversation with the fat quartermaster, who was describing, with a great deal of pardonable egotism, the chalking of the floor of the ball-room, in which he had been chiefly instrumental. But Lord Royster was evidently pre-occupied with his own thoughts, and quite inattentive to the quartermaster; his eyes roved about the room, seeking, as it soon appeared, for some fit object on whom to play a practical joke.

At a late hour in the evening he went up to Mrs. Perkins and asked her to waltz. Mrs. Perkins, who had been anticipating this honour, would certainly have preferred a quadrille; but rather than not dance at all with a lord, she gave her consent. Lord Royster had then retired, and returned abruptly to claim her hand just as the waltz was commencing. They began, but had hardly taken a few turns before Mrs. Perkins was obliged to stop quite out of breath. She persevered, however, until most of the waltzers had stopped to rest, and she and Lord Royster found themselves almost alone on the floor. During another pause, Mrs. Perkins was too busy panting and gasping, and trying to inflate her exhausted lungs, to be very well conscious of what was going on around her.

Gradually, however, in spite of her flustered condition, it dawned upon her, that she and her partner were attracting an unusual share of observation.

People had stopped dancing, and were gazing most decidedly and uncompromisingly upon Lord Royster and Mrs. Perkins; some were smiling, and stifled laughs began to be heard. All this seemed very unaccountable to the good lady. She scanned her own dress—nothing was out of order. At last her eye fell upon her partner with more detailed observation than she previously had time to bestow, and then the mystery was explained. During his absence, Lord Royster had changed his dress, and made a complete "*guy*" of himself.[221] The back of his dress-coat had a large patch in it, he wore a vest made of a piece of old stair-carpet, and an immense hollyhock,[222] by way of *bouquet*, was fastened in his button-hole. All this Mrs. Perkins noted in a moment. She had been made the victim of a practical joke. She overwhelmed Lord Royster with a torrent of reproaches. But this was by no means a sufficient vent for her rage. She looked round the whole circle of the company (most of whom found it impossible any longer to conceal their merriment), as if seeking for some one individual on whom to pour out her fury. Her eye lighted upon the colonel's lady, against whom her feelings of bitterness had received the climax, upon the latter declining to touch her hand in the last quadrille.

"Ho, indeed, mum; and so we're too proud to touch the 'ands of our fellow-creatures, and yet you call yourself a Christian, I supposes. I wonders where you expects to go to, mum. A colonel's lady—really, I thought you wos a duchess at the very least! I've been a-watching you with your stuck-up airs the w'ole h'evening; and it seems I'm not good enough to be introduced to you, nor to touch the tip of your little finger. And so I've been asked here to be insulted and made game of—eh? but—don't think I want to int*e*rude myself on your acquaintance, mum, not I, indeed; though I 'ad once the 'onour of bein' at a ball, at the Mansion 'Ouse, in London.[223] I know I ain't fit company for a *colonel's lady*. Oh, no! indeed. I shan't defile the h'air longer with my presence. Perkins" (in a very shrill voice), "do you call yourself a man, and are you agoin' to stand there and let me be h'insulted any longer." Here,

[221] "Guy" still meant an ill-dressed person, a fright, a figure of fun.

[222] The North American hollyhock (*Iliamna rivularis*) is a perennial plant that can reach six feet in height.

[223] The official residence of the Lord Mayor of London.

Mrs. Perkins threw herself on her husband, with tears of rage, and tore the poor man's hair, and buffeted him about the face, perhaps unconsciously, in her paroxysm, and from the force of habit.

Mrs. Floyd, who was a tall, handsome, and highly-bred woman, presented a very striking contrast to Mrs. Perkins while the latter uttered this tirade. Her cheek had flushed as she listened to such unusual language, but her features never relaxed from their calm and haughty look, as if she felt how utterly beneath her dignity it would be to permit Mrs. Perkins to ruffle her temper. She only said, in a tone of bitter irony,

"Lord Royster, had you not better look after *your friend*, she seems discomposed."

But the old Colonel, who, however good-natured, was somewhat hasty, waxed indignant at this escapade of Lord Royster, which had resulted in a personal insult to his wife.

"Lord Royster," he said, "what is the meaning of this disgraceful masquerade? Your conduct is unbecoming an officer and a gentleman. Consider yourself under an arrest."

Montreal, 1851

CONCLUSION OF CAPTAIN ARDMORE; OR, THE ROSE OF CHAMBLY.

> "Love is not love,
> Which alters when it alteration finds,
> Or bends with the remover to remove."
> SHAKSPERE

> "The bayonets earthward are turning,
> And the drum's muffled breath rolls around,
> But he hears not the voice of their mourning,
> Nor awakes to the bugle's sound."
> THE OFFICER'S FUNERAL.[224]

Two years had elapsed since I first made Captain Ardmore's acquaintance. It was summer, and his marriage with Miss Vane was appointed to take place in two weeks. But in that short period much may happen. In the interval Captain Ardmore was stricken down by fever, which proved to be typhus. I hardly ever left his bed-side. Often and often he wandered in his mind, and at such times he called on a female name which was not that of Miss Vane. This name so often on his lips was *Patience Gray*. With it was joined the word Chambly; and in his delirium he confounded Harriet Vane and Patience Gray together, and spoke of his approaching marriage sometimes with one, sometimes with the other. I never should have sought to discover the secret partially revealed by these disconnected words, had he not, of his own accord, made me his confidant.

One morning, when his consciousness had quite returned, he directed me to a secret drawer, and requested me to give him a small locket which it contained. It enclosed the miniature likeness of a beautiful young woman. He wept over it and kissed it with emotion, and then asked me frankly if I had not gathered enough from the words let fall in his delirium to guess the name of the original, and obtain some idea of the real state of affairs. I

[224] Lyrics of a song written by Caroline Norton (1808-1877).

confessed that I had. "Then," said he, pressing my hand feebly, "I will tell you all, that when I am gone you may tell *her* I made her the poor amends of dying repentant." I did not believe my friend was dying, and I told him so, but he persisted in thinking otherwise. Having once begun to unburthen his heart of the secret, he seemed to find a relief in returning often and often to the subject. His confession was in substance as follows:—

I have already told the reader that Captain Ardmore had been stationed in command of a troop at Chambly, a pretty village on the river Richelieu, about fifteen miles from Montreal. Patience Gray, though only a farmer's daughter, was beautiful and intelligent, and by no means uneducated. Her father was one of those steady persevering emigrants who form the strength and promise of a new country. He had quitted Scotland poor and friendless, and through his own efforts, had become an independent thriving land-owner.

Patience was the favourite of her father, and of the whole village as well, for her meek and gentle nature did not rouse the feelings of envy so common among rustic beauties. She was
1858 called, *par excellence*, "the Rose of Chambly." Her father had given her the best education his means and situation afforded, and the cheapness of American literature had enabled him to amass a tolerable library, which proved to Patience an endless source of profit and amusement. The leisure granted by the seclusion of her village life, and the absence of those petty trivial gaieties, which occupy so much of the time of young ladies in cities, gave her ample opportunities for reading, as well as other rational and refined pursuits.

Patience was an enthusiastic lover of nature, as most well brought-up young people are, and the efforts she made to pourtray her emotions and impressions, either with the pencil or the pen, were in obedience to the impulses of the strong youthful soul in the absence of sympathy, striving to record its feelings of happiness, and conceptions of beauty. She was too true and natural a being to be otherwise than lovely. Her beauty was of that earnest contemplative expressive kind, which neither dazzles nor astonishes, but wins imperceptibly and surely. Not that Patience was deficient in those personal charms which influence so mysteriously the most philosophic of men. No one could have passed over lightly her fair golden hair, her large, clear, blue, almond-shaped eyes, her figure medium-shaped, so lithe and graceful, the springy elastic step of health and youth, not to be acquired from the most fashionable teachers of *deportment*; yet Patience was one of those women of whom it might be truly said—

> "I must have love thee,
> Hadst thou not been fair."[225]

Fate, destiny, or what you will, had determined that Captain Ardmore and Patience Gray, two beings, so distant in rank and station, so congenial in tastes, sympathies, and sentiments, should become acquainted. Captain Ardmore was returning one day from the fort from an angling excursion; he had just arrived at a rude bridge, formed by a huge pine, which had fallen across a singularly wild and picturesque stream. The dense covert of alder bushes prevented him from seeing the spot where he intended to cross until he came suddenly and unexpectedly upon it. He had barely time to note that his abrupt appearance had startled a female figure midway on the precarious bridge, ere a faint scream and a splash told that the person had lost her balance and fallen into the water, in this place dammed up into a broad and deep pool. In an instant the young officer had plunged in, and two or three vigorous strokes enabled him to reach Patience Gray as soon as she rose to the surface. In less time than I have taken to recount it, she was borne safe to land, having sustained no greater injury from her immersion than the fright.

Mr. Gray thanked the rescuer of his child, as man should do his fellow-man, and as the officer viewed the meeting between father and daughter, a tear of sympathy moistened his eyes. Never had he felt more keenly the applause of conscience, that true reward of every noble action; and when he came to grow more acquainted with Patience, and found in her no mere common-place country-girl, his visits to the cottage began to be more frequent and more prolonged.

His long absences were remarked and commented upon at the mess-table, and his brother-officers grew merry over Ardmore's good fortune in becoming acquainted with the belle of Chambly.

[225] From "Deck Not with Gems," a poem (and song) by Thomas Haynes Bayly (1797-1839).

Some gave him credit for an honourable attachment, and wondered not a little at what they considered his infatuation (for spectators can be very stoical on the love affairs of their neighbours); but Lord Royster, whose gross nature led him to scoff at the idea of generous disinterested love uniting two people of different grades in society, vowed that "*Awdmoah*" should not have it all his own way with the prettiest girl in Chambly, and offered to lay a bet that he would cut him out.

"No time like the present," said an officer. "If I'm not mistaken, *les voilà*, Miss Gray and another girl listening to the *tattoo*. I'll bet a dozen of champagne you don't go up and introduce yourself at once." The windows of the mess-room looked out on the parade ground, and Patience and a young female companion happened this evening to be among the few who usually assembled to listen to the music of the fife and drum. In spite of his impudence, Lord Royster in his perfectly sober moments would have thought twice before he undertook this adventure, involving as it did the chance of a quarrel with Captain Ardmore, whose *penchant* for the rustic beauty was so well known. Now, however, heated and flustered with wine, the challenge implying a covert insinuation of timidity was an inducement more than sufficient, and with a heavy oath he accepted the wager, and sallied forth more than half intoxicated from the mess-room. He crossed the parade-ground, and never doubting that his attentions could be ill received by two country-girls, he accosted them in the most familiar manner. The girls, alarmed at his swaggering gait and thickness of speech, endeavoured to elude him, upon which Lord Royster thought proper to resort to a little gentle violence to vanquish what he considered their affectation of shyness.

"Good gwacious, my pwetty deah," he said, as he threw his arm round the waist of Patience Gray, "what's the use of bein' so disagweeable; I won't eat you; just one kiss and I'll let you go; now why will you struggle so?"

At this instant Lord Royster's wrist was seized from behind with a vice-like grasp, which forced from him an exclamation of pain, and turning he beheld Captain Ardmore, his features working with the powerful efforts he made to restrain his passion.

"Come, come, Ardmore," cried Lord Royster, attempting a jocular tone; "damn it, you mustn't have it all your own way with the girls, even if you are commanding officer."

With difficulty Captain Ardmore restrained the strong impulse to stretch Lord Royster at his feet, but he only said, in a deep concentrated tone which showed the inward struggle,

"Cornet Lord Royster, if you do not immediately withdraw, by heaven I will order out a file of men and place you under arrest."

The discomfited Lord sneaked away. Captain Ardmore turned to support the half-fainting Patience Gray.

No wonder if this second instance of heroism gave the climax to the feeling of affection which had long been strengthening in the heart of the ardent and grateful girl. In the eyes of Patience, Captain Ardmore was a hero, a demi-god, the incarnation of one of those ancient paladins of chivalry of which she had read and dreamed, the most perfect and romantic ideal of a lover which she had ever dared blushingly to invest with the hues of her exuberant fancy in secret communing with her own thoughts.

Then began, for those two young beings, that brief, delightful, delusive, but not the less *enrapturing* phase of existence, comprehended in "first love," that oasis in the desert of life on which all like to turn a backward gaze and lingeringly dwell upon; and when Captain Ardmore, no less infatuated than herself, breathed, in one of their *tête-à-tête* strolls, at the witching evening hour, beside the murmur of the Richelieu rapids, vows of lasting and honourable love, Patience responded to them with such perfect childish touching confidence in her lover's sincerity, such content in the present, and such faith in the future, that had she then *died*, she would have "*carried with her all her illusions, buried herself like an Eastern king with all his jewels and treasures, at the summit of human happiness*."[226]

At length came the *route* for Montreal. Why attempt to describe the parting scene, or the feelings of Patience as she saw the troop defile past her father's house, and caught the last glimpse of her gallant lover, the possessor of her heart, and heard the last faint echoes of the bugles playing that beautiful Scottish air, "We'll maybe return to Lochaber nae mair."[227]

[226] Footnote by Allan: "I cannot forbear inserting the beautiful passage from Balzac to which I am indebted for the above: '*Oh, mourir jeune et palpitant! Destiné digne d'emporter avec soi toutes ses illusions, s'ensevelir comme un roi d'orient, avec ses pierreries et ses trésors, avec toute la fortune humaine.*'" The quote is from Balzac's *Physiologie du mariage*.

[227] A poem (and song) by Allan Ramsay (1686-1758), which was very popular with the British troops during the Napoleonic Wars.

Such is a summary of Captain Ardmore's confession to me; he made no attempt to extenuate his weakness, his fickleness, his crime; and oh! as he lay there shorn of his strength and beauty,—*he*, so lately the gay, the gallant, the handsome,—I did not feel inclined to judge him harshly, as the reader may well suppose. I was rather disposed to seek for pleas which he himself would not have admitted in self-justification. I could well imagine a host of conventional considerations founded on his rank in life, his duty to his family, the effect of time and absence, and the gaieties of Montreal, the implied rather than expressed pity of his brother officers at Ardmore's making a *mésalliance*, and though last, not least, the charms of Miss Vane, and the palpable efforts she had made to win him, and triumph over her rustic rival; all these considerations, though they did not acquit him, pleaded in extenuation of his fault.

It was the evening, I think, of the same day, and Captain Ardmore had become again slightly delirious. I was sitting sadly by his bedside, when his servant entered, and said a lady wished to see me. At first my thoughts reverted to Miss Vane, but it needed only
1858 one glance to enable me to recognise in the applicant the original of the miniature. Yes, it was *Patience Gray*, but how changed from what she must have been when that likeness was taken. She who had been neglected and forgotten, had no sooner heard of the serious nature of Captain Ardmore's illness than she had come to pray to be admitted to watch over him as a nurse.

No; Patience Gray was not a girl of spirit. She had never ceased to love her faithless lover; she did not know how to repay oblivion with oblivion. Her heart was plastic to the first impression of love, but that first impression could not be effaced; and now that he was ill she flew on the wings of her disinterested affection to stand, if possible, between him and death, forgetful of broken vows, of personal pride, of conventionality, of what the world might say, of the danger of infection. This girl, hitherto so shy and timid, had grown heroic, had left her home, and come to Montreal in obedience to the mighty love which dwelt in her heart, inspired by one sole pure and holy motive,—her desire to save the man for whose life she would have given her own, the man who had forgotten her, and who was about to be married to another.

She begged so hard to be admitted, I knew not how to refuse her. "Oh, yes, she could, she would restrain all ebullition of feeling;

she could control herself." At length, with the doctor's sanction, she was permitted to enter; for the patient was always speaking of and expressing a wish to see her.

He was asleep when she entered. When he awoke he did not know her, and confounded her with Miss Vane. "Send for the carriage, Harriet, and we will go home." For days he remained in this half-conscious state. Then he rallied a little, and it was not thought advisable she should appear, lest a recognition should prove too great a shock. On Sunday morning he awoke perfectly conscious, and said to me, "I have only one wish, that I could know that Patience had forgiven me." "She has, she has," I exclaimed, my heart full to bursting; "she has been here nursing you." I could say no more; but Patience had come from behind the curtain, and they were locked in each other's arms.

I was ignorant enough to hope that he was better, but the doctor coming in, shook his head; unfavourable symptoms had appeared during the night, he had not two hours to live. *He* knew it; but she, Patience, who would undertake to convince her of the heart-rending truth?

"Patience, dear Patience! I had but one wish: to see you, to 1858
know that you forgave me, before—"

"Hush! hush!" she exclaimed, with quivering lips, while she laid her cheek to his; "there is nothing to—to forgive—you must not speak—the doctor said you must be kept quiet—you must not speak, love! it will exhaust you, and prevent your—." She could not speak the word "*recovery*;" the flood-gates of her grief burst open; she sank down weeping on her knees by the bed-side. The sound of distant military music was heard. It was one of the regiments going to church, and the lively tune formed a jarring contrast to the grief and sadness within that chamber. Captain Ardmore's features lightened up as he heard the approaching sound. He made a faint effort to beat time with the left hand; the right was clasped in both those of Patience Gray. Suddenly, the hand dropped,—he became perfectly still,—the lower jaw fell. And thus he lay without a sign of life, except the heavy laboured breathing! Oh, God! how inexpressibly painful is this last struggle when all hope is gone, and we can only pray that every breath which the beloved draws may be the last! At length, this sound ceased; all was over. The gallant spirit of Captain Ardmore had passed away for ever; yet still Patience reclined motionless by the bed-side, pressing the dead hand between her own, from time to time carrying it mechanically to her bosom.

Miss Vane had been sent for. She did not arrive till after Captain Ardmore's death. The sight of the inanimate body was too great a shock for her, and she was removed in strong convulsions. But, strange to say, since the death, Patience had become quite calm. Hers was "*a grief too big for tears.*"

A few days, and that most magnificent of sad spectacles—a soldier's funeral—took place. Troops are lining the streets, the soldiers step slowly with reversed arms, and ever and anon is heard the roll of the muffled drum, and the plaintive swell of that most mournfully beautiful of dirges, "*the Dead March in Saul*;"[228] and more eyes than mine are moist as the coffin, surmounted by sword and helmet, is borne past, followed by the charger of the deceased,[229] and at the grave more than one soldier of the firing-party drew his cuff across his eyes, to wipe away the blinding tear, which hindered him in the discharge of his military duty.

Patience Gray had been residing with her father at a relative's house in Montreal. Every one had noticed with wonder the strange calm which had come over her since Captain Ardmore's death. Those who loved her would rather have seen her grieve, as she had done previously to that event. She appeared to be sinking into a state of mental insensibility which made them tremble for her intellect. Thus she remained until the day of the funeral, when, to the astonishment of all, she seemed to rouse from her apathy, and insisted on being present at the church, and afterwards following the procession to the grave-yard in a carriage.

They yielded, in the hope that even this sad excitement would benefit her, but she seemed quite indifferent to, and unconscious of, all that was going forward, until the first volley was fired over her lover's grave. *Then* she raised herself, and sate erect in the carriage, while a gleam of intelligence passed over her hitherto inanimate features, listening eagerly. There came another, and yet another discharge, and then the whole fatal truth flashed back upon her mind with overwhelming force. She uttered one loud piercing cry, and fell senseless into the arms of her agonized father.

[228] The "Dead March" is part of Act Three of *Saul* (1739), the oratorio by Handel (1685-1759).

[229] A charger was a horse trained for battle.

She recovered only partially the use of her fine intellect. Never, from that time till the day of her death, which happened a year afterwards, did she give any tokens of violent emotion, or vivid recollection.

Far different was it with Miss Vane. Her grief had been of that violent character which rarely lasts. As the grass began to grow above Captain Ardmore's grave, so did the memory of the gallant soldier wax faint with Miss Vane. In three months, she began again to be seen in public; in six, she was going to parties as usual, and flirting openly with Lord Royster, to whom the *on dit* reported her to be engaged.[230]

Shortly after the death of Captain Ardmore, his brother-officers caused a tablet to be erected in the church to his memory, with a medallion profile in *basso-relieve*, and a touching inscription beneath, recording the feelings of esteem and respect which the virtues of the deceased had inspired. One day after service, I happened to be just behind Miss Vane, who was leaning on Lord Royster's arm, and heard her distinctly say, as they stopped before the tablet, "Yes, it's a good likeness; but they might have made it a little more ornamental." And to this man, on whose effigy she was gazing, she had been betrothed. He had been buried on the very day appointed for their marriage.

Just one year from Captain Ardmore's death, in the same church where the tablet was erected to his memory, did Miss Vane become the bride of Lord Royster. On that very day, by a strange coincidence, Patience Gary was *buried* at Chambly. While the bells at Montreal rang a merry peal for the wedding of Miss Vane, a knell was tolled for *the Rose of Chambly!*

I could have wished, somehow, that Captain Ardmore had been buried at Chambly, and that the dust of the aristocratic lover and the village maiden had mingled together on the banks of that river, near which their short dream of love and happiness was spent. I should have fancied when I visited the spot that I heard, in the rapids of the Richelieu, a dirge of invisible spirits for those two young beings so prematurely cut off from the world.

[230] "On dit" (French for "they say") means "rumour."

ANDREW LEARMONT SPEDON

The Highlandmen's Hunt; or, The Tale of the Black Hog

(1866)

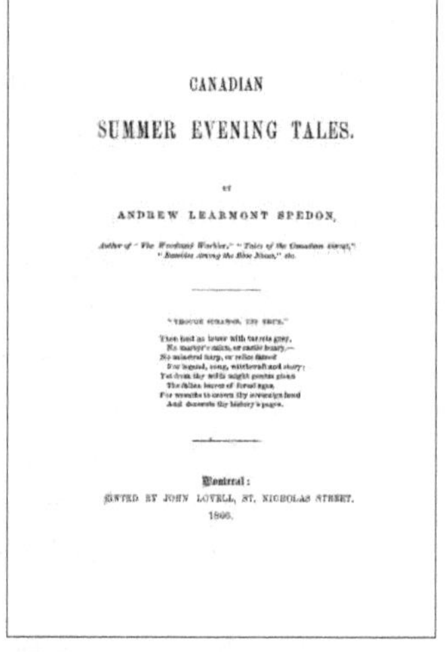

CANADIAN

SUMMER EVENING TALES.

BY

ANDREW LEARMONT SPEDON,

Montreal:

PRINTED BY JOHN LOVELL, ST. NICHOLAS STREET.

1866.

The author: Andrew Learmont Spedon was born in Edinburgh on 21 August 1831, but immigrated with his parents to Quebec in 1833. In 1837, is family moved to Beechridge and, in 1852, to St Jean Chrysostome, where he attended the Huntington Academy of Chateauguay. He later became a teacher there. His journey to Europe in the late 1860s included a pilgrimage to Walter Scott's residence (Abbotsford) to the building of which his father (a stonemason) would have contributed. He published several books of poetry, short stories, and travelogues in the next 15 years: *The Woodland Warbler* (1857); *Tales of the Canadian Forest* (1861); *Rambles among the Blue-Noses; or, Reminiscences of a Tour through New Brunswick and Nova Scotia, during the Summer of 1862* (1863); *Canadian Summer Evening Tales* (1866); *Sketches of a Tour from Canada to Paris, By Way of the British Isles* (1868), *The Canadian Minstrel* (1870), *Tales for Canadian Homes* (1872). In 1873, he moved to Durham (today, South Durham), in the Eastern Townships, where he founded a newspaper. He sold it in 1882, and moved to Hamilton, Bermuda, where again founded a newspaper, the *New Era*. He died in Paget, Bermuda on 26 September 1884.

The text: First published in Spedon's *Canadian Summer Evening Tales* (Montreal: John Lovell, 1866), 23-33, from where the following has been taken. At the end of his preface, the author located and dated the tales as follows: "St Jean Chrysostome, Chateauguay Co[unty], C[anada] E[ast], May, 1866."

I'm nae a "Chew," old Tonald said;
I'se love the pork, but hate the swine;
An' if the diel pe in him's head,
I'll chew him if he enters mine.

About the year 1814, a number of Highland emigrants settled in the vicinity of Chambly, C.E.,[231] on a tract of land in the seigniory of Sir John Johnston, the noted loyalist and warrior.[232] Finding the soil to be somewhat low, and not easily drained, they removed to a newly-surveyed district, adjoining Beech Ridge, now in the county of Chateauguay, C.E., and constituted the "Scotch Settlement," which place, for several years, was known by the name of "Egypt," the very settlement in which I unfortunately spent too many years of my life.[233]

They were a friendly and social people, but very simple and illiterate, and retained nearly all their national characteristics. They were Presbyterians, but full of bigotry and superstition, believing more in the *darkness* of witchcraft than in the *light* of reason and common sense. They were, indeed, a singular people, and their eccentricities could furnish material for many a ludicrous story. The following is only a specimen:

At Beech Ridge lived an eccentric individual, by the name of John Gray. John was a Lowland Scotchman, of large, muscular growth. His habits were social, but extremely coarse; his actions were slow, but sure, and very eccentric at times; he had a rusty kind of a voice, and as a whole, like the gnarled oak, he was of more value than beauty, and but little polished, either mentally or physically.

[231] Canada East was the name of Quebec between 1841 and 1867. Before 1841, it was called Lower Canada.

[232] Actually, Sir John Johnson (1741-1830), a Loyalist who moved to Canada during the American Revolutionary War. He owned land in both Upper Canada and Lower Canada. The seigniory mentioned here is Monnoir, today part of the city of Marieville, about 10 km east of Chambly (and 40 km from Montreal).

[233] The communities of Beechridge and "Scotch Settlement" were part of Williamstown, the territory of which is today divided between Sainte-Clotilde and Saint-Urbain-Premier. Spedon grew up in Beechridge, and his father (who died in 1846) is buried in the Beechridge Presbyterian Church, Sainte-Clotilde, Quebec. The settlement was known as "Egypt" because of the popular Scottish (and Irish) legends according to which the Gaels where of Egyptian origin, and their founding hero, Queen Scota (or Scotia) was the daughter of an Egyptian pharaoh.

Jenny, his wife, was even more eccentric in her way. Order and taste had no place in the catalogue of her household virtues; she was always happy, and ever looking forward to be happier; she felt as contented in her fantastic "Joseph" of medley patch-work, as the Queen of Sheba in her purple robes.[234] And, although at variance with the laws of taste, she was as likely to have potatoes, porridge, and pea-soup for supper as anything else. Their family were the living representatives of both parents, and, like the iron ore, of more value than attraction. They were also happy in their homespun, and knew but as little of the world as the world knew of them. Their shanty was a rough building of round logs, ten feet by fifteen, earthen floor, bark roof, and containing an orifice at the top to let the light in, and the smoke out. During their first winter in the woods, one corner of the hut was partitioned off for their cow, the other was the domestic residence of a large sow. Even in this apparently miserable abode, they lived happy, and though they were destitute of the luxuries of higher life, they knew not the rippled temper of being either whimsical or fastidious in food and clothing. However, they had promised themselves a glorious feast on the hog, of both roast and boil, during the spring work.

Spring at length arrived, and the day came when the fattened hog was destined to yield up the ghost, and the evil spirit thereof, and become transformed into the nutritious element of human life—to lend vigour to the muscles of John and family during their hard spring labour. But whilst John was attempting to seize hold of the animal, it sprang suddenly from its stronghold and long confinement, carried away the shanty door from off its hinges, like the gates of Gaza,[235] and gambolled around the door-yard in wanton frolic, and was followed by John and family. The animal, at length smelling the foul play, and believing its pursuers to be in earnest, galloped off into the woods, and never favoured them with even a transient visit.

Late in autumn of the same year, one of the "Egypt" Highlanders was hunting in the same woods in the vicinity of

[234] Joseph was also a slang term for "coat," in general. The Queen of Sheba appears several times in the Old Testament, but she does not wear purple robes.

[235] In Judges 16: 3, Samson "took the doors of the gate of the city, and the two posts, and went away with them, bar and all, and put them upon his shoulders, and carried them up to the top of an hill that is before Hebron."

Norton Creek,[236] and came in contact with a large sow, having a numerous progeny, half-grown, feeding on beech-nuts, and as fat and fierce as the ancient boars of the Scottish hills. They were none other than the swinish stock and interest of John Gray. But Donald, believing them to be wild boars of the forest, attacked them, and succeeded in killing one of the litter. He carried his booty home, informed one of his neighbours thereof, a relative of his own, whom he desired to accompany him to the place, in order to procure their winter stock of bacon.

On the following morning, they equipped themselves in the Highland costume of kilt and philibeg, bonnet and feathers, with dirk, musket, powder-flask, and flagons of "peat-reek."[237] Darting through the forest, they soon arrived at the spot where Donald had seen the boars. They traversed the woods for some time, keeping a sharp "look-out" for the "*pores*," but no "*pores*" were to be seen or heard. At length, having taken a good swig of the bottle, they purposed to follow the bank of the Norton Creek, and ascertain if any marks of the "*pores*" were visible in the mud.

Whilst scrambling over a shelving rock on the bank, Duncan observed a black animal run into a large crevice or burrow beneath the rock.

"Oh, Tonald, mun, haste ye, come here; Ise pe finding the nest o' the pores, an' seed ane as plack as a craw," cried Duncan.

Donald hastened to the spot, examined the orifice, peered into the dark cavern, and imagined he heard the "pores" snoring soundly asleep.

"She's pe the 'pores' nest for sure," exclaimed Donald.

"Weel, Tonald," said Duncan, "Ise pe thinkin' mysel' the pores pe in ped sleepin' as sound as a pat in the lum."[238]

"Noo, Tuncan," said Donald, "ye'll pe stan' at the hole wi' yer tirk, and mysel' 'ill gang in an' gie the tam pores a ploody prog o' my steel."

Duncan stationed himself at the mouth of the den, dirk in hand, ready to give a good prog to the first animal that attempted to venture out. Donald crept quietly into the den. Groping around him, he caught hold of one in its lair, and gave it a mortal prog.

[236] A stream as well as an area near today's Sainte-Clotilde (see note 233).

[237] The philibeg is a small kilt; the dirk is a Scottish dagger; "peat-reek" is homemade whiskey or moonshine.

[238] "Lum" is a Scottish term for a chimney.

Another as likewise disposed of, and he continued to grope around for the others. Meanwhile, Duncan stood ready for action, staring obliquely into the hole, and heard Duncan engaged at his savage work.

"She's nae pe squeel," said he to himself, "she's pe pedded asleep i' her plankets."

At this moment he was suddenly aroused into action at the sight of a black, shaggy animal behind him, carrying a dead pig in its mouth, and apparently about to rush into the hole. Believing it to be the sow-pig, or "*sow-pore*," as he termed it, he plunged his dagger into its side as it attempted to enter. Then, gripping firmly hold of its tail, with the Herculean strength of a Celtic hero, he endeavoured to drag back the monster from its stronghold.

"I say, Tuncan, what pe stop the light?" cried Donald.

"Suppose the tail o' the sow-pore pe prake, ye'll pe verra soon know what pe stop the light," exclaimed Duncan.

"Haud on, Tuncan, then," cried Donald, "Ise pe seeing his eyes."

"Oh, Tonald, Tonald, haste ye, gie the sow-pore a prog in the een. Pe hurry man, she's pe soon gaun frae me, an' as sure as the teil, ye'er as teid as a herrin',"[239] shouted Duncan, holding on with both hands to its short tail, gasping and grinning like a hag struggling in the grips of a demon.

At this instant, Donald plunged his dirk into one of the eyes which were flashing red-hot like a fire-ball. It was a lucky prog for poor Donald. Immediately it let drop its victim, and backed out. Duncan instantly sprang on the animal and dealt one dig of his dirk into its head. No sooner done, than it bounded off into the woods, with Duncan straddled over its back, Gilpin-like,[240] holding fast to its mane, and at every opportunity plunging his dirk into its body, and yelling on Donald to follow up.

Donald hastened out of the den, and with utter astonishment beheld, at a distance, the black animal scampering off through the brushwood, with Duncan mounted upon its back, his hat off, and his black, shaggy hair flapping about his neck, shouting vociferously on Donald.

[239] "Een" means "eyes" in Scottish English, "teil" is "devil," while "dead as a herring" is a Scottish expression.

[240] The hero of the enormously popular comic ballad "The Diverting History of John Gilpin" (1782) by William Cowper, who is forced to ride a runaway horse.

The animal, from its burden and the loss of blood, soon slackened its speed; Donald bounded forward, and in short time the "sow-pore" was dispatched as their victim.

"Pless my soul and pody, Tuncan," exclaimed Donald, "she's no pe o' the same preed I kilt yesterday."

"Weel," said Duncan, "May pe she'll pe the French preed o' pores; an' tho' she's pe as plack an' ugly as the teil himsel, may pe she'll pe goot for the pacon."

"Weel, weel," said Donald, "if she pinna rost, she's may pe goot for the poil, tho' she's pe as teugh as the teil."

Having carried back the "sow-pore," they entered the cave, being determined to root out the rest from their lair, but found nothing more than the two animals that Donald had killed, and the one that was brought by the sow-pore. Leaving these within the cave, they tied the feet of the sow-pore together. Attaching a pole thereto, they shouldered their black booty, and started homewards in triumph.

As they moved along the rough forest road of Beech Ridge, in the vicinity of John Gray's shanty, his wife, Jenny, beheld, with surprise and horror, the two tall, black, boney Highlanders, in full costume, with blood-stained faces, marching with regular step, carrying the sow-pore between them at shoulder height.

Jenny had heard in Scotland many a wild story about the savage Indians of America, how that many of them went perfectly naked, others with only a blanket about them, that they painted their faces with the blood of their white victims, and had feathers growing out of their heads; that they carried hatchets, bow and arrows, and long knives, to kill the white people with, and, worse than all, that they skinned their victims alive, then roasted and ate them, and afterwards made tobacco-pouches out of their skins.

What a host of horrors haunted the mind of poor Jenny Gray at that moment. She had never before seen a Highlander in full costume, and when she beheld the two heroes she believed them to be none other than savage Indians carrying one of their white victims to the place of rendez-vous. Terrified and bewildered, almost frantic, she and the others of the family present, hurried off towards John, who was working convenient[241] to the shanty.

"*Oh, John, John, John*," exclaimed Jenny, wringing her hands together in bewildered horror, "*the Indians are coming upon us to kill*

[241] Close by.

us a', an' they've a man carrying between them that they're gaun tae kill an' eat, it may be at oor shanty. Oh, John, what'll we do? what'll we do?"

"*The Indians!* d'ye say?" ejaculated John, starting up, "*O Guid guide us*, whaur aboots are they, Jenny?"

"*Oh, yonder; yonder, they're commin', an' as sure as daith, John, it's oor Geordie they hae; I ken him by his black coat, an' they're gaun tae eat him at oor house. Oh, heaven preserve us a'. Bless my soul, we'll a' be deid men in a few minutes. Oh, John, let us rin tae the wuds; rin, rin, my wee bit bairnies, rin—rin for yer life.*"

"*Rin, then,*" said John, wildly starting forth; and therewith, Jenny and her bairns, with the exception of Geordie, their eldest son, who was absent at the time, fled like a gang of furies to the woods, without ever looking back to see whether John or the Indians were following.

John, however, at once had recognised them to be Highlanders, and he hailed them as they approached.

"*What on airth are ye carrying thare, gentlemen?*" interrogated John.

"A sow-pore," said Donald.

"*A what?*" interrogated John.

1866 "A sow-pore," repeated Donald, "that we hae kilt for the pacon."

"A French sow-pore," added Duncan.

"*A soo-pore!*" exclaimed John, laughingly, "I never heard o' sic a name gien either to ony beast or body sin' I was born; may be it'll be some idiom o' yer Gaelic gibberish nae doot, but I wad ca' it naethin' else but a muckle bear."

"*A pear,*" exclaimed Donald, "*py cosh, I never seed a pear afore.*"

"*Pless my soul,*" said Duncan, "*an' it pe a pear. I thocht it pe a pore, an' a sow-pore o' the French preed.*"

The whole adventure was related to John, who suggested at once that the hogs that Donald had seen might be his old sow and a litter. Consequently, it was agreed that they should go in quest of the forest brood. Accordingly, on the following morning, they returned to John's shanty, where Jenny, having been made aware of the facts, and who the savage-looking foresters were, was also in readiness to accompany John and them to the woods in search of the old sow and its young ones. Jenny's hunting-dress consisted of many pieces, various colours, and varied textures, from the muslin white of her wedding garb, to the woollen grey of the Canadian forest; one stocking was black, the other white; a shoe and moccasin were foot companions, whilst the head-piece was the dimpled skeleton of John's wedding castor.

Having arrived at the cave, they discovered that the animals which Donald had dirked were two cubs—the other, one of the litter which Bruin had designed for her young ones.

In the course of an hour's research, the old sow and six of her brood were discovered, and eventually shot. They were shortly afterwards conveyed to John's shanty, where each of the two Highlanders received one the of the young "pores" for his trouble. Thus were they all providentially provided with bacon and bear meat for the winter. But while Duncan lives he will never forget his ride on the bare back of the bear, and how he barely escaped with his life. Neither will my readers, I hope, forget the story of the Highlandmen's Hunt, and the Tale of the "Sow-Pore."

May Agnes Fleming

A Dark Conspiracy

(1867)

The author: May Agnes Early was born in Saint John, New Brunswick, on 15 November 1840, the daughter of an Irish ship's carpenter. She was the eldest of five children, but she and her brother James Patrick (fourteen years younger than her) were the only siblings who survived. She sold her first story to the New York *Sunday Mercury* while still a schoolgirl at the Convent of the Sacred Heart in Saint John. She became a teacher at the Roman Catholic School in Saint John in 1856. She published many other stories and serialised novels and novellas, both in the US and Canada, usually under the pen name "Cousin May Carleton." In 1865, she married William John Fleming, soon after which she started signing her works "May Agnes Fleming." She published a long series of very popular novels and was known as the best-selling Canadian author of the 1870s. She was seen as a master of crime fiction and was often compared with her British contemporary, Mary Elizabeth Braddon. Her novels often included strong female characters. The Flemings left New Brunswick and moved to Brooklyn, New York, in 1875. She died there on 24 March 1880.

The text: Originally published as "Tom's Revenge" and signed May Carleton in a Philadelphia monthly, *Peterson's Magazine* 52: 6 (December), 413-417. It was reprinted under the author's real name with the title "A Dark Conspiracy" in *Norine's Revenge, and Sir Noel's Heir* (New York: G.W. Carleton & Co., 1875), 379-392. Fleming made some changes in the first lines (Tom Maxwell's declaration of aversion toward Fanny), corrected typos, improved the punctuation and, close to the end, she changed the name of the city from "C——" to "New York." The following is from the later version published in a volume tht included a novel, a novella, and this short story. Punctuation has been changed in the third paragraph to make it more comprehensible.

"In love with her—*I* want to marry her!" cried Tom Maxwell in a fine fury. "I tell you I hate her, and I hope she may die a miserable, disappointed, cantankerous old maid!"

Striding up and down the floor, his face flaming, his eyes flashing, his very coat-tail quivering with rage—a Bengal tiger, robbed of her young, could not have looked a much more ferocious object. And yet ferocity was not natural to Tom Maxwell—handsome Tom, whose years were only two-and-twenty, and who was hot-headed and fiery, and impetuous as it is in the nature of two-and-twenty to be, but by no means innately savage. But he had just been jilted, jilted in cold blood; so up and down he strode, grinding his teeth vindictively, and fulminating anathema maranathas[242] against his fair deceiver.

"The miserable, heartless jilt! The deceitful, shameless coquette!" burst out Tom, ferociously. "She gave me every encouragement that a woman could give, until she drew me on by her abominable wiles to make a fool of myself; and she turns round and smiles and puts her handkerchief to her eyes and is 'very sorry,'"—mimicking the feminine intonation—"'and never dreamed of such a thing, and will be very happy to be my friend; but for anything further—oh! dear, Mr. Maxwell, pray don't think of it!' Confound her and the whole treacherous sex to which she belongs! But I'm not done with her yet! I'll have revenge as sure as my name is Tom Maxwell!"

"As how?" asked a lazy voice from the sofa. "She's a woman, you know. Being a woman, you can't very well call her out and shoot her, or horsewhip her, or even knock her down. A fellow may feel like that—I often have myself, after being jilted; but still it can't be did. It's an absurd law, I allow, this polite exemption of womankind from condign[243] and just punishment; but it is too late in the day for chaps like you and me to go tilt[244] against popular prejudices."

It was a long speech for Paul Warden, who was far too indolent generally to get beyond monosyllables. He lay stretched

[242] A formula of excommunication in the Catholic Church.

[243] (Formal) proper, deserved.

[244] Short for "go tilt a lance" (from *Don Quixote*).

at full length on the sofa, languidly smoking the brownest of meerschaums, and dreamily watching the smoke curl and wreath around his head. A genial, good-looking fellow, five years Tom's senior, and remarkably clever in his profession, the law, when not too lazy to exercise it.

Tom Maxwell paused in his excited striding to look in astonishment at the speaker.

"You jilted!" he said, "You! You, Paul Warden, the irresistible!"

"Even so, *mon ami.* Like measles, and mumps, and tooth-cutting, it's something a man has to go through, willy nilly. I've been jilted and heart-broken some half-dozen times, more or less, and here I am to-night not a ha'penny the worse for it. So go it, Tom my boy! The more you rant and rave now, the sooner the pain will be over. It's nothing when you're used to it. By-the-way," turning his indolent eyes slowly, "is she pretty, Tom?"

"Of course!" said Tom, indignantly. "What do you take me for? Pretty! She's beautiful, she's fascinating. Oh, Warden! it drives me mad to think of it!"

"She's all my fancy painted her—she's lovely, she's divine," quoted Mr. Warden; "but her heart, it is another's, and it never—[245] What's her name, Tom?"

"Fanny Summers. If you had been in this place four-and-twenty hours, you would have no need to ask. Half the men in town are spooney[246] about her."

"Fanny. Ah! a very bad omen. Never knew a Fanny yet who wasn't a natural born flirt. What's the style—dark or fair, *belle* blonde, or *jolie* brunette?"

"Brunette; dark, bright, sparkling, saucy, piquant irresistible! Oh!" cried Tom, with a dismal groan, sinking into a chair, "it is too bad, *too* bad to be treated so!"

"So it is, my poor Tom. She deserved the bastinado,[247] the wicked witch. The bastinado not being practicable, let us think of something else. She deserves punishment, and she shall have it; paid back in her own coin, and with interest, too. Eh? Well?"

For Tom had started up in his chair, violently excited and red in the face.

[245] ". . . she never can be mine." The first two lines of the very popular poem "Alice Gray" by William Mee.

[246] Enamoured in a silly, gushy manner.

[247] A beating with a stick (originally on the soles of the feet).

"The very thing!" cried Tom. "I have it! She shall be paid in her own coin, and I'll have most glorious revenge, if you'll only help me, Paul."

"To my last breath, Tom; only don't make so much noise. Hand me the match-box, my pipe's gone out. Now, what is it?"

"Paul, they call you irresistible—the women do."

"Do they? Very polite of them. Well?"

"Well, being irresistible, why can't you make love to Fanny Summers, talk her into a desperate attachment to you, and then treat her as she has treated me—jilt her?"

Paul Warden opened his large, dreamy eyes to their widest, and fixed them on his excited young friend.

"Do you mean it, Tom?"

"Never meant anything more in my life, Paul."

"But supposing I could do it; supposing I am the irresistible conqueror you gallantly make me out; supposing I could talk the charming Fanny into that deplorable attachment—it seems a shame, doesn't it?"

"A shame!" exclaimed poor Tom, smarting under a sense of his own recent wrong; "and what do you call her conduct to *me*? It's a poor rule that won't work both ways. Let her have it herself, hot and strong, and see how she likes it—she's earned it richly. You can do it, I know, Paul; you have a way with you among women. I don't understand it myself, but I see it takes. You can do it, and you're no friend of mine, Warden, if you don't."

"Do it! My dear fellow, what wouldn't I do to oblige you; break fifty hearts, if you asked me. Here's my hand—it's a go."

"And you'll flirt with her, and jilt her?"

"With the help of the gods. Let the campaign begin at once, let me see my fair, future victim to-night."

"But you'll be careful, Paul," said Tom, cooling down as his friend warmed up. "She's very pretty, uncommonly pretty; you've no idea how pretty, and she may turn the tables and subjugate you, instead of you subjugating her."

"The old story of the minister who went to Rome to convert the Pope, and returned a red-hot Catholic. Not any thanks. My heart is iron-clad; has stood too many sieges to yield to any little flirting brunette. Forewarned is forearmed. Come on, old fellow," rising from his sofa, "if 'tis done, when it is done, 'twere well 'twere done quickly."

"How goes the night?" said Tom, looking out; "it's raining. Do you mind?"

"Shouldn't mind if it rained pitchforks in so good a cause. Get your overcoat and come. I think those old chaps—what-do-you-call-'em, Crusaders? must have felt as I do now, when they marched to take Jerusalem. Where are we to find *la belle* Fanny?"

"At her sister's, Mrs. Walters, she's only here on a visit; but during her five weeks' stay she has turned five dozen heads, and refused five dozen hands, my own the last," said Tom, with a groan.

"Never mind, Tom; there is balm in Gilead yet.[248] Revenge is sweet, you know, and you shall taste its sweets before the moon wanes. Now then, Miss Fanny, the conquering hero comes!"[249]

The two young men sallied forth into the rainy, lamp-lit streets. A passing omnibus took them to the home of the coquettish Fanny, and Tom rang the bell with vindictive emphasis.

"Won't she rather wonder to see you, after refusing you?" inquired Mr. Warden, whilst they waited.

"What do I care?" responded Mr. Maxwell, moodily; "her opinion is of no consequence to me now."

Mrs. Walters, a handsome, agreeable-looking young matron, welcomed Tom with a cordial shake of the hand, and acknowledged Mr. Warden's bow by the brightest of smiles, as they were ushered into the family parlor.

"We are quite alone, this rainy night, my sister and I," she said. "Mr. Walters is out of town for a day or two. Fanny, my dear, Mr. Warden; my sister, Miss Summers, Mr. Warden."

It was a pretty, cozy room, "curtained, and close, and warm;"[250] and directly under the gas-light, reading a lady's magazine, sat one of the prettiest girls it had ever been Mr. Warden's good fortune to see, and who welcomed him with a brilliant smile.

"Black eyes, jetty ringlets, rosy cheeks, alabaster brow," thought Mr. Warden, taking stock; "the smile of an angel, and dressed to perfection. Poor Tom! he's to be pitied. Really, I haven't come across anything so much to my taste this month of Sundays."

[248] A common literary reference to Jeremiah 8: 22 ("Is there no balm in Gilead; is there no physician there?").

[249] From Handel's oratorio of *Judas Maccabaeus* (1746).

[250] From a very popular song, "What Are the Wild Waves Saying?" with lyrics by Joseph Edward Carpenter (1813-1885) and music by Stephen Glover (1812-1870).

Down sat Mr. Paul Warden beside the adorable Fanny, plunging into conversation at once with an ease and fluency that completely took away Tom's breath. That despondent wooer on the sofa, beside Mrs. Walters, pulled dejectedly at the ears of her little black-and-tan terrier, and answered at random all the pleasant things she said to him. He was listening, poor fellow, to that brilliant flow of small talk from the mustached lips of his dashing friend, and wishing the gods had gifted him with a similar "gift of the gab," and feeling miserably jealous already. He had prepared the rack for himself with his eyes wide open; but that made the torture none the less when the machinery got in motion. Pretty Fanny snubbed him incontinently, and was just as bewitching as she knew how to his friend. It was a clear case of diamond cut diamond—two flirts pitted against each other; and an outsider would have been considerably puzzled on which to bet, both being so evenly matched.

Tom listened, and sulked; yes, sulked. What a lot of things they found to talk about, where he used to be tongue-tied. The magazine, the fashion-plates, the stories; then a wild launch into literature, novels, authors, poets; then the weather; then Mr. Warden was travelling, and relating his "hair-breadth escapes by flood and field,"[251] while bright-eyed Fanny listened in breathless interest. Then the open piano caught the irresistible Paul's eyes, and in a twinkling there was Fanny seated at it, her white fingers flying over the polished keys, and he bending above her with an entranced face. Then he was singing a delightful love-song in a melodious tenor voice, that might have captivated any heart that ever beat inside of lace and muslin; and then Fanny was singing a sort of response, it seemed to frantically jealous Tom; and then it was eleven o'clock, and time to go home.

Out in the open air, with the rainy night wind blowing bleakly, Tom lifted his hat to let the cold blast cool his hot face. He was sulky still, and silent—very silent; but Mr. Warden didn't seem to mind.

"So," he said, lighting a cigar, "the campaign has begun, the first blow has been struck, the enemy's ramparts undermined. Upon my word, Tom, the little girl is uncommonly pretty!"

[251] When they first met, Desdemona listened to Othello's tales of "most disastrous chances;/ Of moving accidents by flood and field;/ Of hair-breadth 'scapes." (*Othello*, I, iii, 133-135).

"I told you so," said Tom, with a sort of growl.

"And remarkably agreeable. I don't think I ever spent a pleasanter *tête-à-tête* evening."

"So I should judge. She had eyes, and ears, and tongue for no one but you."

"My dear fellow, it's not possible you're jealous! Isn't that what you wanted? Besides, there is no reason, really; she is a professional flirt, and understands her business; you and I know just how much value to put on all that sweetness. Have a cigar, my dear boy, and keep up your heart; we'll fix the flirting Fanny yet, please the pigs!"[252]

This was all very true; but, somehow, it wasn't consoling. She was nothing to him, Tom, of course—and he hated her as hotly as every; but, somehow, his thirst for vengeance had considerably cooled down. The cure was worse than the disease. It was maddening to a young man in his frame of mind to see those brilliant smiles, those entrancing glances, all those pretty, coquettish, womanly, wiles that had deluded him showered upon another, even for that other's delusion. Tom wished he had never thought of revenge, at least with Paul Warden for his handsome agent.

"Are you going there again?" he asked, moodily.

"Of course," replied Mr. Warden, airily. "What a question, old fellow, from you of all people. Didn't you hear the little darling telling me to call again? She overlooked you completely, by-the-by. I'm going again, and again, and yet again, until my friend, my *fides Achates*,[253] is avenged."

"Ah!" said Tom, sulkily, "but I don't know that I care so much for vengeance as I did. Second thoughts are best; and it struck me, whilst I watched you both tonight, that it was mean and underhand to plot against a woman like this. You thought so yourself at first, you know."

"Did I? I forget. Well, I think differently now, my dear Tom; and as you remark, second thoughts are best. My honor is at stake; so put your conscientious scruples in your pocket, for I shall

[252] An old slang idiom, "[If (it should)] please the pigs" means "if circumstances allow" or "God willing."

[253] Though it should be "fidus Achates," i.e., "my faithful/loyal Achates" (Achates was Aeneas's friend and supporter in Virgil's *Aeneid*), this literary phrase for an epitome of friendship and constancy was often rendered in this form, with the noun *fides* (loyalty, faith) instead of the adjective.

conquer the fascinating Fanny, or perish in the attempt. Here we are at my boarding-house—won't you come in? No. Well, then, good-night. By-the-way, I shall be at the enemy's quarters to-morrow evening; if you wish to see how ably I fight your battles, show yourself before nine. By-by!"

Mr. Maxwell's answer was a deeply bass growl as he plodded in his way; and Paul Warden, running up to his room, laughed lightly to himself.

"Poor Tom! Poor, dear boy! Jealousy is a green-eyed lobster,[254] and he's a prey to it—the worst kind. Really, Paul, my son, little black eyes is the most bewitching piece of calico[255] you have met in your travels lately; and if you wanted a wife, which you don't, you couldn't do better than go in and win. As it is—Ah! it's a pity for the little dear's sake you can't marry."

With which Mr. Warden disrobed and went to bed.

Next evening, at half-past eight, Tom Maxwell made his appearance at Mrs. Walters, only to find his *fides Achates* there enthroned before him, and basking in the sunshine of the lovely Fanny's smiles. How long he had been there Tom couldn't guess; but he and Fanny and Mrs. Walters were just settling it to go to the theatre the following night. There was a bunch of roses, pink-and-white, his gift, Tom felt in his bones, in Fanny's hand, and into which she plunged her pretty little nose every five seconds. It was adding insult to injury, the manifest delight that aggravating girl felt in his friend's society; and Tom ground his teeth inwardly, and could have seen Paul Warden guillotined, there and then, with all the pleasure in life.

That evening, and many other evenings which succeeded, were but a repetition of the first. An easy flow of delightful small talk, music, singing, and reading aloud. Yes, Paul Warden read aloud, as if to goad that unhappy Tom to open madness, in the most musical of masculine voices, out of little blue-and-gold books, Tennyson, and Longfellow, and Owen Meredith;[256] and

[254] From a famous anecdote about Mr. Layfield, a mid-18th-century actor who, while on stage playing Iago in Shakespeare's *Othello*, uttered "lobster" instead of "monster."

[255] Slang for a woman. To calico meant to court women or associate with them.

[256] Owen Meredith was the pseudonym of Robert Bulwer-Lytton (1831-1891), a British diplomat who would become Viceroy of India (1876-1880). As Owen Meredith, he was a popular poet in the 1850s and 1860s.

Fanny would sit in breathless earnestness, her color coming and going, her breath fluttering, her eyes full of tears as often as not, fixed on Paul's classic profile. Tom didn't burst out openly—he made no scene; he only sat and glowered in malignant silence—and that is saying everything for his power of self-control.

Two months passed; hot weather was coming, and Fanny begun to talk of the heat and the dust of the town; of being home-sick, for the sight of green fields, new milk, strawberry-patches, new-laid eggs, and pa and ma. It had been a very delightful two months, no doubt; and she had enjoyed Mr. Warden's society vey much, and gone driving and walking with him, and let him take her to the theatre, and the opera, and played for him, and sung for him, and danced with him, and accepted his bouquets, and new music, and blue-and-gold books; but, for all that, it was evident she could leave him and go home, and still exist.

"It's all very nice," Miss Summers had said, tossing back her black ringlets; "and I have enjoyed this spring ever so much, but still I'm glad to get home again. One grows tired of balls, and parties, and the theatre, you know, after awhile, Mr. Warden; and I am only a little country-girl, and I shall be just as glad as ever for a romp over the meadows, and a breezy gallop across the hills once more. If you or Mr. Maxwell," glancing at that gloomy youth sideways out of her curls, "care much for fishing, and come up our way any time this summer, I'll try and treat you as well as you have treated me."

"But you haven't treated us well, Miss Fanny," Mr. Warden said, looking unspeakable things. "You take our hearts by storm, and then break them ruthlessly by leaving us. What sort of treatment do you call that?"

Miss Summers only laughed, and looked saucy; and danced away, leaving her two admirers standing together out in the cold.

"Well, Tom," Mr. Warden said, "and so the game's up, the play played out, the curtain ready to fall. The star actress departs to-morrow—and now, what do you think of the performance?"

"Not much," responded Tom, moodily. "I can't see that you have kept your promise. You've made love to her, I allow, *con amore*, confoundedly as if you meant it, in fact; but I don't see where the jilting comes in; I can't see where's my revenge."

"Don't you?" said Paul, thoughtfully lighting his cigar. "Well, come to think of it, I don't either. To tell you the truth, I haven't had a chance to jilt her. I may be irresistible, and I have no doubt I am, since you say so; but, somehow, the charm don't seem to work with our little favorite. Here I have been for the last two months just as captivating as I know how; and yet there's that girl ready to be off to-morrow to the country, without so much as a crack in the heart that should be broken in smithereens. But still," with a sudden change of voice, and slapping him lightly on the shoulder, "dear old boy, I don't despair of giving you your revenge yet!"

Tom lifted his gloomy eyes in sullen inquiry.

"Never mind now," said Paul Warden, airily; "give me a few weeks longer. Lazy as I am, I have never failed yet in anything I have seriously undertaken; and, upon my word, I'm more serious about this matter than you may believe. Trust to your friend, and wait."

That was all Mr. Warden would deign to say.

Tom, not being able to do otherwise, took him at his word, dragged out existence, and waited for his cherished revenge.

Miss Summers left town next day, and Tom, poor, miserable fellow, felt as if the sun had ceased to shine, and the scheme of the universe become a wretched failure, when he caught the last glimmer of the lustrous black eyes, the last flutter of the pretty black curls. But his Damon[257] was by his side to slap him on the back and cheer him up.

"Courage, old fellow!" cried Mr. Warden; "all's not lost that's in danger. Turn and turn about; your turn next."

But, somehow, Tom didn't care for revenge any more. He loved that wicked, jilting little Fanny as much as ever; and the heartache only grew worse day after day; but he ceased to desire vengeance. He settled down into a kind of gentle melancholy, lost his appetite, and his relish for Tom and Jerrys,[258] and took to writing despondent poetry for the weekly journals. In this state Mr. Warden left him, and suddenly disappeared from town. Tom didn't know where he had gone, and his landlady didn't know;

[257] Another epitome of friendship, from the ancient Greek legend of Damon and Pythias.

[258] A cocktail made with brandy, rum, sugar, and eggs, served hot. It was created in the 1820s by Pierce Egan, the author of the popular book *Life and London* and the play based on it, *Tom and Jerry, or Life in London*, both of which follow the adventures of two friends given to drinking, gambling, and partying.

and stranger still, his bootmaker and tailor, to whom he was considerably in arrears, didn't know either. But they were soon enlightened.

Five weeks after his mysterious disappearance came a letter and a newspaper, in his familiar hand, to Tom, while he sat at breakfast. He opened the letter first and read:

In the Country.

"Dear Old Boy—I have kept my word—you are avenged gloriously. Fanny will never jilt you, nor any one else again!"

At this passage in the manuscript, Tom Maxwell laid it down, the cold perspiration breaking out on his face. Had Paul Warden murdered her, or worse, had he married her? With a desperate clutch Tom seized the paper, tore it open, looked at the list of marriages, and saw his worst fears realized. There it was, in printers' ink, the atrocious revelation of his bosom friend's perfidy.

"Married, on the fifth inst., at the residence of the bride's father, Paul Warden, Esq., of New York to Miss Fanny Summers, second daughter of Mr. John Summers, of this town."

There it was. Tom didn't faint; he swallowed a scalding cup of coffee at a gulp, and revived, seized the letter and finished it.

"You see, old fellow, paradoxical as it sounds, although I was the conqueror, I was, also, the conquered. Fanny had fallen in love with me, as you foresaw, but I had fallen in love with her also, which you didn't foresee. I might jilt her, of course, but that would be cutting off my own nose to spite my friend's face; and so—I didn't! I did the next best thing for you, though,—I married her; and I may mention, in parenthesis, I am the happiest of mankind; and as Artemus Ward remarks, 'My wife says so too.'[259]

[259] Artemus Ward was the penname of Charles Farrar Browne (1834-1867), an American humorist and stand-up comedian. "My wife says so too" was one of his catchphrases.

"Adieu, my boy. We'll come to town next week, where Fan and I will be delighted to have you call. With best regards from my dear little wife, I am, old fellow,

"Your devoted friend,

"PAUL WARDEN."

Mr. and Mrs. Warden did come to town next week; but Mr. Maxwell didn't call. In point of fact he hasn't called since, and doesn't intend to, and has given his friend Paul the "cut direct."[260] And that is how Paul Warden got a wife, and Tom Maxwell his revenge.

[260] To give someone the cut direct (or the dead cut) meant (in contemporary slang) to deny knowing someone.

JOHN RUTHERFORD

Charlie Chatterton

(1868)

The author: John Rutherford (1829-1889) was born in the West of Ireland, lived in Liverpool from 1843 to 1864, when he moved to London and became a journalist. He was in Canada in the mid- to late 1860s, investigating the Fenian movement. He lived in Montreal and he got attached to what he called "the land of his adoption," writing several "Canadian poems" and a "Montreal story." His first book, *Charlie Chatterton*, was published in Montreal in 1868. Back in England, he wrote for both *Cornhill Magazine* and the *Pall Mall Gazette*, befriending Frederick Greenwood, the founder of the latter periodical, to whom he dedicated his second book, *The Troubadours; their loves and their lyrics* (1873)—two of the eleven chapters were reprinted from *Cornhill Magazine* (where they appeared in 1872). His third book (for which he is perhaps best remembered) was *The Secret History of the Fenian Conspiracy*, 2 vols (London: C. Kegan Paul, 1877), much of which deals with the Fenians in Canada. A book that certainly deserves more attention is his last, *Sketches from Shady Places* (London: Smith, Elder, & Co., 1879), "all drawn from life," in which he shows again his talent as an investigative reporter. The last book, as well as several pieces of journalism, were signed "Thor Fredur" (an anagram of Rutherford).

CHARLIE CHATTERTON,

A MONTREAL STORY;

WITH

Canadian and other Poems,

BY

JOHN RUTHERFORD.

Montreal:

PRINTED BY JOHN LOVELL, ST. NICHOLAS STREET.

1868.

The text: First published in *Charlie Chatterton, a Montreal Story; with Canadian and Other Poems* (Montreal: John Lovell, 1868), 9-47. The volume is dedicated "To His Friends at Home, and in Canada, the Land of His Adoption." The following is from the 1868 original (the text has not been reprinted since).

Chapter I.

Smythe's my name—S-m-y-t-h-e, not Smith—I am particular as to this, as I wish it to be distinctly understood that I have no connection with the notorious John Smith, or any of his class. And, having taken you thus far into my confidence, I don't mind telling you, also, that I am at present boarding at No.——, Bleury Street,[261] with Mrs. Blotcher. I say Mrs. Blotcher, for, although there is a Mr. B., he is one of those meek, mild, submissive kind of mortals who may be described as "neither fish, flesh, fowl, nor good red herring,"—seldom visible to the naked eye, except at meal times, when he generally manages to take a pretty good cargo on board, asking no questions for conscience and his wife's sake. Viewed domestically, Blotcher would have perfectly obeyed the command—husbands, submit yourselves unto your wives—had such a command existed. Rising every morning, summer and winter, at 5:30, Blotcher first proceeds to light the stove, and having infused a cup of tea, carries it to Mrs. B. in bed—saws the wood, cleans the knives and forks, and having swallowed his breakfast in solemn silence, he wipes the children's noses and disappears quietly through the back door till dinner time. Viewed professionally, Blotcher is a clerk. For fifteen long years he has occupied the same high-legged stool, in the chambers of Messrs. Gripper & Holdem, Attorneys, in Little St. James Street,[262] during the whole of which time he was never known to be absent a single hour from business, or ever to have asked or received an advance of salary; on which account he is looked upon by the firm as a most estimable and exemplary man, and is an especial favorite with the junior partner, Mr. Holdem.

But things are generally pretty evenly balanced in this world, and if Mr. Blotcher's salary is light, so are also his duties. From his earliest infancy, Blotcher has cherished an inveterate hatred towards flies, and bluebottles are his special aversion. Woe to the

[261] A street in downtown Montreal, which at the time separated the Golden Square Mile (where the richest families, mostly Scottish, lived) to the west, and an area called Little Dublin (today, Chinatown) to the east.

[262] Today, Rue Saint-Jacques in Old Montreal.

unhappy one which ventures to light upon his desk, for down comes the ruler upon it, almost invariably resulting in a deep indentation in the mahogany, and the escape of Mr. Bluebottle. One hot summer's day in July, however, he had been particularly successful, having succeeded in killing six. I observed that he was in very high spirits that day; he wiped the children's noses a great deal oftener than appeared to be at all necessary, and seemed to be at peace with himself and all mankind.

The long days of winter are not, moreover, without their enjoyments for Blotcher; and keeping the stove warm during office hours, seems to him to constitute the whole duty of man. But business is business, and Messrs. Gripper & Holdem are not entirely devoid of it. Occasionally a client will drop in, at which times Blotcher is always to be found with some lengthy deed, which he is supposed to be engrossing. Seldom is he off his guard, in this respect, for he has a quick ear for all comers. Once, and only once, did his acuteness fail him; for catching sight of a Brobdingnagian bluebottle on the ledge of the office door, he rushed to deal him a mortal blow with the ruler, when the door being suddenly opened from behind, down fell the weapon with all the force of Blotcher's arm upon Mr. Gripper's nose. Horror-struck with the result, Blotcher retreated slowly to his tripod, followed by Mr. Gripper, who, in great wrath, demanded an explanation of his strange conduct; nor was he particularly well satisfied with poor Blotcher's mumbling explanation and apology.

"Now, Sir," said Gripper, after his wrath had somewhat subsided, "understand, once for all, that there must be no more tom-foolery of this kind in our office. Has any one called during any absence?"

"Yes, Sir,—Mr. Sheephead."

"What did he call about?"

"He called about an account due him by a Mr. Bolter."

"Aw, very good—did you ask him if he applied to Bolter himself for payment, in the first instance?"

"Yes, Sir, I did."

"And what did Bolter say?"

"He told him to go to the devil."

"And what did Sheephead say he did then?"

"Why, Sir, he said he came to you."

O! Blotcher, Blotcher, you should open your mouth as seldom as possible, except at meal times, for as sure as you do, you are certain to put your foot in it. And for this, and the bluebottle affair, Blotcher would assuredly have got the sack, but for the consideration Gripper had for his large wife and family, which reminds me that I have yet to introduce you to Mrs. B.

Well, she is a rum 'un.[263] On her stocking soles, I should say she measures five feet eight inches. Her head, which appears like a dumpling stuck upon her shoulders, is ornamented, in front, by a nose of a decidedly celestial tendency, and most suspicious brilliancy of hue. Her tongue wags with a persistency suggestive of perpetual motion. Where she was born or to what country she belongs, it would be difficult for any one to say; for when Blotcher married her, she had been the widow of a sergeant in a cavalry regiment, and had been in nearly every quarter of the globe. Charlie Chatterton, one of the boarders, who is a clerk in a dry goods store in St. Paul Street,[264] says he doesn't believe that she was ever born at all, in the regular way, but that she must either have been got up by subscription, or got at a raffle, and I am almost disposed to agree with him. How Blotcher could have summoned courage to propose to her, remains to this day a mystery to all his friends. But it is generally believed that he had no hand in the matter at all. Be this as it may, however, sure enough it is, that besides wearing the continuations,[265] Mrs. B. is a fruitful vine; for in addition to four military encumbrances,[266] a chest of drawers, and a wash tub, which she brought to Blotcher as dowry on her marriage day, she had added six pledges of various degrees of ugliness to the Blotcher family. Indeed the house never is without a baby; for no sooner does Mrs. B. have one off her hands than she invariably produces another. And although I am no great authority in such matters, I have shrewd suspicions that another infliction of the same kind is shortly in store for Blotcher.

[263] The adjective "rum" ("odd," "peculiar") is mostly British.

[264] In the Old Port area of Old Montreal, Saint-Paul is the city's oldest street.

[265] Slang term for trousers.

[266] Slang term for children (here, children Mrs. Blotcher had had with the cavalry sergeant).

Of the boarders generally there is not much to be said. With the exception of Charlie Chatterton, they are an ordinary, common-place lot enough, and when assembled, as usual, in the sitting-room of an evening, to enjoy a pipe, the conversation is not unfrequently made up of a relation by each, of the fabulous number of boarding houses he has tried, in the vain expectation of finding something like the comforts of a home, and the supposed quantities of superannuated cow and bad butter which he had consumed. But, however varied their experiences may be in regard to these important points, it is wonderful to observe the unanimity of opinion which exists amongst them with regard to the boarding house cat, and its powers of adopting the "appropriation clause."[267] In one instance, it had taken to wearing rubbers; in another, the sudden disappearance of hair oil, combs and brushes, could only be accounted for upon the supposition that it had taken to cultivate its whiskers. But the most remarkable instance of feline kleptomania is that related by Tom Simpkins, confidential clerk in the large soap and tallow works of Messrs. Hogg & Lard, Griffintown,[268] where the cat actually smoked, and had taken a fancy to a favorite meerschaum pipe, to the coloring of which, Tom had for many months given his whole mind; and as all acknowledged that no loss they had sustained could be compared to this in cruelty and heartlessness, a universal vote of sympathy was passed for him.

Having no special grievances to record from my own experience in this way, I was generally wont to slip up with Charlie Chatterton to his room, where, recharging our pipes, we usually managed to have a quiet chit-chat on things in general. One important decision we soon came to, however, and which I must not fail to record, was that in future we should room together; and this we could easily manage, as Charlie occupied a large front room in which was a vacant bed.

It was on the 10th of last month that we finally resolved on this. Well do I recollect the date, for Blotcher got awfully drunk that night, and there was no end of a row in the kitchen,

[267] Allusion to the government appropriation of money from the selling of church lands in Upper and Lower Canada. Although this had been provided in the Clergy Reserves Act from 1840, the process of secularization lasted throughout the second half of the nineteenth century.

[268] At the time, an Irish working-class neighbourhood, south-west of downtown Montreal.

in consequence. Slipping down stairs, I beheld Blotcher lying prostrate upon the floor, in an exceedingly maudlin state, and Mrs. B. standing over him flourishing a potatoe smasher above his head, and vowing that she would put "an existence to his period."[269] Blotcher, poor soul, lay helpless as a child; but after her wrath had expended itself a little, he raised himself slowly upon his elbows, and said:

"Look here, Shusan—I tell you what is, Shusan; you've scrashed my faish, and pulled my hair, and kicked me, in my own housh, and if you do anyshing more, you'll—you'll roush the Bri'sh Lion!"[270]

"Shut up, you fuddled old idiot," roared his spouse, "and pack off to bed, and if ever I catch you going to the Axe and Anchor in Craig Street[271] again, I'll break every bone in your body."

Thus was Blotcher finally put to bed, and, with the exception of occasional groans, distinctly heard all over the house, peace and quiet once more reigned in No.——, Bleury Street.

Chapter II.

From the first day on which I saw Charlie Chatterton, I took quite a fancy to him; he appeared to be a light-hearted, easy-going sort of fellow, decidedly good looking, and altogether of a presentable sort. But it was not until after we begun to room together, that I learned much of his history, or found out his various peculiarities and little foibles. Not that he was by any means reserved—quite the reverse. One very cold evening, at the beginning of this month, whilst we were sitting together over the stove, Charlie took his meerschaum from his mouth, and after expelling a prodigious volume of smoke he said to me:—

"Well, Smith."

[269] The correct expression is, of course, "put a period to his existence."

[270] In the 19th century, the figure of the "British Lion" (which no foe would want to "rouse") was being pushed forward as the embodiment of British belligerence and a counterpart to the more easygoing John Bull.

[271] Today, Rue Saint-Antoine, separating today Downtown Montreal from Old Montreal.

"Smythe," I said.—"S-m-y-t-h-e, Smythe's my name, and I beg that you will remember this in future, as I am very particular on this point."

"All right, old fellow; I'll try not to make that mistake again. Well, Smythe, I've been thinking that since we have managed to tumble together in this sort of way, and are likely to be chums for the winter, at least, the sooner we get acquainted with each other the better. For my own part, I have not much to relate. You already know that I come from London, Ont.[272] Before I left home, the governor[273] was everlastingly down upon me for my want of business habits, and nothing would satisfy him short of my going to Montreal, to get what he was pleased to term "a brushing up." So here I am, a full fledged boarder in the house of Blotcher & Co. I easily obtained a situation, for my bosses do a large account with my father. But I have a most disgustingly small salary; something like midshipman's half pay, you know, Smythe,—nothing a year, and find yourself.[274] But, I dare say, it's as much as I'm worth. However, I manage to keep things straight at home with the old lady, who, every now and again, pops a ten dollar bill into her letters, so that one way and another I manage to get along pretty comfortably. She's one of the right sort, Smythe, and I'm sure you'd like her,—at least, I know *I* do.—Just shove another piece of wood into the stove—it's awful cold; there, that's a good fellow. By-the-way, the governor gave me no end of introductory letters to some of the big wigs here, which he said I was to be sure to deliver. Here they are,"—taking out his pocket-book and counting them—"one, two, three, four, five.—Now, as I have been in Montreal five weeks already, I think it is time I should be looking some of them up. Well, here goes for No. 1, to Donald Claymore, Esq., No,——, Beaver Hall Square.[275] That's rather a fashionable sort of place, isn't it, Smythe?"

"Yes," said I, "it is, and I can tell you—you must be on your p's and q's if you mean to put in an appearance there."

[272] At the time, London, Ontario, which was incorporated as a city in 1855, had a population of about 18,000.

[273] Nineteenth-century slang term for one's father.

[274] A expression several times repeated in 19th-century literature, its origin being probably in "The Reefer's Tale" (later republished as "The Modern Munchausen") by the pseudonymous Peregrine Reedpen.

[275] A very fashionable address at the time. In the 1980s, Beaver Hall Square was first truncated with the enlargement of the René-Lévesque Boulevard, and then renamed Place-du-Frère-André.

"Any nice girls, Smythe?"

"Of course there are," said I. "Why, man, Fanny Claymore is the belle of the city."

"You don't say so?"

"I do say so," said I, "and I mean it, too. And what's more, I can tell you, he'll be a lucky fellow who gets her; for, besides her good looks, she is a most amiable creature, I'm told, and the old gentleman, her father, is reported to be highly metallic.[276] You must have seen her often in the carriage in St. James Street,[277] though you did not know her."

St James Street, Montreal, 1872

"Well, well, I'll look them up some day soon," said Charlie; "and now, Smythe," said he, "it's your turn to unfold your tale, so out with it, and pass the tobacco."

"Well, it won't take long to do either," said I. "Smythe, Fitz Smythe's my full name, though I've dropped the Fitz since coming here. I belong to a very old family, the Smythes of Smythe Hall, Co. Wicklow, in Ireland. My father, of whom you may have heard, was for many years Colonel of the —th Hussars; but is now retired on half pay, and as there is a large family of us, and my father's estates are very much embarrassed, I have been forced to shift for myself. For three years I remained in Dublin, hoping, through his influence with the Lord Lieutenant, to procure some government

[276] Slang for rich ("metal" was slang for money).

[277] Today, Rue Saint-Jacques. At the time, Little Saint-James Street (see note 262) ran east from Place d'Armes (see note 213), while Great Saint-James Street ran west.

appointment, or failing this, that something would turn up. In these expectations, however, I was disappointed, and both my patience and funds becoming exhausted, I resolved to pack up my all, which did not amount to much, and with what little assistance I could get from my father, try Canada for it. And although you see me here, in the humble capacity of a clerk in the iron store of Crowbar & Hatchett, there is one thing I'm determined never to forget, and that is, that I am a gentleman. No, Charlie, I shall never forget that. None of your saloon bars, gin slings, or other liquid abominations for me. And if you are a wise man you'll do the same, and I have no doubt that we shall manage to knock out as much fun and rational amusement together as will enable us to pass the winter very agreeably. But there's the supper bell—I don't know how you feel, but I'm dreadfully peckish."

Chapter III.

My conversation with Charlie respecting the Beaver Hall people, appeared to have made a deep impression upon his mind; for I observed a marked difference in his deportment when together of an evening. He smoked furiously, though generally in silence, appeared moody and indisposed for conversation upon topics which formerly interested him; and when I endeavoured to lead off upon any topic, all that I could get out of him was an occasional ah—yes, or no. This was so different from the previous state of things between us, that I resolved to have the matter cleared up in some way or other; and having a shrewd idea of the tack upon which he had gone,[278] I said to him in an off-hand kind of way:

"What a beautiful place this Montreal is, especially in the neighbourhoods of St. Catherine Street[279] and Beaver Hall Square." I felt certain that the mention of this last named place would elicit something from him; nor was I mistaken, for it seemed to act like a charm upon Charlie.

[278] To go upon a tack, an expression meaning to take a certain approach (especially a completely new one).

[279] The main thoroughfare in Montreal.

"Oh, yes," he said, "it is a charming place. I have walked all round it several times lately. By-the-way, Smythe, did you say Fanny Claymore was fair or dark?"

I replied that I had no recollection of having said that she was either, but that if it would afford him any comfort to know, she was fair, exceedingly fair, in every sense of the term.

"By Jove!" said he, "it must have been her then whom I saw at the window. I had my letter of introduction in my pocket, but could not get up sufficient courage to go in and deliver it. I must do it, however; for I have had a letter from my father, in which he says that he has learned, in course of correspondence with Mr. Claymore, that I had not made my appearance either at his house or at his store; and that he was much surprised at my not having done so."

"You should call at once, by all means, Charlie," said I, "as from all that I have heard of the Claymores, they are very nice homely people, and I think you may fairly reckon upon meeting with a very cordial reception. I would give a thousand dollars, my boy, to be in your shoes, but no such luck is at all likely to come my way."

Now I must tell you that amongst the many discoveries I had made of Charlie's peculiarities since our associating together, I had remarked in him a highly nervous temperament, together with a strong tendency to spooneyism;[280] and that anything in the shape of a lady's bonnet, with a pretty face in it, was sure to set his heart in a flutter. So that it was not without some misgivings that I looked forward to what might be the result to him of his introduction to the Claymores. The following day he had fixed for the delivery of his introductory letter at Beaver Hall Square. "There is" (says Shakespeare) "a tide in the affairs of men which, taken at the flood, leads on to fortune."[281] And who is there amongst us who cannot look back to some such turning point in his life. This was Charlie's, and how he availed himself of it the sequel will show.

Mr. Claymore was, as might be supposed, absent in the city when Charlie called at the Square, the following day. The carriage was at the door, and Mrs. C. stood ready dressed in the hall, waiting for Fanny, who was to accompany her on a drive. This was awkward for Charlie, who had prepared a very neat and elegant

[280] See note 246. While "spooney" was an early-19th-century creation, "spooneyism" was even more recent.

[281] In *Julius Caesar* (IV, iii, 216-217).

speech for the occasion, not one syllable of which could he now remember. So, fumbling nervously in his pockets for his letter, which, to his utter dismay, he found he had left behind; with a face of the deepest crimson, and a voice choking with emotion, he walked or rather sidled up to Mrs. Claymore, and stammered out, "I beg your pardon, mum, but I'm the young man from London."

"Oh! you are, are you?" said she, "and pray, what brings you here at this particular time? Thomas," addressing the footman, "show this young man down to the kitchen. I shall return in about a couple of hours, when I shall talk to him."

"Step this way, my good fellow," said Thomas, trying to look as important as possible. But Charlie's troubles were not at an end; for although there was no lion in his path, sure enough there was a favorite Scotch terrier waiting for his young mistress's appearance, to accompany her in the carriage, and down went Charlie's foot upon his tail, whereupon the brute set up such a howling as brought Miss Fanny down at the double quick.

"Poor Sancho, poor fellow, and did that stupid clodpole tread upon you, poor,—good doggie. Mamma," said Fanny, "is that the young man you expected from London, whom I saw go down stairs just now?"

"Well, I suppose so, my dear," said Mrs. C.; "he says he's from London, so I presume it is he; but, as you know, I cannot spare time to talk to him at present. I have sent him down stairs; he can wait until we return."

"Yes, certainly," replied Fanny, "and serves him right, for treading on Sancho. I always thought these English servants were particularly sharp, but that young man seems to be a regular clown. I fear he will never do to wait at table, mamma."

Meanwhile, Mrs. Claymore, Fanny and Sancho, stopped into the carriage, and poor Charlie found himself sitting on a wooden chair by the side of the kitchen stove.

"So you're the cove[282] wot's come to look after the place, are you?" said Thomas.

"What place?" said Charlie, having somewhat recovered himself, and beginning to feel nettled.

"Oh! come now, none of yer gammon,[283] young man; you can't play off that game on me, my boy. Have a glass o' beer and

[282] British slang for fellow.

[283] Nonsense.

look pleasant. Cookie, have you any cold mutton to give us? We always takes our luncheon at this time, you know, and a jolly good 'un, too. The Hemperor and Hempress is generally hout at this time hevery day, so don't be frightened. You can peg away[284] as hard as you like for the next two hours, if you like. There's no one comes at this time o' day except the bobbie on his beat. But if you expect to get this situation you've made a mess of it, to start with, let me tell you, young man. Why, bless you, you might as well have knocked the young missus herself down, as have tramped on the tail of that vile whelp. I've got the sack myself for something of the same sort; but it's a long story and I'll tell you all about it some other time. Take off your beer, man. Why, you're not eating a bit. And so you've just come from London, have you? I'm blowed if I would have thought so from yer haccent. My last guv'nor was Sir Horace Hunter, Baronet. He was a good 'un, he was. We came out here with the Guards,[285] and I left him through some absurd misunderstanding about a diamond ring, which, somehow or another, went a-missing, and couldn't be found. I might have remained with this here family long enough, but for that cursed terrier. But I doubt you won't like this place, if you have been
accustomed to a nobleman's family."

"I doubt either you or I have made some great mistake," said Charlie, looking mournfully into his glass, which stood before him untouched.

"Not a bit of it," said Thomas, "it's Molson's best.[286] But if you prefer 'arf an' 'arf you can 'ave it hall the same. Cookie, hand us out a bottle o' stout. Don't let us do the shabby thing by our friend."

"No, no," said Charlie, getting very excited. "Why, man, I never was in service in my life, and don't want any situation, and if you will just step upstairs with me to the dining room for a minute, I'll explain."

"Explain the d——l," roared Thomas; "if you ain't been in service and don't want no situation, what in the dickens are you, and what brings you here? You've come to the wrong shop, my

[284] Slang for "work at it, work steadily;" also "dig in, eat."

[285] The Canadian Grenadier Guards, which had already had a long history, but whose ranks were swollen in 1862, during the American Civil War.

[286] Molson's Brewery was established in Montreal in 1786. Its headquarters were at the time this story was published (and still are today), on St. Mary Street (Notre-Dame Est).

chicken, if you think you'll trap me into any burglary business. No, no, my lad, 'not for Joseph.'"[287]

It was in vain that Charlie endeavoured to convince him that he had no burglarious intentions. Thomas was inexorable, and commenced shouldering him rather roughly to the door.

"I'll call and see Mr. Claymore myself," said Charlie. "Yes, I'll call at seven o'clock this very evening, and inform him of the manner in which you have used me."

"Did you say that seven o'clock was the hour," said Thomas, very sarcastically, "at which we were again to be favored with your company, young man?"

"Yes, I said seven o'clock; are you deaf, sir?" said Charlie.

"All right," replied Thomas; "then I'll take good care to have all the silver plate locked up at that time." As Thomas continued standing at the door, looking savagely after him, Charlie, expecting every moment that he would call out "police," took to his heels, and never stopped until he found himself once more safe within the four walls of Blotcher's house.

1868

Chapter IV.

When Charlie appeared at the supper table that evening, I noticed that he looked unusually cross and out of sorts, and when I asked him how he had found all his friends at Beaver Hall Square, and particularly how he liked Fanny, he looked absolutely savage.

"Don't talk to me, Smythe," he finally said. "I feel very unwell to-night, and intend going early to bed," which I advised him to do at once, in the belief that a good night's rest was all he required to set him to rights. There was no social pipe or chat that night, and it was the first really unpleasant evening I spent with him since I had formed his acquaintance. What on earth could be the matter with him, I was utterly unable to imagine. I thought of all sorts of possible and impossible causes for his altered mood. Could he have been such an idiot as to have rushed into a declaration of love to Fanny, upon the strength of his introductory letter, and

[287] An expression of strong refusal, originating in a popular song from the 1860s.

met with such a reception as any sane man might have expected? Nothing short of some such mad proceeding on his part seemed adequate to account for his thoroughly woebegone and dejected looks. It was not, however, until several days after, that I learned all the particulars of his unfortunate escapade, and I am free to confess that the source from which I derived my information was none other than our servant Betsy, who, having at one time been a fellow servant with the cook at Beaver Hall Square, had had the whole affair communicated to her, upon the express understanding that she wasn't "to say nothing to nobody about it." I could scarcely refrain from laughing while Betsy was telling me of it; but when she further informed me that the cook had rated Thomas soundly for what she considered his harsh treatment of Charlie, on account of her being herself in want of a young man, and having made up her mind that Charlie would suit her to a T, I could no longer control myself, and tears of laughter rolled over my cheeks. From the sublime to the ridiculous there is but a step, and this step Charlie had taken with a vengeance. How he was to escape from the very awkward position in which he had placed himself, was to me by no means clear. Something, however, must be done. So I set my brains to work forthwith to find out what that something was to be, and how it was to be gone about without wounding poor Charlie's already lacerated feelings. With the knowledge I possessed of his highly nervous and excitable temperament, and of the difficulty of ministering to a mind diseased, I determined, after due reflection, to go gently about the matter. So, having first taken from Betsy a pledge of solemn silence to every one else on the subject, I proceeded up stairs to our room, where I found my poor fellow-boarder lying upon his face across his bed. He had scarcely uttered a word to me from that unfortunate day, and even now took no notice of my entrance.

"Charlie, Charlie," said I, "get up, man—what's the good of lying there. Here's a letter for you."

"Who is it from?" said he.

"Well," I said, "since you have asked me such a ridiculous question, all that I can say is that it appears to be from some acquaintance of yours in town, though I would not be quite sure of that either, as the postmark is very illegible."

"Oh, from some one in town you think, is it?" he said, beginning to look up. "Who can it be from? Let me have a look at it, Smythe;" and a minute more found him deeply engrossed in what appeared to be a very business-like letter, the contents of which, as he proceeded with it, I could almost read in his face.

"Come, don't keep all the fun to yourself," said I, "tell us all about it. It contains no bad news, at all events, if I may judge from your looks." So he at once proceeded to read it to me.

No.——, St. Francois Xavier Street,[288]

December, 1868.

"MY DEAR SIR,

Having ascertained from Mrs. Claymore that a person had called at my house, stating that he had come from London; and suspecting from the correspondence I have lately had with your father, who furnished me with your address, that this person may have been none other than yourself, I beg you will do me the favor to call upon me, at the above address, when I will explain to you the nature of the circumstances which led to your meeting with such a reception as I understand you then met with.

I am,

Yours very truly,

DUNCAN CLAYMORE."

No great persuasion was necessary to induce Charlie at once to comply with this request. And, truth to tell, I was as anxious to get the matter set at rest as himself; for of late his society had been far from agreeable. He called accordingly on Mr. Claymore, who received him most cordially at his place of business, and explained to him how that, having discharged his present footman, he had requested an applicant for the situation who had recently arrived in the city from London, England, to see Mrs. Claymore, in whose hands he generally left all such domestic matters—and that they all regretted exceedingly the unfortunate mistake which had taken place. Mr. Claymore wound up by inviting Charlie to dinner on the following Friday, at six o'clock; and so he trotted home as happy as a sand boy.[289]

That dinner party was destined to be a memorable event in Charlie's life. Friday came, and so far Charlie was equal to the

[288] Rue Saint-François-Xavier in Old Montreal, one of the oldest streets in the city.

[289] There was a common expression about being "as happy (or jolly) as sand-boys." Sand-boys (who were usually adult men) sold sand to pubs, which used it to cover their floors; they were often paid in alcohol, hence the idea that they were always merry.

occasion; for a good sized parcel had arrived for him which the label outside showed beyond a doubt to be for Charles Chatterton, Esq., from the fashionable clothing establishment of Dressem & Snip, in Notre Dame Street, and which, on being opened by him on his return from business, proved to contain a very handsome dress suit, a satin necktie, and a pair of lavender kids.[290]

"Why, Charlie, you look quite killing," said I to him, when he had finished dressing; "positively you are quite irresistible, and if you play your cards well, I shall expect to see a case in-*fanny*-ti-cide in the papers to-morrow! Go in and win, my boy; 'faint heart never won fair lay,' you know." So Charlie jumped into the cab which was waiting for him, and was duly deposited at Mr. Claymore's door.

"What name, sir?" said Thomas, looking very hard at Charlie.

"Mr. Chatterton," replied Charlie, in a somewhat low tone of voice.

"Mr. Chatterbox," roared the flunky, as he opened the door and ushered Charlie into the drawing-room, amidst an ill suppressed titter from the assembled guests.

Thomas, as has been already stated, had received notice to leave, and this was not the only mistake of the kind he made during the evening, whether intentional or not, I cannot say. But certain it is that a worthy couple, a gentleman and his wife, the latter a stout elderly lady, who, in proceeding up stairs, had her dress trodden on by her husband, forcing from her the angry exclamation—"Lor', man, Davie, get off my dress," were, from this circumstance, announced by Thomas as "Lord and Lady Davie." These, and the following particulars, I obtained from Charlie upon his return, on the distinct understanding that I was not to chaff[291] him about it. I will not, however, recount all his misadventures on that occasion. Suffice it to say that he returned home that evening a regular dried up dry-goods man—in short, a complete *Fanny*-tic. We sat up that night talking until it was very late, or, I should say, early; for it was nearly one o'clock ere we retired to bed, and in course of our conversation, I learned that Charlie had made most praiseworthy attempts to render himself agreeable to the family. On dinner being announced, Charlie could scarcely believe his ears when Mr. Claymore stepped up to him with the request that he would take

[290] Very fashionable kid gloves, the colour of lavender. Notre-Dame Street, where the fictional store is located, is one of the oldest and longest streets in the city. The best-known portion of it runs through Old Montreal.
[291] Slang term for "tease."

Fanny down stairs.—Besides his devotions to Fanny during the evening, he was also most lavish in his attentions to Sancho, on the principle of "love me, love my dog." But Sancho really was a most loveable brute, and the perfect picture of a Sky terrier,[292] with a coat like a door mat. By dint of coaxing, Charlie managed to get him upon his knee, for Sancho seemed to remember their last meeting, and to entertain a wholesome dread of him. Whilst talking to Fanny, Charlie commenced patting Sancho upon what he believed to be his head, and commenting eulogistically upon the beauty of his eyes, &c., and it was not until he was brought up in the midst of his *tete-a-tete* by a loud laugh from Fanny, which she was unable to suppress, that he perceived he had made a mistake, and had been lavishing his encomiums upon the creature's tail—a tail of which he now began to think he was never to hear the end; but Fanny's ready wit came to his rescue, and soon put him again at his ease.

Chapter V.

Matters continued to move on in the ordinary way at Blotcher's, nothing occurring amongst us in any way worthy of notice, with the exception of Blotcher's coming home occasionally in an obfusticated state,[293] and the reproduction of the usual kitchen pantomime. On one occasion, however, he fell on the ice and broke his leg, which lamed him for life. As for Charlie, he became each day more and more particular in matters relating to his personal appearance. The growth of his moustache, and the parting of his back hair were causes of particular solicitude to him. He had also taken to writing amorous ditties, several of which he submitted to me for my opinion, and all of which I advised him to put into the fire as speedily as possible. One day, after dinner, he said to me, "I say, Smythe, what's the correct thing for a fellow to say when he intends to pop the question?"

"Well," said I, "Charlie, this is really too much of a good thing. You don't mean to tell me you have already arrived at this stage of the proceedings?"

[292] Actually, Skye terrier (from the Isle of Skye, in Scotland), a very shaggy type of terrier and one of Queen Victoria's favourite breeds.
[293] Slang for drunk (variant of "obfuscated").

"No, no," he said, "I merely want to know, in case of accidents. You know a fellow never knows what may happen; so it is always as well to be prepared."

"I fear, then, you must take your preparatory lesson from some one else," said I, "for I have resolved never again to interfere in such matters. You remember Duclois, the young French Canadian, to whom I introduced you some time ago. Well, he came once to me with the same request as you now make, telling me that he was paying his addresses to a very pretty young English girl; but, being very deficient in his knowledge of our language, he was quite at a loss what to say to her. Without thinking much about it, and as much to get rid of the subject as anything else, I said to him: 'Oh, just say to her, that if you were her guardian angel, you would watch over her always.' The poor fellow seemed delighted. 'Oh!' said he, 'that ees gode, 'tees ver' mooch gode.—I directly go.' So off he went instanter; and what do you think I afterwards learned he said to her? I'm sure you would never guess. Getting down upon his knees before his lady love, he exclaimed: 'Oh! Madame, eef I was your angel in de gardain, I would wash you always ovare.' No, no, Charlie, I will run no such risk with you. But let me merely say, that many who cannot summon the courage to face up, *viva voce*,[294] on such occasions, do so by letter, either in prose, or in verse; though generally in the former."

"Oh! aw," said Charlie, "I'm no great hand at letter writing, but I *can* do something in the poetical way, though *you* don't seem to think so, but I will prove it to you before you are a day older."

And sure enough he kept his word, in a way, for about two o'clock the following morning, I was awakened from a profound sleep by his shouting in the room, "Oh! I've got it, I've got it."

"Well, then, I hope you'll keep it," said I, "for the beggar has been troubling me all night."

"No, no," said he, "that's not what I mean. I've got some ideas in my head."

"I'm exceedingly glad to hear it," I replied, "for I was not aware of the fact before."

"Have you got a mucifer latch, Smythe?"

"If it is a lucifer match you want,[295] you had better say so at once; you will find some in my coat pocket;" and having thrown

[294] Latin for "out loud."

[295] "Lucifer matches" (sometimes simply "lucifers") were a famous (though faulty) type of match. The name survived and was long used as a common term for matches even though the original lucifers had been off the market since the late 1830s.

on his overcoat, he lit the lamp and proceeded to secure his grand ideas on paper. These he showed me in the morning, in the form of a couple of verses which appeared to be the production of a lunatic rather than of a sane person. They ran as follows:—

"I dreamt of thee, dear Fanny, last night,
As the lady whom I adore,
And these few lines to thee to indite,
I jumped out of bed on the floor.

Oh! Fanny dear, oh! Fanny dear,
I vow I'll love thee ever,
And for thy sake, I greatly fear
I've lost my heart and liver."

Through my strict supervision and carefulness to prevent the dispatch of these, and indeed all such like productions, and with as few contretemps as might be expected in the case of a nervous man like Charlie, matters continued to progress favorably at Beaver Hall Square. Charlie was now in his twenty-first year, and the sly dog had never told me that on attaining his majority he was to come into possession of a legacy of forty thousand dollars left him by an uncle who had been an indigo planter in India. But old Claymore knew this well, so that when Charlie actually did "pop the question" to Fanny, and was referred by her to papa, he found the course clear, with nothing to do but go in and win. At the marriage I acted as groomsman. Charlie and his beautiful bride went on a tour to Niagara Falls and the States; and on their return the young couple took up their residence at the east end of St. Catherine Street, and many a time do I look in upon them of an evening, when Charlie and I sometimes get together in his sanctum to do a weed.[296] Then do we fight our battles o'er again, and have many a hearty laugh over our sayings and doings in No.—— Bleury Street.

I have now only to add, that shortly after the time when Blotcher slipped on the ice, he slept with his fathers, and Mrs. B—— appointed herself regent until Blotcher the second should reign in his stead.

[296] Nineteenth-century slang for tobacco in general or for a cigar.

Emma Naomi Crawford

Buggins' Mare

(1873)

The author: Emma Naomi Crawford was one of many children born to an Irish physician, Stephen Dennis Crawford, from Donnybrook, Dublin, and his wife Sidney, from County Cork. Her better-known sister, Isabella Valancy, was born in Donnybrook in December 1846. The Crawfords immigrated first to the United States, and Emma Naomi (she was called Naomi by her family) was born in Wisconsin on 8 July 1852. However, they went back to Ireland and a few years later decided to immigrate one more time. They arrived in Upper Canada in 1857 and settled in the new community of Paisley, Ontario. With not enough patients, facing suspicions of financial irregularities, and battling his own alcoholism, Stephen Crawford took his family to Lakeview in 1861. Here, they met Susanna Moodie and Catharine Parr Traill, and Isabella became friends with Traill's daughter, Katie. In 1869, they relocated to Peterborough, but the family was still unable to escape poverty and illness. In 1875, when Stephen Crawford died, he was survived only by his wife, two daughters (Isabella and Naomi), and one son (Stephen Walter), who had left home and was to spend the rest of his life in the Algoma district of Ontario. The two sisters began writing for the periodical press to make ends meet, but Naomi died of consumption on 20 January 1876, in Peterborough, Ontario. Isabella Valancy lived until 12 February 1887, publishing poetry and novels and leaving behind many unpublished manuscripts. Though she died in poverty, she was later recognised as one of the greatest Canadian poets of the nineteenth century.

The text: The only time it was published before was in *The Favorite* 1: 9 (8 March 1873), 130. It was signed with her full name, followed by "of Peterboro', Ont."

Further reading: Alice Crawford. "New Information about Isabella Valancy Crawford and Her Family." *Canadian Poetry* 69 (Fall/Winter 2011), 87-88.

Buggins was extremely proud of her, and she undoubtedly was, as his friend and confident, Spunge, had remarked when advising her purchase, "a nice little beast." She was a bright sorrel in color, a fast trotter by nature, and by name "Two-Forty."[297] As I have said, Buggins was very proud of her. She had won races for him, to celebrate which triumphs champagne suppers to her owner's entire acquaintance seemed some way indispensable, and sometimes lost them. She had ruined two of three former owners,—the first a young farmer, with, perhaps, more spirit than discretion, her third birthday being celebrated by the execution of a mortgage on his property, and who speedily went to destruction in a racing cutter; the second, a widow lady of business habits, who bought her as a speculation, and sold her at a handsome profit to the third, a sporting barber, who never was known to pay any attention to business after her purchase, until one morning when, the sheriff having paid a not quite unexpected visit the day before, he was found with one of his long-idle razors in his hand,
1873 and a corresponding gash in his throat.

Naturally, after that pleasing occurrence, "Two-Forty" went up in sporting circles with a bound. The animal which could ruin two men in three years was a prize to be eagerly sought for by all young fellows of spirit. Every one went to see her. Chubb (the richest man in Cackleford, a lawyer, and a judge of horseflesh) said he would give the safest mortgage in his possession for her, she had a largely-attended reception every morning, the small boys betted largely as to her probable purchaser, the local poet wrote some stanzas in her honor, and finally, at her sale by auction, and after a brisk competition, Buggins became her owner, and should have been a happy man.

But he wasn't.

True, he had, figuratively speaking, snatched her from the very claws of Chubb, whom he hated; for did not Mr. Archer, Kitty's

[297] "Two-forty (on a plank road)" was slang for someone really fast. The expression came from the sport of *trotting* (today known as harness racing), in which one horse pulls a two-wheeled cart occupied by the driver, either at a pace or at a trot. More exactly, it came from the exploits of Top Gallant, the first horse who ran the mile in 2:40 minutes. At the time Crawford was writing, the expression was still popular, though the record had been broken several times, and the record holder was Flora Temple (1845-1877), the so-called "Queen of the Turf," with 2 minutes and 19 ¾ seconds.

father, approve highly of Chubb as a suitor for that bewitching damsel, and as highly disapprove of him, Buggins, in the same position? True, his friends had spoken of him—particularly Spunge, who soon after borrowed ten dollars from him—as a "sharp fellow" and a "knowing rascal." But he was not happy.

He bought a racing cutter, which was usually on loan, also a large sleigh, which was ditto. He occasionally was allowed by "Jim," the gentleman who cared for the precious animal, to take a seat in the vehicle under which she took exercise, and enjoyed himself immensely, or thought he did, which was very much the same thing. He paid her a daily visit, under the protection of "Jim," also, and, watched by him with a derisive smile, stroked her arched neck, and retreated swiftly towards the door, sometimes leaving a portion of his coat-collar between her strong white teeth, invariably followed by her dainty heels in close proximity to his head.

Buggins had but two cares, the mare and Mr. Chubb, and which was the heavier and more carking[298] it would have been difficult to decide. He was engaged (privately) to Kitty Archer, and Chubb wished to be (publicly). He was only well off, Chubb was rich. Mr. Archer spoke of Chubb as a "fellow who had some go in him," and of himself, Buggins, as "that sap-headed young fool, Buggins."

Everything taken into consideration, this was a trying state of affairs. He spent hours daily in pondering over these unfortunate circumstances. He was really fond of Kitty, and Kitty said she was fond of him. Chubb paid Kitty every attention, escorted her everywhere, worshipped publicly and privately at her shrine, made her presents which, by reason of their richness, were seriously detrimental to the peace of mind of her dearest friends, and made himself agreeable to her father, who was about his own age, while Buggins could do little but gaze admiringly at her, write her frantic notes (which were, as a rule, intercepted by her father), and make himself gloomily conspicuous wherever they met. How he had found courage at any time to propose to her he could not tell, nor had he the least idea of how and when their rather unsatisfactory engagement might end.

At last a crisis arrived.

On New Year's Eve he sat alone in his apartment at Mrs. Smiler's residence, which combined a perfectly Spartan simplicity

[298] Burdensome, troublesome (archaic).

of arrangement with "the comforts of a real English home" (see advertisement). He was reading a letter, written on the regulation pink paper, and directed to "Charlemagne Buggins, Esq." His round blue eyes dilated with horror and astonishment as he read:

"Dear Charlie,

"I'm just distracted. Only think! that horrible Chubb has proposed to me, and pa, the spiteful old tyrant, has accepted him! We are to be married in three weeks, and I'm sure I don't know what to do. I'm going to the picnic ball at Southbridge to-night, and as Chubb's away on business, pa gave me leave to go with the Harris girls. I'll be waiting at the corner next the old church at half-past seven, and you may bring a cutter there and drive me to Southbridge. I want to talk things over with you.

"Kitty.

"P.S.—I'll never marry Chubb."

Buggins fell into profound thought, a very unusual circumstance with him, and for some time sat gazing absently into the fire. At length he rose, burned this note, and, putting on his overcoat, and slouching his cap guiltily over his eyes, departed from the roof of Smiler, and betook himself "down town."

* * * * * * *

"You must be awfully clever, Charlie," said Miss Archer admiringly, "and I'm sure no one would think so to look at you."

This candid speech was made as they flew, Buggins and she, along the quiet country road leading to Southbridge. They were seated in his racing cutter, and were drawn by "Two-Forty."

"I had some trouble in getting the mare," said Buggins, glancing retrospectively at that animal, who was scudding along with a too evident forgetfulness of the cutter and its occupants. "Jim wouldn't let me have her, so I had to give him a dollar and send him down town, and, as soon as he was gone, I got a boy who was hanging round to help me, and between us we got her harnessed, and here we are."

"Two-Forty" was in high spirits, so lively, in fact, that at an early stage of their drive Buggins had seen the advisability of "giving her her head," and now, with the reins hanging in graceful festoons over the dash-board, they careered along, Buggins grasping the side of the cutter with one hand and Kitty with the other.

Buggins was cheerful, exultant, with a proud consciousness of having outwitted the tyrant Archer. He had Kitty by his side, a marriage license in his pocket, and while Mr. Archer read the evening paper, and thought of the absent Chubb, they were speeding towards the residence of his friend, the Rev. Thomas Jolly, at Southbridge, as fast as "Two-Forty" could take them.

They didn't talk much, the pace was too rapid for that, but Charlie looked at Kitty in silent delight, and Kitty looked at Charlie, and drew comparisons between him and Chubb not to Chubb's advantage.

About a mile further on, the steeple of the church over which the Rev. Thomas ruled as pastor glittered in the moonlight, and Kitty said tremulously:

"Pa and Chubb will storm fearfully, but I'm not a bit frightened, for they can't unmarry us, can they, Charlie, though I'm not of age?"

"Of course not!" said Charlie, "but——"

Further remark was impossible. Round a curve in the road dashed a cutter drawn by a white horse, and driven by a fur-coated gentleman. "Two-Forty's" nerves were delicate, and the sudden appearance of this equipage rather disturbed her. She likewise was fond of a race. She took in the situation at a glance. There was a rival trotter to beat, a clear road to do it in, and a gentleman incapable of offering a successful resistance to her plans holding the reins. She paused, she snorted, she turned, and, with ears laid back, retraced her steps hastily. No low-bred white horse should pass "Two-Forty."

Buggins tightened the reins, Miss Archer screamed, "Two-Forty" started at a maddening pace back to Cackleford. Buggins shouted, Miss Archer wept, faster and faster went "Two-Forty," pursued by the white horse.

On they went for about a mile. Every moment brought them nearer danger and Cackleford, every moment brought them farther from the Rev. Thomas Jolly and happiness! Again "Two-Forty" saw something ahead, again she paused, only to start off with a bound, as she heard the bells jingling behind her.

Buggins leant forward, trying to catch a glimpse of the approaching sleigh. It was a large double one, coming furiously on, and at the same moment he saw with horror that the road just ahead narrowed considerably, and that an immense drift on one side and a fence on the other made it almost an impossibility that they could pass. If he could only turn the mare, they might pass the pursuing cutter!

He shouted frantically at "Two-Forty," and tugged at the reins. "Two-Forty" replied with her heels, injuring the dash-board beyond repair in so doing. The fur-coated gentleman, now about ten yards behind, shouted, "Hi! take care there!" in a voice familiar to Buggins.

It was too late. There was a crash, a snort from "Two-Forty," a shout from the occupant of the sleigh, a piercing scream from Kitty, and Buggins rose bodily in the air. He came down, however, with even more haste, and, unobtrusively entering the drift, was enabled to observe from its cool recesses the effect of the unexpected meeting upon the rest.

On the road lay a confused mass of struggling horses, broken sleighs and gentlemen, and by the fence lay a smaller mass, very quiet, supposed by Buggins to be Kitty. The white horse was standing quietly by, while its master in a frenzied manner was rushing to and fro; and far away, on the road to Cackleford, "Two-Forty" was careering along, apparently in the best health and spirits.

"Is that Chubb?" shouted a voice from under the cutter. "Come and help me out, can't you?"

"Why it's Archer!" cried he of the fur-coat, and dashed madly into the struggling heap, returning triumphantly, after a sharp tussle with the cutter, with Mr. Archer, very angry, very much shaken, and quite breathless.

"Are you hurt, sir?" enquired the false-hearted Chubb anxiously, helping the horses to their feet, and very much excited.

"No!" said Mr. Archer, "Is that the fool who ran into us by the fence there?"

Chubb strolled leisurely towards the fence, and stooped to examine the heap.

"It's a woman!" he exclaimed, and then, as he raised the heap in his arms, "Good heavens! it's Kitty!"

"Kitty!" cried Mr. Archer. "Why she ran off with Buggins to be married, and I'm after them to stop it. It can't be Kitty!"

But it was! She had fainted, and after ten minutes spent in rubbing her hands in snow, she opened her eyes, to find herself in her father's sleigh, that gentleman ejaculating softly though profanely over Buggins, and Chubb turning the horses toward Cackleford.

Buggins trembled. Kitty was lost to him forever, and he would be left to extricate himself from the drift. Should he speak? Should he take help from the hand of Chubb?

"Oh, pa!" exclaimed Kitty, as Mr. Archer tucked the robes carefully round her shivering little shoulders, "where's Charlie?"

"I'm here!" cried Buggins feebly from the drift.

"Oh, you are, are you?" cried Archer delightedly; "well, stay there, you sneaking young villain!"

"I can't get out!" shouted Buggins, as Chubb, with a cheerful smile, cracked his whip encouragingly to the white horse, which immediately started.

"Don't leave him there, pa!" cried Kitty tearfully.

"Don't be a fool, Kitty!" responded the old gentleman, and then to Buggins, as the horses broke into a swift trot:

"Next time you want to run off with a girl, don't confide in her father's stable-boy, even if he does help to harness your horse! Good-night!"

And Buggins was left alone with his despair, the sleigh-bells jingling merrily in the distance, and the moon shining derisively down upon him.

He never saw Kitty Archer again, but Mr. and Mrs. Chubb return from Europe next week, and life holds nothing for Buggins now.

And "Two-Forty" is again for sale—cheap!

John Arthur Phillips

Thompson's Turkey

(1873)

1873

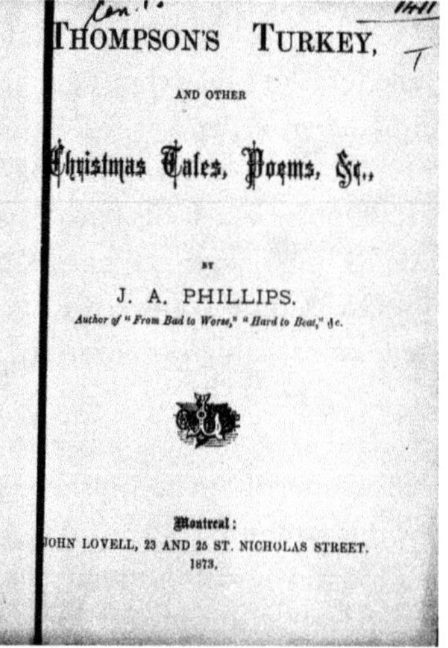

THOMPSON'S TURKEY,

AND OTHER

Christmas Tales, Poems, &c.,

BY

J. A. PHILLIPS.

Author of "From Bad to Worse," "Hard to Beat," &c.

Montreal:

JOHN LOVELL, 23 AND 25 ST. NICHOLAS STREET.

1873.

The author: John Arthur Phillips was born on 25 February 1842 in Liverpool. He was educated in Barbados and became a journalist in New York in January 1865, working with Charles Graham Halpine ("Miles O'Reilly"), editor of the *Citizen.* He moved to Canada in 1870, settling in Montreal, where he joined the staff of the *Montreal Star* and was editor of *The Hearthstone* and *The Favorite*, both weekly literary magazines, helping to launch the careers of the Crawford sisters. In 1873 he returned to the *Star*, until 1875, when he became city editor of the *Sun* and married Ivy Sarah Parson. In 1877 he joined C.R. Tuttle in preparing his *Illustrated History of the Dominion* and worked on it for the next four years. In the meantime, he relocated to Ottawa in 1878, where he became editor of the *Citizen.* He was also the Ottawa correspondent for *Quebec Chronicle* and, for the last 14 years of his life, for *Montreal Gazette.* He was a conservative in politics and was known by fellow journalists as "Captain" or "Cap Phillips." He died on 8 January 1907, in the press room of the House of Commons. At the time of his death, he was also known as the author of the patriotic (pro-British) song "The Flag for Me." He published several volumes of short stories and poetry, including *Thompson's Turkey and Other Christmas Tales* (1873), *Hard to Beat* (1877); *The Ghost of a Dog* (1885); *Out of the Snow and Other Stories* (1886).

The text: First published in Phillips's *Thompson's Turkey and Other Christmas Tales, Poems, &c* (Montreal: John Lovell, 1873), 9-42. It must have appeared in December 1873, since Phillips's preface is dated 1 December 1873. The use of hyphens in compound adjectives (which are sometimes used and sometimes left out in the original text) has been made consistent here.

Chapter I.

How Thompson Got the Turkey

It wasn't Thompson's fault.

I take this the earliest possible opportunity, to give it as my free, candid and disinterested opinion that it wasn't Thompson's fault. I am quite well aware of the fact that there were people before the time who said it was Thompson's fault; I am quite well aware of the fact that there were people at the time who said it was Thompson's fault; I am quite well aware of the fact that there were people after the time who said it was Thompson's fault; I am quite well aware of the fact that there are people who even at the present day maintain that it was Thompson's fault; but I never did believe it was Thompson's fault, and I never will.

The fact is Thompson couldn't help it.

I know very well there were people at the time who said that Thompson could have helped it; I know very well that there were people after the time who said Thompson could have helped it; I know very well there are people now who still assert that Thompson could have helped it; but I never did believe Thompson could help it, and I never will.

And, after all, what was it that people said was Thompson fault; and what was it that people said Thompson could have helped doing?

Why, getting married; that was all!

I never could see, and I never will see that it was Thompson's fault to get married; other people do it, why shouldn't Thompson? I never could see, and I never will see that Thompson could have helped it; other people can't help it, and why should Thompson?

And then everybody wanted to marry Winnie Dumsic, why shouldn't Thompson? But, Winnie—her name was Winnetta, but we always called her Winnie for short—didn't want to marry everybody; she didn't even want to marry me, although I was ready and willing to marry her several times over if necessary; she didn't want to marry old Flailflax, the wealthy linen draper, although he did own a big house on the mountain side,[299] and was reported to have so much money in the bank, that an extra vault had had to be built on purpose to hold it all; she didn't want to marry young Grunter, the pork packer, although he was always as sleek and smooth as if just freshly rubbed with some of his own grease, and his father was said to have left him enough money to pack every pig in Canada, himself included; she didn't want to marry the Rev. Mr. Maypole, the new curate of St. Fashionable's, although he was so upright, and dressed so nicely, and read prayers "beautifully"—so the other girls said—and gave the old women snuff to brace up their nerves—the girls all said that was "so charitable"—and did a thousand and one things which always made unmarried curates so agreeable to the female portion of the congregation of St. Fashionable's; the fact is Winnie wanted to marry Thompson, and she did it.

Young ladies sometimes will do such things, whether their parents like it or not; and, therefore, as Winnie had made up her mind to marry Thompson, she did marry him, and I say it wasn't Thompson's fault, and he couldn't help it.

There were other reasons why Thompson couldn't help it. Winnie Dumsic was one of the sweetest, most lovable little bits of femininity that ever set a poor male mortal crazy; she was so rosy, so joyous, so artless, so natural, so piquant, so winning that nobody could help loving her; I couldn't, how could Thompson?

Then she and Thompson had grown up together from childhood; even when she was a little thing in short frocks and frills round her pantalets nobody could help stealing apples, and cakes, and sweetmeats, and other things for her, and tearing their clothes climbing for flowers to please her, and fighting each other on her account, and wanting to kiss her and being too bashful to do it; I couldn't, and how could Thompson?

She always looked to me like a lump of sugar, and I was not at all astonished when Thompson put her in his cup of life to sweeten it for all time; I wasn't astonished, but everybody else was.

You see this was the way of it. Winnie was rich; old Dumsic, her father, was a large dealer in small-wares, pins and needles and such things, and a good deal of money had stuck to old Dumsic's fingers by the aid of pins and needles and such things. He was a

[299] In other words, a house situated in the Golden Square Mile (see note 261).

proud man, was old Dumsic; very fond of his only child, and very fond of talking of his "connections in the old country"—Rumor said he had been a pot-boy[300] in Dublin in his youthful days, but Rumor might have lied as she very often does; and everybody knows that every Irishman, out of Ireland, is either an Irish king, or the descendant of one. It has often struck me that kings in Ireland must have been very plentiful at some time, and that they must have been amongst the earliest immigrants, which would, of course, account for so many of their descendants being found on this side of the Atlantic; be that as it may, Dumsic was the lineal descendant of an Irish king, so he said, and had a right to be proud, which he was, whether he had the right or not.

Being proud, Dumsic, of course, would not hear of Thompson for a son-in-law, for Thompson was poor; in fact, Thompson was only a clerk in old Dumsic's store, and although Dumsic and Thompson's father had been great friends, and Dumsic himself had been very kind to Thompson since his father's death, still he would not have dreamed of giving Winnie to him.

Nor was poverty his only objection to Thompson; no, that might have been overcome; but it was Thompson's name, that could not be overcome.

You see old Dumsic had studied genealogies and derivations very deeply—that was how he found out that he was the descendant of an Irish king—and he informed Thompson that his name was very plebeian: in fact, old Dumsic went so far as to say that there was no such thing as a Thompson with a p. He argued, and with considerable show of correctness, that the name, as a surname, was derived from the christian name Thomas, and had been originally written Thomas' son, and applied to a younger member of the family as indicating that he was a son of the original Thomas; that on the general adoption of surnames the apostrophe and one s were dropped, and the name written Thomason, which in due course of time had become changed to Thomson, or Tomson; but Thompson—with a p—he looked on as a base impostor of a name, and triumphantly asked "how did the p get in?"

Of course, Thompson did not like to hear his name abused, and retaliated on Dumsic by telling him that his, Dumsic's, name was originally Drumstick, and that the r, t and k had been knocked out of the name at various stages of its transmission from the

[300] A waiter; a boy carrying pots of ale in a public house.

Irish king to the present owner; but that only made Dumsic mad, and when Thompson told him that he loved Winnie, and asked his consent to their union when he was able to support her—for he was a proud fellow, was Thompson, and didn't want to marry Winnie for her money, but because he loved her—old Dumsic poured out all the vials of his wrath, and vowed that if she married Thompson he would cut her off with a farthing, so that the p in her name should not even stand for a penny.

That was a terrible time for Thompson; of course he lost his place in old Dumsic's store; and, of course, old Dumsic forbid his seeing or speaking to Winnie again; and, of course, Winnie and Thompson used to meet each other on the sly and vow eternal constancy and all that sort of thing; and, of course, they used to write to each other every day, and I used to deliver the notes without old Dumsic suspecting me—for he rather liked me and thought I was going to marry Winnie, but Winnie didn't love me and did love Thompson, and although I liked Thompson very well, I didn't care to marry a girl who loved him and didn't love me.

Thompson soon got another place, but it was not as good as the one he had lost, and the chances of matrimony seemed further off than ever; but things are often nearest to us when they seem furthest off. It was summer when old Dumsic discharged Thompson, and the lovers agreed to wait five years for each other; but, somehow as the cold weather came on, and it was not so pleasant waiting in Viger Garden, or Victoria Square[301] to meet each other, both parties suddenly changed their minds, and one morning early in December Thompson entered my office in a very excited manner and asked me to come and see him married.

Thompson and I were always very friendly, although we did love the same girl; it wasn't his fault if Winnie cared for him and not for me, so I couldn't blame Thompson, could I? So I went to see them married, and gave away the bride, I did, and I kissed her next after Thompson, I did; and it made me feel as if a frozen poker had been run down my back when I thought it was the

[301] Both are in the southern part of Downtown Montreal, though almost a mile apart. Victoria Square (which got its name in 1860) is a long public space that looks today (despite the addition of high-rises) quite similar to the way it looked in the mid-1870s. On the other hand, the Viger Garden, famous in the 19th century for its greenhouses and its musical concerts, has been replaced by Viger Square, on the concrete roof of an expressway. The project of its redevelopment has been on the books for a long time.

last time I would ever kiss her. But I didn't let them see that I felt it, and offered to take Winnie's note to her father asking for forgiveness and deliver it in person.

It was as great a refresher to me as a shower bath to see old Dumsic get mad when I told him what had happened; he turned so red in the face I thought he would go off in a fit of apoplexy, and I half wished he would, for I knew he had made a will leaving Winnie his heiress, and if he died right off he would not have time to alter it; but he didn't know enough to die decently, he must live to make himself disagreeable, and so, after a while he recovered himself, and the first things he said was:

"Phillips, you're a fool."

I told him that possibly he might be correct, but I did not think it polite to state it quite so plainly. He did not mind that at all, but repeated the obnoxious expression prefacing the word fool with a very objectionable adjective which made me so angry that for a moment a desperate desire to seize him by the throat, choke him to death, and say he died of apoplexy on hearing the news, came over me; but I thought of the marks I should leave on the neck, of the coroner's jury, of a trial for murder, of a rope and other unpleasant things, and stifling my indignation contented myself with saying "you're another."

But if I stifled my wrath old Dumsic didn't stifle his; he raved terribly, and used shocking bad language for so old a man; he swore he would never forgive Winnie, that he would drive Thompson to despair, and so many more dreadful things, that I was forced to leave him, and the old fool made a new will that same day and took himself off on an express train that night no one knew whither.

Poor Thompson had a hard time of it at first; his salary was small, and Winnie had been accustomed to so many luxuries that it seemed a shame to deprive her of. But they both put their shoulders bravely to the wheel, and it was astonishing how well they got on. Winnie would not hear of boarding, and determined to keep house herself. They got the upper part of a house in a cheap and quiet by-street and it was surprising how nicely and cosily they fitted it up, considering their limited means. Thompson always used to say that he could never have done it but for the timely aid of a kind friend; but Thompson, although a good fellow, is rather foolish on some subjects, and sometimes talks about things that he ought not to speak of to everybody.

How happy they were; how much they loved each other, and how they cheered and helped each other nobody knows better than I; and nobody felt it more than I did the first evening I spent

Victoria Square, Montreal, 1870

with them and sat by the fire crying, half with pleasure, half with pain, like the great fool that I am, and swearing all the time that it was a splinter from the crackling wood which had flown into my eye and made it water. Very happy and very contented they were, and very hard Thompson worked to sustain his humble home.

He wasn't a fool, wasn't Thompson; far from it, he was a clever sort of chap, and could do lots of things besides wait behind a counter and sell ribbons and things to young ladies. He was a well educated fellow, was Thompson, and could write poetry so nicely that the girls were always wanting him to write in their Albums; and so, when old Dumsic discharged him, Thompson thought he would turn his talents to account and he sent some of his writings to the American papers, for the Canadian papers were willing enough to publish, but very unwilling to pay, and as Thompson was writing for bread and butter he could not afford that kind of business.

Very nice stories did Thompson write, and his *nom de plume* of "Phontoms"—anagram of Thompson, for he would stick to his name—soon got to be well known and liked. But at first he got very little pay for his productions, and what he did get, added to his salary, was scarce enough to keep Winnie and himself, even with the exercise of great economy.

It was about three weeks before Christmas that they were married and commenced housekeeping, and Winnie had set her heart on giving a "party" at Christmas and asking some of her old friends to come and witness her triumphs of housekeeping; but it was a great undertaking, and had to be calmly considered and gone about in a serious manner.

Dinners are expensive things, and economical as she tried to be, Winnie found that the plainest fare she could afford to set before the half dozen friends she had invited would make a deep hole in her scanty purse; and very little would be left to provide refreshments for those who had been asked to come after dinner and spend the evening.

"I don't see how I can manage it," said Winnie, pushing back her hair and looking up from a little red book, in which she had been making some entries, at her husband who was busy writing at the centre table; "Do you think we could do without any dessert, Charlie, dear!" I forgot to mention before that Thompson's other name was Charles, but I suppose it don't make much difference.

"Do without dessert, darling? well, it wouldn't look very well for Christmas; but you know best, if we can't afford it, don't do it. I have given you all the money I have, and I won't run in debt; a man in debt never belongs to himself, and I mean to belong to myself if nothing else does."

"Nothing else?" inquired an arch voice, as a pair of loving arms were wound round his neck and a dainty little form threw itself into his lap with an impetuous rush which sent all the papers flying.

"Well nothing worth speaking about; of course, you don't count now, you are part of me, and the law does not recognize you as a good and chattel."

"But do you recognize me as a good? I don't like to be called a chattel."

"The best good in the world to me;" and then there was a little joyous squeeze, and a great deal of nonsense was said, and the ink bottle escaped being overturned on the new table cover by a miracle before common-sense conversation was resumed. They were very nonsensical people, were Thompson and his young wife, and they were not yet through their honeymoon you must remember.

"But about the dinner, Charlie," resumed Winnie presently. "I've stretched the money as far as it will go and if I have dessert there won't be enough for the turkey; we ought to have a turkey, oughtn't we?"

"I suppose so; people do generally have a turkey for Christmas dinner; but if we can't afford it we must do without it. I wish we had the one I have described in that Christmas story I sent to Harpers."[302]

"We can't eat a turkey out of a Christmas story," said Winnie, sententiously. "We might as well try an entire banquet out of 'The Arabian Nights' at once."

"Then Phil"—Winnie always would abbreviate my name somehow—"and the others must be content with roast beef and plum pudding; I'm going to make a plum pudding, Charlie, for it wouldn't be Christmas without it."

"Say you are going to try to make one, puss, but don't expect me to eat any of it; I have too much respect for my digestive organs."

"Then you shan't have a bit of it, sir, for your impudence, and Phil shall have the whole of it."

"Poor Phil, I pity him," sighed Thompson with mock concern for which he got the tiniest possible slap on the ear and the sweetest possible kiss on the lips.

"Now then, puss, jump down and let me go on with my writing," and so the turkey was dropped for the time being.

But Thompson did not forget it; he thought of it several times the next day, and determined to stretch a point, if possible, and get a turkey if only to surprise and please Winnie.

Luck favored Thompson, and two days before Christmas he received a polite note from Harpers enclosing a cheque for twenty-five dollars for the accepted Christmas story, and offering to purchase more of his productions.

[302] The publisher Harper & Brothers (started by James Harper in 1817 in New York City) oversaw three periodicals: *Harper's New Monthly Magazine* (founded in 1850), *Harper's Weekly* (1857) and *Harper's Bazar* (1867). It was common practice to refer simply to the name of the publishing company when it owned several magazines. Many Canadian authors contributed stories to all three publications of Harper & Brothers.

This was the largest sum he had ever received for an article, and a proud man was Thompson as he walked into a neighboring broker's office and got his cheque cashed. "One ten and the rest in ones, if you please," said Thompson, thinking how he would surprise Winnie by presenting her with the turkey, and then raining one-dollar bills on her afterwards. The broker gave him the money, and smiled quite pleasantly as he said,

"Making your fortune fast now, eh, Thompson, my boy? That's right. A merry Christmas to you," and Thompson felt himself grow half an inch taller as he walked out.

It was a busy day at the store that day, and it was quite late when Thompson took down his overcoat to start for home where he knew tea was ready and Winnie anxiously expecting him; he was a little late already, and, besides, he had the turkey to buy.

"Wait a minute, Thompson," called out the junior partner as Thompson passed the office, "I have something to say to you before you go."

And so he had to wait another five minutes; but the "something" proved very pleasant to hear, for the junior partner told him that the head of the firm—who was the junior partner's father—was very much pleased with the way he had conducted himself since he had been in the employ of the firm, and presented him with a cheque for fifty dollars, and promised him an increase of one hundred dollars salary next year.

Happy Thompson! He almost kissed the junior partner on the spot, and with difficulty restrained himself from executing a little impromptu dance of joy; but he managed to stammer out a few words of thanks and reserved his terpsichorean performance until he should have reached home.

"That's right," said the junior partner approvingly to what Thompson had said, "you always take an interest in your employers' business, and be sure they will take an interest in you. Here," he continued to a cash-boy who was passing, "take that to the cashier and ask him to give me small bills, ones or twos, for it. I am going off to Toronto to-night, Thompson," he went on as the boy departed on his errand. "I shall eat my Christmas dinner there, and be away three or four days; look after the store for me a bit while I am gone."

"The cashier says he aint got no small bills, sir," said the cash-boy returning and holding out a ten-dollar bill to the junior partner.

"That's very provoking," said that gentleman, "I have nothing but tens and twenties and I want to buy some car tickets. Do you happen to have any small bills, Thompson?"

Of course Thompson had, and he handed ten of them to the junior partner, buttoned up the ten-dollar bill with the cheque and his other money, and went on his way rejoicing to buy the turkey.

Chapter II.

How the Turkey Got Thompson

It was a hard turkey to buy, and took some time to select. Thompson had never done any marketing before, and had an idea that it was a very easy matter to walk into the market, select a turkey, pay for it and carry it off with him; but when he got there he saw so many turkeys it was quite distracting to make a selection, and the clatter of the poultry vendors so confused him that he had nearly invested in a scraggy looking goose when he was touched on the shoulder and a laughing voice said at his elbow,

"Ha, ha, Mr. Married Man, doing your own marketing already; where is the gude wife?"

"Oh, Mrs. Westerville, I am so glad to see you. I was just—that is I want to—well I was trying to buy a turkey."

"And very nearly purchased a goose. O you men are not fit to be trusted marketing by yourselves; why didn't Winnie come with you?"

"You see I intend this for a surprise."

"And you would have surprised her I have no doubt, if you had taken her home a goose and called it a turkey. Let me make your purchases for you."

"Oh, thank you. I am afraid I shall make a mess of it if I try it alone."

"Of course you will; men always do. And how is Winnie? I haven't seen her since your marriage. Oh what naughty people you were to get married on the sly, and not even send me a piece of wedding cake."

"Winnie is quite well, thanks, and will be glad to see you if you don't mind calling in rather queer quarters. We are not very rich, you know, and poor people can't be very particular where they live."

"Never mind your 'queer quarters,' Mr. Poor Man, I'll come and see you if you will give me your address. There, will that turkey do?" holding out a large plump bird which she had poked in the breast, and pinched in the back, and pulled by the legs, and squeezed by the bill, and satisfied herself was young and tender.

"That will do very nicely indeed, thank you. What is the price?" to the stall keeper.

"Seven and sixpence."

"A dollar and a half!" cried Mrs. Westerville in pretended astonishment.[303] "It's downright robbery. I paid a dollar for one only yesterday; these market people always take advantage of you men, they see you know nothing about it, and cheat you in the most barefaced manner."

After a little haggling the turkey was purchased for a dollar and a quarter, and Thompson having bought some vegetables which he thought Winnie might want for dinner, and some grapes which he intended for her own special eating, changed one of his ten-dollar bills so as to get plenty of small change again, and having loaded himself up like a pack horse trotted homeward happy.

Very much delighted was Winnie, and very sceptical about the quality of the turkey until told that Mrs. Westerville had bought it, and then she suddenly subsided before the superior wisdom of that matron of nearly a year's standing. Very much delighted was Winnie, and a very pleasant, happy evening they passed, she sitting on his lap eating grapes and occasionally holding one between her rosy lips and making him take it from them with his—I told you they were a very silly couple; and very animated was Winnie with her details of the grand preparations—in a small way—which she had made for the eventful Christmas; very merry and joyous she was, and a little inquisitive too, for she asked Thompson more than once where he had got all the money from to buy "turkeys"—

[303] According to the Currency Act of 1853, pounds, shillings, and pence, as well as dollars and cents, were recognized as Canadian currency. The exchange rate varied from one province to another, but the price of the turkey in Phillips's story indicates that, in 1873 in Montreal, one pound was worth exactly 4 dollars, one shilling (one twentieth of a pound) 20 cents, and sixpence (half a shilling) 10 cents.

she said turkeys, although there was but one—"and grapes, and vegetables and all manner of things."

But he was a dark and mysterious Thompson that night, and for the first time in his life deceived his darling a little; for he was a plotting and a scheming Thompson also, and was laying a deep plan for surprising his little wife the next night; and so he answered evasively that he had "found that he had more money than he expected, and could afford a little extra expenses," and so put her off with a kiss. Very happy and very merry were they, and many a little joke was cracked about the turkey.

Next morning Thompson was up bright and early and off to business with a light heart; and several times during the day he caught himself whistling snatches of gay little songs as he attended on the customers who thronged the store. A little before dinner time he got his cheque changed by the cashier, receiving as many small bills as that gentleman could spare—it was wonderful how much Thompson seemed to want small bills—and four tens.

As soon as the clock struck twelve he ran out ostensibly to dinner, but that was surely only an excuse, for he had told Winnie he would be too busy to come home and that he would get something to eat down town. Nowhere near home, nor any restaurant did Thompson go, but right to old Dumsic's store in Notre Dame street, and entered it as large as life just as if he was going to buy the whole store and pay for it on the spot.

But he didn't want the whole store, he only wanted a very small portion of some of the goods in the store; for be it known that amongst the "small wares" in which old Dumsic dealt were sundry articles of jewellery, and one of these articles, a dead gold[304] brooch with a small amethyst in it, Thompson had set his heart on possessing and presenting to Winnie as a Christmas present. Very glad were his old fellow clerks to see him, and many a merry little joke was passed about his "changed appearance since he became a double man," and other kindred pleasantries; and when he pulled out two ten-dollar bills to pay for the brooch—the price was twelve dollars and a half—one of the clerks began to chaff him and asked if he had "struck a mine," or "robbed a bank," or "made them himself," and such like playful questions. And when he went to the cashier's desk to get his change there

[304] "Dead gold" refers to the unburnished surface of gold, also called "matte gold."

sat old Dumsic himself, who had returned suddenly that morning from nobody knew where, looking as cross as he could, and he never said a word to Thompson, or as much as look at him; but he put on his spectacles and peered very suspiciously at the bills as if he thought they were bad, and he grunted in a disappointed sort of way as he threw them into the drawer and counted out the change. Very cross and savage indeed did old Dumsic look, but Thompson never heeded him, his heart was too full of joy for him to mind how old Dumsic looked; and he went whistling gaily out of the shop and turned into a tobacconist's, where he was known, and enquired the price of a handsome little meerschaum cigar holder which he wished to present to a stupid, blundering, foolish sort of a friend of his whom he was pleased to think himself under some sort of obligation to.

He changed another ten-dollar bill at the tobacconist's, and after he had received the change counted out twenty-five dollars in one-dollar bills and put that away carefully in one pocket, and laughed slily as he did so, did that artful Thompson, and put the remaining twenty-two dollars—two tens, and a two into another pocket; then he went back to business, and every now and then during the afternoon he chuckled to himself in a satisfied sort of way.

As Thompson had not gone home to dinner he was allowed an hour and a half for supper, and he went off sharp at six whistling all the way and in the best possible humor with himself. But all the good spirits in which he had been all day were as nothing to his uproarious hilarity when he heard Winnie's little shriek of delight at the production of the brooch, and saw her look of wonder when he pelted the one-dollar bills at her, one at a time to make them last longer; and then she climbed on his lap and made him tell her all about it; and beautiful castles in the air they built of the great things which they were to do when Thompson had become a world renowned author and made an immense fortune—authors always do make immense fortunes, in books you know, although they very seldom do in real life.

Very merrily and gaily they chatted away without thinking of supper, and Thompson's hour and a half was almost all gone when he suddenly remembered that he was very hungry and fell to with a good appetite.

But Thompson was not destined to enjoy his supper that night, for he had scarcely taken two bites out of the round of toast when there was a great knocking at the door, and on Winnie's opening it three men pushed past her and entered the room.

Thompson knew them in a moment, and rose in astonishment; they were old Dumsic, a detective—whom Thompson knew by sight—and a policeman in uniform.

"What does this intrusion mean?" asked Thompson looking with surprise at the intruders, while Winnie, with that instinctive feeling which women have that one they love is in danger, came to his side and put her arm around him as if to shield him.

"There he is," said old Dumsic savagely, "catch him before he runs away."

"I'm very sorry, Mr. Thompson," said the detective, who was a mild-eyed, gentlemanly-looking man, "will you step outside for a minute?" and he glanced at Winnie.

"No, he won't," she interrupted, before Thompson could speak: "Whatever you have to say you can say before me. What is it?"

"There is a little trouble about some one passing counterfeit bills," said the detective, "and he's wanted down at the Station;" somehow he didn't like to tell that brave-looking little woman that a charge of passing counterfeit bills had been made against her husband.

"Tell the truth," said old Dumsic sharply, "he's arrested for passing counterfeit notes; the woman he bought a turkey from last night has made a charge against him, and he passed two on me to-day. I'll make an affidavit to-morrow. The rascal to steal my daughter and then try to rob me; he ought to be hung."

"It's all a confounded lie," shouted Thompson taking a step towards old Dumsic in so fierce a manner as to make that gentleman skip nimbly behind the policeman. "I know nothing about any counterfeit bills; all the money I have had for the last two days I got from Mr. Stamps, the broker, and from the cashier of our store."

"Well, perhaps you'll be able to make it all right, sir," said the detective kindly; "but if you'd take my advice you wouldn't say much now. I may have to use it as evidence against you."

"Use whatever you please," said Thompson savagely. "I've got nothing to conceal in the matter. Take me anywhere you please at once and let me explain this matter."

"Oh, yes," said old Dumsic peeping cautiously from behind the policeman, "he can explain, of course! He can explain where he got the money to buy turkeys"—*he* said turkeys too, although there was but one—"and give dinner parties, and buy brooches, and throw bank notes about like this," and he pointed to the heap of dollar bills which Winnie had left on the table.

"I will explain nothing, except before the proper authorities," said Thompson calmly: "I am ready to go at once. I scarcely thought, Mr. Dumsic," he continued, turning to that gentleman, "that your spite against me would have carried you as far as this. May God forgive you the injustice you do me, and the pain you cause your own flesh and blood."

"It isn't him," said the detective, "it's the poultry dealer who made the complaint; she found out this morning that the bill was bad, and I went to the store to find you. The cashier told me you were here, and as I was coming along I met Mr. Dumsic who told me you had passed two counterfeits on him; he hasn't made any charge yet."

"Yes, I have," cried old Dumsic, "I make it now, and I will swear to it to-morrow morning."

"Let us go," said Thompson reaching for his hat. "I want to get this thing settled at once. Cheer up darling," he continued to Winnie, "it is nothing serious, I will be back soon."

"Do you think I am going to let you go alone? No, Charlie; I'm your wife, and wherever you go I go with you. I know this is a base, wicked calumny, a plot to separate us, but it shan't; no matter where they take you, they must take me too."

Her face was very pale, but her lip never trembled, and her eyes shone bright and trusting up to Thompson's.

"Stay where you are," said old Dumsic speaking to Winnie, and looking at her for the first time. "I am your father, I will take care of you, you shan't go to prison with this fellow."

"Father, I always tried to be a good dutiful daughter to you; I loved you dearly until you endeavored to make my life miserable and forced me to an act of disobedience; I am happy now in the love of the man who loves me, and I cannot and will not leave him."

She disengaged herself from Thompson's arms and quickly put on her bonnet and cloak.

"Come, we are ready now. Can you go round by St. Urbain's street?"[305] she asked the detective. "I have a friend there I should like to consult."

"All right, ma'am," replied the detective, "we can make it in the way."

"You'll go quietly, sir?" he inquired of Thompson.

"Certainly."

"Come along then," he said, and walked out of the room followed by Thompson and Winnie, which conduct so astonished the policeman who was a Frenchman, and had understood nothing of what had passed and who had come to assist at arresting somebody, that he seized old Dumsic by the collar and led him off in triumph.

Chapter III.

How the Turkey Got Eaten

I do like to enjoy a good smoke. I don't know anything more calculated to make a man feel at peace with his washerwoman and the rest of mankind than to lie in an easy chair, with one's slippered feet duly elevated, and slowly and luxuriously inhale peace, comfort and bliss through the medium of a well-seasoned pipe, after having partaken of a good hearty supper. I always did take especial pleasure in my after-supper smoke, and on this particular Christmas Eve of which I have been writing, I derived more than my usual comfort from my favorite clay; for it was charged with primest of Latakia,[306] and I had my most particular friend and boon companion, Jack Rainforth, sitting opposite me pulling away industriously at an ancient briar,[307] and varying his occupation occasionally by mixing a little warm brandy and water and telling funny stories.

He was a wonderful fellow, was Jack, and knew a little of everything; he was a bit of a lawyer, and a bit of a doctor, and something of an author, and had been a strolling player, and could

[305] A long street, running north-south, east of downtown Montreal and less fashionable.

[306] A type of pipe tobacco, originally produced in Latakia, Syria.

[307] A pipe made from the root of a briar or other thorny plant.

tell lots of funny stories about "the profession" as he called it,[308] and was always full of good humor, so that it was quite a treat to have him for a companion. I always considered it a treat to have Jack with me, and thought myself particularly lucky this evening to have him all to myself so that I could enjoy him alone and not have to share him with others. Jack was just telling me a capital story about a dog which belonged to a friend of his when there was a sudden knock at the door, and before I had time to call out "come in," it opened and Thompson, and Winnie, and the detective entered.

I never was more astonished in my life, and sat stupidly staring at them with my feet still on the table, quite forgetting that I had dropped one of my slippers and that there was a great hole in the toe of my sock, until Thompson's voice roused me.

"Phil, old fellow," he said, "I have been arrested for passing counterfeit money, and am on my way to the police station, will you come with me; perhaps I shall want a friend to help me out of the scrape."

"Go with you, old boy, why of course I will," I cried, trying in my excitement to pull on my pipe under the delusion that it was a boot and burning my toe so that it made me jump. "But what do you mean? tell me all about it."

Then Thompson told us what has been related in the last chapter, and we all stood silent for a moment when he had finished, looking at each other; it was Jack who spoke first, and his words made us all start.

"Where is the cashier?" asked Jack fixing his eye on the detective.

"He was at the store half an hour ago," answered the detective looking as blank as a blank cartridge after it has been exploded.

But it wouldn't do, Jack kept his eye on him and saw that he saw that Jack saw that he saw what Jack meant.

"You won't find him there now," said Jack. "You gave him warning by calling at the store, and by this time he is on his way to Rouse's Point.[309] You all go down to the Station and wait for me, I will just go round by the store and then join you. Come with me, Phil."

[308] "Strolling players" were members of travelling theatre groups in Elizabethan times, but in the Victorian era the term (as well as the designation of "the profession") was also associated with vaudevilles and the circus.

[309] Rouses Point, New York, is a village located one mile south of the Canada-US border.

Jack and I went to the store where Thompson was employed, and found one of the other clerks at the cashier's desk.

"Where is Mr. Moyson," that was the cashier's name, I asked.

"He's been gone about half an hour, sir; he said he didn't feel well, and left me in his place for the rest of the evening."

"Did he lock the safe?" asked Jack.

"No," said the clerk, rather surprised at the question, "he counted what money he had taken and put it away, leaving me to lock up when I got through."

"Just look in the safe and see if the money is there," said Jack.

The clerk looked very much astonished, but turned to the safe, and in a minute he came back with a blanched face, and said,

"I think Mr. Moyson has taken it home with him; it isn't there."

"I think he has," replied Jack dryly. "Do you know where he lives?"

"No.——, McGill College Avenue."[310]

"Thank you," and Jack hurried out of the store. "It's just as plain as it can be," he continued, when we were on the street, "this 1873 fellow has been planting a lot of bad bills by the aid of his position, and he gave those tens to Thompson; and now, seeing that his game is up he has collared all the cash he can lay his hands on and bolted." Jack used a great deal of slang sometimes, especially when he was excited.

"Perhaps he hasn't gone yet, he might be at his boarding house packing up," said I.

"I intend going there at once," replied Jack hailing a sleigh.

We reached McGill College Avenue, and found a sleigh waiting before Moyson's boarding house.

"All safe," whispered Jack, "now for a touch of diplomacy." As he said this he walked up to the carter who was waiting for Moyson; and after a few words of conversation I saw the man put something Jack gave him into his pocket, get up in his seat and drive off. Jack then gave some instructions to our carter, and we waited for Moyson's appearance.

He did not keep us long but came running down in a great hurry, threw a carpet-bag into the sleigh and was just about jumping in when Jack caught him roughly by the shoulder and said,

[310] A short street in downtown Montreal, running north-south between Sherbrooke and Sainte-Catherine; it was a very recent street, as the area on which it was built had been ceded to the city by McGill University in 1856.

"You're my prisoner!"

He reeled as if he had been struck a heavy blow, and his teeth fairly chattered as he stammered out,

"What do you mean?"

"All right, my tulip," said Jack—it was wonderful to see how naturally Jack played the policeman, that is, the kind of policeman one sees on the stage; "*You* know well enough what I want you for; those flash notes of the Bumptown Bank,[311] you've been shoving lately—it's all right, my beauty, tumble in;" it really was extraordinary how Jack picked up all his slang.

"Who are you, and how dare you stop me?" said Moyson gaining heart a little. "You have no warrant for my arrest."

"Who am I, eh? I am Detective Rocks of the Bumptown force," and he turned back the lappel of his vest and showed a large reporter's badge—for Jack had been a bit of a reporter amongst other things—which Moyston mistook for a detective's shield, "and as for warrants there's half a dozen out for you, here's one if you would like to see it, my buttercup," and he pulled out a large and official looking paper which he flourished before the cashier's eyes; but he never glanced at it, one look at the supposed shield was enough, and he stood perfectly stupefied with fear.

"Now then, look alive, my blooming morning glory" cried Jack pushing him into the sleigh, "we'll make you all comfortable for a few years at government expense, my full blown sunflower." Jack's facility for finding names for him was surprising.

"Wait a minute," cried Moyson as we drove off, "I'll give you"—and he whispered something in Jack's ear.

"Will you?" said Jack. "Honor bright."

"Honor bright," replied Moyson, "I've got the money in my pocket."

"All right," said Jack, "we'll have to go to the station, just for form sake, you know, but I'll get you discharged and then you can go."

"How can you get me discharged if I once am in the station?"

"Oh, the easiest thing in the world; when I see you in the light I say I find I have made a mistake in the dark and arrested the wrong man; you come the indignant dodge, threaten to have

[311] "Flash notes" are counterfeit bills; "Bumptown" is Phillips's sobriquet for Montreal, a city he discusses in a series of "Bumptown Papers," signed "James Bumpus" and published in *The Hearthstone* in March-April 1872.

me dismissed for arresting an innocent citizen and all that sort of thing; nobody there knows you: I admit that I haven't a warrant for your arrest—you not being the man I want and off you go, don't you see!"

"Yes I see it now, all right."

"All right it is," said Jack *sotto voce.* "I'm glad you see it, for if you had resisted I don't know how I should have got you to the station; I suppose it will be all right when I do get you there, although I don't know but what I have made myself amenable to the law for burglary, or something, passing myself off as a detective and arresting a peaceable citizen; anyhow I'll chance it;" somehow Jack would use slang even when talking to himself.

It was a funny sight when we reached the station; there was the French policeman making a charge against old Dumsic for passing counterfeit money and resisting the police, for old Dumsic had resisted considerably as the damaged condition of the policeman's face showed; and there was old Dumsic tearing and swearing like a wild man, and threatening everybody with destruction if he was not instantly released. But when the Sergeant ordered old Dumsic

to be searched and two counterfeit ten-dollar bills were found in his pocket, matters began to look serious, and old Dumsic would probably have been locked up if Jack and I with Moyson had not happened to arrive at the time, just as the detective entered with Thompson and Winnie.

Of course it did not take very long to explain matters to the Sergeant, and Moyson's capture threw an entirely new light on the subject of Thompson's passing the counterfeit bills; for when he was searched a large number of counterfeits were found on him, and seeing there was no chance of escape—for Jack soon undeceived him about his being a detective—he confessed that he had given the bad bills to Thompson, and also that when the junior partner had sent to him for change he had kept the good bill and substituted another.

It was quite evident that there was no ground for a charge against Thompson, but as a warrant had been issued, he had to be taken up to the house of the magistrate, who, on a representation of the case being made, accepted bail for his appearance on the day after Christmas.

Old Dumsic sat on a bench in the Police Station and abused that French policeman for a good half hour, which must have been very entertaining to the man, who did not understand a word of English; and the man fully explained how the mistake of arresting him occurred, in French, which was all a mystery to old Dumsic, who was quite ignorant of that language. At last old Dumsic got tired of that kind of conversation, and, having deposited a sufficient sum as his bail to appear and answer the charge of assault, left the station and went home; but a great change seemed to have come over him, and he appeared to be arguing something over to himself as he went along.

I suppose it is scarcely necessary to say that the Christmas dinner next day was a great success. Of course Jack was there and had a story all ready to tell about a friend of his who had got into a scrape very similar to the one Thompson had got into buying his turkey; and very handsome the turkey looked when it was brought on the table lying helplessly on its back with its legs in the air; and very merry and jolly we all prepared to be.

But the funniest thing of all happened just as Thompson had his knife raised to carve the turkey, for the door suddenly opened, without any previous warning, and in walked old Dumsic looking a little ashamed of himself I thought, but doing his best to smile 1873
pleasantly. He walked right up to Thompson and, offering his hand, said,

"Charlie, I've come to the conclusion that I have been in the wrong, and as I can't prevent your marrying Winnie now, I give my consent. Home don't feel like home at all without Winnie, and I want to have her back. Oh, you shall come too," he continued to Thompson. "I'm going to turn over a new leaf to-day and what I can't cure, I'm going to endure, and not make myself a fool about it."

Then Winnie looked at Thompson, and Thompson nodded his head, and she tripped up to her father and gave him a sounding kiss, and Thompson shook hands with him and made him sit down to dinner, and the very first cut of the turkey was given to old Dumsic.

It was quite wonderful to see how old Dumsic thawed, just as quick as an icecream pyramid when a red hot poker is applied to it; and awfully jolly he got too, and he and Jack told stories that kept everybody laughing, and old Dumsic had ordered a basket of wine in, and I am afraid Jack and he drank rather too much, for they vowed eternal friendship after all the others had left the table;

and Dumsic told Jack he didn't believe he was the descendant of an Irish king at all, and that he would not be at all surprised if his name had originally been Drumstick as Thompson said, and that a very jolly old Drumstick he felt, which everybody knows Dumsic would never have done if he had been quite sober. And the fun we had after the friends who had been invited for the evening arrived, was too much for me to tell, and there was old Dumsic running about making love to all the girls, and declaring he wanted to get married again.

That was last Christmas, and I am going to dine with Thompson again this year, but he doesn't live in "queer quarters" now, but with old Dumsic, who has given him an interest in the pin-and-needle business; and there is to be something more than a Christmas party for there is to be a christening too, and the young gentleman's name is to be Phil after his godfather, and Dumsic after his grandfather, so I will finish my story by wishing long life and happiness to Philip Dumsic Thompson, Esq.

GRANT ALLEN

Our Scientific Observations on a Ghost

(1878)

The author: Grant Allen was born on 24 February 1848 near Kingston, Ontario, on Wolfe Island, the largest of the Thousand Islands (in the Saint Lawrence River), where his mother's family (originally from Lower Canada) had settled several generations before. His father, Reverend Joseph Antisell Allen was an immigrant from County Tipperary, the first Anglican minister on the island and a professor at Queen's University (Kingston). Allen was homeschooled. Soon after he was dismissed because he had published two articles arguing in favour of Canada's union with the US (in November 1866), his father took his family to the US and, via France, to England. Allen graduated from Merton College, Oxford, and, in the mid-1870s, he was teaching at a college in Jamaica. In 1876, he returned to England and published a book on *Physiological Aesthetics* (1877). He soon found fiction a more suitable medium and, during the last two decades of his life, he was one of the most prolific novelists and short-story writers in the English-speaking world. He is especially remembered today as a supporter of Herbert Spencer's theories and a pioneer of detective fiction. He died on 25 October 1899 in a village in Surrey.

The text: First published in *Belgravia* 36 (July 1878), 45-59, where it was signed "J. Arbuthnot Wilson," which soon became Allen's usual pseudonym. It was reprinted in Grant Allen's *Strange Stories* (London: Chatto and Windus, 1884), 321-340. When asked to tell the story of his literary beginnings, Allen recalled the following: "One day it happened that I wanted to write a scientific article on the impossibility of knowing one had seen a ghost, even if one saw one. For convenience sake, and to make the moral clearer, I threw the argument into narrative form, but without the slightest intention of writing a story. It was published in *Belgravia* under the title of "Our Scientific Observations on a Ghost," and was reprinted later in my little volume of "Strange Stories." A little while after, to my immense surprise, Mr. Chatto wrote to ask me whether I could supply him another story, like the last I had written, for the *Belgravia Annual*. I was rather taken aback at this singular request, as I hadn't the slightest idea I could do anything at all in the way of fiction. Still, like a good journalist, I never refuse an order of any sort." The text below follows the book version (one minor difference between the 1878 text and the one in the book will be mentioned in a note). Typographical errors have been corrected.

Further reading: Will Abberley. "Criminal Chameleons: The Evolution of Deceit in Grant Allen's Fiction." *Mimicry and Display in Victorian Literary Culture: Nature, Science and the Nineteenth-Century Imagination.* Cambridge: Cambridge University Press, 2020. 86-115.

"Then nothing would convince you of the existence of ghosts, Harry," I said, "except seeing one."

"Not even seeing one, my dear Jim," said Harry. "Nothing on earth would make me believe in them, unless I were turned into a ghost myself."

So saying, Harry drained his glass of whisky toddy, shook out the last ashes from his pipe, and went off upstairs to bed. I sat for a while over the remnants of my cigar, and ruminated upon the subject of our conversation. For my own part, I was as little inclined to believe in ghosts as anybody; but Harry seemed to go one degree beyond me in scepticism. His argument amounted in brief to this,—that a ghost was by definition the spirit of a dead man in a visible form here on earth; but however strange might be the apparition which a ghost-seer thought he had observed, there was no evidence possible or actual to connect such apparition with any dead person whatsoever. It might resemble the deceased in face and figure, but so, said Harry, does a portrait. It might resemble him in voice and manner, but so does an actor or a mimic. It might resemble him in every possible particular, but even then we should only be justified in saying that it formed a close counterpart of the person in question, not that it was his ghost or spirit. In short, Harry maintained, with considerable show of reason, that nobody could ever have any scientific ground for identifying any external object, whether shadowy or material, with a past human existence of any sort. According to him, a man might conceivably see a phantom, but could not possibly know that he saw a ghost.

Harry and I were two Oxford bachelors, studying at the time for our degree in Medicine, and with an ardent love for the scientific side of our future profession. Indeed, we took a greater interest in comparative physiology and anatomy than in physic proper; and at this particular moment we were stopping in a very comfortable farm-house on the coast of Flintshire[312] for our long vacation, with the special object of observing histologically a peculiar sea-side organism, the Thingumbobbum Whatumaycallianum, which is found so plentifully on the shores of North Wales, and which has been identified by Professor Haeckel[313] with the larva of that famous marine ascidian[314] from whom the Professor himself and the remainder of humanity generally are supposed to be undoubtedly descended. We had brought with us a full complement of lancets and scalpels, chemicals and test-tubes, galvanic batteries and thermo-electric piles; and we were splendidly equipped for a thorough-going scientific campaign of the first water. The farm-house in which we lodged had formerly belonged to the county family of the Egertons;[315] and though an Elizabethan manor replaced the ancient defensive building which had been wisely dismantled by Henry VIII., the modern farm-house into which it had finally degenerated still bore the name of Egerton Castle. The whole house had a reputation in the neighbourhood for being haunted by the ghost of one Algernon Egerton, who was beheaded under James II. for his participation, or rather his intention to participate, in Monmouth's rebellion.[316] A wretched portrait of the hapless Protestant hero hung upon the wall of our joint sitting-room, having been left behind when the family moved to their new seat in Cheshire, as being unworthy of a place in the present baronet's splendid apartments. It was a few remarks upon the subject of Algernon's ghost which had introduced the question of ghosts in general; and after Harry had left the room, I sat for a while slowly finishing my cigar, and contemplating the battered features of the deceased gentleman.

As I did so, I was somewhat startled to hear a voice at my side observe in a bland and graceful tone, not unmixed with aristocratic

[312] A county in the northeast of Wales.

[313] Ernst Haeckel (1834-1919), a famous German zoologist and Darwinian, who discovered thousands of new species.

[314] Also knowns as a sea squirt.

[315] An English aristocratic family, originally from Cheshire. They expanded into Flintshire in the 1590s.

[316] The Monmouth Rebellion (1685) against Catholic King James II (1685-1688) was led by the Protestant James Scott, Duke of Monmouth, illegitimate son of King Charles II (1660-1685). Monmouth was defeated and beheaded.

hauteur, "You have been speaking of me, I believe,—in fact, I have unavoidably overheard your conversation,—and I have decided to assume the visible form and make a few remarks upon what seems to me a very hasty decision on your friend's part."

I turned round at once, and saw, in the easy-chair which Harry had just vacated, a shadowy shape, which grew clearer and clearer the longer I looked at it. It was that of a man of forty, fashionably dressed in the costume of the year 1685 or thereabouts, and bearing a close resemblance to the faded portrait on the wall just opposite. But the striking point about the object was this, that it evidently did not consist of any ordinary material substance, as its outline seemed vague and wavy, like that of a photograph where the sitter has moved; while all the objects behind it, such as the back of the chair and the clock in the corner, showed through the filmy head and body, in the very manner which painters have always adopted in representing a ghost. I saw at once that whatever else the object before might be, it certainly formed a fine specimen of the orthodox and old-fashioned apparition. In dress, appearance, and every other particular, it distinctly answered to what the unscientific mind would unhesitatingly have called the ghost of Algernon Egerton.

Here was a piece of extraordinary luck! In a house with two trained observers, supplied with every instrument of modern experimental research, we had lighted upon an undoubted specimen of the common spectre, which had so long eluded the scientific grasp. I was beside myself with delight. "Really, sir," I said, cheerfully, "it is most kind of you to pay us this visit, and I'm sure my friend will be only too happy to hear your remarks. Of course you will permit me to call him?"

The apparition appeared somewhat surprised at the philosophic manner in which I received his advances; for ghosts are accustomed to find people faint away or scream with terror at their first appearance; but for my own part I regarded him merely in the light of a very interesting phenomenon, which required immediate observation by two independent witnesses. However, he smothered his chagrin—for I believe he was really disappointed at my cool deportment—and answered that he would be very glad to see my friend if I wished it, though he had specially intended this visit for myself alone.

I ran upstairs hastily and found Harry in his dressing-gown, on the point of removing his nether garments. "Harry," I cried breathlessly, "you must come downstairs at once. Algernon Egerton's ghost wants to speak to you."

Harry held up the candle and looked in my face with great deliberation. "Jim, my boy," he said quietly, "you've been having too much whisky."

"Not a bit of it," I answered, angrily. "Come downstairs and see. I swear to you positively that a Thing, the very counterpart of Algernon Egerton's picture, is sitting in your easy-chair downstairs, anxious to convert you to a belief in ghosts."

It took about three minutes to induce Harry to leave his room; but at last, merely to satisfy himself that I was demented, he gave way and accompanied me into the sitting-room. I was half afraid that the spectre would have taken umbrage at my long delay, and gone off in a huff and a blue flame; but when we reached the room, there he was, *in propriâ personâ*, gazing at his own portrait—or should I rather say his counterpart?—on the wall, with the utmost composure.

"Well, Harry," I said, "what do you call that?"

Harry put up his eyeglass, peered suspiciously at the phantom, and answered in a mollified tone, "It certainly is a most interesting phenomenon. It looks like a case of fluorescence; but you say the object can talk?"

"Decidedly," I answered, "it can talk as well as you or me. Allow me to introduce you to one another, gentlemen:—Mr. Henry Stevens, Mr. Algernon Egerton; for though you didn't mention your name, Mr. Egerton, I presume from what you said that I am right in my conjecture."

"Quite right," replied the phantom, rising as it spoke, and making a low bow to Harry from the waist upward. "I suppose your friend is one of the Lincolnshire Stevenses, sir?"

"Upon my soul," said Harry, "I haven't the faintest conception where my family came from. My grandfather, who made what little money we have got, was a cotton-spinner at Rochdale, but he might have come from heaven knows where. I only know he was a very honest old gentleman, and he remembered me handsomely in his will."

"Indeed, sir," said the apparition coldly. "*My* family were the Egertons of Egerton Castle, in the county of Flint, Armigeri;[317] whose ancestor, Radulphus de Egerton, is mentioned in Domesday as one of the esquires of Hugh Lupus, Earl Palatine of Chester. Radulphus de Egerton had a son——"

"Whose history," said Harry, anxious to cut short these genealogical details, "I have read in the Annals of Flintshire, which lies in the next room, with the name you give as yours on the fly-leaf. But it seems, sir, you are anxious to converse with me on the subject of ghosts. As that question interests us all at present, much more than family descent, will you kindly begin by telling us whether you yourself lay claim to be a ghost?"

"Undoubtedly I do," replied the phantom.

"The ghost of Algernon Egerton, formerly of Egerton Castle?" I interposed.

"Formerly and now," said the phantom, in correction. "I have long inhabited, and I still habitually inhabit, by night at least, the room in which we are at present seated."

"The deuce you do," said Harry warmly. "This is a most illegal and unconstitutional proceeding. The house belongs to our landlord, Mr. Hay: and my friend here and myself have hired it for the summer, sharing the expenses, and claiming the sole title to the use of the rooms." (Harry omitted to mention that he took the best bedroom himself and put me off with a shabby little closet, while we divided the rent on equal terms.)

"True," said the spectre good-humouredly; "but you can't eject a ghost, you know. You may get a writ of *habeas corpus*, but the English law doesn't supply you with a writ of *habeas animam*.[318] The infamous Jeffreys[319] left me that at least. I am sure the enlightened nineteenth century wouldn't seek to deprive me of it."

"Well," said Harry, relenting, "provided you don't interfere with the experiments, or make away with the tea and sugar, I'm sure I have no objection. But if you are anxious to prove to us the existence of ghosts, perhaps you will kindly allow us to make a few simple observations?"

[317] Armigeri were people who had the right to use a coat of arms.

[318] While *habeas corpus* means literally "that you have a body," *habeas animam* would translate as "that you have a spirit."

[319] Geoffrey Jeffreys (1645-1689), often called "the Hanging Judge," famous especially for the harshness with which he treated those accused of having participated in the Monmouth Rebellion.

"With all the pleasure in death," answered the apparition courteously. "Such, in fact, is the very object for which I've assumed visibility."

"In that case, Harry," I said, "the correct thing will be to get out some paper, and draw up a running report which we may both attest afterwards. A few simple notes on the chemical and physical properties of a spectre will be an interesting novelty for the Royal Society, and they ought all to be jotted down in black and white at once."

This course having been unanimously determined upon as strictly regular, I laid a large folio of foolscap[320] on the writing-table, and the apparition proceeded to put itself in an attitude for careful inspection.

"The first point to decide," said I, "is obviously the physical properties of our visitor. Mr. Egerton, will you kindly allow us to feel your hand?"

"You may *try* to feel it if you like," said the phantom quietly, "but I doubt if you will succeed to any brilliant extent." As he spoke, he held out his arm. Harry and I endeavoured successively to grasp it: our fingers slipped through the faintly luminous object as though it were air or shadow. The phantom bowed forward his head; we attempted to touch it, but our hands once more passed unopposed across the whole face and shoulders, without finding any trace whatsoever of mechanical resistance. "Experience the first," said Harry; "the apparition has no tangible material substratum." I seized the pen and jotted down the words as he spoke them. This was really turning out a very full-blown specimen of the ordinary ghost!

"The next question to settle," I said, "is that of gravity.—Harry, give me a hand out here with the weighing-machine.—Mr. Egerton, will you be good enough to step upon this board?"

Mirabile dictu![321] The board remained steady as ever. Not a tremor of the steelyard betrayed the weight of its shadowy occupant. "Experience the second," cried Harry, in his cool, scientific way: "the apparition has the specific gravity of atmospheric air." I jotted down this note also, and quietly prepared for the next observation.

"Wouldn't it be well," I inquired of Harry, "to try the weight in vacuo?[322] It is possible that, while the specific gravity in air

[320] A sheet of paper of 8.5 x 13.5 inches.

[321] Latin for "wonderful to tell" (the expression comes from Virgil).

[322] Latin for "in a vacuum."

is equal to that of the atmosphere, the specific gravity in vacuo may be zero. The apparition—pray excuse me, Mr. Egerton, if the terms in which I allude to you seem disrespectful, but to call you a ghost would be to prejudge the point at issue—the apparition may have no proper weight of its own at all."

"It would be very inconvenient, though," said Harry, "to put the whole apparition under a bell-glass: in fact, we have none big enough. Besides, suppose we were to find that by exhausting the air we got rid of the object altogether, as is very possible, that would awkwardly interfere with the future prosecution of our researches into its nature and properties."

"Permit me to make a suggestion," interposed the phantom, "if a person whom you choose to relegate to the neuter gender may be allowed to have a voice in so scientific a question. My friend, the ingenious Mr. Boyle,[323] has lately explained to me the construction of his air-pump, which we saw at one of the Friday evenings at the Royal Institution. It seems to me that your object would be attained if I were to put one hand only on the scale under the bell-glass, and permit the air to be exhausted."

"Capital," said Harry: and we got the air-pump in readiness accordingly. The spectre then put his right hand into the scale, and we plumped the bell-glass on top of it. The connecting portion of the arm shone through the severing glass, exactly as though the spectre consisted merely of an immaterial light. In a few minutes the air was exhausted, and the scales remained evenly balanced as before.

"This experiment," said Harry judicially, "slightly modifies the opinion which we formed from the preceding one. The specific gravity evidently amounts in itself to nothing, being as air in air, and as vacuum in vacuo. Jot down the result, Jim, will you?"

I did so faithfully, and then turning to the spectre I observed, "You mentioned a Mr. Boyle, sir, just now. You allude, I suppose, to the father of chemistry?"

"And uncle of the Earl of Cork,"[324] replied the apparition, promptly filling up the well-known quotation. "Exactly so. I knew

[323] Robert Boyle (1627-1691), one of the founders of modern chemistry.

[324] "The father of chemistry and uncle of the Earl of Cork" is a famous (and probably apocryphal) inscription on Boyle's tombstone in Dublin (though Boyle was buried in London). Moreover, when Boyle died, his elder brother was still earl, which means Boyle was never "uncle of the Earl of Cork" (his nephew inherited the title seven years after Boyle's death).

Mr. Boyle slightly during our lifetime, and I have known him intimately ever since he joined the majority."

"May I ask, while my friend makes the necessary preparations for the spectrum analysis and the chemical investigation, whether you are in the habit of associating much with—er—well, with other ghosts?"

"Oh yes, I see a good deal of society."

"Contemporaries of your own, or persons of earlier and later dates?"

"Dates really matter very little to us. We may have Socrates and Bacon chatting in the same group. For my own part, I prefer modern society—I may say, the society of the latest arrivals."

"That's exactly why I asked," said I. "The excessively modern tone of your language and idioms struck me, so to speak, as a sort of anachronism with your Restoration costume—an anachronism which I fancy I have noticed in many printed accounts of gentlemen from your portion of the universe."

"Your observation is quite true," replied the apparition. "We continue always to wear the clothes which were in fashion at the time of our decease; but we pick up from new-comers the latest additions to the English language, and even, I may say, to the slang dictionary. I know many ghosts who talk familiarly of 'awfully jolly hops,' and allude to their progenitors as 'the governor.' Indeed, it is considered quite behind the times to describe a lady as 'vastly pretty,' and poor Mr. Pepys, who still preserves the antiquated idiom of his diary, is looked upon among us as a dreadfully slow old fogey."[325]

"But why, then," said I, "do you wear your old costumes for ever? Why not imitate the latest fashions from Poole's and Worth's,[326] as well as the latest cant phrase from the popular novels?"

"Why, my dear sir," answered the phantom, "we must have *something* to mark our original period. Besides, most people to whom we appear know something about costume, while very few know anything about changes in idiom,"—that I must say seemed

[325] An "awfully jolly hop" meant an exciting ball. Samuel Pepys (1633-1703) is famous for his diary (kept between 1660 and 1669), first published in 1825.

[326] Henry Poole & Co is a Savile Row tailoring firm, established in 1806. Charles Frederick Worth (1825-1895) was an English fashion designer, who founded the House of Worth in Paris in 1858.

to me, in passing, a powerful argument indeed—"and so we all preserve the dress which we habitually wore during our lifetime."

"Then," said Harry irreverently, looking up from his chemicals, "the society in your part of the country must closely resemble a fancy-dress ball."

"Without the tinsel and vulgarity, we flatter ourselves," answered the phantom.

By this time the preparations were complete, and Harry inquired whether the apparition would object to our putting out the lights in order to obtain definite results with the spectroscope. Our visitor politely replied that he was better accustomed to darkness than to the painful glare of our paraffin candles. "In fact," he added, "only the strong desire which I felt to convince you of our existence as ghosts could have induced me to present myself in so bright a room. Light is very trying to the eyes of spirits, and we generally take our constitutionals between eleven at night and four in the morning, stopping at home entirely during the moonlit half of the month."

"Ah, yes," said Harry, extinguishing the candles; "I've read, of course, that your authorities exactly reverse our own Oxford rules. You are all gated, I believe, from dawn to sunset, instead of from sunset to dawn, and have to run away helter-skelter at the first streaks of daylight, for fear of being too late for admission without a fine of twopence. But you will allow that your usual habit of showing yourselves only in the very darkest places and seasons naturally militates somewhat against the credibility of your existence. If all apparitions would only follow your sensible example by coming out before two scientific people in a well-lighted room, they would stand a much better chance of getting believed: though even in the present case I must allow that I should have felt far more confidence in your positive reality if you'd presented yourself in broad daylight, when Jim and I hadn't punished the whisky quite as fully as we've done this evening."

When the candles were out, our apparition still retained its fluorescent, luminous appearance, and seemed to burn with a faint bluish light of its own. We projected a pencil through the spectroscope, and obtained, for the first time in the history of science, the spectrum of a spectre. The result was a startling one indeed. We had expected to find lines indicating the presence of sulphur or phosphorus: instead of that, we obtained a continuous band of pale luminosity, clearly pointing to the fact that the apparition had no known terrestrial element in its composition. Though we felt rather surprised at this discovery, we simply noted it down on our paper, and proceeded to verify it by chemical analysis.

The phantom obligingly allowed us to fill a small phial with the luminous matter, which Harry immediately proceeded to test with all the resources at our disposal. For purposes of comparison I filled a corresponding phial with air from another part of the room, which I subjected to precisely similar tests. At the end of half an hour we had completed our examination—the spectre meanwhile watching us with mingled curiosity and amusement; and we laid our written quantitative results side by side. They agreed to a decimal. The table, being interesting, deserves a place in this memoir. It ran as follows:—

Chemical Analysis of an Apparition.

Atmospheric air . . .	96·45	per cent.
Aqueous vapour . . .	2·31	„
Carbonic acid . . .	1·08	„
Tobacco smoke . . .	0·16	„
Volatile alcohol . . .	A trace	
	100·00	„

1878

The alcohol Harry plausibly attributed to the presence of glasses which had contained whisky toddy. The other constituents would have been normally present in the atmosphere of a room where two fellows had been smoking uninterruptedly ever since dinner. This important experiment clearly showed that the apparition had no proper chemical constitution of its own, but consisted entirely of the same materials as the surrounding air.

"Only one thing remains to be done now, Jim," said Harry, glancing significantly at a plain deal table in the corner, with whose uses we were both familiar; "but then the question arises, does this gentleman come within the meaning of the Act?[327] I don't feel certain about it in my own mind, and with the present unsettled state of public opinion on this subject, our first duty is to obey the law."

[327] The Vivisection Act.

"Within the meaning of the Act?" I answered; "decidedly not. The words of the forty-second section say distinctly 'any *living* animal.' Now, Mr. Egerton, according to his own account, is a ghost, and has been dead for some two hundred years or thereabouts: so that we needn't have the slightest scruple on *that* account."

"Quite so," said Harry, in a tone of relief. "Well then, sir," turning to the apparition, "may I ask you whether you would object to our vivisecting you?"

"Mortuisecting, you mean, Harry," I interposed parenthetically. "Let us keep ourselves strictly within the utmost letter of the law."

"Vivisecting? Mortuisecting?" exclaimed the spectre, with some amusement. "Really, the proposal is so very novel that I hardly know how to answer it. I don't think you will find it a very practicable undertaking: but still, if you like, yes, you may try your hands upon me."

We were both much gratified at this generous readiness to further the cause of science, for which, to say the truth, we had hardly felt prepared. No doubt, we were constantly in the habit of maintaining that vivisection didn't really hurt, and that rabbits or dogs rather enjoyed the process than otherwise; still, we did not quite expect an apparition in human form to accede in this gentlemanly manner to a personal request which after all is rather a startling one. I seized our new friend's hand with warmth and effusion (though my emotion was somewhat checked by finding it slip through my fingers immaterially), and observed in a voice trembling with admiration, "Sir, you display a spirit of self-sacrifice which does honour to your head and heart. Your total freedom from prejudice is perfectly refreshing to the anatomical mind. If all 'subjects' were equally ready to be vivisected—no, I mean mortuisected—oh,—well,—there," I added (for I began to perceive that my argument didn't hang together, as 'subjects' usually accepted mortuisection with the utmost resignation), "perhaps it wouldn't make much difference after all."

Meanwhile Harry had pulled the table into the centre of the room, and arranged the necessary instruments at one end. The bright steel had a most charming and scientific appearance, which added greatly to the general effect. I saw myself already in imagination drawing up an elaborate report for the Royal Society, and delivering a Croonian Oration,[328] with diagrams and sections complete, in illustration of the "Vascular System of a Ghost." But alas, it was not to be. A preliminary difficulty, slight in itself, yet enormous in its preventive effects, unhappily defeated our well-made plans.

"Before you lay yourself on the table," said Harry, gracefully indicating that article of furniture to the spectre with his lancet, "may I ask you to oblige me by removing your clothes? It is usual in all these operations to—ahem—in short, to proceed *in puris naturalibus*.[329] As you have been so very kind in allowing us to operate upon you, of course you won't object to this minor but indispensable accompaniment."

"Well, really, sir," answered the ghost, "I should have no personal objection whatsoever; but I'm rather afraid it can't be done. To tell you the truth, my clothes are an integral part of myself. Indeed, I consist chiefly of clothes, with only a head and hands protruding at the principal extremities. You must have noticed that all persons of my sort about whom you have read or heard were fully clothed in the fashion of their own day. I fear it would be quite impossible to remove these clothes. For example, how very absurd it would be to see the shadowy outline of a ghostly coat hanging up on a peg behind a door. The bare notion would be sufficient to cast ridicule upon the whole community. No, gentlemen, much as I should like to gratify you, I fear the thing's impossible. And, to let the whole secret out, I'm inclined to think, for my part, that I haven't got any independent body whatsoever."

"But, surely," I interposed, "you must have *some* internal economy, or else how can you walk and talk? For example, have you a heart?"

"Most certainly, my dear sir, and I humbly trust it is in the right place."

"You misunderstand me," I repeated: "I am speaking literally, not figuratively. Have you a central vascular organ on your left-hand side, with two auricles and ventricles, a mitral and a tricuspid valve, and the usual accompaniment of aorta, pulmonary vein, pulmonary artery, systole and diastole, and so forth?"

[328] Delivered upon being awarded the Croonian Medal by the Royal Society.

[329] Latin for "in a purely natural state" (usually understood to mean "naked").

"Upon my soul, sir," replied the spectre with an air of bewilderment, "I have never even heard the names of these various objects to which you refer, and so I am quite unable to answer your question. But if you mean to ask whether I have something beating just under my fob (excuse the antiquated word, but as I wear the thing in question I must necessarily use the name),[330] why then, most undoubtedly I have."

"Will you oblige me, sir," said Harry, "by showing me your wrist? It is true I can't *feel* your pulse, owing to what you must acknowledge as a very unpleasant tenuity in your component tissues: but perhaps I may succeed in *seeing* it."

The apparition held out its arm. Harry instinctively endeavoured to balance the wrist in his hand, but of course failed in catching it. We were both amused throughout to observe how difficult it remained, after several experiences, to realize the fact that this visible object had no material and tangible background underlying it. Harry put up his eyeglass and gazed steadily at the phantom arm; not a trace of veins or arteries could anywhere be seen. "Upon my word," he muttered, "I believe it's true, and the subject has no internal economy at all. This is really very interesting."

"As it is quite impossible to undress you," I observed, turning to our visitor, "may I venture to make a section through your chest, in order, if practicable, to satisfy myself as to your organs generally?"

"Certainly," replied the good-humoured spectre; "I am quite at your service."

I took my longest lancet from its case and made a very neat cut, right across the sternum, so as to pass directly through all the principal viscera. The effect, I regret to say, was absolutely nugatory. The two halves of the body reunited instantaneously behind the instrument, just as a mass of mercury reunites behind a knife. Evidently there was no chance of getting at the anatomical details, if any existed, underneath that brocaded waistcoat of phantasmagoric satin. We gave up the attempt in despair.

"And now," said the shadowy form, with a smile of conscious triumph, flinging itself easily but noiselessly into a comfortable arm-chair, "I hope you are convinced that ghosts really do exist. I think I have pretty fully demonstrated to you my own purely spiritual and immaterial nature."

[330] A small pocket, in which a pocket watch was often worn.

"Excuse me," said Harry, seating himself in his turn on the ottoman: "I regret to say that I remain as sceptical as at the beginning. You have merely convinced me that a certain visible shape exists apparently unaccompanied by any tangible properties. With this phenomenon I am already familiar in the case of phosphorescent gaseous effluvia. You also seem to utter audible words without the aid of a proper larynx or other muscular apparatus; but the telephone has taught me that sounds exactly resembling those of the human voice may be produced by a very simple membrane. You have afforded us probably the best opportunity ever given for examining a so-called ghost, and my private conviction at the end of it is that you are very likely an egregious humbug."

I confess I was rather surprised at this energetic conclusion, for my own faith had been rapidly expanding under the strange experiences of that memorable evening. But the visitor himself seemed much hurt and distressed. "Surely," he said, "you won't doubt my word when I tell you plainly that I am the authentic ghost of Algernon Egerton. The word of an Egerton of Egerton Castle was always better than another man's oath, and it is so still, I hope. Besides, my frank and courteous conduct to you both to-night, and the readiness with which I have met all your proposals for scientific examination, certainly entitle me to better treatment at your hands."

"I must beg ten thousand pardons," Harry replied, "for the plain language which I am compelled to use. But let us look at the case in a different point of view. During your occasional visits to the world of living men, you may sometimes have travelled in a railway carriage in your invisible form."

"I have taken a trip now and then (by a night train, of course), just to see what the invention was like."

"Exactly so. Well, now, you must have noticed that a guard insisted from time to time upon waking up the sleepy passengers for no other purpose than to look at their tickets. Such a precaution might be resented, say by an Egerton of Egerton Castle, as an insult to his veracity and his honesty. But, you see, the guard doesn't know an Egerton from a Muggins: and the mere word of a passenger to the effect that he belongs to that distinguished family is in itself of no more value than his personal assertion that his ticket is perfectly *en règle*."[331]

[331] French for "in (good) order."

"I see your analogy, and I must allow its remarkable force."

"Not only so," continued Harry firmly, "but you must remember that in the case I have put, the guard is dealing with known beings of the ordinary human type. Now, when a living person introduces himself to me as Egerton of Egerton Castle, or Sir Roger Tichborne of Alresford,[332] I accept his statement with a certain amount of doubt, proportionate to the natural improbability of the circumstances. But when a gentleman of shadowy appearance and immaterial substance, like yourself, makes a similar assertion, to the effect that he is Algernon Egerton who died two hundred years ago, then I am reluctantly compelled to acknowledge, even at the risk of hurting that gentleman's susceptible feelings, that I can form no proper opinion whatsoever of his probable veracity. Even men, whose habits and constitution I familiarly understand, cannot always be trusted to tell me the truth: and how then can I expect implicitly to believe a being whose very existence contradicts all my previous experiences, and whose properties give the lie to all my scientific conceptions—a being who moves without muscles and speaks without lungs? Look at the possible alternatives, and then you will see that I am guilty of no personal rudeness when I respectfully decline to accept your uncorroborated assertions. You may be Mr. Algernon Egerton, it is true, and your general style of dress and appearance certainly bears out that supposition; but then you may equally well be his Satanic Majesty in person—in which case you can hardly expect me to credit your character for implicit truthfulness. Or again, you may be a mere hallucination of my fancy: I may be suddenly gone mad, or I may be totally drunk,—and now that I look at the bottle, Jim, we must certainly allow that we have fully appreciated the excellent qualities of your capital Glenlivat.[333] In short, a number of alternatives exist, any one of which is quite as probable as the supposition of your being a genuine ghost; which

[332] Allusion to the Tichborne case, a cause célèbre from the 1860s and 1870s. Roger Tichborne presumably died at sea in 1845. Two decades later, in 1866, an Australian man claimed to be the real Roger Tichborne. He travelled to England and was immediately accepted by Lady Tichborne as her long-lost son. In 1874, a criminal court decided that he was not the vanished heir and sentenced him to prison, where he remained at the time of the publication of Allen's story.

[333] The Glenlivat distillery had closed in 1852. In the 1860s, George Smith renamed his distillery (rebuilt in the village of Minmore) "Glenlivet." Harry might be confusing the two names or he is referring to an old bottle.

supposition I must therefore lay aside as a mere matter for the exercise of a suspended judgment."

I thought Harry had him on the hip, there: and the spectre evidently thought so too; for he rose at once and said rather stiffly, "I fear, sir, you are a confirmed sceptic upon this point, and further argument might only result in one or the other of us losing his temper. Perhaps it would be better for me to withdraw. I have the honour to wish you both a very good evening." He spoke once more with the *hauteur* and grand mannerism of the old school, besides bowing very low at each of us separately as he wished us good-night.

"Stop a moment," said Harry rather hastily. "I wouldn't for the world be guilty of any inhospitality, and least of all to a gentleman, however indefinite in his outline, who has been so anxious to afford us every chance of settling an interesting question as you have. Won't you take a glass of whisky and water before you go, just to show there's no animosity?"

"I thank you," answered the apparition, in the same chilly tone; "I cannot accept your kind offer. My visit has already extended to a very unusual length, and I have no doubt I shall be blamed as it is by more reticent ghosts for the excessive openness with which I have conversed upon subjects generally kept back from the living world. Once more," with another ceremonious bow, "I have the honour to wish you a pleasant evening."

As he said these words, the fluorescent light brightened for a second, and then faded entirely away. A slightly unpleasant odour also accompanied the departure of our guest. In a moment, spectre and scent alike disappeared; but careful examination with a delicate test exhibited a faint reaction which proved the presence of sulphur in small quantities. The ghost had evidently vanished quite according to established precedent.

We filled our glasses once more, drained them off meditatively, and turned into our bedrooms as the clock was striking four.

Next morning, Harry and I drew up a formal account of the whole circumstance, which we sent to the Royal Society, with a request that they would publish it in their Transactions. To our great surprise, that learned body refused the paper, I may say with contumely. We next applied to the Anthropological Institute, where, strange to tell, we met with a like inexplicable rebuff. Nothing daunted by our double failure, we despatched a copy of our analysis to the Chemical Society; but the only acknowledgment accorded to us was a letter from the secretary, who stated that "such a sorry joke was at once impertinent and undignified." In short, the scientific world utterly refuses to credit our simple and straightforward narrative; so that we are compelled to throw ourselves for justice upon the general reading public at large. As the latter invariably peruse the pages of "Belgravia," I have ventured to appeal to them in the present article, confident that they will redress our wrongs, and accept this valuable contribution to a great scientific question at its proper worth. It may be many years before another chance occurs for watching an undoubted and interesting Apparition under such favourable circumstances for careful observation; and all the above information may be regarded as absolutely correct, down to five places of decimals.

Still, it must be borne in mind that unless an apparition had been scientifically observed as we two independent witnesses observed this one, the grounds for believing in its existence would have been next to none. And even after the clear evidence which we obtained of its immaterial nature, we yet remain entirely in the dark as to its objective reality, and we have not the faintest reason for believing it to have been a genuine unadulterated ghost. At the best we can only say that we saw and heard Something, and that this Something differed very widely from almost any other object we had ever seen and heard before. To leap at the conclusion that the Something was therefore a ghost, would be, I venture humbly to submit, without offence to the Psychical Research Society,[334] a most unscientific and illogical specimen of that peculiar fallacy known as Begging the Question.[335]

[334] Here, in the 1878 version, Allen wrote "without offence to Messrs. Crookes and Wallace." William Crookes (1832-1919), a chemist and physicist, and Alfred Russell Wallace (1823-1913), the evolutionary biologist, were among the scientist interested in spiritualism. The Society for Psychical Research (Crookes and Wallace were among the founders) was created in 1882, in time for the 1884 edition of *Strange Stories*.

[335] A logical fallacy (*petitio principii*), in which the argument is based on premises that assert the conclusion, instead of supporting it.

Susie Frances Harrison

Crowded Out

(1886)

The author: Susan (called Susie) Frances Riley was born on 24 February 1859 in Toronto, the daughter of a hotel manager. She trained as a musician, first working as a pianist and singer, and, for two decades starting in 1902, as principal of the Rosedale branch of the Toronto Conservatory of Music. She was a gifted composer, the author of several pieces of classical and folk music, as well as of an opera (which does not survive). She was also a very active music critic, writing for periodicals and giving lectures. Since 1877, she had been married to J.W.F. Harrison, a church organist and choirmaster (born in England in 1847), whom she had met in Montreal, where she lived from 1875 to 1879. Her first child, a son, was born in 1878; the second, a daughter, in 1881, after the Harrisons had relocated to Toronto. From 1883 to 1887, they lived in Ottawa, where Susie's husband was musical director of Ottawa Ladies' College. In Ottawa, she published her first book, *Crowded Out!* (1886), in which the title story is inspired by her fruitless attempts to have her writings published in London. She was a prolific journalist and poet, and she had two novels published, in 1898 and 1914. Perhaps her most popular publication was the 1887 *Canadian Birthday Book*, an anthology of poems written by both English and French Canadians. For most of her life, she used the pseudonym "Seranus" (based on a publisher's misreading of her given names handwritten as "S. Frances"). She died in Toronto on 5 May 1935.

The text: First published in *Crowded Out! And Other Sketches*. By Seranus. Ottawa: The Evening Journal Office, 1886, 5-10. It was reprinted, with some changes in punctuation but with all the original typographical errors, in the New York periodical *The Theatre* 5: 13/117 (May 1889), 294-296. The text below follows the original version from the 1886 book, but some of the improved punctuation from *The Theatre* has also been used. Typographical errors have been corrected.

Further reading: Jennifer Chambers. "Whos' In and Who's Out: Recovering Minor Authors and the Pesky Question of Critical Evaluation." *Home Ground and Foreign Territory: Essays on Early Canadian Literature*. Ed. Janice Fiamengo. Ottawa: University of Ottawa Press, 2014. 257-274.

I am nobody. I am living in a London lodging-house. My room is up three pairs of stairs. I have come to London to sell or to part with in some manner an opera, a comedy, a volume of verse, songs, sketches, stories. I compose as well as write. I am ambitious. For the sake of another, one other, I am ambitious. For myself it does not matter. If nobody will discover me I must discover myself. I must demand recognition, I must wrest attention; they are my due. I look from my window over the smoky roofs of London. What will it do for me, this great cold city? It shall hear me, it shall pause for a moment, for a day, for a year. I will make it to listen to me, to look at me. I have left a continent behind, I have crossed a great water; I have incurred dangers, trials of all kinds; I have grown pale and thin with labor and the midnight oil; I have starved, and watched the dawn break starving; I have prayed on my stubborn knees for death and I have prayed on my stubborn knees for life—all that I might reach London, London that has killed so many of my brothers, London the cold, London the blind, London the cruel! I am here at last. I am here to be tested, to be proved, to be worn proudly, as a favorite and costly jewel is worn, or to be flung aside scornfully or dropped stealthily to—the devil! And I love it so this great London! I am ready to swear no one ever loved it so before! The smokier it is, the dirtier, the dingier, the better. The oftener it rains the better. The more whimsical it is, the more fickle, the more credulous, the more self-sufficient, the more self-existent, the better. Nothing that it can do, nothing that it can be, can change my love for it, great cruel London!

But to be cruel to *me*, to be fickle to *me*, to be deaf to *me*, to be blind to *me*! Would I change then? I might. As yet it does not know me. I pass through its streets, touching here a bit of old black wall, picking there an ivy leaf, and it knows me not. It is holy ground to me. It is the mistress whose hand alone I as yet dare to kiss. Some day I shall possess the whole, and I shall walk with the firm and buoyant tread of the accepted, delighted lover. Only to-day I am nobody. I am crowded out. Yet there are moments when the mere joy of being in England, of being in London, satisfies me. I have seen the sunbeam strike the glory along the green. I know it is an English sky above me, all change, all mutability. No steady cloudless sphere of blue but ever-varying glories of white piled cloud against the gray. Listen to this. I saw a primrose—the first I had ever seen—in the hedge. They said "Pick it." But I did not. I, who had written there years ago,—

> I never pulled a primrose, I,
> But could I know that there may lie
> E'en now some small or hidden seed,
> Within, below, an English mead,
> Waiting for sun and rain to make
> A flower of it for my poor sake,
> I then could wait till winds should tell,
> For me there swayed or swung a bell,
> Or reared a banner, peered a star,
> Or curved a cup in woods afar.[336]

I who had written that, I had found my first primrose and I could not pluck it. I found it fair, be sure. I find all England fair. The shimmering mist and the tender rain, the red wallflower and the ivy green, the singing birds and the shallow streams—all the country; the blackened churches, the grass-grown churchyards, the hum of streets, the crowded omnibus, the gorgeous shops,—all the town. God! do I not love it, my England? Yet not my England yet. Till she proclaim it herself, I am not hers. I will make her mine. I will write as no man has ever written about her, for very love of her. I look out to-night from my narrow window and think how the moonlight falls on Tintern, on Glastonbury, on Furness.[337] How it falls on the primrose I would not pluck. How it would like to fall on the tall blue-bells in the wood. I see the lights of Oxford St. The omnibuses rattle by, the people are going to see Irving, Wilson Barrett, Ellen Terry.[338] What line of mine, what bar, what thought or phrase will turn the silence into song, the copper into gold? * * * * I come back from the window and sit at the square centre table. It is rickety and uncomfortable, useless to

[336] From her poem "To Maurice Thompson," first published in *Rose-Belford's Canadian Monthly and National Review* 8: 5 (May 1882), 537-538.

[337] The famous ruins of three monasteries in Great Britain: Tintern Abbey (in Wales, made famous by one of Wordsworth's poems), Glastonbury Abbey (in Somerset), Furness (in Cumbria).

[338] Some of the most famous English actors of the era: Henry Irving (1838-1905), Wilson Barrett (1846-1904), Ellen Terry (1847-1928). Oxford Street is a major thoroughfare in Westminster, London.

write on. I kick it. I would kick anything that came in my way to-night. I am savage. Outside, a French piano is playing that infernal waltz. A fair subject for kicking if you will. But, though I would, I cannot. What a room! The fire-place is filled with orange peel and brown paper, cigar stumps and matches. One blind I pulled down this morning, the other is crooked. The lamp glass is cracked, my work too. I dare not look at the wall paper nor the pictures. The carpet I have kicked into holes. I can see it though I can't feel it, it is so thin. My clothes are lying all about. The soot of London begrimes every object in the room. I would buy a pot of musk or a silken scarf if I dared, but how can I?

I must get my bread first and live for beauty after. Everything is refused though, everything sent back or else dropped as it were into some bottomless pit or gulf.

Here is my opera. This is my *magnum opus*, very dear, very clear, very well preserved. For it is three years old. I scored it nearly altogether, by *her* side, Hortense, my dear love, my northern bird! You could flush under my gaze, you could kindle at my touch, but you were not for me, you were not for me! * * * * My head droops down, I could go to sleep. But I must not waste the time in sleep. I will write another story. No; I had four returned to-day. Ah! cruel London! To love you so, only that I may be spurned and thrust aside, ignored, forgotten. But to-morrow I will try again. I will take the opera to the theatres, I will see the managers, I will even tell them about myself and about Hortense—but it will be hard. They do not know me, they do not know Hortense. They will laugh, they will say "You fool." And I shall be helpless, I shall let them say it. They will never listen to me, though I play my most beautiful phrase, for I am nobody. And Hortense, the child with the royal air, Hortense, with her imperial brow and her hair rolled over its cushion,[339] Hortense, the *Châtelaine* of *Beau Séjour*, the delicate, haughty, pale and impassioned daughter of a noble house, that Hortense, my Hortense, is nobody!

Who in this great London will believe in me, who will care to know about Hortense or about *Beau Séjour*? If they ask me, I shall say—oh! proudly—not in Normandy nor in Alsace, but far away across a great water dwells such a maiden in such a *château*.

[339] A fashion made popular by Alexandra, Princess of Wales (1844-1925): the hair was combed over a hollow cushion; the addition of false hair was often necessary.

There by the side of a northern river, ever rippling, ever sparkling in summer, hard, hard frozen in winter, stretches a vast estate. I remember its impenetrable pinewood, its deep ravine; I see the *château*, long and white and straggling, with the red tiled towers and the tall French windows; I see the terrace where the hound must still sleep; I see the square side tower with the black iron shutters; I see the very window where Hortense has set her light; I see the floating cribs on the river,[340] I hear the boatmen singing—

Descendez à l'ombre,
Ma jolie blonde.

And now I am dreaming surely! This is London, not *Beau Séjour*, and Hortense is far away, and it is that cursed fellow in the street I hear! The morrow comes on quickly. If I were to draw up that crooked blind now I should see the first streaks of daylight. Who pinned those other curtains together? That was well done, for I don't want to see the daylight; and it comes in, you know, Hortense, when you think it is shut out. Somebody calls it *fingers*, and that is just what it is, long fingers of dawn, always pale, always gray and white, stealing in and around my pillow for me. Never pink, never rosy, mind that; always faint and shadowy and gray.

* * * *

It was all caste. Caste in London, caste in *Le Bas Canada*,[341] all the same. Because she was a *St. Hilaire*. Her full name—*Hortense Angélique De Repentigny de St. Hilaire*—how it grates on me afresh with its aristocratic plentitude. She is well-born, certainly; better born than most of these girls I have seen here in London, driving, walking, riding in the Parks. They wear their hair over cushions too. Freckled skins, high cheek-bones, square foreheads, spreading eyebrows—they shouldn't wear it so. It suits Hortense—with her pale patrician outline and her dark pencilled eyebrows, and her little black ribbon and amulet around her neck. *O, Marie, priez pour nous qui avons recours à vous*![342] Once I walked out to *Beau Séjour*. She did not expect me and I crept through the leafy ravine to the pinewood, then on to the steps, and so up to the terrace.

[340] Floating cribs are a traps for fish, which are captured and kept alive inside.

[341] French for Lower Canada (see note 231).

[342] French for "O Mary, pray for us who have recourse to you" (though this is from the novena in honour of the immaculate conception and Harrison left out the words "conceived without sin").

Through the French window I could see her seated at the long table opposite Father Couture. She lives alone with the good Père. She is the last one of the noble line, and he guards her well and guards her money too.

"I do remember that it vill be all for ze Church," she has said to me. And the priest has taught her all she knows, how to sew and embroider, and cook and read, though he never lets her read anything but works on religion. Religion, always religion! He has brought her up like a nun, crushed the life out of her. Until I found her out, found my jewel out. It is Tennyson who says that. But his "Maud" was freer to woo than Hortense,[343] freer to love and kiss and hold—my God! that night while I watched them studying and bending over those cursed works on the Martyrs and the Saints and the Mission houses—I saw him—him—that old priest—take her in his arms and caress her, drink her breath, feast on her eyes, her hair, her delicate skin, and I burst in like a young madman and told Father Couture what I thought. Oh! I was mad! I should have won her first. I should have worked quietly, cautiously, waiting, waiting, biding my time. But I could never bide my time. And now she hates me, Hortense hates me, though she so nearly learned to love me. There where we used to listen to the magical river songs, we nearly loved, did we not Hortense? But she was a *St. Hilaire*, and I—I was nobody, and I had insulted *le bon Père*. Yet if I can go back to her rich, prosperous, independent—What if that happen? But I begin to fancy it will never happen. My resolutions, where are they, what comes of them? Nothing. I have tried everything except the opera. Everything else has been rejected. For a week I have not gone to bed at all. I wait and see those ghastly gray fingers smoothing my pillow. I am not wanted. I am crowded out. My hands tremble and I cannot write. My eyes fail and I cannot see. To the window! * * * * The lights of Oxford St. once more; the glare and the rattle without, the fever and the ruin, the nerves and the heart within. Poor nerves, poor heart; it is food you want and wine and rest, and I cannot give them to you. * * * *

Sing, Hortense, will you? Sit by my side, by our dear river St. Maurice, the clear, the sparkling.[344] See how the floating cribs sail

[343] "What, has he found my jewel out?" is a line from "Maud" (x, i, 1), first published in *Maud: And Other Poems* (1855) by Alfred Tennyson (1809-1892).

[344] One of the most important tributaries of the Saint Lawrence; it flows north to south, through La Tuque, Shawinigan, and Trois-Rivières.

by, each with its gleaming lights! It is like Venice I suppose. Shall we see Venice ever, Hortense, you and I? Sing now for me,

Descendez à l'ombre,
Ma jolie blonde.

Only you are a *petite brune*, there is nothing *blonde* about you, *mignonne*, my dear mademoiselle I should say, if I were with you of course, as I used to do. But surely I *am* with you, and those lights are the floating cribs I see, and your voice it is that sings, and presently the boatmen hear and they turn and move their hands and join in—Now all together,

Descendez à l'ombre,

* * * * * * *

It was like you, Hortense, to come all this way. How did you manage it, manage to cross that great water all alone? My poor girl, did you grow tired of *Le bon Père* at last and of the Martyrs and the Saints and the Jesuit Fathers? But you have got your amulet on still I hope. That is right, for there is a chance—there is a chance of these things proving blessings after all to good girls, and you were a good girl Hortense. You will not mind my calling you Hortense, will you? When we are in *Le Bas Canada* again, in your own seigneurie, it will be "Mademoiselle," I promise you. You say it is a strange pillow, Hortense? Books, my girl, and manuscripts; hard but not so hard as London stones and London hearts. Do you know I think I am dying, or else going mad? And no one will listen even if I cry out. There is too much to listen to already in England. Think of all the growing green, Hortense, if you can, where you are, so far away from it all. Where you are it is cold and the snow is still on the ground and only the little bloodroot is up in the woods. Here where I am Hortense, where I am going to die, it is warm and green full of color—oh! such color! Before I came here to London, you know London that is going to do so much for me, for us both, I had one day—one day in the country. There I saw—No! they will not let me tell you, I knew they would try to prevent me, those long gray fingers stealing in, stealing in! But I *will* tell you. Listen, Hortense, please. I saw the hawthorne, pink and white, the laburnum—yellow—not fire-color, I shall correct the Laureate there,[345] Hortense, when I am better, when I * * publish! * * * It is dreadful to be alone in London. Don't come, Hortense. Stay where you are, even if it is cold and gray and there is no color. Keep your amulet round your neck, dear! * * * * I count my pulse beats. It is a bad thing to do. It is broad daylight now and the fingers have gone. I can write again perhaps. * * The pen * * * The paper * * * * The ink * * * * God. Hortense! There is no ink left! And my heart—My heart—Hortense!!!

Descendez à l'ombre,
Ma jolie blonde.

[345] "Laburnums, dropping-wells of fire" is a line in Tennyson's 1850 *In Memoriam* (lxxxii). Tennyson was at the time Poet Laureate (since 1850). The blossoms of the laburnum tree are yellow.

Roger Pocock

A Useless Man

(1886)

The author: Henry Roger Ashwell Pocock was born in 1865 in Tenby, in South Wales, and spent part of his childhood on board the former HMS *Wellesley*, refitted as a training ship for the Wellesley Nautical School (on the River Tyne), which was training unruly young boys for the navy, under the command of his father, Charles Ashwell Boteler Pocock, (1829-1899), who had retired from the Royal Navy at half pay with the rank of commander because of his eyesight. His sister, the future famous actress Lena Ashwell (1872-1957) was born on board the ship. He was educated at Ludlow Grammar School, in Shropshire, and at the School of Submarine Telegraphy in Penge, Surrey. In 1882, his father took the family to Canada, renting a house near Brockville, Ontario. Roger was soon sent to Guelph Agricultural College, which he left in 1883 to take up various jobs. His brother-in-law found work for him on the far side of Lake Superior, carving out the roadbed for the Canadian Pacific Railway. The "useless man" in the story below is clearly based on the writer himself, while the narrator is inspired by his boss, Mr. Middleton. He held numerous other jobs in 1883-1884, until, on 3 November 1884, he enlisted in the North-West Mounted Police, in Winnipeg. He took part in the campaign against Louis Riel's North-West Rebellion in 1885 and he lost his toes to frostbite in March of that year. He started walking in February 1886 and, while still convalescing, he began writing stories.

The text: First published in *The Week* 3: 32 (8 July 1886), 515-516. It was signed "Coyote."

Further reading: Geoffrey A. Pocock, *Outrider of Empire: The Life and Adventures of Roger Pocock* (Edmonton: University of Alberta Press, 2007).

I was sent to survey a three-mile section of the Canadian Pacific Railway, on the Bay of St. Ignace, Lake Superior.[346] The lay of the land was that of a house roof, and it was at the foot of an eight-hundred-feet cliff. Most of the roadway was cut out of solid rock, with here and there a bridge over a ravine, or a tunnel under a spur of rock, to break monotony.

The work was half finished, when I was visited by the District Engineer, bringing with him a boy whom he proposed to leave to my tender mercies. The apprentice was described as an interesting and amiable youth, and had improved the occasion by scaling the precipice overhead. He had succeeded in getting lost, and we were organising a search party, when he favoured us with his presence and was introduced. He presented an interesting and rather torn-up appearance, and was dressed in brown corduroy. He was of slender build, with very marked, irregular features, an exquisite skin, and soft, expressive eyes. He began our acquaintance by expressing doubts as to whether the rock formation was plutonic or metamorphic, exhibiting some very poisonous berries which he described as having an agreeable flavour, and borrowed five dollars.

Next day, we went to work and measured out one of the big rock-cuts. I tried Eustace with the chain, the measure, the rod, and in all these he showed, and cheerfully admitted, the grossest incompetence. His talent for making blunders was marvellous, and the cause was—thinking. Often, when his negligence stopped the work of the party, I feared to rouse him from meditations that might benefit the human race. In climbing, he was slow and heavy; in locating, he was blind and obtuse. I set him to mark the stakes, and blessed him when he forgot their sequence. Before evening I saw that he was entirely useless.

Whenever he had a chance he would go up among the cliffs and get lost. When he did turn up he was generally more or less damaged from falls, and always laden with amethysts, herbs, ore, sketches, and ideas. He would favour me with his ideas on anatomy, speculative astronomy, submarine navigation, boating, statuary,

[346] Nipigon Bay, north of St. Ignace Island (the second-largest island in Lake Superior).

and other kindred topics. He would draw plans, and sometimes, on the sly, write verses. He never inflicted these on me, and I forgave him, because he was a good listener. In the evenings I tried him at "estimates," but he would make little digressions, estimating the velocity of the earth, or drawing heads on the waste paper, and proved incompetent. He was at home with logarithms but stuck at a common fraction: I did the estimates alone.

Notwithstanding the fact that he hindered my work, I grew to like the boy. He would ask questions that set my hair on end, without showing effort or seeking effect. Once he asked me if I thought him a coward, and I could not say; but when a stone from one of the blasts knocked the paint-pot out of his hand, he only observed that that was a wasteful method of blasting.

A day came that I had dreaded for many weeks: the Black Cape had to be measured. I postponed the job until the afternoon, walking up and down brooding over the difficulty. I told my party that one of us must be lowered down the cliff, and swinging out below the dread brink of the precipice, must paint a conspicuous white mark at a point that I should name. The narrowness of the ledge from which the work must be done, the weakness of the rope, the difficulty of keeping a clear head in such a place, all made the operation exceedingly dangerous. I could not do the work myself, for my presence was required below; my men were too heavy, and Eustace— "Mr. B——, I'm going down the cliff." Eustace was standing before me, very pale, his eyes glittering. Presently he had gone away, and I saw him sitting on a log at some distance, trembling violently. I didn't think Eustace was so sensitive. After dinner I told my chainman: "Sinclair, you must do that cliff business." The three started the ascent to the ledge by ropes and ladders. The rodman went first and Eustace after him. The rope was being attached to a small cedar, as I adjusted my tripod, and looked through the instrument. I had prepared my lense, and bade them lower away. In the inverted picture presented by my lenses I saw a human form, lowered by a rope, swing into view. "Lower, five feet, lower yet, one foot up, three to the right, a little to the right, more, an inch higher, a little to the left still. Right, place the mark there." I finished signalling these directions with my hands, and leaving the instrument looked towards the cliff. The men above were in great distress, and the voice came up from below: "Cease lowering, hold on, I say!" It was Eustace swinging in mid-air, and the cedar was yielding! A moment of confusion. I shouted directions, they responded, the navvies looked up and joined the shouting. The cedar was crashing down the cliff with an avalanche of stones. The men on the ledge and Eustace were hidden by the dust. The men above were safe, but Eustace!—

From out of the cloud of dust I heard his voice: "Have you got any more cedars up there?"

When the dust cleared, the cedar was floating on the lake below, but Eustace was hanging on the face of the cliff, below the impending ledge. How he got out of the rope I don't know, or how he hung where there was no apparent crack in the face of the rock, I cannot tell. I recovered the rope, and took it up to the ledge, drawing up and attaching one of the guide-ropes that aided the ascent. Some men were piling blankets and sacks upon the rocks below, in order to break the fall. Hastily we lowered the rope, and called to Eustace. From below he was seen to swing outwards from the cliff, holding only by one foot and hand. His last support gave way, and he fell into space. A tremendous wrench threatened to drag us from the ledge. He had caught the rope, and was hanging

in mid-air, swinging in space. They were calling us to lower away, and the last yard was in our hands. "How much more?"—"Twenty feet." We gave up the hold of one man, and lowered the rope a bit; we gave up the second man, and one bore the strain alone. The strain was more than that one man could bear. "Look out!" There was a dull thud, a cry of expectation, and then three ringing cheers. When I descended to the lake, Eustace thrust a scrap of stone into my hand. "What's this? I found it where the mark was to be made."—"Why, it's silver!"

Next day, Eustace told me that he thought it would be advisable to go down to the "Landing" and have his teeth doctored: "Because I have neuralgia, you know; and really the diet here does not suit me."

I have had many a worse investment than the shares of a certain mine, found on the face of a cliff by a thoroughly useless man.

Duncan Campbell Scott

The Little Milliner

(1887)

The author: Duncan Campbell Scott was born on 2 August 1862 in Ottawa. He studied at a boarding school (Stanstead Wesleyan College, in Stanstead, Quebec, where his father was a Methodist minister until 1878, when he was dismissed) and soon afterwards (in 1879), due to the precarious situation of his family, he joined the Indian Branch of the Department of the Interior (soon reorganised as the Department of Indian Affairs in 1880) as a temporary junior clerk. He was a talented pianist, but a new friend he acquired in 1883 (Archibald Lampman) encouraged him to write poetry and short stories. His first published short story was "The Ducharmes of the Baskatonge," in the February 1887 issue of *Scribner's Magazine.*

The text: First published in *Scribner's Magazine* II: 4 (October 1887), 493-498, together with "The Desjardins" and "Josephine Labrosse" as part of a series entitled "In the Village of Viger." Reprinted in the volume *In the Village of Viger* (Boston: Copeland and Day, 1896), 13-29, from which the following has been taken. Contractions have been restored to the original from the magazine (for example, "wouldn't") instead of the peculiar forms from the volume (for example, "would n't"), while other errors have been corrected, following subsequent editions (for example, "Villeblanc sobered up and looked sadly" instead of "Villeblanc sobered up and look sadly").

Further reading: Gerald Lynch. "In the Meantime: Duncan Campbell Scott's *In the Village of Viger.*" SCL/ÉLC *Studies in Canadian Literature/Études en Littérature Canadienne* 17: 2 (Summer 1992), 70-91.

It was too true that the city was growing rapidly. As yet its arms were not long enough to embrace the little village of Viger, but before long they would be, and it was not a time that the inhabitants looked forward to with any pleasure. It was not to be wondered at, for few places were more pleasant to live in. The houses, half-hidden amid the trees, clustered around the slim steeple of St. Joseph's, which flashed like a naked poniard in the sun. They were old, and the village was sleepy, almost dozing, since the mill, behind the rise of land, on the Blanche had shut down. The miller had died; and who would trouble to grind what little grist came to the mill, when flour was so cheap? But while the beech-groves lasted, and the Blanche continued to run, it seemed impossible that any change could come. The change was coming, however, rapidly enough. Even now, on still nights, above the noise of the frogs in the pools, you could hear the rumble of the street-cars and the faint tinkle of their bells, and when the air was moist the whole southern sky was luminous with the reflection of thousands of gas-lamps. But when the time came for Viger to be mentioned in the city papers as one of the outlying wards, what a change there would be! There would be no unfenced fields, full of little inequalities and covered with short grass; there would be no deep pools, where the quarries had been, and where the boys pelted the frogs; there would be no more beech-groves, where the children could gather nuts; and the dread pool, which had filled the shaft where old Daigneau, years ago, mined for gold, would cease to exist. But in the meantime, the boys of Viger roamed over the unclosed fields and pelted the frogs, and the boldest ventured to roll huge stones into Daigneau's pit, and only waited to see the green slime come working up to the surface before scampering away, their flesh creeping with the idea that it was old Daigneau himself who was stirring up the water in a rage.

New houses had already commenced to spring up in all directions, and there was a large influx of the laboring population which overflows from large cities. Even on the main street of Viger, on a lot which had been vacant ever since it was a lot, the workmen had built a foundation. After a while it was finished, when men from the city came and put up the oddest wooden house that one could imagine. It was perfectly square; there was a window and a door in front, a window at the side, and a window upstairs. There were many surmises as to the probable occupant of such a diminutive habitation; and the widow Laroque, who made dresses and trimmed hats, and whose shop was directly opposite, and next door to the Post Office, suffered greatly from unsatisfied curiosity. No one who looked like the proprietor was ever seen near the place. The foreman of the laborers who were working at the house seemed to know nothing; all that he said, in answer to questions, was: "I have my orders."

At last the house was ready; it was painted within and without, and Madame Laroque could scarcely believe her eyes when, one morning, a man came from the city with a small sign under his arm and nailed it above the door. It bore these words: "Mademoiselle Viau, Milliner." "Ah!" said Madame Laroque, "the bread is to be taken out of my mouth." The next day came a load of furniture,—not a very large load, as there was only a small stove, two tables, a bedstead, three chairs, a sort of lounge, and two large boxes. The man who brought the things put them in the house, and locked the door on them when he went away; then nothing happened for two weeks, but Madame Laroque watched. Such a queer little house it was, as it stood there so new in its coat of gum-colored paint. It looked just like a square bandbox which some Titan had made for his wife; and there seemed no doubt that if you took hold of the chimney and lifted the roof off, you would see the gigantic bonnet, with its strings and ribbons, which the Titaness could wear to church on Sundays.

Madame Laroque wondered how Mademoiselle Viau would come, whether in a cab, with her trunks and boxes piled around her, or on foot, and have her belongings on a cart. She watched every approaching vehicle for two weeks in vain; but one morning she saw that a curtain had been put up on the window opposite, that it was partly raised, and that a geranium was standing on the sill. For one hour she never took her eyes off the door, and at last had the satisfaction of seeing it open. A trim little person, not very young, dressed in gray, stepped out on the platform with her apron full of crumbs and cast them down for the birds. Then, without looking around, she went in and closed the door. It was Mademoiselle Viau. "The bird is in its nest," thought the old postmaster, who lived alone with his mother. All that Madame Laroque said was: "Ah!"

Mademoiselle Viau did not stir out that day, but on the next she went to the baker's and the butcher's and came over the road to Monsieur Cuerrier, the postmaster, who also kept a grocery.

That evening, according to her custom, Madame Laroque called on Madame Cuerrier.

"We have a neighbor," she said.

"Yes."

"She was making purchases to-day."

"Yes."

"To-morrow she will expect people to make purchases."

"Without doubt."

"It is very tormenting, this, to have these irresponsible girls, that no one knows anything about, setting up shops under our very noses. Why does she live alone?"

"I did not ask her," answered Cuerrier, to whom the question was addressed.

"You are very cool, Monsieur Cuerrier; but if it was a young man and a postmaster, instead of a young woman and a milliner, you would not relish it."

"There can be only one postmaster," said Cuerrier.

"In Paris, where I practised my art," said Monsieur Villeblanc, who was a retired hairdresser, "there were whole rows of tonsorial parlors, and every one had enough to do." Madame Laroque sniffed, as she always did in his presence.

"Did you see her hat?" she asked.

"I did, and it was very nice."

"Nice! with the flowers all on one side? I wouldn't go to St. Thérèse with it on." St. Thérèse was the postmaster's native place.

"The girl has no taste," she continued.

"Well, if she hasn't, you needn't be afraid of her."

"There will be no choice between you," said the retired hairdresser, maliciously.

But there was a choice between them, and all the young girls of Viger chose Mademoiselle Viau. It was said she had such an eye; she would take a hat and pin a bow on here, and loop a ribbon there, and cast a flower on somewhere else, all the time surveying her work with her head on one side and her mouth bristling with pins. "There, how do you like that?—put it on—no, it is not becoming—wait!" and in a trice the desired change was made. She had no lack of work from the first; soon she had too much to do.

At all hours of the day she could be seen sitting at her window, working, and "she must be making money fast," argued Madame Laroque, "for she spends nothing." In truth, she spent very little—she lived so plainly. Three times a week she took a fresh twist from the baker, once a day, the milkman left a pint of milk, and once every week mademoiselle herself stepped out to the butcher's and bought a pound of steak. Occasionally she mailed a letter, which she always gave into the hands of the postmaster; if he was not there she asked for a pound of tea or something else that she needed. She was fast friends with Cuerrier, but with no one else, as she never received visitors. Once only did a young man call on her. It was young Jourdain, the clerk in the dry-goods store. He had knocked at the door and was admitted. "Ah!" said Madame Laroque, "it is the young men who can conquer." But the next moment Monsieur Jourdain came out, and, strangely enough, was so bewildered as to forget to put on his hat. It was not this young man who could conquer.

"There is something mysterious about that young person," said Madame Laroque between her teeth.

"Yes," replied Cuerrier, "very mysterious—she minds her own business."

"Bah!" said the widow, "who can tell what her business is, she who comes from no one knows where? But I'll find out what all this secrecy means, trust me!"

So the widow watched the little house and its occupant very closely, and these are some of the things she saw: Every morning an open door and crumbs for the birds, the watering of the geranium, which was just going to flower, a small figure going in and out, dressed in gray, and, oftener than anything else, the same figure sitting at the window, working. This continued for a year with little variation, but still the widow watched. Every one else had accepted the presence of the new resident as a benefaction. They had got accustomed to her. They called her "the little milliner." Old Cuerrier called her "the little one in gray." But she was not yet adjusted in the widow's system of things. She laid a plot with her second cousin, which was that the cousin should get a hat made by Mademoiselle Viau, and that she should ask her some questions.

"Mademoiselle Viau, were you born in the city?"

"I do not think, Mademoiselle, that green will become you."

"No, perhaps not. Where did you live before you came here?"

"Mademoiselle, this gray shape is very pretty." And so on.

That plan would not work.

But before long something very suspicious happened. One evening, just about dusk, as Madame Laroque was walking up and down in front of her door, a man of a youthful appearance came quickly up the street, stepped upon Mademoiselle Viau's platform, opened the door without knocking, and walked in. Mademoiselle was working in the last vestige of daylight, and the widow watched her like a lynx. She worked on unconcernedly, and when it became so dark that she could not see she lit her lamp and pulled down the curtain. That night Madame Laroque did not go into Cuerrier's. It commenced to rain, but she put on a large frieze[347] coat of the deceased Laroque and crouched in the dark. She was very much interested in this case, but her interest brought no additional knowledge. She had seen the man go in; he was rather young and about the medium height, and had a black mustache; she could remember him distinctly, but she did not see him come out.

The next morning Mademoiselle Viau's curtain went up as usual, and as it was her day to go to the butcher's she went out. While she was away Madame Laroque took a long look in at the side window, but there was nothing to see except the lounge and the table.

While Madame Laroque had been watching in the rain, Cuerrier was reading to Villeblanc from *Le Monde*.[348] "Hello!" said he, and then went on reading to himself.

"Have you lost your voice?" asked Villeblanc, getting nettled.

"No, no; listen to this—'Daring Jewel Robbery. A Thief in the Night.'" These were the headings of the column, and then followed the particulars. In the morning the widow borrowed the paper, as she had been too busy the night before to come and hear it read. She looked over the front page, when her eye caught the heading, "Daring Jewel Robbery," and she read the whole story. As she neared the end her eyebrows commenced to travel up her forehead, as if they were going to hide in her hair, and with an expression of surprise she tossed the paper to her second cousin.

"Look here!" she said, "read this out to me."

---

[347] A type of linen originally from Frisia.

[348] A popular French-language newspaper published in Montreal. It was called *Le Nouveau Monde* from 1867 to 1881. It became *Le Monde canadien* in 1897. It folded in 1899.

The second cousin commenced to read at the top.

"No, no! right here."

"'The man Durocher, who is suspected of the crime, is not tall, wears a heavy mustache, has gray eyes, and wears an ear-ring in his left ear. He has not been seen since Saturday.'"

"I told you so!" exclaimed the widow.

"You told me nothing of the kind," said the second cousin.

"He had no ear-ring in his ear," said the widow—"but—but—but it was the *right* ear that I saw. Hand me my shawl!"

"Where are you going?"

"I have business; never mind!" She took the paper with her and went straight to the constable.

"But," said he, "I cannot come."

"There is no time to be lost; you must come now."

"But he will be desperate; he will face me like a lion."

"Never mind! you will have the reward."

"Well, wait!" And the constable went upstairs to get his pistol.

He came down with his blue coat on. He was a very fat man, and was out of breath when he came to the little milliner's.

"But who shall I ask for?" he inquired of Madame Laroque. 1887

"Just search the house, and I will see that he does not escape by the back door." She had forgotten that there was no back door.

"Do you want a bonnet?" asked Mademoiselle Viau. She was on excellent terms with the constable.

"No!" said he, sternly. "You have a man in this house, and I have come to find him."

"Indeed?" said mademoiselle, very stiffly. "Will you be pleased to proceed?"

"Yes," said he, taking out his pistol and cocking it. "I will first look downstairs." He did so, and only frightened a cat from under the stove. No one knew that Mademoiselle Viau had a cat.

"Lead the way upstairs!" commanded the constable.

"I am afraid of your pistol, will you not go first?"

He went first and entered at once the only room, for there was no hall. In the mean time Madame Laroque had found out that there was no back door, and had come into the lower flat and reinspected it, looking under everything.

"Open that closet!" said the constable, as he levelled his pistol at the door.

Mademoiselle threw open the door and sprang away, with her hands over her ears. There was no one there; neither was there any one under the bed.

“Open that trunk!” eying the little leather-covered box.

“Monsieur, you will respect—but—as you will.” She stooped over the trunk and threw back the lid; on the top was a dainty white skirt, embroidered beautifully. The little milliner was blushing violently.

“That will do!” said the constable. “There is no one there.”

“Get out of the road!” he cried to the knot of people who had collected at the door. “I have been for my wife’s bonnet; it is not finished.” But the people looked at his pistol, which he had forgotten to put away. He went across to the widow’s.

“Look here!” he said, “you had better stop this or I’ll have the law on you—no words now! Making a fool of me before the people—getting me to put on my coat and bring my pistol to frighten a cat from under the stove. No words now!”

“Monsieur Cuerrier,” inquired Madame Laroque that night, “who is it that Mademoiselle Viau writes to?”

1887 “I am an official of the government. I do not tell state secrets.”

“State secrets, indeed! Depend upon it, there are secrets in those letters which the state would like to know.”

“That is not my business. I only send the letters where they are posted, and refuse to tell amiable widows where they go.”

The hairdresser, forgetting his constant fear of disarranging his attire, threw back his head and laughed wildly.

“Trust a barber to laugh,” said the widow. Villeblanc sobered up and looked sadly at Cuerrier; he could not bear to be called a barber.

“And you uphold her in this—a person who comes from no one knows where, and writes to no one knows who——”

“I know who she writes to——” The widow got furious.

“Yes, who she writes to—yes, of course you do—that person who comes out of her house without ever having gone into it, and who is visited by men who go in and never come out——”

“How do you know he went in?”

“I saw him.”

“How do you know he never came out?”

“I didn’t see him.”

“Ah! then you were watching?”

"Well, what if I was! The devil has a hand in it."

"I have no doubt," said Cuerrier, insinuatingly.

"Enough, fool!" exclaimed the widow—"but wait, I have not done yet!"

"You had better rest, or you will have the law on you."

The widow was afraid of the law.

About six months after this, when the snow was coming on, a messenger came from the city with a telegram for Monsieur Cuerrier—at least, it was in his care. He very seldom went out, but he got his boots and went across to Mademoiselle Viau's. The telegram was for her. When she had read it she crushed it in her hand and leaned against the wall. But she recovered herself.

"Monsieur Cuerrier, you have always been a good friend to me—help me! I must go away—you will watch my little place when I am gone!"

The postmaster was struck with pity, and he assisted her. She left that night.

"*Accomplice!*" the widow hissed in his ear the first chance she got.

About three weeks after this, when Madame Laroque asked for *Le Monde*, Cuerrier refused to give it to her.

"Where is it?"

"It has been lost."

"*Lost!*" said the widow, derisively. "Well, I will find it." In an hour she came back with the paper.

"There!" said she, thrusting it under the postmaster's nose so that he could not get his pipe back to his mouth. Cuerrier looked consciously at the paragraph which she had pointed out. He had seen it before.

"Our readers will remember that the police, while attempting to arrest one Ellwell for the jewel-robbery which occurred in the city some time ago, were compelled to fire on the man in self-defence. He died last night in the arms of a female relative, who had been sent for at his request. He was known by various names—Durocher, Gillet, etc.—and the police have had much trouble with him."

"There!" said the widow.

"Well, what of that?"

"He died in the arms of a female relative."

"Well, were you the relative?"

"Indeed! my fine fellow, be careful! Do you think I would be the female relative of a convict? Do you not know any of these names?" The postmaster felt guilty; he did know one of the names.

"They are common enough," he replied. "The name of my aunt's second husband was Durocher."

"It will not do!" said the widow. "Somebody builds a house, no one knows who; people come and go, no one knows how; and you, a stupid postmaster, shut your eyes and help things along."

Three days after this, Mademoiselle Viau came home. She was no longer the little one in gray; she was the little one in black. She came straight to Monsieur Cuerrier to get her cat. Then she went home. The widow watched her go in. "Now," she said, "we will not see her come out again."

Mademoiselle Viau refused to take any more work. She was sick, she said; she wanted to rest. She rested for two weeks, and Monsieur Cuerrier brought her food ready cooked. Then he stopped; she was better. One evening Madame Laroque peeped in at the side window. She saw the little milliner quite distinctly. She was on her knees, her face was hidden in her arms. The fire was very bright, and the lamp was lighted.

Two days after that the widow said to Cuerrier: "It is very strange there is no smoke. Has Mademoiselle Viau gone away?"

"Yes, she has gone."

"Did you see her go?"

"No."

"It is as I said—no one has seen her go. But wait, she will come back; and no one will see her come."

That was three years ago, and she has not come back. All the white curtains are pulled down. Between the one that covers the front window and the sash stands the pot in which grew the geranium. It only had one blossom all the time it was alive, and it is dead now and looks like a dry stick. No one knows what will become of the house. Madame Laroque thinks that Monsieur Cuerrier knows. She expects, some morning, to look across and see the little milliner cast down crumbs for the birds. In the meantime, in every corner of the house the spiders are weaving webs, and an enterprising caterpillar has blocked up the key-hole with his cocoon.

Roger Pocock

Lost

(1888)

The author: Pocock was an adventurer, whose life can hardly be contained in a few lines. After he recovered from the frostbite and snow-blindness of the 1885 campaign with the North-West Mounted Police, he wandered through Canada and the US as a travelling salesman, a prospector, or a journalist. In 1898, he organised and led an expedition to Klondike, but it failed to reach the destination and one member died. He set a record for long-distance horse-riding on the Outlaw Trail in 1899 (from Fort MacLeod, Alberta, to Mexico City). He published accounts of this in *Lloyd's Weekly Newspaper*. He served in the Boer War, as a volunteer in the National Scouts; back in London, he accompanied a Danish expedition to Greenland. *The Illustrated Mail* sent him to Russia in 1904, during the war with Japan. He founded the Legion of Frontiersmen (which still exists): he started with ads in the press, looking for men with guns and experience of "real frontier work," to guard the empire's borders in times of peace and serve as mounted riflemen in time of war. More than 10,000 men enrolled and trained by 1914. Pocock was no longer in the Legion, but he, too, served in WWI as a corporal in the County of London Defence Corps. He was promoted captain, seeing service in Military Intelligence and the Royal Air Force. He continued to take part in expeditions (not of all of which were organised by him) until the last days of his life. He died on 12 November 1941.

The text: It appeared as "Lost. The Story of a Strange Adventure," in *Tales of Western Life, Lake Superior and the Canadian Prairie*. By H. R. A. Pocock (Ottawa: Printed by C. W. Mitchell, 1888), 96-114. The book was dedicated "To the 'Riders of the Plains,' the Gallant North-West Mounted Police." In his "Preface," Pocock confessed to "an attempt . . . to describe certain phases of Western Life and Scenery in Canada, and to present some of the peculiarities which distinguish western from more civilized communities elsewhere. It must not however be supposed that men and women in the North-West are of necessity picturesque and barbarous; for indeed the towns and villages are complete models of their kind, the women have harmoniums and social differences, choir practices, and an exhaustive knowledge of their neighbours' affairs; the men look after the politics and the weather, go to church when not too lazy, and are sometimes depraved enough to carry umbrellas. . . . But this book is not about the citizens and the farmers . . . I have ventured to describe only the portions of the community that do not live in the routine of civilized life, to tell the truth about them, to do justice to them, to represent as far as possible the action of law and other circumstance upon such elements; to describe them before they are all gone" (v-vi).

I was sent by the Officer Commanding with a despatch to Pipeclay Creek, the telegraph line being down; and, since there were no 'jumpers' (little sleighs) in the Post, I travelled mounted, trusting that the weather would hold steady until I got back. I was well provided against the cold with a buffalo coat, fur cap, two pairs of riding breeches, three of stockings, and good moose moccasins. No one would have suspected any danger on that jolly winter day. The thermometer was steady at forty degrees below zero,[349] the sun bright, and the air sparkling with tiny points of light, while the snow beside the trail shone like a sheet of gems. Breathing that clear air set all one's blood racing, and it seemed like a draught of spring water in one's throat. The frost from my breath soon made long icicles from my moustache; the film spread across my eyes and had to be brushed off every few minutes; my cap, and the breast of my coat were sparkling with frost, and the horse was all white with rime. But a chap doesn't mind cold with good furs, an easy Mexican saddle, and a fine broncho like mine under him. Sometimes trotting a mile or so, but walking usually, and keeping Buck held in lest he should play out, I came at about noon to Brown's 'stopping place;' and, having rubbed down, watered, and fed my horse, I got Mrs. Brown, who is a fair cook although a half-breed, to make me some dinner. There must have been something wrong with the food, for it made me uneasy all the afternoon with something like colic.

It must have been four o'clock, and I had made some miles since dinner, when I saw that the weather was changing; and, although the sun still shone in a clear sky, the air became hazy, and breaths of wind began to sift up the snow in places. I tried to

[349] Forty degrees below zero is the same on the Fahrenheit and the Celsius scales.

take my bearings, although I knew that there was not so much as a stone for twenty miles ahead, but the horizon was already hidden; and, in a few minutes after I first feared a change, there set in the wildest blizzard I had ever seen. The wind swirled in fierce eddies, the snow lashing my face like a thousand whips; and where I could catch sight of the ground I saw that the trail was fast drifting over, and even Buck's fresh tracks were covered almost as soon as he made them. Seeing that there was no hope unless I kept the trail, I dismounted to lead Buck, who would do nothing but back up against the wind; and I might have got on even then but for the colic, that seemed to take all the strength out of me. Instead of warming I tired, and the snow was now so soft that there was great difficulty in making any headway. After a time my cheeks began to freeze; and my hands getting wet in attempting to thaw them with snow, they got so numb that I couldn't dry them, and froze too. At last I mounted and left the way to Buck's instinct; and as a last resort fired off the seven rounds in my revolver in case there were any freighters near; but I could hear no sound except the wind howling all round, and began to give up hope.

I had read in dime novels of men lost on the prairie cutting their horses open and getting inside; but I guess that they only do that in dime novels, for a chap who would serve an old friend like Buck in that fashion deserves to freeze stiff. I could see where the sun was setting, and knew that my proper course was south; but which way did the sun set—North West? I knew it ought to set there at that season, and so I must keep it to the right. Or was I to keep to the right of it? And which was my right? Before the sun set I believe I turned my face from it in order to go towards it.

I remembered as the night set in that if I fell asleep I should never wake; so I rode on swaying from side to side of the saddle, so drowsy that I could hardly remember to keep my knees tight against the horse's sides. I beat my hands together until the arms ached, but could not warm them; and, sometimes I slid down to the ground to walk until I could get my eyes open. I suppose the storm went down after the sun set, because I remember the night was very calm, and the stars unusually bright. There was a light on the horizon that seemed to come from a shack, for there appeared to be barns near it, and a hay rick. I tried all night to get to the light, but it seemed to keep just at the same distance off, and at last melted away.

It must have been at about noon the next day that I remember sitting still in the saddle, and there being bushes all round; and Buck went along a step at a time scraping away the snow with his hoofs, with his head down. I seemed to think that I was wanted somewhere, and yet could not tell where to go. I set Buck off at the trot; and kept traveling some time, until the plain was all left behind and I saw Chief Mountain[350] right ahead and made for a Pass beside it.

Soon I came to the Pass, and went in until the mountains shut in the view all around. The tops seemed to get higher and higher, and the gorge deeper and blacker, until the mountains actually began arching overhead, but miles high. I stopped still, and kept watching until I saw them join overhead; and then they all fell with a crash over me and I was buried. First I was broad awake; but a delicious sleep seemed to creep up me until I was nearly covered as it were with cold still water. But there was a beating going on in my brain; and, while the sleep crept up my face and covered me, it crashed harder and harder, and then something seemed to close in over my eyes with a little throbbing, and I was dead.

I seemed to awaken without any body, and I had no size or weight, but only just *me.* I was hanging in awful eternity all dark and cold and full of horror. I was hanging on what seemed a thread of light, but I could not feel or see it. The ray or thread seemed to slant away forever upwards and downwards, and I was frightened lest I should fall off although there was nothing to fall to. But the most awful thing was being *alone.* I had never been *alone* in my life before, and it was so awful that for months after I could never think of it without terror. Then somehow I felt I was moving at a frightful speed as it were on an orbit like the earth does. Each time I passed round the circle *something* passed going in the opposite direction to me. And that other thing was ME, but not the *me* I had been before I died, but as it were another half of me I had never come across before. Each time we crossed something of knowledge passed between us. At first it used to be millions of years between our meetings, but the time between got shorter and shorter until I had hardly time to understand one meeting before another came. Once it seemed that one of a set of ten rounds was missed, and it was a horrible aching loss repeated every tenth round. At last I felt that I gained whole worlds of knowledge at

[350] In the US state of Montana, on the border with Alberta, Canada.

each meeting, and kept waiting for them with fear, but yet felt that I existed for nothing else. And then they came so quickly that I had not time to expect them, for they were like crashes falling on me quicker and quicker and destroying me. At last they blended one with another with such a feeling as though the sun were to be suddenly blown out at noon; and that instant I was joined with the other *me* in one, knowing all things in Heaven and Earth, all things that ever were, or are, or shall be; and I said it was like the blowing out of the sun, for everything in the past, the present, or eternal future, everything in all Space and all Time was but ONE WORD—and the name of that one word was GOD!

We talk of the ordinary Being we call God as being great: but I tell you that then I was greater than any god I had known enough to think about. I don't want to be disrespectful to Him mind, because I know that He is greater than any ordinary god I could imagine, so grand and terrible and good that I feel now as though I could cry with shame at ever having said as much as a common damn. It may seem a queer thing for a man like me to be writing on such a subject; but I am a very different sort of chap since that dream, and I want to tell the World about the awful things I saw.

As to what followed you must wait Reader until there is a Heavenly Language to write it down in. I saw God with these eyes, I saw Him as I would see you if you were standing before me now; but I could no more tell what He was like than—than blow out the sun. It was not meant that I should, or I should have been given a way to do it, so I will go on with my story.

When I awoke I was lying on the snow with my buffalo coat open, and Buck with one hoof on my breast, and gently licking my forehead with his rough tongue. I talked to him as I lay there, and he looked down in my face just as though he were trying to speak. I wish men would show as much feeling for a chap when he's down in his luck. I recollect distinctly saying "Are you dead too, Buck, old chap?" Then my head seemed to get quite clear, and I stood up. "Say Buck, we're dying—at least I am. We have got to get home again somehow—which way shall we go, old man?" Buck took a long look all round, then sniffed and looked at me as much as to say "Well you'd oughter know." "I don't Buck, though," I said, "you see we're lost us two. Wait a bit we'll have a smoke and a bit of fire anyhow." I had matches and tobacco, and when

I got the pipe lit I felt splendid. Then I took the despatch, and committed it to memory, and used the paper to light a fire of twigs from the poplar bush near by. I was not so badly frozen as I had thought, and the pain of thawing out braced me so that I began to feel hungry. There was no food to be had, so I chewed one of my mitts instead. I had eased Buck of the saddle, and found his back was not a bit sore, which surprised me considering the length of time he must have had it on. I found he had been keeping himself alive by scraping away the snow with his hoofs to get at the long grass near the bush, and in the hollows. I took a whisp of grass and rubbed him down until he began to feel quite comfortable, and to dance round as though he had been in the stable a week. I suppose he did this to cheer me up, for he couldn't have been so merry after having no oats since noon the day before.

By the time we got finished it was quite dark; so for fear of freezing if I slept, and knowing I must do all I knew how to get back to the Post, I steered North by the Pole Star, but could go no faster than a walk on account of the snow. For some hours we kept on, and I repeated all the poetry I could think of to keep up our spirits; and even got off two or three songs, which were not up to much for I am a poor singer. By and by I concluded I would try my hand at praying, that being the most appropriate thing on such an occasion. But I could only think of the Lord's Prayer, and part of the Ten Commandments, which I soon finished. Then I tried to recall my catechism, but I got it all mixed up. By the time I had got to Keeping one's tongue from picking and stealing[351] I thought I had better quit. After that my mind began to be hazy again, and I knew that the delirium must be coming on, but could do nothing to prevent it. I repeated the multiplication table to try and keep my head clear, but it was no use, and I had the wildest fancies imaginable, so magnificent sometimes that I wonder that my mind could have imagined them. I seemed to be one Hero, a great ideal man, who had saved England by his own splendid daring in time of War; that some time in the twentieth century the Masses rose up and overthrew the Government, and in the Revolution London was on fire, but Hero came and overthrew the mob government, and put out the fire. After that he build up

[351] The sentence in the Church of England Catechism the character was confused about is the following: "To keep my hands from picking and stealing, and my tongue from evil speaking, lying, and slandering" (part of the answer to the question "What is thy duty towards thy Neighbour?").

the old Empire again, only more magnificent than men had ever dreamed of in the past; that he built up a great new London with a Capitol covering a mile square in the middle, adorned with a Cathedral whose dome soared up nine hundred feet into the sky; that he converted all nations to the Christian Faith, and caused a great re-union of all the churches; that he taught the world a new architecture, new sciences, new methods of art, and how to bring all the laws of Nature to be servants of Man; and at last how he was killed in a great battle in which England was fighting the whole world in defence of Freedom, aided by her colonies and the United States; and his death shook the whole earth.

The next thing I can recall was watching the Aurora in my natural senses, and I suppose the same night. There was a grand display that night—First came streamers of the common white, four bands abreast, and extending across the whole sky. When they got overhead they seemed to be only a hundred feet overhead. In a minute all the four bands changed into snake-like strips of red fire, squirming about, and moving at a terrible speed, while behind them seemed to be a pale green ground. The huge, fiery snakes were so bright and sharp that more than once I thought I heard the queer rustling crackling sound that the Aurora make sometimes, but I may be mistaken. I was surprised at this, because I thought that that kind of Aurora, which I had seen once before, was only seen in the spring and fall.

Buck was again scraping away the snow; and I set him off at a trot and went on for some time. Then it was broad daylight, and Buck was going at the keen jump when we came it seemed to the top of a hill; below me lay the city of Montreal just as you see it from the Mountain. Buck balked and wouldn't go down the hill; and as I had brought no spurs on the trip for fear of freezing my feet, I was obliged to swear at him until he started. When we got down into the town I made a break for home, for Mother lives in Montreal, and had been there since we came from England years ago. I reached the house, and tied the horse to the garden railing; then stole in quietly at the front door, and found her in the drawing-room sitting by the fire darning a stocking, just as I see her now while I am writing this; and I stole up behind her and kissed her.

Then the scene changed, and I was on the deck of my Father's old ship, with a regular Atlantic gale blowing; on the quarter deck stood Father just as I had seen him many a time; and the waves washed over the vessel again and again, and had we not all held on to bolts and shrouds we should have been washed overboard. A try sail[352] was set to keep her steady, and the ship could stand not a rag of canvass more. But Father seemed to have lost his senses, and sent both watches aloft to make sail as though we had a summer breeze, instead of a storm that looked as if it was to be our last. However I went aloft too; and was on the yard-arm with the men, while the sail we were working at was flapping angrily in our faces. Then I felt a sharp blow on the breast and face from the canvass, and heard Father cry out, and the next moment I was falling through space, and then many fathoms deep in the cold sea. I struck out, and came up far in the wake of the ship: and was beaten hither and thither by the confused rush of the waves, that seemed to grin at me with the faces of the dead, all white as drifting snow. The gulls wheeled screaming in the air above, the wild waves circled round me like the vortex of the Maelstrom, and then all was still as death. I could hear a voice calling, but not make out what was said; and then I thought it was the voice of the Sergeant Major of my Troop calling out: "Now then—what are you about? Who told you to dismount—eh?" I knew that I must have been bucked off my horse in the Riding School, and that all the rest were waiting for me to mount again, but still I could not as much as open my eyes. There was a moving to and fro, and I felt myself carried on a stretcher to the Hospital. The next thing I was conscious of was the rumbling and jolting of wheels, the tramp of feet, and the awful music of the Dead March.[353] I knew I was being buried alive, and I even thought I could hear my Mother crying behind, yet couldn't move or speak, or give any sign of life. I fought and fought but could make no sign, and presently felt to my horror that I was dozing off again. I made one great struggle, and felt I could break my body to pieces rather than not be heard—then there was a low rushing sound, and I was awake.

The prairie round me was hazy, the wind was sweeping up the snow with low melancholy gusts, the sky was grey with clouds, and, as I watched, a heavy storm set in—not cold, but one of those moist heavy falls of snow, that with wind are taken for blizzards by

[352] The main (fore-and-aft) sail on any mast in the Royal Navy was called a "trysail" in the 19th century.

[353] See note 228. The riding school of the NWMP, mentioned above, was in Regina.

many people. I watched the storm for a long time sitting quite still in the saddle, but then the delirium must have set in, for I became first a Russian Arch Duke and then a Montana Cow-boy.

After that I remembered very little of what happened; and, as the yarn is being dragged out to a much greater length than was intended, I will pass over the next three or four days, during which I must have become very feeble both in brain and body. I was stupid and dull, and my brain never fully cleared for a moment; but from what I can learn I must have travelled a long distance without knowing it. The weather must have been mild or I would have been frozen stiff; and somehow I must have been looked after all that time, just as they say Providence looks after a chap when he's drunk. But one thing I will never forget as long as I live. I had been travelling down hill I thought, all one night, full of strange fancies. At last I imagined a party of Mounted Police was approaching up the trail, and I was glad to see them even though it was in a dream. As I rode straight towards the phantoms, expecting I suppose that the dream would dissolve as soon as I got close, I saw one of them open his mouth to speak. I heard a human voice speaking to me as in a mist; then I felt my body fall with a crash to the ground—and I remember no more.

* * * * * * *

They say it was weeks and months before the doctors knew that I should live; a watch was kept by me in hospital night and day for forty five days, and on the forty sixth day I awoke in my right mind, and found my old chum himself sitting by the bedside. And you bet I feel mean after all that to think of the life I led before I was frozen; and that I thank the Great God who showed himself to me in my delirium, for making me a better lad, even at the expense of the most splendid physique that ever man had.

I am now at home with mother; and I wish you as good a nurse if ever you should happen to get stove-up[354] reader.

I hope it will not be considered an impertinence on the part of McNeill's chum to add a few words to this strange story.

I was one of the party sent out after the missing man, and was given charge of the party as a special favour on account of being McNeill's chum. He is a universal favourite, a man intended

[354] Or stoved-up; slang for run-down, worn-out, exhausted.

by nature to be more respected in the world than is usually the case with a hair-brained buck-policeman.[355] He has both talent and originality; and, if not cursed with a roving disposition and a love for whiskey, might have risen to eminence.

We found him riding slowly down a main trail with his arms crossed upon his breast and his head down. His buffalo overcoat was spread under the saddle to ease and warm the horse at the expense of the rider, and it was his red serge jacket that first attracted our attention at a distance of perhaps two miles. As he came near he regarded us with a fixed stare, but showed no sign of recognition. When he got within a horse's length I called him by name: His whole body seemed to shrink and recoil at the sound, and then he fell with a crash from the saddle insensible. We carried him to the nearest Police Post, he having travelled nearly 150 miles during the seven days he was lost, and tended him with great care all the way. It was a long time before he recovered his faculties, and many months before he was fit to travel. In the meanwhile my time had expired, and not wishing to re-engage I delayed my return to the Eastern Provinces until my chum was fit to travel with me, he having been invalided pending his claim for a pension. On our arrival at Montreal he went home, and has since been sometimes better sometimes worse, but shows some sign of a permanent recovery. His lungs were injured by the frost, but I have no fear that he is really suffering as he says from Consumption; and his fine brain seems in some respects deteriorated. I think that he will be tempted by the coming summer when he sees the ice melt and the sun shine out over the trees, and recover in time some of his old zest for life, and be himself again.

This narrative is intended to represent some of the phenomena attending prolonged exposure to cold. Instances have been comparatively frequent of the recovery of persons frozen who have been for days protected by a covering of snow; but hitherto the Author has not been able to find in the Medical Records on the subject any instance of delirium from frost; unless that of one of the Arctic explorers who found cold affected his men like drunkenness can be accepted as a precedent. The minor detail of the following story is from personal experience, as also the phenomena of exalted delirium; but for the main outline of

[355] "Buck" means of the lowest rank.

the theme the Author is indebted to an unfortunate member of the Mounted Police, who while on duty in Alberta was for seven days lost in winter, and during that period had neither food nor shelter, nor any association with men. His recovery was due to a fine constitution, and he is now fit for the ordinary occupations of life, although sadly disfigured, and deprived of that keen zest of life, and ambition, and capability which formerly characterised him. In another instance in the records of the Mounted Police, a man was, although only delirious for two hours at most, slightly impaired as regards the brain, and suffered for some time from injuries to two vital organs. No two cases of this nature would be alike, depending as they do so much upon the temperament of the individual, and the surrounding circumstances. Phenomena of this nature are fortunately so rare that the Medical Faculty have even in Canada few facilities for observation. There appears to be an interesting field of study here for future development.

Edward William Thomson

The Privilege of the Limits

(1891)

The author: Thomson was born on 12 February 1849 on a farm in what was then Peel County, Ontario (now part of the Greater Toronto Area). His father came from a family of old settlers (his grandfather had fought in the War of 1812 and had been a member of the Legislative Assembly of Upper Canada). His mother came from a successful Irish family (her brother was Michael Hamilton Foley, postmaster-general of Canada in the cabinet of John A. Macdonald before the Confederation). Thomson was educated at the Brantford Grammar School and at the Trinity College Grammar School in Weston (now in Port Hope), but at the age of 14, he was sent to Philadelphia, to join the wholesale business of an uncle. In October 1864, he enlisted in the 3rd Pennsylvania Cavalry and took part in several battles of the American Civil War. He was discharged in August 1865 and returned to Canada, but was again a soldier in 1866 and saw action against the Fenians at Ridgeway. He trained to be a civil engineer and became a land surveyor, but in 1878 he changed careers and joined the staff of the Toronto *Globe*. He was a surveyor again, in Manitoba, in the early 1880s, but by 1885 he was back with the *Globe*. In 1891, he moved to Boston, where he worked as revising editor of *The Youth's Companion*. In 1902, he returned to Canada, where he remained (until 1922) the Ottawa correspondent of the *Boston Transcript*. He wrote stories and poems (including a few about his Civil War experiences) for magazines, some of which he collected in *Old Man Savarin and Other Stories* (1895, with a new edition in 1917) and *When Lincoln Died and Other Poems* (1909). He died in Boston on 5 March 1924.

The text: First published in *Harper's Weekly* 35: 1805 (25 July 1891), 558. Reprinted in *Old Man Savarin and Other Stories* (Toronto: William Briggs, 1895), 29-44. The following is the 1895 version, which includes a few spelling changes.

"Yes, indeed, my grandfather wass once in jail," said old Mrs. McTavish, of the county of Glengarry,[356] in Ontario, Canada; "but that wass for debt, and he wass a ferry honest man whateffer, and he would not broke his promise—no, not for all the money in Canada. If you will listen to me, I will tell chust exactly the true story about that debt, to show you what an honest man my grandfather wass.

"One time Tougal Stewart, him that wass the poy's grandfather that keeps the same store in Cornwall[357] to this day, sold a plough to my grandfather, and my grandfather said he would pay half the plough in October, and the other half whateffer time he felt able to pay the money. Yes, indeed, that was the very promise my grandfather gave.

"So he was at Tougal Stewart's store on the first of October early in the morning pefore the shutters wass taken off, and he paid half chust exactly to keep his word. Then the crop wass ferry pad next year, and the year after that one of his horses wass killed py lightning, and the next year his brother, that wass not rich and had a big family, died, and do you think wass my grandfather to let the family be disgraced without a good funeral? No, indeed. So my grandfather paid for the funeral, and there was at it plenty of meat and drink for eferypody, as wass the right Hielan' custom those days; and after the funeral my grandfather did not feel chust exactly able to pay the other half for the plough that year either.

"So, then, Tougal Stewart met my grandfather in Cornwall next day after the funeral, and asked him if he had some money to spare.

"'Wass you in need of help, Mr. Stewart?' says my grandfather, kindly. 'For if it's in any want you are, Tougal,' says my grandfather, 'I will sell the coat off my back, if there is no other way to lend

[356] A historic county, settled by Scottish loyalists (mostly Highlanders) beginning with 1784. Today, the former county survives in the form of two townships, North Glengarry and South Glengarry, on the border with Quebec. Thomson used "McTavish" in other stories and a couple of times as his own pseudonym.

[357] A city in Ontario, on the border with both Quebec and the US state of New York.

you a loan;' for that was always the way of my grandfather with all his friends, and a bigger-hearted man there never wass in all Glengarry, or in Stormont, or in Dundas, moreofer.[358]

"'In want!' says Tougal—'in want, Mr. McTavish!' says he, very high. 'Would you wish to insult a gentleman, and him of the name of Stewart, that's the name of princes of the world?' he said, so he did.

"Seeing Tougal had his temper up, my grandfather spoke softly, being a quiet, peaceable man, and in wonder what he had said to offend Tougal.

"'Mr. Stewart,' says my grandfather, 'it wass not in my mind to anger you whatefer. Only I thought, from your asking me if I had some money, that you might be looking for a wee bit of a loan, as many a gentleman has to do at times, and no shame to him at all,' said my grandfather.

"'A loan?' says Tougal, sneering. 'A loan, is it? Where's your memory, Mr. McTavish? Are you not owing me half the price of the plough you've had these three years?'

"'And wass you asking me for money for the other half of the plough?' says my grandfather, very astonished.

"'Just that,' says Tougal.

"'Have you no shame or honor in you?' says my grandfather, firing up. 'How could I feel able to pay that now, and me chust yesterday been giving my poor brother a funeral fit for the McTavishes' own grand-nephew, that wass as good chentleman's plood as any Stewart in Glengarry. You saw the expense I wass at, for there you wass, and I thank you for the politeness of coming, Mr. Stewart,' says my grandfather, ending mild, for the anger would never stay in him more than a minute, so kind was the nature he had.

"'If you can spend money on a funeral like that, you can pay me for my plough,' says Stewart; for with buying and selling he wass become a poor creature, and the heart of a Hielan'man wass half gone out of him, for all he wass so proud of his name of monarchs and kings.

[358] Three historic counties (see also note 356), which form today the municipality of the United Counties of Stormont, Dundas and Glengarry (divided into several townships). They also provided the name of the Stormont, Dundas and Glengarry Highlanders, a reserve infantry regiment of the Canadian Army.

"My grandfather had a mind to strike him down on the spot, so he often said; but he thought of the time when he hit Hamish Cochrane in anger, and he minded the penances the priest put on him for breaking the silly man's jaw with that blow, so he smothered the heat that wass in him, and turned away in scorn. With that Tougal Stewart went to court, and sued my grandfather, puir mean creature.

"You might think that Judge Jones—him that wass judge in Cornwall before Judge Jarvis that's dead—would do justice. But no, he made it the law that my grandfather must pay at once, though Tougal Stewart could not deny what the bargain wass.

"'Your Honor,' says my grandfather, 'I said I'd pay when I felt able. And do I feel able now? No, I do not,' says he. 'It's a disgrace to Tougal Stewart to ask me, and himself telling you what the bargain was,' said my grandfather. But Judge Jones said that he must pay, for all that he did not feel able.

"'I will nefer pay one copper till I feel able,' says my grandfather; 'but I'll keep my Hielan' promise to my dying day, as I always done,' says he.

"And with that the old judge laughed, and said he would have to give judgment. And so he did; and after that Tougal Stewart got out an execution. But not the worth of a handful of oatmeal could the bailiff lay hands on, because my grandfather had chust exactly taken the precaution to give a bill of sale on his gear to his neighbor, Alexander Frazer, that could be trusted to do what was right after the law play was over.

"The whole settlement had great contempt for Tougal Stewart's conduct; but he was a headstrong body, and once he begun to do wrong against my grandfather, he held on, for all that his trade fell away; and finally he had my grandfather arrested for debt, though you'll understand, sir, that he was owing Stewart nothing that he ought to pay when he didn't feel able.

"In those times prisoners for debt wass taken to jail in Cornwall, and if they had friends to give bail that they would not go beyond the posts that wass around the sixteen acres nearest the jail walls, the prisoners could go where they liked on that ground. This was called 'the privilege of the limits.' The limits, you'll understand, wass marked by cedar posts painted white about the size of hitching-posts.[359]

[359] A post to which a horse or other animal is hitched.

"The whole settlement was ready to go bail for my grandfather if he wanted it, and for the health of him he needed to be in the open air, and so he gave Tuncan-Macdonnell of the Greenfields, and Æneas Macdonald of the Sandfields, for his bail, and he promised, on his Hielan' word of honor, not to go beyond the posts. With that he went where he pleased, only taking care that he never put even the toe of his foot beyond a post, for all that some prisoners of the limits would chump ofer them and back again, or maybe swing round them, holding by their hands.

"Efery day the neighbors would go into Cornwall to give my grandfather the good word, and they would offer to pay Tougal Stewart for the other half of the plough, only that vexed my grandfather, for he wass too proud to borrow, and, of course, every day he felt less and less able to pay on account of him having to hire a man to be doing the spring ploughing and seeding and making the kale-yard.[360]

"All this time, you'll mind, Tougal Stewart had to pay five shillings a week for my grandfather's keep, the law being so that if the debtor swore he had not five pound's worth of property to his name, then the creditor had to pay the five shillings, and, of course, my grandfather had nothing to his name after he gave the bill of sale to Alexander Frazer. A great diversion it was to my grandfather to be reckoning up that if he lived as long as his father, that was hale and strong at ninety-six, Tougal would need to pay five or six hundred pounds for him, and there was only two pound five shillings to be paid on the plough.

"So it was like that all summer, my grandfather keeping heartsome, with the neighbors coming in so steady to bring him the news of the settlement. There he would sit, just inside one of the posts, for to pass his jokes, and tell what he wished the family to be doing next. This way it might have kept going on for forty years, only it came about that my grandfather's youngest child—him that was my father—fell sick, and seemed like to die.

"Well, when my grandfather heard that bad news, he wass in a terrible way, to be sure, for he would be longing to hold the child in his arms, so that his heart was sore and like to break. Eat he could not, sleep he could not: all night he would be groaning, and all day he would be walking around by the posts, wishing that he had not passed his Hielan' word of honor not to go beyond a post;

[360] Scottish term for a vegetable garden (literally, a cabbage garden).

for he thought how he could have broken out like a chentleman, and gone to see his sick child, if he had stayed inside the jail wall. So it went on three days and three nights pefore the wise thought came into my grandfather's head to show him how he need not go beyond the posts to see his little sick poy. With that he went straight to one of the white cedar posts, and pulled it up out of the hole, and started for home, taking great care to carry it in his hands pefore him, so he would not be beyond it one bit.

"My grandfather wass not half a mile out of Cornwall, which was only a little place in those days, when two of the turnkeys came after him.

"'Stop, Mr. McTavish,' says the turnkeys.

"'What for would I stop?' says my grandfather.

"'You have broke your bail,' says they.

"'It's a lie for you,' says my grandfather, for his temper flared up for anybody to say he would broke his bail. 'Am I beyond the post?' says my grandfather.

"With that they run in on him, only that he knocked the two of them over with the post, and went on rejoicing, like an honest man should, at keeping his word and overcoming them that would slander his good name. The only thing pesides thoughts of the child that troubled him was questioning whether he had been strictly right in turning round for to use the post to defend himself in such a way that it was nearer the jail than what he wass. But when he remembered how the jailer never complained of prisoners of the limits chumping ofer the posts, if so they chumped back again in a moment, the trouble went out of his mind.

"Pretty soon after that he met Tuncan Macdonnell of Greenfields, coming into Cornwall with the wagon.

"'And how is this, Glengatchie?' says Tuncan. 'For you were never the man to broke your bail.'

"Glengatchie, you'll understand, sir, is the name of my grandfather's farm.

"'Never fear, Greenfields,' says my grandfather, 'for I'm not beyond the post.'

"So Greenfields looked at the post, and he looked at my grandfather, and he scratched his head a wee, and he seen it was so; and then he fell into a great admiration entirely.

"'Get in with me, Glengatchie—it's proud I'll be to carry you home;' and he turned his team around. My grandfather did so, taking great care to keep the post in front of him all the time; and that way he reached home. Out comes my grandmother running to embrace him; but she had to throw her arms around the post and my grandfather's neck at the same time, he was that strict to be within his promise. Pefore going ben[361] the house, he went to the back end of the kale-yard which was farthest from the jail, and there he stuck the post; and then he went back to see his sick child, while all the neighbors that came round was glad to see what a wise thought the saints had put into his mind to save his bail and his promise.

"So there he stayed a week till my father got well. Of course the constables came after my grandfather, but the settlement would not let the creatures come within a mile of Glengatchie. You might think, sir, that my grandfather would have stayed with his wife and weans, seeing the post was all the time in the kale-yard, and him careful not to go beyond it; but he was putting the settlement to a great deal of trouble day and night to keep the constables off, and he was fearful that they might take the post away, if ever they got to Glengatchie, and give him the name of false, that no McTavish ever had. So Tuncan Greenfields and Æneas Sandfield drove my grandfather back to the jail, him with the post behind him in the wagon, so as he would be between it and the jail. Of course Tougal Stewart tried his best to have the bail declared forfeited; but old Judge Jones only laughed, and said my grandfather was a Hielan' gentleman, with a very nice sense of honor, and that was chust exactly the truth.

"How did my grandfather get free in the end? Oh, then, that was because of Tougal Stewart being careless—him that thought he knew so much of the law. The law was, you will mind, that Tougal had to pay five shillings a week for keeping my grandfather in the limits. The money wass to be paid efery Monday, and it was to be paid in lawful money of Canada, too. Well, would you belief that Tougal paid in four shillings in silver one Monday, and one shilling in coppers, for he took up the collection in church the day pefore, and it wass not till Tougal had gone away that the jailer saw that one of the coppers was a Brock copper,—a medal,

[361] Old preposition meaning "within, inside."

you will understand, made at General Brock's death,[362] and not lawful money of Canada at all. With that the jailer came out to my grandfather.

"'Mr. McTavish,' says he, taking off his hat, 'you are a free man, and I'm glad of it.' Then he told him what Tougal had done.

"'I hope you will not have any hard feelings toward me, Mr. McTavish,' said the jailer; and a decent man he wass, for all that there wass not a drop of Hielan' blood in him. 'I hope you will not think hard of me for not being hospitable to you, sir,' says he; 'but it's against the rules and regulations for the jailer to be offering the best he can command to the prisoners. Now that you are free, Mr. McTavish,' says the jailer, 'I would be a proud man if Mr. McTavish of Glengatchie would do me the honor of taking supper with me this night. I will be asking your leave to invite some of the gentlemen of the place, if you will say the word, Mr. McTavish,' says he.

"Well, my grandfather could never bear malice, the kind man he was, and he seen how bad the jailer felt, so he consented, and a great company came in, to be sure, to celebrate the occasion.

"Did my grandfather pay the balance on the plough? What 1891
for should you suspicion, sir, that my grandfather would refuse his honest debt? Of course he paid for the plough, for the crop was good that fall.

"'I would be paying you the other half of the plough now, Mr. Stewart,' says my grandfather, coming in when the store was full.

"'Hoich, but YOU are the honest McTavish!' says Tougal, sneering.

"But my grandfather made no answer to the creature, for he thought it would be unkind to mention how Tougal had paid out six pounds four shillings and eleven pence to keep him in on account of a debt of two pound five that never was due till it was paid."

---

[362] These copper medals were produced by a private company soon after General Brock's death in 1812. There were used for a while as half-penny coins in Upper Canada, until they were declared unlawful when American troops started minting them and flooded the Canadian market. A story very similar with this passage, entitled "How a 'Brock Copper' Cancelled a Debt of $500" (signed by "T. S. Wood, Picton, Ontario) appeared in the *Canadian Antiquarian and Numismatic Journal* of April 1878 (and a much abridged notice of the same in the *American Journal of Numismatics* of October 1878).

Robert Barr

A Society for the Reformation of Poker Players

(1892)

The author: Robert Barr was born on 16 September 1849 in Glasgow. In 1854, his family immigrated to Wallacetown (today a hamlet in the municipality of Dutton/Dunwich, in Southwestern Ontario), then moved on a farm near another hamlet, Muirkirk (today part of Chatham-Kent). In 1866, he joined volunteer units preparing to stop the Fenian raids (an event he narrated in the 1893 novel *In the Midst of Alarams*). Barr attended Toronto Normal School (his experiences there formed the basis for the 1907 novel *The Measure of the Rule*) and became first a teacher and then principal of the Central School in Windsor. He started contributing anecdotes to *Grip* in Toronto in the 1870s, signing them "Luke Sharp," which was to remain his preferred pseudonym for the rest of his life. He became a reporter, and then editor, of the *Detroit Free Press* (where he was joined by two of his brothers). The *Detroit Free Press* was at the time extremely popular for its humor and witticisms. In 1881, Barr was sent to London to open a (weekly) British edition of the paper. In 1892, with Jerome K. Jerome, he founded the *Idler*, a popular monthly. In London, Barr published at least one novel or collection of short stories every year. He specialised in parodies (especially of detective stories), but also wrote novels focusing on social issues, such as *The Mutable Many* (1896) and *The Victors* (1901). When he died, on 21 October 1912, he was one of the best-known Canadian authors.

The text: First published in *In a Steamer Chair and Other Ship-Board Stories* (New York: Frederick A. Stokes), 193-207. The volume appeared in June 1892. The following is from the original of 1892.

O Unseen Hand that ever makes and deals us,
        And plays our game!
That now obscures and then to light reveals us,
        Serves blanks of fame
How vain our shuffling, bluff and weak pretending!
'Tis Thou alone can name the final ending.

The seductive game of poker is one that I do not understand. I do not care to understand it, because it cannot be played without the putting up of a good deal of the coin of the realm, and although I have nothing to say against betting, my own theory of conduct in the matter is this, that I want no man's money which I do not earn, and I do not want any man to get my money unless he earns it. So it happens, in the matter of cards, I content myself with euchre and other games which do not require the wagering of money.

On board the Atlantic steamers there is always more or less gambling. I have heard it said that men make trips to and fro merely for the purpose of fleecing their fellow-passengers; but, except in one instance, I never had any experience with this sort of thing.

Our little society for the reformation of poker players, or to speak more correctly, for the reformation of one particular poker player, was formed one bright starlight night, latitude such a number, and longitude something else, as four of us sat on a seat at the extreme rear end of the great steamer. We four, with one other, sat at a small table in the saloon. One of the small tables on a Transatlantic steamer is very pleasant if you have a nice crowd with you. A seat at a small table compares with a seat at the large table as living in a village compares with living in a city. You have some individuality at the short table; you are merely one of a crowd at the long table. Our small table was not quite full. I had the honor of sitting at the head of it, and on each side of me were two young fellows, making five altogether. We all rather prided ourselves on the fact that there were no ladies at our little table.

The young Englishman who sat at my right hand at the corner of the table was going out to America to learn farming. I could, myself, have taught him a good deal about it, but I refrained from throwing cold water on his enthusiastic ideas about American agriculture. His notion was that it was an occupation mostly made up of hunting and fishing, and having a good time generally. The profits, he thought, were large and easily acquired. He had guns with him, and beautiful fishing-rods, and things of that sort. He even had a vague idea that he might be able to introduce fox-hunting in the rural district to which he was going. He understood, and regretted the fact, that we in the United States were rather behind-hand in the matter of fox-hunting. He had a good deal of money with him, I understood, and he had already paid a hundred pounds to a firm in England that had agreed to place him on a farm in America. Of course, now that the money had been paid, there was no use in telling the young man he had been a fool. He would find that out soon enough when he got to America. Henry Storm was his name, and a milder mannered man with a more unsuitable name could hardly be found. The first two or three days out he was the life of our party. We all liked him, in fact, nobody could help liking him; but, as the voyage progressed, he grew more and more melancholy, and, what was really serious, took little food, which is not natural in an Englishman. I thought somebody had been telling him what a fool he had been to pay away his hundred pounds before leaving England, but young Smith of Rochester, who sat at my left, told me what the trouble was one day as we walked the deck. "Do you know," he began, "that Henry Storm is being robbed?"

"Being robbed?" I answered; "you mean he has been robbed."

"Well, has been, and is being, too. The thing is going on yet. He is playing altogether too much poker in the smoking room, and has lost a pile of money—more, I imagine, than he can well afford."

"That's what's the trouble with him, is it? Well, he ought to know better than to play for bigger stakes than he can afford to lose."

"Oh, it's easy to say that; but he's in the hands of a swindler, of a professional gambler. You see that man?" He lowered his voice as he spoke, and I looked in the direction of his glance. By this time we knew, in a way, everybody on board the ship. The particular man Smith pointed out was a fellow I had noticed a good deal, who was very quiet and gentlemanly, interfering with nobody, and talking with few. I had spoken to him once, but he had answered rather shortly, and, apparently to his relief, and certainly to my own, our acquaintance ceased where it began. He had jet black beard and hair, both rather closely clipped; and he wore a fore and aft cap,[363] which never improves a man's appearance very much.

"That man," continued Smith, as he passed us, "was practically under arrest for gambling on the steamer in which I came over. It seems that he is a regular professional gambler, who does nothing but go across the ocean and back again, fleecing young fellows like Storm."

"Does he cheat?" I asked.

"He doesn't need to. He plays poker. An old hand, and a cool one, has no occasion to cheat at that game to get a young one's money away from him."

"Then why doesn't someone warn young Storm?"

"Well, that's just what I wanted to speak to you about. I think it ought to be done. I think we should call a meeting of our table, somewhere out here in the quiet, and have a talk over it, and make up our mind what is to be done. It's a delicate matter, you know, 1892
and I am afraid we are a little late as it is. I do believe young Storm has lost nearly all his money to that fellow."

"Can't he be made to disgorge?"

"How? The money has been won fairly enough, as that sort of thing goes. Other fellows have played with them. It isn't as if he had been caught cheating—he hasn't, and won't be. He doesn't cheat—he doesn't need to, as I said before. Now that gambler pretends he is a commercial traveler from Buffalo. I know Buffalo down to the ground, so I took him aside yesterday and said plumply to him, 'What firm in Buffalo do you represent?' He answered shortly that his business was his own affair. I said, 'Certainly it is, and you are quite right in keeping it dark. When I was coming over to Europe, I saw a man in your line of business who looked very much like you, practically put under arrest by the purser for gambling. You were travelling for a St. Louis house then.'"

"What did he say to that?"

"Nothing; he just gave me one of those sly, sinister looks of his, turned on his heel, and left me."

[363] A deerstalker hat (the term is also used today for the military "garrison cap").

The result of this conversation was the inauguration of the Society for the Reforming of a Poker Player. It was agreed between us that if young Storm had lost all his money we would subscribe enough as a loan to take care of him until he got a remittance from home. Of course we knew that any young fellow who goes out to America to begin farming, does not, as a general rule, leave people in England exceedingly well off, and probably this fact, more than any other, accounted for the remorse visible on Storm's countenance. We knew quite well that the offering of money to him would be a very delicate matter, but it was agreed that Smith should take this in hand if we saw the offer was necessary. Then I, as the man who sat at the head of the table, was selected to speak to young Storm, and, if possible, get him to abandon poker. I knew this was a somewhat impudent piece of business on my part, and so I took that evening to determine how best to perform the task set for me. I resolved to walk the deck with him in the morning, and have a frank talk over the matter.

When the morning came, I took young Storm's arm and walked two or three turns up and down the deck, but all the while I could not get up courage enough to speak with him in relation to gambling. When he left me, I again thought over the matter. I concluded to go into the smoking room myself, sit down beside him, see him lose some money and use that fact as a test for my coming discourse on the evils of gambling. After luncheon I strolled into the smoking room, and there sat this dark-faced man with his half-closed eyes opposite young Storm, while two others made up the four-handed game of poker.

Storm's face was very pale, and his lips seemed dry, for he moistened them every now and then as the game went on. He was sitting on the sofa, and I sat down beside him, paying no heed to the dark gambler's look of annoyance. However, the alleged Buffalo man said nothing, for he was not a person who did much talking. Storm paid no attention to me as I sat down beside him. The gambler had just dealt. It was very interesting to see the way he looked at his hand. He allowed merely the edges of the cards to show over each other, and then closed up his hand and seemed to know just what he had. When young Storm looked at his hand he gave a sort of gasp, and for the first time cast his eyes upon me. I had seen his hand, but did not know whether it was a good one or not. I imagined it was not very good, because all the cards were of a low denomination. Threes or fours I think, but four of the cards had a like number of spots. There was some money in the center of the table. Storm pushed a half-crown in front of him, and the next man did the same. The gambler put down a half-sovereign, and the man at his left, after a moment's hesitation, shoved out an equal amount from the pile of gold in front of him.

Young Storm pushed out a sovereign.[364]

"I'm out," said the man whose next bet it was, throwing down his cards.

The gambler raised it a sovereign, and the man at his left dropped out. It now rested between Storm and the gambler. Storm increased the bet a sovereign. The gambler then put on a five-pound note.

Storm said to me huskily, "Have you any money?"

"Yes," I answered him.

"Lend me five pounds if you can."

Now, the object of my being there was to stop gambling, not to encourage it. I was the president pro tem. of the Society for the Reformation of Poker Players, yet I dived into my pocket, pulled out my purse under the table and slipped a five-pound note into his hand. He put that on the table as if he had just taken it from his own pocket.

"I call you," he said.

"What have you got?" asked the gambler.

"Four fours," said Storm, putting down his hand.

The gambler closed up his and threw the cards over to the man who was to deal. Storm paused a moment, and then pulled toward him the money in the center of the table and handed me my five-pound note.

When the cards were next dealt, Storm seemed to have rather an ordinary hand, so apparently had all the rest, and there was not much money in the pile. But, poor as Storm's hand was, the rest appeared to be poorer, and he raked in the cash. This went on for two or three deals, and finding that, as Storm was winning all the time, although not heavily, I was not getting an object lesson against gambling, I made a move to go.

[364] A sovereign was a British coin worth one pound; a half-sovereign was worth 10 shillings (half a pound); a crown was worth 5 shillings (a quarter of a pound); and the half-crown mentioned a couple of lines above was worth two shillings and sixpence (one eighth of a pound).

"Stay where you are," whispered Storm to me, pinching my knee with his hand so hard that I almost cried out.

Then it came to the gambler's turn to deal again. All the time he deftly shuffled the cards he watched the players with that furtive glance of his from out his half-shut eyes.

Storm's hand was a remarkable one, after he had drawn two cards, but I did not know whether it had any special value or not. The other players drew three cards each, and the gambler took one.

"How much money have you got?" whispered Storm to me.

"I don't know," I said, "perhaps a hundred pounds."

"Be prepared to lend me every penny of it," he whispered.

I said nothing; but I never knew the president of a society for the suppression of gambling to be in such a predicament.

Storm bet a sovereign. The player to his left threw down his hand. The gambler pushed out two sovereigns. The other player went out.

Storm said, "I see your bet, and raise you another sovereign." The gambler, without saying a word, shoved forward some more gold.

"Get your money ready," whispered Storm to me.

I did not quite like his tone, but I made allowance for the excitement under which he was evidently laboring.

He threw on a five-pound note. The gambler put down another five-pound note, and then, as if it were the slightest thing possible, put a ten-pound note on top of that, which made the side players gasp. Storm had won sufficient to cover the bet and raise it. After that I had to feed in to him five-pound notes, keeping count of their number on my fingers as I did so. The first to begin to hesitate about putting money forward was the gambler. He shot a glance now and again from under his eyebrows at the young man opposite. Finally, when my last five-pound note had been thrown on the pile, the gambler spoke for the first time.

"I call you," he said.

"Put down another five-pound note," cried the young man.

"I have called you," said the gambler.

Henry Storm half rose from his seat in his excitement. "Put down another five-pound note, if you dare."

"That isn't poker," said the gambler. "I have called you. What have you got?"

"Put down another five-pound note, and I'll put a ten-pound note on top of it."

"I say that isn't poker. You have been called. What have you got?"

"I'll bet you twenty pounds against your five-pound note, if you dare put it down."

By this time Storm was standing up, quivering with excitement, his cards tightly clenched in his hand. The gambler sat opposite him calm and imperturbable.

"What have you got?" said Storm.

"I called you," said the gambler, "show your hand."

"Yes; but when I called you, you asked me what I had, and I told you. What have you got?"

"I am not afraid to show my hand," said the gambler, and he put down on the table four aces.

"There's the king of hearts," said Storm, putting it down on the table. "There's the queen of hearts, there's the knave of hearts, there's the ten of hearts. Now," he cried, waving his other card in the air, "can you tell me what this card is?"

"I am sure I don't know," answered the gambler quietly, "probably the nine of hearts."

"It is the nine of hearts," shouted Storm, placing it down beside the others.

The gambler quietly picked up the cards, and handed them to the man who was to deal. Storm's hands were trembling with excitement as he pulled the pile of banknotes and gold towards him. He counted out what I had given him, and passed it to me under the table. The rest he thrust into his pocket.

"Come," I said, "it is time to go. Don't strain your luck."

"Another five pounds," he whispered; "sit where you are."

"Nonsense," I said, "another five pounds will certainly mean that you lose everything you have won. Come away, I want to talk with you."

"Another five pounds, I have sworn it."

"Very well, I shall not stay here any longer."

"No, no," he cried eagerly; "sit where you are, sit where you are."

There was a grim thin smile on the lips of the gambler as this whispered conversation took place.

When the next hand was dealt around and Storm looked at his cards, he gave another gasp of delight. I thought that a poker player should not be so free with his emotions; but of course I said nothing. When it came his time to bet, he planked down a five-pound note on the table. The other two, as was usual, put down their cards. They were evidently very timorous players. The gambler hesitated for a second, then he put a ten-pound note on Storm's five-pounds. Storm at once saw him, and raised him ten. The gambler hesitated longer this time, but at last he said, "I shall not bet. What have you got?"

"Do you call me?" asked Storm. "Put up your money if you do."

"No, I do not call you."

Storm laughed and threw his cards face up on the table. "I have nothing," he said; "I have bluffed you for once."

"It is very often done," answered the gambler quietly, as Storm drew in his pile of money, stuffing it again in his coat pocket. "Your deal, Storm."

"No, sir," said the young man, rising up; "I'll never touch a poker hand again. I have got my own money back and five or ten pounds over. I know when I've had enough."

Although it was Storm's deal, the gambler had the pack of cards in his hand idly shuffling them to and fro.

"I have often heard," he said slowly, without raising his eyes, "that when one fool sits down beside another fool at poker, the player has the luck of two fools—but I never believed it before."

Ethelwyn Wetherald

A Modern Lear

(1892)

The author: Agnes Ethelwyn Wetherald was born on 26 April 1857 in Rockwood, Ontario, a village near Guelph, where her father, William Wetherald (1820-1898) operated a boarding school for boys. After a brief stint as school superintendent in Pennsylvania, her father took the family back to Canada and became a Quaker preacher. Ethelwyn was educated in Quaker schools, both in the US and Canada. She published her first poem at the age of 17 in *St. Nicholas Magazine* and her first story at the age of 23, in *Rose-Belford's Canadian Monthly*. She began a career as a journalist in 1886, using the pseudonym "Bel Thistlewaite" in the Toronto *Globe*, and she published the novel *An Algonquin Maiden* (co-written with Graeme Mercer Adam) the same year. She held the position of "Women's editor" at the *Globe*. She moved to London, Ontario, where she wrote for the *London Advertiser* and for the monthly *Wives and Daughters*. She was quite prolific in Canadian and American periodicals, to which she contributed articles, poems, and short stories. Her first volume of poetry was *The House of the Trees* (1895), after which she became editorial assistant for *Ladies' Home Journal*, published in Philadelphia. She also contributed to the editing of a series of volumes of *The World's Best Literature*, but she decided to leave Philadelphia and return to Canada. She published six more volumes of poetry, but she never collected her short fiction. She never married, but she adopted a daughter (born in 1911). She spent most of her life on a farm in Chantler, near Fenwick, on the Niagara Peninsula. She died on 9 March 1940, in Pelham Township, Ontario.

The text: First published in *New England Magazine* New Series 6: 5 (July 1892), 603-606. It was signed with her real name.

If there is anything upon which a vast amount of fine language has been needlessly expended, that thing is personal influence. In my opinion—an opinion based on thirty years of most convincing experience—personal influence, though talked of as much as the late Mrs. Harris, is as unsubstantial a myth.[365] The philanthropist who has begun by trying to reform the world, and ended by seriously asking his conscience whether he has altered the views of any soul in it beside himself, will understand me.

My benevolent efforts were expended wholly in behalf of my father. My mother was a New England housekeeper of the old-fashioned sort—a woman who blushed with mortification if unexpected company found her with less than five kinds of cake, with tarts, pies, and doughnuts galore. Her preserves were always made "pound for pound," and her hams, pickles, and jellies were the admiration of the neighbourhood. Under this regimen, my sister Rhoda and I grew up to be a pair of sickly dyspeptics, and at about the age of twenty married two brothers similarly afflicted.[366] My youngest sister Cordelia incurred the lasting displeasure of our parents by eloping at the age of seventeen with a blacksmith's son. She was a self-willed little tomboy, and though we did not exactly feel that her loss was our gain, still people of a delicate nature, like my sister Rhoda and myself, could hardly be expected to grieve too much after one of such tendencies as Cordelia's. My mother dying a few years ago, my father divided his property between Rhoda and myself. He had no son to work his farm, he was too old to work it himself, and he did not wish to be bothered with overseeing hired labor. Joseph and I begged him to make our house his permanent home, but Jacob and Rhoda were equally urgent, and it ended in his dividing his time about equally between us. But he hadn't been at our house more than three days before he began finding fault with his food.

"Seems to me, Jane," he said, "this bread ain't just like what your mother used to make."

[365] Mrs. Harris is a very influential character in Dickens's *Martin Chuzzlewit,* though she lives entirely in the imagination of another character, Sarah Gamp.

[366] Dyspepsia means indigestion.

"I'm thankful to say it ain't," said I. "This is unleavened bread. Yeast is rank poison."

"It's pretty hefty," said he, lifting a piece in his hand as if trying to guess its weight. "Don't let that slice fall on your toes, Joe. I've known less than that to lame a man for life."

"The merit of this whole wheat bread," said I, "is that it contains all the elements necessary for the nutrition of the system."

Another time he said, "Jane, why don't you cook some meat? I'm perishin' for want of it."

"Meat!" I exclaimed. "Are we carnivorous beasts, that we should prey on other animals, and make our bodies a burying-ground for their remains?"

"Burying-ground!" he said dismally. "The fact is, I ain't half such a cheerful object as a burying-ground—there ain't any bumps or fulness about me."

"This sort of talk is distasteful to me," said I.

Breakfast was perhaps my father's worst meal. The many wholesome preparations of grain, such as cracked wheat, oatmeal, cornmeal, and hominy, appealed to him in vain.

"We consider this excellent brain food," my husband said cheerfully one morning, as he took a second help of Graham mush.

"'Tain't brain food I want," said father, "it's stomach food. If I was a horse, I wouldn't mind livin' on bran and chopped stuff. Don't you ever have any milk?"

"No," said Joe smartly, "we don't. If I was a calf, I wouldn't mind livin' on milk."

"You shall have some milk, father," said I, rising to get it. "It's a bilious food, but it contains all the elements that make up the human frame."

"How are tea and coffee in the way of elements?" he asked in a miserable way.

"They are nothing but stimulants," I exclaimed, glad to find he took even this slight interest in the subject. "There is nothing in them to build up the body."

"Well," he said dolefully, "I don't know as I'm looking for anything to build my body up. I've got past that. If I can only find somethin' to *prop* it up, somethin' to keep it from cavin' in, I'll be satisfied."

If it were not that people who live hygienically are good-natured, my father's querulous discontent would have been a sore trial to us. One day at dinner, after Joseph had said our usual form of grace, my father exclaimed rudely, "Ye may well say the Lord *make* us thankful, Joe, for if he didn't make us thankful no power on earth could." That same day he asked for pie.

"Do you know what pie is?" asked Joe; and I explained: "Pie is a deadly compound of fruit, fat, flour, and fire."

"All them things is good, Jane," said my father, "taken in moderation."

"We don't want them in this house," said Joe. "I ain't goin' to be bothered with dyspepsia in moderation."

Not long after I was horrified to behold my two delicate children munching candy. "Grandpa gave it to us," they said, smiling stickily at me.

"Father," I exclaimed, "this is too bad! Candy is made up wholly of carbonaceous materials—none of the nitrogeneous or phosphatic elements enter into it, and it is a severe tax upon the excretory organs."

He said nothing, but turned away and took out his pipe, indifferent also to the fact that tobacco is a poisonous narcotic. I was out of patience with him. I felt relieved when he expressed his intention of going over to stay with Rhoda and Jake for a month.

Rhoda and I are back and forth a good deal, and I soon heard how things were going there. She and Jake are far more advanced than Joe and I are. They consider the use of cooked food a sinful pandering to animal appetite. For breakfast they usually have a little ground wheat, moistened with berry juice, or canned pears or something of that sort. Dinner consists of a little uncooked oatmeal, with figs or dates, and occasionally nuts. They have no supper. My father soon observed that this was a fortunate thing, as three such meals a day would have finished them off long ago. Rhoda quoted father as saying that if he had to live on two meals a day of raw provisions he meant to have enough of those. When, therefore, my sister went into the dining-room one day to set the table with apples, raisins, and rye meal, she was astonished to find it already spread with covered dishes, containing uncooked potatoes, carrots, turnips, cabbage, and onions. She and Jake ate some of the cabbage. The other vegetables they held not fit to eat, because they had grown and ripened underground.

"Underground," said father, who was eating everything before him with savage rapacity, "underground ain't such a bad place. I've often thought I'd better go there myself and settle down." That afternoon Rhoda said she really believed he *would* die. The turnips and carrots seemed to disagree with him. She made him drink cup after cup of hot water, just as near the boiling point as he could bear it. I ran over with ginger and mustard, which I use only in case of sickness, and heard his feeble voice refusing the seventh cup of hot water. "No, thank ye, Rhody," he said, "my stomach can stand a good deal; it can stand to be flattened out with chicken feed and greens, but it hain't no mind to be drowned out nor scalded out."

"I knew those underground vegetables were bad for you," said my sister. "It's a solemn example."

"Is it?" said father. "Well, I tell you what it is, girls, I want some beef-steak for my supper to-night, tender and juicy, and plenty of it. That's what I want."

Rhoda uttered a shriek, and sat down and shuddered. "Never in this house," she exclaimed.

"I'm afraid to, father," I said. "You might over-eat again, and you would then surely die. Meat of any sort fires the blood."

The old man looked first at Rhoda, then at me, saying things which I will not repeat. It distressed us to be spoken to in this way, but allowance must always be made for the fretfulness of old age. The poor man never seemed wholly to recover from the raw potatoes and turnips. He grew weaker and weaker till he took to his bed altogether. During his illness he maintained a curious aversion for anything in the shape of gruel or fruit, and astounded one good lady who brought him a basket of delicious grapes by stripping bunch after bunch, and throwing them, three or four at a time, hard at her, now at my sister or myself, now at the walls and windows. He called it "grape shot," I remember, and laughed in demoniac glee at our protests. After this he sank into unnatural calm, and thinking that his end was approaching we sent for the minister. A portion of Scripture was read, and prayer offered. Then the good man approached his bedside, and asked him what would satisfy the deepest desire of his nature.

"Pork and beans!" exclaimed father, with sudden force.

"I was not alluding to creature comforts," said the minister confused.

"But I am," was the tart response, "and I intend to allude to 'em till I get 'em." The glitter of delirium reappeared in his eye, and the house re-echoed with shrieking demands for pork and beans. Our nearest neighbor, whose sleep was disturbed by this strange outcry, came in next day with a dish containing the loathsome viands. "Oh, you'll kill him," said Rhoda.

"He'll kill himself," said she, "with this awful shrieking. If he's going to die anyway, he'd better die in peace. She went into the sick room with her pork and beans, and a slice of home-made bread and butter, and came back presently with an empty plate. A great stillness brooded over the house. I looked in at the invalid half an hour later, and found him peacefully sleeping, with a sweet smile on his face.

From this moment, incredible as it may seem, father steadily improved. Of course the mind has a great influence over the body, but I did not suppose that a masculine love of having his own way could triumph over the pernicious effects of the most abhorred of culinary products.

As soon as he was able to walk, father came back to our house, making some unpleasant remarks, as he came, about jumping from the fire back into the frying pan. But convalescents are proverbially irritable, and I took no notice. "What you need now, in your present weak condition," I said, "is a liberal supply of all the elements necessary to renovate the system." And for supper that night I provided him with a generous slice of brown bread, made of the whole grain, and a large sauce dish of dried apples. He began to eat in silence. I could see he was weak yet from his sickness, for presently a tear trickled down his cheek, and moistened the bread. "You are thinking of mother," I said, "but you should not grieve after her. Death is common to all. It is a wise provision of Nature."

"Don't talk to me about provisions, Jane," said he.

At that moment the door was softly pushed open, and a rosy-cheeked young woman looked in and made a rush across the room at father. "Dear old dad," she cried, throwing her arms around him; "dear, blessed, old dad, you will forgive me, won't you? Oh, you must forgive me. I'll not let go of you till you do."

"Why, Cordely," said father, "is that you?" He was so weak he could only sit still and look at her, while his lip quivered. "Of course, if you're happy," he added, "I hain't a word to say agin' the match."

"Do I look very miserable?" she asked, a smile playing among the dimples in her red cheeks. Then she crossed and shook hands with me, and kissed me, looking a little shy and frightened. Suddenly her face grew grave and sad. She took a chair by father's side. "I didn't hear of mother's death till after it was all over," she said, "and then my baby wasn't expected to live and I couldn't leave the little fellow. But when I heard you were sick I told Ed I couldn't stand it to be estranged from you any longer. And so we've come back here to live, and I'm going to try and make amends for all the pain I've caused you." She took his wrinkled old hand between both of hers, and kissed it and cried over it. Then she jumped up. "Why," she exclaimed, "I've brought you over a little chicken broth, piping hot,—and I nearly forgot all about it." She brought in a small covered tin pail, whisked the dried apples and brown bread off the table, without so much as by your leave, and the next moment that poor sick man, who had no more craving for food than a canary, was stimulating an artificial appetite on a stew made of the most gross of animal substances (a chicken will eat what a pig will not) with bits of toasted white bread floating in it!

But this was nothing to what followed. Two days later was Thanksgiving, and Cordelia invited father, Rhoda, Jake, Joe, and myself over to her place for dinner. Of course, we did not wish to disoblige her by not going. Jake and Joe promised to be very careful what they ate. Rhoda said if it wouldn't offend Cordelia she'd like to take a little ground wheat over, which she could eat with cranberry or apple sauce; but I persuaded her it would be best to conform a little more than that, and we decided to eat a very little of one vegetable, choosing one with no pepper nor butter in it, and afterwards some nuts and raisins. Father seemed a good deal excited over the affair, but he didn't say anything till we got there. The air in the dining-room was simply nauseating with odors of sage and onions, nutmeg, allspice, and lemon, roast goose, and mince pies.

"Now, Ed," said Cordelia to her big blacksmith husband, "be sure and give father the upper part of the leg, a wing, and part of the breast, with plenty of dressing. I'll help the gravy and vegetables."

"Father," said Rhoda, "it may be well to remember that none of those things contain the elements of—"

"I don't want no elements," roared father. "Curse the elements! What I want is a square meal."

"And that's just what we calculate to give you," said the blacksmith with a loud laugh. The wild excess and wanton extravagance of the meal were talked over by Rhoda and me for many a day. As for father, he continues to live with Cordelia and her husband. We expected he would go into a decline, but he appears marvellously well and cheerful. It's wonderful what a man of naturally strong constitution will survive.

Sara Jeannette Duncan

Peter Linnet's Interview

(1893)

The author: Sara Jeannette Duncan was on born on 22 December 1861 in Brantford, Ontario. She trained as a teacher, but she became a journalist in 1884 (she signed her first articles for the Toronto *Globe* as "Garth," and then "Garth Grafton") and was soon a well-known columnist and editor, both for Canadian newspapers (the *Week*, for which she wrote essays, the *Globe*, where she began by writing a column entitled "Other People and I," and was later editor of a section entitled "Woman's World," and the *Montreal Star*, for which she reported from Ottawa as parliamentary correspondent) and, in 1885-1886, for the *Washington Post*, where she edited the literary section. In 1888 she circumnavigated the world with another journalist (Lily Lewis) and used her notes both for articles published during the trip and for her first novel, *A Social Departure*. In 1890 she married Everard Charles Cotes, a British civil servant working at the Indian Museum in Calcutta. Duncan remained based in India until 1921; she was editor of the *Indian Daily News* (1894-1897) and managing editor of the Eastern News Agency. Starting with her fourth novel, *A Daughter of To-Day* (1894) she signed her books "Mrs. Everard Cotes." At the turn of the 20th century, she was widely recognised as an important Anglo-Indian novelist, but today her best-known novel is *The Imperialist* (1904), the only one she ever wrote that is set entirely in Canada. She died on 22 July 1922 in Ashtead, England. Her only short-story collection, *The Pool in the Desert* (1903) includes, in reality, a single short story and two novellas. Many other short stories and sketches by Duncan have remained uncollected in periodicals.

The text: First published in *Cosmopolitan* 15 (October 1893), 732-737. It was signed with her full name. The following is the original from the magazine.

His obscure American name was Linnet, Peter Linnet. It was not to be found in any of the blue-books,[367] nor amongst the members of the board of trade, nor, as a general thing, upon the Government House list. His attention was not given to minutes and resolutions, or to the price of gunny-bags,[368] or, as a rule, to society. He was not even known to the income-tax collector, for reasons that might have been obvious to anybody. His business was with the souls of the heathen, and he lived up-country.

It was not a paying business, from our point of view. Years ago Peter Linnet put all he had into it, and we would consider the money irrecoverably sunk. The little white church and school-house at Rubblebad did not represent a fraction of the cost of building them. They were, to be sure, immovable security, but I doubt whether even government would have advanced him a thousand rupees on them, takkavi,[369] to buy more of the good seed Peter Linnet went up and down his district sowing broadcast. Perhaps, too, government would have doubted the probability of a harvest. Peter Linnet never doubted. And that was as well, for any lack of faith upon his part would have bankrupted him. He was not, you see, a missionary whose future was the care of the denomination that sent him out, and for him there was neither stipend nor pension realizable "here below." Peter Linnet was a missionary on his own account, and I think he rather scouted the denominations. My impression is that he was a "brother" of sorts, but the district called him "ma bap."[370]

He lived up-country, but every now and then he made what he called a "raid" upon Calcutta. The cause, like all other causes, stood upon a financial basis, and whenever the basis showed signs of being undermined Peter Linnet would journey to the capital,

[367] Books containing the names of all employees of a department of the government.

[368] Another name for burlap bags used to carry all kinds of products; in India, they were usually made of jute.

[369] Duncan inserted a note here: "Vernacular term for advances made to the peasants by government, to buy seed-grain."

[370] Duncan's footnote: "My father and my mother." The term is used for anyone with a parental role, including a benefactor.

engaging much in prayer, in the train going down, that the Lord would soften the hearts of the Calcutta rich. He would remind the Lord—it was a quaint way he had—that the fall in the exchange value of the rupee must benefit somebody, and pray that he might be directed, when he arrived, to the right persons, as he could not well depend upon his own knowledge of finance. It was truly wonderful, to Peter Linnet, how the Lord would interfere in the matter, and how seldom the busy men of the city, or the desk-worn sons of the secretariats, refused him the ten-rupee note which he had privately determined to be a fair price for the blessing of the cause. He could not possibly know that after a long and persevering series of fashionable ladies bent upon the extraction of subscriptions for benevolent raffles, a venerable person like himself, simple and trustful and without guile, might involuntarily leave his own blessing behind him. Not that the Calcutta broker understood the blessing to come from either source. His way of putting it probably was that he had paid the old gentleman off to be left in peace, and he thought it cheaply done at ten rupees. And he did not at all connect being left in peace with some still remembered words the old gentleman might have repeated as the office-bearer showed him down-stairs—"My peace I leave with you." . . . However, never mind.

Calcutta had so often been kind to Peter Linnet and his cause, that he was as deeply perturbed as profoundly surprised, one day, to find it cold. He had come down with great expectations, based on his past receipts and his present record. He had ideas of business for a missionary, and he brought his record with him always, in a note-book—so many children educated, so many sick healed, so many souls saved. This time the numbers were particularly gratifying, and his old heart throbbed as he noted them down in a hand that was growing a trifle shaky. He had a new plea to put forward, too—famine threatened, many of his people were hungry. He wished he could make the plutocrats of Calcutta understand how hungry, but he concluded, with a sigh, that his good friends of the capital were much too well fed. He would be obliged to appeal to their imagination; but he fancied he could do that. His children of the district were eating the leaves of trees. Yes, he didn't boast of his eloquence, but he fancied he could do that.

And Calcutta had repulsed him. For the first time in many—perhaps it was because of the many!—his card failed to bring a sala'am. The sahib was busy or had gone out, and the man at the door was not too respectful. Peter Linnet pushed back his old, green-lined sola topee,[371] mopped his forehead and looked sharply through his spectacles at the inscrutable durwans.[372] He disbelieved the first one or two, but presently incredulity began to give way to disappointment, and the old man opened his umbrella and trudged away, without a word. Perhaps he had neglected, for once, to ask for divine direction to the firms that profited by the depreciated rupee; at all events, he didn't seem to find them. And one of his best friends, in the Department of Public Works, had given him only a good cigar and the assurance that the friend himself was unable to send his sick wife and his nine-year-old boy to England that hot weather, because of the parlous state of the rupee, and that, much as he would like to subscribe to Mr. Linnet's good work, he felt morally compelled to pay his debts first. Peter Linnet told the man in the Public Works department to be of good cheer—the Lord would provide; and shook his head when the man replied, flippantly, "Or the secretary of state." The cigar merited no rebuke, however, and the missionary took his discouragements pleasantly away.

He talked of his troubles in the second-rate boarding-house he shared with young Eurasian shopmen, and almost all the other boarders contributed an eight-anna bit apiece,[373] to lighten them, which, Peter Linnet assured the donors, he did not measure by its purchasing power—it might be as the mustard seed, planted in the name of the Lord.[374] There was a coffee-colored wag in the boarding-house, however, who contributed nothing but an irrelevant suggestion, coupled with a wink, over the curry, to all the other boarders who were looking in his direction. "I say, padre,"

[371] Duncan's footnote: "Pith-hat." Also known as pith helmet.

[372] Duncan's footnote: "Doorkeepers." More exactly, the durwan is a live-in doorkeeper.

[373] The anna is a former Indian coin, worth one sixteenth of a rupee.

[374] Allusion to a parable repeated in three of the gospels, for example: "The kingdom of heaven is like to a grain of mustard seed, which a man took, and sowed in his field: Which indeed is the least of all seeds: but when it is grown, it is the greatest among herbs, and becometh a tree, so that the birds of the air come and lodge in the branches thereof" (Matthew 13: 31-32).

said he, "you ought to write your name down at Government House.[375] They won't like it if you don't."

It had never occurred to Peter Linnet to write his name down at Government House before, but he pondered the idea. He would not wish to seem disrespectful. He was not of the world; neither, indeed, could he be. But should we not render unto Cæsar the things that are Cæsar's? He told the coffee-colored youth that he was much obliged for the hint, and the youth winked again. And that very morning, after making his solicitations in the new departmental buildings in the next street, the Rev. Peter Linnet walked in between the big yellow lions on the gate-posts, and up the broad, red, palm-bordered drive, to the public portal of the viceroy's Calcutta palace and wrote his name in the register of their excellencies' presumed acquaintances.

Then a very natural and probable thing happened. Peter Linnet, coming home to his dinner after a particularly disheartening day among the tea firms, found a large, square envelope, addressed to him, and inside the envelope a card informing him that the A. D. C.-in-waiting[376] was commanded by his excellency the viceroy to invite the Rev. Peter Linnet to an evening party, on the 10th of February, at 9.30 o'clock. To say that the old missionary was pleased would not to be to say enough. He was as happy as a schoolboy. He read the invitation as definitely, distinctly, an invitation to him. It was no small honor; but the honor, he chid himself gravely, was not his—not his. Doubtless, his excellency had heard of the good work at Rubblebad, and wished to obtain details from headquarters. When he went down to dinner, he considerably astonished the facetious young man by again thanking him for his suggestion about calling at Government House. "The viceroy has since invited me to come and see him," added Mr. Linnet, "and I hope much good will arise out of it."

When the evening came, Peter Linnet brushed his seamy frock-coat very carefully and put a new note-book in his breast-pocket, in which were carefully tabulated all the records of his mission from the beginning—the children educated, the sick healed, the souls saved. This year he had a new entry, which

[375] Built in 1803, it was the official residence of the Viceroy of India between 1858 and 1911, when the capital was moved to Delhi. It is now known as Raj Bhavan and is the residence of the governor of the state of West Bengal.

[376] A.D.C. is an acronym for "aide-de-camp."

he surveyed with much satisfaction—the number of men and women and little ones preserved from death by starvation. Peter Linnet meant, respectfully, but firmly, to call his excellency's attention very especially to that. In his excitement he could eat no dinner at all before starting. "The Lord will keep me up," he said to himself, for, even to an independent American missionary of Peter Linnet's temperament, a viceroy is a very formidable person. He passed from a fever lest he should be too early into a fever lest he should be too late, and when he was deposited, at last, upon the red carpet of the wide outer hall of Government House, his legs trembled under him and he was obliged to sit down, for a moment, on one of the round, gilt-backed sofas, to compose himself. He saw a number of young men standing about, some in uniform, some buttoning their gloves, and he noticed that they were usually joined by ladies in very dazzling evening dress, who disappeared along one of the corridors, arm in arm with them. "It seems to be quite a large party," said the missionary to himself, and hobbled after them—he was short and a little lame—feeling unaccountably depressed.

1893 Upstairs, Peter Linnet became even more deeply impressed with the size of the party. The gentlemen in uniform had multiplied, and so had the ladies in long, silken trains. After he had stumbled over two of these, in his anxiety to find the viceroy, the missionary shrunk into a palm-decorated corner. The band was playing near him, so near that he began to feel conscious of a headache, and moved away. He found that he did not know exactly where to go. The long, pillared room was so brilliantly lighted, so full of music and movement and people—people he felt as remote from as he would be in Rubblebad. The wide doors gave upon verandahs in which more people still were moving about duskily, and the room opened into others which made a mingled vista of palm fronds and dainty gowns. The missionary thought he would like a chair, but all those near him were occupied and he did not quite dare to walk the length of the room in search of one. To his relief, he noticed, presently, that the party was not wholly European; a rajah waddled past him in pink brocade and pearls, and an elderly zamindar,[377] in a long, tight, black coat and a neatly-rolled white turban, came and stood within three feet of him. Peter Linnet felt sometimes that he understood Indians better than Anglo-Indians.

[377] Duncan's footnote: "Landholder."

"Can you tell me, worthy one," said he to the zamindar, in Hindustani, "where the greetings to the Burra Lord Sahib are being offered?"

"Certainly, your honor. But upon these tamashos[378] are no greetings offered. The guests come and go at their pleasure. Is it that you wish to speak with the Burra Lord Sahib?" It was beyond the politeness of even a zamindar to disguise incredulity here.

"It is for that purpose that I am invited."

"Then, it is necessary first to see a secretary-sahib, or a young officer-sahib with blue silk upon his coat. There is one, and yonder is another," and the zamindar bowed himself away.

Peter Linnet rubbed his hands and bided his time. When a secretary should seem to be disengaged, he would go up and ask to be presented to the viceroy. In the meantime, he began to be conscious of glances and to remember how very old his coat was. His face gathered anxious wrinkles as he thought how the time was going. He looked at his silver watch and said to himself that he had not been out of bed at this hour for twenty years. Then he caught a secretary on the wing from the refreshment table to the verandah, who stared at him.

"I should be glad, sir, if you would introduce me to his excellency. I have not yet had the opportunity of thanking him for his kind invitation."

"Aw! Quite unnecessary, I assure you. Never done!" and the secretary was hastening away, but Mr. Linnet detained him.

"But I have also a little matter of business to talk of with his excellency—"

The secretary raised his eyebrows, and put up his eye-glass.

"What are you, officially?" he enquired.

"A minister of the gospel, sir."

"Oh—unattached, I presume. I mean—not on the establishment?"

"I am my own establishment, sir."

"Precisely. And what is the name of your station?"

"Rubblebad."

"Haw! Rubblebad! I was once at Rubblebad. Get it hot there, don't you, in June? Pretty place, though, with the river an' all."

"River, sir? There is no river at Rubblebad."

[378] Duncan's footnote: "Grand occasions."

"Ah; to be sure! N'more there isn't! But you do get it hot there, don't you? Don't wonder you like to run down to Calcutta, now and then. Oh, very hot at Rubblebad!"

The secretary said this over his shoulder, as he joined a passing native, whom he clapped familiarly on the back and addressed as "Maharajah, old chap!"

"I didn't make him understand," thought the little missionary, patiently; and he moved back a step or two, away from the dazzling candelabra, and stood, with his hands clasped behind his back, waiting for another opportunity. It seemed a very long time before one came. Then the head of a department, who knew the cause and its apologist, came by, looking for his wife. It was growing late and tomorrow's minutes were heavy upon his official anticipation. Peter Linnet hurried forward and held out his hand.

"Why, padre!" said the civilian, taking it, with some embarrassment.

"Yes, my good friend. You are surprised to see me? But I have business here—I have business here! I must see the viceroy. Would you do me the kindness to take me to him?"

"Oh—I am not the proper person, padre. The A. D. C.'s look after all that, you know. But if I were you, I'd write to him—I would, indeed. Good night, padre—there's my wife; I mustn't let her escape again!" and before the missionary was well aware of it, he was once more abandoned to the rustling crowd on the floor and the portrait of Lord Canning on wall.[379]

Peter Linnet felt the note-book in his pocket weigh heavily upon his soul. If he hesitated longer, this golden opportunity might be lost, and the Rubblebad mission might never again come under the attention of a viceroy of India. The little ones of his district were still anhungered,[380] though he and all that were his had deprived themselves of meat for a month, that the lambs of the flock might feed. So many more children were to educate, so many more sick were to heal, so many more souls were to save! The old man glanced at the other excellency—the one on the wall—who regarded him with impotent, but friendly eyes, and took courage. Then he went hesitatingly up the room, to where the crowd was thickest, and asked a youngster in the artillery to point him out the viceroy.

[379] George Canning (1812-1862), Governor-General of India during the last six years of his life.

[380] Archaic term for being oppressed with hunger.

"Beside the pillar, talking with General Gilbert—that dark-eyed chap with the orders. See?"

"Thank you," said Peter Linnet.

Then he somewhat feebly pushed his way toward his viceregal host, tripping over the ladies' dresses, catching his own baggy trousers in the officer's spurs, and wondering at the dimness of his sight.

"Your excellency," he said aloud, while yet some distance off, feeling tremblingly for his note-book, "your excellency—" but, at that, he staggered faintly and fell prone upon the train of the wife of the presidency magistrate, who stood perfectly still, with great presence of mind, while he recovered himself. There was a parting in the crowd and a little polite consternation; and a couple of Sikh body-guardsmen quickly helped him out. An A. D. C. hurried down to see him into his ticca-gharry,[381] and came back, pulling his pretty moustache, with that smile of semi-shocked amusement which an A. D. C. has for occasions of violated conventionality.

"Oh, the old fellow's all right now," said he to another A. D. C. "Just a little too much champagne, I fancy; wanted to come back, but told him he really mustn't! One glass will do for a Methody,[382] any day. Did his excellency happen to notice?"

"No!" replied the other.

"Tant mieux!"[383]

[381] Duncan's footnote: "Hired conveyance."

[382] Slang term for a Methodist.

[383] French for "so much the better."

Charles G. D. Roberts

"The Young Ravens that Call upon Him."

(1894)

1894

The author: Charles George Douglas Roberts was born on 10 January 1860, in Douglas, New Brunswick, a suburb of Fredericton, where his father was canon of Christ Church Cathedral. He was homeschooled until the age of 14, after which he went to high school and college (University of New Brunswick) in Fredericton, earning a B.A. in 1879 and an M.A. in 1881. He started publishing poetry in 1878 and, in 1880, his first collection, Orion and Other Poems was published in Philadelphia. He was a teacher until 1883, when he went to Toronto, working briefly as editor of The Week, and in 1885 he starting teaching at the University of King's College, in Windsor, Nova Scotia. He continued publishing poetry, but also started writing short stories, especially for the American periodicals. In 1897 he moved to New York (without his wife and children), where he wrote and published several novels, guide books, children's books, and poetry. In 1907, he moved to Europe (first in Paris, then Munich, finally London, which was his home from 1912 to 1925). He enlisted in the British Army during WWI. He returned to Canada in 1925 and eventually settled in Toronto, where he began writing mostly poetry. He was knighted in 1935. He died on 26 November 1943 in Toronto.

The text: First published in Lippincott's Monthly Magazine 53 (May 1894), 675-677. It was reprinted, unchanged, in Roberts's collection Earth's Enigmas (Boston and New York: Lamson, Wolffe and Company, 1896), 52-61.

Further reading: D.M.R. Bentley. "'The Thing Is Found to Be Symbolic': Symboliste Elements in the Early Short Stories of Gilbert Parker, Charles G.D. Roberts, and Duncan Campbell Scott." Dominant Impressions: Essays on the Canadian Short Story. Eds. Gerald Lynch and Angela Arnold Robbeson. Ottawa: University of Ottawa Press, 1999. 27-52.

Thomas Hood. "Charles G.D. Roberts's Cosmic Animals." Other Selves: Animals in the Canadian Literary Imagination. Ed. Janice Fiamengo. Ottawa: University of Ottawa Press, 2007. 184-205.

It was just before dawn, and a grayness was beginning to trouble the dark about the top of the mountain.

Even at that cold height there was no wind. The veil of cloud that hid the stars hung but a hand-breadth above the naked summit. To eastward the peak broke away sheer, beetling in a perpetual menace to the valleys and the lower hills. Just under the brow, on a splintered and creviced ledge, was the nest of the eagles.

As the thick dark shrank down the steep like a receding tide, and the grayness reached the ragged heap of branches forming the nest, the young eagles stirred uneasily under the loose droop of the mother's wings. She raised her head and peered about her, slightly lifting her wings as she did so; and the nestlings, complaining at the chill air that came in upon their unfledged bodies, thrust themselves up amid the warm feathers of her thighs. The male bird, perched on a jutting fragment beside the nest, did not move. But he was awake. His white, narrow, flat-crowned head was turned to one side, and his yellow eye, under its straight, fierce lid, watched the pale streak that was growing along the distant eastern sea-line.

The great birds were racked with hunger. Even the nestlings, to meet the petitions of whose gaping beaks they stinted themselves without mercy, felt meagre and uncomforted. Day after day the parent birds had fished almost in vain; day after day their wide and tireless hunting had brought them scant reward. The schools of alewives, mackerel, and herring seemed to shun their shores that spring. The rabbits seemed to have fled from all the coverts about their mountain.

The mother eagle, larger and of mightier wing than her mate, looked as if she had met with misadventure. Her plumage was disordered. Her eyes, fiercely and restlessly anxious, at moments grew dull as if with exhaustion. On the day before, while circling at her viewless height above a lake far inland, she had marked a huge lake-trout, basking near the surface of the water. Dropping upon it with half-closed, hissing wings, she had fixed her talons in its back. But the fish had proved too powerful for her. Again and again it had dragged her under water, and she had been almost drowned before she could unloose the terrible grip of her claws. Hardly, and late, had she beaten her way back to the mountain-top.

And now the pale streak in the east grew ruddy. Rust-red stains and purple, crawling fissures began to show on the rocky face of the peak. A piece of scarlet cloth, woven among the fagots of the nest, glowed like new blood in the increasing light. And presently a wave of rose appeared to break and wash down over the summit, as the rim of the sun came above the horizon.

The male eagle stretched his head far out over the depth, lifted his wings and screamed harshly, as if in greeting of the day. He paused a moment in that position, rolling his eye upon the nest. Then his head went lower, his wings spread wider, and he launched himself smoothly and swiftly into the abyss of air as a swimmer glides into the sea. The female watched him, a faint wraith of a bird darting through the gloom, till presently, completing his mighty arc, he rose again into the full light of the morning. Then on level, all but moveless wing, he sailed away toward the horizon.

As the sun rose higher and higher, the darkness began to melt on the tops of the lower hills and to diminish on the slopes of the upland pastures, lingering in the valleys as the snow delays there in spring. As point by point the landscape uncovered itself to his view, the eagle shaped his flight into a vast circle, or rather into a series of stupendous loops. His neck was stretched toward the earth, in the intensity of his search for something to ease the bitter hunger of his nestlings and his mate.

Not far from the sea, and still in darkness, stood a low, round hill, or swelling upland. Bleak and shelterless, whipped by every wind that the heavens could let loose, it bore no bush but an occasional juniper scrub. It was covered with mossy hillocks, and with a short grass, meagre but sweet. There in the chilly gloom, straining her ears to catch the lightest footfall of approaching peril, but hearing only the hushed thunder of the surf, stood a lonely ewe over the lamb to which she had given birth in the night.

Having lost the flock when the pangs of travail came upon her, the unwonted solitude filled her with apprehension. But as soon as the first feeble bleating of the lamb fell upon her ear, everything was changed. Her terrors all at once increased tenfold,—but they were for her young, not for herself; and with them came a strange boldness such as her heart had never known before. As the little weakling shivered against her side, she uttered low, short bleats and murmurs of tenderness. When an owl hooted in the woods across the valley, she raised her head angrily and faced the sound, suspecting a menace to her young. When a mouse scurried past her, with a small, rustling noise amid the withered mosses of the hillock, she stamped fiercely, and would have charged had the intruder been a lion.

When the first gray of dawn descended over the pasture, the ewe feasted her eyes with the sight of the trembling little creature, as it lay on the wet grass. With gentle nose she coaxed it and caressed it, till presently it struggled to its feet, and, with its pathetically awkward legs spread wide apart to preserve its balance, it began to nurse. Turning her head as far around as she could, the ewe watched its every motion with soft murmurings of delight.

And now that wave of rose, which had long ago washed the mountain and waked the eagles spread tenderly across the open pasture. The lamb stopped nursing; and the ewe, moving forward two or three steps, tried to persuade it to follow her. She was anxious that it should as soon as possible learn to walk freely, so they might together rejoin the flock. She felt that the open pasture was full of dangers.

The lamb seemed afraid to take so many steps. It shook its ears and bleated piteously. The mother returned to its side, caressed it anew, pushed it with her nose, and again moved away a few feet, urging it to go with her. Again the feeble little creature refused, bleating loudly. At this moment there came a terrible hissing rush out of the sky, and a great form fell upon the lamb. The ewe wheeled and charged madly; but at the same instant the eagle, with two mighty buffetings of his wings, rose beyond her reach and soared away toward the mountain. The lamb hung limp from his talons; and with piteous cries the ewe ran beneath, gazing upward, and stumbling over the hillocks and juniper bushes.

In the nest of the eagles there was content. The pain of their hunger appeased, the nestlings lay dozing in the sun, the neck of one resting across the back of the other. The triumphant male sat erect upon his perch, staring out over the splendid world that displayed itself beneath him. Now and again he half lifted his wings and screamed joyously at the sun. The mother bird, perched upon a limb on the edge of the nest, busily rearranged her plumage. At times she stooped her head into the nest to utter over her sleeping eaglets a soft chuckling noise, which seemed to come from the bottom of her throat.

But hither and thither over the round bleak hill wandered the ewe, calling for her lamb, unmindful of the flock, which had been moved to other pastures.[384]

[384] The title of Roberts's is from Psalm 149, in an 1844 translation of the Old Testament: "sing praises on the harp to our God: who covers the heaven with clouds, who prepares rain for the earth, who causes grass to spring up on the mountains, and green herb for the service of men; and gives cattle their food, and to the young ravens that call upon him" (7-9).

Charlotte Augusta Fraser

Who Was He?

(1894)

The author: Very little is known of Charlotte Augusta Fraser (she also signed "A.C.F.," "Caroline Augusta Fraser," "C. A. Frazer"), who was likely born in 1849. Her Scottish immigrant parents had arrived in Canada in 1846. Her father was a Presbyterian minister to First Nations people of Canada East. Charlotte was the third child, born after her family moved to Canada West. In the 1880s, the family was in Montreal, where Charlotte worked as editor of the Children's Department of the *Montreal Star*. She became a member of the American Folk-Lore Society and she gathered tales of Highlanders from Ontario. She published a novel, *Atma* (1891) and, with her friend Margaret Ridley Charlton (1858-1931), two books of fairy tales: *A Wonder Web of Stories* (1892) and *With Printless Foot: A Holiday Book of Fairy Tales* (1894). She published several stories and articles in *The Canadian Magazine*. She died in Montreal in 1896.

The text: First published in *The Canadian Magazine* 3: 5 (September 1894), 480-488.

WHO WAS HE ?

BY MISS C. A. FRASER

THE following story, it may be, labors under a great disadvantage in being a narrative of fact, and also in being Canadian, Canada not being generally supposed to have acquired as yet the nameless mystery and sense of eld, likely to result in occurrences weird or strange. Nevertheless, it is an absolutely true tale which I am about to tell, and the events befell myself, a Canadian, a good many years ago, in one of the oldest and busiest parts of Ontario.

I was travelling, by rail, from Hamilton to visit friends in the country. I suppose that my journey was, in its commencement, quite uneventful, for I have no slightest recollection of it, until at a junction depôt, I suddenly loom up in my memory as an angry and slightly excited young person, vigorously upbraiding the railway officials, the government and the universe generally, regarding a matter of errant luggage. I do not in the least recall, at this date, what the difficulty really was, but I infer from my own demeanour that my conscience was entirely clear, and that the defection was owing to no heedlessness of mine. That the situation was beyond hope of immediate remedy I also infer from the same conditions. I would not have been so recklessly eloquent had there been a loophole of escape. Whether the officials were too guilty to defend themselves, or too indifferent, I cannot tell. On this point "the haunts of memory echo not," but I seem in the glimpse I get now, peering through the vista of years, to have the floor, and to be improving the occasion to the utmost of my ability, when suddenly comes an interruption.

A stranger had been carelessly regarding me. I had been aware of his standing there, a little to my left, apart and alone; but he was, at first glance, a very prosaic-looking individual, commonplace, I imagined, in fact, and he not being invested with badge or other token of office, I had not intentionally included him in my audience, and was only vaguely conscious of his presence, until now, when stepping forward and removing his cigar, he quietly offered a suggestion. I do not now know what it was, and it does not especially matter. I remember only the shock with which I awakened to a sense of my own volubility, and to my instant collapse.

He was of middle height, narrow-chested, and afflicted with a cough. He had a light-brown beard, not long, nor carefully trimmed. He looked tolerably well-to-do, but was not, in appearance at least, a city man. I have seen many merchants in small towns of just the same style and manner. His only pronounced characteristic was his expression, which was not the expression of such a merchant, especially while on a trip either of business or pleasure. He looked unhappy: in fact he looked bored, and at the moment of proffering me advice, he had the air of being constrained to do what cost an unwelcome effort. Apart from the look of *ennui* which he wore, and which might be readily attributed to physical weakness overcome by the discomfort of even a short journey, he had an intensely pre-occupied air. Even when a few hours later he conversed with me pleasantly enough, I remember, little interested in him as I was, being struck with this. I can see his face now distinctly with that strange absence of mind written upon it. It approached the expression of a clair-

The following story, it may be, labors under a great disadvantage in being a narrative of fact, and also in being Canadian, Canada not being generally supposed to have acquired as yet the nameless mystery and sense of eld, likely to result in occurrences weird or strange. Nevertheless, it is an absolutely true tale which I am about to tell, and the events befell myself, a Canadian, a good many years ago, in one of the oldest and busiest parts of Ontario.

I was travelling, by rail, from Hamilton to visit friends in the country. I suppose that my journey was, in its commencement, quite uneventful, for I have no slightest recollection of it, until at a junction depôt, I suddenly loom up in my memory as an angry and slightly excited young person, vigorously upbraiding the railway officials, the government and the universe generally, regarding a matter of errant luggage. I do not in the least recall, at this date, what the difficulty really was, but I infer from my own demeanour that my conscience was entirely clear, and that the defection was owing to no heedlessness of mine. That the situation was beyond hope of immediate remedy I also infer from the same conditions. I would not have been so recklessly eloquent had there been a loophole of escape. Whether the officials were too guilty to defend themselves, or too indifferent, I cannot tell. On this point "the haunts of memory echo not,"[385] but I seem in the glimpse I get now, peering through the vista of years, to have the floor, and to be improving the occasion to the utmost of my ability, when suddenly comes an interruption.

A stranger had been carelessly regarding me. I had been aware of his standing there, a little to my left, apart and alone; but he was, at first glance, a very prosaic-looking individual, commonplace, I imagined, in fact, and he not being invested with badge or other token of office, I had not intentionally included him in my audience, and was only vaguely conscious of his presence, until now, when stepping forward and removing his cigar, he quietly offered a suggestion. I do not now know what it was, and it does not especially matter. I remember only the shock with which I awakened to a sense of my own volubility, and to my instant collapse.

He was of middle height, narrow-chested, and afflicted with a cough. He had a light-brown beard, not long, nor carefully trimmed. He looked tolerably well-to-do, but was not, in appearance at least, a city man. I have seen many merchants in small towns of just the same style and manner. His only pronounced characteristic was his expression, which was not the expression of such a merchant, especially while on a trip either of business or pleasure.

[385] From Tennyson's (see also notes 343 and 345) poem "The Two Voices" (first published in *Poems* in 1842).

He looked unhappy; in fact he looked bored, and at the moment of proffering me advice, he had the air of being constrained to do what cost an unwelcome effort. Apart from the look of ennui which he wore, and which might be readily attributed to physical weakness overcome by the discomfort of even a short journey, he had an intensely pre-occupied air. Even when a few hours later he conversed with me pleasantly enough, I remember, little interested in him as I was, being struck with this. I can see his face now distinctly with that strange absence of mind written upon it. It approached the expression of a clairvoyant entering a trance. And the nonchalant, matter-of-fact manner of the man was oddly at variance with it. It is difficult to describe him. When I attempt to do so, I find myself using contradictory terms which seem to be necessitated by the exigencies of the task of picturing to the imagination of others a face in which an intensity of thought, resulting almost in trance, was no more strikingly portrayed than an expression of fretful ennui. He was distinguished from the little crowd around him in no other way, and attracted, seemingly, no observation. I would hardly have seen him, would certainly not have looked twice to catch the second time a slight sense of the oddness of his look, had he not spoken to me.

The conclusion of his counsel was to the effect that, as I must wait for a later train than that by which I had intended going, I had better betake myself to one of two small hotels which stood side by side at a few yards' distance. I remember thanking him hastily, putting some inquiry as to train time, and rapidly "making tracks" for the nearer of the two quiet-looking country inns which he had indicated. I had a novel and newspapers. It was a warm day in May, and I found a pleasant little sitting-room, into which non but myself intruded during the time spent in waiting. So that by reading, resting, and a short walk abroad, the time slipped by easily enough, and when towards sic o'clock, I again found myself on the platform waiting the arrival of the evening train, I had entirely recovered my equanimity, and having somewhat altered my plans in a manner to meet the difficulties engendered by a failure to arrive at a previously appointed hour, I hastened to claim my luggage and have it checked for a station seven miles further on than the one that had been intended for my destination.

In the light of later events I wish that I had been less devoted to the interests of myself and my luggage, and had sooner spared even a faint and passing regard for my nonchalant fellow traveller, for such it turned out he was to be. As I was eagerly scanning a pile of trunks and boxes, I turned my head to find him at my side. Except that the cigar had disappeared, he was the same wearied, bored individual; and in the same tone of resignation to duty, he said:

"You had better hand over your checks to the baggageman, and let him find your things."

"But there is no one in the baggage room," I replied, "and it is close on train time. I am afraid of being late."

He looked up and down the platform. "There he is," he said; "I will send him to you."

He walked away, and a few moments later a baggage man, or some equivalent, made the necessary alterations in the checking of my trunks, and I resumed my occupation of gazing up the track. I saw my helpful friend engaged in the same way, but when, a few minutes later, I seated myself in the car, carefully selecting a window which would give a view of familiar landscapes, I had forgotten all about him.

Just as the shadows were lengthening into evening dusk, a number of people walked into the car. A car further back had been detached from the train at some little wayside station just reached, and its occupants filed in, finding seats here and there. Amongst them was the stranger. He was coughing violently when he entered, and looked more than ever tired and worn. He hesitated on reaching my seat. The car was pretty well filled, and I immediately made a move, which invited him to sit down. Out of regard for his cough, I asked if he would prefer the window shut, the air being now agreeably cool, but he said he would not and sat still, gazing past me at the pleasant fields and dainty foliage of early summer time. I looked at him more attentively then, than I had hitherto done, and his face imprinted itself on my memory. If I were skilled with the pencil I could draw it now; the features were such that a moderately exact description would enable any artist to depict them—an ordinary face, but for its expression.

As I watched him the fancy seized me that he was blind, an utterly untenable idea, considering that he was seated, slightly stooped forward, the better to see the country through which we were flying. This look of not seeing did not prevent the impression which I got of very keen and earnest thought, which, however, did not find its subject matter in his present environment. I have seen this curious conjunction of expressions in another face quite recently, but both were portrayed with much less intensity. And in the lives of the two persons who wore that look, there lurked, I must believe, a mysterious tragedy.

Have some of my readers ever mistaken a wax figure for nature, and gazed upon it as upon a fellow-being, to awaken with an unpleasant sense of repulsion to its lack of life? Some thing of that I experienced as I looked upon my companion's impassive countenance, which yet, like the cold wax, was shaped to express thought and emotion. I felt uncomfortable, and I think that I wished that he would go away, notwithstanding that I had myself invited him to sit down.

The conductor called the name of a station, Newton, and the stranger, turning to me, said, in that quietly sympathetic manner in which he always spoke: "The next station is yours?"

"No," I replied, "I shall only get off for a minute to get another ticket. My friends will not expect me by this train, and it is much too far for me to go alone to their house. I shall go on to Fairbank, and if I wish, someone will drive me out here to-morrow."

"You had better speak to the conductor about it," he said, "I am afraid that the train will not stop long enough to admit of your procuring a ticket."

The conductor was near, and he beckoned him, and finding the conjecture correct, I was enabled to make some arrangement which dispensed with the necessity for a ticket.

My new acquaintance resumed his former attitude, looking steadily past me out of the window, but he had grown conversational. My mention of Fairbank had unlocked his speech.

"I used to know Fairbank very well," he said musingly, "but it is long since I have been there."

I at once became conversational also, for I did not know Fairbank well, having been there only once before, and I felt some interest in the place, having promised to visit friends there before my return home. I said as much, and he responded in the same way, as if talking to himself.

"I have not been there for six years. I left it on May 24th, 18—. I was born and brought up and married there."

He did not speak for a few minutes, and then, as if recounting something only half remembered, and not too keenly interesting, he went on:—

"I have a little daughter there. My wife died of consumption six months before I left, and my little girl is with her mother's friends."

The thought occurred to me at once of course, that he was then on unfriendly terms with his wife's relatives, else why refrain so long from seeing his child. We were nearing Fairbank, and wishing to continue the conversation I made some remark about the interest, verging on historic, which clung about the little town. He did not reply in a similar strain, however, but still harping on his family ties, went on softly:—

"I have not seen her since. We called her Cora. She was only four when I left, but she is in good hands. They are good people."

He spoke the last sentence almost with emphasis, so that I reconsidered my former assumption as to his straightened relations with these connections of his. But then why allow so long a time elapse without seeing this little Cora? Why pass the place by this evening and make no sign of even a wish to alight at the depôt for which we were now slowing perceptibly? One's mind is apt to get bright and inquisitive towards the end of a journey, the result, I fancy, of enforced silence for successive hours, and my thoughts busied themselves now with conjecture. Had this man who evidently cherished no ill-will to his friends, yet so grievously sinned against them that they would have none of him? That could hardly be, for the infliction of such a punishment as complete estrangement from his only child would certainly awake in him at the very least, a sense of injury, no trace of which was apparent as, with a very faint smile visible on his face, he recalled old days.

"I knew every foot of ground about here, and every man, woman and child in the place. You will hear my name often, for I have a good many cousins about, who bear it. My name is Cheyne, Henry Russel Cheyne."

I was collecting my belongings, some of which I had to detach from the rack overhead. My friend did not offer any assistance—he was too much engrossed in his reminiscences—but when he arose to let me pass out, he walked after me to the car door, and, finding that a light shower was falling, he volunteered to raise my umbrella, my own hands being fully occupied with the small paraphernalia with which womankind makes life a burden while *en route.*

In handing it to me, he roused for a moment to a more active interest than he had yet displayed.

"You will not find any cabs here at this hour," he said, "but speak to the station master. He will send you over to ——'s hotel."

I interrupted him laughingly: "Oh, I am not going to a hotel; I have friends here. Thanks, and good-bye."

That was all, and I never saw my travelling acquaintance of the clairvoyant mien again. Not a very thrilling episode, was it? But all the strangeness is yet to come.

In the excitement of an unexpected arrival at the pleasant house where my friends, Mr. and Mrs. Gabriel, an elderly couple without children, lived, I forgot him, until the following afternoon, when a slight circumstance revived my interest in the unsatisfactory condition of his domestic ties.

Mrs. Gabriel had a very delightful house. It was a red brick cottage with verandah all around it. It was very large in area, square, and having on each of three sides a door opening upon the verandah. One of these doors led into the drawing-room, a large room with low ceiling, and always dimly lighted by reason of the verandah and its flowering vines and creepers. Mrs. Gabriel's work table stood nearly all the time upon the verandah, where the light was better, and I used to sit upon the steps there with work or book. She persuaded me to remain a week with her before returning to Newton to carry out my first intention.

It was very pleasant. The lilacs about the house were in bloom: the weather was charming: all the girls came to call on me, and we drove to return their calls, as Mrs. Gabriel believed herself unable to walk, and had, moreover, a delightful little carriage and very safe horse.

On the first afternoon of my stay with her, however, she could not come out. The roomy, shady drawing-room was filled with ladies, mostly elderly, who, with a very business-like air, discussed means and methods of aiding in the payment of a large church debt. Mrs. Gabriel nearly bustled with the importance of presiding over the proceedings.

As a stranger, I was not interested, but remained, feeling that it was expected of me, and I would, no doubt, have been sufficiently wearied, had not relief come in the form of an exceedingly pretty little girl, very prettily dressed, too, who, perceiving my admiration, and sympathizing, probably, in my boredom, presently sidled up to me. I was and am exceedingly fond of children, and this little damsel was really extraordinarily pretty, and, as I discovered, to my amusement, funnily vain, and adorned with little coquettish mannerisms, which somehow did not repel, because, notwithstanding her assumption of being very grown-up, she was yet exceedingly childish. And then, she was so very pretty. Not the baby prettiness of flaxen curls, dimples, and unformed features: my little co-sufferer was, I fear, not of the kind of which poets tell. She was really very like a fashion-plate. Faces in fashion-plates are all on the same model, only that some have fair hair, and others dark. They all have the same classic little heads, and small, correct profiles, and the head and face are the same, whether it be of child or matron. It is a style not often seen, which makes its adoption for fashion-plate use objectionable. But rare as it is, this little girl had it. She was both delightful to view, and amusing by reason of the fashion plate association of ideas. She was very lively, and chatted away easily.

"My name is Cora Cheyne," I presently heard, and instantly replied in some surprise: "I thought that Mrs. King was your mother." 1894

"Oh, no; I call her mamma, because I have always lived with her. But she is my grandmamma. My papa and mamma are both dead."

I heard this last speech with a little shock of indignation. I felt my sense of justice awakened in defence of my whilom railway acquaintance. Whatever his offence, he surely could not deserve that his only child be taught to believe him dead.

Cora went on: "I hope that you are coming to our house. Mamma means to ask you to come on Wednesday afternoon. I have a great many things to show you."

And when her mamma, or her grandmother, for that was really the relationship, invited me to spend the following afternoon with her, I gladly consented. Curiosity was thoroughly aroused, although I was ashamed to recognize that such was the case. I spoke to Mrs. Gabriel of the pleasure with which I looked forward to spending several hours in the beautiful garden and extensive lawn to which she had drawn my attention during a former visit to her.

"I was glad," she cried, "to see you amused with little Cora, for our proceedings could not have been interesting to you."

"Yes," I replied, "she is a dear, funny little girl," and then, because my mind was full of the small mystery which I had unearthed, I added at a venture:—

"I know her father."

Mrs. Gabriel looked at me in slight surprise, caused, probably, by my positive tone.

"Her father is dead, my dear," she said gently. "He has been dead for some years now. It was very sad; he died soon after his wife, leaving just this little girl; but," she added, after a pause, "she is in good hands."

The similarity of her concluding remark to one dropped by the stranger on the train, did not escape my attention, but I merely responded by asking a question:—

"What makes you sure that Mr. Cheyne is dead, Mrs. Gabriel?"

"Oh, my dear," she replied, "it does not admit of question. I saw him in the coffin, and, indeed, I almost saw him die. He had a lingering illness, unlike his wife. It was lung disease in both cases, but she was only a few weeks unable to go about, while he had been coughing for quite two years before she fell ill. We all knew them well: they belong to people so well known about here, you know. But when did you think that you met some one like him?"

"On the railway train when coming here," I replied, and proceeded to give her a detailed account of my journey, and the slight assistance given by a stranger. As I was talking, her husband entered, and she turned to him.

"——— thinks that she met Cora Cheyne's father while on her way here," she said, smiling a little sadly, "and I have just been telling her of his death."

"Strange," he responded, "I was thinking of him as I came along the street just now. He died just six years ago this month, and I was one of the pall-bearers at his funeral. It was a very different May from this, very cold, a flurry of snow had fallen the day before. Yes, Henry Russel Cheyne died six years ago."

I think my jaw dropped with horror. Until now no one had spoken the full name. "It had been 'Cora's father' with both Mrs. Gabriel and myself, and the mystery in my mind had been a commonplace one of family estrangement. A horror which I did not care to investigate seized my mind. With whom had I been talking on that pleasant May evening?

"What is the matter, my dear?" asked my kind hostess.

"Oh, nothing," I replied. "May I have a light all night in my room, Mrs. Gabriel? I think I am nervous, and I will make sure of its safety before I fall asleep."

Fear of fire was one of Mrs. Gabriel's idiosyncrasies, and she entered a vigorous protest against my proposal, assuring me that by keeping me awake, an unwonted light would only increase nervous agitation. It was quite her favorite theme, peril by fire, and the digression lasted until we parted for the night.

When alone I reasoned with myself and partly got rid of the uneasy, startled sensation which had seemed to make sleep impossible. I told myself that most positively the man with whom I had talked, who had made in my little difficulties such practical suggestions, was certainly a living, breathing person. Either by some extraordinary coincidence, there had lived in this small town, two men of precisely the same name, one leaving the place on the very same day of the other's death, or, much more probably, Henry Russel Cheyne had not died at all. There had been some motive for pretending a death when actually none had taken place, and I determined that, all things considered, any investigation that I could personally conduct through Mrs. Gabriel or little Cora, would be perfectly justifiable in the present light of events. And in the character of a private and self-appointed detective, I betook myself on the appointed afternoon to Mrs. King's house. I went alone, Mrs. Gabriel being engaged, taking work with me, as I had been invited for a very informal visit, after a manner much in vogue in Fairbank. Little Cora was at school when I arrived, and Mrs. King and I made a pleasant tour of the garden, lawn and poultry yard together. She was, I should think, about sixty years of age, very tall and upright in bearing, with keen, dark eyes, and a bright complexion. She was a very religious woman and much respected in the neighborhood, where she had spent her whole life, and where she had been twice married, the first time to a brother of my friend, Mr. Gabriel.

When we re-entered the house, I found that she had two large drawing-rooms, one of which she called the sitting-room. It seemed to be her favorite apartment, and in it were hung a number of water-color sketches by a young relative in New York, in whom she was much interested, and she pointed them out with evident pride. Among them on the wall were portraits and photographs.

The mystery of Cora's father had taken the background in my thoughts during our stroll, but it suddenly assumed lively proportions, when I heard Mrs. King say:—

"This is Cora's mother."

I turned hastily from the picture at which I was looking closely, to see that she held in her hand a circular frame which she had taken from its place.

I went to her side. It had been enlarged from a smaller picture at a time when the photographer's grasp of his art left much to be desired, and the portrait was not pleasing. It was distinct enough, however, and my mental comment was that Cora certainly did not take her looks from her mother. But what I said was: "Have you a portrait of her father, Mrs. King?"

"Yes," she answered, "and a very good one. It is a photograph also, but taken in Buffalo less than a year before his death."

And restoring to its peg the one she held, she took down its companion picture, and carrying it to a better light, held it up to view.

1894

I looked in silence for a minute, with a tide of thoughts rushing through my mind, and then, extending my hands, I received it from her, and turned away, in an involuntary fear lest she should read my mind. I daresay that it was well that I did so, as some of the horror I felt must have been reflected in my face. For the man whose well-executed portrait looked at me from the circular gilt frame in my hand, was my fellow-traveller, who had called himself Henry Russel Cheyne!

I feared that my voice must betray my excitement when I at length ventured to speak:—

"Mrs. King," I asked, "Where was Mr. Cheyne's home at the time of his death?"

"Here," she replied, quietly and laconically. "He died almost where you are standing. There was a partition at that time dividing this room, and I had a bed carried there, because it was more cheerful for him. He had been ailing long, but after his wife's death, he became rapidly worse.

For want of anything better to say, and because I wished her to continue talking, I asked:—

"Did he know that he was dying?"

"Oh, yes," she answered, and added softly, "but he had been long ready. His death-bed was, like that of his wife, very beautiful.

Only three days before the end, he tried to make Cora understand: but she was then only four years of age, and would not listen. She pounded his pillows, thinking that she made him more comfortable, and slipped off the bed as she talked, to arrange the phials and flowers that stood on a table beside him. He only smiled to me, and said that perhaps it was better so. But he loved little Cora very much."

I thought drearily of the vague indifference with which Henry Russel Cheyne, on that evening train, had spoken of this little daughter, and I tried to imagine the scene in which he had, with pathetic yearning, striven to take of her an eternal farewell.

I do not know how far I might have pursued my inquiries had not an interruption come, in the form of Cora herself, pretty, presumptuous, and self-assured as ever. She assumed little airs of authority, and proceeded to play the part of hostess at once, her grandmother becoming absorbed in silent admiration, in which, notwithstanding my amusement and disapproval, I could not help participating.

I returned to Mrs. Gabriel's early, in a very thoughtful mood. I found her knitting by lamplight, her husband seated at the other side of her work-table, reading.

I sat down and waited for him to lay aside his paper. As soon as he did so, I began: "Mr. Gabriel, was Cora Cheyne's father a poor man?"

"By no means. He was in very comfortable circumstances. All that he had will be Cora's. Mr. King, her step-grandfather, and myself are executors. She will be a small heiress I fancy, for Mrs. King is a wealthy woman through her first marriage, to my brother, and is tolerably certain to leave nearly everything to Cora."

I tried to form some theory of motive and conduct which would explain the extraordinary circumstance of a feigned death, which implied a lifetime's entire and complete separation from home, kindred, and fortune. If all that he had was in executors' hands, and he still living, he was penniless and friendless. My thoughts shaped into another question:—

"What advantage would accrue to Cora, Mr. Gabriel, by her father's premature death?"

"She could gain nothing by it," he replied, and I fancied that he spoke more stiffly, as if wearied of my obstinate persistence in what appeared to him a silly delusion. "She cannot, of course, have anything until she is of age. She has a very happy home, in which she is an only and idolized child, but her position there would have been the same had he lived. He was greatly esteemed by Mr. and Mrs. King."

"His death left her an orphan, then, did it not," I asked, "without altering her outward circumstances, which were fortunate and secure in any case?"

"That is the state of the case," said Mr. Gabriel, "and I think that to-morrow you must come with me for a walk. I will take you to the burying-ground, and you shall read the inscription on the tombstone of this man who interests you so much."

"That will be the best way," exclaimed Mrs. Gabriel, "and then I think, dear, that you must try to get rid of this fancy of yours. I really believe that you must have fallen asleep on the train and dreamed it."

That this solution would involve a belief in my being endowed with second sight did not seem to occur to my good friend, but I gathered from her words, as well as from her husband's tone, that they were unwilling to have more of my mystery.

Unforeseen circumstances prevented the walk to the little cemetery next day, but a year or so later, being in Fairbank again, I went there by myself and read the record of the death of Henry Russel Cheyne on the day which my railway acquaintance of the same name had given as the date of his leaving the little town never to return.

And now I have related the strange circumstances which disturbed me so much at the time, and which, after discussing with a few friends, I allowed to sink into forgetfulness, until a short time ago, when they were suddenly and most oddly recalled to vivid recollection. I was in conversation with a young cousin of my own, whose age would nearly correspond with Cora's, if Cora be still living. Amy chatted away about her school days, she having just graduated from an Ontario college. I was only half listening, until suddenly, in some recital of school-girl escapade, the name of Cora Cheyne cropped up.

"Cora Cheyne!" I exclaimed, "where was she from, Amy?" I once knew a little girl of that name in Fairbank."

"Yes, she was from Fairbank," my cousin answered. "But she was only a short time at our college, and I did not know her very well."

"Was she very pretty, Amy?" I asked. "She was a remarkably beautiful little girl when I saw her."

"Was she?" in a tone of slight surprise. "I don't know. I never thought of it. She was so very delicate, and looked so sickly. And," she added, after a pause, "she was such a queer girl, we did not take to her at all. She was always seeing ghosts."

I did not say anything, but I "thought the more," and it seemed to me that in these days of psychical research, it were well to make known this curious episode of my own experience.

It may serve no purpose save to amuse an idle half-hour, for I know that my repeated asseverations will fail to win most people to a belief in the truth of so strange a tale, but I would like to think that some one among my readers will take it seriously enough to ponder the enigma, and perchance solve it. It may not convince any one of the existence of apparitions. It has never convinced me. I am a staunch unbeliever in spiritualistic phenomena, and even this experience, which I consider extraordinary, has never affected my incredulity.

STEPHEN LEACOCK

My Financial Career

(1895)

The author: Stephen Butler Leacock was born on 30 December 1869, in Swanmore, a village in Hampshire, England. His family immigrated to Ontario in 1876, his father trying his hand at farming a few times, until he left for Winnipeg in 1878 to take advantage of the Manitoba boom. He was unsuccessful and turned to alcoholism. The family, which soon grew to eleven children, was supported financially by Leacock's paternal grandfather from England. Leacock graduated from Upper Canada College in 1887. Leacock studied at the University of Toronto, graduating in 1891. He had already started teaching at Upper Canada College, where he remained until 1899, when he started postgraduate studies at the University of Chicago, where he obtained his PhD in economics in 1903. In 1900 he married Beatrix Hamilton. He taught at McGill University in Montreal until his retirement in 1936. He died on 28 March 1944 in Toronto. Leacock published articles and humorous stories in college newspapers, having a first story ("That Ridiculous War in the East") published in *Grip* on 6 October 1894. His extremely successful career as a humorist began in earnest the following year with "My Financial Career." His short fiction was collected in the early 20th century, most notably in *Literary Lapses* (1910), *Nonsense Novels* (1911), *Sunshine Sketches of a Little Town* (1911), *Arcadian Adventures with the Idle Rich* (1914), followed by non-fiction and memoirs, such as *My Discovery of England* (1922), *My Discovery of the West* (1937), *My Remarkable Uncle* (1942).

The text: It was first published in the *[New York] Life* 25: 641 (11 April 1895), 238-239, and it was signed. Reprinted in *Literary Lapses: A Book of Sketches* (Montreal: Gazette Printing Company, 1910), 5-9, from which the following has been taken. However, the spelling "check" and "check book" from the 1910 book has been replaced with "cheque" and "cheque book" from the magazine original.

Further reading: Beverly J. Rasporich. "The Leacock Persona and the Canadian Character." *Mosaic: An Interdisciplinary Critical Journal* 14: 2 (Spring 1981), 76-92.

David Staines, ed. *Stephen Leacock: A Reappraisal.* Ottawa: University of Ottawa Press, 1986.

When I go into a bank I get rattled. The clerks rattle me; the wickets rattle me; the sight of the money rattles me; everything rattles me.

The moment I cross the threshold of a bank and attempt to transact business there, I become an irresponsible idiot.

I knew this beforehand, but my salary had been raised to fifty dollars a month and I felt that the bank was the only place for it.

So I shambled in and looked timidly round at the clerks. I had an idea that a person about to open an account must needs consult the manager.

I went up to a wicket marked "Accountant." The accountant was a tall, cool devil. The very sight of him rattled me. My voice was sepulchral.

"Can I see the manager?" I said, and added solemnly, "alone." I don't know why I said "alone."

"Certainly," said the accountant, and fetched him.

The manager was a grave, calm man. I held my fifty-six dollars clutched in a crumpled ball in my pocket.

"Are you the manager?" I said. God knows I didn't doubt it.

"Yes," he said.

"Can I see you," I asked, "alone?" I didn't want to say "alone" again, but without it the thing seemed self-evident.

The manager looked at me in some alarm. He felt that I had an awful secret to reveal.

"Come in here," he said, and led the way to a private room. He turned the key in the lock.

"We are safe from interruption here," he said; "sit down."

We both sat down and looked at each other. I found no voice to speak.

"You are one of Pinkerton's men, I presume," he said.

He had gathered from my mysterious manner that I was a detective. I knew what he was thinking, and it made me worse.

"No, not from Pinkerton's," I said, seeming to imply that I came from a rival agency.

"To tell the truth," I went on, as if I had been prompted to lie about it, "I am not a detective at all. I have come to open an account. I intend to keep all my money in this bank."

The manager looked relieved but still serious; he concluded now that I was a son of Baron Rothschild or a young Gould.[386]

"A large account, I suppose," he said.

"Fairly large," I whispered. "I propose to deposit fifty-six dollars now and fifty dollars a month regularly."

The manager got up and opened the door. He called to the accountant.

"Mr. Montgomery," he said unkindly loud, "this gentleman is opening an account, he will deposit fifty-six dollars. Good morning."

I rose.

A big iron door stood open at the side of the room.

"Good morning," I said, and stepped into the safe.

"Come out," said the manager coldly, and showed me the other way.

I went up to the accountant's wicket and poked the ball of money at him with a quick convulsive movement as if I were doing a conjuring trick.

My face was ghastly pale.

1895 "Here," I said, "deposit it." The tone of the words seemed to mean, "Let us do this painful thing while the fit is on us."[387]

He took the money and gave it to another clerk.

He made me write the sum on a slip and sign my name in a book. I no longer knew what I was doing. The bank swam before my eyes.

"Is it deposited?" I asked in a hollow, vibrating voice.

"It is," said the accountant.

"Then I want to draw a cheque."

My idea was to draw out six dollars of it for present use. Someone gave me a cheque book through a wicket and someone else began telling me how to write it out. The people in the bank had the impression that I was an invalid millionaire. I wrote something on the cheque and thrust it in at the clerk. He looked at it.

"What! are you drawing it all out again?" he asked in surprise. Then I realized that I had written fifty-six instead of six. I was too

[386] Allusion to Jason "Jay" Gould (1836-1892), American robber baron, and his descendants.

[387] While we're in the mood, while we feel inspired (the expression is today rather obsolete).

far gone to reason now. I had a feeling that it was impossible to explain the thing. All the clerks had stopped writing to look at me.

Reckless with misery, I made a plunge.

"Yes, the whole thing."

"You withdraw your money from the bank?"

"Every cent of it."

"Are you not going to deposit any more?" said the clerk, astonished.

"Never."

An idiot hope struck me that they might think something had insulted me while I was writing the cheque and that I had changed my mind. I made a wretched attempt to look like a man with a fearfully quick temper.

The clerk prepared to pay the money.

"How will you have it?" he said.

"What?"

"How will you have it?"

"Oh"—I caught his meaning and answered without even trying to think—"in fifties."

He gave me a fifty-dollar bill.

"And the six?" he asked dryly.

"In sixes," I said.

He gave it me and I rushed out.

As the big door swung behind me I caught the echo of a roar of laughter that went up to the ceiling of the bank. Since then I bank no more. I keep my money in cash in my trousers pocket and my savings in silver dollars in a sock.

Harriet Julia Campbell Jephson

The Judge's Widow

(1895)

The author: Harriet Julia Campbell was born on 14 May 1854 in Quebec City, the daughter of a barrister. She studied art in Rome and, in 1873, she married Commander Alfred Jephson of the Royal Navy. She spent most of her remaining life (she died on 26 November 1930 on the Isle of Wight) in England. She contributed to several British periodicals (especially articles on Canadian society) and she often illustrated her own texts. Alfred Jephson was knighted in 1891 and Harriet became Lady Jephson, a name with which she signed her books and articles afterwards. Apart from *A Canadian Scrap-Book*, her best-known publication is *A War-Time Journal* (London: Matthews, 1915).

The text: First published as "The Judge's Widow. A Study in Human Nature. By Lady Jephson," in *Windsor's Magazine* 1 (June), 709-712. Reprinted in *A Canadian Scrap-Book* (London: Marshall Russell, 1897), 109-127. The following is the book version. There is only one minor difference between the two (the last sentence appears in a paragraph of its own only in the book).

Madame Le Gros lived on "The Cape," Quebec, in a large cut-stone house, which faced the Governor's gardens.[388] One section of the Quebec people described her as "that poor dear frivolous Madame Le Gros." Others, who were inclined to frivolity and amusement, called her "that dear delightful charming old lady."

She was the wife of a great local magnate and one learned in the law. The magnate was many years older than his wife, so that when she was a frisky dame of sixty or thereabouts, he was nearing

[388] Le Jardin du Gouverneur (or the Governor's Garden) is in Old Quebec, on the shore of the Saint-Lawrence River, near Cap Diamant (or Cape Diamond).

ninety, and had arrived at the state described by Shakespeare as: "*sans* teeth, *sans* eyes, *sans* taste, *sans* everything."[389]

In due course of time the magnate was gathered to his fathers, and his widow grieved for him very truly and warmly. Nevertheless, she was particular to see that her mourning was becoming, and that Plover & Pie sent home exactly the right allowance of crape suitable to an inconsolable widow. All the winter following the judge's death, Madame Le Gros received only intimate friends, and her historic card parties were discontinued. By way of recreation she drove up and down John Street[390] every afternoon, muffled in her crape and wearing an expression to match her weeds;[391] nevertheless, her human joyous nature took a pleasure hardly known to herself in the brightness of all about her. She noted the smartest tandems and the prettiest sleighs, whose fur robes were richest, and whose sleigh bells were best mounted. Mrs. May's new sealskin met with her warmest admiration, and pretty Dollie Duncan's snow-shoeing costume she voted *chic* and delightful. She wondered whether Captain Sumner was really going to fall in love with Miss Hammond, and if Mdlle. de la Rue were trifling with that poor young subaltern's affections. Then she turned her attention to the Cameron children, and kissed her hand to them all effusively. She even stopped her sleigh at Blank's the confectioner's, and ordered "lollipops" for their benefit. Afterwards she looked in for Vespers at the French cathedral, and drove home well content.

When, however, Madame had dined, and found herself night after night *tête-à-tête* in her comfortable drawing-room with her ancient and uninteresting companion, she began to wish that card parties and grief were not incompatible. She scanned the *Quebec Chronicle* for news, and scolded Mademoiselle for her stupidity in having heard no gossip that day. She played a mild game of draughts, drank a glass of hot punch, fondled her pug, yawned, was intolerably bored, and went early to bed. The following autumn a few choice friends were admitted nightly for whist, and before the winter closed Madame's receptions were as crowded as ever—Madame meanwhile abating no sign of external grief, and wearing her crape of the prescribed depth.

[389] In *As You Like It* (II, vii, 166).

[390] Today, Rue Saint-Jean; it is one of the oldest streets in Quebec City.

[391] "Weeds" is an old slang (but originally literary) term for garments; hence, "widow's weeds" is a term for mourning clothes.

Madame Le Gros was a wonderfully well-preserved woman. Her enemies (and she had many) accounted for the freshness and smoothness of her skin by declaring that she slept with beefsteaks tied to her cheeks. Her nut-brown hair was declared to emanate from the barber's shop, or to owe its colouring to his skill; but slander erred in both instances, as it very often does. She had been a beauty in her youth, and she retained a large share of this gift in her age, but she was innocent of dye or "aids to beauty."

I shall never forget my first acquaintance with Madame Le Gros. In my own home the Sunday card parties had been severely condemned, and the old lady alluded to as a sad instance of aged depravity. I had always nourished a keen curiosity to see the inside of the Wicked House, and, above all, longed to find myself face to face with the wicked person, and one day an unsuspicious friend took me there unknown to my mother.

How my heart beat as I crept after her up the softly-carpeted staircase; and what a sensation of guilty pleasure thrilled me at the thought that I was periling my soul in the House of Rimmon.[392]
1895 In my own mind, from piecing together casual remarks and dwelling upon them, I had conjured up in my imagination a being in whom horns and a tail were marked characteristics. The subject fascinated me beyond description. It seemed to me valiant to imitate Christian and face Apollyon on his own ground, and I remembered well how Christian had resisted the blandishments of Mrs. Light-Mind and Mrs. Love-the-Flesh.[393] My astonishment and disappointment were great when I was introduced to an ordinary-looking, handsome old lady (who sat tatting at the window),[394] and learnt that she was Madame Le Gros.

"Well, my dear," said Apollyon, "so you are little Margaret MacGregor! How is your pretty mother? Did she send a message

[392] Another name for Baal in the Old Testament; Naaman asks God's pardon for going to his house of worship with his master even after knowing Rimmon was a false idol: "In this thing the Lord pardon thy servant, that when my master goeth into the house of Rimmon to worship there, and he leaneth on my hand, and I bow myself in the house of Rimmon: when I bow down myself in the house of Rimmon, the Lord pardon thy servant in this thing" (2 Kings 5: 18).

[393] All are characters (Apollyon is a demon) in the John Bunyan's popular Christian allegory *The Pilgrim's Progress* (1678). So are those mentioned a few lines below, when the references to Christian resume.

[394] Tatting is the craft of making knotted lace with the help of a handheld shuttle.

to me? No? Never mind! Perhaps we shall be on good terms in heaven all the same."

"Oh, no! Madame," I said, shocked at such levity. "You won't go to heaven if you play cards and wear a wig. Mamma says so." Madame laughed heartily. "In the first place I don't wear a wig," said she, "and you may tell your mother so, with my love; and in the second place I never see any harm in cards, but a great deal of harm in speaking ill of my neighbours, and that you may tell your mother, too, my child."

Then she praised my blue eyes and golden hair, and said I should keep up the reputation of my family for good looks, and I listened, not altogether displeased, but fearful lest I, like Hope and Christian, should become entangled in the meshes of Flatterer's net. Such remarks as these were strongly reprobated in my own family. "Perhaps," I thought, with a thrill of excitement, "this was Madame Bubble, and if so, I must follow Standfast's example and resist her enticements mightily."

"My eyes are green and my hair is mud-coloured. Mamma says so," said I stoutly.

Madame Le Gros laughed again, and said something in French to my friend which I did not understand.

"If it prefers to be called ugly, it shall be," she said, stroking my head. "And now go and play me a tune, my dear, something martial like the 'Marseillaise.' *What* did you say? The piano out of tune, Mademoiselle. How can you talk such nonsense, when no one has played on it for over a year! Very nice, indeed, my child! Now you can come here and I will show you my famous screen. When I am dead and gone you can think of me and it together. Draw out the screen, please, Mademoiselle—so, with the light well on it, that we may see the pictures."

The piece of furniture alluded to was original enough, and it owed its embodiment to Madame Le Gros' *bizarre* and unconventional mind. It was a white, wooden framework, in which were set numerous photographs and an occasional letter and autograph.

"Now, my love," said Madame, "this is the history of Canadian society and politics for many a long day. Here you will find the Governors and their wives, commanders-in-chief, military and naval, great statesmen, judges, even two Royal Princes who have visited Quebec. You will perceive that all are signed and dated. Here is Mr. McGreevy, who was assassinated years ago, and Sir Etienne Cartier, and there is Lord Monck, and yonder a bishop.[395] That is a famous general, Sir Garnet Wolseley, and this one here is a Canadian author, Fennings Taylor.[396] I was promised a photograph of Her Gracious Majesty once, *that* would have made my screen complete, but the man who was going to send it from England died, unfortunately. Now sit and look at all these wonderful people whilst I talk to Mrs. Carr; and, Mademoiselle, fetch the child some chocolates to discuss meanwhile.

By this time, whether influenced by Madame's charm or chocolates I cannot say, but I had altogether shifted my ground in the Pilgrim's Progress. Instead of regarding Madame Le Gros as Apollyon, or even Mrs. Love-the-Flesh, I felt convinced that she was none other than Godly-Man, assailed by those demons, Prejudice and Ill-will. I munched my chocolates, gazed as bidden at the screen, and fancied myself on Mount Innocence.[397]

The room was low-ceilinged and eminently cosy in shape and arrangement. A fire burned in the grate, and deep arm-chairs covered with old-fashioned chintz were placed on either side of it. The walls were lined with low bookcases latticed in brass wire, and on the top of the bookcases stood blue china plates, a fat Chinese figure—whose tongue kept bobbing about alarmingly—and several gigantic Oriental vases. No books or magazines lay on the tables, for Madame Le Gros never read anything but the daily newspaper. She said she liked to originate ideas for herself, not imbibe them cut and dried out of books. I had heard my mother allude to this idiosyncrasy, and I wondered whether report had erred again, as it had anent the wig. At all events, I determined to find out.

---

[395] Madame Le Gros is clearly mixing up Thomas McGreevy (1825-1897), a prominent Canadian politician, born in Quebec, and who was still alive, and Thomas D'Arcy McGee (1825-1868), who was assassinated in Montreal. Like McGee, George-Etienne Cartier (1814-1873) was one of the Fathers of the Canadian Confederation. The Viscount Monck (1819-1894) served as governor-general of Canada before after the Confederation of 1867.

[396] Garnet Wolseley (1833-1913) was a British officer (rising to the rank of field marshal in 1894) who was in Canada in 1865-1867 and 1870-1871, contributing to the defeat of the Fenian Raids and the Red River Rebellion. John Fennings Taylor (1817-1882) was known mostly for his three volumes of *Portraits of British Americans, with Biographical Sketches* (1865-1868).

[397] Characters and setting from the second part of *Pilgrim's Progress*. Godly-man resides on Mount Innocence and his garments remain white no matter how much dirt Prejudice and Ill-will throw at him.

"Madame," said I, "is it true that you don't like books and never read them?"

"Quite true, my dear, quite true. For once rumour has spoken gospel truth. It is reading too many books nowadays, take my word for it, that makes the majority of people exactly alike. All cut out after the same pattern—all their ideas running in parallel grooves! They read 'Télemaque' and 'Henri Quatre' and 'Charles Douze,' Cæsar and Ovid and Virgil (and I know not what besides),[398] as girls and boys, and when they have consumed the prescribed amount of mental diet they are as stupid and gorged as a boa-constrictor. They have no individuality of thought left, no originality—they can only assimilate. My education was neglected when I was young, and that is why I am not an utterly dull old woman."

Distilled poison again dropped into my ears! I trembled guiltily. What would my governess say to such unorthodoxy?

"But, Madame, what books are these, then, and who reads them?"

"They are books on all subjects, my dear, and were the poor Judge's. He did not agree with me over that matter, which was just as well, as it gave rise to discussion, and prevented our married life from being dull. He was a wonderful reader, my love; but I think he might have been a still greater man had he trusted his own brains where judgment were concerned, and not leant so entirely on these fusty old legal commentaries. How d'ye do! How d'ye do!" as she smiled and bowed from her window. In a stage aside: "I'm sure I don't know *who* you are! Well, to be sure! that new colonel's wife is always driving about with—but fie upon me now, I'm talking scandal, and what will my father confessor say? I don't mind innocent gossip, but *scandal* is quite a different thing. Must you be going, Mrs. Carr? Wait a bit! Let me tell you how I punished that impertinent little upstart, Mademoiselle Labouchère. I met her at church last Sunday and she walked home with me afterwards, and all the way she made rude and unkind speeches about her

[398] *Les Aventures de Télémaque* is a 1699 novel by Fénelon; *Histoire de Charles XII* (1731) is a biography by Voltaire; Caesar's *De Bello Gallico* as well as the poems of Ovid and Virgil were studied in most schools in the Western world until at least the end of the 19th century. "Henri Quatre" might refer to Shakespeare's play (in two parts) about the English king Henry IV, but, since the other modern examples are all French, it probably refers to Voltaire's epic *Henriade*.

neighbours. When we found ourselves opposite my house, she looked up at my windows and said, 'I don't like your curtains at all, Madame Le Gros; they are anything but artistic' (my beautiful new ones from England, indeed!); 'they look terribly crude and glaring from the street.' So I replied with dignity: 'I am sorry, Madame, that you don't approve of the effect from *out*side, because assuredly you will never be in a position to judge from the *in*side. I wish you good-morning, Madame,' and I sailed into my house."

With which specimen of Madame Le Gros' repartee we took our departure.

Lily Dougall

Thrift

(1895)

The author: Lily Dougall was born on 16 April 1858 in Montreal, as the youngest of nine children. Her father was a Scottish merchant and journalist, the editor of the *Montreal Witness*. Her mother was the daughter of John Redpath (1796-1869), a prominent Montreal industrialist, among whose many business interests had been the construction of the Lachine and Rideau canals. After studies in Canadian private schools, Lily Dougall studied in Scotland, at the University of Edinburgh and the University of St Andrews. She published her first short story in 1889 and continued to contribute to periodicals in Britain (*Temple Bar, Longman's Magazine, Chambers's Journal*) and the US (*Atlantic Monthly*). In 1891, she published her first novel, *Beggars All*, set in England. Her next novels, including *What Necessity Knows* (1892), which was well received, were set in Canada. So are the twelve short stories collected in 1897 as *A Dozen Ways of Love*. After 1900, she lived mostly in England and published mostly theological works. She never married. She died on 9 October 1923 in Cumnor, a village near Oxford, in England. She is regarded as a feminist, thanks in part to the strong, independent heroines of her fiction. She had a long relationship with her assistant and life partner, Sophie Earp. They shared a home and they are buried together. *A Dozen Ways of Love* is dedicated to Sophie Earp.

The text: First published in the *Atlantic Monthly* 76: 454 (August 1895), 217-223. It was reprinted in Lily Dougall's *A Dozen Ways of Love* (London: A. and C. Black, 1897), 59-75. There are many spelling and punctuation changes in the 1897 version, as well as other minor changes which are being followed here. Single quotation marks, however, have been restored to the original double quotation marks from the magazine version More significant changes are discussed in the footnotes.

Further reading: Joanna Dean. *Religious Experience and the New Woman: The Life of Lily Dougall*. Bloomington: Indiana University Press, 2007.

The end of March had come. The firm Canadian snow roads had suddenly changed their surface and become a chain of miniature rivers, lakes interspersed by islands of ice, and half-frozen bogs.[399]

A young priest had started out of the city of Montreal to walk to the suburb of Point St. Charles. He was in great haste, so he kilted up his long black petticoats and hopped and skipped at a good pace. The hard problems of life had not as yet assailed him; he had that set of the shoulders that belongs to a good conscience and an easy mind; his face was rosy-cheeked and serene.

1895

Behind him lay the hill-side city, with its grey towers and spires and snow-clad mountain. All along his way budding maple trees swayed their branches overhead; on the twigs of some there was the scarlet moss of opening flowers, some were tipped with red buds and some were grey. The March wind was surging through them; the March clouds were flying above them,—light grey clouds with no rain in them,—veil above veil of mist, and each filmy web travelling at a different pace. The road began as a street, crossed railway tracks and a canal, ran between fields, and again entered between houses. The houses were of brick or stone, poor and ugly; the snow in the fields was sodden with water; the road——

"I wish that the holy prophet Elijah would come to this Jordan with his mantle," thought the priest to himself.[400]

This was a pious thought, and he splashed and waded along conscientiously. He had been sent on an errand, and had to return to discharge a more important duty in the same afternoon.

The suburb consisted chiefly of workmen's houses and factories, but there were some ambitious-looking terraces. The priest stopped at a brick dwelling of fair size. It had an aspect of flaunting respectability; lintel and casements were shining with varnish; cheap starched curtains decked every window. When the priest had rung a bell which jingled inside, the door was opened by a young woman. She was not a servant, her dress was furbelowed

[399] Apart from other minor differences, the magazine version had a single sentence here, beginning "It was that moment in the end of March when the firm Canadian snow. . ."

[400] In the 1895 version, the priest's thoughts continued: "or Joshua, or Moses."

and her hair was most elaborately arranged. She was, moreover, evidently Protestant; she held the door and surveyed the visitor with an air that was meant to show easy independence of manner, but was, in fact, insolent.

The priest had a slip of paper in his hand and referred to it. "Mrs. O'Brien?" he asked.

"I'm not Mrs. O'Brien," said the young woman, looking at something which interested her in the street.

A shrill voice belonging, as it seemed, to a middle-aged woman, made itself heard. "Louisy, if it's a Cath'lic priest, take him right in to your gran'ma; it's him she's expecting."

A moment's stare of surprise and contempt, and the young woman led the way through a gay and cheaply furnished parlour, past the door of a best bedroom which stood open to shew the frills on the pillows, into a room in the back wing. She opened the door with a jerk and stared again as the priest passed her. She was a handsome girl; the young priest did not like to be despised; within his heart he sighed and said a short prayer for patience.

He entered a room that did not share the attempt at elegance of the front part of the house; plain as a cottage kitchen, it was warm and comfortable withal. The large bed with patchwork quilt stood in a corner; in the middle was an iron stove in which logs crackled and sparkled. The air was hot and dry, but the priest, being accustomed to the atmosphere of stoves, took no notice, in fact, he noticed nothing but the room's one inmate, who from the first moment compelled his whole attention.

In a wooden arm-chair, dressed in a black petticoat and a scarlet bedgown, sat a strong old woman. Weakness was there as well as strength, certainly, for she could not leave her chair, and the palsy of excitement was shaking her head, but the one idea conveyed by every wrinkle of the aged face and hands, by every line of the bowed figure, was strength. One brown toil-worn hand held the head of a thick walking-stick which she rested on the floor well in front of her, as if she were about to rise and walk forward. Her brown face—nose and chin strongly defined—was stretched forward as the visitor entered; her eyes, black and commanding, carried with them something of that authoritative spell that is commonly attributed to a commanding mind. Great physical size or power this woman apparently had never had, but she looked the very embodiment of a superior strength.

"Shut the door! shut the door behind ye!" These were the first words that the youthful confessor heard, and then, as he advanced, "You're young," she said, peering into his face. Without a moment's intermission further orders were given him: "Be seated; be seated! Take a chair by the fire and put up your wet feet. It is from Father M‘Leod of St. Patrick's Church that ye've come?"

The young man, whose boots were well soaked with ice-water, was not loth to put them up on the edge of the stove. It was not at all his idea of a priestly visit to a woman who had represented herself as dying, but it is a large part of wisdom to take things as they come until it is necessary to interfere.

"You wrote, I think, to Father M‘Leod, saying that as the priests of this parish are French and you speak English——"

Some current of excitement hustled her soul into the midst of what she had to say.[401]

"'Twas Father Maloney, him that had St. Patrick's before Father M‘Leod, who married me; so I just thought before I died I'd let one of ye know a thing concerning that marriage that I've never told to mortal soul. Sit ye still and keep your feet to the fire;
1895 there's no need for a young man like you to be taking your death with the wet because I've a thing to say to ye."

"You are not a Catholic now," said he, raising his eyebrows with intelligence as he glanced at a Bible and hymn-book that lay on the floor beside her.

He was not unaccustomed to meeting perverts; it was impossible to have any strong emotion about so frequent an occurrence.[402] He had had a long walk and the hot air of the room made him somewhat sleepy; if it had not been for the fever and excitement of her mind he might not have picked up more than the main facts of all she said. As it was, his attention wandered for some minutes from the words that came from her palsied lips. It did not wander from her; he was thinking who she might be, and whether she was really about to die or not, and whether he had not better ask Father M‘Leod to come and see her himself. This

[401] The sentence was more elaborate in the 1895 version: "She seemed to be hurried into the midst of what she had to say by some current of excitement that pushed her onward, as a hurricane compels the speed of bodies that fly before it."

[402] In the 1895 version, the sentence continued after a semi-colon: "her manner of treating him had already made clear that religious help was not the object of this appointed interview."

last thought indicated that she impressed him as a person of more importance and interest than had been supposed when he had been sent to hear her confession.

All this time, fired by a resolution to tell a tale for the first and last time, the old woman, steadying as much as she might her shaking head, and leaning forward to look at the priest with bleared yet flashing eyes, was pouring out words whose articulation was often indistinct. Her hand upon her staff was constantly moving, as if she were about to rise and walk; her body seemed about to spring forward with the impulse of her thoughts, the very folds of the scarlet bedgown were instinct with excitement.

The priest's attention returned to her words.

"Yes, marry and marry and marry—that's what you priests in my young days were for ever preaching to us poor folk. It was our duty to multiply and fill the new land with good Cath'lics. Father Maloney, that was his doctrine, and me a young girl just come out from the old country with my parents, and six children younger than me. Hadn't I had enough of young children to nurse, and me wanting to begin life in a new place respectable, and get up a bit in the world? Oh, yes! but Father Maloney he was on the look-out for a wife for Terry O'Brien. He was a widow man with five little helpless things, and drunk most of the time was Terry, and with no spirit in him to do better. Oh! but what did that matter to Father Maloney when it was the good of the Church he was looking for, wanting O'Brien's family looked after? O'Brien was a good, kind fellow, so Father Maloney said, and you'll never hear me say a word against that. So Father Maloney got round my mother and my father and me, and married me to O'Brien, and the first year I had a baby, and the second year I had another, so on and so on, and there's not a soul in this world can say but that I did well by the five that were in the house when I came to it.

"Oh! 'house'!—— d'ye think it was one house he kept over our heads? No, but we moved from one room to another, not paying the rent. Well, and what sort of a training could the children get? Father Maloney he talked fine about bringing them up for the Church. Did he come in and wash them when I was a-bed? Did he put clothes on their backs? No, and fine and angry he was when I told him that that was what he ought to have done! Oh! but Father Maloney and I went at it up and down many a day, for when I was wore out with the anger inside me, I'd go and tell him what I thought of the marriage he'd made, and in a passion he'd get at a poor thing like me teaching him duty.

"Not that I ever was more than half sorry for the marriage myself, because of O'Brien's children, poor things, that he had before I came to them. Likely young ones they were too, and handsome, what would they have done if I hadn't been there to put them out of the way when O'Brien was drunk, and knocking them round, or to put a bit of stuff together to keep them from nakedness?

"'Well,' said Father Maloney to me, 'why isn't it to O'Brien that you speak with your scolding tongue?' Faix![403] and what good was it to spake to O'Brien, I'd like to know? Did you ever try to cut water with a knife, or to hurt a feather-bed by striking at it with your fist? A nice good-natured man was Terry O'Brien—I'll never say that he wasn't that,—except when he was drunk, which was most of the time—but he'd no more backbone to him than a worm. That was the sort of husband Father Maloney married me to.

"The children kept a-coming till we'd nine of them, that's with the five I found ready to hand; and the elder ones getting up and needing to be set out in the world, and what prospect was there for them? What could I do for them? Me always with an infant in my arms! Yet 'twas me and no other that gave them the bit and sup they had,[404] for I went out to work; but how could I save anything to fit decent clothes on them, and it wasn't much work I could do, what with the babies always coming, and sick and ailing they were half the time. The Sisters would come from the convent to give me charity. 'Twas precious little they gave, and lectured me too for not being more submiss'! And I didn't want their charity; I wanted to get up in the world. I'd wanted that before I was married, and now I wanted it for the children. Likely[405] girls the two eldest were, and the boy just beginning to go the way of his father."[406]

She came to a sudden stop and breathed hard; the strong old face was still stretched out to the priest in her eagerness; the staff was swaying to and fro beneath the tremulous hand. She

[403] Irish minced oath (instead of "faith"). It is pronounced "feks."

[404] "Bit and sup" is a (mostly Irish) phrase meaning "(a little) food and drink."

[405] In the sense, now obsolete, of "sensible."

[406] The sentence continued in the 1895 version, after a semicolon: "but he had ten times more spirit in him."

had poured out her words so quickly that there was in his chest a feeling of answering breathlessness, yet he still sat regarding her placidly with the serenity of healthy youth.

She did not give him long rest. "What did I see around me?" she demanded. "I saw people that had begun life no better than myself getting up and getting up, having a shop maybe, or sending their children to the 'Model' School to learn to be teachers,[407] or getting them into this business or that, and mine with never so much as knowing how to read, for they hadn't the shoes to put on——

"And I had it in me to better them and myself. I knew I'd be strong if it wasn't for the babies, and I knew, too, that I'd do a kinder thing for each child I had, to strangle it at its birth than to bring it on to know nothing and be nothing but a poor wretched thing like Terry O'Brien himself——"

At the word "strangle" the young priest took his feet from the ledge in front of the fire and changed his easy attitude, sitting up straight and looking more serious.

"It's not that I blamed O'Brien over much, he'd just had the same sort of bringing up himself and his father before him, and when he was sober a very nice man he was; it was spiritiness he lacked; but if he'd had more spiritiness he'd have been a wickeder man, for what is there to give a man sense in a rearing like that? If he'd been a wickeder man I'd have had more fear to do with him the thing I did. But he was just a good sort of creature without sense enough to keep steady, or to know what the children were wanting; not a notion he hadn't but that they'd got all they needed, and I had it in me to better them. Will ye dare to say that I hadn't?

"After Terry O'Brien went I had them all set out in the world, married or put to work with the best, and they've got ahead. All but O'Brien's eldest son, every one of them have got ahead of things. I couldn't put the spirit into him as I could into the littler ones and into the girls. Well, but he's the only black sheep of the seven, for two of them died. All that's living but him are doing well, doing well" (she nodded her head in triumph), "and their children doing better than them, as ought to be. Some of them ladies and gentlemen, real quality. Oh! ye needn't think I don't know the difference" (some thought expressed in his face had

[407] Called "Normal School" in the 1895 version (the two terms are synonymous).

evidently made its way with speed to her brain)—"my daughter that lives here is all well enough, and her girl handsome and able to make her way, but I tell you there's some of my grandchildren that's as much above her in the world as she is above poor Terry O'Brien—young people that speak soft when they come to see their poor old grannie and read books, oh! I know the difference; oh! I know very well—not but what my daughter here is well-to-do, and there's not one of them all but has a respect for me." She nodded again triumphantly, and her eyes flashed. "They know, they know very well how I set them out in the world. And they come back for advice to me, old as I am, and see that I want for nothing. I've been a good mother to them, and a good mother makes good children and grandchildren too."

There was another pause in which she breathed hard; the priest grasped the point of the story; he asked—

"What became of O'Brien?"

"I drowned him."

The priest stood up in a rigid and clerical attitude.

"I tell ye I drowned him." She had changed her attitude to suit his; and with the supreme excitement of telling what she had never told, there seemed to come to her the power to sit erect. Her eagerness was not that of self-vindication; it was the feverish exaltation with which old age glories over bygone achievement.

"I'd never have thought of it if it hadn't been O'Brien himself that put it into my head. But the children had a dog, 'twas little enough they had to play with, and the beast was useful in his way too, for he could mind the baby at times; but he took to ailing—like enough it was from want of food, and I was for nursing him up a bit and bringing him round, but O'Brien said that he'd put him into the canal. 'Twas one Sunday that he was at home sober—for when he was drunk I could handle him so that he couldn't do much harm. So says I, 'And why is he to be put in the canal?'

"Says he, 'Because he's doing no good here.'

"So says I, 'Let the poor beast live, for he does no harm.'

"Then says he, 'But it's harm he does taking the children's meat and their place by the fire.'

"And says I, 'Are ye not afraid to hurry an innocent creature into the next world?' for the dog had that sense he was like one of the children to me.

"Then said Terry O'Brien, for he had a wit of his own, 'And if he's an innocent creature he'll fare well where he goes.'

"Then said I, 'He's done his sins, like the rest of us, no doubt.'

"Then says he, 'The sooner he's put where he can do no more the better.'

"So with that he put a string round the poor thing's neck and took him away to where there was holes in the ice of the canal, just as there is to-day, for it was the same season of the year, and the children all cried; and thinks I to myself, 'If it was the dog that was going to put their father into the water they would cry less.' For he had a peevish temper in drink, which was most of the time.

"So then, I knew what I would do. 'Twas for the sake of the children that were crying about me that I did it, and I looked up to the sky and I said to God and the holy saints that for Terry O'Brien and his children 'twas the best deed I could do; and the words that we said about the poor beast rang in my head, for they fitted to O'Brien himself, every one of them.

"So you see it was just the time when the ice was still thick on the water, six inches thick maybe, but where anything had happened to break it the edges were melting into large holes. And the next night when it was late and dark I went and waited outside the tavern, the way O'Brien would be coming home.[408]

1895

"He was just in that state that he could walk, but he hadn't the sense of a child, and we came by the canal, for there's a road along it all winter long, but there were places where if you went off the road you fell in, and there were placards up saying to take care. But Terry O'Brien hadn't the sense to remember them. I led him to the edge of a hole, and then I came on without him. He was too drunk to feel the pain of the gasping. So I went home.

"There wasn't a creature lived near for a mile then, and in the morning I gave out that I was afraid he'd got drowned, so they broke the ice and took him up.[409] And there was just one person that grieved for Terry O'Brien. Many's the day I grieved for him, for I was accustomed to have him about me, and I missed him like, and I said in my heart, 'Terry, wherever ye may be, I have done the best deed for you and your children, for if you were innocent you

[408] In the 1895 version, the sentence ends "I went to the tavern myself to fetch O'Brien home."

[409] This was followed by another sentence in the 1895 version: "And I had a little money laid by, and I buried him well."

have gone to a better place, and if it were sin to live as you did, the less of it you have on your soul the better for you; and as for the children, poor lambs, I can give them a start in the world now I am rid of you!' That's what I said in my heart to O'Brien at first—when I grieved for him; and then the years passed, and I worked too hard to be thinking of him.

"'And now, when I sit here facing the death for myself, I can look out of my windows there back and see the canal, and I say to Terry again, as if I was coming face to face with him, that I did the best deed I could do for him and his. I broke with the Cath'lic Church long ago, for I couldn't go to confess; and many's the year that I never thought of religion. But now that I am going to die I try to read the books my daughter's minister gives me, and I look to God and say that I've sins on my soul, but the drowning of O'Brien, as far as I know right from wrong, isn't one of them."

The young priest had an idea that the occasion demanded some strong form of speech. "Woman," he said, "what have you told me this for?"

The strength of her excitement was subsiding. In its wane the afflictions of her age seemed to be let loose upon her again. Her words came more thickly, her gaunt frame trembled the more, but not for one moment did her eye flinch before his youthful severity.

"I hear that you priests are at it yet. 'Marry and marry and marry,' that's what ye teach the poor folks that will do your bidding, 'in order that the new country may be filled with Cath'lics,' and I thought before I died I'd just let ye know how one such marriage turned; and as he didn't come himself you may go home and tell Father M'Leod that, God helping me, I have told you the truth."

The next day an elderly priest approached the door of the same house. His hair was grey, his shoulders bent, his face was furrowed with those benign lines which tell that the pain which has graven them is that sympathy which accepts as its own the sorrows of others. Father M'Leod had come far because he had a word to say, a word of pity and of sympathy, which he hoped might yet touch an impenitent heart, a word that he felt was due from the Church he represented to this wandering soul, whether repentance should be the result or not.

When he rang the bell it was not the young girl but her mother who answered the door; her face, which spoke of ordinary comfort and good cheer, bore marks of recent tears.

"Do you know," asked the Father curiously, "what statement it was that your mother communicated to my friend who was here yesterday?"

"No, sir, I do not."

"Your mother was yesterday in her usual health and sound mind?" he interrogated gently.

"She was indeed, sir," and she wiped a tear.

"I would like to see your mother," persisted he.[410]

"She had a stroke in the night, sir; she's lying easy now, but she knows no one, and the doctor says she'll never hear or see or speak again."

The old man sighed deeply.

"If I may make so bold, sir, will you tell me what business it was my mother had with the young man yesterday or with yourself?"

"It is not well that I should tell you," he replied, and he went away.

[410] In the 1895 version, the priest added, "but first, are you in distress?"

Duncan Campbell Scott

Paul Farlotte

(1896)

The author: Scott's career took off in the late 1880s and early 1890s. Two of his poems were included in the influential anthology *Songs of the Great Dominion* (1889); in 1892, he, Lampman and William Wilfred Campbell started writing the column called "At the Mermaid Inn" in the Toronto *Globe*; in 1893, he published his first poetry collection, *The Magic House and Other Poems* (seven more appeared during his lifetime). In 1894, he married violinist Belle Botsford; in 1896, he collected his short stories in the volume *In the Village of Viger* (two other collections appeared in the 20th century). He died on 19 December 1947 in Ottawa. His reputation has been seriously tainted by his support for the residential school system and for the forced assimilation of Canadian First Nations people.

The text: The only short story in the collection *In the Village of Viger* (Boston: Copeland and Day, 1896) that had not been published earlier in a magazine. It is from that volume (pp 119-135) that the following was taken.

Near the outskirts of Viger, to the west, far away from the Blanche, but having a country outlook of their own, and a glimpse of a shadowy range of hills, stood two houses which would have attracted attention by their contrast, if for no other reason. One was a low cottage, surrounded by a garden, and covered with roses, which formed jalousies for the encircling veranda. The garden was laid out with the care and completeness that told of a master hand. The cottage itself had the air of having been secured from the inroads of time as thoroughly as paint and a nail in the right place at the right time could effect that end. The other was a large gaunt-looking house, narrow and high, with many windows, some of which were boarded up, as if there was no further use for the chambers into which they had once admitted light. Standing on a rough piece of ground it seemed given over to the rudeness of decay. It appeared to have been the intention of its builder to veneer it with brick; but it stood there a wooden shell, discolored by the weather, disjointed by the frost, and with the wind fluttering the rags of tar-paper which had been intended as a protection against the cold, but which now hung in patches and ribbons. But despite this dilapidation it had a sort of martial air about it, and seemed to watch over its embowered companion, warding off tempests and gradually falling to pieces on guard, like a faithful soldier who suffers at his post. In the road, just between the two, stood a beautiful Lombardy poplar. Its shadow fell upon the little cottage in the morning, and travelled across the garden, and in the evening touched the corner of the tall house, and faded out with the sun, only to float there again in the moonlight, or to commence the journey next morning with the dawn. This shadow seemed, with its constant movement, to figure the connection that existed between the two houses.

The garden of the cottage was a marvel; there the finest roses in the parish grew, roses which people came miles to see, and parterres of old-fashioned flowers, the seed of which came from France, and which in consequence seemed to blow with a rarer color and more delicate perfume. This garden was a striking contrast to the stony ground about the neighboring house, where only the commonest weeds grew unregarded; but its master had been born a gardener, just as another man is born a musician or a poet. There was a superstition in the village that all he had to do was to put anything, even a dry stick, into the ground, and it would grow. He was the village schoolmaster, and Madame Laroque would remark spitefully enough that if Monsieur Paul Farlotte had been as successful in planting knowledge in the heads of his scholars as he was in planting roses in his garden Viger would have been celebrated the world over. But he was born a gardener, not a teacher; and he made the best of the fate which compelled him to depend for his living on something he disliked. He looked almost as dry as one of his own hyacinth bulbs; but like it he had life at his heart. He was a very small man, and frail, and looked older than he was. It was strange, but you rarely seemed to see his face; for he was bent with weeding and digging, and it seemed an effort for him to raise his head and look at you with the full glance of his eye. But when he did, you saw the eye was honest and full of light. He was not careful of his personal appearance, clinging to his old garments with a fondness which often laid him open to ridicule, which he was willing to bear for the sake of the comfort of an old pair of shoes, or a hat which had accommodated itself to the irregularities of his head. On the street he wore a curious skirt-coat that seemed to be made of some indestructible material, for he had worn it for years, and might be buried in it. It received an extra brush for Sundays and holidays, and always looked as good as new. He made a quaint picture, as he came down the road from the school. He had a hesitating walk, and constantly stopped and looked behind him; for he always fancied he heard a voice calling him by his name. He would be working in his flower-beds when he would hear it over his shoulder, "Paul;" or when he went to draw water from his well, "Paul;" or when he was reading by his fire, some one calling him softly, "Paul, Paul;" or in the dead of night, when nothing moved in his cottage he would hear it out of the dark, "Paul." So it came to be a sort of companionship for him, this haunting voice; and sometimes one could have seen him in his garden stretch out his hand and smile, as if he were welcoming an invisible guest. Sometimes the guest was not invisible, but took body and shape, and was a real presence; and often Paul was greeted with visions of things that had been, or that would be, and saw figures where, for other eyes, hung only the impalpable air.

He had one other passion besides his garden, and that was Montaigne.[411] He delved in one in the summer, in the other in the winter. With his feet on his stove he would become so absorbed with his author that he would burn his slippers and come to himself disturbed by the smell of the singed leather. He had only one great ambition, that was to return to France to see his mother before she died; and he had for years been trying to save enough money to take the journey. People who did not know him called him stingy, and said the saving for his journey was only a pretext to cover his miserly habits. It was strange, he had been saving for

[411] Michel de Montaigne (1533-1592), French author of famous *Essais*. He was born in a small town near Bordeaux, in his family's chateau.

years, and yet he had not saved enough. Whenever anyone would ask him, "Well, Monsieur Farlotte, when do you go to France?" he would answer, "Next year—next year." So when he announced one spring that he was actually going, and when people saw that he was not making his garden with his accustomed care, it became the talk of the village: "Monsieur Farlotte is going to France;" "Monsieur Farlotte has saved enough money, true, true, he is going to France."

His proposed visit gave no one so much pleasure as it gave his neighbors in the gaunt, unkempt house which seemed to watch over his own; and no one would have imagined what a joy it was to Marie St. Denis, the tall girl who was mother to her orphan brothers and sisters, to hear Monsieur Farlotte say, "When I am in France;" for she knew what none of the villagers knew, that, if it had not been for her and her troubles, Monsieur Farlotte would have seen France many years before. How often she would recall the time when her father, who was in the employ of the great match factory near Viger, used to drive about collecting the little paper match-boxes which were made by hundreds of women in the village and the country around; how he had conceived the idea of making a machine in which a strip of paper would go in at one end, and the completed match-boxes would fall out at the other; how he had given up his situation and devoted his whole time and energy to the invention of this machine; how he had failed time and again, but continued with a perseverance which at last became a frantic passion; and how, to keep the family together, her mother, herself, and the children joined that army of workers which was making the match-boxes by hand. She would think of what would have happened to them then if Monsieur Farlotte had not been there with his help, or what would have happened when her mother died, worn out, and her father, overcome with disappointment, gave up his life and his task together, in despair. But whenever she would try to speak of these things Monsieur Farlotte would prevent her with a gesture, "Well, but what would you have me do,—besides, I will go some day,—now who knows, next year, perhaps." So here was the "next year," which she had so longed to see, and Monsieur Farlotte was giving her a daily lecture on how to treat the tulips after they had done flowering, preluding everything he had to say with, "When I am in France," for his heart was already there.

He had two places to visit, one was his old home, the other was the birthplace of his beloved Montaigne. He had often described to Marie the little cottage where he was born, with the vine arbors and the long garden walks, the lilac-bushes, with their cool dark-green leaves, the white eaves where the swallows nested, and the poplar, sentinel over all. "You see," he would say, "I have tried to make this little place like it; and my memory may have played me a trick, but I often fancy myself at home. That poplar and this long walk and the vines on the arbor,—sometimes when I see the tulips by the border I fancy it is all in France."

Marie was going over his scant wardrobe, mending with her skilful fingers, putting a stitch in the trusty old coat, and securing its buttons. She was anxious that Monsieur Farlotte should get a new suit before he went on his journey; but he would not hear to it. "Not a bit of it," he would say, "if I made my appearance in a new suit, they would think I had been making money; and when they would find out that I had not enough to buy cabbage for the soup there would be a disappointment." She could not get him to write that he was coming. "No, no," he would say, "if I do that they will expect me." "Well, and why not,—why not?" "Well, they would think about it,—in ten days Paul comes home, then in five days Paul comes home, and then when I came they would set the dogs on me. No, I will just walk in,—so,—and when they are staring at my old coat I will just sit down in a corner, and my old mother will commence to cry. Oh, I have it all arranged."

So Marie let him have his own way; but she was fixed on having her way in some things. To save Monsieur Farlotte the heavier work, and allow him to keep his strength for the journey, she would make her brother Guy do the spading in the garden, much to his disgust, and that of Monsieur Farlotte, who would stand by and interfere, taking the spade into his own hands with infinite satisfaction. "See," he would say, "go deeper and turn it over so." And when Guy would dig in his own clumsy way, he would go off in despair, with the words, "God help us, nothing will grow there."

When Monsieur Farlotte insisted on taking his clothes in an old box covered with rawhide, with his initials in brass tacks on the cover, Marie would not consent to it, and made Guy carry off the box without his knowledge and hide it. She had a good tin trunk which had belonged to her mother, which she knew where to find in the attic, and which would contain everything Monsieur Farlotte had to carry. Poor Marie never went into this attic without a shudder, for occupying most of the space was her father's work bench, and that complicated wheel, the model of his invention, which he had tried so hard to perfect, and which stood there like a monument of his failure. She had made Guy promise never to move it, fearing lest he might be tempted to finish what his father had begun,—a fear that was almost an apprehension, so like him was he growing. He was tall and large-boned, with a dark restless eye, set under an overhanging forehead. He had long arms, out of proportion to his height, and he hung his head when he walked. His likeness to his father made him seem a man before his time. He felt himself a man; for he had a good position in the match factory, and was like a father to his little brothers and sisters.

Although the model had always had a strange fascination for him, the lad had kept his promise to his sister, and had never touched the mechanism which had literally taken his father's life. Often when he went into the attic he would stand and gaze at the model and wonder why it had not succeeded, and recall his father bending over his work, with his compass and pencil. But he had a dread of it too, and sometimes would hurry away, afraid lest its fascination would conquer him.

Monsieur Farlotte was to leave as soon as his school closed, but weeks before that he had everything ready, and could enjoy his roses in peace. After school hours he would walk in his garden, to and fro, to and fro, with his hands behind his back, and his eyes upon the ground, meditating; and once in a while he would pause and smile, or look over his shoulder when the haunting voice would call his name. His scholars had commenced to view him with additional interest, now that he was going to take such a prodigious journey; and two or three of them could always be seen peering through the palings, watching him as he walked up and down the path; and Marie would watch him too, and wonder what he would say when he found that his trunk had disappeared. He missed it fully a month before he could expect to start; but he had resolved to pack that very evening.

"But there is plenty of time," remonstrated Marie.

"That's always the way," he answered. "Would you expect me to leave everything until the last moment?"

"But, Monsieur Farlotte, in ten minutes everything goes into the trunk."

"So, and in the same ten minutes something is left out of the trunk, and I am in France, and my shoes are in Viger, that will be the end of it."

So, to pacify him, she had to ask Guy to bring down the trunk from the attic. It was not yet dark there; the sunset threw a great color into the room, touching all the familiar objects with transfiguring light, and giving the shadows a rich depth. Guy saw the model glowing like some magic golden wheel, the metal points upon it gleaming like jewels in the light. As he passed he touched it, and with a musical click something dropped from it. He picked it up: it was one of the little paper match-boxes, but the defect that he remembered to have heard talked of was there. He held it in his hand and examined it; then he pulled it apart and spread it out. "Ah," he said to himself, "the fault was in the cutting." Then he turned the wheel, and one by one the imperfect boxes dropped out, until the strip of paper was exhausted. "But why,"—the question rose in his mind,—"why could not that little difficulty be overcome?"

He took the trunk down to Marie, who at last persuaded Monsieur Farlotte to let her pack his clothes in it. He did so with a protestation, "Well, I know how it will be with a fine box like that, some fellow will whip it off when I am looking the other way, and that will be the end of it."

As soon as he could do so without attracting Marie's attention Guy returned to the attic with a lamp. When Marie had finished packing Monsieur Farlotte's wardrobe, she went home to put her children to bed; but when she saw that light in the attic window she nearly fainted from apprehension. When she pushed open the door of that room which she had entered so often with the scant meals she used to bring her father, she saw Guy bending over the model, examining every part of it. "Guy," she said, trying to command her voice, "you have broken your promise." He looked up quickly. "Marie, I am going to find it out—I can understand it—there is just one thing, if I can get that we will make a fortune out of it."

"Guy, don't delude yourself; those were father's words, and day after day I brought him his meals here, when he was too busy even to come downstairs; but nothing came of it, and while he was trying to make a machine for the boxes, we were making them with our fingers. O Guy," she cried, with her voice rising into a sob, "remember those days, remember what Monsieur Farlotte did for us, and what he would have to do again if you lost your place!"

"That's all nonsense, Marie. Two weeks will do it, and after that I could send Monsieur Farlotte home with a pocket full of gold."

"Guy, you are making a terrible mistake. That wheel was our curse, and it will follow us if you don't leave it alone. And think of Monsieur Farlotte; if he finds out what you are working at he will not go to France—I know him; he will believe it his duty to stay here and help us, as he did when father was alive. Guy, Guy, listen to me!"

But Guy was bending over the model, absorbed in its labyrinths. In vain did Marie argue with him, try to persuade him, and threaten him; she attempted to lock the attic door and keep him out, but he twisted the lock off, and after that the door was always open. Then she resolved to break the wheel into a thousand pieces; but when she went upstairs, when Guy was away, she could not strike it with the axe she held. It seemed like a human thing that cried out with a hundred tongues against the murder she would do; and she could only sink down sobbing, and pray. Then failing everything else she simulated an interest in the thing, and tried to lead Guy to work at it moderately, and not to give up his whole time to it.

But he seemed to take up his father's passion where he had laid it down. Marie could do nothing with him; and the younger children, at first hanging around the attic door, as if he were their father come back again, gradually ventured into the room, and whispered together as they watched their rapt and unobservant brother working at his task. Marie's one thought was to devise a means of keeping the fact from Monsieur Farlotte; and she told him blankly that Guy had been sent away on business, and would not be back for six weeks. She hoped that by that time Monsieur Farlotte would be safely started on his journey. But night after night he saw a light in the attic window. In the past years it had been constant there, and he could only connect it with one cause. But he could get no answer from Marie when he asked her the reason; and the next night the distracted girl draped the window so that no ray of light could find its way out into the night. But Monsieur Farlotte was not satisfied; and a few evenings afterwards, as it was growing dusk, he went quietly into the house, and upstairs into the attic. There he saw Guy stretched along the work bench, his head in his hands, using the last light to ponder over a sketch he was making, and beside him, figured very clearly in the thick gold air of the sunset, the form of his father, bending over him, with the old eager, haggard look in his eyes. Monsieur Farlotte watched the two figures for a moment as they glowed in their rich atmosphere; then the apparition turned his head slowly, and warned him away with a motion of his hand.

All night long Monsieur Farlotte walked in his garden, patient and undisturbed, fixing his duty so that nothing could root it out. He found the comfort that comes to those who give up some exceeding deep desire of the heart, and when next morning the market-gardener from St. Valérie, driving by as the matin bell was clanging from St. Joseph's, and seeing the old teacher as if he were taking an early look at his growing roses, asked him, "Well, Monsieur Farlotte, when do you go to France?" he was able to answer cheerfully, "Next year—next year."

Marie could not unfix his determination. "No," he said, "they do not expect me. No one will be disappointed. I am too old to travel. I might be lost in the sea. Until Guy makes his invention we must not be apart."

At first the villagers thought that he was only joking, and that they would some morning wake up and find him gone; but when the holidays came, and when enough time had elapsed for him to make his journey twice over they began to think he was in earnest. When they knew that Guy St. Denis was chained to his father's invention, and when they saw that Marie and the children had commenced to make match-boxes again, they shook their heads. Some of them at least seemed to understand why Monsieur Farlotte had not gone to France.

But he never repined. He took up his garden again, was as contented as ever, and comforted himself with the wisdom of Montaigne. The people dropped the old question, "When are you going to France?" Only his companion voice called him more loudly, and more often he saw figures in the air that no one else could see.

Early one morning, as he was working in his garden around a growing pear-tree, he fell into a sort of stupor, and sinking down quietly on his knees he leaned against the slender stem for support. He saw a garden much like his own, flooded with the clear sunlight, in the shade of an arbor an old woman in a white cap was leaning back in a wheeled chair, her eyes were closed, she seemed asleep. A young woman was seated beside her holding her hand. Suddenly the old woman smiled, a childish smile, as if she were well pleased. "Paul," she murmured, "Paul, Paul." A moment later her companion started up with a cry; but she did not move, she was silent and tranquil. Then the young woman fell on her knees and wept, hiding her face. But the aged face was inexpressibly calm in the shadow, with the smile lingering upon it, fixed by the deeper sleep into which she had fallen.

Gradually the vision faded away, and Paul Farlotte found himself leaning against his pear-tree, which was almost too young as yet to support his weight. The bell was ringing from St. Joseph's, and had shaken the swallows from their nests in the steeple into the clear air. He heard their cries as they flew into his garden, and he heard the voices of his neighbor children as they played around the house.

Later in the day he told Marie that his mother had died that morning, and she wondered how he knew.

Edith Eaton

The Story of Iso

(1896)

1896

The author: Edith Maude Eaton (or Sui Sin Far, her usual penname) was born on 15 March 1865 in Macclesfield, England. Her father was an Englishman and her mother was Chinese. The family emigrated to the United States soon after her birth, but returned to England in 1868. They again left the Old World in 1872 and settled in Montreal, where her father began working for the Grand Trunk Railway. In 1883, she began working as a typesetter for the *Montreal Daily Star*. She began contributing articles to various newspapers and periodicals, while also working as a stenographer and legal secretary. Her first article was "A Trip in a Horse Car," in the *Dominion Illustrated* (13 October 1888). She continued to live in Montreal but, in 1896, she took a trip to New York, after she which she started contributing her first short stories (written in Montreal) to American periodicals.

The text: First published in the (Kansas City) *Lotus* (August 1896), 117-119, and signed "Sui Seen Far." *The Lotus* was a 'little review' edited by Walter Blackburn Harte.

Further reading: Martha H. Patterson. "Sui Sin Far and the Wisdom of the New." *Beyond the Gibson Girl: Reimagining the American New Woman, 1895-1915.* Urbana and Chicago: University of Illinois Press, 2005. 102-124.

"A talking woman will come to a sad end," said old Tai Wang dolorously.

"Why so, Tai?" questioned my cousin. "Don't you think that a little sharp exercise of the tongue benefits the general health?"

"No, not when the tongue belongs to a woman," answered Tai. "Listen and I will tell you the story of Iso:

"Iso lived in the Chinese country outside Kiahing,[412] among the mulberry-trees and rice-fields. Her parents were poor, but respectable, and as a great number of children, mostly boys, had been born to them, they were much esteemed by their neighbours, for in China it is believed that none but the eminently virtuous are blessed with many sons.

"Iso was the eldest, and after reaching the age of six she was seldom seen without a chubby baby strapped on her back, and thus she moved about washing dishes, sewing, and performing other necessary tasks. But even when a child her tongue got her into trouble.

"Once, when her mother bade her take the boys out, she led them to a place where they could amuse themselves with weeds, rock-work, and small ponds, and seated herself with the baby on a grassy mound. To her then came a woman called Mai Gwi Far.

"'Dear me!' said Mai Gwi Far, looking around; 'what a number of little brothers you have! Your father and mother must be very good.'

"'Yes,' said Iso, 'they are good, but they are not good just because they have given me so many brothers. I love my brothers now that I have them, but if they were not here, I should not want them. I would not be so often hungry and my bones would not ache from working so hard. If Kuang Ing Huk[413] offers my parents so many children and they accept them without considering whether they can keep the new ones without taking the rice from those they already have, I can not see why they should be praised for doing so. To me they would seem wiser and better if they had fewer children.'

"These words so horrified Mai Gwi Far that she ran with great haste to Iso's father and told him of the unfilial disposition of his daughter. Iso, being then thirteen years of age, was too old to be whipped, so her father took her and locked her up in a room and kept her there without food for a day and a half, which was indeed a mild punishment for one whose tongue babbled so much foolishness.

[412] Jiaxing, a city about 100 km south-west of Shanghai.

[413] Guanyin, the goddess of mercy in Chinese Buddhism and Chinese folk religion.

"One morning Iso was sent to sweep the tomb of her grandfather and to pull up the grass and weeds which might be growing around his grave. In the afternoon the whole family would meet at the tomb for the purpose of worshipping the dead. Iso carried with her a quantity of incense-sticks and different kinds of food, such as fish, pork, fowl, and vegetables; these she placed around the grave; also some cups of tea.

"Just as she was finishing her task a 'red-headed' stranger came her way and spoke to her in the Chinese language. Iso, only too glad to have the opportunity to rattle her tongue, answered back; consequently the 'red-headed' stranger filled her mind with many senseless ideas; and when her relations came to burn mock money and offer food to the departed spirit who was supposed to partake of the spiritual essence of the offering, Iso refused to worship, saying that she did not believe that the spirit of her grandfather cared whether she worshiped at his grave or not, and if it did care, it was not worth worshipping.

"Ever after that day Iso was regarded with suspicion and aversion by the members of her family, and once, when she returned from marketing with a cat following at her heels, her father became so incensed that he ordered her to leave his presence forever, and so she would have done had not her mother put in soft words. The coming of a cat to a house is regarded by the Chinese as an omen of approaching poverty.

"Negotiations for the marriage of Iso were commenced ere Iso was sixteen. A go-between who had been engaged by a respectable family in the neighbourhood tendered a proposal of marriage to her father, which proposal was in behalf of the eldest son of the family. The young man being considered eligible, Iso's father consulted a fortune-teller, and was told that the signs were favourable for a happy marriage; the betrothal was then sealed by the families exchanging cards. Iso's family were given a card on which a dragon was painted, and the family of the young man received a card with a phenix. Presents were sent and the material for the bridal dress was brought, and, forty-eight hours before the time fixed for the marriage, Iso was told that she must prepare to become a bride.

"Now, instead of thanking her parents for providing her with a suitable husband, as any proper and dutiful daughter would have done, Iso tossed her head at the news and said: 'I can not marry any man whom I do not know well. Let him come here and see me; let me become acquainted with him before marriage, and after the passing of two months I will tell you whether I will become his wife or not. My husband must be pleasing to me, and whether or not he will be so no one can judge save myself; for we all look through different glasses.'

"It is impossible to describe the anger of Iso's parents when they heard such monstrous ideas expressed. Her father said: 'You are mad; nevertheless, you shall marry the man I have chosen for you and at the time appointed.'

"So Ting Sean, Iso's father, hushed up his daughter's words and preparations for the bridal went on, and the event might have been consummated had not one of Iso's little brothers repeated her sayings to a young friend, and thus they were carried to the family of Hop Wo, Iso's betrothed.

"Who would allow a son to marry a woman with a tongue like Iso's? The proposal of marriage was withdrawn, the engagement declared broken. Ting Sean had the mortification of seeing the daughter of his enemy, Lee Chu, borne as bride through the streets to the home of Hop Wo. As to Iso, she was everlastingly disgraced; there were no more proposals of marriage for her and she died in a strange land, far away from China—the country which heaven loves."

"How did that come about?" inquired my cousin.

"Some 'red-headed people' took her across the sea, and right glad were her parents to be rid of the shame of her presence. That is the story of Iso, the girl who talked too much."

"And it's a very good story, too, Tai," said my cousin. "She who is called in China 'The woman who talks too much' is called by us 'The new woman.'"

Lucy Maud Montgomery

The Goose Feud

(1897)

The author: Lucy Maud Montgomery was born an only child on 30 November 1874 in Clifton (now New London), Prince Edward Island. She was raised in Cavendish (a small farming community on the north shore of the island) by her maternal grandparents, after the untimely death of her mother and after her father relocated to Saskatchewan. She visited her father and his new family in 1890, and remained with them for a year, but she was utterly disappointed by the sojourn in the prairies and decided to return to Prince Edward Island. In 1891, she published a poem in the Charlottetown *Patriot* and three articles in various newspapers. She attended Prince of Wales College in Charlottetown for a teaching degree from 1893 to 1895 (she wrote about it in her 1927 article, "The Day before Yesterday") In 1894, she published a short play and other pieces in the college paper. She taught in rural PEI, but in 1895 starting attending literature classes at Dalhousie University in Halifax (1895-1896). In 1895, she published her first short story, "A Baking of Gingersnaps," in *The Ladies' Journal* of Toronto. She had several pieces published in 1896, while she was also teaching in Belmont, PEI, but the real start of her writing career was in 1897, when she contributed several short stories to Canadian and American magazines and newspapers.

The text: First published in *Arthur's Home Magazine* 66: 4 (April 1897), 225-230, where it was signed "Maud Cavendish" (at the end of the text). It was reprinted in the *Western Christian Advocate* 22 July 1908, 16-17, signed "L.M. Montgomery." The 1908 version has improved the spelling and punctuation of the original; a few words were dropped and others added; some paragraphs were rearranged; these minor changes have been used here. More important changes are discussed in the footnotes.

If any one had ever told Mary Parker and me that the day would ever come when we would not speak to each other, we would have laughed the statement to scorn. We had been friends from babyhood. We lived next door to each other when we were girls, and when we married our homes were still side by side, so that we carried our friendship unbroken into our married life.

Our husbands were almost as intimate as we were.[414] Our children[415] played together as much at one place as the other. We had a little footpath past the barns and across the fields from house to house, and it was kept well trodden. Never a day passed but I went over to Mary's house, or she came to mine. We worked in partnership in nearly everything; nothing seemed complete to one unless the other was in it. We expected to go on like this till our deaths, and then be buried close together in the little graveyard.

One spring, when Mary and I were talking over our plans for the summer, she said she was going to try her hand at keeping geese. We had always kept turkeys before. I knew what kind of things geese were around a place, and I tried to talk her out of it. But she was quite set on it, so I gave it up; for I didn't suppose it mattered much.[416] I even helped her select the eggs for setting, and the mother goose when she bought one. When every egg hatched out I was as pleased over her good luck as she was herself.

Mary's goslings were all right till they began to grow up, and then she began to have trouble. She put yokes on them, but that didn't prevent them from getting into the grain or wandering away to places where foxes could get them.

I thought to myself that she wished often enough she had kept to the turkeys, but she would never give in to that. Mary is pretty obstinate in a quiet way when she takes a notion.

We had our wheat in the barn field next to the line fence that year. It was the best field of wheat in Meadowby. We had had poor

[414] The 1897 version has a longer sentence here: "Our husbands, before our marriages, had been merely friendly acquaintances, but soon, through our example, they became almost as intimate in their own way as we were in ours."

[415] The beginning of the sentence was longer in 1897: "Our children, as they came, one by one, grew up and played..."

[416] One full sentence from 1897 was dropped here in 1908: "It never came into my mind that such a thing as a goose could ever make trouble between Mary and me."

luck with our wheat for three years back, so that we were all the prouder of this. William took every man and woman who came to the place out to show them that wheat and expatiate on it. One day I found all Mary's geese in the wheat. They had been in a good while and had made a fearful havoc. I was mad enough, but I drove the geese home and calmly told Mary she must keep them out of our wheat.

She looked worried and said she was sorry; she would see it didn't happen again. She said she had had a real hard time to keep them out of their own grain—she couldn't very well keep them shut up all the time.

A week later I found the geese in again. It exasperated me more than I would have thought possible. I sent one of the children to take them home this time, and I sent a note to Mary, too. I know I'm inclined to be too rash and quick-tempered, and I suppose that note was not very conciliatory. But if Mary thought it was sharp she never let on, but was as friendly as ever.

One afternoon I was sitting in the kitchen, reading,[417] when

I heard steps on the veranda, as if some one were in a big hurry and very decided. I had just got up, when Mary came in without knocking. She hadn't a thing on her head, and her hair was all blown. She had her under lip between her teeth, and her eyes were snapping. In each hand she carried a half-grown goose, quite dead and all blood-stained.

Thinking it over now, I suppose she must have looked pretty ridiculous, but just then I was too much taken by surprise to notice that.[418] She flung the geese down before me as hard as she could and said:

"There! I suppose that is your work, Lizzie Mercer!"

Her voice was just shaking with rage, and she looked ready to tear me in pieces. I never knew Mary had such a temper. I always thought her very quiet and gentle.

I knew the minute I saw those geese just what had happened as well as if I had been told. My oldest boy, Henry, had found those fatal geese in the wheat again, and had taken the affair into his own hands without consulting me, for he knew I wouldn't have

[417] In the 1897 version, the narrator was "reading a paper and thinking what to get for tea."

[418] The phrase "to notice that" replaces "to do more than stare at her" from the 1897 version.

allowed him to lay a hand on one of Mary's geese for anything, much as I hated to see them destroying the wheat. Henry was always too hot-headed, like his mother, and never stopped to think of the consequences of anything he did.

I was as sorry as any one could be to see how Mary's geese had been stoned and mangled. And if she had not spoken the way she did, so insulting, as if I were to blame for it all, I should have given Henry cause to remember it to his death, besides paying for the geese, of course. But Mary wouldn't listen to a word. She went on like a crazy person.[419] She said things I couldn't endure, so I answered her back, and we had a dreadful quarrel. I'm not blaming Mary a bit more than myself. It makes me ashamed now to think of what I said. We stormed at each other over the dead bodies of those geese, getting more and more unreasonable. At last Mary bounced out in an awful temper, and left me in one just as bad. I kept angry all night. But when I grew calm again, I repented of my behavior and felt pretty bad about it. Mary and I had never quarreled before, so I didn't know how it was likely to end. I knew Mary was pretty stubborn.[420] But I said to myself, that as Mary had begun the quarrel, it was her place to end it. I wouldn't give in first.[421] But she made no sign, even though she must have found out that I was not really to blame about the geese.

I felt dreadfully over it for a long while, and then I got cranky and didn't care. I said if Mary could get along without me, I could get along without her. We never spoke all that summer. There were always plenty of friendly folks to tell me the things Mary had said about me, and keep me stirred up and bitter. It did not occur to me that they might have carried my remarks to her with a like result.

But I could not deny I missed her. It made my heart ache to look at the footpath and see it all overgrown with grass. As for the wheat, I grew to loathe the sight of it, and a goose made me feel savage.

At first our families took no part in the trouble. Our husbands laughed at us, and tried to coax us to make it up. They were as friendly as ever, and so were the children. They played together as usual, and I was better to Mary's children than my own. I used

[419] Another sentence from 1897 was dropped here: "I suppose the memory of the note was rankling in her too."

[420] In 1897, Mary was "pretty set in her ways."

[421] Another sentence from 1897 was dropped here: "Perhaps she thought I was to blame on account of that note."

to give them cakes every time they came into the house, and Mary did the same when mine went over there. I believe I had a hope that the children might bring about a reconciliation in time, when another dreadful thing happened.

Our husbands fell out, too. They were discussing our quarrel over the line fence one day, and got into a dispute about it. Each one upheld his wife, of course. They had a dreadful time. Every old family scandal for the last three generations was cast up. They even taunted each other with long-forgotten school-day faults. O, I don't know what they didn't say. When William came in and told me what had happened I cried all night about it. I didn't know till then how much hope I had cherished things would come out right with Mary and me yet. But now I felt sure they never would.

The men were even more unreasonable than we were. They wouldn't even let the children go and come. The poor little things wouldn't speak to each other because their parents did not. I took that to heart more than anything. Nobody had talked much about Mary and me, but when it got to be a family affair people took it up. Somebody called it the "goose feud,"[422] and the name stuck. It had a double meaning, I've no doubt, and the poor dead birds were not the only geese meant.

The minister took in hand to better it, and he called one day.[423] That didn't do any good. He seemed to blame me too much. I was too proud a woman to take it. Then they went to the Parkers with no better success.

The next Sunday he preached a sermon about neighbors and Church members living in harmony from the text, "Live peaceably with all men." He meant well, for a better man never lived. But it only made things worse. I felt that every one was looking at me to see how I took it, and that touched my pride. Mary looked hard enough to bite a nail in two when she went out of church. As for William and Francis Parker,[424] they were so provoked at the minister that they wouldn't go to church for over two months.

Things went on like that for two years. It seemed to me more like fifteen. Sometimes I asked myself if our friendship had been all a dream. Nothing seemed real but our estrangement. I had

[422] The two words had capital initials in the 1897 version.

[423] In the 1897 version, "he and his wife called" (which matches the last sentence of this paragraph).

[424] Here (and only here), the name of Mary's husband appeared as "Frances" in the 1908 version. It is "Francis" in the 1897 original.

given up all thought of making up. The thing had hardened too long. I got over missing Mary, pretty much, just as we get over missing some one dead, because it has to be got over.[425]

There was no footpath now, and Francis Parker had put up a high snow fence back of their house that shut it from us altogether. I thought many a hard thing about Mary, but I was honest enough to own up that it was as much my fault as hers.[426]

It was two years in July since our quarrel, and the fall after that an epidemic of scarlet fever broke out in Meadowby. It was of the most virulent type.[427] My children took it first, but they all recovered. But other people didn't escape so well. It was a sad time. There was hardly a house in Meadowby without some one dying or dead in it. It was more fatal among the children, of course. It made my heart ache to see all the new, little graves in the churchyard.

Some one told me that Mary was in a terrible fright lest her children should take it.[428] She had seven; the youngest was four years old. They had all grown too fast and were delicate. People said Mary had got it into her head that not one of them would live if they took it.

Then the next piece of news was that Mary had it herself, and she was pretty low. The other women went to see her. I felt it was dreadful of me not to go. But my pride was too stubborn to bend. Then Fred, and the twins, and Lizzie—called after me—all took it at once, and Mary had to get up and wait on them before she was fit.[429] She had no help, and there was none to be had in the village. The neighbors went in when they could spare the time but most had their hands full at home.

[425] A short sentence was dropped here from the 1897 version: "There's always a dull ache."

[426] Three full sentences from the 1897 text did not make it into the 1908 text: "Sometimes I wondered what would happen if I were to walk over to Mary's some day and ask her to forgive me. I pictured out our interview if she would, and I never really had any serious idea of doing it. I suppose I thought more of that affair than of anything else in those two years."

[427] Here, the 1897 version had another sentence: "Lottie Carr came home from town with it and it spread from her."

[428] Another sentence was dropped here: "She did everything to keep them from infection."

[429] The last part of the sentence was reworked in 1908. The 1897 version had "and Mary had to get out of her sick bed before she was fit and wait on them and do her work."

Nobody knows what I suffered in those two weeks. All my old love for Mary came back when I heard of her trouble, and I wanted to go right to her aid. But I could not bring myself to do it.[430] Sometimes I spoke about going. William never said a word, either to discourage or encourage. I knew that he was ashamed of his fracas with Francis Parker long ago, and would have given almost anything to have it wiped out. But he was even prouder than I was. I knew he would never put out the hand of reconciliation, but he would not put hindrances in my way if I felt inclined to. I didn't go, however, though I kept thinking of it.[431]

One morning Mrs. Corey called in on her way from Mary's, where she'd been all night. She said Mary's "baby," little Dora, was down with the fever, and was very bad.[432] I didn't say much, but when Jane Corey had gone I went upstairs to my room and sat down on a trunk by the window. It was higher than the snow fence, and I could see right over to Mary's. The house looked so forlorn and desolate. The doctor's horse was tied at the gate. It was the second week in November and everything was gray and brown. I remember just how Mary's windows looked through the bare boughs of the garden.

1897 I knew Mary was just wrapped up in Dora.[433] If anything happened to the baby it would almost kill her. The tears came into my eyes as I pictured her bending over Dora's sick bed. I cried and cried, but I couldn't make up my mind to go—I was afraid Mary would repulse me.[434]

[430] The 1897 text had four extra sentences here, which were not kept in 1908: "I wanted my eldest daughter Annie to go and stay at Mary's. But she cried and said she couldn't. They seemed worse than strangers, she said. Oh, I worried dreadfully about it."

[431] In the 1897 version, the narrator "thought of it day and night." This is then followed by two sentences that were dropped in 1908: "I went a great deal to other houses and helped wait on the sick, and sit up, and sometimes lay out the dear little dead bodies. All the sorrow and suffering around me helped to soften my heart."

[432] In the 1897 text, Mrs. Corey said that Dora "was worse than she'd ever seen a child."

[433] The paragraph begins with an extra sentence in the 1897 text: "I went over it all again sitting there."

[434] The end of this paragraph was reworked; several sentences were dropped in 1908 and were replaced by this last sentence. This is how it read in 1897: "I tried to put myself in Mary's place and see how I'd act if she came to me. It was satisfactory, but I was afraid to try it. I had found out how hard Mary could be and I was afraid she would repulse me. That would kill me. I cried and cried, but when Sophia Reed came in at tea time I hadn't made up my mind. She said it was her opinion. . ."

Just after tea Sophia Reed called in and said it was her opinion that Dora wouldn't live through the night. That decided me. As soon as Sophia had gone, I put on my bonnet and shawl and went out. Nobody knows how queer I felt. I stood for a spell on the veranda to collect my thoughts. I noticed every little thing. The air was quite sharp. The sky was curdled all over with little rolls of violet gray clouds, with strips of faint blue between. There had been a scad[435] of snow in the afternoon and the ground was grayish white. It had melted about the door and was sloppy. The hens and turkeys were pecking around. The apple-trees were ragged brown, but the other trees were bare, and the leaves lay around in heaps, with snow in their crinkles. William was fixing the pump. He didn't say anything as I went by, though he must have guessed where I was going.

I went past the barns and struck into the old footpath. The little feathery heads of bleached grass stuck up wetly through the snow. Mary's turkeys were roosting on the snow fence. When I got to the door my heart was beating so that I could hardly breathe.

I opened the door and went in. A thin, dragged-out woman, with tears glistening on her cheeks, was stirring something on the stove. At first I could hardly believe it was Mary. She looked up as I opened the door. Those few seconds seemed to me as long as the two years that had gone. She just said, "Lizzie!"

Then she was clinging to me and crying.[436] I soothed and petted her until she got calmer, and then I made her go and have a sleep, for she hadn't closed an eye for over thirty-six hours. By this time Henry was at the door. I had told him to come and get my orders if I didn't come back. I sent word to Annie that I wasn't coming home that night, and that she must look after things and get her father's supper.

Dora didn't seem any worse, in spite of Sophia Reed's forebodings. Mary woke up at 9 o'clock quite refreshed, and we sat up with Dora and talked everything over. Mary said I could have no conception of what she had suffered from remorse and loneliness. She said she'd started more than once to come over and make up, and then the memory of something those kind folks had told her I'd said would rise up and stop her. I believe her feelings were a pretty exact copy of my own.

[435] Canadian term for "a large quantity."

[436] In the 1897 version, the sentence continued: "and I don't know what I said or did."

About 12 Dora suddenly took a bad turn. I told Francis he must start right off for the doctor. Mary had borne up well, but now she seemed to lose all command of herself. She shrieked, and cried, and caught hold of Francis. She said he wasn't to think of going and leaving us two women alone with a dying child. She went on like that and we couldn't pacify her. Then, all at once, William walked in.[437] I don't know how he knew the fix we were in. I believe he must have been hanging around outside. He said he'd go for the doctor.[438] Francis and he went out to the barn together to harness the horse. I never knew what they said, but the next day they were working together as if nothing had happened.

Mary and I had a serious time that night. It almost seemed that we would lose Dora. But just as a long, red streak showed itself against the eastern sky the doctor said the crisis was past and Dora would live. Mary and I knelt by the bed with our arms around each other. The reddish gold of the sunrise fell over Dora's white face like a promise of hope. In the tears of joy we shed over her living baby we washed out the last stain of bitterness from our hearts.

THE GOOSE FEUD

If any one had ever told Mary Parker and me that the day would ever come when we would not speak to each other we would have laughed the statement to scorn. We had been could ever make trouble between Mary and me. I even helped her select the eggs for setting and the mother goose when she bought one. When every egg but one hatched out I was

Illustration from *Arthur's Home Magazine*

[437] These two sentences were different in the 1897 text: "She went on like that for as much as fifteen minutes. Just as Francis and I were trying to soothe her and get her to listen to reason, William c[a]me in."

[438] The following sentence began differently in 1897: "He didn't say another word, but Francis. . ."

LUCY MAUD MONTGOMERY

The Knuckling Down of Mrs. Gamble

(1900)

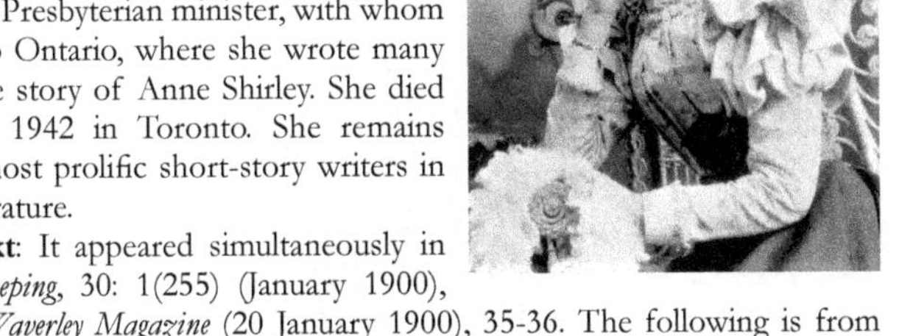

The author: In 1898, she moved back to the PEI community of Cavendish to live with her grandmother, by then a widow, and remained there until 1911. Her first book, published in 1908, is also her best known: *Anne of Green Gables*. In 1911, she married Ewen Macdonald, a Presbyterian minister, with whom she moved to Ontario, where she wrote many sequels to the story of Anne Shirley. She died on 24 April 1942 in Toronto. She remains one of the most prolific short-story writers in Canadian literature.

The text: It appeared simultaneously in *Good Housekeeping*, 30: 1(255) (January 1900), 3-8, and in *Waverley Magazine* (20 January 1900), 35-36. The following is from *Good Housekeeping*.

Mrs. Gamble was knitting by the west window of the kitchen. It was already quite dark in the big, spotless room, for the kitchen of the Gamble farmhouse was on the north side, and was shadowed west and north by a grove of firs.

Outside it was a chill, colorless November dusk; overhead the gray sky was faintly flushed with a transient pink, and lower down, between the dark boughs of the firs and far away over the dull hills, Mrs. Gamble could see the sullen, crimson bars of an autumn sunset. The cherry tree at the corner of the house was tossing its bare boughs weirdly, and shriveled brown leaves went scurrying up and down the garden in uncanny dances before the breath of viewless winds.

Mrs. Gamble dropped her knitting on her lap and leaned forward to look out of the window, through the firs, to that red glow of fading sunset. She was a tall, stout woman of perhaps sixty, for there were many gray threads in the smooth, thick waves of somewhat coarse auburn hair that framed her strong-featured face. Amelia Gamble had never used spectacles in her life, and her light gray eyes were as keen and penetrating as they had ever been, and a good deal harder. She drew her black shawl closer about her square shoulders and shivered a little.

"It's dreadful cold and bleak out tonight," she said aloud. She had a habit of talking to herself, for she was a woman who hated to be alone, and was given to many devices for circumventing unwelcome solitude. "I shouldn't wonder if we had snow before morning. It would be a relief to see those long, bare hills covered over. I hope it won't rain, anyhow. I hate fall rains. I wish James was home, or that some one would drop in for company. It makes me feel nervous, someway, to be alone in this big house. I must be getting old and silly when I get such notions in my head!"

She went and poked up the fire. She would have some cheerful light anyhow. Amelia Gamble had been brought up to consider it shameful waste to light a candle before it was absolutely dark, and she had never departed from the traditions of her childhood. Then she went to the other window. It looked out on the long valley of the village, at the head of which the Gamble homestead stood on the hill. The main road wound through the valley, and here and there along the dun slopes early lights twinkled. Mrs. Gamble's cold eyes swept down the length of the valley, and then fell on a beshawled figure coming up the lane between the rows of bare sweetbrier bushes.

"That's Lorilla Johnson," said Mrs. Gamble. "I'd know that wobbly walk o' hers anywhere. I dunno 's I'm glad to see *her*, for all I've been wishing some one would step in. She's a gossip and a pry, and that tongue of hers is hung in the middle. It's queer how some folks aren't happy unless they're forever poking their noses into something that don't concern them."

She had been moving swiftly about during this monologue, pushing chairs into place and lighting a lamp. When Lorilla's sharp, imperative little rat-a-tat came at the door Mrs. Gamble opened it, and bade her caller a semi-cordial good evening. But Lorilla Johnson was not to be daunted by a cool reception. It was her maxim to make herself at home under all circumstances, and when she had laid off her hat and shawl, and ensconced herself comfortably in the rocker, she produced from her satchel a long, gray, woolen sock, and began to knit, her tongue keeping time to the click of the needles. She was a thin woman, with a long, colorless face, and pale blue eyes, and had a disagreeable little laugh. Mrs. Gamble disliked her, and Lorilla knew it, but had her own way of taking revenge.

"I knew James wouldn't be back till late," she said, "so I thought I'd run up and keep you company for an hour or so. Don't you find it rather lonesome here by spells?"

"Not particularly," was the curt response. "There's too much to do for that. Fine ladies, with nothing to do, may find time to be lonesome, perhaps, I never could."

Lorilla smiled and shifted her tactics. She understood Amelia Gamble.

"That's so," she assented smoothly. "Fact is, it's a marvel to me how you ever manage to keep up with your work so well. It's a great thing to have your good health. Now me—I'm never well two days at a time. I've a cough now. There's a good deal of sickness round the Center. Dr. Richardson is kept pretty busy, I guess. All the Dales are down with diphtheria."

Lorilla stopped for breath, and Mrs. Gamble narrowed her lips down hardly as she stooped to pick a stray wisp of yarn from the yellow painted floor.

"It there's anything going, the Dales will have it, I'll be bound," she said. "When they are well they go gadding around until they catch something. Where'd they get the diphtheria?"

"Over Carleton way, they say. I s'pose you know Florrie has it too!"

It was the most effective shot in Lorilla's locker, and her lead-colored eyes watched Mrs. Gamble keenly as it was fired. The result disappointed her. Mrs. Gamble started slightly, but showed no other sign of emotion.

"Spencer's Florrie?"

"Yes. Of course, I s'posed you knew; she took down with it Monday. Dr. Richardson says she's pretty bad. I guess Jessie is about worn out. Have you been to see them, Mrs. Gamble?"

A braver woman then Lorilla Johnson might have quailed before the flash of Amelia Gamble's gray eyes.

"You know as well as I do, Lorilly Johnson, that I've never been to see Jessie Gamble at any time, and don't ever expect to go. She's nothing more to me than any stranger, nor her husband either."

"Mrs. Gamble! Your own son!" faltered Lorilla, deprecatingly.

"He's been no son of mine ever since he married Jessie Greene. I gave him his choice between us, and he made it and must abide by it. I'm sorry to hear Florrie is ill, just as I'd be sorry for anybody's child. Is she dangerous, did you say?"

"The doctor hasn't much hope of her, I believe. Spencer's just distracted, so they say, and Jessie, too. She's their only one, and they're just wrapped up in her. Like as not it's want of proper nursing is the trouble. Jessie isn't much of a hand in sickness, I suppose—never had any experience—and she can't get anyone. People are scared, you know. Diphtheria isn't a thing to be trifled with."

"Jessie Greene never had any faculty for managing, anyhow," said Mrs. Gamble, coldly. "There never was a Greene that had—or any constitution, either. Florrie was always a sickly child. Don't you find it chilly in that corner, Lorilly? Move nearer the fire."

Lorilla understood that Mrs. Gamble considered the discussion of Spencer Gamble's family troubles closed, and nothing more was said on the tabooed subject. When she finally went away Mrs. Gamble sped the parting guest without any regret.[439]

"I wish she'd stayed away," she muttered, "or held her tongue about Spencer's folks when she did come. I don't want to be told anything about them. Lorilly Johnson is always trying to twit me underhand about that affair. Florrie Gamble isn't anything more to me than any other Lawton child. There's James now"—as her quick ear caught the rumble of wheels coming down the hard frozen lane. "I'm sure I'm glad. I don't know what has got into me to-night—I seem to get all of a tremble when I'm left alone."

She had the supper table set for her husband by the time he came in, with his arms full of parcels, which he deposited silently on the dresser. James Gamble was a tall, stoop-shouldered old man, with dim, blinking eyes and long straggles of thin gray hair and whiskers. There was something meek and deprecating about his whole appearance. Lawton gossips said that James Gamble never dared to have an opinion of his own in the presence of his wife.

---

[439] "Welcome the coming, speed the parting guest" is a line from Alexander Pope's translation of Homer's *Odyssey* (XV, 84).

Supper was a silent meal, neither of the two seeming disposed to talk. As Mrs. Gamble passed her husband his second cup of tea, he cleared his throat tentatively and stirred the tea with the air of a timid man who wants to say something.

"Melie, did you hear that Spencer's Florrie was down with the diphthery?" he said, hesitatingly. "I heard it down at Shattuck this afternoon."

"Yes, I heard it," answered Mrs. Gamble, coldly. "Lorilly Johnson was here this evening and said so."

"Spencer was in at Morton's store while I was there," James Gamble faltered between nervous swallows of tea. "I heard him telling Tom Keefe about Florrie. He said they hadn't much hopes of her. He seemed awful down-hearted over it."

His wife made no reply. Her face was emotionless and her cold gray eyes gazed unblinkingly at the light. James Gamble moved his chair about restlessly.

"They do say over Shattuck way—I heard Tom Keefe and Bob Sharp talking of it when they didn't know I was around—that Spencer and Jessie ain't very well off this winter. It took most all Spencer's wages to pay the doctor's bills for that sick spell of Jessie's in the summer. Well, it just amounted to this: they appeared to think that Spencer's folks didn't have enough to eat or enough to warm themselves with."

"I suppose," said Mrs. Gamble in a hard, dry voice, "if you heard that about any stranger you'd take them a load of stuff. I suppose you could do as much for Spencer's folks."

"It ain't the same thing," said her husband, huskily, "and Spencer wouldn't take it if I did—you know that, Melie. He's too proud to take for charity what is his by right. He looked peaked and miserable enough himself, and he'd a bad cough too. It just seemed to rack him in pieces like."

A sudden change swept over Amelia Gamble's face, quite marvelous in the transformation it wrought. The hard lines seemed to melt away, the mouth softened. A whole flood of repressed mother love glorified her cold gray eyes. She bent forward insistently.

"Did you tell him to do anything for it?" she asked eagerly. "Did you recommend that emulsion Julius Hackett was taking?"

"I wasn't speaking to him at all, Melie—you know that well enough. He never looked my way."

"Spencer always took coughs so hard," said Mrs. Gamble anxiously, "and he never would take care of himself. I suppose he's run himself down slaving and slaving—and nothing but sickness to contend with."

"Perhaps you might go down and see them to-morrow," suggested her husband timidly. "You'd do as much for a stranger, Melie."

"I don't doubt I would; but you've said yourself this isn't the same thing. Jessie Greene said one that she hoped neither you nor I would ever darken her door; and she can't complain that we have—or ever will," said his wife defiantly.

"You don't know for sure whether she ever said such words or not, Melie. It might have been nothing but gossip. And if she did, I daresay she was provoked to it. *You* said enough about her; I daresay it all went to her ears."

"It's lately you've begun to take her part," said Mrs. Gamble sarcastically. "*I* wasn't the only one who said things, James Gamble."

"I know you weren't, Melie," he said humbly. "Only I kind of think now—maybe we were foolish to raise such a row. Of course, I ain't saying I don't still think it was a big mistake for Spencer to marry a Greene, but when he did we might as well have made the best of it. This house is big enough for half a dozen families, goodness knows. We're left all alone in our old age and it's all because we were cantankerous with Spencer. We were too unreasonable, Melie."

It was not often James Gamble dared to speak so plainly to his wife. He expected some biting sarcasm in reply but Mrs. Gamble made no response.

Her husband lighted a candle, seated himself near the fire, and tried to read. She washed and put away the dishes, then sat down near him and gazed into the glowing fire.

Was it true, she wondered uneasily, that Spencer and his wife were not so well off in the matter of food and fuel as were others?

Her thoughts traveled remorselessly back over the past as she sat there. Spencer had been her only, idolized son. It had been for him that James Gamble and his wife had toiled and economized—that his inheritance of land and money might surpass any other in Lawton. Everything they had done was with an eye to Spencer's future benefit. When they had built the new house Mrs. Gamble had insisted that it should be large and handsome, so that when Spencer should bring there a wife he might bring her to no mean or narrowed home. And to think that after all he had married Jessie

Greene! It was five years ago. James Gamble and his wife had opposed it bitterly. But Spencer Gamble was his mother's son. His obstinacy was fully equal to hers. When she had plainly given him his choice between her and Jessie Greene he had not hesitated.

James Gamble had been furious with the temper of a usually meek man, roused at last. He told his son that he would disown him if he married Jessie Greene; and Spencer Gamble had married her, taken her to a tiny house at Lawton Center, and between him and his parents fell a long and unbroken silence.

He struggled along somehow and managed to make a living by hiring out in summer and doing odd jobs in winter. It was not what Spencer Gamble had been used to and he felt the difference keenly.

Amelia Gamble's heart broke when her son went out from her roof to return no more, but she made no sign. Lawton people said she was the hardest woman they had ever known. She never even looked at Jessie or Spencer when she met them. This cold November evening, it was five months since she had seen her son—for after his marriage he had not even attended Lawton church. Instead he had gone with Jessie to the little Methodist church over at Shattuck, and this was another of the grievances of Mrs. Gamble, senior.

There had never been a moment in all the five long, lonely years that her heart has not yearned secretly over him, although she never admitted it. Now, as she sat over the dying embers, she confessed to herself at last that she had been hard and unjust. As her husband said, it would have been wiser to have made the best of it. After all, poor as the Greenes were, nothing except her poverty and some disreputable relatives could have been urged against Jessie herself. She might have learned to love her for Spencer's sake. The house was big enough for them all. It would have been pleasant to have had Spencer's wife for company and Spencer's golden-haired little girl playing about the old place.

And now little Florrie was dying and Spencer was ill. Mrs. Gamble wiped away some unaccustomed tears. The fire had gone out and the room was getting very cold.

At the next morning's breakfast table Mrs. Gamble broke a long silence so abruptly that her husband started.

"James, I'm going to walk down to the Center after breakfast and see Spencer's folks. I suppose if some of us have got to knuckle down it's my place to do it. Anyhow, I won't have much peace of mind if I don't go. I daresay Jessie'll shut the door in my face."

"I'm sure she won't do anything of the kind," said her husband eagerly, an expression of relief coming out strongly on his thin, pinched features. "She'll be glad enough to see you, no doubt." We ought to have done it long ago. Better take a basket along with you, Melie—maybe, if Jessie's had to wait on Florrie, all by herself, she'll have got behindhand with other things."

It was a generous basket that Mrs. Gamble packed, albeit with a grim face. She kept that same grim face on as she walked down the valley road. Snow had come in the night, and was still falling softly. The plowed fields were stretches of snowy dimples, and the barn roofs were like sheets of marble. The spruces stood up along the road feathered over whitely, and every twig on the beeches was outlined in pearl. The far away hills loomed dimly through the misty veil of snowflakes.

To Mrs. Gamble it seemed as if the very cows in the barnyards, blinking their mild eyes at her over the fences, with broad-rayed flakes clinging to their sides, knew her errand. The faces she saw looking at her from the windows seemed to wear significant smiles. A neighbor's hearty greeting seemed over-charged with sinister meaning. More than once she was on the point of turning back. Could it be possible that she, Amelia Gamble, was going to "knuckle down" to Jessie Greene—a Greene from Shattuck, at that?

Yet she went steadily on till she found herself standing before the door of Spencer Gamble's tiny house at the Center. From the windows of a house opposite she saw Lorilla Johnson's pale, curious face peering out. In spite of herself, Mrs. Gamble smiled. Spurred on by the consciousness of being watched by Lorilla, she rapped sharply at Spencer's door—and then stepped back, with a vague impulse to run from the spot in spite of a dozen Lorillas.

Spencer himself, hollow-eyed and unshaven, opened the door. Amazement, incredulity, and alarm, chased each other over his haggard face. He was too surprised to speak, and stood dumbly in the doorway.

"Come, Spencer, ain't you going to ask me in?" said his mother, crisply. "I haven't walked all the way down here in the snow for nothing. How is Florrie—and Jessie?"

She brought the last word out with a choke. It broke the back of her pride, but it was a hard blow. Spencer stepped back embarrassed.

"Of course—come in, mother. Jessie—Florrie—they're well—no, I mean—" Mrs. Gamble pushed past him and went in. There was nobody in the neglected kitchen. She stalked to the door of the little bedroom off it, and peered in grimly. Jessie Gamble, bending over her child's cot, started with dismay as she saw her mother-in-law. She looked thin and heart-broken. When Spencer Gamble had married her she had been the prettiest girl in Shattuck. Now, the color was all gone from her long cheeks, her soft, fairish-brown hair was falling loosely on her neck, and her large, wistful brown eyes were full of fear and sorrow.

Something—pride, coldness, disappointment, or whatever it was—gave way in Mrs. Gamble's heart at that moment. She did not say anything, but she held out her arms, and the next moment the younger woman was sobbing in them.

It was half an hour before Mrs. Gamble came out to the kitchen, which Spencer was clumsily trying to restore to order. She had her bonnet and shawl off, and was trying a big apron about her substantial waist.

"Jessie's clean tuckered out, Spencer. She's gone to sleep in there, and I'm going to look after Florrie. I believe she'll pull through. Doctor Richardson don't know everything. I never had much opinion of him, anyway. If you haven't had time to do much cooking, you'll find something eatable in that basket, I dare say. I knew you'd be all sort of upset, so I brought it along. Then I want you to go home and tell father I won't be back to-day, and he must cook his own meals. You needn't be afraid to," she added, seeing the doubt on her son's face, "he'll be glad to see you again, Spencer."

When the doctor came that night it was to find Florrie out of danger.

"It's all owing to you, mother," said Jessie, humbly. "If you hadn't come to-day I believe Florrie would have died. I was so weak and sick myself I couldn't do right for her. I haven't been real strong since the summer."

A month later the house at the Center was locked up and the windows boarded over. Spencer Gamble and his wife and child had moved to the big house on the hill.

EDITH EATON

The Smuggling of Tie Co

(1900)

The author: In 1897, soon after her first short stories were published, Edith Eaton spent a spell as a journalist in Jamaica, where her sister worked. From 1898 to 1912 (at her physician's recommendation, as she suffered from a weak heart) she lived in the United States, wandering first throughout the West Coast (San Francisco, Los Angeles, Seattle), working as a stenographer and publishing stories and articles, and, after 1910, in Boston. She collected some of her stories in 1912, in *Mrs. Spring Fragrance* (published in Chicago). The same year, she returned to Montreal, where she died on 7 April 1914.

The text: First published in *The Land of Sunshine* (July 1900), 100-104. *The Land of Sunshine* was "the magazine of California and the West," was published in Los Angeles and was edited by Charles F. Lummis. It was signed "Sui Sin Fan" and gave the place of abode of the author (at the end of the story) as "Seattle, Washington." It was later included in *Mrs. Spring Fragrance* (Chicago: A. C. McClurg, 1912), 184-193. There are some minor changes (especially with respect to punctuation) in the 1912 version, and they have been followed here. A more significant change is mentioned in a footnote.

Amongst the daring men who engage in contrabanding Chinamen from Canada into the United States Jack Fabian ranks as the boldest in deed, the cleverest in scheming, and the most successful in outwitting Government officers.

Uncommonly strong in person, tall and well built, with fine features and a pair of keen, steady blue eyes, gifted with a sort of rough eloquence and of much personal fascination, it is no wonder that we fellows regard him as our chief and are bound to follow where he leads. With Fabian at our head we engage in the wildest adventures and find such places of concealment for our human goods as none but those who take part in a desperate business would dare to dream of.

Jack, however, is not in search of glory—money is his object. One day when a romantic friend remarked that it was very kind of him to help the poor Chinamen over the border, a cynical smile curled his moustache.

"Kind!" he echoed, "Well, I haven't yet had time to become sentimental over the matter. It is merely a matter of dollars and cents, though, of course, to a man of my strict principles, there is a certain pleasure to be derived from getting ahead of the Government. A poor devil does now and then like to take a little out of those millionaire concerns."

It was last summer and Fabian was somewhat down on his luck. A few months previously, to the surprise of us all, he had made a blunder, which resulted in his capture by American officers, and he and his companion, together with five uncustomed Chinamen, had been lodged in a county jail to await trial.

But loafing behind bars did not agree with Fabian's energetic nature, so one dark night, by means of a saw which had been given to him by a very innocent-looking visitor the day before,[440] he made good his escape, and after a long, hungry, detective-hunted tramp through woods and bushes, found himself safe in Canada.

He had had a three months' sojourn in prison, and during that time some changes had taken place in smuggling circles. Some ingenious lawyers had devised a scheme by which any young Chinaman on payment of a couple of hundred dollars could procure a father, which father would swear the young Chinaman was born in America—thus proving him to be an American citizen with the right to breathe United States air. And the Chinese themselves, assisted by some white men, were manufacturing certificates establishing their right to cross the border, and in that way were passing over in large batches.

That sort of trick naturally spoiled our fellows' business, but we all knew that "Yankee sharper" games can hold good only for a short while; so we bided our time and waited in patience.

[440] The passage about the help Fabian received from a visitor was added in the 1912 version.

Not so Fabian. He became very restless and wandered around with glowering looks. He was sitting one day in a laundry, the proprietor of which had sent out many a boy through our chief's instrumentality. Indeed, Fabian is said to have "rushed over" to "Uncle Sam" himself some five hundred Celestials, and if Fabian had not been an exceedingly generous fellow he might now be a gentleman of leisure, instead of an immortalized Rob Roy.[441]

Well, Fabian was sitting in the laundry of Chen Ting Lung & Co., telling a nice-looking young Chinaman that he was so broke that he'd be willing to take over even one man at a time.

The young Chinaman looked thoughtfully into Fabian's face. "Would you take me?" he inquired.

"Take you?" repeated Fabian. "Why, you are one of the 'bosses' here. You don't mean to say that you are hankering after a place where it would take you years to get as high up in the 'washee, washee' business as you are now?"

"Yes, I want go," replied Tie Co. "I want go to New York and I pay you fifty dollars and all expense if you take me, and not say you take me to my partners."

"There's no accounting for a Chinaman," muttered Fabian, but he gladly agreed to the proposal and a night was fixed.

"What is the name of the firm you are going to?" inquired the white man.

Chinamen who intend being smuggled over always make arrangements with some Chinese firm in the States to receive them.

Tie Co hesitated, then mumbled something which sounded like "Quong Wo Yuen" or "Long Lo Toon," Fabian was not sure which, but he did not repeat the question, not being sufficiently interested.

He left the laundry, nodding goodbye to Tie Co as he passed outside the window, and the Chinaman nodded back, a faint smile on his small, delicate face lingering until Fabian's receding form was lost to view.

It was a pleasant night on which the two men set out. Fabian had a rig waiting at the corner of the street; Tie Co, dressed in citizen's clothes, stepped into it unobserved, and the smuggler and

[441] Rob Roy MacGregor (1671-1734) is a famous Scottish outlaw and Jacobite soldier. Rob Roy is also the hero of an eponymous 1817 novel by Walter Scott (see also note 134).

would-be smuggled were soon out of the city. They had a merry drive, for Fabian's liking for Tie Co was very real; he had known him for several years, and the lad's quick intelligence interested him.

The second day they left their horse at a farmhouse where Fabian would call for it on his return trip, crossed a river in a row-boat before the sun was up, and plunged into a wood in which they would remain till evening. It was raining, but through mud and wind and rain they trudged slowly and heavily.

Tie Co paused now and then to take breath. Once Fabian remarked:

"You are not a very strong lad, Tie Co. It's a pity you have to work as you do for your living," and Tie Co had answered:

"Work velly good! No work, Tie Co die."

Fabian looked at the lad protectingly, wondering in a careless way why this Chinaman seemed to him so different from the others.

"Wouldn't you like to be back in China?" he asked.

"No," said Tie Co decidedly.

"Why?"

"I not know why," answered Tie Co.

Fabian laughed.

"Haven't you got a nice little wife at home?" he continued. "I hear you people marry very young."

"No, I no wife," asserted his companion with a choky little laugh. "I never have no wife."

"Nonsense," joked Fabian. "Why, Tie Co, think how nice it would be to have a little woman to cook your rice and to love you."

"I not have wife," repeated Tie Co, seriously. "I not like woman, I like man."

"You confirmed old bachelor!" ejaculated Fabian.

"I like you," said Tie Co, his boyish voice sounding clear and sweet in the wet woods. "I like you so much that I want go to New York, so you make fifty dollars. I no flend in New York."

"What!" exclaimed Fabian.

"Oh, I solly I tell you, Tie Co velly solly," and the Chinese boy shuffled on with bowed head.

"Look here, Tie Co," said Fabian; "I won't have you do this for my sake. You have been very foolish, and I don't care for your fifty dollars. I do not need it half as much as you do. Good

God! how ashamed you make me feel—I who have blown in my thousands in idle pleasures cannot take the little you have slaved for. We are in New York State now. When we get out of this wood we will have to walk over a bridge which crosses a river. On the other side, not far from where we cross, there is a railway station. Instead of buying you a ticket for the city of New York I shall take train with you for Toronto."

Tie Co did not answer—he seemed to be thinking deeply. Suddenly he pointed to where some fallen trees lay.

"Two men run away behind there," cried he.

Fabian looked round them anxiously; his keen eyes seemed to pierce the gloom in his endeavour to catch a glimpse of any person; but no man was visible, and, save a dismal sighing of the wind among the trees, all was quiet.

"There's no one," he said somewhat gruffly—he was rather startled, for they were a mile over the border and he knew that the Government officers were on a sharp lookout for him, and felt, despite his strength, if any trick or surprise were attempted it would go hard with him.

"If they catch you with me it be too bad," sententiously remarked Tie Co. It seemed as if his words were in answer to Fabian's thoughts.

"But they will not catch us; so cheer up your heart, my boy," replied the latter, more heartily than he felt.

"If they come, and I not with you, they not take you and it would be all lite."

"Yes," assented Fabian, wondering what his companion was thinking about.

They emerged from the woods in the dusk of the evening and were soon on the bridge crossing the river. When they were near the center Tie Co stopped and looked into Fabian's face.

"Man come for you, I not here, man no hurt you." And with the words he whirled like a flash over the rail.

In another flash Fabian was after him. But though a first-class swimmer, the white man's efforts were of no avail, and Tie Co was borne away from him by the swift current.

Cold and dripping wet, Fabian dragged himself up the bank and found himself a prisoner.

"So your Chinaman threw himself into the river. What was that for?" asked one of the Government officers.

"I think he was out of his head," replied Fabian. And he fully believed what he uttered.

"We tracked you right through the woods," said another of the captors. "We thought once the boy caught sight of us."

Fabian remained silent.

Tie Co's body was picked up the next day. Tie Co's body, and yet not Tie Co, for Tie Co was a youth, and the body found with Tie Co's face and dressed in Tie Co's clothes was the body of a girl—a woman.

Nobody in the laundry of Chen Ting Lung & Co.—no Chinaman in Canada or New York—could explain the mystery. Tie Co had come out to Canada with a number of other youths. Though not very strong he had always been a good worker and "very smart." He had been quiet and reserved among his own countrymen; had refused to smoke tobacco or opium, and had been a regular attendant at Sunday schools and a great favorite with mission ladies.

Fabian was released in less than a week. "No evidence against him," said the Commissioner, who was not aware that the prisoner was the man who had broken out of jail but a month before.

Fabian is now very busy; there are lots of boys taking his helping hand over the border, but none of them are like Tie Co; and sometimes, between whiles, Fabian finds himself pondering long and earnestly over the mystery of Tie Co's life—and death.

CPSIA information can be obtained
at www.ICGtesting.com
Printed in the USA
BVHW050934300123
657338BV00002B/3